THE MERCENARIES

The Mercenaries

BY

Quentin Grady

ISBN-10: 0-9994434-0-8
ISBN-13: 978-0-9994434-0-8

CONTENTS

Preface

The Mercenaries is the fifth book of the *Tales of the Ghost Eagle* series. Book 5 was originally intended to cover two years of the war: 1757–1758. It turned out that 1757 was more of a tipping point in the war than I realized. I will talk more about England and France later. The year 1757 was also a tipping point for Corrinne and Philippe and Charles and Henri and Anamosa. As the author, after so many books and pages, you get to know your characters as you would close friends. Often enough, when they are presented with difficult and unknown situations, they react as you might expect this close friend of yours to react. You know them that well. Unless…they are confronted with unexpected, dangerous, and deadly circumstances and realize they have made a big mistake. In that instance, you just trust their instincts.

Early in 1756, Lady Corrinne with her twin babies and Anamosa were forced to return to Boston after being discovered by agents of Colonel Wilhelm von Kleinfels. She believed it would be safer living in Boston among friends. For a time, this was true. But the renewed sense of safety was short-lived. First Corrinne's beloved maidservant Mathilde was poisoned at a flower market in broad daylight on the streets of Boston. Another enemy tried to burn down their house. Lord Charles VanderMeer survived two assassination attempts, one by poison, then an attack by an assassin armed with a blunderbuss. The second attack left him paralyzed from the waist down. Clearly, Boston was not safe.

Lord and Lady VanderMeer flee again, this time to the French fortress-port of Louisbourg on Île Royale, north of Halifax. This was supposed to be a temporary haven before going on to somewhere else. Question was, where? Back to Québec City or Montréal? And when? Leave now or a year from now? The occult *beast* was still in pursuit. The House of Brunswick had a list of enemies that wanted them dead. So, while they'd planned to take a breather in Louisbourg, the rest of the world was making decisions based upon war.

The year 1756 ended with a war officially declared between France and England halfway through the year. England was confronted with a series of defeats in Europe and America on land and at sea. The Great Lakes and the lands south and west of the Allegheny River were now dominated by the French. The conduct of the war had polarized. It was French versus English regulars in the American colonies. And England's ally, Prussia, versus everyone else on the European continent. France's only objective in Europe, beyond defending its borders and protecting its monarchy, was to invade and capture the English Electorate of Hanover. So important Hanover was to the crown of England, George II sent his son, the Duke of Cumberland, to Hanover with orders to defend it.

Hanover? The people of England and Parliament were perplexed by this. Hanover was a German state! What provokes the endless requirement for England to spend treasure or send troops in the defense of Hanover?

Enter Lord William Pitt. He was the leading member of Parliament of his time, a great orator and a populist. A man of the people. He loathed fighting land wars in Europe. Why? *For what gain?* he would argue. He publicly criticized the king's decision to defend Hanover. Pitt was hated by the royals, especially George II, but loved by the English people. Under pressure from the city populations and the newspapers, essentially everyone, George II reluctantly promoted Lord William Pitt to the post of Secretary of State for the Southern Department, a position of power in England, second only to the prime minister. This position made William Pitt responsible for the American colonies, the jewel of the empire. In December of 1756, Lord William Pitt accepted the position from the Duke of Devonshire, an otherwise impotent Prime Minster, and informed the man, "My Lord, I am sure I can save this country, and no one else can."

Lord William Pitt's promotion in leadership to be the primary decision maker for the conduct of the war was a *game changer*. His strategy was simple. Pitt regarded France as a global competitor and England's primary enemy. If England defeats France in North America, it defeats France as a global power, *forever!* His primary target was the fortress-port of Louisbourg on Île Royale, in North America. If Louisbourg falls, all New France will fall within a year, he declared to senior army and navy officers and members of Parliament. In January 1757, Lord Pitt wrote missives to the army and the navy commanders, ordering them to adopt his plan to achieve this victory without delay.

French spies ascertained the English decision to invade Louisbourg, although given Lord Pitt's oratory skills, it was not exactly a secret. But France did not want to deploy its regular troops to Louisbourg while Prussian armies were marching around Europe. France began hiring mercenaries eagerly supplied by the numerous German states of the decaying Holy Roman Empire, to support the defensive needs of New France. These mercenaries were soldiers, but they were also used as assassins for hire. There were plenty of employers among the warring powers who had specific targets for them.

In North America, General John Campbell, 4th Earl of Loudoun, remained the undisputed commander-in-chief of the American theater of war despite his failures in 1756. He read with contempt Lord William Pitt's missive declaring Louisbourg as the primary target. He did not care what this "commoner" ordered. Lord Loudon considered the siege of Louisbourg to be an effort of extraordinary complexity.

No, Lord Loudon intended to pursue his favorite strategy. A direct march north up the Hudson River Valley, moving past the city of Albany, across Lake George and Lake Champlain, capture the French Fort Carillon and Fort Saint-Frédéric along the way, or bypass them altogether, and allow the Americans to encircle these French strongholds. Montréal was only a week's march after that. That city would capitulate in a matter of days. Then he would march east on the Saint Lawrence River, lay siege, and invest Québec City. This strategy would require an army of regular redcoats of around fifteen thousand. Lord Loudon already had them staged and billeted with eleven thousand in the port of New York and another four thousand in Halifax.

In Québec City, Governor-General Pierre de Vaudreuil and General Louis-Joseph de Montcalm planned to attack Fort William Henry at the south end of Lake George. But when to attack paralyzes the adversarial military leaders with indecision. The biggest disagreement was the degree to which native warriors would be used in the assault on Fort William Henry. Having learned a bitter lesson at Fort Oswego, General Montcalm wanted the native participation kept to a minimum. Governor Vaudreuil, born and raised as a Canadian, intended to use the native warriors as his own private army. He invites and encourages thousands to become involved with promises of great rewards. At the earlier defeat of Fort Oswego, Montcalm had learned that controlling the actions of even a few hundred of these primitive warriors was almost impossible. This European general and aristocrat could not conceive the brutal massacre awaiting him when a few thousand of them descend on the surrendered defenders of Fort William Henry. Yet General Montcalm was responsible for the safety of his prisoners and he was naïve to think otherwise.

Captain Louis-Antoine Comte de Bougainville was an aide-de-camp of General Montcalm during this war. He was a scientist, had authored books on calculus, and later would be celebrated as a world explorer who, like Captain Cook, circumnavigated the globe. During 1757, he was personally involved in the American battles. His journals describe the hideous repercussions of the English surrender, when the native allies of the French collected their "reward" as promised by Governor Vaudreuil. Captain Bougainville's descriptions are difficult to read. While I did not include many of the atrocities he described, I have no reason to doubt his eye-witness accounts. What I added to the story as experienced through the eyes of the characters was intentionally minimized. But it is safe for the reader to presume that what occurred was indeed much worse.

As *The Mercenaries* unfolds, Lady Corrinne and her twin children, Marcus and Calypso, along with Anamosa, seek and receive shelter inside the stout walls of the Fortress of Louisbourg. The good news is that Ensign Henri Gerrard and a light battalion of Québécois marines are there, too. Captain LaTour prepares to transport the paralyzed Lord Charles VanderMeer to France in a winter crossing of the Atlantic on the *Falcon Queen*, then overland to Amsterdam, to deliver his lordship safely to his father, Louis Ernest, Duke of Brunswick-Wolfenbüttel. In the west, Scout Captain Philippe Gerrard commands the *coureur de bois* scout companies in General Louis-Joseph de Montcalm's army, using Fort Carillon on Lake Champlain as his base. Philippe is unaware that Corrinne is now residing in Louisbourg. She has written him multiple letters. But Philippe's mail is being intercepted by someone in Québec City. Receiving no letters from Philippe in reply, Corrinne feels more isolated and lonelier than ever before.

Of course, the persistent deadly threat of the vulnax wraith pursues them all with relentless hatred. Its unsleeping thoughts dwell on learning Lady Corrinne's location and, most importantly, the location of the châsse carrying the bone relics. But the wraith cannot "see" the châsse over water! Is the châsse on an island? Or is it aboard a ship? It will also use mercenaries as servants and sends them to Louisbourg.

The ghost eagle does not sleep either. It can "see" the demon and any of its servants. It is not intimidated.

This book brings new twists to the story that were a welcome surprise to me. There are new characters, too. New allies. I hope you enjoy it.

Book 6 is being written.

Quentin Grady

ILLUSTRATIONS

Acadia 1754 Map. From Wikimedia Commons.
https://upload.wikimedia.org/wikipedia/commons/9/93/Acadia_1754.png
(accessed November 23, 2017).

Siege of Fort William Henry Map. Parkman, Francis. 1897. *Montcalm and Wolfe, Volume 1*. Little, Brown, and company.

Rade de Brest Map. From Wikimedia Commons.
https://commons.wikimedia.org/wiki/File:017_004a.jpg
(accessed November 23, 2017).

Île Royale map, Châsse Panel, and the cover illustrations
by Yoko Matsuoka.
http://www.m-y-designs.com/

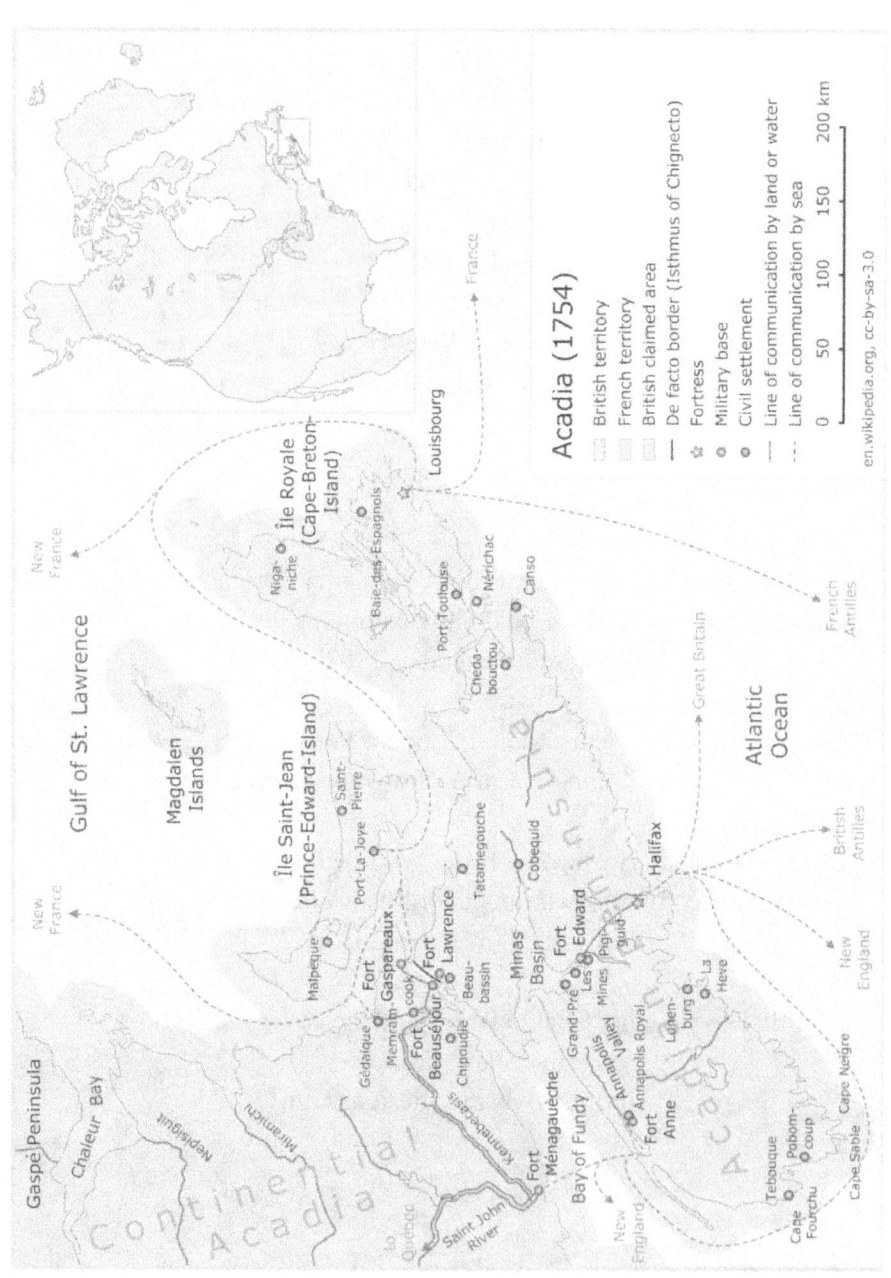

Acadia 1754

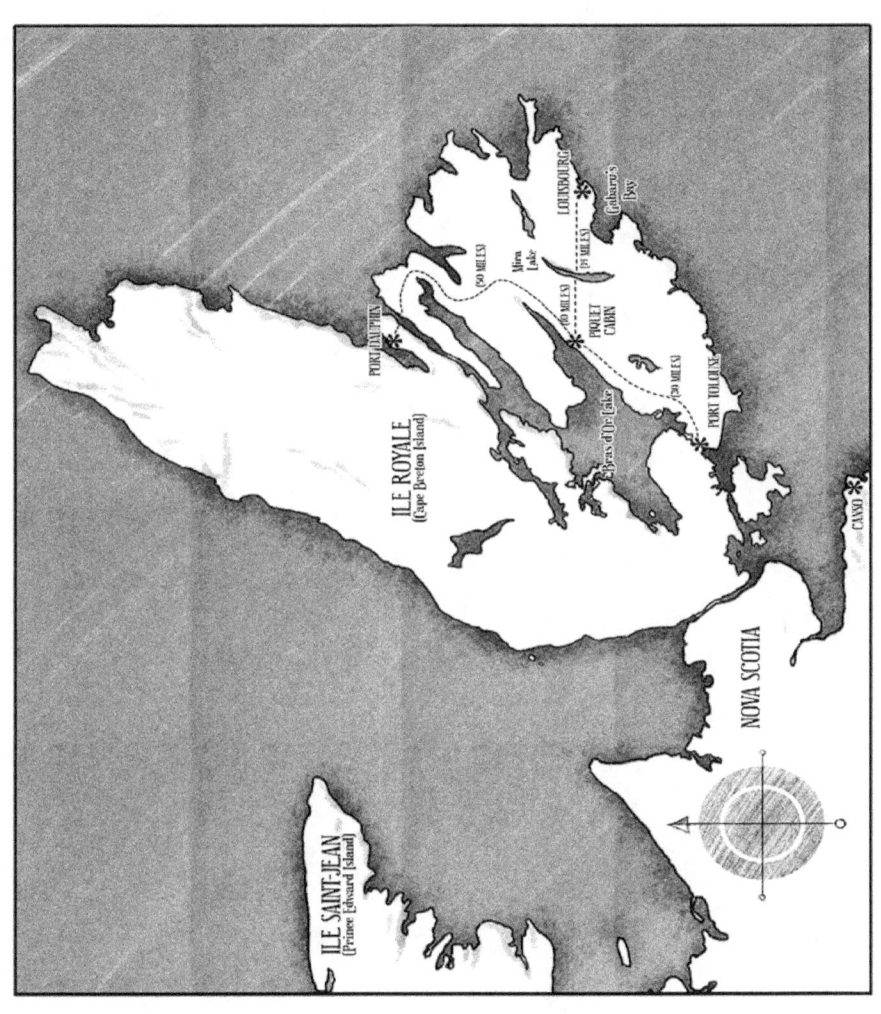

Île Royale

PROLOGUE
STRAIT OF CANCEAU
NOVEMBER 1756
The Eagle Decision

The *ghost* found its powers of sight weakened after the slaying of Archbishop Nicolet. Before the final confrontation with the demon, someone else must embrace this spiritual persona. But who? And how? The *ghost* had no idea how to communicate this need to the woman, but it must find a way. The *ghost* must get close to her, to within a few paces. It must contact her, to warn the woman of the demon's presence. The danger was not over.

The ghost sensed the woman's presence was on land. Saltwater lay between them. Saltwater dulled his ability to discern details. And it was getting colder. Winter had gripped the land, turning water into ice. Food would now become scarce. The white eagle was difficult to dominate as the animal's strong instincts for survival pulled its attention always towards the direction of the breeding place.

Odors rose from the water channel, carried inland by the wind. It had the scent of fish. The water barrier was not that wide. He could see land on the other side. But every time they banked to get closer, to see if they might glide across, the white eagle would balk and maintain the angled bank until it was flying again in the opposite direction.

The *ghost* increased its dominance. The white eagle tucked its wings and dove straight down at the ground. The acceleration disconcerted the *ghost*, and he lost control. It was the eagle's decision, not his, to pull out of this dive. Sometimes, if the dive did not begin from too high an elevation, the eagle would allow herself to bounce off the ground. To the *ghost*'s surprise, he could feel the pain of striking the ground. So too did the eagle, of course. Evidently to make the point: *I can hurt you.* That was even more disconcerting! She had done this more than once. Fortunately, the eagle did not do it this time. She spread her wings to stop the dive.

1

The *ghost* had learned a female eagle's strength of will was much stronger than that of a male's. The *ghost* could not interpret her puzzling thoughts, but her emotions were always quite clear. She'd learned how to cope with his intrusiveness. Her unspoken message was strong.

Force me to do this and we will die together.

The *ghost* endeavored to be gentle with her, to beguile her behavior to do what he wanted. But the eagle grew weary from enduring the cold dry air. It refused to even bank in the direction of the water. It was useless to keep trying. Resigned, the *ghost* withdrew its dominance altogether and allowed the raptor to fly with greater speed in the direction of the breeding grounds.

Lady Corrinne and Charles VanderMeer had been lucky the day they arrived in Louisbourg. Lucky when they arrived in Halifax with an invented identity. Lucky when they docked in Boston and had the fortuitous meeting with Thomas Hancock. The VanderMeer ship, *William's Queen*, was flying the Dutch flag with the sixteen-foot-long banner of the House of Brunswick fluttering in the wind atop its main mast. It received a perfunctory welcome by the French authorities when it entered Louisbourg's harbor. Despite the welcoming cheers of the citizens and soldiers as they neared the quay wall to anchor, France was at war. Any ship flying a flag that was not French was viewed with suspicion by Governor Augustin de Drucour and his military commanders. But *William's Queen* had visited before. Captain LaTour was known to them. And Captain LaTour had just completed a vital and extremely dangerous mission of espionage in Boston that involved Ensign Henri Gerrard. So Drucour was perplexed to see this same ship now returning under the flagship banner of the senior Dutch royal house and carrying Lord and Lady VanderMeer and their three children.

Before Drucour met with the VanderMeers, Ensign Gerrard presented the governor with the sealed, coded missives given to him from the "baker" in Boston; the French spy known as *Parliament*. Drucour was the only person in New France who possessed the solution to this cipher. Before dealing with the Dutch royals in his harbor, he decoded the missive. He was staggered to learn the English amassment of regular troops in Halifax had grown to over five thousand, that twice that many were still billeted in the port city of New York, and that they intended to land and lay siege to Louisbourg in the coming spring of 1757, maybe in April. Drucour had expected this, but not so soon. Louisbourg was not ready. It did not have sufficient strength of troops-in-arms to withstand a heavy siege. Drucour needed more metropolitan regiments assigned to the garrison and a fleet of warships from the French navy. He coded urgent messages to France.

The next morning, Drucour gave the VanderMeers the private audience they had requested.

"Please excuse this delay in a proper welcome, your lordship. My duties as governor and the pressing issues of war take precedence. In this vein, I must ask you first, what is your purpose for being here?"

"You have the coded missive." Charles' tone suggested the purpose was obvious. "I am delivering vital intelligence to France. And I also desire temporary sanctuary for Lady VanderMeer and our children."

Drucour was not expecting this. "Sanctuary? From who?"

Hours of polite questioning and confidential explanations ensued. Charles and Corrinne had previously decided to tell the governor the truth… *Well, some of it.* That the marriage between them was a masquerade, contrived to disguise their work as spies for France while living in Boston, where publicly they managed a trading insurance company for the Dutch Republic.

In truth, the VanderMeers did no spying at all. But they had needed an excuse as to why they personally brought Ensign Gerrard back to Louisbourg with them. It sounded plausible enough.

Corrinne volunteered that her real husband was Captain Philippe Gerrard of the Troupes de la Marine. That he was fighting in the army of General Louis de Montcalm.

"It is important to maintain this fictional marriage if we are ever to return to Boston. A few of the marines here in Louisbourg might recognize me…maybe not. But I will deny this as a coincidental resemblance if I am confronted."

"The truth of our relationship *must* remain a secret, Governor," Charles asserted more strongly. "This is a state secret between the Dutch Republic and France. I ask you to accept this."

Accept this? The governor almost balked at the man's temerity. By their mutual admission, Lady Corrinne was not even Charles VanderMeer's real wife. *These children are not his either!* Yet Governor Drucour was persuaded that Charles VanderMeer was indeed the son and heir to the Duke of Brunswick, pending confirmation from France.

"As you wish, Lord VanderMeer. I will acknowledge Lady VanderMeer as your wife," he conceded politely, then added, "for the time being."

"I anticipate my identity will be validated by your government." Lord Charles VanderMeer's tone of voice suggested a relationship of importance existed between the Duke of Brunswick and certain French ministers, and that he, Charles VanderMeer, was the linchpin in this relationship. Governor Drucour conceded if this elaborate façade was true, the highly valuable connection to the French government must not be damaged.

But added to the depressing news about redcoats amassing in Halifax, the appearance and revelations from Lord and Lady VanderMeer were unsettling. Their presence in Boston had never been revealed to him before! And they demanded to maintain themselves as Lord and Lady VanderMeer, as they might later return to Boston to continue spying.

I should have been told!

"Lord VanderMeer, I intend to send a courier ship to my superiors in France. I will seek guidance from the Minister of Marine concerning what you have told me. Based on your assurances, my lord, I expect to hear something positive by year's end."

Charles nodded. "Thank you for this gracious consideration, Governor. I must continue my sail to Europe in the meantime to counsel with my father. As the heir to the Duchy of Brunswick, I have enemies in my own country who would do us harm. An attempt was made to assassinate me in Boston, which resulted in my paralysis. That is why I brought my family away with me. Yet my family will be in greater danger if they accompany me without the proper preparations. I need time to decide on matters of their safety. Before I depart Louisbourg, I want to be sure Lady VanderMeer and my children have your sanctuary. With your permission and assistance, of course."

Drucour balked again. *Now I am to be a host?*

Lord and Lady VanderMeer waited quietly as Governor Drucour evaluated all they had told him.

Drucour deliberated. Lord VanderMeer would be leaving. If invasion and siege were approaching, Lady VanderMeer's presence here mattered little in Louisbourg's fate. In truth, her exposure to this danger might lend support to his request for more troops. He took a deep breath.

"But of course, your lordship. I am honored to safeguard Lady VanderMeer."

Governor Drucour arranged for his new *guests* to find accommodations among the civilian faubourg. He solicited Julien Fizel, a local militia captain and one of Louisbourg's more wealthy citizens, a man of property and commerce. He made the necessary introductions and compelled the merchant to help. The VanderMeers were offered a two-story stone and masonry house in the eastern faubourg owned by the merchant. The house was on the highest ground of the fortress and not too far from the Queen's Bastion. It had a garden to cultivate and would provide privacy.

At high tide the same day, Drucour dispatched a fast courier schooner to France, carrying the encoded missive of the ominous intelligence learned from *Parliament*. The courier dispatches to France included a separate encoded missive to Jean-Baptiste de Machault, the Minister of Marine, requesting validation of Lord and Lady VanderMeer's identities and asking for recommendations and directions from his superior.

A second courier with an encoded dispatch was carried by horse, south to Port Toulouse on the Canceau strait, with orders to skate up the frozen Saint Lawrence River to Québec City. This dispatch would inform Governor Vaudreuil of the build-up of regular troops in Halifax. In this communication was no mention of Lord and Lady VanderMeer.

After moving from the ship into the new house, Corrinne let it be known it was her intention to build a permanent residence somewhere in the faubourg. She solicited civilian builders to submit plans. She further announced the VanderMeers intended to promote more trade between France and the Dutch Republic in Louisbourg. This was simply to subdue the exaggerated rumors pervasive in a cloistered community starving for news without much to talk about. Corrinne had no intention of staying in Louisbourg permanently, even if the winters were not so harsh, which they were. Leaving Louisbourg was only a question of when to leave, how to leave, and where to go. But she kept all this to herself.

There followed a tearful departure two days later when Charles boarded *William's Queen* to sail back to Amsterdam to see his father.

It was overcast, blustery, with a drizzly rain that intermittently turned to sleet. Marie-Louise de Drucour lamented to Corrinne the weather that day was typical for Louisbourg in the winter months. She would learn it was not an exaggeration. The governor's wife graciously offered to stay with the children—Anamosa, Marcus, and Calypso—warm and safe inside the stone house arranged for them by her husband. This allowed Corrinne to stand at Frédéric Gate at the center of the quay wall to wave good-bye. The gate was the main entrance to the fortress and the faubourgs for the ships at anchor in the harbor. Frédéric Gate marked the coming or going of any passengers who boarded or disembarked from their ships while in Louisbourg.

The governor's wife urged Corrinne to dress warmly. Corrinne wore a long winter coat with a fur collar, under which she wore a tight-weave woolen dress that draped over fur-lined heavy boots. A scarf was wrapped around her head, ears, and under her chin. Another scarf was wrapped horizontally to cover her nose and mouth. Her gloved hands were further protected inside a muff. Even so, when she walked to stand at Frédéric Gate, she was already freezing and trembled in gusts of wind that surged across the harbor.

Captain LaTour weighed anchor and put to sea with the tide.

Corrinne watched the sails unfurl. Tears froze to her cheeks as she waved good-bye to Charles. They were not married, but for two years pretended they were. Charles gave her emotional support. They endured the terrifying visitations by the wraith. Corrinne could not imagine what she would have done if Charles had not applied his remarkable analytical abilities to help sort out the mystery behind this deadly curse.

Lord Charles VanderMeer, artist, jeweler, and primary heir to the Duchy of Brunswick, suffered the icy weather sitting in his wheeled chair near the helm. With tears streaming down his cheeks, he waved back at the woman who was not really his wife. It was never his intention, but over the last two years he'd fallen deeply in love with Corrinne. He never overtly expressed these feelings, of course, but he thought she knew.

Fully sailed, the *Queen* glided swiftly over the water.

They would never meet again.

La Rochelle, France

Captain Beauregard LaTour of the Dutch ship, *William's Queen*, had selected the French port of La Rochelle as the sailing destination for the dangerous winter crossing of the Atlantic Ocean. Foremost, because La Rochelle just happened to be on the exact line of latitude as Louisbourg, making the course almost a straight line eastward. The ship carried little cargo. The transit was fast, just ten days. The one day of bad weather the ship encountered along the way was manageable, which lessened any discomfort to Lord Charles VanderMeer.

Captain LaTour worried about the nobleman's health, reflected in the man's sagging mood. When Lady VanderMeer was around, Charles was usually cheered by her inexhaustible optimism. Of course, Lord VanderMeer was paralyzed from the waist down, so anything he attempted to do alone was a struggle. The members of the crew were always anxious to help. LaTour could tell, however, this was wearing on the man's pride. Lord VanderMeer was highly intelligent, polite, and also the owner of the ship. The captain tried to mitigate the depression by engaging Charles in conversation as often as he could, taking all his meals with him, making certain the man's hygiene was attended to daily. But this seemed to have a negative effect on Lord VanderMeer's disposition, as if all the care and attention only emphasized his helplessness.

The ship was flying the orange-white-blue Dutch tri-color on the stern and the banner of the House of Brunswick atop the mainmast. Upon sailing into the harbor of La Rochelle, these colors and the banner drew immediate attention from the port authorities and the French navy. A saluting cannon was fired. Signal flags were raised inside the fort. Captain LaTour recognized the flag-order to advance no further into the harbor. He reefed most of the sails and circled outside the main anchorage until a harbor pilot was rowed out to him and taken aboard. Captain LaTour was directed to a privileged spot in the harbor, there to anchor. The French anchored a thirty-six-gun heavy frigate nearby as a show of respect.

The air was chilly, but the skies were clear. Captain LaTour had Lord VanderMeer brought topside in his wheeled chair so he could observe and participate in the welcoming activities. A large harbor launch rowed toward them. From their manner of dress, he counted three dignitaries aboard.

They would no longer be alone. Lord VanderMeer used their remaining private moments to hand Captain LaTour some letters.

"Captain, please ensure these missives are couriered privately and as quickly as possible."

"Of course, your lordship."

The missives bore the mark of Lord VanderMeer's signet ring pressed into the sealing wax. One was addressed to the Minister of Marine in Paris, Jean-Baptiste de Machault d'Arnouville, explaining his current situation and asking the minister to intercede for him with Governor Augustin de Drucour in Louisbourg, requesting sanction and strong protection for Lady VanderMeer and her children. One was to his father, Louis Ernest, Duke of Brunswick, announcing his arrival in France and detailing the route he planned to take in an overland coach from La Rochelle to Amsterdam. And the third was to Lady Corrinne VanderMeer in Louisbourg, explaining he'd arrived in La Rochelle and the arrangements he was requesting for her with Minister Machault. Charles had no doubt Minister Machault would make certain Corrinne and the children were adequately protected.

"I've asked the recipients addressed in my correspondence to reward the couriers if the seals are not broken. I do not want these letters intercepted."

"I will make certain of this. Do not be concerned, your lordship."

The dignitaries came aboard and once they certified that Lord VanderMeer was who he claimed to be, offered accommodations per his station inside the fort.

"I will have my naval surgeons attend you as well," the harbor admiral offered.

"I plan to stay but one night before continuing my journey to Amsterdam. I will leave by overland coach in the morning. If you please, Admiral, could you also recommend a coach company I can trust. I request an armed escort. My father, the Duke, will send a cavalry escort to meet me somewhere on the road along the way."

All of Lord VanderMeer's excess baggage was brought topside, much of it paintings. The painting he'd finished of Anamosa during the crossing he left on board in the care of Captain LaTour to deliver back to Lady Corrinne. Except for his personal bags, everything else would follow him in a separate wagon.

"With permission, lordship, I will join you later at the fort. I have ship's business to manage."

"Captain, you do not have to go with me any further."

Captain LaTour squinted at this ridiculous comment. He shook his head. "My lord, you are my friend. I promised to take you to Amsterdam and I will go with you on this road journey to be certain you get there safely."

After Lord VanderMeer was moved aboard the harbor launch, Captain LaTour informed the crew they would be paid. A cheer went up.

"Those of you who wish to visit families in Le Havre or anywhere else, feel free to go, but return by the end of January. At the end of January, I plan to have the ship dragged from the water to dry dock and conduct maintenance much as we did last year. Victorio will be in charge while I am away. In the meantime, I need six volunteers to stay with the ship for watch rotation at twice the pay."

The ship's business completed, Captain LaTour arrived at the harbor fort only a few hours after Lord VanderMeer. He found Charles already bathed and resting comfortably in a bed inside the fort.

LaTour was impressed. "You've been cleaned and put to bed already? No food or drink?"

"I need the rest more." Charles pulled a dangling cord next to his bed. "But if you are hungry, let us dine here in the room."

Servants appeared in response to the bell. Charles ordered fresh baguettes, butter, fruit, various fromages, and a bottle of Bordeaux to share.

"If I may, what did the naval surgeons tell you?"

"Oh, they confirmed my paralysis is permanent," Charles replied lightly. "They meant well. They are used to dealing with men paralyzed by war. But they also warned I have suppurating sores on the bottoms of my feet that need to be cleaned and bandaged every day to prevent the rot."

LaTour suppressed his frown.

The servants abruptly returned. Charles had a bed tray and LaTour had a small table set before him. Once they were gone, Charles continued.

"It will be a long journey. We will stop only for a few hours at each relay stable to change driver and horses. The admiral organized an army ambulance coach for me. It has three beds in the carriage, a large one for me, and two that fold-up during the day—one for you and one for the attending surgeon ordered to go with me. There will be nine cavalry mounts assigned to escort the ambulance and my baggage wagon."

"*Nine* cavalry mounts?" Captain LaTour was impressed. "That's a guard of honor."

"My father is Captain-General of the Netherland armies." Charles smiled. "The French want to retain the Dutch Republic as a neutral friend. Do not be alarmed, but they are worried another assassination could be attempted on me during this journey."

*

Word spread around the naval fortress that Lord Charles VanderMeer, primary heir to the House of Brunswick, had arrived. He had never been seen before in person, at least not in France. Because of the war, this large coastal harbor and fort had a resident company of army courier cavalry, ready to carry dispatch pouches and important missives in several directions. The most secret and urgent of these missives were transported by a relay of such couriers. There were also spy networks that carried intelligence about the French to destinations in England and central Europe.

Within a few hours, eight of these special couriers were dispatched with the following news: *Lord Charles VanderMeer arrived alone in La Rochelle, France, and is now traveling by overland coach to Amsterdam.* A relay of couriers on galloping horses would soon reach Paris. Others would continue to Berlin and Prague. A few would go to the largest rival houses in the German states, to people who asserted a claim to any of the duchies of Brunswick, Lüneburg, and Wolfenbüttel in Bevern. One such person was Lord Brockaert Eschwege of Hesse.

Delivery of couriered messages was a permissible interruption of the royal persons at any time of day or night. Lord Eschwege stopped breaking his fast and accepted the sealed missive from the sweating courier. He read the short report and gave the courier a silver ounce before dismissing him.

His wife saw a thoughtful, quiet mood descend on Lord Eschwege as he gazed out the window.

"Something important, I trust?" she inquired from her seat at the other end of the long dining table.

"Um, yes. Lord Charles VanderMeer arrived in La Rochelle and will be visiting his father in Amsterdam in less than a week."

"The same man you met in Boston?"

"The very same man, I must presume."

A knowing smile flitted across her face. "Then an opportunity for our cause?"

"There is that, at the least. Except Lord VanderMeer arrived alone. Lady VanderMeer gave birth to twins. I wonder if they are still in Boston... I remember a report claiming she had left that city. Last year, a different report, stating she had returned. If Lord VanderMeer left Boston, I presume he would not leave his wife and children behind. But she does not accompany him."

"Maybe she remained in La Rochelle?"

"Maybe, but that fact would be in the missive. Lord VanderMeer must tell his father of their location. The Duke will want to know." Lord Eschwege pushed back his chair and stood. "I leave for Amsterdam right away. As the primary heir, Lord VanderMeer will be required to receive visitors. I intend to be among the first."

*

On a well-traveled road halfway between Paris and Amsterdam, surrounded by farms and vineyards, the overland coach from La Rochelle was met by two full companies of Dutch cavalry commanded by a colonel. Sent by Louis Ernest, Duke of Brunswick, they had received special permission from the Austrian ambassador to take cavalry across the Austrian Netherlands. The Dutch had brought a similar ambulance carriage, another oversized passenger carriage for the three doctors and one nurse, plus two cargo wagons for Lord VanderMeer's baggage.

Lord VanderMeer was pleased by the appearance of the Dutch. The French surgeon alighted from the ambulance to confer with the Dutch army surgeons.

"Give me that bag." Charles pointed at a bag hanging overhead among the thick corded netting. He fumbled through it and took out a purse full of gold and silver coins and counted out two gold pieces to give to his surgeon. Then ten silver ounces for the French cavalry.

Charles handed the ten coins to Captain LaTour.

"Give two coins to the captain and one to each of the troopers. They guarded my life. Please do this privately and give them my personal thanks. I will pay the surgeon."

That is the kind of man he is, LaTour thought. There was no precedent for Lord VanderMeer to be so generous.

The transfer of bags and passengers took twice as much time as a relay stop. The Dutch physicians insisted Lord VanderMeer be completely bathed before he was settled into the ambulance bed. The Dutch escort had even brought a bathtub with them.

The Dutch colonel commanding the cavalry was not keen on bringing Captain LaTour with them, but Lord VanderMeer overruled the colonel's preference, using an officious tone of voice LaTour rarely heard. If Charles was uncomfortable wearing the title of a royal, when it came time to assert himself, he did not hesitate. The colonel snapped to attention and saluted.

For the remainder of the three-day journey to Amsterdam, Captain LaTour rode in the passenger coach, only checking on Charles when the horse teams were changed. They talked quietly, lest they be overheard.

"One of the doctors is asking me questions," LaTour confided, "about Lady Corrinne's location and where our journey began. To be polite, I answered that Lady Corrinne did not sail with you. That we started in

Boston. He also questioned how you came to be paralyzed. I said it was an assassination attempt in Boston, but I did not have any more details. He did not seem to believe me, so I suggested he should ask you instead of me. After stating, *I will tell his lordship of your interest*…that seemed to shut him up."

Charles sighed. "My father will ask me too. And I must tell him, of course. I expect he will keep Corrinne's location a secret…at least for a while. It will eventually become known. I warned her in my letter she should return to Québec City or Montréal until the war is over. She certainly cannot come here."

"What about you?"

"The doctors do not feel my current vigor will tolerate another long journey. And they are right."

LaTour did not want to ask the obvious questions. The pause became prolonged.

Charles nodded. "Yes, Captain, it is as you think. I will not be leaving Amsterdam again. Even if I had the strength, my father would not allow it. He is aware of the assassination dangers. I explained all of this to Corrinne."

This information depressed LaTour. He did not press Charles further until they arrived at the ducal palace in Amsterdam. By then Charles had developed a fever and was hurried to bed.

Captain LaTour was shown to a room in the palace. He had never slept in a bed so big or a room so large in his life. It was intimidating. He was not permitted an audience with Lord VanderMeer until three days had passed and only because Charles ordered that his captain be brought to the room.

When LaTour stood at the bedside of Lord VanderMeer, he made jokes about the size of the room and bed, how much food was wasted on him, how he could not go to a privy without someone watching him, and that a small group of noblemen had gathered at the palace, all of whom pestered him with questions.

"I remain in my room most of the day to avoid them. Fortunately, it is big enough for me to take long walks. It is not as large as this one…but it has enormous windows and a small library. My lord, there are three valets helping me to dress and undress! I am attended by *two* women when I bathe, which appears to be required of me every single day whether I want it or not! I am humbled by all of this attention."

Charles' face was covered in beads of fever sweat, but he offered a tired, amused smile. He coughed a few times and cleared his throat.

"Are the women pretty? You've but to ask and they will sleep with you."

"God's balls! I would not dare to ask! But they *are* pretty. Is this a common practice for guests?"

Charles waved a hand to dismiss the servant standing near the door. When the door closed, he continued in lower tones.

"Among the royals, the practice is all too common. Most of them are amoral. The women can refuse, of course, but they would be dismissed from service." He pointed to a chair. "Sit my friend, I have more to tell you. My father confers with his brother Ferdinand in Brunswick. There is a need for general officers with field experience. Ferdinand has plenty. He will likely fight for Prussia. He is a favorite of Frederick II. My father and his brother actually fought against one another in the same battle in the last war. They are probably planning a way to avoid this from happening again. My father is expected to return later today. You can plainly see that my fever has gotten worse. The sores on my left foot have been claimed by rot. My toes are already black. The doctors want to amputate my left leg, below the knee. In fact, they want to amputate both legs as they expect there may be rot infecting my right foot already. They want to do this today, but I refused."

LaTour was saddened and alarmed. "But my lord, you cannot—"

Charles held up a palm. "I wish to talk with my father first. The surgery alone could kill me. All the doctors can think to do is bleed me for the fever, ply me with opiates I do not need, or cut away pieces of my body."

LaTour winced. "My lord, I…"

"Captain, I will be lucky to last two to three more months. I am at peace with this knowledge. With the time I have left, I want to plan for Lady Corrinne, Anamosa, Marcus, and Calypso. By the adoption and birthing records in Boston, they will forever carry my name. Philippe knows the truth, of course, as do you. Keeping my name could create advantages for them someday, but there could also be dangers. I explained this to Lady Corrinne in my letter."

Charles waved the captain closer and began speaking in whispers.

"Tell me about the men waiting to see me. What are their names?"

"They asked all kinds of questions about your health. I only remember one of them…a Lord Eschwege…and that was because he claimed to have met you in Boston."

"Lord Eschwege!" Charles' gaze sharpened. "I did meet him in Boston! Captain, you are in danger! Many of these men waiting to see me are enemies.

They want to know two things. How soon will I *die* and the location of Lady Corrinne so they can send an assassin for her and the children! They will never learn it from me, so they will try to learn it from you. And they are not above abducting you and using torture. Eventually someone at the palace will tell them. But you still have time."

"God's balls," LaTour whispered.

"Indeed. You need to leave here and go back to your ship as quickly as possible, or at least get across the border into France." Charles leaned out of his bed and pulled open the drawer of the bedside table. He withdrew three sealed letters. "Take these with you. One is for Corrinne. One is for Thomas Hancock's agent in London, a letter inside a letter. It asks him to forward my letter to Boston. Get an audience with Minister Machault in Paris, give him the third letter and tell him what you know. He will likely have orders for you."

The conversation stopped. Lord VanderMeer rested back upon the pillows. His elevated sense of alarm made his heart beat faster. He was breathing more heavily now. It was an effort to talk.

LaTour was uncertain. "My lord, are you in pain?"

Charles shook his head. "Not in pain. It's the fever. It exhausts me."

The captain placed a hand on the bed. "I do not want to leave you here alone…among these enemies."

Charles blinked slowly a few times, lost in thought. He abruptly extended his hand to the captain. LaTour took hold of it.

"I do not think it wise for you to see me again, Captain. I intended to present you to the Duke. My father would like you. And you would like him. But the Duke might ask you to stay longer and he would refuse you permission to leave. So, no. You are in grave danger. This is a good time to say good-bye."

"Good-bye?!" LaTour had just got into the room! He was not prepared for good-bye!

Charles VanderMeer's grip tightened on the captain's hand. His eyes were luminous.

"In my life, I have never met a captain more courageous or as honorable as you. But we have another common enemy, a *thing* far more malevolent than the men in the foyer downstairs. You know of what I speak. It is looking for Lady Corrinne because it suspects the châsse is with her. It has servants, too. They will also learn where she is."

Captain LaTour's hand developed a sudden tremor. "My lord…it is difficult for me…to even think on this…*thing*."

"I know, Captain. I understand. But your ship rests at anchor in La Rochelle's harbor. The men downstairs will shrug at learning this information. But the *wraith* will send its servants to board your ship to conduct a search for the châsse and question your crew. Or worse. You must return to the *Queen*, put to sea, and find another port. Go to the islands if you like. You have plenty of money. I grant you the freedom to sail where you please."

Captain LaTour was shaken by the thought. *The servants may board the* Queen*!?*

"What about Lady Corrinne? The *thing* will send its servants to Louisbourg, too. She must be warned…or taken somewhere else."

"Yes, Captain. I've explained all of this in my letters to her. That is why you must meet with Minister Machault in Paris on your return. Maybe he can order you to go to Louisbourg for some reason? Perhaps as a special courier? But I am tiring. I want you to go back to your room, gather up your belongings, go to the stable, select the fastest horse possible, and flee back to France." Charles saw uncertainty in the captain's eyes. "Captain LaTour, that is my final *order* to you."

Captain LaTour nodded. He cleared his throat once, twice.

Charles let go of the captain's hand and leaned over to the table drawer again. He pulled out the leather purse full of coins and held it out to the captain.

LaTour considered the offer of money absurd. He shook his head in refusal.

"Go on. Take it. The room servants will pilfer it all anyway."

LaTour reluctantly accepted the small sack. It was heavy.

"My lord, tell me there's a chance you will survive these amputations," he managed to croak, "and that we will see one another again. I beg you, sir."

"Of course there is a chance, Captain! God willing, there is *always* a chance. But right now, you must depart. Be discreet. Leave without announcement, lest you are followed."

LaTour felt awkward about leaving so abruptly.

"It's all right, Captain. You brought me here safely just as you promised. My father will protect me now. Remember to hug the children next time you see them, and give my love to Lady Corrinne. Buy presents to give to them from me. Now please! Bid me farewell."

After another long hesitation. Upon seeing Lord VanderMeer's gesture that he should leave, Captain LaTour nodded sadly.

"Dieu soit avec vous. Adieu, Mon Seigneur."

Captain LaTour did exactly as Lord VanderMeer ordered. It did not take too long. He did not have much baggage. The leather pouch of gold and silver coins came in handy for bribing the stable master. Before another hour passed, he was on a strong, healthy cavalry horse and moving west towards the French border.

On the road, he obsessed about what he had learned. He'd not anticipated that his ship and crew might be in danger too. He could not put to sea until they returned at the end of January. And the crew was scattered all over France seeing family. Maybe he could petition the port authorities to place armed marines aboard? Perhaps he could pay them for this? Or maybe he could get this ordered in writing from Minister Machault? *A better idea.*

It wasn't until he stopped at a travelers' inn for the night that he realized something was missing from the satchel he carried. His ship's log—detailing the sail from Boston to La Rochelle—was gone! In frustration, he dumped the satchel on the bed and overturned his clothing bag on the floor. It was not there. This log included entries about the visit to Louisbourg. For a few moments, he thought about going back for it. But the palace was eight hours of cold, hard riding and many miles behind him.

LaTour kicked the empty satchel across the room. He had brought the log with him just so something like this would *not* happen. *I should have checked that I had it before I left!* he lamented. *By now they all know where she is! I must get to Minister Machault!*

News spread quickly through the aristocracy in the Dutch Republic and other German electorates. Lord Charles VanderMeer, the primary heir to the House of Brunswick-Wolfenbüttel, was paralyzed. And he had returned to Amsterdam without his wife and children.

Lord Brockaert Eschwege was the first to arrive at the Duke's palace. Within hours of his arrival, he was secretly petitioned by agents of three different German great houses, all requesting his services. Brockaert knew the royals preferred a layer of separation between themselves and any foul assassination they planned. They desired plausible deniability. Knowing these aristocrats would never reveal their incriminating request to anyone else, Brockaert accepted a commission from all three houses who petitioned him on that same day! According to the doctors, Lord VanderMeer would soon be dead from the rot of his wounds without anyone's assistance. With this unexpected boon, Brockaert started working on where Lady VanderMeer rested her head each night. It was a mystery. No one seemed to know. Brockaert was certain Captain LaTour knew, since his ship brought Lord VanderMeer across the Atlantic. When Captain LaTour rebuffed all his questions along that vein, Brockaert bribed the captain's room servant, promising a reward in gold.

"Search Captain LaTour's belongings at the first opportunity. Look for any type of diary or a ship's journal and bring it to me."

This took a few days as the captain seemed reluctant to leave his room. It was unlikely the search would produce anything, but it was worth a gold coin as a bribe before someone else did the same thing. To his surprise, the servant returned in three days with not just any journal, but the *William's Queen* logbook! Brockaert almost hooted aloud at this stroke of good fortune! He must act with haste before the captain discovered the logbook was missing. Lord Eschwege left the palace without announcement or explanation.

Brockaert was on horseback and long gone before Captain LaTour returned to his room from his private discussions with Lord VanderMeer.

Lord Eschwege was full of optimism. This journey to the ducal palace had been productive. He'd learned two important things. First, Lord VanderMeer would not survive his paralysis. He was already infected with the rot. There was no need to attempt an assassination. The veteran military surgeons were specific and very certain. "If Lord VanderMeer does not die this month, he will certainly die before the end of January. It matters not if we amputate his legs. The rot has spread into his blood."

With Lord VanderMeer's death, the commission from the three great houses was already half-earned. But the second revelation was the most fortunate. The ship's log detailed the exact location of Lord VanderMeer's wife and children: the fortress-port of Louisbourg on Île-Royale. Brockaert was the first to know this invaluable information. And France was already soliciting mercenaries for that garrison. It would be easy to use that public solicitation as the means to insert his agents into the fort. It would take time to get there, a lot of money, and a skilled, ruthless assassin. Brockaert knew just the right man for this. Someone he had used before.

Brockaert rode hard for the rest of the day until he reached his home and told his wife the good news. The next morning, Lord Eschwege packed another bag, this time for a week of travel and had his carriage take him to the town of Darmstadt in Hesse. A French minister there remained in residence just to facilitate contracts for mercenaries. Once there, Brockaert sent a message by special courier to Captain Bergen Stoecklin, asking the officer to meet with him in Darmstadt without delay. He knew the man would come. While he waited, Brockaert contacted the local French minister, who managed the mercenary contracts, and offered to augment the garrison at Louisbourg, Île-Royale. In just one early morning meeting, Lord Eschwege received the lucrative contract. France evidently felt an urgency to make decisions quickly.

All Brockaert needed now was Captain Stoecklin!

Darmstadt, Hesse

Captain Bergen Stoecklin was a Swiss commander of a company of mixed mercenaries, seventy-two men in all. Sixteen were Swiss and the rest hailed from various German states. The captain was forty-two, a hardened mercenary veteran of multiple wars, rebellions, and colonial conflicts since the age of nineteen. He was also a pitiless assassin. He did not often accept such work, maybe once a year or less. And then only for the wealthiest and more powerful great houses of the electorate state members of the Holy Roman Empire. He preferred assassination work. He could do it alone and pick the time and place. He needed only to get close enough to the target, and it was over. He could make more money killing a single person than he could serving as a mercenary for a great power over an entire fighting season and with much less risk to his life. But assassinations had dangers, too. Principally, revenge from the family affected. He'd learned from experience to act with anonymity. He always devised a deceit to avoid blame and always fashioned an easy path of escape after a murder.

Captain Stoecklin saw a bounty of opportunities in this new war declared between France and England in 1756. There were armies marching every which way in Europe. Assassinating someone could be as simple as fighting alongside that person. This method came with a perfect explanation for the sudden death. *The victim died from violent acts by the enemy.* In one ironic battle in an earlier war, he stormed an enemy line by force and stabbed his intended victim, his commanding officer, once the objective was achieved. Ironically, he was paid in gold by the opposing house who hired him *and* received a decoration for bravery by the house he'd served at the same time.

But Bergen Stoecklin recognized he could get himself killed. War was exceedingly dangerous, filled with random, violent events. As they say, just be in the wrong place at the right time. So far, he'd avoided serious injury and death. But one could not tempt fate too often. Stoecklin had seen highly decorated soldiers become convinced they were protected from death by divine intervention, go on to do something foolish, reckless, and fatal on a battlefield. He mocked such notions. He did not believe in luck, spiritual or otherwise. He was a realist. He was also a mathematician, with a talent for equations and numbers, which he had discovered to his surprise as a young man. The mathematical statistics of a soldier's life expectancy resulted in a calculated prediction that Stoecklin's own days of war-fighting should have ended already. A high statistical probability existed that his death was overdue. Stoecklin desired just one more lucrative assassination in this new war.

Like a wish come true, a courier brought him the wax-sealed missive from Lord Brockaert Eschwege of Hesse. The message promised a great "reward"—more than he had ever earned before—for performing a confidential mission.

Captain Stoecklin knew exactly what those words meant. He hastened to meet with Lord Eschwege in Darmstadt.

Unknown to Captain Stoecklin, two years earlier, Lord Brockaert Eschwege had been commissioned by Queen Anne, regent of the Dutch Republic, and mother to William V, who was still not old enough to ascend the throne. For personal reasons, Queen Anne wanted someone else to head the House of Brunswick-Wolfenbüttel. She intended to have the Duke assassinated. The revelation of Lord VanderMeer's existence complicated that plan. Lord Eschwege was commissioned by the queen to investigate the legitimacy of Lord Charles VanderMeer, a previously unknown heir to the Duke of Brunswick. If he was legitimate, Lord Eschwege was offered a larger fee to arrange the immediate death of Lord VanderMeer and any offspring that existed. Lord Eschwege learned Lord VanderMeer was not only married, but also Lady Corrinne VanderMeer was pregnant! But before Eschwege could successfully act on this knowledge, Lady VanderMeer and her children vanished from Boston.

Now he had another chance.

Anxious as Captain Stoecklin was to meet with Lord Eschwege, the Swiss officer intended to be cautious. He'd learned the victim was Lord Charles VanderMeer, the primary heir to the Duchy of Brunswick-Wolfenbüttel. And that Lord VanderMeer may have a daughter, which was unconfirmed. Lord Eschwege had acquired a long list of enemies. Stoecklin wasn't eager to have his name placed on that same list simply by association with Lord Eschwege. Then again, as this would be his last assassination, and given the prospect of the copious amount of money promised, maybe he could tolerate a few more enemies in his life? After this, he planned to retire to the Swiss Alps.

They met at the ancient ducal palace and sat across a table in one of the private quarters. After a few cordialities, the servants were dismissed and the tone of the conversation became blunt and to the point, as if discussing the slaughter of cattle.

"Lord Charles VanderMeer will soon be dead. I want the rest of his line extinguished."

"Where are they?"

"In the fortress-port city of Louisbourg on Île-Royale in New France."

"*Louisbourg*?! The amount of time it takes just to get there, perform this service, and get back will be four to six months—at a minimum! And there are dangers from storms while crossing the Atlantic. And avoiding the English naval blockade."

"You will be generously compensated for your time," Lord Eschwege countered. "I will arrange your contract with the French. They will provide warship transportation for your company of men. They number seventy or so, yes? You will be paid by the French as mercenaries for Louisbourg's Volontaire-Étrangers Regiment. But you, personally, will be paid much more for my work that awaits you there."

"I am anxious to hear the amount, but I have other conditions. I want a ship from a neutral country, preferably a Dutch ship, *not French*, arranged for my return. The captain should have specific orders to facilitate my transport. I will not do anything until I see this ship in the Louisbourg harbor and personally contact its captain. He must have orders to remain in port but sail immediately when I am aboard."

Lord Eschwege made notes on a writing pad. He was not going to let anything stand in the way of this agreement.

"Agreed. Before you sail for Louisbourg, I will give you the name of the ship coming for you and the estimate of its arrival. But I cannot promise you can bring all your men back with you. Maybe only a few."

"The objective is Lady VanderMeer?"

"Yes. You will need to find her when you get there. I have no intelligence on that, but she is there. Act discreetly. Give her no warning. She is undoubtedly guarded."

"So, there is Lady VanderMeer, and I hear a rumor of a daughter?"

Lord Eschwege nodded coldly. "Yes, the daughter must die, too. And Lady VanderMeer's twins…a boy and girl. They should be…almost two years of age by now. Them as well. The children are next in line as heirs."

"Two years of age? Babies?!" Captain Stoecklin's immediate inclination was to refuse.

Lord Eschwege frowned. "Your tone surprises me, Captain. Is this a problem?"

"Would it be a problem for you?"

Eschwege blinked. "Yes! It certainly would. But I am not a professional assassin. And you will be well-paid for this."

"I certainly *will*," Stoecklin replied loudly. This murder would be the most horrific he ever committed. "The commission?"

Their negotiations did not last long. Stoecklin insisted he be paid a third of the enormous fee in advance. Eschwege agreed but in return insisted that Captain Stoecklin and his men must depart for the port of Rochefort on the west coast of France without delay.

"My men need a few days to prepare."

"I give you three days. The French will provide wagon transport to Rochefort for your men, starting from here in Darmstadt."

*

Louis Ernest, Duke of Brunswick, rushed back to his ducal palace in Amsterdam, one of several he maintained throughout the Dutch Republic. He was anxious to see his son, Charles VanderMeer, now reported to be sick in bed and paralyzed. He had been conferring with his brother, Prince Ferdinand, for almost two weeks, discussing the war between England and France, the anticipated line of march and spring campaign objectives of the warring armies. They met with dozens of ambassadors and modified their diplomatic positions to keep the Dutch Republic neutral during this conflict. It would not be easy.

Prince Ferdinand of Brunswick-Lüneburg would accept command as a field marshal in the Prussian army. This would align the House of Brunswick with Prussia against the French, while Louis Ernest commanded the armies of the Netherlands and remained neutral.

The passionate arguments advanced by the competing powers in the middle kingdoms were complex. The larger great houses were taking sides with the Austrians, the Prussians, or the French. But even if they were not allied to one of the great powers, they still pursued claims to a variety of electorate titles within the Holy Roman Empire, citing birthrights by lineage going back five hundred years or more. And the Duchy of Brunswick was one of the most coveted.

Louis Ernest was very fond of his son. He looked so much like the boy's mother, a girl Louis had loved deeply, a girl who died long ago. Louis was barely a teenage boy when he met Mariel, a young girl whose father was one of the many people who tended the palace gardens. Mariel was just a few months younger than Louis. Tiny in stature, slender, with straight blond hair and huge blue eyes, she was a commoner and enamored instantly by the obvious interest of the handsome royal who came upon her by chance while out riding his horse. Louis was smitten by the girl's interest. He went out of his way to see her again and again after that chance meeting. He was awkward and clumsy, like any teenage boy. But Mariel was charmed. They kissed and touched. Their desire grew. Then in the twilight hours of a warm summer evening, lying beside one another in a field of sweet-smelling garden grass, surrounded by the groomed beds of flowers, Louis professed his love for Mariel. She did anything he asked from that moment forward.

Months later, when she became heavy with child, Louis did everything he could to get her the best doctors, the royal ones. He professed his intention to wed Mariel. Louis' outraged father, Albert II, refused him permission to marry a commoner. He threatened Louis with the loss of his privileged aristocratic status. Louis quickly vowed obedience to his father, under the condition no harm would ever come to Mariel. She must be protected. "And your tryst must be kept a secret," Albert II demanded of his son in return. Thus, in secret, Louis married his one true love anyway, in a church. The secret marriage was never officially sanctioned nor even acknowledged by Albert II. To the devastation of Louis, young Mariel died during the difficult childbirth of a baby boy, who she named Charles just before she hemorrhaged. Albert II considered the girl's death a fortunate outcome. He considered the baby boy another royal bastard and established the fictitious last name of VanderMeer for the baby. Albert II arranged for a generous financial stipend for the rest of Charles' life. And that was that.

And that should have been the end of it. Except Louis had married Mariel in the *Church*. And the *Church* kept records.

Louis Ernest had never married again. He could not get over losing Mariel. And he had not acknowledged any heir, until the secret that was Charles VanderMeer became widely known. Charles was reputed to be the only heir in the Duke's line, until more recent news arrived, announcing that Charles had children.

The middle kingdoms were not pleased.

For now, Duke Louis Ernest was undisputed, although not unchallenged, as the Duke of Brunswick-Wolfenbüttel. Duke Louis Ernest had many cousins. Every year, the lines of claim to the Duchy of Brunswick were adjusted by deaths, by war, and through marriage. Many royals would not hesitate to arrange an assassination attempt of a rival claimant, so long as it did not start a war. But since war had already started, there could be little risk in such murders. Blame could easily be attributed to many people in many places. Louis Ernest had tolerated this threat every day of his life. He had no choice. It was a deadly concern. He took precautions.

But it was not tolerable that his son, Charles, had been attacked. Someone tried to assassinate him in Boston and more than once. They had almost succeeded the last time. And with Charles' paralysis and the creeping rot, they still might succeed.

Traveling back to Amsterdam with the Duke was Colonel Rutger van Boekel, his long-time aide-de-camp, unofficial secretary, confidential best friend, most trusted advisor, and remarkable problem solver. Rutger van Boekel was a man of many talents, someone who could accomplish almost any task the Duke gave him to do. One such task had been researching the validity of Charles VanderMeer's marriage to Lady Corrinne. He found records. The marriage was recorded by the Church. But the records were ambiguous. However, the Duke was pleased that Charles finally married. So Rutger did not assert his suspicions.

Colonel van Boekel had not dressed in a complete army uniform in over ten years, not since he'd served with the Duke in the last war. He did not plan to wear another one in the future, unless a task required it of him. Most of the time, he dressed in the guise of a wealthy Dutch merchant. It made it easier to do the things he was asked to do.

At the Duke's direction, the carriage moved faster down the road. It swayed violently back and forth as it approached Amsterdam. The Duke and his confidential aide held tightly to the hand stirrups bolted above the windows inside the carriage house.

"What do the doctors say about your son?" van Boekel shouted over the sound of galloping horse hooves.

The Duke grimaced and shook his head. "Nothing good. They say he has only weeks to live."

"Is there something I can do?"

"I am sure there will be once I sit and talk with Charles. It's been almost four years since I last saw him. He came alone to Amsterdam. I was hoping to meet his wife and children."

"I expect Queen Anne will try to take advantage of this."

"Of course. When is she not trying to take advantage of me? God knows what lies she has insinuated to William."

Louis Ernest was the Commander of the Netherland Armies and a close advisor to Prince William V of Orange, son of Anne, the Queen Regent. Prince William was only eight years old. His father, William IV, was dead.

The young prince looked up to Louis Ernest as a father figure, much to the displeasure of Queen Anne.

When the carriage arrived at the palace, the Duke went directly to Charles' bedchamber, even before he purified his appearance. He was not prepared to see the feverish, sickly man, drenched with perspiration lying in the bed. Charles no longer resembled the vibrant young artist he used to be. He had lost a lot of weight.

The smell in the room was atrocious. The Duke barked orders at the servants.

"Fan the miasma out of this room. Open the windows. Clean up this bed, and bathe my son!"

He took a seat by the bed and grasped Charles' hand.

"I'm here, Charles. I'm here. Everything will get better from now on."

Charles opened his eyes and smiled weakly at his father. "I am sorry to come back to you in such a condition. I'd hoped to bring Lady Corrinne with me. But it was too dangerous."

"Don't apologize. I thank God you are back. Are they feeding you correctly?" The Duke frowned as he looked about him and then spoke angrily. "They are certainly not caring for your condition, from what I see."

By now a dozen servants had flooded into the bedchamber. Windows were opened, but only a little. It was still winter. A fan line was set up to circulate the air outside. A movable deep bathtub was wheeled into the room and was being filled with buckets of hot water. Other servants stood waiting by the wall with fresh bedding, some held soap and towels for the bath.

Two doctors now appeared and apprised the Duke of his son's condition. With every statement they made, Louis Ernest looked to Charles and confirmed it was his opinion, too.

The house chamberlain led a flock of stewards forward. "*Het spijt me*, my lord. We must lift your son from the bed to prepare him for the bath."

"But first we must examine the condition of his legs and skin," one of the doctors added.

The Duke's grasp on Charles' hand tightened. "They want me to leave the room," he said apologetically.

Charles smiled weakly. "Better if you do. What happens now is not a pleasant sight. Please come back when I am more presentable. I've much to tell you."

The Duke stood. "I've much to tell you, too."

"Oh, wait! Back there, leaning against the wall." Charles abruptly pointed toward the back of the bedchamber. "In one of the valises, there is a portrait of Lady Corrinne. I brought it for you."

"A portrait?" The Duke was pleased. His expression changed to intense curiosity. He went to the back of the room. There were a dozen different valises filled with paintings. "Which one?" He began to open them one at a time.

"You will know her the moment you see her," Charles promised.

Eventually, the Duke came upon a portrait that made him stare in awe. It was a woman of extraordinary beauty. *This must be her.*

Lady Corrinne was sitting in a chair, her head turned slightly to the left, gazing at the painter. Her expression confident. A slight smile to her lips, inviting, pleased with the person who was looking at her. She wore a richly colored dress of a deep verdant green. Her blond hair was braided and gathered up. A gold circlet, an ancient Celtic style, set with a large purple jewel in the center, crowned her head. Around her neck hung a necklace with a teardrop-shaped diamond. But it was her deep green eyes the Duke found to be the most compelling. Her gaze was suggestive of welcome and warmth. Charles had captured the nuanced expression of a woman waiting for someone. It was a portrait of love.

Louis Ernest carried the portrait canvas carefully by the edges over to the bed. It was three feet wide and five feet high. He held it so they could both admire the work.

"She is stunning, Charles."

"Thank you. I know. I painted this for you, Father. It is a gift."

"I am honored! I will have it framed and hung before this day is over!"

When the servants pulled back the covers, the Duke winced at seeing the blackened feet. It was indeed the rot. The stench was overpowering.

"I will return to you again in a few hours." He turned to leave and heard Charles moan as they began to lift him from the bed.

The Duke carried the portrait with him to his chambers and laid it upon the bed. He sent for the resident portrait artist.

Three valets appeared. They attended and undressed him from his traveling clothes. Another bathtub was wheeled into the room and filled with hot water. The Duke eased himself into the wonderful warmth of the water, but he did not relax for very long. The valets assisted with the soaping and washing. Before an hour passed, he was clean, dried, and dressed in the formal attire befitting his station as the Duke of Brunswick. By then, the palace artist arrived.

Together, they admired the quality of Corrinne's portrait.

"This painting was done by a master," the artist complimented. "Who is the portrait of?"

"For the time being, her identity will remain a secret. Even to you," he added with emphasis. "But I want this framed immediately so it can be mounted on the wall."

"Yes, Your Grace. Where would you prefer it be displayed?"

The Duke pondered this question. "Place it in the center of the hallway, outside of the state dining room. We will take down one of the older relics to make room."

"Yes, Your Grace." Most of the portraits on those walls were of deceased individuals, but of royal blood. The artist would not have dared to remove any without express orders.

"Get the framing done right away. I want her placement to be prominent in that hallway, today! I will go down and select one of the older ones to be moved somewhere else."

The Duke pulled a chord to order food brought to him. Both the household chamberlain and the house butler answered the call.

The household chamberlain spoke first. "Your Grace, Lord VanderMeer has been bathed and is resting in fresh bedding. He claims he would like to design a wheeled chair for his use."

"He is an artist and a designer. Bring Lord VanderMeer whatever materials he needs to make his drawings and arrange for the proper craftsmen to visit with him...Furniture makers or carpenters, I presume?"

"Yes, Your Grace."

The butler spoke next. "You rang, sir."

"Bring some noonday food to eat. And locate Colonel van Boekel. Have him join me."

"Yes, Your Grace."

The chamberlain cleared his throat. "There are eleven people waiting who seek an audience with you." He handed the Duke the list of names.

Louis Ernest scanned the names. He'd met with each of them with his brother, Ferdinand. Now they wanted to talk with him *alone*.

A manipulative bunch, every one of them. They must have ridden cavalry horses to follow me here so soon.

"I will see them later today. Organize them by order of importance... but I will see the English ambassador first...then the French...and then the Prussian. In that order. Inform my son I will dine with him tonight."

As the chamberlain and butler left, Rutger van Boekel entered.

"All three ambassadors await me. Let's eat and discuss what they will ask."

*

Two hours later, Louis Ernest walked down the hallway adjoining the state dining room and studied the different portraits. Rutger was with him.

"Not a very happy looking tribe, are they?"

"They seem to say, *I've not had a good toss in bed in over a century.*" In private, Rutger took liberties with the Duke that others would not dare.

The Duke grunted and smiled.

The palace portrait artist followed them at a respectful distance. He moved the newly framed painting of Lady Corrinne on a hall trolley, covered and protected by a white sheet of fresh canvas. He'd scavenged an ornate gilded frame from a damaged painting. It encompassed this new one perfectly. Behind the artist were four workmen with tools and ladders to use in hanging the portrait.

Louis Ernest finally stopped.

"She does not look happy," Rutger remarked as they assessed the painting in front of them. "Maybe she was tossed only once?"

"Yes, I would say so." The woman in the portrait was rather plain-looking. The Duke read the brass-engraved plaque beneath the portrait. "*Rosine Elisabeth Menthe, wife to Duke Rudolph Augustus in 1681.* Hmm, seventy-five years ago. I've not heard her name mentioned before." He turned to the artist. "Was she important?"

The artist hurried forward. "No, Your Grace. Madame Rudolphine, as she was addressed, was a commoner. It was a morganatic marriage, arranged only a few months after the Duke's first wife died."

"Then no surviving family to offend by moving this one?"

"Not in my opinion, Your Grace. She had no claim to any title or land after Duke Rudolph passed."

"Then lower the duchess. Move her somewhere else...respectful, but less conspicuous."

The artist gave orders to the workmen to mount the new portrait. When it was up, the Duke, Rutger van Boekel, and the artist stood across the hallway to study it. The painting was new, so the colors were still vibrant. Even if that were not the case, the realism captured by the brush of the artist was unmatched. The palace artist suspected the painter had mixed his color pigments with glass that was milled into a fine powder. This would make the colors catch the light. The painting stood out, conveying more majesty than any other portrait up or down the hallway.

Rutger was strangely quiet. He had not said anything as the painting was raised.

Louis Ernest smiled broadly. "She is magnificent, yes?"

The palace artist nodded with admiration. "This painter possesses exceptional skills, Your Grace. Everyone will want to know the painter's name…most certainly the name of the lady in the portrait. I expect they will ask me, and when I do not reply…"

The Duke frowned with annoyance. "Don't become choleric! Everyone will find out, eventually." He repeated his earlier assertion in tones that came from the general in the man. "But not from me, and not from you. It will officially remain a secret, unless I deem otherwise."

"Y-yes, sir."

The Duke looked at Rutger. "You've not said anything." The man's expression was one of surprise. "Rutger?"

"Your Grace, may I speak with you privately."

Addressed so formally by a man who was allowed to eschew formality when in private, the Duke immediately directed the artist and workmen to move away from them.

"What is wrong?"

"Your Grace, I am at a loss how to say this. I know Lord VanderMeer was the artist, and I can only assume *that* is a portrait of his wife. But I tell you with all sincerity, that woman looks exactly like Madame Margaux-Lyneth Dubonnet, wife of Colonel Gustave Dubonnet de Arras. He is the commander of the Auvergne Regiment, forted near Amiens."

"What?!" The Duke was taken aback. "That is impossible! Do you imply my son painted an imitation? You are mistaken!"

"No, my lord. I believe Charles VanderMeer painted his wife, Lady Corrinne, as he asserts. And this is her portrait. General Hollenberg saw her in Boston, when you sent him to investigate. He described Lady Corrinne to me, and you too, if you recall. I do not say this carelessly. I met Madame Dubonnet three years ago when you sent me to confer with Minister d'Argenson in

Amiens. He hosted a dinner for about a hundred guests. Madame Dubonnet sat directly across the table from me at that dinner. We conversed together at length. She was very charming, very intelligent, very engaging, and very beautiful. So much so, I *never* forgot her. She made an impression on me."

As he spoke, Rutger gestured at the portrait, repeating the movement several times for emphasis.

"My lord, I swear to you. Madame Dubonnet looks exactly as Lady VanderMeer was described to us…down to the color of the blond hair and the green of her eyes. This cannot be a coincidence."

Louis Ernest shifted his attention to the portrait, then to Rutger, and back again to the portrait. Rutger's words—*this cannot be a coincidence*—resonated in his mind. *This needs to be resolved right away*, the Duke decided.

"Colonel van Boekel, I want to meet personally with Madame Dubonnet as soon as possible. I can go west but must remain in Dutch territory. Pick someplace discreet, where we will not create too large a distraction."

"As you wish, Your Grace."

The Duke pointed at the portrait. "And we will take Lady Corrinne with us when the time comes. Tell the artist to take her portrait down and create something to protect it when we carry it with us. But not in this heavy frame."

*

Early in the morning, a day later, Rutger van Boekel rode west out of Amsterdam with a seven-man cavalry escort selected from the Duke's horse regiment. The colonel wore elements of his Dutch army uniform, the pants, but not the coat, his sash, his sword, but most importantly his gilded gorget with House of Brunswick coat-of-arms, symbols of his military rank, and engraved with the word *ambassadeur*. Rutger had already selected the small Dutch village of Aanwas as the place for this meeting. It was ten miles north of Antwerp, yet still within Dutch territory. He had been there before. The road through it was well-traveled and safe.

They reached Aanwas by midday the second day and rested the horses. His cavalry escort remained there. He gave the officer in charge orders to reconnoiter one of several local lodges to find a discreet but secure place for a meeting. The next morning, Colonel van Boekel rode alone into Antwerp and called upon an Austrian general he knew who provided a two-man escort of cavalry to the French border, another two days of riding away. His nose was nearly frostbitten from the winter winds.

At the French border, he presented his credentials to the French officer in command of a small detachment of border troops. After some polite questions and answers, he continued his way without an escort, towards Amiens. The road to Amiens was also well-traveled with the movement of small companies of French troops, all marching towards France's eastern border. It was apparent the French army was repositioning its strength for the next fighting season.

He reached Amiens after a cold, hard day of riding when his horse suddenly came up lame. He got off the mount and walked it the rest of the way to the military stables. He identified himself, stating official business with the Auvergne Regiment and requested attention for his horse. Because of his rank, clearly presented on the gorget, his horse was stabled. The officer in charge said his presence would be announced to the regimental commander. He was directed to the hotel reserved for people conducting official business.

Rutger van Boekel collapsed into a bed and slept for ten hours. He awoke before sunrise the next morning, ordered a bath, and dressed in fresh clothes while his others were cleaned. He broke his fast and couriered a message to Colonel Gustave Dubonnet, commander of the Auvergne Regiment. The message was short, identifying who he was and reminded the colonel of the last time they met. To that he added:

I carry a very important message from his excellency, the Duke of Brunswick. It is of a personal nature for you and your wife. It is imperative I meet with you as soon as it can be arranged.

This was the part of Rutger's mission that had the greatest uncertainty. His message would be verbal. To contact a regimental colonel would be considered presumptuous in times of peace, much worse if France was at war. If the French received him with the slightest suspicion, it could lead to his arrest as a spy. But the message would induce a reaction, of that he was certain. *Now, all I must do is wait.* He chose to do that in the atrium.

*

Colonel Gustave and Madame Dubonnet were breaking their fast together when a courier delivered a sealed missive to the mansion.

Gustave set aside his fork, broke the seal on the letter with a knife, and read the message.

"Well, this is interesting." He passed it to his wife for her to read.

The words—*and your wife*—in the message provoked the intuition and intense curiosity of Margaux-Lyneth. She clearly remembered the flattering gaze of this intelligent Dutch officer from a dinner three years earlier. *Why is Colonel van Boekel here to see Gustave? And representing the Duke of Brunswick!*

"This is important, Gustave," she asserted abruptly. "We must go to see this ambassador. And meet with him privately."

"What?! Privately? No, I will simply bring him to my headquarters."

"No! This meeting must be conducted in private."

I should never have shown her this, Colonel Dubonnet rued. He'd seen his wife's moods shift like this, many times. She was impulsive and unpredictable. One of the reasons he loved her.

"Madame, you don't even know what this is about!"

"Neither do you, Gustave! France is at war. And you just received a personal message from the Duke of Brunswick. He is commander of the Dutch armies, yes? So why is the commander of the Auvergne Regiment getting a personal message from the head of a foreign government?"

Gustave experienced a moment of déjà vu, not unlike the cavalry attack on his flank that collapsed his line during the last war.

"*Mon Dieu*, Madame! We've only just broken our fast. It is too early in the day to accuse your husband of treason!"

Margaux smiled indulgently. "Gustave, you know what I mean. I do not think this meeting should be conducted in public. That is all. Colonel van Boekel is patiently waiting for us at the ambassadors' hotel. Let's go to him now."

"Now?!"

"Yes. This day holds no other surprises. Meeting with the Dutchman will give us things to talk about later."

There was a tiny attention bell on the table. It tinkled merrily when she rang it.

The chamberlain responded. "*Oui*, Madame?"

"Maurice, have our carriage brought around."

"*Oui*, Madame."

"Margaux! The message was addressed to me!"

Madame Dubonnet exhaled loudly, stood, and walked to the other side of the room.

"The message said *and your wife*," she reminded him pointedly, then examined her face and hair in the mirror. "Now don't be petulant. We are going together."

Colonel Dubonnet sprang to his feet, annoyed. "I say no!"

Margaux-Lyneth walked over, pressing her body against her military husband. She smiled, kissed, and lightly licked his lips.

"And I say, we are going together. And you will let me, Gustave, because you love me, and later I will make you very happy!"

Colonel Gustave Dubonnet de Arras had been wounded three times in battle. He was celebrated by his men for his courage and bravery. His wife obtained his surrender in only five minutes. He gazed into her compelling green eyes.

"God help me, I do love you."

*

Rutger was sitting in the open atrium of the hotel with a dozen other residents, sipping coffee and reading the two-day-old shipping newspaper from the port of Le Havre. Suddenly, the hotelier hurried towards the main entrance with his concierge in tow and began fawning over the unexpected arrival of the commander of the Auvergne Regiment, Colonel Gustave Dubonnet, and his elegant wife.

Madame Dubonnet accepted the polite greetings and compliments while her eyes danced over the room. Spotting the Dutch officer, she smiled broadly and swept towards him, her husband in tow.

Rutger was dressed as a civilian merchant again, but he wore his gorget, so it could be seen. He stood up and snapped his heels together in attention.

"Colonel Dubonnet, it is my pleasure to see you again." They shook hands. "And Madame Dubonnet." He bowed and said, while raising her fingertips to his lips, "I am once again utterly enchanted."

"Colonel van Boekel! You flatter me too much. Such a welcome surprise," she said.

The hotelier and concierge hovered nearby.

"*S'il vous plaît*," Colonel Dubonnet said quietly, "*café et croissants*."

Rutger pulled out a chair for Madame Dubonnet at the table he'd chosen because it offered relative isolation in one corner of the atrium. Once they were seated, the fourth chair was removed, and the table was quickly reset.

"Thank you both for agreeing to see me so soon after my ambiguous request. I will not waste your time or gracious indulgence. First, let me affirm that I am an ambassador and speak on behalf of Duke Louis Ernest of the House of Brunswick-Wolfenbüttel. He ordered my confidential mission to see you. It concerns a matter deeply personal to the Duke."

At that moment, the concierge and two waiters arrived with the coffee and croissants. They began to pour and serve before retreating to a respectful distance.

"Did you journey by carriage?" Margaux asked to fill the lull.

"By cavalry horse, Madame. From Amsterdam, it was five days of cold riding. Fortunately, it did not snow. I arrived last night. By carriage, it would likely take seven days."

The servants left the table area.

"And your mission?" Colonel Dubonnet asked pointedly.

"Yes, Colonel. But I must first tell you a story. The day before I left Amsterdam, the Duke invited me to see a portrait of the wife of Lord Charles VanderMeer. Have you heard of that name?"

They had not.

"Lord Charles VanderMeer is the Duke's only child and his heir. The portrait of Lord VanderMeer's wife was presented to the Duke by his son as a gift. The portrait is magnificent to see. The woman I saw in this portrait…is identical in appearance"—he gestured one hand respectfully—"to Madame Dubonnet. Yet, this woman resides in the fortress port of Louisbourg on Île Royale."

Margaux-Lyneth set down her cup. "She resembles me? What is the woman's name?"

"Her given name is Corrinne. She is addressed as Lady Corrinne VanderMeer."

Margaux-Lyneth looked at her husband. Emotions flew across her face.

Gustave reached out his hand. "My love, what is wrong?!"

"We were young, maybe two years of age, when we were separated. I cannot recall my real parents. I cannot recall the place. But I do remember my sister's name. It was Corrinne," she replied in a choked-up voice. She looked off in the direction of the window. "I used to talk with her while looking in the mirror, pretending she was still with me. But I gave that up long ago."

They talked for almost two hours. Rutger told them what he knew of Lord and Lady VanderMeer, explaining his knowledge was recent history, no more than three years old. He offered the details of how they purportedly met and where they were married. He spoke of Charles' artistic talents, how the Duke had decided long ago to keep the relationship with his son a secret, for Charles' protection. Gustave had questions regarding that. Rutger explained what he could, but added it would be better for the Duke himself to reveal more.

"Madame Dubonnet, the history of Lady Corrinne's childhood family has been difficult, near to impossible for me to determine, as the Duke asked me to do three years ago. I am hoping…if she is indeed your sister…I am hoping that you have information you might share?"

"A moment, Colonel," Gustave interjected. "Before my wife starts sharing information with you, and while we appreciate this remarkable story, which has obviously provoked strong emotions in my wife…what is it you want?"

"A very good question." Rutger nodded thoughtfully. "His Excellency asks to meet with you both. And he will bring the portrait of Lady VanderMeer with him for you to see."

"And his son?" Margaux asked quickly.

"Unfortunately, Lord VanderMeer is very ill and lies in bed in Amsterdam. That is the reason he is not with me here today. The Duke will travel to Aanwas, a town inside Dutch territory, but only ten miles north of Antwerp. The Duke cannot leave the Dutch Republic while war persists. He invites you to meet with him in that town."

"Impossible," Gustave replied immediately. "I cannot be absent from my regiment."

"I will go," Margaux added without hesitation.

"No, you will not, Madame! We are at war!"

"Gustave, unless this is a miraculous coincidence, the lady in the portrait is my sister. That alone gives me reason to go. But this also means I am related to the Duke of Brunswick, by my sister's marriage to his son. As are you, I presume. We, you, France, cannot refuse an invitation from the Duke of Brunswick. The travel will be through the Austrian Netherlands, France's ally, then on into the Dutch Republic, neutral in this war. I will go."

Gustave threw his napkin on the table. Margaux had overstepped. She was not going anywhere, not without him. He played another card.

"Colonel van Boekel, if the Duke of Brunswick requests a meeting with us, I must first receive permission from my commanding general, Minister d'Argenson, and since this concerns Lord VanderMeer's wife residing in Louisbourg, I am certain the Minister of Marine, Jean-Baptiste de Machault, must also be consulted. That will take time. There will be questions."

"I understand. This is an unusual request," Rutger replied in a respectful voice. "Please inform your ministers that the Duke of Brunswick will consider this a personal favor." This last was stated in a tone to suggest the Duke would, indeed, be offended if the ministers did not agree to his wishes. "And Madame, the Duke hopes to meet with you before his son dies."

CHAPTER 3
LOUISBOURG, ÎLE-ROYALE
DECEMBER 1756
Marquis de Vauban

The militarization of the port of Halifax on Nova Scotia began in 1749. It was England's answer to the fortress-port of Louisbourg, two hundred miles to its northeast. It placed English naval forces within two days of sailing to meet the enemy when the next war came. There would always be a next war with France. Indeed, it came.

The recent intelligence on the English army staging in the port of Halifax over the fall of 1756 was not much of a surprise to the French governors of New France. The surprise was the rapid growth of this troop consolidation, now alleged to be five thousand regular redcoats with another ten thousand in the port of New York. Ensign Henri Gerrard had brought this intelligence back to Louisbourg after receiving it from the French spy in Boston. A force of that size was now a threat to Québec City by river assault, just as much as an invasion landing was to Louisbourg. Governor Vaudreuil in Québec City reacted by sending a coded letter back to Governor Drucour, ordering the return of the Québécois' marine battalion. They were only on loan. Presumably, Governor Drucour could not refuse. Drucour did not speak to his subordinates regarding Governor Vaudreuil's letter, nor did he send back an acknowledgement.

Governor Drucour held a council of war to discuss the possible English intentions based on this new information. It didn't take long, and the consensus was unanimous. If the English could organize a naval fleet with troop transport ships of sufficient size and numbers by April, Louisbourg was the likely target for the summer fighting season. It was closer to Halifax. Naval support would be much easier. The English would make a landing in Gabarus Bay, as they had in 1745, and begin a siege with forces estimated to be four times the size of the current Louisbourg garrison. Based upon the expanded troop strength, if the English made a successful landing in

Gabarus Bay, Louisbourg would fall, just like it had in 1745. Unless France sent naval and troop relief.

As word of the war council's assessment spread throughout Louisbourg, the civilians of the faubourgs demanded to know the governor's intentions. Drucour assured them that the Minister of Marine, Jean-Baptiste de Machault, Comte d'Arnouville, already planned to send more troops to reinforce the garrison, as weather permitted. There would also be a fleet of warships deployed to defend the harbor.

Drucour's assurances were exaggerated. In truth, the governor was not in possession of any direct communications from Minister Machault regarding Louisbourg's defense, other than France's long-standing intention to defend its most important port in America—should the time come to do so.

To add substance to the governor's overconfident words, he ordered the garrison to further strengthen the fortifications already built for defense in Gabarus Bay. The men of the garrison groaned and grumbled. They knew better. They could cut down all the trees for a mile in every direction to build more fortifications. The problem was, there were not enough troops in the fort to get behind the existing logs, let alone any new ones; certainly not with the numbers needed to be effective. But good soldiers that they were, they did as they were ordered.

In parallel to his public face, Governor Drucour sent more coded missives by courier ship to the Minister of Marine, urgently requesting reinforcements, munitions, and a full naval squadron to be based in the harbor at the beginning of the 1757 fighting season.

Minister Machault will comply, he assured himself. *He's received the new intelligence on the troop strength in Halifax and New York. He knows the threat is imminent.*

But privately, Drucour still worried. With formal war declared in Europe, the huge land armies of the great powers would be maneuvering when the fighting season began. History had proven that France worried more about defending its eastern borders, and the king's throne, than any of its colonies in America.

If the current winter ends early, the fighting season could begin by April! January, February, March... That was only three months away! Troops? Ships? Time estimates? Drucour had not heard anything. If plans for the relief of Louisbourg existed, they had to be in progress now to be successful.

*

"Louisbourg will not survive a siege, unless reinforced!"

This startling consensus by the senior officers in the war council reminded Ensign Henri Gerrard of an opinion from a certain garrison colonel he'd befriended a year earlier. Standing together atop Lighthouse Point back then, the veteran officer had gestured sweepingly at all the cannon and stone defenses of the fort. "The fortress is impressive, yes?" he confided to Henri. "Do not state this to your men, but you should appreciate that for all its stone bastions and cannons, Louisbourg will not survive a formal siege longer than three months."

What? Would not survive? The colonel was serious! How could that be?

Henri was unaware of the basis for the colonel's opinion. Henri had crawled up and down and across every bastion and battlement in the fort numerous times out of curiosity. He considered it impregnable. He was stunned to hear this mighty fortress could be subdued in only three months! Plus, he had labored for a year, month over month, until his hands were bleeding, to create the outer defensive works at Gabarus Bay. Now to accept that if the English established a landing anywhere on Gabarus Bay, Louisbourg's fate was sealed? This was a fortress, miles in length, with stone walls and stone bastions, packed with heavy cannon in strategic locations, and invested by thousands of soldiers! It would be supported by the French navy, which was part of the plan for its defense. To assert the fort's loss by siege was inevitable as soon as the first English boot touched the beach? It did not seem plausible.

After the council ended, Henri visited this same garrison colonel in his private quarters and reminded him of their conversation a year earlier atop Lighthouse Point.

"The war council consensus seems rushed and implausible, Colonel. What do I not see?"

But the senior officer logically affirmed his year-old prediction. "Ten thousand redcoats led by competent officers can surround this fortress in less than two months. If they blockade the harbor entrance and bring enough siege cannons, they will simply shell us into surrender."

"But how can you be so certain? I mean, why did we invest all our effort to fortify the bastions and construct the outer breastworks in Gabarus Bay if the outcome favors the English no matter what we do?"

"An excellent question, Henri."

The colonel rose from his desk and retrieved two books from a heavy trunk containing his personal library. The first and second volumes of a tome written by the famous French fortification genius, Sébastien Le Prestre, Marquis de Vauban.

"Here, Volume I, 1704, *Treatise on Sieges and the Attack on Fortresses.* And Volume II, 1706, related to the defense of these same fortresses. You may borrow these books. You've never had any formal military training. It is time you study and understand such things. These texts are familiar to every senior officer in European armies, be they English, French, Prussian, Austrian, or otherwise. Come back and see me when you have absorbed the text and performed the lessons contained therein, and we can talk more about it."

"Yes, sir. Thank you, sir."

Ensign Henri Gerrard had read a lot of books during his deployment at Louisbourg. Many of them he borrowed from Corrinne, which she had borrowed from the governor's library. But he came to conclude the most important books he would read were these texts written by Vauban. They were ornate and beautifully bound, of course. But they were not books of history or poetic verse. These were texts on accepted military doctrine. They took longer to read and were scientific, based on mathematics. It required Henri relearn his algebraic geometry, scalars, and gave him practice with a ruler and compass.

To assess his mastery of the concepts taught, he made an accurately scaled map of the Louisbourg fortress and its surrounding topography down to Gabarus Bay to give him something to mark up; the final work belonging to him alone. He carefully studied the lesson-like descriptions. He performed the calculations as they related to Louisbourg's fortifications and did the measurements as suggested. The diagrams in the books were beautiful. The sketches inside the text included many of the most famous fortifications in Europe. They were far more sophisticated than anything built at Louisbourg. Nevertheless, Marquis de Vauban, step by step, detailed the siege methods to use to overcome even the most formidable of these magnificent structures. The conclusion was always the same. Follow the rules, and no matter how strong the fort is made, given enough time, it will fall. The only hope was for a relief force to come to the fort's aid to break the siege. If the fort is built on land, that meant an army, or the navy, if the fortress was a port.

When Henri's map was complete, he presented it to Corrinne, and endured her perceptive questions as a test of the conclusions. Regrettably, she agreed with the marquis!

"The Marquis de Vauban was a genius," she stated with admiration. "Why do you frown?"

Shortly after Christmas, Henri returned the books to the colonel.

"Thank you, sir."

"Back so soon? So, what did you learn?"

"As you predicted, applying the tactics to Louisbourg as the Marquis de Vauban outlines in his texts, Louisbourg will fall, in three months or less, as you said. Unless the English walk slow, or it rains a lot."

The colonel heard lingering doubt in the young officer's voice.

"You do not say this with any conviction. Why?"

"Marquis de Vauban has not considered the fighting acumen of a garrison. Personally, I think we will give better than we get."

"Really? Well, I think so, too, Ensign." The veteran smiled sympathetically, recalling that time in his youth when he was also this fearless. "But first, do you trust the integrity of Vauban's rules or not? Yes? No?"

"Not to be impertinent, Colonel, why did we spend so much time and effort building the outer works at Gabarus Bay?"

"You've said the word yourself. *Time!*" The colonel emphasized this declaration with a pound of his fist. "It's all about time! Gabarus Bay is the place the English landed when they last lay siege to Louisbourg, which they did successfully in 1745, using an amateur force of men. They will land there again. Our objective in a siege will be to forestall the enemy every way we can. To make the English pay a bloody price for any landing and every advance on land. Make them pause to recover from their wounds. The strength and defense of those outer works will earn us extra *time* for the French navy to come to our aid. But even if the English blockade the harbor, which they will do, we can still win. Many things can happen. The weather may change for the worse. It's happened before. The English sailors may become ill. That has happened before. If the siege becomes prolonged, the English may run out of food, or gunpowder, or ammunition. If we can last until the winter months, and the fighting season ends, winter weather will force the English to withdraw. The longer we hold out, the better our chances of breaking the siege. However, even if we survive this year, the

English will learn from their mistakes and try again next year…if they want Louisbourg bad enough. Which seems to be the case."

Henri shook his head. "Then no matter the valor of our garrison, the end is still inevitable?"

"The garrison could fight with the valor of the Seraphim. If the English decide any sacrifice is justified to invest the Fortress of Louisbourg, it will fall. *Unless,* France responds with similar sacrifice in men and ships to prevent the fall. That is the simple rule of siege warfare. Marquis de Vauban describes how to conduct a siege with efficient, mathematical precision. Given enough *time*, all wars come to an end. That could happen too…but I doubt it will be this year or next."

Henri left the colonel dispirited. The fort's strategy brought to mind the fatalistic lesson Sentry Cheever had taught him. *If three men with bayonets come at you together, what can you do to survive?*

*

A few days into the new year, Governor Drucour received another missive from Governor Vaudreuil in Québec. This one was not encoded. This one was written in large, florid script. There had been no reply to his previous letter to Drucour and Vaudreuil was angry. This letter included separate pages of official orders addressed to Major Péan. The major was ordered to march the battalion home, that sleds would be provided to transit the frozen river if necessary. They would be staged and waiting for the marines near the river mouth at the fishing port of Gaspé. Vaudreuil ordered Péan to march south to Port Toulouse and arranged for any type of vessel to transport the battalion to Gaspé.

To Governor Augustin de Drucour, Vaudreuil demanded correspondence in reply, citing specifics of the Québécois marines' departure from Louisbourg.

The rumor that another letter arrived from Governor Vaudreuil spread around the garrison. Only a few senior officers besides Drucour knew the contents verbatim. An opinion in the resulting gossip emerged that the Québécois marines had been ordered to march as soon as possible. By coincidence, the Fortress of Louisbourg was experiencing a rare period of sunshine. Good weather, like bad weather, passed overhead in a curiously circular pattern. Theories claimed you could tell this by the constantly shifting direction of the winds or the accompanying clouds, if any. Nautical experience suggested this welcome respite of sunshine could last for several days…but sometimes less. It was a perfect time for the marines to start their journey back to Québec City, or so they hoped. But Québec City was over six hundred fifty miles away as a bird flies!

Major Péan was abruptly summoned to see Governor Drucour. Vaudreuil's disrespectful letter put Governor Drucour in a very foul mood, according to his aides. Without permission, Major Péan brought his staff of marine officers with him: a captain, three lieutenants, and three ensigns, one of whom was Ensign Gerrard. Péan thought the larger presence of officers might dilute the governor's venom. It did not. Governor Drucour was still fuming from the terse context of Vaudreuil's letter.

They came to attention.

Surrounded by his officers, Drucour's expression soured further at the smugness he falsely perceived in the major's face.

"I have the impression, Major Péan, that your governor considers me his subordinate. What is your opinion?"

Drucour handed the entire letter to the marine major, including the pages detailing Péan's new orders.

Péan read it quickly. He was elated to read his personal orders. *Holy shit! We can leave today if we want!* But Péan wisely suppressed his joy. He addressed the governor with flattery.

"I do not believe this poorly worded missive is meant to be disrespectful. Unlike you, my lord governor, I think Governor Vaudreuil is intimidated by the troop build-up in Halifax. They do not need ships to attack Québec City. They can march overland and cross a river. Letters I received from my wife relates that General de Montcalm is preoccupied by a belief the English will move north in a winter invasion of Lake Champlain, using snow shoes, skates, and sleds. They can move very fast on the lake ice, crossing both lakes in four days, all the way to the Richelieu River. Montréal sits directly at the end of that river. It would fall quickly. Montcalm is outnumbered three to one and possibly worse if you count the augmented troops, the Americans. All the regular metropolitan troops are in a defensive stance behind the walls at Fort Frédéric or Fort Carillon. If Montréal falls, this leaves Québec City isolated and defenseless. It has only a small garrison of gendarmerie to use as a military force. The city is still protected by the frozen river to the east. The English regulars cannot come that way, not yet. But the American scout companies could skate down this river. That is the greater threat. I conclude this is the reasoning behind Governor Vaudreuil's decision. He wants us to return now…before the river thaws."

Henri was stunned by what he just learned. Not about the English threat. He was still absorbing the revelation that Major Péan was married!

How do I not know this? Is she the woman he kissed in Québec City?

Péan had never mentioned anything about having a wife!

Unknown to anyone else in the room, Governor Drucour had received a second missive, one from Jean-Baptiste de Machault, the Minister of Marine. It arrived on a courier schooner out of Brest just a day earlier than Vaudreuil's offensive communiqué. The good news, Minister Machault confirmed reinforcements were indeed planned and would be conveyed soon by ships. The promised troops were mercenaries. Drucour was not pleased to hear that. He did not like mercenaries. But troops of any kind at this point were welcome. Machault indicated a fleet of ships would be deployed and based in the harbor for the duration of the fighting season. That was very good news. Drucour was encouraged to hear something so positive. Except, the French government was fickle in its conduct of war. Drucour would not presume any part of Machault's promises were reliable, until he physically saw the mercenaries and the warships sail into the harbor.

But there was also annoying news from Machault. The minister validated everything asserted by Lord and Lady VanderMeer. Machault ordered that Lady VanderMeer must be protected. Because of the war, serious threats had arisen against the House of Brunswick. Actions taken by enemies of the Duchy of Brunswick could extend even to the port of Louisbourg. In stiff words, the minister said he would hold Drucour directly responsible for her safety.

Directly responsible!? Drucour felt besieged already. First by the English troop build-up with Louisbourg as its primary objective. Second, by the dictatorial words of Governor Vaudreuil, as if Drucour had no choice but to obey. And now Minister Machault's warning to protect Lady VanderMeer.

Even with Major Péan's diplomatic explanation of Vaudreuil's missive, Drucour was not mollified. Vaudreuil knew that if Louisbourg fell, Québec City was next. Vaudreuil just didn't care. Just as Drucour didn't care what happened to Lady VanderMeer. He had bigger problems. But his wife, Marie, cared. That trumped any of his feelings.

"You may keep the pages outlining your orders, Major. I give you leave to act on them at your discretion. Present your plan of march for my approval. By this afternoon!"

Péan wanted to do a dance of celebration, but he remained respectful. "Yes, sir."

Drucour suddenly thought of a way to irritate Governor Vaudreuil.

"One more topic for discussion. Minister Machault has directed me to safeguard Lady VanderMeer until he can arrange for her departure. I am directed to assign a personal guard with this responsibility. I order you to select a platoon of your marines to remain in service to the Louisbourg garrison in that capacity. You may inform Governor Vaudreuil of Minister Machault's direction in this regard. I want a list of the marines assigned to this task by name and rank, with the name of the officer in charge. Present this to me with your plan of march. Any questions?"

"No, sir."

"You are dismissed."

*

Like everyone else in the faubourgs, Corrinne had heard rumors of the war council's assessment. Louisbourg was the primary target for invasion by the English. Accompanying that news was the depressing prediction the fortress would fall only a few months after a siege began. Like Henri, she thought the assessment to be overly generous, that is, until Henri came by and laid out the elegant artistry of his personal siege map on her table. He had detailed it with angles and trench lines to explain exactly how the siege would be conducted. He explained how all of this came from a book written by the famous French fortification architect, Marquis de Vauban. She could see the genius behind the architect's conclusions and said so.

"It is plain to me that Louisbourg will fall to the English."

Henri was not pleased with her opinion.

"But…but Vauban never considers the valor of the defending garrison! He claims it is an unpredictable variable and does not matter. That at best, it only adds to the time length of the siege. I do not agree his conclusion is unequivocal. What if we win the battle? It could happen!"

Corrinne smiled at Henri's certainty, the educated, articulate way he explained his beautiful map and its calculations. But whether or not Louisbourg was in the English battle plans, Corrinne planned to leave this place anyway, by April at the latest, most likely to Québec City, preferably Montréal. For that, she needed Philippe to come and get her. And since he had not answered any of her letters, all she could do right now was hope, wait, and pray.

Corrinne's best friend in Louisbourg, Marie-Louise de Drucour came by to see her. Marie was like a walking Boston newspaper. Her husband told her everything, but she could tell no one else. She badly needed someone to be her confidant. Corrinne was the only person Marie trusted to keep a secret, or any other information she gleaned from her husband.

After Marie fussed over Anamosa and the twins, the two women sat at the table and sipped tea together.

"Thank you for bringing me this wonderful sunshine," Corrinne said, cheered by her friend's presence.

"I've much to tell you. Yesterday, Augustin received another letter from Governor Vaudreuil. It was not coded. It was terribly rude and disrespectful. Vaudreuil demanded the Québécois marines return to Québec City without delay. Agustin summoned and met with Major Péan just a few hours ago. He gave him the written orders from Vaudreuil. The marines are leaving us."

"But…but that does not make any sense. It is winter! The river is still frozen!"

"Well, the Québécois marines plan to march from this fortress tomorrow morning," Marie stated firmly. "They are going to Port Toulouse and from there to Gaspé."

"Tomorrow morning!? They are marching *tomorrow*?"

"Well, that is the rumor. The marine barracks are bursting with activity. They are packing wagons full of supplies. Augustin was ordered in another missive from Minister Machault to have you *guarded*. Augustin ordered the marines to do this."

"What?" Corrinne grappled for words. "Guarded?! From who?"

Marie had no answer for this question and looked surprised. "I thought you could tell me."

Machault must know something, Corrinne thought. *There must be a letter from him to me!*

Corrinne decided to learn, firsthand, the truth to all these rumors and the intentions of the marines…and Henri. After Marie left, she sent a messenger to Major Péan with an invitation to dinner.

*

Major Péan had his officers follow him back to his quarters.

"You heard the governor, our departure is at my discretion. I am pleased to announce the Québécois marines will leave tomorrow morning. It is a seventy-mile slog through snow and mud on the primitive road to Port Toulouse.

Once there, we will organize any available river transport to take us across the strait of Canceau to Gaspé. Sleds are waiting for us there."

Péan outlined his plan of march to Port Toulouse, wagons for the food, ammunition, and tenting. He assigned each officer duties for this preparation.

"Regarding the platoon to remain behind with the garrison to protect Lady VanderMeer, we will first ask for eleven volunteers before we select the unfortunate individuals."

Henri did not hesitate. "I volunteer."

Péan ignored this offer. "Everyone is to pack lightly. They may be forced to carry these packs all the way to Québec City. If there are no sleds in Gaspé, we will march overland to the south side of the river and use the scouting road to march the rest of the way. From Gaspé, it is a four hundred mile walk! There are only a few villages along the southern river bank. It is still winter! Bring snow shoes and ice skates."

Péan dismissed the officers, leaving him alone with Ensign Gerrard.

"A lot of marines will die during this march," Péan admitted sadly. "They always do." He turned his attention to Henri. "Now tell me why you want to stay in this icy dungeon of a fort?"

Henri was slow to reply. "The war council assessment. If the English decide to attack Louisbourg, the fortress will fall to them, like it did the last time."

"So what? That's war! Not even your extraordinary good luck can stop that from happening. And it's a good reason to leave this place."

"Except Lady Corrinne, the twins, and Anamosa will still be here. If the time comes that Louisbourg's fall is imminent, I want to be here to help them escape capture."

"There is a whole garrison here to protect them! You and eleven marine volunteers will not make any difference."

Henri remained silent.

The major fumed, sensing Henri disagreed.

"Are you still suffering from a head injury? All right, think about this. Must I remind you Québec City is where your red-headed girlfriend— *Madeleine?*—where Madeleine lies naked in a bed, diddling herself, and moaning your name!"

"I know!" Henri had thought about Madeleine…a lot. "And I disagree with you. It's about Lady Corrinne, the twins, and Anamosa. We could be the difference for them if a siege comes. I've already mapped how the siege will be conducted. The English will follow Vauban's rules. I will have ways planned to get out of this trap…should it come to that."

"Vauban's rules!?" Major Péan shook his head. "Henri, let me point out for the hundredth time, how fucking naïve you are. You base your expertise at rescuing Lady VanderMeer and her children in the middle of the chaos and carnage that will ensue as this fortress falls on your personal courage and the genius of a man who died fifty years ago?"

"Lady Corrinne is my father's wife," he said in a tone that stated he should not have to say this. "Marcus is my brother. Calypso is my sister. And I love Anamosa! Whether I choose to volunteer or not, they would still be here. I choose to stay with them. I will find a way," Henri said the last sentence with conviction, his expression had turned somber. This blunt admission, about family, was something Henri never talked about. Major Péan exhaled wearily. It was useless to try and change Henri's mind.

"Then think about this, Ensign. This is war. When this fortress comes under siege…and it will, you and all the other volunteers will be in danger just like every other soldier in this garrison. But the marines only take orders from you. There will be *deadly* consequences in every decision you make."

"I know."

This mutual acknowledgement punctured the tension in the discussion.

"What should I do now?"

"We are leaving the marine barracks empty. It will get filled by reinforcements, probably mercenaries. Get eleven volunteers and find a new place to billet them. Since they may die under your command, pick something decent. Maybe one of the large rooms under the Dauphin Bastion. Don't worry about who occupies it now. I will get Governor Drucour to approve it."

"Is there something else I can do to help you prepare for the march?"

"Well, since you've made the journey to Port Toulouse a few times, pull out that coveted map you made and walk me down the road."

Henri was only too happy to do that. He pulled out a map roll from the leather knapsack at his back.

Their discussion had just begun when they were interrupted by a loud knock on the door of their quarters. Major Péan, still smoldering over Henri's foolish obstinacy, winced with irritation.

"Enter!"

One of Péan's aides, a corporal, came into the room and saluted. "Major, a messenger just delivered this to my post." He held out a small roll of paper tied with a bow of blue ribbon. "He said to give it to you."

"Probably an invitation to another one of Madame Drucour's depressing soirees," he groused.

Major Péan had been snubbed by nearly every available female in the faubourgs. The parties were no longer entertaining, except as a place to drink brandy till one was drunk. But even that had become tedious.

"Dismissed."

The corporal saluted and left.

What Péan read made him frown. "Did you do this?" Péan held out the paper.

"Do what?" Henri read it. "No."

"Lady VanderMeer invites me to dinner…for the first time! Tonight, of all nights!"

"Maybe it's a farewell dinner."

"After all this time…I should refuse," Péan thought aloud. He saw Henri grimace. "Oh, don't worry. I'll go."

*

This place was supposed to be a haven, Corrinne lamented in a rare lapse of optimism. It was midafternoon. She was sitting in her favorite chair in the second-floor bedroom that looked out over the harbor waters.

It is more like exile, she noted, feeling lonely and isolated. An exile much worse than when she was hiding at Winter House in the village of Old Saybrook in southern Connecticut. At least there she had visits from Sentry Cheever, who brought her messages from Charles back in Boston. *No letters from Charles in this place*, she rued. *Not yet. And who would bring them? No letters from Philippe, either.*

It would be dark soon. The children were napping. She needed to wake them up before the sun set, so they would sleep through the night after dinner.

Dinner? Her invitation had been impulsive.

What is my purpose? What questions do I ask the major that I do not already know the answers to?

The English were amassing troops in Halifax, intending to attack and invest the fortress. No surprise there. They might do this in the spring. She needed to be gone from Louisbourg by then. That was her plan anyway. The fortress would fall if it was surrounded. Henri had already proven that to her.

Another reason to be gone by then. Marie-Louise made another trip to the house to say she just learned Ensign Gerrard had volunteered to stay behind along with eleven marines. Knowing how Anamosa felt about Henri, Marie guessed Anamosa was Henri's reason for staying.

Marie added in a more confidential tone. "I thought you should know."

But Corrinne wondered why, indeed, would Henri volunteer to stay? No matter what Henri wanted, he would first follow orders. *He was certainly drawn to that girl...Madeleine...in Québec.* Since arriving, Corrinne received two precious letters from Michelle, Henri's mother. Michelle had related the intimate tête-à-tête Henri once had with Madeleine. She reminded Corrinne that Madeleine was writing to Henri constantly and asked about him all the time. *Well, that's none of my concern. Henri is a grown man.*

Major Péan, however, was a contradiction. She had known this officer since arriving in New France with Philippe. *Mon Dieu! That was so long ago!* Yet this would be the first time she ever sat down to dine with Major Péan. She knew him as a man of poor moral character. He had been a corrupt administrator, working as the commander of the gendarmerie and reporting to Intendant Bigôt. But Major Péan was certainly not a coward. As a marine officer, facing the enemy in the field, he'd been commended for valor... more than twice. He once fouled the aim of Intendant Bigôt's pistol just as the intendant attempted to shoot her. It missed. Unfortunately, the ball grazed Philippe's head instead. But that was not Péan's fault. The major had a weakness, however; a blind spot. It was a big one.

There was a woman in Québec City by the name of Angélique des Méloizes. She was Major Péan's wife. Angélique was a member of the elite, aristocratic class of New France. She was beautiful and avaricious, which was why she married Major Péan. He had access to money, a lot of it, while he worked for Intendant Bigôt. And when he was absent in his duties as a marine officer, all the major's monies flowed to her. Angélique and Corrinne knew one another and were about the same age. But other than a respectful nod if meeting by chance in public, they had never spoken a single word to one another. Angélique considered Corrinne to be a peasant courtesan of the lowest class. Corrinne was *certain* that Angélique was a whore, because Angélique had slept with Intendant Bigôt when Major Péan was deployed on military missions. Not that Corrinne cared at all about what this woman did.

Michelle's recent letter had a few pages of the gossipy news of Québec City. Corrinne begged for such gossip to alleviate her boredom in Louisbourg.

According to Michelle, Angélique des Méloizes was now rumored to be sharing Governor Vaudreuil's bed.

First Bigôt and now the governor. *Interesting.* Of course, this could never be a topic of dinner conversation with the major. She doubted Michel Péan even knew about it.

Corrinne gazed at the glorious sunset reflecting off the harbor waters. She could not recall the last sunny day, or any sunny days after arriving in Louisbourg, until this one. They were lucky to have weather this lovely in early January.

If it is this sunny tomorrow, I will take the babies out for a walk. We will probably have a marine escort with us. Marcus will like that.

Corrinne hired a maidservant for the evening, someone who could prepare everything. She was one of the women who served Governor Drucour's table.

The major replied to the invitation and requested they dine at the hour of seven. And precisely at seven there was a knock at her door.

Both Major Péan and Henri had dressed in their cleanest uniforms. They looked very handsome, she had to admit.

"Welcome, Major Péan, Ensign Gerrard."

"*Bonsoir*, Lady VanderMeer," the major replied with a generous bow. "Thank you for this welcomed invitation."

Corrinne smiled. "We've all known one another for a long time, so let's leave the formalities behind for the evening. Please call me Corrinne."

"I am honored, Corrinne. Please call me Michel."

The maidservant encouraged Corrinne to have three chairs around the table already set for the dinner.

Péan spoke. "My lady, I appreciate your indulgence to begin the evening at seven. As you probably heard, the marines start their march to Québec City in the morning. We still have much to do in preparation."

"I prefer to dine early, Major…er, Michel."

The server filled their glasses with wine.

Corrinne raised her glass. "To your successful return to Québec City. May your journey be safe. I envy you."

With the sound of strange voices heard from downstairs, Anamosa could not contain Marcus and Calypso from going down to see who was there. When they appeared, climbing down the steps, Corrine rushed to them to guard against a fall. She took hold of Marcus, helped him to the floor and carried Calypso in her arms back to the table. Anamosa went directly to Henri and accepted his hug and kisses on both cheeks, her face beaming.

Like Henri, Major Péan had risen from his chair at the appearance of the children. Except Anamosa was no longer a child. He was stunned by her beauty, an extraordinary young maiden. He bowed to her in greeting.

"Mademoiselle. You have grown. You charm me with your presence."

Anamosa politely embraced and kissed the major on his cheeks.

Péan found the girl's subtle perfume mesmerizing. *Something she learned from Lady Corrinne, no doubt.*

Corrinne felt herself bristle at the embrace, but gathered Péan was being courteous. "Well, it appears my children have joined us for dinner. Please sit and let us continue."

The extra three chairs were brought to the table. Corrinne set Calypso on the floor and to her surprise and astonishment, the little girl walked straight to the major. He gave her a friendly nod and smile. Without warning, or permission, she climbed up onto his lap, placed her hands on his cheeks and gave him a tiny kiss! Then she smiled at him.

"*Bonjour,*" she said in a tiny voice.

Major Péan was instantly captivated by the marvelous gesture of affection from this beautiful creature he'd never met before.

"*Mon Dieu*! I am kissed by an angel. I am blessed," he reacted with sincere appreciation. "*Bonjour* to you too, Calypso."

Calypso smiled again, then turned her body towards the table and made herself comfortable on the major's knees.

"I am to be a chair for the evening…delightfully so."

Corrinne could not believe Calypso's comfort with the major. "Well, it appears my daughter finds you appealing. It must be the uniform," she added drolly. "I must warn her about soldiers!"

Péan was smiling joyously. "I am without words at this honor. My goodness! Lady Corrinne, Lady Anamosa, and Lady Calypso! I am surrounded by the most beautiful women in New France…and for certain in all of Louisbourg."

At Corrinne's gesture, the server placed hors d'oeuvres on the plates. Calypso did not hesitate and started eating from the cheeses and sweetbreads. Michel Péan was only too happy to help her.

"Thank you for your generous compliment, Michel. But I think it proper that the beauty of Angélique des Méloizes be mentioned first."

Péan's smile did not falter. "Of course, of course," he agreed. "I think Angélique would forgive me for this wonderful flirtation. Who could blame me?"

Anamosa had pulled a chair next to Henri and was smiling happily. Marcus pulled his chair next to hers. He concentrated on eating.

"Major, I must confess," Henri said, "after all our time together, I was not aware you were married."

"I make it a point never to discuss personal matters. Lady Corrinne's praise is accurate. Angélique is very beautiful. But my marines have an unfortunate habit of making crude comments about women. I would have stabbed several of them with my sword by now if I allowed such discussions to take place."

Corrinne decided to change the subject. "Michel, I am keen to understand why Governor Vaudreuil recalled you so abruptly. It is the middle of winter, after all."

Péan's eyes shifted to the maidservant.

"My servants do not gossip."

Major Péan used the same explanation he gave to the governor.

Corrinne contemplated the conjecture. "Is that possible?"

"Possible? Yes. But I do not feel the English possess the fortitude for a winter campaign."

"The rangers fight in the winter," Henri stated.

"As you say. But the number of those American scouts is small, less than half a battalion. They might raid, they do that often enough, but little more. They could still be a reason for Vaudreuil to want us back. My experience is that he usually has several reasons for his decisions. But whatever his reason, I am happy about this one! Spending the rest of the winter in Québec City versus Louisbourg? No comparison. Québec is the place to be."

"And the decision for a marine guard to remain behind to protect me? From where does that idea spring?"

Péan's smile towards Calypso relaxed just long enough to answer. "It was a directive by Minister Machault. I presumed it was a request made by Lord VanderMeer. He must believe you require protection from something."

The great houses, Corrinne concluded. *They must have learned where I am. And if they know, things even more evil will know, too.*

"My lady," Major Péan said, seeing Corrinne's expression turn serious, "I anticipate you already know Ensign Gerrard has gallantly volunteered to command the marines who have been assigned with the mission of your safety. And he has been decorated for his courage several times, which I have personally witnessed."

"You were there too, Major! So were a lot of marines." Henri did not like acclaim.

Péan looked at Calypso and confided, "You should know that I was considered the bravest of them all."

Calypso understood none of what he said. But she smiled and nodded.

"Will you do me a favor, Major?"

"Anything, my lady."

"I have not received a reply to any of the letters that I've sent to Philippe. Mail comes here from Québec almost every week. I am concerned. He has not answered me."

Again, Péan glanced at the maidservant.

"She is *trusted*," Corrinne assured him.

"I will be frank. First, I do not know the reason. But Captain Gerrard is probably at Fort Carillon with his *coureur de bois* scouts. Mail has come to Louisbourg from both lake forts to a few of my marines who have brothers in the militia. There is no question that mail flows in both directions. Knowing the people in Québec City as I do, including those who inspect and route all the mail, I would guess your mail to Captain Gerrard is being sorted out from delivery."

Corrinne's anger was visible. "Who would do that and why?"

"I can think of a few people who know both you and Captain Gerrard and would make it their business to know your business. Your guess at their identities would be better than mine. I cannot confirm anything, because I truly do not know. Your letters are undoubtedly somewhere, but I don't know the first place to look for them."

"Neither do I, Michel. But you are the one going back to Québec. Will you help me?"

"Of course, he will," Henri interjected quickly, so the major could not hesitate.

Major Péan was surrounded by three beautiful females, who, at that moment, were all looking at him. Even Marcus had stopped eating. *Help* was a word they all understood.

"I am a decorated hero," Péan spoke softly to Calypso. She smiled up at him. "This is the type of thing heroes do every day. Of course, I will help you. But this march is problematic. I may not get to Québec City for a month."

"That's sooner than I will! I say we eat dessert before the babies go to bed. Let's eat cake!"

*

Early the next morning, Major Péan dispatched his captain and a sergeant on horseback to Port Toulouse ahead of his march. He gave his second-in-command a purse.

"Do not run out of money," he warned the captain. "Take care of your horses. Report to the naval officer in charge of Port Toulouse. Give him this missive from me." He handed over a wax-sealed envelope. "Your mission is to remain sober and solicit the Port Toulouse boatmen for transport to Gaspé. We will follow you in less than a week. I want no delays in getting off this island."

"They might just keep going," the major said to Henri as they watched the two marines ride out the Dauphin Gate, carrying full packs. "Not that I could blame them."

The marines were divided into two divisions of sixty men each. One group in front of the four horse-drawn sledges, wheels tied to the sides in case the road became clear of snow. The second division of marines came last. The marines were ambling around their lines, anxious to get going.

Péan had just returned from saying his farewells to Governor Drucour.

"Here is the governor's authorization to occupy the small barracks in the Dauphin Bastion. Give it to the master-at-arms. Let him clear out the room."

Péan shouted orders to Color Sergeant Cabrelle to get the men back in lines for march.

"I still cannot believe Color Sergeant Gosse volunteered to be your second. How did you tempt that grenadier to do it?"

"He approached me and volunteered. He said Louisbourg is closer to France than Québec City. And if Louisbourg should fall and should he survive, the English would send him back to France."

A corporal brought Major Péan a saddled horse.

The major said proudly, "All the marine officers have horses to ride, even Color Sergeant Cabrelle. The voyageurs will bring the horses back with the wagons. It was a trade...I gave my word to deliver Drucour's hand-written reply to Governor Vaudreuil and got horses to ride." He turned and saw the marines line up in marching ranks. "Color Sergeant Cabrelle! Move them out!"

Major Péan got up on his horse.

Henri saluted the officers and men of the first group of marines. As they passed by, a few of them made lewd comments to Henri about where he could find the cleanest whores. He shouted his thanks.

Major Péan reached down and shook Henri's hand. "Do your duty, Ensign. Make us proud. Stay alive!"

Henri saluted. "Good luck, Major." It became awkward to say anything more.

Major Michel Péan stared hard at the young officer, as if memorizing his face. Then he nodded once and spurred his horse.

Henri watched Major Péan ride away to lead his column of marines from the front, like Péan always did. Henri considered the major one of the bravest officers he ever met. And Henri experienced a disturbing thought, that he might never see him again. The major's words lingered in his thoughts.

This is war, Ensign! There will be deadly consequences in every decision you make.

The second division of marines began marching past. Henri saluted and heard more friendly jeers shouted out to him. In a few more minutes, they were gone.

"What do we do now, sir?"

He turned to the intimidating hulk of Color Sergeant Gosse.

"I say we move into our new barracks!"

Color Sergeant Gosse saluted.

*

The absence of his fellow marines left Henri feeling hollow. He decided to walk out to one of the battlements, picking one that would not have many sentries who might plague him with questions he could not or would not answer.

The skies were clear. The winds were brisk and coming into port from the east, from the Atlantic. The air was damp and chilling. Henri was bundled up against the cold, wearing extra underwear, a long coat, scarves, and gloves. He decided to walk out to the cannon battery at Black Rock Point, *Cap Noir* as it was labeled on the nautical charts. It was the most isolated battery in the fort, far to the east of any other battlement and armed with only three cannons. But it had the best view of the sea approaches to the harbor entrance and could give alarm if a British cruiser ventured too close. It was constantly manned. On a clear day, like this was, a sentry could spot an approaching vessel, miles away. On the overcast and foggy days of winter, which was most of the time, the battery watch did little more than huddle around their coal stove to keep warm, crouched under the common tarp to stay dry.

The watch sergeant was surprised to see the marine officer trudging up the steep granite incline. He cursed and started kicking his men to stand up and look alert.

"Ensign Gerrard? What brings you out here?"

"I just want a place to sit and think for a while. Lend me your watch glass."

"Think? You cannot *think* inside a warm barracks?"

Henri frowned. "Are you telling me to leave?"

"No, sir!" The sergeant quickly handed over his watch glass. "You're going up there? To think?"

"Yes." Henri climbed up the stairs, chiseled out of the rock, to sit beside the small navigation light at the top of the precipice.

"Your thoughts will freeze up there, sir!"

Henri grinned. Normally, he only visited Black Rock Point when on duty. But the daytime skies were clear. He scanned the sea horizon for a few sweeps with the watch glass before settling down behind the rocky overhang beneath the navigation light and out of the wind. He became entranced with staring at the far horizon.

The governor had approved him staying behind and was pleased Henri volunteered. He began thinking about Major Péan's advice...*Deadly decisions make for deadly consequences.* Henri commanded the marines now.

It was only because he was staring at a fixed spot on the horizon did he suddenly discern three tiny masts that sailed into his line of sight.

He sat up straight and peered with concentration. It was a ship! But whose?

"Sergeant LaCorne! I see a ship on the horizon."

Shit! How does he do that? The sergeant trained the other watch glass in the same direction. It took a few seconds to fix on it.

"I see it, sir." The sergeant scrambled up the steps to stand next to the marine ensign. "Starboard side to us. It's on a southwesterly course."

"I agree. Make sure to enter this in your log." Henri calculated the distance. "Let's say we are fifty feet above sea level, times one and five tenths, equals seventy-five. Take the square root of seventy-five…that makes it a little over eight miles away."

Sergeant LaCorne looked at him with surprise. "Does that always work?"

Henri nodded. "Yes. That is the approximate distance. But the formula only works on a clear day when you can see the horizon. Still, that is probably an English cruiser out there. They know this formula, too. That's why they are staying right on the edge of the horizon. It makes them hard to see while on their patrols. Good to know, yes? I'd wager they will come a lot closer to us at night. A good lesson to remember."

CHAPTER 4
ROCHEFORT CITADEL
JANUARY 1757
The Mercenaries

The Hessian officer, Colonel Wilhelm von Kleinfels, professed loyalty to Frederick II, King of Prussia, France's former ally, but its enemy in the current war. Now allied to England, Prussia supplied regiments to them for the defense of Hanover. German mercenary regiments were also supplied to France because Prussia was only one of the many German states, albeit the most powerful. There were over thirty moderately large German territories in what was collectively referred to as the Holy Roman Empire, or the HRE. This quilt-work of feudal states was established centuries earlier during the rule of Charlemagne and occupied the center of Europe ever since splitting apart or being absorbed into larger states through war or hegemony. The great powers of the time referred to these states as the HRE, because it was the accepted way to refer to a place described by the French philosopher Voltaire as "something neither Holy, nor Roman, nor an Empire." They were all independent, or tried to be. They all had standing armies of various sizes, including Hesse. But unless they owned a gold mine, and the majority did not, the only income these lesser states could expect were the monies received from the wealthier powers of Europe in soliciting their professional soldiers.

German mercenaries were the finest in Europe. They were so coveted that these smaller German states might fight as allies in one fighting season, and as enemies in the next. If the money offered was high enough, sometimes regiments from the same German state fought as enemies and allies at the same time. Such was the condition of the perpetual land wars in Europe.

But whether the great powers of Europe were allies or enemies, year over year, they could agree on one thing. God help them all if the German states ever unified into one country.

Frederick II, king of Prussia, was obsessed with creating this German nation.

Colonel Wilhelm von Kleinfels of Hesse had sworn his allegiance to Prussia, but he responded to requests to supply mercenaries to fight for the French. Such a request came from the French Minister of Marine, Jean-Baptiste de Machault. Fulfilling this contract would maintain his unique position as a secret messenger between the warring powers of France and Prussia. King Frederick II was not opposed to Hesse providing its mercenaries to make money.

As long as these mercenary regiments are deployed in America, not in Europe.

Colonel von Kleinfels was physically very weak. He'd not half the strength he had a year earlier. He now walked with a limp and used a cane. His left hand had been amputated. The vulnax wraith had abandoned its full possession of Wilhelm von Kleinfels' enfeebled and crippled body for another servant, Alain Marcoux, a much younger man. Alain Marcoux, however, stood accused of the infamous assassination of Archbishop André Nicolet in Québec City. A change in name was necessary, and so it was done with a simple pronouncement.

Colonel von Kleinfels informed the French that Hessian Lieutenant-Colonel Karl Krieger would command and train this new regiment of soldiers for the French.

The vulnax wraith now fully possessed Lieutenant-Colonel Karl Krieger. But there was a certain danger in the possession of this host. Krieger might command mercenary troops in battle. What if the host was slain? The vulnax would be trapped in the dead body until an opportunity arose to possess another. The interval of time for this opportunity to occur was uncertain. Possession could occur only if a potential host had close contact with the corpse. But the dead host could be buried on the battlefield, or the body dismembered or obliterated by a cannon ball.

The vulnax commanded Colonel von Kleinfels to have a second gold-threaded pouch created. The potent bone shards from the ancient mountain tomb in Sankt Goarshausen were then divided evenly between the two pouches, one to be worn by Kleinfels, and one worn by Krieger. This provided better assurance that the crucial relics continued to exist.

Colonel von Kleinfels went to Berlin, available for summons at the convenience of the Prussian sovereign. He made frequent forays to Amsterdam to supervise the spies hired to monitor Lord VanderMeer in the ducal palace.

Unless tasked by the vulnax, his other priority was carrying messages between Frederick II and the French Minister of Marine, Jean-Baptiste de Machault.

Rochefort Citadel, France

The citadel of Admiral Dubois de la Motte was at the mouth of the La Charente River in the port of Rochefort, France. It was well defended with heavy naval guns and warships in the anchorage. From this place, the revered seventy-three-year-old French admiral launched sorties of ships and men to defend New France. English success in sea battles against this extraordinary naval officer had not improved with de la Motte's advanced age; just the opposite. But winning sea battles was not enough. France had a superior navy, for now, but England was building warships at an accelerated pace and had surpassed the French numbers. No matter the command superiority of French naval officers, this war would come down to numbers and attrition. France could win all the battles at sea, but it would soon run out of seaworthy ships. They were not replacing the ones they lost in battle fast enough.

Admiral de la Motte knew to win this war against England, France would have to invade the island. The English island nation was defended by the waters around it; the huge natural moats of the English Channel and the North Sea. Invasion had always been the plan in every previous war for hundreds of years. Yet, invasion had never happened.

The admiral regretted he had lived so long, because his country was losing this latest war. England was already invading New France with superior numbers of troops. France willingly deployed hundreds of thousands of troops in the field to defend the French borders in Europe. But only a meager number of metropolitan troops were deployed to defend New France. Unless something changed, France would lose its premier colony. After hundreds of years of successful colonization, Admiral de la Motte considered this an unthinkable and unacceptable outcome. Land was eternal. French claims in the North American continent represented two-thirds of the available land. It was the largest colonial territory in the world. New France was the symbol of the French empire. This war between France and England would determine future global dominance. Which of them would dominate the seas? Which of them would dominate the American continent? One of them would lose. That meant one of these ancient thrones of power would fall.

"New France must be defended at all cost, lest France's historical destiny as a global power be forever diminished," Admiral Dubois de la Motte complained to the Minister of Marine.

Financier Jean-Baptiste de Machault, Minister of Marine, the man responsible for the survival of the colonies, a man educated in statesmanship and economics, had performed his own assessment. He saw this same outcome coming, too. He had received urgent missives from Augustin de Drucour, Governor of Louisbourg, about the English troop build-up in New York and Halifax.

The Rochefort citadel was designated by Minister Machault as the place where new regiments of German mercenaries, contracted by France, would be formed up, trained, and deployed in the American war. Admiral de la Motte would direct their deployment to the right places in New France.

In an unscheduled meeting in late December, Minister Machault was called upon by Lord Brockaert Eschwege, a Dutch royal who was also contracting German mercenaries.

"Your lordship, I have assembled under a French contract two companies of soldiers, seventy-two men, a mix of trained Swiss and German veterans. They are commanded by a Swiss officer, Captain Bergen Stoecklin, who has over twenty-five years of experience. True, this is a small assemblage of veterans, but they are contracted and ready to deploy to Louisbourg. By now they are bivouacked near the Rochefort citadel. They only require a French warship for transport."

This was good news to Minister Machault, coming at the end of a deplorable month filled with bad news. Indeed, seventy mercenaries was a small force of soldiers, but any type of help for Governor Drucour would be welcomed.

"This transport can be arranged immediately. What else?"

"Captain Stoecklin is proficient in recruiting mercenary veterans. After he has seen to the proper integration of his men within the Louisbourg garrison, he must return to the German states and continue his recruiting efforts for me. I need a ship to transport Captain Stoecklin back from Louisbourg. Out of his concern for the English blockade, Captain Stoecklin insisted I give him the name of a Dutch ship, along with the name of its captain who will provide him this transport. He feels a neutral Dutch flag will minimize chances of his capture by the English. And I happen to know of a ship flying Prince William's flag, currently anchored in La Rochelle that meets this requirement.

Its captain and crew are French. I understand the captain confidentially reports to Admiral de la Motte. It seems predestined for this assignment."

Captain LaTour? Minister Machault was scheduled to meet with Captain LaTour the next day. The captain had just returned from escorting Lord Charles VanderMeer to Amsterdam.

Before the day was over, Minister Machault had written the orders to Admiral de la Motte to provide for the ships in question.

Lord Eschwege had Captain LaTour's name and his ship, *William's Queen,* committed to give Captain Stoecklin return transport from Louisbourg. This run of good luck was extraordinary! He commissioned a coach company to provide relay transportation to Rochefort to personally deliver the good news to Captain Stoecklin.

*

Lieutenant-Colonel Karl Krieger, *né* Alain Marcoux, had spent every day at the Rochefort citadel for the past three months as the new recruits flowed in from the east; most of the new recruits were deserters from the defeated armies among the warring German states.

One morning in early January, Krieger sat up in bed and swung his legs over to the cold stone floor. His quarters were small but adequate. The room was beneath the fort's main battlements and above the troop barracks on the ground floor.

It was still dark outside. He gripped his throbbing head and massaged his temples to ease the ache. The vulnax used Krieger's sleep to visit the dreams of his other servants. Consequently, Krieger never really slept. Rather than dreams, what he experienced was more like dark visions arising from a fever-ridden delirium. He awoke exhausted and the resulting morning headaches were almost debilitating until he massaged away the pain. Except, it never really went away, only subsided into a dull ache that never disappeared, even hours later. The vulnax was always there, in his head. Krieger retained lucid memories of what the wraith had done during his coma-like sleep. He understood what he must accomplish on any day. The training of the mercenaries he commanded was secondary.

This time the vulnax had visited the dreams of Wilhelm von Kleinfels, the Hessian colonel the vulnax once fully possessed. The man was crippled by a stroke brought on by the strain of that possession. His physical condition was too weak for anything too strenuous. But he could still gain an audience with the King of Prussia, Frederick II, as the accepted messenger between the king and the French Minister of Marine, Jean-Baptiste de Machault. And Machault was a confidential friend of Lord VanderMeer, the man who knew the location of the châsse. To that end, Kleinfels was an important servant. In the vulnax's visitation, Kleinfels was told to arrange another audience with the Minister of Marine under any pretense. Even anecdotal information about Lord VanderMeer might be useful in locating the châsse.

But these meetings were not informal. There had to be a specific objective involved, and a message initiated by the Prussian sovereign, Frederick II. Colonel von Kleinfels had to suggest something for the king to say. The arrangements would take time.

The British were expected to launch an offensive against either Québec City or Louisbourg in the summer fighting season of 1757, but French spies had not determined which fortress the British had chosen to attack. With the troops amassed in Halifax, Louisbourg seemed to be the chosen target. Even if the British had decided, it would be a guarded secret. The English would never acknowledge the objective, and the French would never admit to knowing anything. Just a few weeks of sailing advantage by the warring navies could determine success. Therefore, Krieger and his mercenary regiment would not learn where they were sailing until after they boarded the transport ships.

A normal crossing of the Atlantic took three to six weeks, depending on the winds and the weather. The transit courses to and from the naval port of Brest were patrolled constantly by a squadron of English cruisers attempting to intercept sorties. As the war entered its third year, this coverage now extended south to Port Louis at Lorient. But the French naval port of Rochefort at the mouth of Le Charente River was not so closely watched. Not yet. It was the perfect place to have a mercenary regiment billeted and made ready to deploy with a minimum of delay.

Lieutenant-Colonel Krieger's regiment was approaching half-strength. New recruits reported for evaluation every day. He was two months away from his goal. But when he learned two fully trained companies of mercenaries had recently camped outside of the citadel, he was interested to know their purpose. He rode out with his second-in-command, Major Sauer, to meet the commander of these companies.

Captain Bergen Stoecklin greeted the arrival of the two mounted Hessian officers warily.

"What do they want?" he questioned under his breath.

He saluted the Hessian uniform the colonel wore more than the seniority of the epaulets on the uniform. After introductions, Colonel Krieger inquired as to the disposition of Captain Stoecklin's troops.

"My men are under contract by the French already. We've come to Rochefort for immediate transport."

"To where?'

Stoecklin was not going to tell him this outright. "I will learn the destination when I am aboard the ship. But somewhere in America. I presume that means Québec City or Louisbourg."

Colonel Krieger's eyes widened. The fortress port of Louisbourg was a place where the whore queen might be hiding. It was also a direct line of sail to the west from Rochefort.

"If you will allow, Captain, I would like to add three of my men to your command. I will have a full regiment of mercenaries when I deploy. That will take more time for recruitment and training. My men will act as informal liaisons for me in preparation for my arrival. Mostly collecting information. They will follow your orders as all your other men do, of course."

If that was all this colonel wanted, Captain Stoecklin was agreeable. He was paid by the number of men he provided anyway.

Two days later, Lord Eschwege arrived, giving news to Captain Stoecklin about the ship he would use for his return. "Keep this information a secret, Captain."

In another two days, the French navy provided a second-rate ship-of-the-line with fifty-six cannons as the transport to Louisbourg. The mercenaries would billet between the guns, as none of the cannons would be removed for accommodation purposes. Among the seventy-five mercenaries that went aboard, three of them were blood servants of the *vulnax*.

Boston

In the first week of the new year, Rachel Bristol went to bed one night but lay awake as her thoughts dared the notion she might have a new and better life ahead of her. Not that she knew her future, that was still full of uncertainties. But she knew well what lay in her past: the evil association with people possessed by the compelling power of the *vulnax wraith*. Her homicidal older sister Caroline was dead in a showdown with the magistrate's men in Boston. Rachel would not miss her. The stone mason known as Ritter was shot in the head by Lady VanderMeer. He'd been another brooding murderer. Only Carter Trevathan remained. Rachel Bristol had not seen or heard from this manipulative, disgusting merchant since late September. He was a pig. Nor had she been visited in her dreams by the wraith since leaving Boston. It scared her even to think about that *thing*, as if the thought of the wraith would provoke a paralyzing visitation. So, she focused her thoughts on the future. Each new day absent of any invasive haunting produced another blossom of optimism.

The town of Cambridge where she chose to live had been a fortuitous decision. Most of the people in this town of colleges were educated, polite, and espoused modern thoughts in any conversation. Rachel had met and talked with many of them during her nursing duties at a local hospital. These people were different from the coarse mob of illiterates that seemed to dominate Boston. To her surprise, Rachel found herself enjoying each day. Days that soon became weeks. Weeks that now amounted to three months since her hurried escape from Boston late in September 1756.

Across the small room, she could hear the soft, even breathing of Jimmy Cantlin sleeping in his small bed against a wall. Back in Boston, Rachel had worked as a nurse at the Penny Surgeon clinic near the Long Wharf. She had befriended this young boy, one of dozens of homeless boys who wandered the Boston streets. She bandaged a cut on Jimmy's hand one morning and noticed the infatuation in his gaze. She continued to minister to his minor cuts and bruises and watched his infatuation for her intensify over time. Jimmy was twelve back then and came around the Penny Surgeon often, just to be near her. She nurtured his attraction, short of anything intimate, but enough to tantalize and get him to carry messages to Carter Trevathan, or to her sister Caroline at the Marine Society Hospital, or to run other favors for her when asked.

As the plan to slay Lord VanderMeer reached a peak, Rachel decided one day, she needed a plan to flee Boston. She made Jimmy part of it. A solitary woman, particularly one as attractive as Rachel, taking the ferry across the harbor for the first time might be noticed and remembered by the ferrymen at least for a few days. A woman accompanied by a young boy was less remarkable. She captured Jimmy's affections with suggestive innuendos and asked him to come with her, promising him they would live together somewhere new. Jimmy was a member of the street rabble who roamed the streets and markets in gangs, to thieve, pick-pocket, or assault other unfortunates to survive. Some of these boys were killed committing crimes, others taken by exposure or disease before they reached the age of sixteen. Jimmy's only family was a sister, a whore living in squalor somewhere down on the docks. He saw her rarely. And each time, she told him to stay away from her.

The attempted murder of Lord VanderMeer had failed, but had left Lord VanderMeer paralyzed. Boston's respected magistrate, Jack Tasker, was slain by Caroline in the effort. The public murder of a popular Boston magistrate, in the middle of the afternoon, in the middle of a Boston street, provoked an outcry among the populace, demanding justice.

Rachel was not directly involved with Tasker's murder but recognized the time to flee had come. "We need to leave today," she told Jimmy.

From the earlier suggestion of the chance to live with Rachel, Jimmy agreed immediately. "I have nothing to fetch. I am ready to go now."

Rachel fled Boston to avoid the magistrate's men. She guessed right. After capturing and killing Caroline, the magistrate's men started searching for the *sister*.

The city of Cambridge was a place to hide, if only temporarily. It was reputed to be quiet and the people courteous. Jimmy turned thirteen within days of leaving Boston on the ferry. It would become the life Jimmy had only dreamed about.

Rachel had been born Rachel de Propei, one of the two daughters of the Marquis de Propei back in Rouen, France. The Marquis desired no relationship with his daughters after he murdered their mother and had them committed to an institution for the mentally ill. Decades later, Wilhelm von Kleinfels, a Hessian nobleman bought Rachel's freedom, along with that of her sister's, from London's Bedlam asylum where they had been confined. He changed their last name to Bristol before bringing them to Boston.

In Boston, the last name of Bristol was now infamous, associated with the murder of the magistrate and the attempted assassination of Lord VanderMeer. Rachel assumed Jimmy's last name, Cantlin, after crossing the harbor, presenting themselves as brother and sister to the landlady of the apartment they now shared together. New immigrants arriving and settling in the outlying villages of greater Boston was a constant occurrence, nothing new. Rachel found work as a nurse. Jimmy went to a local school. The two newcomers were adjudged to be orderly, polite, and friendly. The brother-and-sister facade was accepted by the landlady and their neighbors. Their false identity was safe. The apartment was only two rooms: a kitchen and a bedroom. They slept in the same room, but Jimmy slept in the separate, smaller bed over in a corner.

Being across the harbor from Boston, Rachel expected her stay in Cambridge would not last very long. She anticipated someone would eventually come looking for her. But to her surprise, life for Rachel and Jimmy consistently improved. She cooked his meals and helped him with his studies. Under Rachel's constant care, Jimmy thrived. And she was no longer tortured by the nightmares. It was as if the wraith had vanished altogether. Could there be a better future for them right here in Cambridge?

Rachel Cantlin, *née* de Propei, *née* Bristol, harbored secrets from Jimmy. She was a skilled assassin and murderer, who would not hesitate to employ the most gruesome, painful poisons to achieve her deadly purposes. She had left multiple victims in her wake already. She was just as homicidal as her dead sister Caroline, only not as impulsive. The quiet and polite Rachel was far more intelligent and calculating. Far deadlier.

That night in early January as Rachel fell asleep with a smile on her lips, across the Atlantic Ocean, in the cities of Paris, Berlin, Prague, and Vienna, word had spread a month earlier of Lord Charles VanderMeer's unexpected arrival in Amsterdam. That a failed assassination attempt had left the primary heir to the House of Brunswick paralyzed from the waist down.

Absent from Lord VanderMeer's arrival in Amsterdam was the châsse containing the bone relics. The wraith had questions to ask all its servants.

Where is the châsse? Where is the ship? Where is the whore queen?

*

The attack occurred a few hours after midnight. Rachel was in a deep slumber when her body arched violently. She remained elevated in a painful balance on her head and heels. She did not come fully awake, ensnared in the dream-like dreadful emptiness, her arms and legs rigid with fear. The vulnax wraith's invisible tendrils slithered over her body, like ravenous centipedes. The tendrils searched for evidence of physical intimacies. Something hooked over Rachel's lips and entered her mouth. She tasted blood. She heard acute, high-pitched tones, insect-like whines. She abruptly recalled memories of past conversations. The perverse prodding and probing proceeded down her body and into her genitals. She dared not resist. It was useless to try. From experience, any type of struggle only provoked a stab of pain.

Find Carter Trevathan! Obey him!

The demand by the vulnax was repeated as the assault went on and on. Minutes elapsed before the onslaught stopped. Her body collapsed on the thin, straw-filled mattress.

Rachel gasped and gulped air as if she'd finally breached the surface from some deep watery blackness. Her throat was sore and dry.

Water!

She'd suffered attacks like this in the past...none of them this bad. She had endured them all. Experience taught her the night visitor could cause her pain, but it could not injure her physically. At least it hadn't yet. All her hopes and expectations for a peaceful future were now dashed.

How could I be so stupid?

Taking several deep breaths, her panting subsided. Her sensibilities returned. Desperately thirsty, she got up and walked on unsteady legs across the room. At the dresser, she lifted the water pitcher with both hands and drank until she could drink no more. The water was as icy cold as the air in the room. She felt a chill on her legs from the wintry draft that always circulated near the floor of the small apartment. It felt more piercing this time. Rachel patted the front of her night shirt. It was wet.

"What?! I've soiled myself?" she mumbled, horrified.

"Rachel? Are you all right?" Jimmy's youthful voice was loud, insistent, but with undertones of anxiousness.

"Yes, Jimmy," Rachel replied in a calm voice. "I'm all right. Just a bad dream. Go back to sleep."

Rachel could not sleep after the assault. She needed time to recover and went out to the kitchen area to sit by the small iron stove they used for heat and for cooking meals. The flue went up through the ceiling. She opened the side door, added a few sticks of wood, stoked the glowing coals with a poker, then eased herself into a wooden chair a few feet away to await the warmth. She ached everywhere. She inspected her torso and arms. Many places were sore to the lightest touch, as if she'd been beaten. There were no marks, but the bruises were there. You just couldn't see them. She knew this from experience, along with the knowledge this invisible bruising healed slowly.

Her eyes welled with tears. As the muted warmth permeated the room, she used a small wash rag to daub at the cloying wetness on her ankles. It came back with dark stains. In the dim light of the stove's fire she recognized the redness.

Blood! She grimaced.

Rachel clawed the night dress above her waist and examined herself. She touched her genitals with care, terrified there may be more invisible bruising. But there was no pain, no visible wounds, nothing to explain the blood. When she wiped the blood away it did not reappear. The bleeding had no origin she could find, but it had stopped.

What did it do? Now Rachel was really scared. This had never occurred before. *And for what purpose? To terrify me further? Why? What have I done wrong? When have I not obeyed?* Her new life in Cambridge had just begun to settle into something almost normal. *Normal?* She scoffed at the notion. *I am foolish to think my life will ever be normal!*

Rachel gazed sullenly into the fire. The command to find Carter Trevathan was specific. She'd dreaded going back to the city where she could be recognized. But she had no choice.

I must go…and soon.

She decided to go that morning. Might as well. The first ferry was hours away. She cooked two of the expensive eggs and buttered some warm bread for Jimmy, who arose as the smell of food wafted through the air. She dressed while he ate. She sensed him staring at her temporary nakedness.

"I must go to Boston for the day," she announced.

Jimmy paused mid-bite and glanced out the window. It was still dark. "The city? Why?"

"There's something I must do. I will be back tonight."

"What if you don't come back? What should I do then?"

Rachel knew if she did not give Jimmy a plausible reason, he would not hesitate to get on a ferry and come searching for her. She could see him asking questions of everyone he knew. And he knew the streets of Boston better than she did. Rachel sat down next to him and took his hands in hers.

"I promised a friend I would visit her in the new year, so she would know I am all right. If I do not do this, she may come searching for me. I plan to catch the sunset ferry back, but there is a small chance I might stay overnight with her. If that is the case, be strong for me. It is not safe for either of us in Boston. And if you go searching for me and get recognized, you will endanger our new lives together. Do you want this to end? No? Good. Neither do I. Don't worry. I am coming back."

"Do you promise?" His tone was vulnerable.

Rachel leaned forward and kissed him lightly on the lips for a second longer than usual.

"I promise," she said. "Now, finish eating and go to school at the proper time. I promise to give you a surprise when I return."

But Rachel was not certain about keeping her promises. She was not certain about anything that might happen that day, nor was she certain about Jimmy.

Jimmy, however, appeared mollified for the time being. He had reached puberty. He had become too protective of her and increasingly needy. He already asked too many questions. And he knew a secret truth about her… about her dead sister, Caroline. That could become a danger to her someday. Hopefully not. Rachel did not want to kill Jimmy. She hoped it would not come to that. Her occasional suggestions of unnamed rewards for his obedience kept him under control, like a dog on a leash. Like this time. At least for now.

*

It was a mile walk to the ferry nearest to Cambridge using a road ending at the landing point adjoining the expansive Phipps' plantation farm. The ferry launch started at first light, if the harbor had not iced over during the night. It would go back and forth constantly after that until sunset. The large whaleboat carried twelve passengers, had four rowers, and cost two pence per person. Early in the morning, the launch was full of day laborers and she was the only female. Everyone was bundled up against the frosty breezes, scarves around their faces, another scarf wrapped over a hat and tied beneath their chins to cover their ears. Rachel wore the same attire. In fact, the scarves gave her adequate protection against being recognized.

The half-mile crossing of the harbor proceeded beneath overcast skies. The passengers were pelted by an intermittent drizzle of frozen rain. Coming back, she would use a different ferry, the one that plied the crossing back and forth to Charlestown, even though the walk from the Charlestown landing back to Cambridge was a cold four-mile slog down muddy roads. It was a precaution to make her face less memorable, less likely to be noticed or recalled.

After landing at Barton's Point, Rachel entered the familiar streets of Boston, which had not changed much. In early January, there were still a few frozen and decaying Christmas wreaths on merchant shop doors. She had reason to leave Boston in a hurry the last time. The magistrate's men were searching for a second female murderer—a nurse. The search probably continued. She avoided the places where she used to work; the Marine Society Hospital on Sudbury Street and the streets near the Penny

Surgeon down by the Long Wharf piers. She knew where Carter Trevathan lived and circuitously made her way to that apartment building, one of many newer buildings adjoining Faneuil Hall. She went up to the third floor and knocked softly on the door.

When Carter opened it, she hardly recognized him for all the weight he'd lost. His face was unshaven, sagging with exhaustion. His clothing was soiled, as if he'd worn it for days. Whatever ailed him had not affected his penchant for tidiness. The apartment looked clean and did not smell. But he certainly did!

Carter stared at her, as if seeing a ghost. "Rachel?"

"Yes."

"I thought you were dead!"

"You smell dead." Without invitation, she pushed past him. "You need a bath," she said tersely.

The nurse in her went straight to the stove and lifted the pail of clean water standing near it and set it to warming.

"You'll need more water for a bath."

"I do not have the strength to carry any more up the stairs," Carter replied with shame.

"When did you last eat?"

"I had some cheese for supper last night."

"Give me money. I will go out and buy food."

Carter pulled out his purse and shook a handful of silver and copper coins into her palm.

Rachel went downstairs and filled the second pail with cold water from the common well out in the back. It was indeed a heavy haul to bring it up the three flights of stairs.

"When that first pail gets hot, put this one on the stove. Wait for my return."

There were some market stands at the end of the street that opened for the morning hour business. With the scarf around her face, she bought four eggs, root vegetables, squash, beans, and a generous cut of fresh beef. From another farmer, she purchased a jug of milk, some butter in a sailor's cup, and was forced to buy the jug and cup. At the baker's stall, she got two fresh loaves of bread wrapped in newspaper and a piece of fishing net to carry it all. To her bundle, she added a small canvas sack of milled flour. It was enough food to last two or three days, maybe longer.

When she returned to the apartment, Carter had already placed the second pail on the stove to heat. The first was steaming on the floor. His mouth started to water at the thought of hot food.

"I am so thankful you came to see me," he said with a tone of relief.

Rachel did not reply. She placed all the food at the center of the round dining table and pulled the small metal bathing tub away from the wall to the center of the kitchen. It was not very deep or long but was wide and high enough to kneel and give one's self a sponge bath.

"Do you have soap?"

Carter pointed to the large bar and scrub brush on the window sill.

"Undress, get into the tub, and kneel down."

As Carter did as he was told, Rachel moved the pail of heated water nearer to the tub. She retrieved some stiff towels hanging on a wall hook. They were a little rancid but would have to do. She used a ladle to take water from the pail. Carter was naked and shivering in the tub.

"I'll start with your hair first. I don't see any lice. You're lucky."

Rachel was vigorous with the soaping and rising. She had him stand, hold out his arms, and thoroughly brush-scrubbed down his arms, legs, back, and torso as she would with any patient, rinsing off the soap with the ladle, letting the tub catch the soapy water. Her touch was not meant to be intimate, but as she washed his crotch, Carter got an erection. She ignored it. She moved a chair next to him, told him to sit, then finished washing each of his feet, scrubbing away the dirt beneath his toenails with the brush. She tossed a towel into his lap that was not wet.

"Dry yourself and get dressed in clean clothes while I cook something to eat. After you're dressed, empty the bathing tub out the window into the gutter drain. Rinse it out with a ladle."

Rachel washed her hands thoroughly with soap and placed a large iron fry pan on the stove. She cut the beef into chunks and added the beans, squash, and roots along with a ladle of clean water. It cooked quickly while she added in small pieces of bread, butter, some milk, a half cup of flour and stirred it all into a thick, gluey stew.

Carter tried to engage her in conversation as she prepared the food, but she did not answer any of his questions.

"This tastes wonderful," Carter said later as he gulped down almost without chewing his first bites of hot buttered bread and stew. "I cannot thank you enough for doing this…and the other things," he added.

Rachel took small bites of the stew and watched him carefully as she decided what to say. After a few mouthfuls, she spoke.

"Just so you understand, Carter, I am here only because *It* visited me last night and told me to come and see you. So, I expect you to tell me why I am here."

Surprise crossed Carter's face and he stopped eating. "Me? What did it tell you?"

"It didn't tell me anything. It raped me first…then told me to find you. Why am I here?"

"Raped you! How does that happen? The thing is…is a ghost!"

"I did not ask how when it was over. But I was bleeding from my vulva. Tell me what it said to you."

Carter explained he'd been harassed repeatedly for two months to learn the destination of VanderMeer's ship.

"It said the ship had stopped somewhere before it crossed the Atlantic. Everyone in Boston claims *William's Queen* went to Amsterdam, even the newspapers. Thomas Hancock believes this to be true. I asked him personally. No one else was closer to the VanderMeers than Hancock. A week ago, my head started pounding with headaches all day, every day. It's punishing me. I don't know what else to do. But the headache stopped as soon as you came into my apartment. That must mean something, yes? You must have something to tell me?"

"I came here as I was told to do," Rachel replied. "That's all it demanded of me."

They fell silent.

"Well, it only asks me the same questions every night. But I do not have any answers."

Rachel decided Carter was telling her the truth. And he was out of ideas. She had to spur him into action.

Carter refilled his plate and kept eating.

"Maybe the VanderMeers left signs of where they went inside their house? Did you search it?"

He shook his head and replied between mouthfuls. "The maids live there still."

"The maids live there?" Rachel repeated. She looked out the window, considering this. "Then the maids certainly know something. If they were allowed to stay in the house, the VanderMeers would have told them something…where they were going…when they were coming back. We killed the maidservant, Mathilde. She was Lady VanderMeer's confidante. The other maids are just as loyal to her, yes? Then Lady VanderMeer may trust them enough to confide in them."

Carter belched loudly. Rachel frowned.

"Pardon me. The maids are not alone. The Scotsman married one of them. Her name is Dian. He lives at the house with her when he's not working. He's a very dangerous man," Carter emphasized. "Captain Martyn married the other one, Molly, her name was. He lives there, too, when he is not away at sea, which is most of the time."

"So? Then you find a way to get inside during the day under some pretense. Threaten and question them."

Carter shook his head again.

"These are not ordinary maids. One of them killed the man I sent to burn down the house two years ago. Remember?"

Rachel grew impatient. "Then you abduct them when they shop for food!"

"They are guarded by two or three heavily armed men any time they leave the house. Capturing one alive is a possibility, but not without risk. You might more easily kill them, but you hardly have an opportunity to question them. You need more men. And it would take you longer to prepare."

Rachel noted his emphasis on the word *you*…as if she were supposed to do something.

"They must follow a routine," she pressed. "When do they shop? Where do they shop? Do they go together or one at a time? Put your education to work on this, Carter!"

"Fuck you!" Carter bellowed. "What do you think I've been doing? This is all I think about! They shop in the morning on Wednesdays and Saturdays. But only one of them, the one called Dian. The other one, Molly, the one with the baby, never leaves the house at all. Even then, the house is still guarded by four men, two in the front and two in the back, day and night."

Rachel reacted to this last bit of news. Squinting, she asked in a low tone, "She has a baby?"

CHAPTER 5
LOUISBOURG, ÎLE ROYALE
JANUARY 1757
Aurorae

Corrinne rose from bed while it was still dark. The hands of the Julien Le Roy standing clock she'd brought with her from Boston indicated thirty-eight minutes past two in the morning. The clock dominated the second-story bedroom of the stone and masonry house she shared with her twin babies and Anamosa. She found the muted ticking sound reassuring. Like a heartbeat, it provided a tempo for her thoughts. She usually awoke between the hours of two and three. The winter nights in the fortress city of Louisbourg seemed to push back the daylight. You could try to sleep your way through them, but they were long; fifteen hours long! Her mind was far too active to sleep so much. And that morning she awoke more restless than usual, sensing a change was near. Maybe it was wishful thinking. Stinging rain, snow, persistent cold, and ice fogs in the winter were normal here. Her hope for better weather was perpetual.

Maybe the skies will clear today?

It had become a morning prayer.

Corrinne began her mundane routine. She stoked the glowing embers of the fireplace and added some wood. Flames licked around the split and quartered logs after a few seconds. Next, she checked on her eighteen-month-old twins, Calypso and Marcus, sleeping together in each other's arms like the innocent little angels they were. They were getting so big. They filled the infant crib.

They need separate beds, she decided. A list took form in her mind. *Today I will hire a carpenter to create them.*

Then just one step sideways to Anamosa, the beautiful Ottawa girl with the striking blue eyes. She knelt on the floor next to the girl's bed.

Corrinne smiled and studied the sleeping girl for a few minutes as she did most mornings. She was endlessly fascinated by Anamosa's serene face, her probing eyes, the tranquility of her moods. Charles had mixed some oils to capture the blue of her eyes. He also made a sketch of her face and intended to paint her portrait during the crossing. Her physical qualities were accented by the silver amulet recently crafted by Charles. It was engraved with eight special symbols and set with a deep purple amethyst at its center. Anamosa wore the amulet constantly around her neck. Ostensibly, it gave her a measure of protection from the evil that sought to do all of them harm. Corrinne wore one too, set with an emerald, so did Marcus and Calypso. They kept taking them off, so they hung at either end of the crib for now. The amulets might seem excessive and superstitious to other people, but Corrinne knew better. She had witnessed the bubbling horror of this evil more than once. If she thought walking around on her knees for an hour each day while making the sign of the cross would help, she would do that, too.

Corrinne sensed a magical quality in Anamosa. They shared so much common history now, plus an unbreakable connection to Philippe and Henri. Anamosa's real father had been an anonymous French fur trader. A man who died soon after her birth somewhere in the hazardous snows and icy waters of the northwest wilderness. At least, that's what the Ottawa believed. No one had ever learned what happened to him. Like so many others, the man simply left one day and never returned.

Anamosa's mother was beautiful, too, so Corrinne had been told. They had never met. Her name was Okeanneh. Philippe Gerrard was just another French fur trader the first day he walked into her village. Okeanneh's gaze was drawn to him instantly. She was the daughter of the Ottawa chief and she expressed her desire. A bargain was quickly arranged. The Ottawa offered exclusive trade in furs for Philippe and his partner, Pierre Dunemoore, but Philippe must marry Okeanneh.

Philippe was attracted to Okeanneh in the same way. Anamosa was six or seven by then. Philippe did not care that Okeanneh had a child. They married, an Ottawa ceremony, in 1752. Tragedy struck when Okeanneh died a few years later, one of the many victims of the deadly assassin, Helmut Colbért, who came from France specifically to kill Phillipe. With Okeanneh's death, Anamosa was alone. But Philippe loved Anamosa. He brought her with him out of the wilderness to Montréal.

How could anyone not love you? Corrinne thought as she stroked the girl's hair.

Philippe and Corrinne had met by chance in the French port of Le Havre, in the summer of 1740. Both were fleeing mortal danger at that moment in time. A meeting by fate in a waterfront tavern in Le Havre. Together, they invented fictional identities and found a way to begin a new life in New France. For a time, supported by one another's presence, they overcame all the obstacles to this new life. Then, abruptly, Philippe's hunger for adventure drew him further west to join the prosperous fur trade. Weeks passed before Corrinne knew this. As soon as she learned he was gone, she experienced an ache, a longing for Philippe stronger than for anyone else in her life. She was deeply in love and bonded to this man long before he met anyone else, long before Philippe realized it himself. *It was our destiny*, she later asserted to him on the night they were married. Every time her thoughts were drawn to these compelling memories, they only reaffirmed this. And she was drawn to thoughts of Philippe every day in dismal Louisbourg.

Corrinne had not seen Philippe in two years.

Ironically, Anamosa was deeply in love Henri, much as a girl so young can feel love. And that was that. At first, Corrinne considered leaving Anamosa in Québec City when she and Philippe decided to flee to Boston. But the girl clung to Corrinne in a way that captured her heart. Anamosa had that effect on people; one could not help but love her. Corrine took Anamosa as her ward and later, in the charade of marriage she invented with Charles VanderMeer, adopted her, giving her the VanderMeer name. Together, the two of them had survived so many deadly trials, Corrinne could no longer imagine life without Anamosa.

The warm glow of the fire on Anamosa's flawless skin was luminous. Corrinne gently smoothed a stray curl away from the girl's brow. Anamosa was much bigger now, taller at least, almost up to her shoulders. Corrinne had never been quite certain of Anamosa's age. Although Okeanneh had never told Philippe Anamosa's exact birthdate and when questioned Anamosa was uncertain of her age, too. She presumed the girl might be eleven or twelve by now, considering how Anamosa's body had started to change in just the last six months. Corrinne concluded there must be truth in the belief that native girls matured much faster than their French counterparts.

Since all was well with the children, Corrinne took a quilt from the bed and went to her chair placed by the second-story window of the stone residence. It provided a generous view of the harbor and the eastern faubourg of the fortress when it was not dark and foggy, as it was this night. The oversized chair was crafted by Victorio and the *William's Queen* carpenter as a farewell gift to her before they sailed away to Amsterdam. These men of the sea were highly skilled. Victorio was the ship's sailmaker, healer, navigator, and engineer, as well as Captain LaTour's second-in-command. The chair had a wood and canvas-stiffened frame, overstuffed with purified strands of dried island hemp. The canvass was stretched and stitched with sail twine, using sailor knots in a manner that fashioned and held a shape. It was intentionally made wide enough for two women to sit side by side. Enough room to allow Corrinne to fold her legs back to one side.

Pulling the thick quilt snug around her neck, she sat with her feet off the cold floor. The outdoor temperature that night was well-below freezing, which she could tell from the frost marks on the window. Not much had changed. It was just as frosty as the day she arrived in Louisbourg months earlier. As Corrinne looked out the window that January morning, she saw nothing new. In fact, she saw nothing at all. In the darkness, the thick fog was visible only by the blurry whiteness coming from the direction of the Louisbourg lighthouse, which was up on a hill, a mile and a half away, across the harbor. On such opaque nights, Corrinne would usually read one of the books she had borrowed from Governor Drucour's library, using only the dim light of a lantern on a side table. She read a lot. There were now two stacks of books piled nearby on the floor.

She pushed around this pile of books and saw no titles she had not read. Sighing with resignation, she leaned her head back and closed her eyes, hoping to doze away some time.

The month of January is almost over! Two more months of isolation and boredom.

At least she wasn't hiding in seclusion like she had in Connecticut. She could go out any time she wanted. Go anywhere she chose. Except there was no place to go and little to see in Louisbourg. It was a walled city full of soldiers and bastions bristling with cannons, guarding a natural harbor big enough to anchor a small fleet of ships. Inside its walls, Louisbourg was half the size of Québec City. But unlike the capital city of New France, outside the fortress walls the landscape was unpopulated, devoid of people expect for the Mi'kmaq, the invisible native allies the citizens of Louisbourg rarely saw. Instead, one saw endless miles of trees on lands covered with a coarse, stony topsoil, very poor for farming. It was perpetually wet, with dozens of small hills amid a bog-riddled wilderness.

Was Louisbourg a safe haven? That's how she and Charles referred to it prior to arriving. *Haven? There's that word again*, she thought. It suggested a welcoming comfort. It was not. Louisbourg was a temporary retreat, just a wayward inn on the longer journey. *To where?*

Louisbourg was no more than a friendly refuge away from Boston and all the treachery and assassination attempts by servants of the Hessian, Colonel Wilhelm von Kleinfels, whose last attack had left Charles paralyzed from the waist down.

Governor Drucour and Julien Fizel had chosen an adequate home for her. It was simple and small, and she was grateful for the privacy of the eastern faubourg. The homes on this side of the city were slightly more spread out. Most of them tended large vegetable gardens as a food source for the fort. Others had livestock sheds for the few cows and goats available for milk, butter, and cheeses.

She opened her eyes for a moment and looked out the window. Still just the blurry white light in the distance. She closed them again.

On the days clear of fog, she could see the entry channel and watch the arrival and departure of ships entering or leaving the anchorage. The view was reminiscent of the third-floor apartment residence she once occupied above the Dunemoore Company warehouse on the river in Montréal…seemingly a lifetime ago. Watching the sailing vessels come and go, Corrinne imagined the world was trying to connect with her, even in this remote place.

Ships brought news. Everyone in Louisbourg was starved for news. Louisbourg was dependent on ships to bring food and supplies. In addition to copious amounts of fish caught year-round, the city thrived on the harbor trade from the visiting ships. This included cross-deck smuggling that occurred routinely among the anchored vessels. Even a few American smugglers who brought high-quality manufactured goods from the New England colonies were tolerated if the taxes and *bribes* were paid. But the advent of formal war declared between England and France in the summer of 1756 had diminished the American trade almost to nothing. Only the cleverest and most earnest smugglers chanced getting beyond the English blockade cruisers. It was extremely lucrative if they did manage to get into the harbor, but they would be hung if caught by the English after leaving.

But Corrinne's greatest disappointment was something she had expected as a reward for living in Louisbourg—letters from Philippe!

Corrinne had written five letters to Philippe since her arrival with high expectations of an overdue, joyous reply. And who knew? Philippe might even show up one day to surprise her! The very thought of this made her heart pound with delicious anticipation. But five letters later and still no reply. The weeks of waiting had now become two months. She invented rational excuses for this. She knew General Montcalm was involved in the fighting in and around Lake George and Lake Champlain. She told herself Philippe had simply not received her letters yet. Yet, Henri sent letters to and received letters from Québec City. Logic told her letters to Philippe would have reached this city, too. And the forts on Lake Champlain were less than a week further at most. It was very frustrating.

Major Péan and the Québécois marines should be nearing Québec City soon. He made a promise to find out about her letters. But even if Péan learned something tomorrow, it might take weeks for him to inform her.

Henri's eleven marine volunteers were guarding her, of course. Corrinne and Henri agreed posting sentries outside of the house was simply not practical, that sentries would only draw needless attention to her. They decided that six marines from the Dauphin barracks would be assigned every day, in eight-hour shifts. They would approach and inspect the house from the outside. In the mid-morning and late afternoon, one of the soldiers would knock on the door to say hello. Corrinne would have something prepared to serve them mid-morning. The soldiers became enamored with the twins and doffed their hats when meeting Anamosa, who charmed these men with just a glance. Corrinne liked the attention. It broke up the boredom. And the soldiers were happy to run errands to the faubourg market and shops for her.

Henri confided to Corrinne about sending letters to Madeleine, the nurse he pined for back in Québec City. Communication with Québec City was very routine, and Madeleine sent more letters to Henri than he sent to her. *Smart girl*. When Henri spoke of Madeleine, she could see the excitement in his eyes. Corrinne had been suspicious of this girl from the moment they were introduced. She had no reason to be suspicious. She did not know why she felt this way. *Maybe I am jealous*, she thought. *Or maybe because Anamosa loves Henri so much*. It was conspicuous to her that Henri never mentioned Madeleine's name when Anamosa was present. Henri was smart…and not insensitive.

Henri remained part of the Louisbourg garrison. He had watches to stand like other junior officers. He would eat dinner at the house at least once a week, sometimes twice. Corrinne would smile at Anamosa's reaction every time he came around. Her usually tranquil expression would expand into brilliant white smiles, not taking her eyes off him. Henri would sometimes bring her presents: beads, hair ribbons, an ivory comb, jeweled hair pins, a silver bracelet, things he would purchase from the smuggling ships. Anamosa would hold each of these precious objects in her hands and kiss his cheeks. She kept them all in a small étui bag on the nightstand by her bed.

Corrinne opened her eyes and looked out the window again. Fog.

Fog. Fog. Fog. Yes, a change in weather would be nice.

Corrinne closed her eyes. This time she dozed, successfully, then awoke again for no reason. She sat up, gazed out the window, and blinked a few times. The beam from the lighthouse appeared much sharper now. She discerned blurry colors in the fog and noticed the mist was moving, to the right, moving east out of the fort and out of the harbor.

The fog is lifting! Thank God!

The fog dissipated right before her eyes. She could now see the house next door...and the night sky above her was bursting with color.

Curtains of sinuous green and golden aurorae rippled in waves across the heavens. Corrinne's mouth dropped open. It was a wondrous, mesmerizing drapery of colored light across the top of the world. She'd seen them before, but that night would turn out to be the best display yet, everything she'd longed to see and more. It made her heart beat fast.

Now this is a change! Dieu merci!

She laid her head on an overstuffed arm of the chair and gave all her attention to the natural wonder. But her reverie was interrupted. The standing clock gonged softly five times. Corrinne automatically counted the gongs. She frowned and shifted in the chair.

Five in the morning. It will still be this dark at seven! The sun would not rise again until after eight, then set again before five. Such were the nine-hour days this far to the north. She was becoming obsessed with the clock.

"Corrinne?"

It happened on all the aurorae nights. Anamosa would appear at the side of the chair, a beautiful apparition. Her white nightgown reflecting the colored ripples.

Corrinne held out her hands. "Come to me, little love."

She pulled back the quilt to encourage the girl to climb into the wide chair beside her. Anamosa rubbed her nose beneath Corrinne's chin before snuggling into the warmth and embrace of her arms. Corrinne gently guided Anna's ice-cold feet into the warmth behind her knees. She kissed Anna's head and caressed the dark luxurious hair. The girl would be asleep again in a minute.

*

Captain Jean Vauquelin of the French privateer *L'Valkyrie* kept his long watch glass fixed on the stern lights of the British ship he was trailing in the heavy fog in waters just northeast of the port of Louisbourg. He was close enough to hear the sounds aboard the English ship. Too close, really. He'd not attempted this tactic before. But the captain was used to taking such risks. It was winter in Louisbourg. This was now the fourth day of heavy fog. Waiting for the fog to clear was unpredictable. It might easily be another day. This delay was unacceptable when delivering vital war missives. The English ship had slowed its speed to just a few knots. So Vauquelin had decided on this risky maneuver. He'd already learned the captain of this English ship was an excellent navigator. *Maybe even better than I am*, Vauquelin mused grudgingly. The English ship was on a blockade patrol going back and forth repeatedly to guard the entrance to the port. This English captain knew these waters and Vauquelin trusted this captain's skills. By following close behind on the same course, when the English ship passed the entrance this time, Vauquelin would turn sharply to the right and gain the safety of the harbor before the English ever knew he was there.

L'Valkyrie was a special ship. A fast schooner, heavy with sail over a shallow draft and lightly armed with only eight small cannons. It had but one purpose, to carry the few passengers as directed by the French Admiralty and deliver the important dispatch pouches to and from the government of New France. It would routinely run the blockades of Louisbourg and up the river leading to Québec City; that is, if it wasn't frozen.

Captain Vauquelin was twenty-nine, a commoner, the son of a French merchant captain. Six feet tall, slender, black hair, blue eyes, a descendent of Celtic peoples of the Brittany peninsula in France. Adventure was in his blood. He had been going to sea since reaching the age of nine, over twenty years ago. He saw action at sea ten years earlier during the War of Austrian Succession, the last war with the English. By the time he was offered command of a French privateer, he had already made over two dozen crossings in command of merchant vessels.

L'Valkyrie was a warship, albeit a small one. But it was a warship with cannons, and he reveled in being its captain and in outsmarting his English counterparts. Skills like Vauquelin's, like that of a musical prodigy, were not seen very often. His boldness had already been noticed by the admiralty of both navies.

That night, Vauquelin's fast schooner had reefed most of its sail to match the speed of the British vessel, so as not to overtake it. *L'Valkyrie* was sailing dark and quiet. No lights, and everything that could make metal-on-metal noise was tied off or padded into silence. His crew was expert in this. The men cupped their hands over one another's ears to cover the sound of their voices. Both ships steered the same southwesterly course. To the right was the coastline of Île Royale. One could not see it for the fog, but the sounds of the seas crashing against the rocks were a constant reminder this coast was a graveyard of ships. The winds were not too strong, but they kept changing direction erratically, a sign to the captain they were on the edge of a change in the weather. Good or bad? They'd know soon enough. In the meantime, he ordered two of his seamen to drop lead lines repeatedly in the water to starboard, one forward and one aft, to measure the depth continuously, lest the swells push them too close to the rocks.

Vauquelin's second-in-command tugged on the captain's coat sleeve. Dimmette, a much older experienced seaman with white hair and a creased face, was highly valued for his knowledge of sailing. He was a bit too cautious for Vauquelin, and the first mate would occasionally challenge his logic. Vauquelin found that valuable. Dimmette considered the young captain brilliant, aggressive, and seemingly gifted by the Creator with extraordinary luck. The crew of *L'Valkyrie* revered their captain.

Vauquelin leaned his head toward the first mate. Dimmette cupped his hands over the captain's ear and whispered, "We're very close to Louisbourg, Captain. At this speed, I estimate we will reach the turn before we hear the English ship's bell toll the half hour. And the fog seems to be thinning. The winds are changing. We are dangerously close to that frigate. If the fog lifts too soon and they spot us, they have time to rake our deck with their stern cannons."

Vauquelin whispered back between cupped hands, "Don't worry. The English are cold and wet like us. I sense them huddled on watch, collars pulled up high on the sides of their faces against the icy spray. They only concentrate on what lies ahead, not what lies behind them. They are watching for those rocky islands near the entrance. By the time we are noticed, we will have turned into port and sailed beyond the Island Battery. Make ready for the starboard turn. I want full sail after that."

Vauquelin could see the blurry loom of white light in the fog off his starboard bow. It lay to the southwest. It was the Louisbourg lighthouse. Above his head, he could just make out the wondrous hazy dance of the green and golden northern lights. The combinations of the white and colored lights reflected eerily within the obscuring fog. Added to the sound of waves lapping along the hull, the roar of the coastal swells breaking upon unforgiving rocks, it was a mystical experience like no other place in the world. The danger was beautiful and exhilarating. Vauquelin loved it. But he dared not let his attention admire the aurorae. Make a mistake in seamanship here, and one would die in the icy waters in minutes.

Vauquelin went aft to stand next to his helmsman. "Be ready to turn to starboard," he whispered to the man.

He trained his watch glass on the stern lights of the English ship. He was familiar with this particular blockade cruiser, the *Anamosa*. He had encountered it twice before, both times he had barely eluded being engaged. The *Anamosa* was half again larger, carried twice as many guns as *L'Valkyrie,* and was one of the few ships that could match his speed and maneuverability. Vauquelin hoped to talk with its captain someday to learn its secret.

*

Captain Conor Martyn of the *Anamosa* had been pursuing the French privateer *L'Valkyrie* for three days without success. The *Anamosa* outgunned the smaller vessel. But this French captain was smart. He would never engage. Instead *L'Valkyrie* ducked into the winter fog bank that lingered off the Cape Breton coast that time of year and went quiet and dark. Martyn zig-zagged through the fog while remaining close to the Louisbourg harbor entrance. This was tedious and dangerous navigation, which he had learned how to do through much experience. His frustration was so acute, he almost considered ramming the French ship if he spotted it. *L'Valkyrie* was a notorious courier. It would make a run for the harbor. The fog would lift if he waited long enough. But two days of fog soon became three and now was close to four.

Time to go home, he decided on this fourth night. He presumed the schooner had probably went north to Port Dauphin by now. He would complete one more slow pass by the lighthouse.

Captain Martyn noted the annoying blur of white light atop a conspicuous rock precipice overlooking the Atlantic. The rock was part of the defensive seawall, one of several battlements and cannon batteries along the ocean coastline of the Fortress of Louisbourg the engineers had built. This point of land was called Cap Noir by the French, sometimes referred to as Black Point Rock. It had cannons, but they were smaller caliber guns, sixteen pounders, not much of a deterrent, but enough to alert the cannoneers at Rochefort Point and the Island Battery, inducing them to aim their twenty-eight-pound naval rifles towards any potential invader.

Black Rock Point was significant because of the rock's size, a huge blister of natural black granite, surrounded by three cannon embrasures constructed with field stone to create a redoubt. The fifty-foot-high prominence was the farthest battlement outside the curtain walls to the east of the Princess demi-bastion, a thousand feet away. This place on the rocky coast had several tiny sea-carved, sandy beaches along the shoreline. Most were ten paces wide or less. At best, these beaches could be used by the English as a landing place for a small scouting force, maybe raiders, or used as a diversion during a larger siege. But it would be a suicidal attempt. Even if a landing was successful, there was little chance of expanding upon any success. The islands and shallows near the entrance to the harbor forced ships to make a wide passage. Black Rock Point sat inside that natural barrier.

Why mark this place with a light?

Every time he sailed by Black Rock Point at night, Martyn asked himself this same question. He obsessed about the light because it made no sense to him. He had sailed the *Anamosa* up and down the dreary Cape Breton coastline, near the Fortress of Louisbourg, more times than he could count. This light was much less bright than the lighthouse. Probably no more than a stout lantern set in a bucket-hole of cement. It could be seen from sea only up to a mile offshore, and even less in the fog. He knew this because he'd measured the distance during one of his earlier patrols, when he was charting the coastline details and noted this in his log. Its short range of visibility made for a very poor navigational signal. Besides, the Louisbourg lighthouse was right there, tall and bright, just a mile and a half away. Tactically, this light would mark the presence of the small cannon battery he could plainly see in the daytime. Yet this rock signal was always illuminated at night, in any kind of weather. Somehow it was important.

So the sentries can find it in the dark? Or maybe it is used by French couriers or smugglers? Martyn speculated. *Perhaps a place where* L'Valkyrie *could send a boat ashore with dispatches…*

One could not see the beaches in this fog. But the crash of the heavy surf could be heard. A small launch would get crushed on the rocks.

Captain Martyn had presumed one possible use for the light in the fog. Taking a bearing on this light and one from the lighthouse and plotting them on the chart would give him a rough check on his position from shore, serving as a range of sorts. It was imprecise, but helped. A sudden notion struck him.

L'Valkyrie *would know this too! And use it like I do!* This speculation spurred his annoyance. *We are at war! That light is a legitimate target!*

"Lieutenant Carson, wake the men. No drums. No quarters. No bells. Do this fast but do this *quietly*! Load the starboard guns and both guns on the stern. We are going to shell Black Rock Point as we pass by."

*

A quarter mile down the sloping landscape leading away from Lady VanderMeer's house, close to the edge of the harbor and the sea, were the seaside defenses of the fortress: the Princess, the Brouillan, and Maurepas bastions. The potent Rochefort Point Battery, recently expanded, was a semicircle of embrasures filled with twenty-eight-pound naval cannons. Outside the enceinte where it joined to the Princess bastion, a thousand feet away from everything else, was the isolated battery at Black Rock Point.

As one of the most junior officers of the Louisbourg garrison, Ensign Henri Gerrard was usually assigned a four-hour officer tour between midnight and eight. In truth, he did not mind this duty. He learned a lot about the soldiers from the different regiments, heard their thoughts, opinions, and good suggestions. Under the cover of night, shivering in the cold, and the persistent rains and fogs, the men were provoked to candor they would not dare espouse in the light of day, and certainly not to an officer. He only censured them if they disparaged another officer by name in his presence.

That night, he started his watch at four in the morning. He was to make his rounds of the guards and sentries in the Maurepas, Brouillan, and Princess bastions, which comprised the main eastern defenses of the fortress. Simply making his presence known was enough to keep the watch alert. That was the idea. In addition, he was tasked with touring the coastal cannon batteries at Pièce la Grave, Rochefort Point, and Cap Noir.

In the ice fogs and wetness of late January, inspecting the guard on the coastal batteries was a very long walk, a shivering circuit of almost two miles if one did it right, which he did. But Henri had walked it numerous times, took an interest in talking to the sentries for a few minutes, listened and laughed at their atrociously lewd jokes, and gave a sympathetic ear to their endless and repetitive complaints about things soldiers had complained about since ancient times: the food, the pay, the cold, no women, what, why, if, when, and how. Before he moved on to the next location, he made certain to mention the importance of what they were doing.

"It's nights like these when the enemy might decide to raid. The nights when we least expect it. That's what I would do," he warned them. "And I would not use any pistols or muskets to announce my arrival. I would use my skinning blade on you." He slapped the knife loudly. They'd seen the great knife on his hip in the daylight. "I'd sneak upon you in the night like a Seneca brave and in one movement put a hand over your mouth, so you could not cry out. One swipe of this razor will cut to the neck bone. You would die quietly, drowning in your own blood…and in great pain."

In the darkness, they could not see the ensign's eyes to tell if he was jesting.

Then Henri singled out one man at random and added. "Except for you, Private. *You* I would rape."

They had all laughed raucously and added jokes of their own.

The soldiers liked Ensign Gerrard.

The very last place he reached two hours later was Cap Noir. It was the worst of the night watches for the cannoneer sentries. Right on the Atlantic coast. Miserable. Very little cover from the weather. The gun crew would usually huddle beneath blankets, sitting side by side around a small iron stove they would feed with the coal brought by wagons to the fort, from mines discovered decades ago in the northern part of Île Royale. They were fortunate to have coal. Out here by the edge of the ocean, wood remained damp and difficult to burn.

The night had begun to clear up by the time Henri approached the point and climbed up the elevated redoubt. The winds were shifting, and the fog was slowly moving out of the harbor. Best of all, the night sky came ablaze with the aurorae. When Henri reached the three cannon embrasures, the crew of five cannoneers plus a sergeant were already staring upward in wonder.

"Sergeant LaCorne."

The sergeant got to his feet and saluted. He knew the voice. "Ensign Gerrard! Welcome. You've brought the aurorae with you!"

"And something else, too."

From inside his heavy cloak, Henri pulled out a small canvas sack he'd been carrying for three hours just for the Cap Noir sentries. It was filled with a dozen sugared croissants he had purchased before he went on watch from the eastern faubourg bakery, the one that still made pastries when sugar was available. These were the first of the day, freshly baked in the ovens. Under his cloak, he had kept them hidden from the other sentries. The pastries remained warm by his body heat as he marched.

"Compliments of Lady VanderMeer. Don't fight over them."

The soldiers made sounds of appreciation and issued compliments about Lady VanderMeer, likely the only time they didn't add something obscene about her, although they never did in front of Ensign Gerrard.

Henri took a watch glass from the sergeant and climbed up the carved stone steps leading to the light atop the imposing granite hillock to better see over the embrasures. The Louisbourg lighthouse would ruin his night vision so he avoided looking at it. He slowly scanned the foggy seas, not expecting to see anything when he caught a momentary blink of a shipboard lantern light.

He was instantly alert. *Wow! The fog really is starting to thin! Who would be out there now? A fishing chaloupe? This early in the morning? In this fog?*

Henri kept watching. The soldiers kept eating.

*

Captain Martyn's plan was to fire each of his eight starboard cannons at the Black Rock light one at a time as they passed perpendicular to the point. The fog would obscure good aim. The seas were not calm. The ship was swaying amid the offshore swells, though not violently. But the rolls were just enough to foul a cannon's aim.

"Just elevate your guns for the range," he told the gun mates. "Point them straight ahead and fire when the seas pause at the crest of a roll when the center of the light blur is in your sights."

He expected the blasts to occur in groups of two or three in a series lasting fifteen seconds or less.

"Each gun captain will make the decision on when to fire. Don't be tempted to fire by the report of the cannon next to you," he warned. "Aim carefully! There will be extra portions of rum in reward for your accuracy."

"And what about the stern cannons, Captain?" the gunner's mate asked.

"Just load them both. Prepare to fire both on my command. I will point out your target when the time comes."

Maybe the battery at Rochefort Point, he mused. *Wake them up too?* Captain Martyn was not sure what the target would be.

"We'll fire the stern guns when we turn to port. The stern will certainly be pointing at something."

*

Henri saw *two* lantern lights blink into view. They were far enough apart to suggest it was two fishing chaloupes or something else. *Something much bigger?*

"Sergeant LaCorne! Something big is out there!"

The sergeant picked up the other watch glass in a hurry and started scanning. The rest of the cannon crew squinted out over the cannon snouts.

"I see one or two lights," the sergeant confirmed. "Fishermen, maybe."

"I don't think so," Henri replied. "They can plainly see the lighthouse. Why would fishermen be out there on a morning like this?"

The lights were moving southwest. They rose and fell in unison with the seas.

"Those lights are on the same ship," Henri declared.

The sergeant frowned. "What kind of ship?"

"Big enough to be a blockade cruiser. And it's close to us. *Load two cannon!*" he ordered tersely. "*One with a ball! And one with grape shot! Aim to fire on those lights at my command!*"

Filled with a burst of adrenal excitement and still chewing on the sugary pastries, the veterans yanked back two of the sixteen-pound guns. They removed the muzzle plugs and loaded and primed them as ordered. This watch was no longer cold and tedious. The cannoneers *loved* firing their cannons. And they could brag about this for weeks!

While that frenzied activity proceeded, Henri watched the lights carefully through the scope. He imagined the shipboard sounds and wondered if it might be a French ship.

The lighthouse is right there! He should have turned by now. Either into the harbor or out to sea. And he's too close to the coast. One rogue wave could push the ship upon one of the rocky islands.

It was not moving too fast. Henri could tell the ship would pass broadside to the Black Rock position in less than a minute.

If it fires at us this close…?!

"Sir! We have the range on the lights! Cannons ready, sir!"

But what if it is French?

*

Corrinne watched the aurorae. This far to the north, on those rare nights here when the sky was clear of any clouds, she was inspired by them. Like her wedding night, when she made love to Philippe on the deck of the *Falcon Queen* under lights just like this. *Our movements were not exactly poetry,* she mused. *But they were delicious!*

Then in the harbor channel, Corrinne noticed three green lights moving in unison in a line. "What the hell is that?"

*

Henri experienced one last moment of doubt, when the two lights he was watching were both extinguished…at the same time!

"FIRE!"

*

Captain Martyn touched the shoulder of the first gun captain.

"Fire when ready." As he uttered those words, two fiery blasts erupted from Black Rock Point. "GET DOWN!"

Captain Martyn threw himself on the deck. An instant later and he would have been dead.

The *Anamosa* gun crews were already crouching on deck so they simply flattened themselves further. The grapeshot crossed over the deck in an angry buzz, a deadly cloud of metal, some of it stopped by the rail, shattering its wood, digging into the masts, and shredding one of the stay sails into rags. The sixteen-pound ball from the other cannon slammed through the deck house behind the helm, ripping away the front of the structure, carrying it over the port side to fall into the sea. Large chunks of oak exploded in several directions. A jagged fragment of wood struck the helmsman in the head, knocking him senseless. The man fell, and the helm started spinning clockwise. The ship began to turn precipitously towards the shore.

Dazed but aware his ship was in danger, Captain Martyn staggered to his feet.

"FIRE!" he shouted and ran aft to the helm.

All eight cannons on the *Anamosa*'s starboard side fired simultaneously.

As Martyn ran aft, he suddenly spotted the black shadow of a ship entering Louisbourg harbor as it caught the illumination of the lighthouse.

It displayed three lanterns with green lenses, arrayed on the deck house, in line with the bow. He cursed. That was *L'Valkyrie!* He grabbed the helm and spun the wheel hard to port.

"Fire at those bloody green lights!" Martyn shouted to his gun captain on the stern and pointed. "There! In the channel!"

The gunner's mate knew he must fire while the ship was turning to port. He would have only one shot from each gun. He could see the strange green lights but did not know the range. He spun the elevation screw on one gun twice and on the second gun four times in an attempt to bracket the range of the target. When the first of the green lights aligned with the sights of the cannons, he fired them both.

The shorter-range ball exploded harmlessly at the center of the semicircle of guns on Rochefort Point, causing chaos among the French gun crews, who'd already come charging half-dressed from their barracks at hearing the Black Rock battery's cannon blasts.

The longer range second ball splashed into the water just aft of *L'Valkyrie*. Two seconds earlier, it would have smashed into the side of the vessel.

*

Captain Vauquelin's mouth hung open. He could not be more surprised by the cannon duel that exploded simultaneously between the *Anamosa* and the cannon battery at Cap Noir. Then another cannon ball from the *Anamosa* splashed into the water not more than ten paces off his stern. A few seconds earlier, a disaster! The captain was lucky again. The three green lantern lights were properly arrayed on his deck house. It was the coded signal to the Island Battery guarding the harbor entrance that this was a French ship entering at night. And Vauquelin fervently hoped the commander of the Island Battery did not suddenly decide he was the enemy and that the green lights were a ruse because of the other cannon exchange. Because at this range, *L'Valkyrie* would disintegrate under a withering broadside from the heavy forty-two-pound guns of the Island Battery. As he planned, Vauquelin had all *L'Valkyrie*'s sails raised and was now speeding into Louisbourg harbor.

Captain Vauquelin was lucky…once more.

*

The Fortress of Louisbourg came fully awake at the sounds of multiple cannons firing during the darkest hour of that cold morning in January. The soldiers and cannoneers also saw the aurorae ablaze in the clear night sky overhead. The fiery sights and sounds of the cannons combined with the aurorae spectacle in the sky was surreal. Other cannons in the bastions fired at nothing in random directions, presuming the fortress was under general attack. Not to be left out, sporadic musket fire broke out everywhere along the bastions and curtain walls as all the sentries shot at any menacing shadows they imagined outside the walls. It took another thirty minutes until all the firing stopped, brought under control by the officers who finally realized the fort was not in any danger.

*

The *Anamosa* had turned left into the fog. It was now invisible. Captain Martyn learned seventeen of his crew were wounded, minor flesh wounds after splinters of wood, large and small, caused gashes in their skin. Two men had broken ribs from the flying debris. But none of his men had been killed. The wounded men would heal quickly beneath their bandages. Not the worst butcher's bill, considering. All of them could return to duty except the helmsman who would lie unconscious for several more hours, and then stagger around concussed for three days afterwards like a drunk. As the injured aided one another, they could hear the muffled cannon blasts and musket fire their broadside had provoked all across the Fortress of Louisbourg.

Captain Martyn gave over the helm to another man after ordering him to steer due east. The first glimmers of light appeared as the new morning pushed through the fog, which was already thinned by the steady winds from the west. It permitted him to see to the bow at least. He walked forward. There were slippery smears of blood all over the deck and on the rails of his ship. Shards of metal grapeshot protruded conspicuously from the masts. Several rigging lines were dangling, swinging with broken tackle blocks, forcing Martyn to raise an arm to avoid getting brained. He heard the occasional moans and stopped to offer compassionate words to the wounded sailors.

Continuous cannon fire was heard for quite some time. Unbeknownst to the men of the *Anamosa*, the Rochefort Point Battery was firing heavy balls in every direction into the fog, suspecting more English ships might be lurking there.

Captain Martyn returned to the helm deck and picked up his speaking trumpet.

"Do you hear that noise?! You caused that! You have all performed bravely this morning! And you lived to tell about it! I am proud of every one of you! Well done. Extra rum rations today…for everyone! The *Anamosa* is going home."

A cheer went up. Captain Martyn had to make log entries and compose his report on this action for submission to the commodore in Halifax. Seeing the green lights arrayed in a line on *L'Valkyrie* gave him new valuable intelligence and a strong, admittedly better, reason why he fired his broadside. That and the completely unexpected blast from Black Rock Point. He may have to change the order of how things happened in that single minute. But the British navy now knew about the green lantern signal. And the light at Black Rock Point was gone…or at least it was out.

Captain Martyn took back the helm, deciding to personally steer his ship towards the east until they were clear of the fog bank and safely into the open seas.

That was one very alert gun captain at Black Rock, he concluded. *He must have spotted my deck lights as the winds thinned the fog. Lesson learned. And* bloody *Captain Vauquelin! He had the* bloody *audacity to trail in my wake! Bloody hell! Well, that lesson will not be forgotten either.*

That latter lesson would not be mentioned in Captain Martyn's report.

*

The *Anamosa*'s powerful broadside pulverized the battery works at Black Rock Point. But the captain's order to fire all the starboard guns in response to the incoming fire also disrupted his plan to fire in a sequence. Of the eight balls that flew, three struck near the light at the top of the rock. The granite mound erupted, sending chunks of broken rock flying in every direction. Two other balls flew high and splatted harmlessly into the boggy ground beyond the battery. The last three balls flew low. Weakened from years of Louisbourg's weather, with repeated rains, freezes and thaws that cracked and split the cements, the sixteen-pound iron balls shattered the brittle structure into fragments. The six-man gun crew was tossed in the air.

His ears still ringing, Ensign Henri Gerrard stood up on wobbly legs with his arms outstretched. He'd been struck in the head by a piece of granite. His hat was gone. His head ached terribly. There was blood running from a scalp wound above his left eye. The light atop the rock was gone. Using the eerie rippling glows and shadows created by the aurorae, Henri lurched forward, feeling his way, stepping over and around obstacles of stone and cement. Two of the three cannons were overturned, knocked from off their mounts. He came upon Sergeant LaCorne whose face was wet with blood, too.

"Is that you, Sergeant?"

"Yes, sir."

"Are you all right? Can you stand? The men need us!"

"Yes, sir!"

Henri pulled the sergeant to his feet and together they searched with their hands outstretched among the rubble that was formerly the Black Rock Point battery. Miraculously, they found the other men groaning but still alive. All of them had head, body, or flesh wounds of varying degrees. One man a broken collar bone. Another a broken arm. But they could all stand. It was a miracle!

"Take hold of the man next to you," Henri ordered. "Help each other walk. We are going to the Royal Hospital!"

The Royal Hospital was a large two-story rectangular building only a block away from the harbor quay wall. An impressive structure, it was not quite as large as the King's Bastion, but the spire at its top was higher.

"Did we hit the ship?"

"Did you hit the ship?! I'll say you did. It was properly lit up by fire and shot! You should be proud! That was the English cruiser we saw when the sun was shining at the beginning of the month! A frigate! Your shots took it completely by surprise. You damaged it! And forced it to turn out to sea to get away."

"A frigate?!"

In the dark, the injured and bloodied cannoneers smiled with satisfaction. Forget about weeks. They were heroes! And they were wounded! They could boast about this for *months*, maybe even till next summer!

The men supported one another under the shoulder and stumbled along the well-worn path leading to the Princess' demi-bastion. They were all bleeding and in some sort of pain. With each step, one of them moaned. Even before they reached the wall by the Princess Bastion, they had to stop and rest twice. One of the men kept passing out. Henri decided he could not let them stop and rest again. The men might be head-shocked from the blast. His own head ached terribly. They all had to stay awake.

The battery at Rochefort Point was still firing its long guns continuously. The large naval rifles were lighting up the night with the cannon blasts. Beautiful bursts of light, sparks, and flame. And the concussive sound with each blast made the men laugh.

"What the hell are they firing at?" Sergeant LaCorne wondered. "More ships?"

"No. You shamed them from their beds," Henri replied. "They had to make some noise, too. But none of them will have any wounds to show for their bravery."

The wounded soldiers laughed again. They liked the idea they had awoken the entire fort. More to brag about.

"Do you think we might be rewarded for this, sir?"

"Rewarded? But I just brought you sugared croissants!" Ensign Gerrard replied in jest.

That brought a chorus of jeers.

"I've shit mine out when a ball hit me," one of them said.

"I puked mine up!" said another.

Henri smiled. Their vulgarity was so easily provoked. He shivered. The cold wind was more penetrating out here in the open.

"Can we rest again, sir? I'm dizzy."

"Me, too," said another man.

He could not let them rest.

"We need to get out of this cold. That's why you're dizzy. The hospital is not much further. Look! It's just there. You can see its lights." Henri must keep them awake. "Nurses are there, remember? And they will have to touch you."

"Touch us?" one replied in a very interested tone. "What…why?"

Henri grinned. "You are all wounded and bleeding. The nurses will touch your bodies anywhere they find blood."

The men were silent for a few seconds as they absorbed this image. Then came sounds of clothing being rustled. In the dark, the cannoneers had started spreading blood from any of their wounds all over the front of their pants.

Their pace quickened.

CHAPTER 6
ROCHEFORT, FRANCE
JANUARY 1757
SIGILLA

When his usual morning headache pain lessened, Lieutenant-Colonel Karl Krieger staggered to his feet. He examined his appearance in the mirror under the lantern light like a man with a hangover. The men of his regiment expected to see him within the hour. He spent every day training and drilling the expanding regiment of troops for the anticipated wilderness battle tactics in America. He washed his face and shaved, pulled a white wig over his short hair, and donned an impeccable Hessian uniform.

Knock. Knock.

On the other side of the door, a corporal knocked gently on the door. The colonel did not answer. Hearing no reply, he repeated the soft knock, then spoke. "Colonel Krieger?"

Again, no answer. This rarely happened. The corporal hesitated a few moments more and returned to his post outside. It was not an emergency. As instructed previously, he would not come back to knock again for another hour.

Krieger inspected his appearance one final time in the mirror before he went down to his regimental headquarters beneath the battlements. Waiting for him were one of his aides, Lieutenant Fürst, along with regimental Color Sergeant Kohring. The subordinates immediately came to attention, snapped their heels together, and saluted.

"Sir!"

He returned the salute. "Why did the corporal of the guard knock on my door?"

"Private Haas just returned from La Rochelle," the lieutenant replied. "He found the ship we seek. It rests at anchor in the La Rochelle harbor."

"Send him to me at once."

The lieutenant's heels clicked together. "Sir!"

The supreme desire of the *vulnax wraith* was to locate the châsse. The reliquary still held a few decayed bones from the corpse of Lord Vaelblez. The new *sigilla* of the *moon, suns, stars* and *water* sealed the châsse. It now made the death of the Great House descendants irrelevant, though it would kill any of them given the opportunity. The châsse *must* be smashed into pieces to break these much stronger seals. The descendants' value now lay in information they could provide to give up the reliquary's current hiding place. If the châsse was in contact with the land, the vulnax's servants would eventually locate it and the vulnax would be able to sense its energy, like it had before. Not now. After so many months, the châsse must be either on a small island or still over water. Over water meant it was aboard Lord VanderMeer's ship. Lord VanderMeer arrived in Amsterdam in an overland coach in December. He was in a wheeled chair, paralyzed from the waist down, the permanent result of the failed assassination attempt. But the man was reported to be alert and coherent. He had taken up residence with his father, the Duke of Brunswick. Getting to him in that palace would be very difficult, probably impossible, and would take too long to find the answer to a simple question.

"Where is Lord VanderMeer's flagship?"

William's Queen was not in Amsterdam. This suggested it had arrived at a different port somewhere in France. A month earlier, servant-soldiers from Krieger's mercenary regiment were ordered to search the French coastal ports, large and small, especially Le Havre, Brest, Lorient, and Toulon. Until now, their searches had proved fruitless.

Then a rumor came down from Amsterdam, that *William's Queen* was anchored in La Rochelle. Colonel Krieger sent a man to see if that was true. Ironically, it was the closest port and the one they visited last. La Rochelle was less than thirty miles away. And purportedly the ship lay at anchor there.

A Hessian private entered the office, saluted, and remained at attention.

"Private Haas, are you certain it was the correct ship?"

"Yes, sir! Its name was *William's Queen*. I rowed out in a boat and read the name on the stern. It was also flying a Dutch royal house banner atop the mainmast."

"How long has it been in port?"

"The harbormaster recorded its arrival the first week of December."

"From what port did it sail?"

"The harbor master claimed it sailed there from America. I took a small rowing boat into the anchorage to find out myself. The watch on deck challenged my approach and pointed a swivel cannon at me. He waved me away without answering any of my questions."

Colonel Krieger calculated if Lord VanderMeer's ship had made another port of call after leaving Boston, that port would have to be along the way, or the arrival in La Rochelle would have been much further delayed. *Someone on the ship will know.*

"You will be going back with me to La Rochelle tomorrow morning. I want to see this ship. You are dismissed."

"Sir!"

Private Haas left. Lieutenant Fürst appeared.

"How many new men today?"

"The regimental count is four hundred seventy-eight," the lieutenant replied. "Four new recruits since yesterday morning."

"Inform Major Sauer to conduct the usual drills. Line maneuvers and marksmanship from individual positions of cover. Keep track of the best marksmen. And arrange a landing galley for our use at dawn tomorrow. Eight horses. Cavalry mounts. You and six other men with experience, including Private Haas. We will be gone for two days, maybe less. I will tell the galley captain where we are sailing after we are aboard. Explain that it will be a short voyage up the coast for training purposes. Send in the new men one at a time."

"Sir!"

Krieger personally evaluated all the candidates for this new regiment. Each day three to ten recruits would show up. He rejected most of them, selecting only the very best, seeking only veterans. He offered pay at twice what they could get from anyone else for such service. When word of this generosity spread through the scores of minor German states, the flow of recruits was constant. His goal was a regiment of seven hundred fifty and preferably a thousand officers and men, if there was time to recruit so many before they deployed to America. Transport to America was not likely to occur until April at the earliest. It was still possible. The intended destination had not been determined.

The new men filed into his office one at a time. The mercenaries were required to be five-year veterans and to have some fluency in French and English. The regiment spoke only German among themselves. Most of the mercenaries were professional soldiers and had served in armies of all these warring countries at some point. Language fluency was not a challenge. The interviews took less than an hour. In the end, he selected two of the four to be added to his regiment. They were both from the Saxony army, recently defeated by Frederick II and absorbed into the Prussian army, from which they deserted. Both were sergeants, veterans of ten and fifteen years. They hated Frederick II. *Ideal recruits.*

Krieger stood, and the two new men saluted crisply. Krieger could feel the presence of the vulnax as if *It* were standing right behind him.

Krieger returned the salutes. "Welcome to the Volontaires-Étrangers Regiment. I expect absolute obedience to orders. Report to First Sergeant Kohring for your pay, uniform, and further assignment. Dismissed."

The vulnax wraith possessed the consciousness of this officer, much as a human would ride a horse, leading by invisible reins. If the human went in the right direction, the vulnax would remain subdued most of the time. But it could surge to dominance in an instant when it chose to do so, spurring the human into acting in specific ways. The wraith cared little about the mercenary training that Krieger considered so important. It was tolerated as a necessity for this body to be transported back to the American continent commanding an enormous strength of arms to pursue the châsse in any manner the wraith chose.

Colonel Krieger's plan was to board the *William's Queen* in La Rochelle and question the crewmembers. The châsse's current location was still a mystery. For too long, a mystery.

For centuries, the vulnax existed by moving freely from one host to the next, as age or death required, though at intervals, sometimes sealed in a tomb or sarcophagus for hundreds of years. But time did not really matter. Eventually, the tomb would be discovered, plundered, and the sarcophagus opened. It would possess a new person. So it had been ever since, at the behest of a priest, he tasted the blood of a dead man as it lay atop a funeral pyre. He'd forgotten who he was back then, exactly why he did this, or how he found the courage to do this. What mattered was he had dipped his human finger into the dead man's head wound and put the finger into his mouth. A surge of power overcame all his senses. Then the pyre was lit by torches and the roaring fire consumed the dead body so completely, even the bones were consumed. All the wraith's current memories stemmed from that moment, and all previous memories concerning this human he once was were consumed in the flames. The wraith never forgot this. Some part of the body of the person it possessed must be preserved after death if memories of the past were to continue.

But it wasn't just memories that must be preserved.

*

The next day at mid-morning, accompanied by seven of his blood servants, Lieutenant-Colonel Krieger led his cavalry troop to the beach area near the fort where a horse transport vessel was waiting. France had created hundreds of such ships of various designs, all intended to support the planned invasion of England. This vessel embodied a design taken from sketches of a Viking war galley used for the transport of horses. It had a center mast with a square-rigged foresail, but the French added a staysail mast at the stern. It would hold twenty horses, plus riders, and twenty oarsmen. This design was not proving as favorable to others because of its low freeboard. If the waves of the open seas were too violent, it might swamp the sides. If the animals panicked, it could induce the vessel to capsize and sink. But if the waters were calm and the galley followed a river or a coastline, going in and out of harbors and quays, the shallow draft was adequate, and it could glide quickly over the waters. The coastal raider was not dependent on just the wind. The oarsmen gave it very good maneuverability.

The front of the vessel supported long heavy planks resting on rollers. Once the vessel beached on a shoreline, the planks were extended up over the bow to create a ramp. Thus, horses could be led ashore quickly.

The captain had selected a landing in the Aytré region south of La Rochelle. This area had a long sandy shore that was shallow with very few rocks and no shoals. The coastal population consisted of small fishing villages and farms. Easily accessible roads were nearby. It was the perfect place to practice a cavalry shore-landing, probably too easy. This was the express purpose for Colonel Krieger's exercise. But the shallowness of this beach made it subject to rapid tidal swings. They planned to use the high tide in the late afternoon for the landing and unloading. The time of sunset was less than an hour later.

Sailing out of the naval arsenal of Rochefort into La Charente River and on into the coastal strait, the length of the journey was only twenty miles to reach the beaches of Aytré. The following winds were favorable. With only eight horses and riders, the ship carried less than half its intended load. Less weight meant more speed. The raider glided swiftly over the coastal waters.

Colonel Krieger stood at the captain's side during the afternoon as they navigated. The captain was amazed at how well this Hessian officer could spot the landmarks. As sunset approached at the hour of six, the destination was in sight.

The flat-bottomed craft slid upon the sandy-muddy shore. The practiced crew pushed the thick planks over the rollers and made a ramp onto the beach. When the horses were ashore, and the men assembled for the ride, Krieger turned back to the captain.

"I will return with my troop tomorrow morning," he informed. "Plan to retrieve us right at this spot when the tide is high again. It will still be dark, but if I find you waiting for me with the ramp extended, you will earn an extra Louis d'Or."

The captain saluted. "I will be waiting right here, Colonel. Look for our lanterns marking the end of the ramps."

It was cold. The troop wore woolen long coats over their mercenary white-and-gray uniforms. The ride from the landing spot to La Rochelle harbor was four miles. Krieger purposely slowed their advance. Lieutenant Fürst carried a directional lantern to light the way. They walked the horses down the road to avoid drawing too much attention to their passing. They reached the southern edge of the outer anchorage at the hour of eight.

"Show me the ship," Krieger ordered Private Haas.

The private led the horses to an overlook of the southern waterfront, across the bay from La Rochelle. They saw the deck lights of at least twenty ships in the anchorage, three of them were large ships-of-the-line.

"That one"—Haas pointed towards a smaller top-sail schooner—"in the center, by itself. I know its deck lights. I rented a cargo boat just down there." He pointed again at a long pier, tethering dozens of rowing vessels. "There are plenty of them large enough for all of us."

There was no moon that night, but the skies were clear.

"Wait here with two men and tend the horses," he ordered Lieutenant Fürst. "The others will come with me. Private Haas, take off your uniform coat and secure us a boat until morning. Get one large enough to carry five, with four oarlocks."

"Yes, sir."

The fort guarding the harbor and anchorage was to the west of them. It was full of French marines, cannoneers, and long barrel naval cannons. Krieger expected the eyes of its sentries to be looking towards the open sea to watch for English cruisers, not the anchorage. Krieger did not want to be noticed by the sentries.

"Speed and quiet will be necessary. Remove anything that will make noise."

Private Haas came back with another lantern and led them to the cargo launch. As ordered, it had four oarlocks. Krieger and his men pushed off from the pier and rowed quietly into the anchorage. It was so dark, the men could hardly tell one ship from another. But under the possession of the vulnax, Krieger could see in the dark better than in daylight. The colonel sat in the stern, and steered with the short tiller to put the cargo launch on the seaward side of *William's Queen* so the profile of the ship was outlined by the distant city lamps of La Rochelle.

They had removed anything that might make a sound. No pistols, no sabers, and carried only bayonets in scabbards. If they were undetected, the ship's watch could be overwhelmed by surprise.

"Two oars," Krieger whispered when they reached the last hundred paces.

The forward-most oars were lifted noiselessly from the water and laid outboard along the benches of the boat. The two oarsmen closest to the colonel continued to dip and pull. The men in front made ready the heavy balls of netting and canvas used as fenders. Just before they came alongside the *William's Queen*, Krieger touched the shoulder of his starboard oarsmen, who immediately elevated his oar to place it soundlessly inside the boat like the others. The cargo launch was alongside, the contact with the hull cushioned by the heavy fenders.

As planned, two of the men climbed silently aboard at the stern. Carrying bayonets in one hand, they began slinking up both sides of the helm deckhouse alert for the watch. Colonel Krieger had warned them explicitly not to kill anyone they found.

The bosun of the *Queen* was alone on his watch. They had posted four anchor watches when they first arrived. This had been reduced to two at night. But after a month of not much occurring, it was relaxed further to one man at night. The harbor waters were calm. The ship was anchored forward and aft and hardly moved.

The bosun used a pile of coiled rope as his pillow and wrapped himself in a woolen blanket against the cold. They'd been in port over a month. Many of the crew were back in Le Havre with families.

Captain LaTour previously announced to the crew he was uncertain where they would sail to next, or even when they would sail. He'd told the crew to come back at the end of January, a time ashore much longer than usual. After that, the plan was to haul the *Queen* up a shipway in La Rochelle harbor, scrape and preserve the hull, and conduct other repairs, only this time by the crew. By the end of February or the middle of March, the captain expected to have a new sailing objective, most likely the Antilles.

Then Captain LaTour had gone to Amsterdam with Lord VanderMeer. Weeks ago, a message arrived from the captain saying he had gone to Paris, ordering Victorio to join him. Now Victorio had gone to Paris. That left the bosun in charge of the ship.

The bosun had sailed ships since he was twelve and the last dozen years with Captain LaTour. He was the best captain the bosun ever knew. This was the best ship he had ever sailed.

La Rochelle was a peaceful port, protected by the French navy in Rochefort and the heavy guns of the harbor fort. These anchor watches were uneventful and boring. Except for the occasional thieves in cargo boats sneaking too close to them, who were easily chased away, there was not much to do. They were empty anyway. Any cargo carried into La Rochelle from the last voyage was offloaded in the first week. The *Queen* sat high in the water. There was plenty of fresh food, though probably too much wine. He'd already drank two bottles that night and had fallen asleep on the helm deck under the starry night sky.

The bosun was snoring loudly when he struggled awake from a choking sensation. He awoke to find himself in the grips of two men, his arms restrained by their knees, his mouth covered with a rag to muffle his screams. He reacted instinctively, freeing an arm, he pulled a knife from his belt and thrust it into the man's belly on his right. The man belched a bloody howl of pain.

But the man on the bosun's left had a bayonet to his throat. The bosun's violent struggle had made the blade bite into the skin, creating a large spurting gash on his neck. The pain was intense.

At that moment, Colonel Krieger was there and laid one hand across the mortal throat wound to temporarily stem the blood flow.

"Hold him still," he hissed to the men. Then he took his own bayonet and stuck it into the victim's knee.

The bosun's body heaved upward from this heightened pain. His yell was muffled. He managed to spit bloody sputum. The throat wound gushed with blood.

"How did you come to La Rochelle? From what port?" Krieger hissed, twisting the blade, popping the bones of the knee. "What port?" he demanded in a louder voice.

The bosun's lips moved soundlessly. He gasped weakly.

"Does this ship carry the châsse?"

No answer.

Krieger twisted the knife viciously back and forth.

The loss of blood from the carotid artery was too great. Seconds later, the bosun's heart stopped.

"I told you not to injure him!" Krieger snarled an instant before he shoved his bayonet through the throat of the offending soldier.

The man died in a gurgle of blood. Now three men lay dead. The other two soldiers, one of them Private Haas, watched in shock, uncertain how to react.

"Strip these bodies of their clothes," he told the private. "Cut off their heads and bag them. Tie weights to the bodies, the bags, and clothes, and drop them over the side. I will conduct a search below by myself."

The vulnax fully dominated Krieger's body. It started all the way forward and searched among the various barrels and piles of canvas in the bow. In the darkness belowdecks, it could see clearly as if it carried a torch. He moved methodically, conducting the search aft into the center hold and into the crew's quarters. Then into the cabin spaces, searching each cabin, under the bunks, into small closets. Next, the galley and the food storage bins, which were not even half full. He spent the most time in the captain's cabin, searching it thoroughly, until he discovered the cleverly disguised chart drawer. He pulled everything out, old charts, rulers, compasses, books of tides, lists of shoals. He wanted to find the chart the captain used for the return voyage from Boston, which would show the course lines he sailed and the ports of call. It wasn't there. He searched further and could not find the captain's logbooks either.

Captain LaTour had taken these important documents with him. And now the man who could have told him where the captain had gone was dead.

Krieger growled with a rage that could be heard up on the main deck. The soldiers looked at one another nervously. But no one dared to go below and see what was wrong.

The vulnax left the captain's cabin and walked forward again, moving slowly, a few steps at a time, back through the sea cabins and the cargo holds, reaching out with his senses, touching the wood with his hands, this time trying to detect the slightest presence of the châsse, possibly a residue from a place where it once rested. But as he entered the bow hold he still felt nothing.

The vulnax knew the new sealing *sigilla* were very strong. He once lay trapped beneath those same signs—trapped for centuries. But were the *sigilla* strong enough to mask the *châsse's* presence? He did not think so. But he wasn't sure. He'd never tried to look beyond the *sigilla,* from the outside. Water was strong enough to cloak the *châsse's* presence. If it was not on this ship, then perhaps it was buried on a small island. If it was an island, the vulnax would have to get very close to the *châsse* to sense it.

But where is it?

They could wait for another crew member to come aboard the next morning. But in calm, flat waters on a quiet night like this, the loud screams of the dying men were certainly heard. There were bloodstains all over the deck. The closest ship anchored near *William's Queen* was a heavily armed naval frigate. The noises would have been noticed. When the sun came up, a launch full of armed sailors would be sent over to investigate. They would assume it was the work of thieves, if the troops were not seen. They needed to be gone and soon.

The châsse is not aboard this ship. Someone in Boston knows where it is. But who?

An animal growl of frustration erupted from Krieger. He ripped one of the four-inch, oaken steps from the forward deck ladder and threw it back into the empty hold. He climbed to the main deck.

All traces of the bodies were weighted to sink in the dark harbor waters. Krieger and his men were gone before the midnight hour. They returned to the beaches of Aytré.

Paris

It took six days of patient waiting in Paris before Captain LaTour was summoned to meet with Jean-Baptiste de Machault, the Minister of Marine.

"My apology for making you wait so long, Captain. There is much going on concerning me, issues other than the war. But tell me about Lord VanderMeer."

LaTour described the poor health of Lord VanderMeer, that the prognosis of his survival was not good. The minister was genuinely saddened to hear this.

"And the Duke of Brunswick?"

"I left the palace before I met him. Lord VanderMeer felt certain if I stayed much longer, I could be coerced by one of the numerous people trying to learn the location of Lady Corrinne. I heeded his advice and left, only to discover that my bedchambers in the ducal palace were scoured. My ship's logbook was stolen from my baggage. From that, someone can determine her location. I worry…well, that an assassin might find a way into Louisbourg. Lady Corrinne needs to be warned."

"I think she already presumes this. I ordered Governor Drucour to have her protected. I will send an additional message to her that we have talked. But I will not…I will refrain from mentioning what you've said about Lord VanderMeer. I must trust he will communicate with her personally. When do you put to sea again?"

"Not until mid-March. My ship is overdue for careening. That will take most of February and maybe into March."

"Where do you go next?"

"I don't know," LaTour replied glumly. "As you are aware, I have two masters. Lord VanderMeer, the owner, is dying. He gave me his leave to go anywhere I wanted. But I am bewildered what to do. My other master is Admiral de la Motte. I am supposed to see him after the careening. I feel certain he will order me to do something for him."

Machault leaned on his elbows and bridged his hands.

"Allow Admiral de la Motte to tell you this, but the admiral will order your ship to sail back to Louisbourg as soon as your careening is completed."

"Louisbourg?" That was news to Captain LaTour. "Why?"

"You may blame me. This is something I arranged. There is a Swiss mercenary captain in Louisbourg who needs to be brought back to France to recruit more mercenaries. He demanded transport by a Dutch ship to minimize being boarded by the English. *William's Queen* fits this need perfectly. I expect your orders will contain more specifics."

"Well," LaTour replied in a fatalistic tone. "Like I said, Admiral de la Motte would have something for me to do. What about Lady Corrinne?"

Machault nodded. "There are other courier ships that will take her a message."

"With the threat of invasion, she will need transport away from Louisbourg…to go somewhere else…maybe Québec City? If I arrive there in late March or early April…"

Machault shook his head. "I anticipate your orders will state you are to bring the Swiss captain back to Brest without delay. But this doesn't stop you from filling up your cargo hold with luxury goods for the famished people of Louisbourg…among whom Lady Corrinne resides."

"Of course."

They were both quiet for several seconds. LaTour could see and sense Minister Machault had become preoccupied with something.

"Minister, if I may intrude, is France winning this war?"

Machault frowned with weariness and returned his attention to the captain.

"Winning? Depends on who you ask. But a better question to ask is does France have the *will* to win this war? Consider the question rhetorical. Is our business finished, then, Captain?"

LaTour stood. "Yes, sir."

Machault came around his desk to shake the captain's hand. "Apologies for my brusqueness, Captain. I am beset with the problems of government."

"I do not want to increase that burden. People I meet speak highly of you. I enjoyed seeing you, Minister. And I always will. Thank you for your time."

Amsterdam

Rutger van Boekel was frustrated with trying to arrange this simple meeting for the Duke of Brunswick in Aanwas. So many French officials of government suddenly wanted to become involved with any discussion concerning the Duke of Brunswick that just agreeing on a date generated relays of couriered messages for over a month, with no agreement. At this rate, it would take another month. Rutger decided to take a great chance and couriered a confidential missive directly to Madame Margaux-Lyneth Dubonnet, apologizing for the clumsiness.

> *Regrettably, it has become difficult to get them all to agree when to do this. It appears it may not be possible until the end of February, or possibly even March. The war and recent French troop movements into the western German states now complicate this even further. So, I propose Madame, that you determine a date that is convenient for*

you. It will only take a few days for the Duke to travel from Amsterdam to Aanwas. When you predict a date to position yourself safely in the city of Antwerp, I will send a messenger to Antwerp from Aanwas to arrange the final ten miles of escort. Please send a confidential reply to me in Amsterdam.

CHAPTER 7
LAKE GEORGE
WINTER 1756
Panther Claw

Fort Oswego was the last remaining British fort on Lake Ontario. In August of 1756, it fell to General Montcalm's forces. The French now commanded the wilderness lands and rivers around the great lakes. Fearing the French would follow up this victory over Fort Oswego to campaign south on the Oswego River, Colonel Webb ordered the 44th Regiment of Foot, still marching on the Oneida Carry, to stop their advance. He ordered them to destroy all the supply forts at either end of the carrying place, all the way back to the Mohawk River.

But they did not stop there. Webb ordered the destruction of the staged supplies of food stocks, ammunition, the wagons, cannons, and the custom-engineered portage-hoisting mechanisms. In less than the space of a week, a resupply capability to Lake Ontario—an effort that took ten years of hard labor to build, not by the English but by the Americans—was destroyed completely. The British had effectively demolished the ability to assert claim to any lands north of the Mohawk River and west to the Ohio River valley. This was viewed as abandonment by the native tribes across the great lakes. New allies from as far away as Detroit now flocked to join with the dominant French.

The French were unopposed, and they knew it.

Governor-General Pierre de Vaudreuil and General Louis-Joseph de Montcalm debated how to exploit this new position of strength in Québec City. It was too late in the year to campaign further in 1756, but there were ways to harass the English during the winter to prepare the way for a spring campaign in 1757. To that end, they argued about the different strategies but agreed they must seize the two remaining forts standing in the way of investing the city of Albany in the New York colony. Fort William Henry was situated at the south end of Lac du Saint-Sacrament, Lake George to the English, and Fort Edward fifteen miles further south on the Hudson River.

If this spring campaign objective was successful, Albany would be threatened. The English might be forced to sue for peace. Presuming the possibility of the fall of the two English forts was realized, French strength-in-arms were too few and too weak to exploit this advantage much beyond a threat to Albany. But did the English realize this? They were, after all, still reeling from the loss of Fort Oswego. It was just another reason for the French to act while there was time. It was one of the rare occasions that Vaudreuil and Montcalm agreed with one another. Under the presumption the English would retreat to winter quarters and wait until spring, they started to plan an attack during the winter.

*

Captain Philippe Gerrard's *coureur de bois* scout companies around Lake Champlain and Lac du Saint-Sacrament became the most formidable raiders in this contested wilderness. Only the native warriors allied to the English, the Mohawk and Oneida, proved equal in confronting the deadly stealth of the *coureurs de bois*. The French met with the Iroquois war chiefs and asserted the French had no design on settling in these lands and no hostile intentions towards the Iroquois tribes...unless the Iroquois attacked first. The only enemy the French sought to defeat were the English-Americans. As a result, an informal truce of sorts now existed between the French and the Iroquois. For a few months, Captain Gerrard's scouting raids around the English forts and trading posts were not impeded by the Mohawk.

In early October 1756, that changed. A group of American fighters entered the conflict and became more prevalent in the lands around Lake Champlain and Lake George. They had scouted around the lakes since the previous year in small groups and grew stronger even before the attack on Fort Oswego. They were wilderness men from New Hampshire and Vermont, called *rangers* by the English. Now they challenged the French everywhere. They were commanded by Robert Rogers, a gifted, charismatic wilderness fighter.

Robert Rogers was born of Ulster Scottish immigrants in Massachusetts, a Presbyterian family who found themselves unwelcome by the current Puritan residents. Since land was plentiful in the Merrimack Valley of New Hampshire, the family migrated and soon became landowners there with many other independence-minded settlers. It was a rugged wilderness with brutal winters. Life was hard for these settlers who nevertheless declared it their home. They learned how to survive, to build sturdy defensible log homes, to grow crops, to herd cattle and raise families. These were families who became deeply familiar and comfortable with the wilderness and its dangers. All of this, while intermittently assailed by the native tribes who claimed these same lands, arguing they had lived upon them for a millennium. But the Scotsmen, too, had passionate tribal roots in their blood and history. Defending homestead lands, be they in Scotland, Ireland, or America, was instinctive. They expected to be challenged. These settlers gave as good as they got. And eventually they got even better.

Rogers was a skilled woodsman of fourteen years when he joined with the English forces during King George's War of 1745. The New Hampshire wilderness fighters were ordered to attack the French and the Wabanaki Confederation of tribes in the northeast, and, in particular, the Abenaki tribal settlements, whose aggressive warriors marauded from their Saint Francis River mission villages just to the north. The fighting and raiding went back and forth over four years until King George's War ended. By then Robert Rogers, John Stark, and other Vermont and New Hampshire men had become hardened veterans, highly skilled in wilderness fighting and just as merciless in retaliation as their enemies.

When the next war with the French was declared, Robert Rogers and other settlers in New Hampshire saw an opportunity to expand their land claims across the Connecticut River further into the west. They explored the lands around Lake Champlain and determined all they had to do was drive the French out of the way. They heeded the call from General John Winslow, another American long serving in the British army. General Winslow was a senior English officer, but behind the red uniform he wore, Winslow was American first; a tough soldier with Pilgrim roots.

Rogers was twenty-four years old when he led two companies of rangers into the disputed lakes and lands surrounding Lake George and Lake Champlain. General Winslow declared him a captain and commanded him to expand his ranger forces to battalion strength.

"Your orders are simple. Harass and take these lands and lakes away from the French!"

Rogers smiled. "That was our intention."

From that point on, the French scout companies led by Captain Philippe Gerrard suffered casualties on an equal basis with these skillful American scouts. It was almost one for one, and most times in revenge. Men were killed and scalped by both sides, and captured prisoners were executed after questioning, often under torture, which steadily grew more appalling, intended as a message, a warning to the other side. The savagery of the acts worsened, building over time.

This savagery coarsens the very nature of a man, Philippe wrote in the journal he'd begun keeping. *The tolerance builds. It blackens the soul. When my men found one of their friends hanging in the air by the wrists, his skin flayed from the body, obvious that the man had died slowly by fire, cooking from the feet up, their rage was not containable. To my everlasting shame, I did not stop them. After centuries of cruelties, they seem anxious to do such things. But to accept this as justifiable human nature? To measure my own humanity by how soon I turn my face from the horror? No. I cannot. This is not a measure of humanity; it is a measure of cowardice. And the sounds? I will be forever haunted. I am shamed and forbade my men from engaging in such acts in the future. But when I am not present, I know it still occurs.*

Scenes of torture were common in the lives of many *coureur de bois* scouts. Most were inured to these memories and indifferent when it happened now. For those whose native loyalties were connected by family, and often more tribal than French, their allegiances were fickle. They could be swayed either way if the argument was persuasive.

Then there were the scouts recruited directly from various tribes, and some who volunteered for revenge or other undeclared reasons. One such man in Philippe's troop of scouts was a warrior named Mkuigen Malsum. His name meant *red wolf* in the Abenaki tongue. And not just any wolf with reddish fur, which by itself would be a very rare sight indeed. But a type of wolf reputed to have an origin from that place after death—a *wendigo*.

But Philippe Gerrard regarded Malsum as just a man, albeit a seemingly sinister man. He was an Abenaki warrior, over forty summers in age, possessed with extraordinary wilderness talents, even when compared to the *coureurs de bois*, rangers, and other natives. He was six feet of sinew and muscle, embodied with endless physical endurance. He knew the lands around the lakes intimately. He knew the distances involved, how long it would take to reach somewhere on foot in a fast walk or at a run, the best places for ambush, the best places of retreat, game runs, fishing shallows, and was considered the best tracker of man or animal. During the months before the arrival of the rangers, when the courage of the *coureurs de bois* tended to be reckless, many skirmishes took place and men on both sides died foolishly.

Malsum and Philippe were more cautious and had saved each other's lives more than once.

Eventually, the instances of death among the scouts became less and less. Philippe was encouraged.

"Maybe they are finally getting smarter," he mentioned quietly to Malsum one day.

Malsum shook his head. "No. It just means the stupid ones are all dead."

Malsum's head was shaved clean on all sides except for a black topknot bush of hair adorned with feathers. Bone ornaments hung from his ears and nose. From head to foot, his body was covered with tattoos of black lines and puzzling symbols. Malsum refused to explain their meaning or how he got them.

The lines on his face were recognizable and the most frightening: tattoos to infer the outlines of his skull and the teeth beneath his lips. It was a death mask. If he stared at anyone for too long, they would grow fearful. Occasionally they would vomit. Truly a *wendigo* in the flesh.

Malsum was the most dreaded member of Captain Gerrard's scouts. In addition to a fluency in most native tongues, Malsum also spoke French and English fluently. Not many people other than Philippe realized the fluency with which the native could speak the white man's languages. With his eyes closed, he could not tell if it was an Englishman with a Scottish accent talking, or a citizen of Québec City. Most of the time, Malsum disguised this ability. He usually spoke French in the halting but polite patois of a native who'd learned just enough French to conduct a trade. If a person wanted a more expressive discussion with Malsum, he would need to speak the Abenaki tongue…fluently.

Philippe found him reading a missive one day. Confronted, Malsum reluctantly admitted he could also read and write in French and English. No one else knew this. Philippe had not mentioned it to anyone, earning more of Malsum's trust.

"My mother was Abenaki," was usually the most Malsum ever admitted when asked a question about his past.

They knew nothing about his father. No one knew what village he came from. The Abenaki grudgingly acknowledged he was one of their own but little more. They seemed to fear him more than they feared the white man. There were so many rumors, the truth became distorted by the speculation. But they all agreed on one thing: Malsum was someone you did not want as an enemy. This reputation was earned. Among the many weapons Malsum carried was a bone-handle knife with a vicious metal blade, sharp and curved backwards like a hook, resembling a panther claw. And that is what Malsum called it: Panther Claw. Eventually this became his warrior name. It was a blade created to cut tough leather hides after they were cured, or anything else that required a precise pattern that needed to be cut for further crafting into useful things: clothing, sacks, scabbards, moccasins, or long strips of leather cord. Malsum did not take trophy scalps. Instead, he would carefully slice away a person's face as his trophy. The victims were usually dead… at least, they were dead when they were discovered. No one had ever seen him do this to anyone who was still alive. But Malsum carried a dried, leathery, blackened skin mask of a human face with him as proof. He would sometimes put this on before interrogating prisoners to get them to talk. And they all talked…with eagerness! Often just seeing the death mask tattoos on Malsum's face was enough.

By circumstance, in one engagement of mid-November 1756, Philippe's troop of forty-six men fell into a trail behind an equal number of rangers. The trail was trampled, one or two days old, judging by the fill in the tracks from the recent snowfall.

"There!" Malsum said suddenly.

He pointed towards a singular trail separated from the others by several paces. The Abenaki warrior knelt and studied it. These were fresh in comparison to the others.

"A day old. Maybe less. One man. Hurt. Uses a stick. Drags one leg."

The *coureurs de bois* spread out and advanced at a fast walk. It did not take long to catch up with the wounded man. And it was a ranger! To capture one alive was a very rare occurrence; the rangers loathed to leave any wounded man behind, and for good reason. This man had broken his right leg below the knee in a fall down an embankment, he would later claim. The entire leg was swollen and had turned purple. It was close to going rotten. Death would follow soon after that. He was scared enough to answer the few questions posed to him.

His name was John Griffin. He'd separated accidentally from the ranger company. He did not elaborate on that.

"They are two days gone from the area," Griffin told them.

He also claimed to be seventeen. But he was barely over five feet tall and very skinny.

Just a boy. Philippe decided. *No more than twelve.*

"Where are you from?"

"Albany, New York. I'm lost, I planned to follow this eastern shoreline of Lake George back to Fort William Henry. But the snow drifts piled high on a lip over the edge of an embankment. It made them hard to judge. I stepped through one and fell. There were rocks at the bottom. That's how I broke my leg. I've been without food for two days."

Griffin was breathing heavily from pain and exhaustion and was weakened and starving; a few days short of dying in Philippe's estimation. And if the temperature dropped any more, he would freeze to death.

When Philippe learned the rangers had left the area, he ordered camp to be made. Sentries were posted by twos in several directions. John Griffin was tied to a tree five paces from the center fire pit where he soon met Malsum. Philippe introduced John Griffin.

"John Griffin, this is Malsum. He will assist me in asking you questions."

There was no need for Malsum to don his skin mask. John Griffin had heard about this man and the gruesome stories about *the face of death*. Upon seeing the fierce visage of the Abenaki for the first time, the boy immediately wet himself.

Malsum sat cross-legged in front of him, Panther Claw clearly visible in one hand. He purposely touched the edges of Griffin's wincing face, examining the cheekbones and the hairline with one finger, as if measuring it.

Griffin answered any question Philippe asked. Just by surviving, seriously injured and alone, it was evident the boy had wilderness skills. But John Griffin was not a ranger and Philippe was not surprised to hear him admit this.

"I was refused by Captain Rogers. Said I was too young. Come back to the island next summer, Captain Rogers told me."

"What island?"

"Ranger Island, on the Hudson River, just west of Fort Edward. Over thirty maybe forty acres. That's where they train. Captain Rogers gave me a list of the ranger orders of march and told me not to come back until I had them memorized. But when they left on this new scout, I waited a day and followed them, to prove I could track them without being seen and survive doing it. I am still learning the rules."

"What rules?"

For a few seconds, John Griffin hesitated. Malsum leaned in close.

"They are in my pack! They are in my pack!"

Griffin's pack had already been dumped out on the ground and rummaged through. Anything of value to a scout had been taken. Philippe looked through the refuse and found a scroll of paper tied with a slender cord, ignored by the others. It was a hand-written list, titled "Ranger Orders of March." Twenty-eight rules. They were in English. Philippe scanned them quickly. The French had nothing written down like this, but Philippe found it remarkable how many of these tactics the *coureurs de bois* performed naturally by instinct and from experience, having learned them through hard lessons. But if this is how the rangers truly maneuvered in the wilderness, the list was valuable intelligence indeed. He turned the page to let Malsum glance at it.

"I'll give this to you later," Philippe said quietly in the Abenaki tongue. Malsum nodded.

"Save me some time, Griffin. What other secrets do you have?" Philippe asked. "Your life will depend on the value of what you tell me. Or how soon your death will be permitted after torture," he warned and tilted his head towards Malsum.

"I-I have no other secrets! I've told you everything there is to know! I swear it!"

Malsum lifted Panther Claw close to the boy's face.

"My middle name is *Dante*," Griffin squealed in fear.

"What?"

"My...my mother was from Sicily...it was her father's name! I have no other secrets!"

"That's all? That's your only big secret?"

"Let me cut off his cock...or one of his fingers. The fingers are probably bigger anyway," Malsum said casually in Abenaki. "How many secrets could this white boy of thirteen summers have? I doubt he's even coupled with a woman."

With a quick slashing movement, Panther Claw cut the lace cords on the front of Griffin's pants.

The boy screamed in terror. The other scouts paid no attention to the scream. They expected it was just one of many screams to come.

"See? I told you! He does not even have hair!" Malsum carefully prodded the boy's cock with the tip of his knife. Griffin squeaked and urinated a few drops. "It's like the head of a frightened turtle. The last joint of his little finger is bigger than this. Perhaps I could cut that?"

Philippe snorted. "No. I have another idea. We'll set his broken leg. Give him some food, and let him go in the morning."

"What! Let him go? Why?"

Philippe looked at Malsum. "The boy knows absolutely nothing. He is not a ranger. I want to send him back with a wild story to tell. See how Captain Rogers reacts to this. And it will give the boy a chance to prove himself."

"Prove himself?" Malsum snickered and prodded the cock again, Panther Claw evoking another *eeek* from the boy. "It will take another five years for that little thing to grow!"

"So be it." Philippe's attention returned to the scroll. "These ranger rules are worth his life. I am going to study them by the light of the campfire." He stood up. "I'll send the surgeon to tend his leg and have someone bring food. I'll give you the scroll to read when I'm done. But I want to keep this list a secret between us."

When Philippe left, Malsum turned his attention back to the boy and accused him in perfect English.

"You lied about your age."

Griffin was astonished to hear this wilderness man speak English.

"Yes! I am only twelve! What are you going to do?" he asked in a plaintive voice.

"Snow Hair will let you go in the morning."

"Let me go?!"

"I am more surprised than you are. I want to cut the skin from your face before we kill you. But Snow Hair says no. You may want to thank him." Malsum leaned close, until their noses touched. "John Griffin, remember my face. Heed my words. Today is not your day to die. If you ever see my face again, it will be your day to die…painfully. Go home! Pray we never meet again. This is not your war, John Griffin. Wait for the next one!"

Fort Carillon, Lake Champlain

The light, powdery snows and persistent cold of the fall and early winter were tolerable and did not prohibit normal travel on the wilderness trails and streams. In the second week of January, the temperature dropped precipitously. It measured well below the freezing point of water according to Captain Louis Antoine de Bougainville's treasured thermometer he kept in a polished wooden box.

Louis Antoine de Bougainville was twenty-seven, brilliant, and highly educated. He had already written and published two books on Integral Calculus. He spent time in England before the outbreak of the latest war and so impressed his English colleagues, he had been elected a member of the British Royal Society. But he wanted to expand his knowledge of the world, so he joined the army and volunteered to serve in New France. Now he was one of General Montcalm's aides-de-camp and was captain of the dragoon regiment in Québec City. Restless even in winter, he had volunteered to stay at Fort Carillon, to go on scouting patrols with his new friend, Scout Captain Philippe Gerrard. He kept a daily journal of his observations in the wilderness. One of them was about the weather. He'd never experienced cold like this and later wrote about its affects in his journal.

> *The cold, dry air came from the north during the night. The denser air billowed down upon Fort Carillon located on the Ticonderoga point of Lake Champlain. It slipped beneath and around the flimsy wooden doorways and shuttered windows, pushing into every corner, coming into the barracks to curl around the double-wide cots shared by pairs of shivering soldiers who slept fitfully. It seized upon any moist air rising from their body heat which precipitated instantly into sticky crystals. Frost fingers lapped around the corners of the blankets and furs. The tiny crystals sucked away more body heat. Any skin exposed for too long would freeze and turn black.*
>
> *The groaning sleepers tucked up their legs beneath the blankets and furs, tightening the corners, pulling up their knees, inserting hands under their arms. It was worse for the unlucky sentries that night, wrapped in blankets or furs over their heads and shoulders, scarves covering their ears and around their nose and mouth. They had to walk constantly to stay warm and stomped their feet to keep the blood flowing. Vaporous breath froze into icicles on their beards and eyebrows.*
>
> *The light of morning found most of the soldiers in the barracks huddled around the cooking hearths, stoked with enough wood to produce as much heat as possible.*

"My thermometer indicates it is twenty-six degrees below the freezing point of water on the Celsius scale!" Bougainville announced to the shivering soldiers as if it were a victory of some sort. "And yet we are still alive! Imagine that?"

One of the men responded cynically. "I don't know what Celsius means, Captain. Does that mean fucking cold? Or really, really fucking cold?"

Bougainville was amused. "I presume it is as cold as your second suggestion."

The first sergeant intruded and prodded the bodies with the toe of his boot.

"Stand up you, slugs! Get moving! Break your fast! All of you! You'll feel warmer when you do."

The cooks dropped hot dollops of mashed squash and beans into wooden bowls. A slice of black bread lay across the top of the mash to hold in the heat.

"Eat it fast."

"What are these black things?"

"Just bits of black bread I added to the mash."

"*Bits of black bread*?" one man complained. "One of mine is squirming!"

"Well, the bugger is probably cold, too. Like I said…eat it fast, before it freezes."

"Don't be concerned. Grubs are a nutritious food," Captain de Bougainville explained to the men with a smile. "The natives eat them all the time."

"Grubs? These are fucking grubs?!"

"I think mine are maggots," said another.

"Do you want some, *sir*?" asked a skeptical voice.

"No, no. *Merci*," Bougainville replied quickly. "I have already eaten."

During the day, construction on the battlements of Fort Carillon proceeded slowly in the bitter cold. The men worked in teams of three, supervised by the engineers. Each hour, two men out of the three chopped wood, sawed logs, cut stone, stirred mortar with a hoe without stopping. They carried and set the cut stone into the wall before the mortar froze. A third man huddled near a fire to stay warm. They all worked in two-hour shifts with one-hour breaks from sunrise to sunset. They recognized this work was important and were encouraged by the officers. All but the most senior officers, captain and above, worked right alongside them. Kettles of water inside the barracks were kept hot, tested first by a man's elbow before they plunged their hands in one, or their feet into another to thaw and warm nearly frozen fingers and toes. The cooks would later claim they forgot which pot held the soup.

They washed, cleaned, and dried their feet every day and pulled on two layers of wool socks lest their feet get frostbite. When not working or standing guard, they slept, too exhausted to play their gambling games with cards and dice. The only comforting thought was the knowledge the English were suffering just as much.

The wilderness began transforming. On the flat unmoving surface of the smaller lakes and ponds, an eerie noise arose during this deep freeze, more easily heard in the chilly stillness of the night. It was a barely perceptible tinkling sound, like the snap of the delicate stem of a wine glass, as the water froze web-like outward from the shore. The devil's harp, some of the *coureurs de bois* called it. Death's music to anyone who lay exposed in the wilderness. Moving waters gave way to ice growth more slowly. The freezing first possessed the shallower streams and creeks, starting near the edges of the broader rivers and the big lakes, until it froze them over to the middle. The cold pushed deeper. The ice thickened to a foot and more. The deadly below-zero air persisted for five days before it warmed to the low single digits and did not warm any further for a long time. Another change in weather rolled over them. The dry air abruptly turned moist. The snow began to fall and fall and fall. Drifts became waist deep.

"At least the winds are minimal," Captain Bougainville offered with optimism to Captain Gerrard.

The next day, it became windy, too.

"This winter will be harsh, just like last year," a veteran groused.

The canoes and bateaux were pulled from the water on the first day of freezing to prevent them from being crushed by the ice. The *coureur de bois* scouts at Fort Carillon inspected and repaired their knee-high, waterproof, fur-lined moccasins fashioned in the same manner as the native peoples had done for hundreds of winters. They restrung their webbed snow shoes with new leather cords. The blacksmiths crafted more ice skates. They had to be custom fit to the feet of each new man. Iron blades crimped over flat pieces of springy birch wood, which would slip over the thick winter moccasins and strapped up around the calves almost to the knee. Using skates, the scouts could travel a lake or river in less than half the time it took in a water craft.

The *coureurs de bois* usually scouted in groups of six to twelve men. Several groups were moving around in the snowy wilderness every day. They brought back reports on the English activity at Fort Edward and Fort William Henry at the south end of Lac du Saint-Sacrament; Lake George as the English called it. They reported that at Fort William Henry, the English were building many boats. They had finished two sloops and another one was under construction. Presumably in preparation for a summer campaign to attack Fort Carillon.

There were also signs of the American rangers scouting around Fort Carillon and Fort Saint-Frédéric. The rangers often captured French soldiers making careless mistakes in traveling between these two forts. The *coureurs de bois* captured prisoners, too. Not rangers, but near Fort William Henry, soldiers went out hunting for food or carried messages to and from Fort Edward.

It was winter. Logistics were difficult. The English and the French knew exactly what their enemies were doing. But neither side knew what the other side planned for the spring. They kept track of the troop strength and troop movements. The officers of both sides did not share any conclusions about this with the common soldiers, for fear they might be captured. But the soldiers speculated among themselves. Prisoner information rose in value as spring approached. And regardless of January's cold and the snow, spring was only two months away.

*

Captain Robert Rogers left his island on the Hudson River with fifty rangers and proceeded to Fort William Henry. Once there he asked its commander, Engineering Major Eyre, for volunteers. Another thirty-three eager men joined the scouts, anxious to learn the wilderness battle skills of the prestigious rangers.

They left late in the afternoon and skated up the ice of Lake George for several hours, their path illuminated only by starlight on the snow. It was very cold, but they remained warm from the physical exertion. Most of the volunteers had skated before, but never like this. Skating a dozen miles only appeared easy. Close to midnight, Rogers called a halt at a place he knew would provide defensive shelter and good cover for a campfire. The volunteers who made it were blistered and exhausted, many of them vomiting from the vigorous pumping sprint. A few had not made it even a mile before turning back to the fort. Half of them straggled into camp over the next two hours because of injuries sustained from nasty falls on the ice. Mostly ankle sprains and minor fractures. Rogers had expected this. It was his way of testing a man's endurance and tolerance to pain. Better to know it now than later. Any volunteer who complained too loudly about his injury would be sent back to Fort William Henry in the morning. They lost about a dozen of the volunteers to this exhaustion.

Presuming they survived the entire scout that lay ahead, the remainder of the volunteers would also lose much body weight before they returned to the fort, where they could proudly brag about patrolling with the rangers. But after what was to come, very few of those who returned would ever volunteer to join a ranger scout again. And only one would be deemed fit enough and tough enough to be invited to join the elite unit.

The rangers were now halfway up Lake George. They camped on the lake's eastern side directly across from the Tongue Mountain ridgeline on the other side of the lake in the west. Sentries were placed by fours in a circle, thirty to forty paces away from the camp, on positions of higher ground. They would be relieved in three hours by four new sentries and three hours after that by another four.

Before the sun rose in the morning, they broke camp and skated across the lake ice to the eastern side. Once there, the skates came off, replaced by snow shoes. Rogers' objective was to reach a place on the western shore of Lake Champlain midway between the two French forts. Once up and over the ridgeline, they circled wide, going three miles inland first to lessen the chance of being seen. They marched with blankets over their head and ears, tied around their waists, with mitten lines down the arms of their coats and attached with knots to prevent losing these vital downy gloves that kept their fingers from freezing. It took two more days of exhausting march through deep snow and across ice-covered streams. Sometimes the ice didn't tolerate the weight of so many men, plunging some of them into freezing water adding to their misery. They arrived with numb and partially frozen fingers and toes, their clothing covered with burrs, cones, dead leaves, and other random debris collected by brushing through the dense forest undergrowth.

Rogers found a good spot to create a defensive circle. They were now five miles north of Fort Carillon and three miles west of Lake Champlain. He found high ground with a depression in the center. Wide enough to encamp all his men with plenty of good outlying sentry positions. He assigned extra sentries to give them an advantage against a night attack from any direction. This would also be the first place of retreat should it become necessary. They used their snow shoes to clear a broad circle, piling banked snow topped with dead branches around the perimeter to make their camp. They dug a half-dozen deep fire pits and heated and ate a meal of salt pork, a wet mash of peas and squash, plus hard navy biscuits, softened with rum-diluted water. They ate a double portion of their food; there was no way of telling when they would eat again. They quickly set up bark-covered lean-tos around the fire pits for protection against the weather. Each of the rangers carried rolls of birch bark with them for just this purpose and arranged spruce boughs for triple beds. Sentries were divided in teams of four and sent deep into the forest darkness, in the usual practice.

He called his subordinate captains, John Stark and Thomas Speakman, plus Lieutenant Kennedy and the senior sergeants together. They all scanned the map Rogers carried with him and preselected familiar places on Lake George for withdrawal and retreat should anyone get separated. Three places. A different one for each of the next three days, the last one at the Lake George narrows.

"You all know these places well. This plan of retreat, should it become necessary, starts tomorrow after we conduct our first ambush. Use these points of rendezvous if you get separated from the rest of us. I expect to learn the strength of forces the French intend to post at these forts during the next two months. Like us, they will have plans for a spring campaign. Those strategies are the most valuable information for us to obtain. Don't scalp them too quickly."

The men laughed.

The ambush plans were explained by the subordinates to the other rangers, with special emphasis for the twenty volunteers that remained. They reviewed the typical orders expected during this battle, how captured prisoners were controlled, the types of withdrawal they would make for different circumstances, and what was expected of each man.

"If you are captured," one veteran sergeant warned the volunteers from Fort William Henry, "you will be questioned most unpleasantly before dying. It will be better for you to get killed and avoid the torture. Get as much sleep as possible tonight when you are not on sentry duty. No way of telling when you will get to sleep again."

Most of the volunteers did not sleep at all that night.

CHAPTER 8
FORT CARILLON
JANUARY 1757
Death on Skates and Snowshoes

Commandant-Captain Paul-Louis de Lusignan commanded both Fort Saint-Frédéric and Fort Carillon during the winter of 1756 and into the early months of the next year. He expected Brigadier General François de Lévis to return from Québec City in the spring. In the meantime, Lusignan took his duties very seriously. He was an older army officer of sixty-five years, finishing a respectable if not distinguished career. Now that the lake was frozen, he found travel between the two lake forts by sleigh both fast and efficient, a short trip of fifteen miles over the ice. If the weather was not bad, Lusignan spent most of his time at Fort Carillon to monitor the construction progress. He expected to get much of the credit for the strength of this fort when it was finished.

On the morning of the nineteenth of January, the commandant called a war council with the officers of Fort Carillon. But he was unaware that a strong force of American rangers was already five miles north of him and setting up a base camp for an attack.

The French officers gathered around a table map, an artistic work of cartography that depicted both Lac du Saint-Sacrement and Lake Champlain, the surrounding lands, the rivers, mountains, the most traveled trails and wilderness roads. It was further detailed with the location of the forts, trading posts, and the tribal villages. The English did not possess a map even half as accurate as this one. But the English knew well enough where the French forts were located. They had firsthand scouted knowledge of the terrain and the best ways to get there. The French recognized that was all an attacker needed to know. The rest was tactics.

Captain Lusignan established the topic for discussion.

"As many of you know, the spring equinox is but two months away. We expect an attack on us this spring, either at Fort Saint-Frédéric or Fort Carillon, or possibly both forts using two forces, one of them being diversionary.

But we do not know when or in what strength the enemy will march. We must assume they know our current strength from the prisoners they have taken over the last several months. We possess similar knowledge about the English. Despite the recent snows and the bitter cold, the British will be positioning more troops and arms corresponding to their war aims. We have been watching the ambitious construction of bateaux, artillery platforms, and cannon sloops at Fort William Henry. Captain Gerrard's scouts will now begin reinforced patrols to evaluate English readiness weekly as a measure of when we should expect their advance. Captain?"

Philippe pointed at locations on the map as he explained his plans. "Tomorrow morning, we deploy three separate groups of scouts to positions here, here, and here. The scout companies will be reinforced with grenadiers and other militia volunteers. Each group will number between thirty and forty men in strength, strong enough for skirmishing if challenged. This is a hundred and eighteen officers and men with enough provisions for a week. We march at first light. One third will circle west, climb up and around the La Chute cascades, and move down Lac du Saint-Sacrament by skate and snow shoe to reconnoiter Fort William Henry atop these hills to the west of that fort." He pointed at the map again. "At the same time, a second group will cross Lake Champlain and skate south down the Long Bay and go up the rivers at its end. Then overland on snow shoes to reconnoiter Fort Edward. I will take the final third across Lake Champlain to reconnoiter the peninsula lands between the Long Bay and Lac du Saint-Sacrament. This is a route the rangers use more often. If there is an engagement by anyone, a messenger will be sent back to the fort. My forces will go forward in support.

"The remainder of the scouts, thirty-two men, will be held in reserve here at the fort to continue their usual patrols and be ready to support our return. The primary objective is to assess the current strength of Fort Edward and Fort William Henry by direct observation and interrogation of captured prisoners, noting the type and count of cannons, the number and types of transport craft and artillery rafts. And by prisoner interrogations, we will piece together and determine the British intentions for future reinforcement and the potential targets of the spring campaign. The second objective will be to confront the American ranger patrols wherever we find them. Ranger prisoners are the most difficult to capture, hence the most valuable."

Philippe answered suppositional questions posed by those gathered and then Captain Lusignan ended the council on an encouraging note.

"All of you are aware of the raids being made by the American rangers, the burning of the outlying farms, the killing of cattle, the prisoner capture, the scalping, the deaths. From this day forward, we will be more aggressive in preventing these incursions. Another two hundred militia and fifty tribal allies arrived at Fort Saint-Frédéric yesterday. Half of them will be coming to Fort Carillon tomorrow. They are here to augment the garrison and permit an increase in patrols beyond what we discussed this morning."

As the war council shuffled to leave, Commandant Lusignan held up a hand to regain their attention.

"*S'il vous plaît*, gentlemen."

The commandant gestured one of his aides forward who carried a heavy sack of mail over a shoulder. He had saved this as a surprise, to hand out before the scout patrols began their journey. A cheer went up from the officers.

Word spread quickly around the fort. The soldiers gathered by units at the usual places, hopeful to hear their names called. The majority never got any mail.

Philippe did not expect anything and was surprised when a sergeant held a letter aloft and waved at him.

"Captain Gerrard!"

"For me?"

"Yes, sir," said the sergeant. The soldier smelled the paper and smiled lewdly. "It's perfumed!"

The *coureurs de bois* began to whistle and moan.

Packed so close together, perfume would usually permeate all the letters. Philippe smiled and accepted it along with the traditional chorus of obscene remarks.

"Your lewdest imaginations would not come even close," he boasted to the men.

He went through the cuisine towards his quarters. The writing of his name on the outside looked familiar.

Michelle?

Opening the folded missive, he recognized Michelle's even and flowing script. Philippe had used the Jesuits as intermediaries and previously arranged for the care of Joshua and Leah Carlisle, the two English children Philippe rescued from the Delaware before bringing them to Montréal. After Archbishop Nicolet's murder, the bishop's son, Father Eric Nicolet, and Michelle offered to be the go-betweens with Corrinne's former chamberlain, a man named Denis, and his wife, Mary. Philippe had arranged a fee to pay Denis and Mary for the care and protection of the English children, until such time when they could be exchanged for French prisoners of war.

Philippe expected this latest letter to be similar to the one from last October, where Michelle assured him of the children's continued safety. There was certainly assurance of that at the beginning of this new letter, along with mention of the growing famine in Montréal and Québec City, and the tragic reports of English raids in the villages along the Saint Lawrence River to the east. But her next page startled him so much he sat down on the first empty stool he reached in the cuisine.

> *Henri wrote to me recently from Louisbourg. He indicated that Corrinne has not received a reply to any of the letters she has sent you since she arrived in Louisbourg last November with the twins and Anamosa.*

November! Philippe's jaw dropped. *Louisbourg? Corrinne is in Louisbourg?!*

> *I wrote to Henri and assured him you are indeed alive and well at Fort Carillon. Henri wrote back that he believes there must be a problem with the mail getting through to you. He asked me to write a separate letter to tell you what has transpired. I have included some pages from his letter to me.*

Philippe had not seen his son's handwriting before. Two pages of precise script, words carefully arranged and spaced to fill each line. This seemed the handwriting of a scholar, as if Henri had practiced this skill all his life. The letter went on for another half page beyond the two, with information concerning Lord VanderMeer and how Corrinne came to take up residence in Louisbourg.

Philippe concluded if Henri's letters were getting through to his mother in Québec, any letters from Corrinne should only take another week, two at most, before reaching him. But none of them had been delivered. *Maybe they are going to Fort Niagara?* That was the only logical reason he could conjure, before he crushed the missive in his fingers as a darker theory loomed.

Has someone intercepted them?

Philippe impulsively rose from the chair and went down to the quarters he shared with Captain de Bougainville. He started packing additional clothing beyond what he would normally carry in a scout.

Captain de Bougainville came into the room and saw the rapt concentration of his friend.

"You're packing a formal uniform for this scout?"

Philippe turned. "I'm not going on the scout tomorrow."

"Not going?!" Bougainville was startled. "What do you mean, *not* going?"

After a short explanation, Philippe permitted his friend to read the pertinent pages of the letter concerning Corrinne.

Philippe added, "I did not know Corrinne was in Louisbourg until today."

"You've received none of her letters?"

"None. You've been in the governor's offices. How are dispatch pouches from Louisbourg received in Québec?"

Bougainville's forehead creased. "Governor Vaudreuil's appetite for mail is voracious. He's ordered that all mail pouches coming to Québec City, from France, or anywhere else for that matter, be delivered directly to his offices first. They are usually collected by Captain Trieste for the governor's personal sorting without exception. Official mail to the governor, or to the government of New France, or from people in the royal court, or any of the ministers, for example, all of those communiques are culled first. The remainder is distributed further. If it involves colony administration, they go back into the dispatch pouch, which is carried over to Intendant Bigôt. Captain Trieste carries the personal missives to his office, which tend to be addressed to specific businesses or individuals. These are sorted and placed in separate destination pouches, usually identified by a fort name, a city, or a Jesuit mission. Those pouches travel with the official dispatches but contain no official mail. Because of the war, if there is any suspicion or doubt about the contents of a missive, the seals are broken and the mail is read."

"By who?"

"After leaving the governor's desk? By any person who has access to these pouches. There would be no one to stop them."

Captain de Bougainville saw Philippe's pained expression. "What are you thinking?"

Philippe decided to confide in him. "For reasons I can explain to you at some other time, years ago Corrinne and I made a deadly enemy of Intendant Bigôt. The intendant attempted to kill her, except I stepped in front of her and the shot from his pistol hit me in the head. His aim was fouled or I would already be dead. The ball only creased my skull. But I was unconscious for two days."

"He shot you!? *Mon Dieu*! Why?"

Philippe's expression turned wry. "Let's just say he does not like us. He is the reason why we left Québec two years ago. And if François Bigôt has learned that Corrinne is in Louisbourg, he will try to do her harm. He is not beyond sending assassins to kill her. I am serious! If her letters to me were intercepted, it suggests something malicious is intended. I *must* go to her aid."

Bougainville was shocked. "Philippe! You cannot just leave! You cannot abandon your duties! That is desertion! You could be shot!"

"She is my wife," Philippe replied sharply. "She comes first for me, before anything else."

Bougainville was speechless. Scout Captain Gerrard was about to desert his post on the eve of the most important scouting mission he had been assigned to undertake to date. Governor Vaudreuil and General Montcalm anxiously awaited this vital information that would decide the targets and timing of their spring campaigns. Bougainville would not let that happen.

"You cannot do this!" Bougainville voice rose. He had to prevent this. "Let us think this through together."

"Think about what? The scout?! My men are capable of completing this mission without me."

"It would still be desertion! Listen to me! Louisbourg is the most formidable fortress ever built in New France. The letter says Lady Corrinne dwells in a house made of stone. She is surrounded by thousands of soldiers, bastions, and cannons. Her safety is personally guaranteed by Governor Drucour. Her well-being is checked daily by your very son! If something was going to happen, it would have happened by now…God forbid the thought. As to your mail, this could be a simple mistake. The letters may be going into the wrong destination pouch by accident. Perhaps Fort Niagara, as you said."

Philippe's eyes turned unfriendly. "Or perhaps the letters are being intercepted purposely. So that I would remain unaware of the danger to her."

Bougainville made a snap decision. "Very well. Instead of you, I will return to Québec City and learn the truth of this."

"She is *my* wife. It is not your responsibility."

"It *is* my responsibility! I am General Montcalm's aide-de-camp. Captain Gerrard, you have admitted your intention to desert. I will not permit you to take this foolish action." Bougainville held up the pages of the missive. "This has distracted you to the detriment of your sworn duty. As aide to General Montcalm, I *order* you to complete your mission." He saw Philippe's expression darken. "Do not protest! Do not say something you may regret! I deem this to be a very serious matter. If your mail is being intercepted, it could be happening to other officers as well. General Montcalm will be outraged to hear this and would ask me to investigate—of that I am certain. So that is what I intend to do. It is more important I personally learn the truth. In fact, it is better I go to Québec City instead of you, just in case there is indeed some sort of malice at play. Knowing you, I postulate your reaction to such knowledge would be much more impulsive than mine. And consider this! What if you did something rash? And what if something happens to you as a result? That would not be good for Lady Corrinne...or the children you have never seen...yes?"

Captain Gerrard's expression began to relax. Bougainville pressed his argument.

"Your sudden presence in Québec City would be conspicuous! And suspicious, yes? Intendant Bigôt could even order your arrest. He has that power! In contrast, my appearance and motives will not be challenged. I am General Montcalm's aide. I have every reason to be in Québec and reason to linger near the governor's offices. I will be more effective than you."

Philippe considered Pierre Dunemoore his most trusted friend. Except for Henri and Captain La Tour, after Pierre he really could not think of anyone else he might trust to act with the same degree of resolve. It came as a surprise to Philippe that he found himself being swayed by the logic and the sincerity of this erudite nobleman, a man he'd known for less than a year. But sincerity alone was not enough.

"These people are my reason for living," Philippe said in low, passionate tones. "And I have not seen Corrinne in two years."

Bougainville's voice became equally low and solemn in response. "I give you my word, Captain Gerrard, if I learn in Québec that Lady Corrinne is in any type of danger, I will personally lead a platoon of my dragoons to go to her assistance. And I have never broken my word."

Phillipe brooded.

Bougainville pressed further. "Captain Gerrard, it is not only your duty to follow orders, but also General Montcalm relies on you personally to lead and complete this mission. The general values and trusts your military opinion on wilderness tactics more than anyone else. He needs your counsel."

Philippe exhaled and sat heavily upon his bed. "All right. If you go to Québec, as you say, I will obtain the information the general needs."

Bougainville breathed a little easier but wanted to be certain he had dissuaded Philippe from desertion. "General Montcalm plans to attack Fort William Henry soon, as early as March. You are now the only officer outside of Québec who knows his intentions other than me."

Philippe decided it might actually be better to give Bougainville a few weeks' head start. Maybe Bougainville would uncover something that would otherwise be hidden from him. Nevertheless, Philippe *was* going to Québec, although not just now.

"I will bring my scouting report to Montcalm…personally."

"Good. So…we have an agreement?"

"When will you leave?" Philippe asked, testing Bougainville's resolve.

"Now. Today. As soon as I pack. I need no one's permission to depart."

Philippe nodded. "All right." They grasped each other's forearms.

And that is exactly what Captain Bougainville did. Shortly after the noon hour, he bade *adieu* to Commandant Lusignan, gathered up whatever dispatches needed to be delivered to Québec City, and was on a personnel sleigh north to Fort Saint-Frédéric. He planned to overnight there and continue north again early the next morning.

Two advance ranger scouts were concealed along the frozen shoreline of Lake Champlain to monitor the number and frequency of sleds going north and south between the two French forts. They had been there two days. They noted six sleds piled with supplies each morning coming down from the north, usually going back empty in the afternoon. There was one solitary sleigh that afternoon making its way north, carrying six people, three of them grenadier guards. They assessed it was probably someone important. Too bad for the rangers. They were not ready for an ambush that day. The next day would be different.

Lake Champlain, north of Fort Carillon

A drizzly cold rain had begun in the middle of the night. Sleep was scarce. The veteran rangers got up without complaint, forced to rekindle the concealed fire pits to dry out their muskets, pistols, and powder before marching out. They broke camp as planned before the sunrise. The wet snow stuck to their snow shoes, building into clumps that needed to be constantly removed, making the march twice as hard. Nevertheless, as planned, Rogers led his troop to the edge of Lake Champlain just as the first glimmers of sunrise light were seen in the east. He divided his forces into three groups, sent one ambush a hundred paces to the north with Captain Stark in charge and left Captain Speakman, a volunteer from Fort William Henry, in charge of the center position. Captain Rogers personally led the remaining two dozen men south of the main position. His ambush was two hundred paces closer but still miles away from Fort Carillon. Then the rangers simply waited for the opportunity to come to them.

Because of the deepness of the snow, heavy supply sleds and sleighs were used to cross the thick ice. They were preferred by the French in the winter. This only made sense. The sleds could carry larger quantities of supplies. They were pulled by horses and moved quickly, hence could be guarded with less men. All good. Except sleds were easily seen on the lake ice and completely vulnerable to the right type of ambush.

The rangers were very experienced in such ambushes. The tactics were simple.

Let the first sleds come from the north or the south. Let them pass by the first ambush position unopposed until they got to the center. Then collapse upon them from three different directions. Try not to kill the enemy. Take them prisoner for interrogation. Overturn and chop the sleds with tomahawks until they were useless. Plunder or set fire to any supplies they could not pilfer.

Fort Carillon

Captain Lusignan had been made a Knight of the Order of Saint-Louis in 1752 in preparation for his retirement, a common reward for dedicated service. He was a capable officer, not very imaginative but mindful of his duties and the dangers of this assignment at the very edge of French territory in a hostile wilderness. Knowing his retirement was near, and the fort nearing completion, he was given to sharing his wisdom with the younger soldiers of Fort Carillon.

"This is where the next important battle with the English-Americans will be fought," he told the younger soldiers of Fort Carillon as they broke their fast that morning, his voice resonating in the excited tones of his youth. "Though it is not likely to occur until the snow and ice is gone," he added in a more logical voice, a tone redolent of an experienced, decorated officer. "There are three hundred militia reinforcements at Fort Saint-Frédéric. This morning, I am sending all our sleds and sleighs to bring them here, as soon as Captain Gerrard's men begin their scout."

Commandant-Captain Paul-Louis de Lusignan was about to be surprised.

Scout Captain Philippe Gerrard was about to be surprised.

Ranger Captain Robert Rogers was about to be surprised.

*

Between Lac du Saint-Sacrament and Lake Champlain's southern Long Bay, an extended peninsula of land between these two bodies of water was created. Long Bay was a slender lake that stretched south thirty miles before it divided into several small rivers and streams all the way to the Hudson River and Fort Edward.

The northernmost point of the ridgeline running down the center of the land peninsula ended in a small peak overlooking Fort Carillon. It was a little over a mile away from the top of the peak to the center of the fort. Only the outflowing water from the La Chute River cascades separated them. If an enemy placed siege cannons or heavy mortars atop that peak, Fort Carillon was very vulnerable. This vulnerability in a siege situation was known to everyone: the English, the Iroquois, the French, including General Montcalm, Captain Gerrard, and Captain Rogers. But getting heavy siege artillery up that hill through the dense forests, against an enemy determined to stop anyone trying to do this, would not be easy. The English debated the necessity of taking this hill just to build a cannon battery to capture this French fort. They could just as easily bombard the fort from a battery position much closer. In the minds of the English, taking the hill was not necessary. In the minds of the French, they hoped the English continued to conclude it was not necessary.

To the peninsula's left was Lake George. It ended where the La Chute River began. The river drained waters through a hook-shaped series of cascades from Lake George into Lake Champlain. To the peninsula's right was Lake Champlain's southern Long Bay. The peninsula stretched for twenty miles, its width varying in places from one to seven miles. The peninsula was the rangers' preferred scouting route to approach the French forts during the summer months. But not in the winter. The French scouts knew the rangers would leave Fort William Henry and skate up the lake ice most of the way before exiting, either east to the peninsula but more likely to the western shore of Lake George.

Captain Philippe Gerrard was certain Fort Carillon was the logical target of the English campaign in 1757. If Captain Gerrard planned to scout Fort Carillon in the winter, he would skate up Lake George. Therefore, he expected the rangers would do this and exit on the western shore. Just to be sure, he planned to scout the Long Bay and the first five miles of peninsula.

Three reinforced *coureurs de bois* scout companies left Fort Carillon that morning and proceeded as planned. One company marched on snow shoes and circled south around the La Chute River cascades. The second company departed on the ice and skated down the Long Bay. Philippe delayed his departure with the third company to create some distance between them, then skated his men to a landing on the peninsula after only a mile and a half. At this place, the width between the Long Bay and Lac du Saint-Sacrament was at its shortest, only the breadth of a mile. His men deployed in different directions, seeking evidence of tracks in the fresh snow. If they found none, they planned to return, spreading out over the width of the peninsula and combing it moving south.

Philippe waited patiently for these initial reports, his mind distracted again and again to stimulating thoughts of Corrinne being so close. *Louisbourg is less than two weeks' travel away!* He thought of how he would see her soon. The memories of lying with her evoked images so sensuous, his heart pounded. But those visions were followed by anger provoked by the ominous disappearance of her letters. This also made his heart pound. His emotions and mood swung back and forth, from thoughts of pleasure to almost rage.

Get your head in this, he reminded himself when the reverie became too strong.

The search of the peninsula was not an hour old when one of his men came down from the center ridgeline above Lac du Saint-Sacrament accompanied by another scout from the western company.

"Rangers!" the western scout said breathlessly. "We found their trail going north and west of the La Chute cascades."

"How many?"

"A lot of snowshoe tracks, way more than fifty. Deep ruts, but filled with the recent snows. At least a day old, maybe two. And no tracks coming the other way. We are searching further to the west in case they have circled back."

"More than fifty?! That's more than half the ranger forces!"

Philippe smiled grimly. *Captain Rogers leads them. They're on more than a scout! Probably doing what we're doing.*

"Then they are already north of Fort Carillon. And that's good! We have the rangers trapped this time!"

Captain Gerrard gave orders. Half of his men would go back up Long Bay, across from the fort and split to set up ambushes.

"Sergeant, take some men and occupy the point below the peak, at the mouth of the La Chute River, across from the fort. Corporal, take some men and occupy the point of land across the lake from the fort. Send out two-man patrols to scout lands around your positions continuously. If the rangers try to retreat on skates down Lake Champlain, intending to enter Long Bay, you are to ambush them from two directions. The rest of you will come with me over the ridge to Lac du Saint-Sacrament. We will cross and combine with the western scout, then go north and search for the rangers." Philippe pointed at a man. "You, skate back to Fort Carillon and inform Captain Lusignan of the ranger presence to his north. He needs to warn Fort Saint-Frédéric." Philippe pointed at another man. "You, go south and find the Fort Edward scout. Join with them and explain what we have discovered. Tell them to continue their mission. Completing their scout of Fort Edward is of primary importance. But warn them the rangers might be coming back down Long Bay before this day is over. If they do, we will be chasing them. We will have them caught between us. Let's go!"

Everyone moved quickly. Philippe took his remaining men up over the ridgeline to the lakeshore. They donned their skates and crossed to the other side of Lac du Saint-Sacrament to unite with the western scout company waiting for them. Captain Gerrard ordered the lieutenant in charge to select a majority of his men to continue south to Fort William Henry.

"Take at least twenty. Most of the rangers are up here, north of Fort Carillon. You will be in less danger down there and will have an opportunity to collect the best intelligence. That is your primary mission. The remainder of your men will join with me."

Understanding the urgency, the forces divided and the *coureur de bois* scouts moved out in opposite directions.

Lake Champlain, north of Fort Carillon

Captain Rogers' ambush had not been set for even an hour when two supply sleds came around a point of land coming north from Fort Carillon, one behind the other. The horses were almost galloping. They went by his position. He was about to attack and drive them into the waiting arms of Captain Speakman in the middle when he spotted a third sled coming around the point of land escorted by two guards mounted on horseback. He waited until the third sled and the guards were abreast of his position before his rangers exploded out on the ice.

As they skated towards the sleds, Rogers saw another four sleds coming around the point. The rangers were spotted. The other four sleds turned around and charged back across the ice to Fort Carillon at a gallop. One of the two mounted guards discharged his weapon and sped after the other four sleds.

"Capture the prisoners alive!" Rogers shouted.

The ambush worked almost perfectly, with only a few wild musket shots fired by the French. Before they could reload, the rangers had skated to them and took seven men prisoner.

"Forget the sleds! Take the prisoners back to shore!"

At the shoreline, the prisoners' hands were bound behind their backs while other rangers fitted the prisoners' feet with snowshoes. Any rangers in skates now switched to snow shoes. A quick interrogation of the prisoners followed. They talked with enthusiasm. The questions revealed there were over two hundred new militia and at least fifty tribal warriors at Fort Saint-Frédéric. Thirty *coureur de bois* scouts were at Fort Carillon. There was also a garrison of more than three hundred fifty regulars. Rogers knew the bushloper scouts would immediately be dispatched to intercept them. But many other troops and militia would follow. They were grossly outnumbered.

This could be bad. "Withdraw west to the morning camp!" Rogers ordered.

They proceeded back up the snow shoe trail from the morning. This trail would be easy to follow by the enemy, but the ground at the camp was high and defensible. Each prisoner was personally assigned a ranger guard who had orders to kill the man if they came under attack.

La Chute River headwaters, south of Fort Carillon

As Philippe and his men reached the first fording point of the La Chute cascades, they all heard the concussive explosion from the signal cannon of Fort Carillon. It warned anyone near the fort that enemy forces were in the area and an attack was possible. Philippe knew the rangers would never attack Fort Carillon. It was too strong. They couldn't do it even if they numbered more than a hundred men. Like his *coureur de bois* scouts, they were raiders and ambushers. The cannon was just a warning, or there would be a lot more cannons firing.

"Either the commandant was informed, or the rangers already ambushed north of the fort. I say they ambushed the morning sleds going to Fort Saint-Frédéric."

Philippe knew the rangers would capture prisoners and question them. That meant the prisoners, faced with the prospect of torture, gave up any information they had to offer. Captain Rogers would know about the militia reinforcements at Fort Saint-Frédéric and the strength of the forces at Fort Carillon. He would also be told the scout companies left that morning to go south to Fort William Henry and Fort Edward.

The French scouts stared at their captain, awaiting his orders.

"The rangers took prisoners. And those prisoners will say the scout companies have already gone south. They will retreat with the prisoners to the west, before they turn south again. The rangers think we are gone! They do not know we came back!" Philippe smiled grimly. "You! Go to the fort and tell Commandant Lusignan of my current position. Tell him to send regulars north on the ice to engage and pursue the rangers. But tell him—and this is important—tell him that I want the rest of my scouts in the fort to rendezvous with me at my current position. Tell the commandant I intend to attack the rangers' flank."

The veteran sprinted away.

Philippe called his officers and senior sergeants around him. He opened his map, spreading it on the back of one of the men so the others could see.

"We are here." He pointed and tapped. "If I were leading the rangers, I would have set my ambush at least three miles further up the ice so any musket shots would not be heard at the fort and to give me time to retreat. Then I would retreat to the west, because I cannot come south."

"They could take a sled for the prisoners and skate down Lake Champlain out of range of the fort," said one of the men. "Maybe head for Long Bay."

"Possibly, but I don't think so. Too dangerous. Like us, they heard the signal cannon at the fort, too. They expect forces from Fort Carillon will be coming up the ice. The rangers want to keep the prisoners alive. That will slow them down. We must find their snow shoe tracks from two days ago when they went north. They are going to come back south the same way, maybe not the same track, maybe further to the west of the original track. But we don't care! This is our garden! Our lands! We know all the best places to set an ambush. Let's find those tracks and set a good trap."

"What about the rest of the company from the fort?" a sergeant asked.

"You stay here with three men to wait for them. No, send one of those men to our ambush positions on the Long Bay, to tell them what we are doing. Tell them to abandon the ambush and find us. When the rest of the scouts come out of the fort, follow our tracks to join with us. We must act with speed!" Philippe declared. "Let's go!"

*

Rogers' rangers arrived at the morning camp site. All the fire pits were reignited. They gathered around them and dried out the powder and the firing ports on their weapons fouled by the morning drizzle. Rogers had left six men behind to watch the shoreline. They came to the camp with a report that a mix of militia, regular troops, and tribal warriors had arrived at the place of ambush. It totaled well over a hundred men and they were now moving cautiously up the snow shoe trail.

"Move out to the south," Rogers ordered loudly. "We will find a defensible position by nightfall. No fires tonight!"

Twenty rangers were left behind to cover this retreat; ten men at hundred pace intervals spread across the trail of withdrawal in a long row. Each ranger carried over sixty rounds of ball shot, some men carried even more, ammunition considered much more valuable than food. They all carried two or three powder horns in addition to knives and a tomahawk. When the enemy was sighted, they would fire, retreat on the run to get behind the next ten men, continue another hundred paces, reload, and wait again. Just before darkness fell they would abandon this tactic of retreat and get to the ranger night encampment as quickly as possible.

That was the plan.

But the temperature had risen that day. Coupled with the intermittent drizzle of the rain, it made the snow drifts cling and difficult to cross, even with snow shoes. Rogers' strategy was to press the speed of march as fast as possible to exhaust anyone coming in pursuit. He found his own men being exhausted by the wet snow. The prisoners had told him that Captain Gerrard's scouts had left that morning to scout Fort William Henry and Fort Edward, with plans to be gone for a week.

"The *coureur de bois* scouts have all gone south. Fortunate for us," he told his officers and senior sergeants when they stopped to rest for ten minutes. "The regulars behind us will never keep up this pace for very long. But the fort commandant will certainly send men to try and cut off our retreat south. There are a series of valleys and ridges ahead of us. We must get by those before we are engaged by the enemy. But if we are engaged, execute all the prisoners."

Finding the advance more arduous and the pace slower than anticipated, Rogers sent a messenger to order the men covering his withdrawal to rejoin the main force. At each of the ridgelines, the rangers sent out a third of his force as flankers to the left and right, then started down a slope spread out in a line. One third of the men took firing positions at the top of the slope they were defending to cover the advance of the remaining third towards the next one. Once the new ridge was reached and occupied defensively, the rest of the rangers would advance, and the tactic would be repeated.

By early afternoon, they had crossed at least a dozen small hills and long ridgelines, with intervening valleys, frozen streams, and rocky outcrops. Rogers could not recall how many ridges there were but knew from prior experience this stretch was the worst of the rugged terrain between them and the lake. They'd also crossed the ice of four different water courses he was certain were feed rivers, all upstream and part of the La Chute River watershed. That meant the very northern tip of Lake George now lay three miles due east of him. Upon reaching Lake George they could switch to skates and easier travel. But these three miles of distance served as a natural barrier with hill and ridgeline climbs, clinging snow and deep drifts, an abattis of sorts, to any French forces seeking to intercept them.

If they were dispatched right away, the French from the fort have a head start on our southerly march, Rogers thought. *Most of them are regulars. With our greater speed of march, we may now be even with them. They are to the east of us and know I will try to get to the lake.*

Rogers pressed on, going further south before he turned east. He wanted to exhaust his pursuers while hurrying his men to traverse the frequent prominences and depressions at the same time. Rogers instinctively knew the physical limits of his men. The rangers were moving about as fast as they could in these winter conditions. This also meant the less fit French troops were moving only half as fast, if that much, and falling behind. If there was any danger, it would already be in front of them, waiting. That's what he would do. For that circumstance, he sent out frequent scouts to make broad checks of the ground ahead.

At the next ten-minute rest period, he called his officers and senior sergeants together to praise their progress and offer words of encouragement.

"If the Fort Carillon commandant sent his regulars to cut us off, they are encountering great difficulties in traversing these ridgelines and valleys, constantly high stepping through this wet snow. They will be fatigued. Unless they take the same precautions we do, no doubt their muskets are soaked and their powder is wet. If they must fight us unexpectedly, they will lose!"

*

Two miles ahead of Rogers' current location, Scout Captain Philippe Gerrard had positioned his force of eighty-six men, a total of fifty-three *coureur de bois* scouts, augmented by the rest of his scout company when they had left the fort, plus a company of grenadiers from the fort. The elite troops had packed away their mitre caps, replacing them with the dark brown and warmer sock caps of the *coureurs de bois*. For once, the white and gray of their uniforms blended well with the snowy terrain. Only half of the grenadier platoon, twenty-three men, had come this far. The rest had become too fatigued and turned back to the fort. The ones who joined with the scouts were hardened veterans, men who did not complain and were anxious to engage with the enemy. Their leader, Lieutenant de Foy, brought word from Commandant Lusignan that over two hundred militia and Abenaki warriors were now pursuing the rear of the rangers.

Philippe considered that information reassuring but of no help to him. The French pursuit was certainly a half day's march behind the rangers, and maybe more. But this fight was going to take place right where he stood, within the next few hours.

Early that morning, Mkuigen Malsum had gone forward to bring back a report of the rangers' progress. Philippe and Malsum were now lying next to one another atop a long ridgeline, running parallel to another, separated by a valley only half a musket shot wide. Philippe knew this valley well. It had a shallow stream meandering its middle, now frozen rock solid. He also knew that the rangers were trying to place as much distance as possible between themselves and their pursuers before turning east to the lake. Once there, they would return to using skates. This valley aligned perpendicular with the rangers' direction of withdrawal. They'd know this from previous raids. The ranger advance would be easier and faster on the frozen stream. The rangers would use this valley.

Philippe had led his troop to a spot where the valley's advantages would come to an end. A place where both ridgelines began to turn sharply westward like a bend in a wagon road. That end was not far ahead. Using his scope, he could see it. The rangers would have to climb and cross this ridge to go east towards Lake George, or be forced westward with the ridgelines.

I would cross here. They will cross here, Philippe decided.

He suspected there were ranger scouts on that opposing ridge already, searching up and down the valley for any signs of an enemy. The *coureur de bois* scouts were well concealed below their captain, waiting for his orders.

Philippe scanned the opposing ridge with his scope while he and Malsum conversed in the Abenaki tongue.

"Rangers climb ridges quickly…much faster than the French militia," Malsum whispered. "The militia will be no help to us. They will not reach the rangers before nightfall. They will not reach this place until morning. The Abenaki…maybe not for another six hours, unless those lazy Abenaki run in the dark through the snow."

"This valley doesn't end. It turns west." Philippe motioned to his left with a finger at the place where the valley seemed to end. "Our ambush will come from this ridgetop. They will try to cross here."

"Our numbers are equal," Malsum cautioned. "They will use most of their men to cover the advance of the others from right over there…at the top of that ridge." Malsum pointed directly across the valley. "And send a large number to flanking positions."

Malsum would never say it, but the rangers were more disciplined than the *coureurs de bois.*

They had both read the rangers' rules of march they had taken from young John Griffin.

Philippe used this to predict what the rangers might do and when they would do it.

"We do not have the numbers to flank them with sufficient strength. At best, we can match them."

What worried Philippe more was that each ranger knew what their *brothers* would do without being told. They followed their rules. They had a creed. His *coureurs de bois* were fearless, instinctive fighters. In small groups, they were the best. But acting as a part of this larger group, individual instinct would not be enough. The outcome of this ambush was not certain.

Philippe considered this for a few moments then looked at Malsum.

"We need to keep the rangers on the ridge until morning. Make them think we are stronger than we are. When the sun goes down, the rangers will try to escape. Our flanks must be stronger than our center."

Philippe slid backwards on the snow down the ridge and called his officers and senior sergeants together to announce what he planned.

"The sun will set in less than three hours. The rangers advance down the valley on the other side of this ridge, but they do not know we are here. Surprise is on our side. Their advance scouts are coming and may be here already. Kill them quietly. We need to prepare positions atop this ridgeline carefully and with good cover. Then remain very still. We wait until the rangers have started their ascent up this slope before we open fire. Expect opposing fire from the other ridgetop. They are expert shots. Make sure your men know this."

Philippe explained how the ranger tactics would be performed during the engagement.

"Our numbers are about equal, so our ability to flank and surround them is limited. They know a large force of French militia are in pursuit, but they do not know the size of the force in front of them. We must make them think our force is much larger!"

Captain Gerrard ordered twenty scouts detailed fifty paces to the left of the main battle line and another twenty, fifty paces to the right. The remaining scouts would be in the middle along with all the grenadiers. The flanking positions were commanded by scout lieutenants.

"Hold your fire no matter what happens in the middle when the fighting begins. Fire only if you are engaged. They will try to flank the middle one way or the other. That will not happen until the sun is down. You must remain hidden until the rangers attempt this flanking movement. I will reinforce you when this occurs. We *must* hold them," Philippe said, "here, all night. In the morning, the militia and Abenaki will fall upon their rear."

The Battle

The rangers had just finished moving down a valley between two ridgelines running parallel with their intended direction of march. It was now time to climb up and over the ridge on their left. Captain Rogers slowly led his men up the ridge to the right until the covering positions were manned. He scanned it with his watch glass. He recalled from memory this next ridgeline was the last. From here, it was downhill to Lake George. And they all wanted to get to the lake and tie on their skates. It bothered him the advance scouts had not reported back to him yet. That happened sometimes. The further the intended path could be determined as safe and clear, the faster they could move.

Or the scouts are already dead and scalped and the enemy awaits us in ambush, Rogers' instinct warned. *If it is going to happen, it will be now. Like right over there.*

It was the middle of winter. His experienced eyes saw no movement on the other ridge. No animals or birds. There was no wind. Just an intermittent rainy drizzle. It was too quiet. Ominously quiet. Intuition had saved his life before. But they still must cross over this ridge.

As the companies of Captains Speakman and Stark closed with him, Captain Rogers reminded all the rangers of the next rendezvous point, the Narrows of Lake George, if they became separated in battle. The ridgetop they occupied was a broad, flat eminence almost fifty paces wide, lots of trees, a good defensive position with plenty of ways for escape. But none of his scouts had returned.

Rogers presumed a second French force from the fort lagged him to the northeast. But presumption was the worst tactic a commander could employ. What if the French were in front of him...waiting? *Better to assume this is the case.*

"Assault formation for this next ridge! I will take the lead on this advance with Lieutenant Kennedy's company." He gave orders to his seconds. "Captain Speakman, deploy flanking platoons. Captain Stark, you hold the middle. Our defensive fall back is right here! Lieutenant Kennedy, get your men ready!"

Flankers spread out left and right, moving beneath the crest of the ridge so they could not be seen. Unbeknownst to them, the positions they selected were directly across from the enemy; their *coureur de bois* reflections. The French scouts lay beneath the crest on their ridge with two French scouts gazing over the top from a well-concealed position.

It only took a few minutes for the assaulting rangers to spread out in a formation with the right spacing to advance. With their muskets at the ready, they advanced in a fast-walking cadence. They had just begun their ascent of the opposing ridge, the top thirty paces above them, when they all heard the ominous clicking sound of muskets being cocked.

"Take cover!" Rogers shouted the words an instant before the line of French muskets fired.

Balls whizzed by and through the rangers on ascent. Lieutenant Kennedy was killed outright. Rogers had a ball crease his head. He fell with his hands gripping the ache, then staggered back to his feet in a crouch, knowing he must command or lose more men.

Captain Stark's men began a furious covering fire, forcing the scouts to remain under cover as they reloaded their weapons. Rogers shouted orders and his men made a running withdrawal back towards the top of the ridge they had just descended. Other men were wounded on the way back.

While the firing continued, Captain Gerrard learned one scout and three grenadiers were killed. Two more men were wounded.

"Slow your fire," he ordered. "Aim carefully. Do not waste ammunition!"

His objective was to hold the rangers in that position.

Half an hour passed, and Captain Rogers gave similar orders to his rangers. The firing subsided to random shots by snipers. *They are not going to counter-attack.* He called his officers and senior sergeants together.

Captain Speakman spoke first. "The French have flanking positions."

"What strength?"

"Unknown. They are across from my flankers. They are not engaging us, and they remain hidden."

"And behind us?"

Captain Stark spoke. "Scouts report the militia is still lagging our march four to five miles away. The Abenaki are coming forward much faster on their own, maybe three miles, maybe less. But no one will be upon us until long after dark."

Captain Rogers could feel the blood from the scalp wound seeping beneath the soaked bandages around his head. He gazed up at the sky for a few moments to focus his thinking.

"If they are regulars, they would have assaulted us by now. Either this French force is not large enough or we are facing the bushlopers, the French scouts. Their marksmanship alone suggests this. The bushlopers are not fools. If it were me, I would try to hold us in this position until the French forces closing from behind get here. Very well, so this is what we'll do."

*

The sun had set. The fighting stopped except for an occasional sniper shot. It was quiet. Too quiet. Philippe ordered his flanking lines stretched out a little more and sent a scout forward from both flanks to reconnoiter. They did not return. After an hour, he concluded the rangers may be trying to escape as per rule ten. He took a mitre hat from the backpack of a dead grenadier and refashioned it into a crude speaking trumpet.

Taking a deep breath, Philippe shouted in English, "Rogers! Captain Rogers! We have you surrounded! More French troops arrive on your perimeter every hour, strengthening my position. Your men are brave. It would be a shame for them to die so senselessly. I promise you quarter and safe treatment if you surrender."

Rogers now knew for certain who he faced. He shouted back, "Go straight to hell, Snow Hair!" The rangers all cheered.

"Fire!" Philippe shouted.

French muskets had aimed as best they could towards the sound of Rogers' voice and now fired in a volley.

One of the balls hit Captain Rogers' flintlock and split the stock of the musket out of his hands. Another ball struck his wrist and hand.

Sporadic musket fire continued again for another hour. When Philippe decided it had gone on long enough, he shouted out again, "Captain Rogers! Fort Carillon is sending more men. In the morning, we will attack without mercy unless you surrender right—"

A huge blast of musket balls came from the ranger line, all aiming for Philippe's voice. Expecting this might happen, Philippe had positioned himself behind a tree. He talked through his mitre trumpet propped in the vee between two trunk branches of the tree he was hiding behind. Good thing, too. A flurry of balls struck the tree up and down its trunk. The grenadier mitre hat was reduced to a smoking, shredded rag. It lay next to him atop the snow, smoldering.

"Rangers shoot pretty good in the dark," Malsum mentioned dryly. "I think they do not like you."

Captain Rogers shouted back to them, "Did yah' enjoy that, Snow Hair?! Not bad shootin', eh? We'll enjoy cuttin' yah' to pieces come morning. Hurry up. We're waiting."

Each time Rogers shouted or shot back only confirmed the rangers were still there. And that was Philippe's purpose. But this conversation would not last much longer.

It was going to be a long night, full of surprises.

*

Captain Speakman led six of his flankers into the valley between his position and the bushloper scouts up on the ridge in front of him. They remained concealed. They'd not fired a single shot during Captain Rogers' original assault. A scout he sent to reconnoiter the ridge had been gone for two hours. Speakman was forced to assume the man was dead. But so was the ranger scout attempting to penetrate his position. It was foolish for either side to send anymore scouts.

Now Speakman led a small assault group to confirm the French were there. It was all part of Captain Rogers' plan to make an escape. The rest of his flankers were waiting for Speakman's signal, their muskets loaded, cocked, and pointing at the ridge crest, as best they could see it.

Captain Speakman took six steps up the ascending slope, inhaled deeply, pulled out his pistol, and fired a ball towards the top. The other five men waited for his order to fire. But the rest of the rangers on the ridge behind him opened fire immediately. An instant later, the French fired back, revealing they were indeed there. Speakman did his best to estimate the number of muzzle flashes.

Two dozen?

"Fire!" he ordered his men, who shot balls upward along the slope.

They intended the French to see this. As planned, Captain Speakman and his men retreated at the run back to the rest of his flankers. Captain Rogers was waiting there for him with thirty additional rangers.

Captain Gerrard heard the exchange of musket fire on his right. He sent ten men to reinforce that flank. *It could be a diversion*, he thought. A minute later, another loud exchange of musket fire convinced him it could be more than a diversion. An attempt to break through? He was down to eighteen men. He sent a messenger to his left flank and ordered ten men sent back to the center.

A messenger arrived from Lieutenant de Foy commanding the scouts on the right flank.

"Captain, my lieutenant says to tell you the English are mounting repeated assaults on his position in strength. He believes they intend to break through. In the dark, casualties are light, but heavy fire is coming up the ascent side of the ridge."

"Tell him to hold his position! Relief is coming!"

Captain Stark could hear the movement at the top of the ridge before him. He had his entire company across the valley and halfway up this opposing slope. Two of his best scouts had crept close to the crest of the ridge only five or six paces from the French flankers and did nothing but wait. Two other scouts crept further to the right until they determined they were beyond the ranger line. One of them went back to inform Captain Stark through whispered words in his ear. Stark sent a messenger back over the ridge to find and inform Captain Rogers.

Captain Rogers had just returned from another assault across the valley where his men had fired muskets at the opposing ridgetop.

After Rogers returned, Captain Speakman led another group down into the valley. A messenger from Captain Stark informed him what was happening at the other flank.

Rogers smiled grimly. He'd been right. The forces facing him were small. But they were Snow Hair's bushloper scouts. He was not out of this yet.

Rogers ordered half of the men to leave quietly and join with Captain Stark.

"Tell him to ascend and take control of the enemy ridgeline but make no advance upon the enemy flank. Keep just enough men there to defend the position until I join with him. Have the rest start breaking into groups of eight and start south to the rendezvous point."

Captain Speakman and his eight men delivered the next volley from the ascent slope, then retreated again to his ridge. So far, there had been few casualties on either side because of the darkness. The firing from the French was intensifying. Forces gathering on the crest had grown in numbers. Much of the musket fire was now directed into the abandoned valley. The dangerous ruse was effective.

Rogers spoke to Speakman over the sound of musket fire.

"Our plan is succeeding. The French strength is now here. Captain Stark has taken the ridge across from his position. The door is open if we hurry. You stay here with ten men and keep firing for another fifteen minutes. I will withdraw with the remainder and go south, cross the valley at Stark's position, and will wait for you at the top of the opposing ridge. When you are ready, run to us as fast as you can!"

They shook hands. Rogers and all but ten of his men sprinted on snow shoes towards the south.

While the remaining men kept firing, Captain Speakman crawled along the line and told each of them, one at a time, what the next step of the plan entailed. Using the flashes of the musket fire, he glanced at his cherished pocket time piece. It was time to go. He went back down to the end of the line and patted the shoulder of the first ranger, who moved to the right, fired one more round, then patted the shoulder of the next ranger before retreating, and so on. Speakman was the last to turn and leave when he abruptly took a musket ball in his gut.

The ranger captain called out, but his calls for help were lost in the continuing thunder of French musket fire. The pain was intense. He staggered away from the ridgeline position towards the main camp. But no one was there. He collapsed against a tree near a smoldering fire pit. He was alone and losing blood.

Suddenly, Abenaki warriors appeared from out of the night. They'd been waiting in ambush, closer than anyone expected. Finding him wounded and dying, they did not bother to kill him, only scalping him before retreating back into the darkness. With blood dripping into his eyes Captain Speakman started to crawl away to hide somewhere else in the darkness until he could no longer crawl.

Then someone was at his side. "Captain Speakman! Captain! It's me! Thomas Brown!"

Thomas Brown was the only ranger remaining that had not gone over the valley to Captain Rogers' position. He had been waiting for Captain Speakman. And when the officer did not show up, like any good ranger, he went back to find him and followed the blood trail back into the main camp and further in the snow.

"Kill me, Thomas," Speakman groaned. "I am dying. I am in great pain. Kill me."

Private Brown gripped his captain's hand. "I cannot kill you, sir," the eighteen-year-old ranger replied with tears streaming down his face. "But I will stay by your side."

The captain spoke of his wife before passing.

Before Brown could leave, the ranger encampment was overrun by Captain Gerrard, his *coureur de bois* scouts, and grenadiers from Fort Carillon.

Philippe ordered his scouts to pursue the rangers, though he expected they were already breaking up into small groups. Indeed, they had.

When he assaulted my flank, I should have assaulted his middle, Philippe reflected bitterly.

The ranger named Brown regarded him with angry, defiant eyes.

"The war is over for you. Take him back to the fort," he ordered the remaining grenadiers.

Philippe looked towards the body of a dead ranger, unfortunately in time to see the man's head chopped off by the hooting Abenaki and several of his *coureur de bois* scouts.

"Stop!"

They regarded him with confused expressions. "Stop what? He is already dead!"

Captain Speakman's head would later be placed on a post as a symbol of victory.

✹

The Escape

Captain Robert Rogers reached Lake George by sunrise and skated on with the remainder of his men to the rendezvous point at the Narrows of Lake George. Once there, they waited for stragglers while Captain Stark skated ahead with two men to Fort William Henry to bring back a sledge large enough to carry the wounded. A day later, Stark returned with the sledge, and the weary ranger force and volunteers returned to Fort William Henry.

Relieved of the stress of the French pursuit, Rogers' body now succumbed to the attentions demanded by the wounds to his head, hand, and wrist. During a brief visit to Fort William Henry and a restless overnight in its pest-ridden hospital, Rogers contracted the smallpox, which had plagued this fort a long time already. Rogers was transported back to the city of Albany, so he could recover from this terrible new malady and his festering wounds. He was kept isolated with other moaning and dying people similarly afflicted, while the healthy offered him water and crusts of bread at arm's length and waited for the diseased to survive or die, as God intended.

Robert Rogers was a hard man to kill by disease, tomahawk, or musket ball. He lived, but he was weakened. It removed his presence from the battlefields of Lake George for the rest of the winter.

*

Captain Philippe Gerrard had received a stinging lesson on rule ten of the "Rules of Ranging," which he later deduced was exceedingly more effective when combined with rules seven and nine. *Made worse by my overconfidence*, he begrudged with bitterness. He set his jaw. *Next time will be different.*

Philippe went forward with his mission, taking the remaining unwounded scouts. He sent messengers over to the peninsula to recall his scout company reconnoitering Fort Edward, urging them to return to Fort Carillon. He continued to the hills west of Fort William Henry and directed the collection of intelligence. He saw a new type of water craft resting upside down on log supports along the shores of Lake George. He would learn it was called a whaleboat, hauled with difficulty over the many miles and intervening hills from the port of Nantucket. The design was now being mimicked by the Lake George shipwrights. They were made of cedar planking, had keels, rounded bottoms, elevated sharp bows, and sterns.

They are fast, turn quickly, and are much more maneuverable than our clumsier bateaux, Philippe noted in his journal. *The rangers will be using these*. Philippe learned the numbers and the command structure of Fort William Henry. *Many of the garrison are sick with smallpox!* He also noted the prisoners claimed most of the British regulars in and around Albany had departed for Halifax. *How many needs further refinement after winter breaks. But it leaves Fort William Henry very vulnerable and without reinforcements.* The same thing was observed at Fort Edward. Captain Gerrard saw the patrols by the English grow larger and more frequent. *Obviously, the fort was warned of our presence by the retreating rangers.*

Philippe ordered a withdrawal before they got trapped by their own mistakes. Despite the disappointing results of the battle with the rangers, Captain Gerrard's companies had collected enough information to complete a report to General Montcalm. Both forts were vulnerable.

Philippe Gerrard would soon be hurrying to Québec City…and hopefully to Corrinne.

The Aftermath

Governor Pierre de Vaudreuil hoped it might be the intelligence he expected on Fort William Henry when a messenger arrived in Québec City from Fort Saint-Frédéric. It was the day after the ranger ambush took place. The news was not good. French prisoners had been taken. The size of the attacking force was inaccurately reported to be a battalion of English grenadiers. The second day, a messenger from Fort Carillon brought news that was the opposite. The attackers were a small force of elite American rangers and they were being opposed by Captain Philippe Gerrard's *coureur de bois* scouts. A winter battle in the forests west of Fort Carillon was in progress. A day later, another messenger arrived directly from Captain Paul-Louis de Lusignan, a commandant who was worried about his own reputation. The battle was over! The report described the successful repulse of the ranger attack. The French casualties in the report were low, but Lusignan tallied only the ones counted from Fort Carillon. Later, the tally would more than double when the casualties from Fort Saint-Frédéric were added to the total. The ranger casualties were exaggerated by adding the battlefield reports from each unit captain, and these were permitted to be duplicated without correction.

English reports made later asserted similar claims, favoring the English, of course.

Governor Vaudreuil found Captain de Lusignan's reported results dispiriting. "This was little more than a skirmish," he remarked to his aide, Captain Trieste, with a frown.

Nevertheless, Governor Vaudreuil recognized he had to make a written report of his own and submit it by courier to the Minister of Marine Machault, before General Montcalm's certain-to-be-less-flattering report was submitted to Minister d'Argenson. The report that arrived first would become the accepted version. Vaudreuil began writing his report the same day he received Captain de Lusignan's report. The main problem was…there was not an undisputed winner! Nor was there anything to claim as having been won!

No one likes losing! Governor Vaudreuil thought. He decided to characterize the battle as an English winter assault on Fort Carillon. That his Canadian forces had successfully repulsed the enemy and counter-attacked, pursuing a *battalion* of English rangers all the way back to Fort William Henry. Only the French soldiers killed by enemy fire were counted. Vaudreuil used the exaggerated numbers of enemy killed and wounded reported by Captain de Lusignan as proof of victory. The real number of French casualties were three times greater than the enemy's. Vaudreuil's own experience told him this would be the case; it was always greater. He would learn the real numbers weeks later. But for now, Governor Vaudreuil sealed his encoded missive and had it skated downriver to Gaspé. There it was added to the dispatch pouch on a fast courier schooner and transported across the Atlantic to the naval port of Brest.

Weeks later, the real numbers would come to light. By then, Vaudreuil and the English generals would all claim a victory in more favorable versions reported to their superiors in Europe. During the brutal, long, slogging, fighting retreat in the skin-freezing winter forests south to Lake George, of the seventy-four rangers involved in the capture of three sleds and seven prisoners, only thirteen rangers were killed, nine wounded, and seven taken prisoner. So fearlessly had these rangers fought against an equally determined enemy elite arrayed against them on familiar ground, that the French suffered fifty-seven dead with numerous more wounded.

The French scouts could be proud for surrounding the elite rangers. And the rangers could be prouder for getting away, scathed though they were. That was no small feat. Much later, when the men who engaged one another made an honest assessment in private, over a flagon of rum or brandy near a warm fire, they would admit this Battle on Snowshoes, as it came to be called, indeed had no winners and no losers. It was a draw. They gained respect for one another.

And these enemies would meet again.

Molly Shreve had never been so happy in her life. She lived in a beautiful house in Boston, was married to a handsome warship captain in the English navy, and most of all, she had a four-month-old baby boy. Conor Martyn II, or Conor Two as she liked to call him. Of course, the house belonged to Lord and Lady VanderMeer. They were just the caretakers. The VanderMeers had fled Boston following the assassination attempt on Lord VanderMeer.

Molly shared the house with another married couple, Dianamora and Sentry Cheever, their closest and dearest friends. Molly and Conor stayed in the master bedroom upstairs, nearest to the nursery. Sentry and Dian stayed downstairs in the second largest bedroom, formerly the bedroom of the beloved maidservant, Mathilde, who was attacked and murdered on the streets of Boston.

Other than the sleeping arrangements, the friends shared everything else in the house as if it were their own: the responsibilities for the cooking, the cleaning, minor repairs, the scullery work, the laundry, the chores, just as any family would do. That is how they thought of themselves: one happy family.

The finances with which to run the household came from a trust fund managed by Thomas Hancock, a prominent Boston merchant and partner of Lord VanderMeer. Hancock was the attorney-in-fact and administered the stipends given to Molly and Dian. He also issued payment for the magistrate's guards watching over the house, two in the front and two in the back. These men did this work on their own time to earn extra money. The last four months had been peaceful. The guards seemed an extravagance. But the house and its occupants had been attacked several times by enemies of the House of Brunswick, so it was asserted. A year earlier, when the VanderMeers attended Mathilde's funeral, an arsonist attempted to burn the house down. Dian had killed this man, or he would have succeeded. It could happen again at any time. It did not matter that the VanderMeers were presently in Europe.

But after four months of harmonious living, Molly believed the menace following the VanderMeers had trailed them back to Europe. It was common knowledge that the maids were the caretakers of the property. This caretaker arrangement would not last forever, of course. The VanderMeers intended to come back to Boston someday. This is what they publicly claimed before they set sail on *William's Queen* for Amsterdam.

Molly's feelings of joy would not last.

*

Boston was digging out of a January winter storm when a courier delivered an envelope addressed to Molly Shreve just after noon. She broke the wax seal and read the single page written in the short, even script of Thomas Hancock. The merchant requested a meeting with Molly, Dian, Sentry Cheever, and Captain Martyn, if the captain was available. He was not. The captain was still out to sea, trading cannon shots with the fort at Louisbourg.

"Mr. Hancock requests a meeting with us?" Molly wondered aloud. This had happened only twice before, and they had always known the reason. She handed the page to Dian. "He does not say what this meeting concerns," she added in a nervous ramble. "He is coming to the house at the hour of seven tonight. It must be important for such a formally written request, don't you think?"

The women looked at one another.

"The VanderMeers?" Dian guessed. "We've not heard anything from them since they sailed."

"Should we invite him to stay for dinner?"

Dian shook her head. "No. I don't think this is a social visit. I'll prepare something light to serve in the library. I will get a message to Sentry to be on time for this. Let's not worry too much. Mr. Hancock is a gentleman."

*

Thomas Hancock called on them precisely at the hour of seven.

"It is so good to see you, Mr. Hancock," Molly greeted with forced cheer. She took his heavy coat and hat while noting the man's mood. "And on such a cold night for a visit."

"*Brrrr!*" Hancock shivered with agreement and smiled back. "But it's always warm and welcoming here."

Dian and Sentry came to the foyer and exchanged welcomes. Molly preceded them to the library where the hearth was aflame with a log. From the cuisine, Dian brought in a tray of warm sweetbreads made from maple syrup mixed with oatmeal. A pot of hot tea was on the small table. Sentry gestured towards a bottle of brandy and four glasses beside the tea.

"Some hot tea for you, Mr. Hancock? Or something a wee bit stronger tah warm your heart?"

"I will have some brandy, if you please…but only if you will join me."

Once everyone had a sip of brandy, Hancock got down to business. His tone turned formal.

"I know you're wondering why I requested this meeting, so I will get right to it. I received a letter from Lord VanderMeer yesterday. He is in Amsterdam staying with his father at the ducal palace. Lady VanderMeer and the children are *not* with him. Because of the repeated attacks on them, he assessed the danger in Amsterdam would be even greater than in Boston. He decided instead to take her to the port of Louisbourg and seek sanctuary for her with the French, temporarily at least, until he makes other arrangements for her safety."

Glances of surprise were traded around the room.

Hancock took another sip. "The Dutch Republic is neutral in this war. Both England and France do not want that to change. The Duke of Brunswick is commander of the Netherland armies. The French were very happy to earn favor with the Duke. So, for now, Lady VanderMeer and the children remain under the protection of the French in Louisbourg. Lord VanderMeer asks that we keep any knowledge of Lady Corrinne's location a secret."

Hancock paused. He waited until he saw each of them nod before he continued.

"Charles asks how all of you are faring. I plan to answer his letter tonight and send it on a courier ship bound for London on the morning tide. So, I prefer the answer to come directly from you. More to the point, have you noticed anything suspicious, anything that might give you cause for concern?"

More glances were traded.

"Molly? Dian?"

"No," Molly answered first. "I was just thinking yesterday how lucky I am to be living in such a beautiful house."

"I've not seen any watchful people on the streets as I shop," Dian offered then she smiled. "Of course, I usually have Sentry looming near me with two other guards whenever I go out."

Sentry was alarmed by the question. "Is there something we should know? Should we be worried, Mr. Hancock?"

"There's nothing I can confirm. I visited with the new magistrate yesterday and asked if he believed any of the villains who intended to do the VanderMeers harm might linger still in the city. He said, after the attack on Lord VanderMeer, two men rode south on horseback through the gate on the neck and were not seen again. And the woman who stabbed Magistrate Tasker, God rest his soul, she was confronted at the Marine Society Hospital and killed. Her name was Caroline Bristol. They believe she had a sister named Rachel who worked at the Penny Surgeon down on the wharf. But, there's been no sign of this Rachel person either."

"Meaning no disrespect, but yah dinnah sound too confident. Are we in danger?"

"You are a perceptive man, Sergeant. I do not foresee any immediate danger. I just feel, after all that has happened, we need to remain on guard. According to Lord VanderMeer's letter, some malicious royals are trying to find Lady VanderMeer when she did not arrive in Amsterdam with him. Let me emphasize…these people are from families rival to the House of Brunswick. They assert a claim to this duchy above that of Charles VanderMeer, the primary heir. These people intend to do her harm…and this includes the children, who are considered heirs, next-in-line after Charles."

Molly's hands went to her mouth. "Oh, my God! No!"

Hancock frowned. "Unfortunately, that is not the worst of it. Lord VanderMeer's health has deteriorated. The royal doctors do not expect him to survive more than a few months."

Dian's frown turned to tears.

Sentry dropped his head in sadness for a few seconds before asking, "These doctors are certain?"

Thomas Hancock stoically tried to absorb the burden of their sadness. But Lord VanderMeer was his friend too. His expression sagged.

"Lord VanderMeer avows this. His legs have the rot. It is spreading. As he penned this letter to me, he claimed the doctors intended to amputate both of his legs. I must assume this has happened by now."

Molly had tears streaming down her face.

"I'm sorry to bring this terrible news. And forgive me for being so blunt. Lord VanderMeer insisted that you know everything. He also wants to assure you the lease-right agreements you signed regarding living here would remain in place. If his lordship does pass on, Lady VanderMeer will still be the landlord and I will remain her attorney-in-fact. The VanderMeers expected to be absent for two years, the property trusts they established provides for this and more. But in my opinion, I do not think they will return until a peace treaty is signed between France and England. There is a lot of sympathy and goodwill in Boston towards the VanderMeers, but too much tragedy and controversy surround them. This only incites speculation. I believe Lady VanderMeer knows this instinctively. It is better for her that she stays away from Boston...for now."

Molly wiped her eyes. "Can we write to Lord VanderMeer?" she asked. "Or get a letter to Lady Corrinne somehow?"

"You might try," Hancock replied in a dubious tone. "Because of the war, your letters would likely be intercepted. If you keep it to a single page, I'm willing to wrap a page inside my business missive. I have an agent in London who communicates regularly with the Dutch Republic. Sending something directly to Lady Corrinne in Louisbourg will be almost impossible. I cannot think of a legal way. But I expect she will try to communicate with you somehow. So be patient."

The room had become very somber. Hancock looked at Sentry Cheever.

"Before I forget, Lord VanderMeer said to ask you about a task... something about Winter House? I'm unsure as to what he refers to."

Sentry felt a chill crawl up his spine at the question. Lord VanderMeer asked him to move the stone vault pieces chiseled with icons of the sun, moon, stars, and water. They were still in the carriage hangar. The stones were custom cut. At the vault behind Winter House, he was to lower them into place. He promised not to reveal his intention or the purpose to anyone else. It was designed and built to contain this...*thing*. Even thinking about this...*thing*...was disturbing. Sentry also knew it was the servants of this wraith responsible for the attacks on the VanderMeers. That some royal houses were planning assassinations only made the situation worse. But it was common knowledge the VanderMeers had left Boston. Would they have a reason to attack the house again?

"It was Lady VanderMeer," Sentry replied to Hancock. "She asked me tah supervise some repairs at *Winter House*. I am waiting for the weather tah improve. I will go down there, maybe in April or May."

"I will reply with that explanation." Hancock made notes. Those gathered remained morose and quiet. "Unless you have more questions, I will take my leave of you." He waited a few seconds. No one knew what to say or ask. "Well…if you think of more questions, get a message to me and I will come back. Otherwise, be at ease. Nothing will change regarding your lease." He saw their depressed expressions and felt the need to say something more. "The VanderMeers are very gracious and generous people. I miss them, too. They were my good friends. You must consider me your good friend, too."

*

Carter Trevathan and Rachel Cantlin met again to devise a plan of diversion. Diversion had worked before when they murdered the maidservant, Mathilde. During her funeral, when everyone was out of the house, they planned to set fire to the mansion-like structure, to drive them out of it to make Lord and Lady VanderMeer more vulnerable. More importantly, to force them to move the châsse into the open. That plan failed because the maid, Dian, had killed the arsonist, Felix, as he came through the backdoor of the VanderMeer house, intending to burn it down.

"There's only two of us left in Boston," Carter stated. "We would be unsuccessful trying to force an entry. Too many guards. We need another diversion, like before, something subtle that provokes no alarm or suspicion. Maybe a business of some sort? One that gives us reason to approach the house?"

"No. That still leaves the guards," Rachel argued. "It must be something that draws the guards away from the house, allowing me to slip inside."

"Yes, exactly. There are four guards. At best, we might induce only half of them to leave, and I am not sure how to get them to do that."

They stared at one another, thinking of ideas.

"Bribe them?" Rachel suggested.

"Too dangerous. These guards are the magistrate's men. They are well paid and very loyal."

"Then we do this on the day the maid Dian shops," said Rachel. "You said two guards go with her? That leaves only two at the house. We need to draw away the one at the back."

"Yes. It has to be a lure that keeps the guard away long enough to allow you to enter, confront her, ask questions, and get answers," Carter mused. "Wait! How about a food cart?"

"A food cart? You mean a street vendor who pushes a cart around?" Rachel asked skeptically. "Who pushes the cart? A cart is too slow. It's too cold. What if it snows? We need to draw the guards away from the house by half a block at least to give us enough time."

Carter had already quickened to his idea. "All right, then a food *wagon*. One that offers much more than a cart and moves along the city streets pulled by horses."

It seemed way too elaborate. "I've never seen a wagon like that. They don't exist."

But Carter was already nodding to himself. "I know! That's why this is a good idea. I will create such a wagon. I will get something going and try it out on the guards. See what happens. We just need to stock all their favorite foods."

"How will you do all that?"

"Don't worry. This is what I do. Give me two weeks, and I will have it up and running. The business does not have to make money, it just has to work."

Rachel agreed to return in two weeks.

Carter went to work.

From the refuse yard of a carriage builder, Carter purchased the shells of four worn out carriage houses that had been scrapped. He had the carriage builder anchor them securely in pairs on the back of two long flatbed wagons. The adjoining sides from the shells were cut and removed completely, and the shells were fastened together securely to form one long carriage house the length of the long flatbeds. Everything was removed from the inside and replaced with cabinetry, cutting tables, and high stools. The wood was bare and unpolished, with enough shelving added along the inside beneath the windows to hold the foods. A small wood stove in the middle was to be used for cooking and heating. The windows were overhung by one long awning, which could be cranked out to form a shelter from the rain or snow, depending. Five windows per side, with a long window over the door where the money would change hands.

It only took the carriage builder four days to complete the work. It went so well, Carter ordered a second carriage just like the first and had paid a double premium in labor for the carpenter's speed. While the construction was proceeding, he hired knowledgeable employees from restaurants to canvass the shops to learn what types of foods people liked. They would work inside the carriage house, to prepare and distribute the food as it was ordered. Next, he found drivers for the horse teams. The wagons would be loaded up with provisions from the shops of various suppliers from around the city by five each morning. He paid market prices at the shop and marked this up by fifteen percent for the convenience. At a minimum, this would include fresh breads, meats, cheeses, pastries, urns of tea, plus new foods added to the menu as requests were made. Payment would be conducted through the window over the half-door in the middle and then customers would receive their food from windows on the left and right.

All the planning kept Carter busy with the challenges of getting this new enterprise launched. He liked challenges of commerce. It filled him with energy. The costs were piling up, but money was plentiful and funded from his still thriving cotton import and cloth manufacturing business. By day six, they were about ready to start. It seemed a shame all of this elaborate design was potentially only to deliver death. The consolation and beauty of it was, no matter what happened, the business could continue. The death-dealing was Rachel's problem.

Death? Carter shook his head to block out these darker thoughts.

"*Food Coach. Food Wagon. Hot Meals,*" he mumbled potential names to himself while breaking his fast, alone, in his favorite restaurant. "*Food Carriage.*" He made a note of that in his pocket journal. "That's what they are. People will easily remember that. That's the new name, *Food Carriage*. And the wagons will have large signs, 'Food Carriage I' and 'Food Carriage II.' Yes. Need to get the signs made." He made another note. "And maybe a slate to hang on the side of the coaches listing the foods available or any new additions to the menus."

They would only serve from the side of the wagon facing away from the street along the curb. Each wagon had a crew of five with one man in charge. Carter gave each of the supervisors a timepiece, a map, and the street routes to follow in Boston, emphasizing they were to be at certain corners at certain times of the day, so the customers would be confident when and where the coaches would appear.

"Follow the street routes exactly…and be on time," he emphasized. "It is important the customer can rely on the time of your arrival, so they will line up beforehand. We will adjust the routes as we learn which corners are the most profitable. You will load up at the hour of five and be open for business down by the docks at the morning hour of six. Carriage I starts at the distillery wharfs in the south, Carriage II at North Battery. You will both work your way towards Faneuil Hall in the middle of the city before going east into the residential areas by noon. We will finish by three, clean up the coaches for the next day, and distribute the profits. The crew of each wagon will split a third of the daily profits they earn on the sales of food. Ten percent to the supervisor, five percent to each one of the crew. That's just for starters. I may raise the bonus percentages later if the profits are good, and I will offer extra bonuses, depending on what customers tell me or what stories the newspapers print. Remember to treat the customers politely," he admonished.

Carter paid for expensive print "stories" at the bottom of the front page of all the newspapers. "Food Carriage Begins Business Tomorrow Morning" the title proclaimed. The story described the innovative new service and included a schedule of times and places.

Carter found the reaction by the citizens and laborers of the city during the first week to be nothing short of remarkable. He had to raise prices to slow down the crush of customers. They were running out of food before noon and had to make provisions for a resupply wagon mid-morning. He was surprised by the success of this endeavor. He had not expected to make much money at all from this, if any. He had only wanted to avoid losing money. But, in fact, he was making a considerable sum. At the end of the first week, he ordered two more flatbed coaches from the same carriage builder. *Might as well grow a business.* The demand was there for it.

By the end of the second week, Boston had come to anticipate the very popular food coaches at certain places and certain times. Carriage I quickly learned which foods were most preferred by the guards at the VanderMeer house. Carter already knew the maid liked to shop at the outdoor markets on Wednesdays and usually left the house at nine in the morning and did not return until the noon hour. Often, she would stop at a restaurant to eat and was usually accompanied by her husband, Sentry Cheever, who carried her purchases, and they were trailed by two of the guards from the house. That left the house with only two guards, one in front and one in back. And the last couple of days, the one at the back had been seen to run out to the food coach on Marlborough Street to buy himself a morning treat.

A third coach was constructed and began operating on Monday morning of the third week. Carter had adjusted the routes and times for this new coach and arranged the schedule of the others to fit his plan. The supervisors now used whistles to announce their presence in a neighborhood. That also helped customer flow.

They were ready.

Tuesday of that third week, Rachel Cantlin came to Carter's apartment in the afternoon to go over the plan for the next day. He walked with her to the back-fence area of the VanderMeer house on Common Street. He had already loosened a particularly wide fence board, so it would swing on one nail to the side. Rachel was slender enough to slip through the hole.

The night visitor had ordered Rachel to take a container of wine with her, laced with at least a cup of her blood, and force the maid at the house to drink it. Carter purchased a small bottle of wine for this purpose and helped her draw the blood from a vein in her arm. Rachel was disgusted by the idea, but did as she was told. She was also told to sleep with Carter and pleasure the man, which disgusted her further, but she did not disobey. Carter was very happy about this.

*

Wednesday morning revealed bad weather, which was freezing cold with an overcast sky. But it was not snowing. Rachel stayed in the apartment until Carter returned from making sure the food coaches rolled off on schedule exactly at six. He showed up at half past the hour with a newspaper wrapped around some buttered biscuits, bread, cheese, and a jug of hot tea. They broke their fast together. Carter did most of the talking.

"Let's review it one more time. Carriage I will come up Summer Street to the intersection with Marlborough precisely at ten. These horses plod along slowly, so you should be able to walk way ahead of them on Summer Street, cross over Marlborough, head up Winter Street to the corner of Common. Stop at this corner and wait until you see the wagon turn left on Marlborough. It turns left, but goes a half block further before it stops. The super blows his whistle, announcing its arrival. The customers are alerted and lining up. It's too cold for people to be going about until the afternoon, so it is a perfect time to do this. You will already be down the fence line. You slip into the yard. Remember to stop and look around the corner of the carriage hangar to make certain the guard has gone to the food coach."

"And if he is not gone…and just sitting there?"

Annoyed by the question, Carter gave her an exasperated look. "Then you kill him with your knife. He will be huddled inside the small guard shack in front of the hangar. There are no windows in it. He won't see you coming. Is that clear?"

Rachel's expression darkened. "If it's just that simple, maybe you should do it?"

Carter ignored her and took a large sip of hot tea. He pointed at the piece of paper on the table upon which he had drawn a rough sketch of the inside of the house. This information he had artfully collected in casual conversation with different doctors, nurses, caterers, contractors, and other visitors to the house during the funeral and wedding, as well as through his own observations.

"You go in this back door, through the mudroom, into the cuisine. There is a second entry door here to the right with a direct hallway to the front entrance. Library to the right. Dining room. Oh, the other maid, Molly, may already be in this cuisine preparing food so be ready to act. If she's not, she is somewhere else in the house, of course, so step quietly. There is a servants' hallway right here near the front door," he said, pointing. "It leads down to other bedrooms, but this last one on the left has a bathing and laundry room with a tile floor adjoining it. She might be in there. If not there, then it is upstairs to the bedrooms. These stairs are carpeted. Your footsteps will be muted. This room is the nursery." He tapped a spot on the makeshift map. "If she is nowhere else, she will be in there...with her baby. You know what to ask?"

"Of course."

"Do not be surprised if *It* overcomes you suddenly. It might decide to do the questioning."

A surge of panic hit Rachel. "Why would it do that?"

"I'm not saying it will for certain," he replied defensively. "Maybe not. I just don't want you to be unprepared if this happens."

"What do I do if it does?"

"Nothing to do. It will take over your will. The goals are the same. Just don't try to fight it. You know what happens when you do."

Rachel exhaled heavily with that unnerving thought. "Yes...I know what happens."

"At nine, I will go to the outdoor market the maid favors and watch for her. If I do not see her by half past the hour, I will come to Summer Street and find you. We will call it off. But if I do not come to retrieve you, you proceed. I will be seen by others standing at my business stand in Faneuil Hall when the hour of ten comes around. I expect it will not take long for word to spread around this town if you are successful. If you encounter unsolvable obstacles, go out the fence the way you came in, down to the ferry, and get across the harbor. If you are unnoticed, we can try again on another day."

They discussed other possible scenarios and posited solutions for another half hour.

Rachel tried to calm herself that the night visitor might fully possess her in the middle of this. *Why even tell me this?* she thought angrily. There was nothing she could do about the possibility. Like Carter said, the goal was still the same. She'd been through worse. It wasn't going to rape her… she didn't think. That would make no sense. Maybe it was better to know it could happen. *Doesn't mean it will.*

Carter left in time to be inside Faneuil Hall before eight. At the hour of nine, Rachel bundled up in her dark gray long-coat, a scarf around her head and face, topped off with a black knitted cap. Accoutrements easily stuffed into the coat packets. She had the slender seven-inch fish knife in a scabbard on her belt, out of sight beneath the coat. In the left coat pocket was a tin cup and the small bottle of red wine diluted with her blood. In the right pocket was a longer, black-knit cap, long enough that—when pulled down—it would cover her head to the neck. Before she came to Boston, she had cut holes in this cap for her eyes and mouth and darned the edges of the cuttings so the holes would not fray further.

She left as soon as she was ready and headed to a place half way up Summer Street where she could loiter inconspicuously and watch for the approach of the food coach when it turned up from the wharves.

Rachel stayed off the main streets of Boston as she wended her way, entering Summer Street from Bishop's Alley. When she got there, she looked left and right. The wind was coming up this street from the wharf area. An occasional rain drop carried on the wind stung a little. Not many people were outside. Those who were walked around in a leisurely manner. Now, all she needed to do was wait until she saw the wagon, or until Carter showed up to say it was off. But she was mentally ready to get this over with, so she hoped that would not happen. She tucked herself inside a doorway of a shop that was closed and waited, glancing left and right, up and down the street, constantly watching for Carter or the wagon to appear turning up from the wharves.

*

Carter was surprised to see so many farmers' stalls open at the market on such a cold day. But it was the scheduled market day. It was crowded. People had to eat. He was bundled up like everyone else, with a scarf covering most of his face. He bought a cup of hot tea to keep his fingers warm and lingered by the stand to return the cup when he was through with it. He stomped his feet to keep them warm.

He looked at his watch. Fifteen minutes past the hour of nine.

She should be here by now, he thought.

And as soon as Carter thought that, he saw the maid named Dian walking arm in arm with Sentry Cheever. She looked the size of a child standing next to him.

God, he's fucking big!

They were followed by two guards and headed to a stall that sold cheese, cream, and eggs. Lingering there, they chatted with the farmer and his wife. When they moved on, Carter looked at his watch again: nine thirty. Obviously, Miss Dian liked to talk. Carter decided to stay with them another fifteen minutes just to be sure. There was a restaurant to one side of the street with a chalkboard advertising hot cakes and maple syrup. That sounded good to him, hopefully they would see it, too. He gave back the cup and thanked the vendor. Then he took a big chance and walked close to Dian and her Scotsman.

He spoke out loud but not directly to them as he walked by, close enough for them to hear.

"Mmmm! Hotcakes!"

He continued walking until he was inside the restaurant before turning around. They were not looking at him, but one of the guards must have heard, as the man was now pointing at the street sign. The restaurant was filling up with customers.

"Just take a seat at any table," a harried but cheerful waitress said.

"Thank you. I will stand here. I'm waiting for someone else."

He looked at his watch after more minutes went by. *Nine forty-five*. He turned to leave and bumped into the imposing form of Sentry Cheever coming through the door with Dian.

Shit! Carter spoke hurriedly. "Excuse me, sir."

"No problem," Sentry said in a voice that matched his size. "Are the hotcakes good?"

"The best in town," he offered and slipped by them.

No question about it now. This was going to happen. Carter hurried back to Faneuil Hall.

Rachel was already halfway up Winter Street watching the wagon making its way slowly to Marlborough. Her gloved hands were ice cold, more from fear than from the weather. The wagon reached the corner. She watched it turn. Simultaneously, the supervisor blew his whistle several times. Rachel stole quickly down the fence line, stopped, and looked left and right. There was no one walking on this street. She tilted the loose board aside and slipped into the yard.

She stepped quickly and leaned against the back of the carriage hangar. She replaced her scarf and knitted cap with the knitted hood with holes cut for her eyes and mouth. Her breath was coming in large vaporous puffs. She took deep breaths of the cold air to calm herself, drew her knife, and moved quietly towards the front of the hangar, stopped again at the corner and glanced quickly around it. There was no sign of any movement. No frosty breath at the entrance of the shack. But she had to be sure.

Rachel stepped quickly again to the half-door of the guard shack, her knife raised and ready to plunge into a throat. It was empty. The guard was gone, as they planned he would be. She moved up the back steps and into the house, shutting the entrance door as quietly as possible. Taking another deep breath, she pushed down on the door lever to the mudroom. It opened just a crack and she looked in. The mudroom was empty, and she did not see anyone in the cuisine. She stepped into the room and up the step into the cuisine, then paused, listening for sounds. Only silence.

The floor creaked as she walked, but it could not be helped. Her knife was drawn and ready. She walked the hallway. The library to the right was empty. She reached the area where the dining room was on her right and glanced around the corner to the left. No one was in the entry foyer or in the hallway leading to the other bedrooms. She glanced up the stairs. No movement. She sprinted across the large foyer.

Moving down the carpeted hallway, she found the door leading to the laundry was open. She did not stop, but hurried into the laundry room. It was empty, too. Disappointed, she returned to the foyer and glanced out a window. There was no movement in the guard shack outside and she could see no one in the distance all the way to Marlborough Street. She turned her attention upstairs. There was no one moving along the open hallway at the top. It all seemed too easy.

The Citadel Fort of Admiral Dubois de la Motte
Rochefort, France

Lieutenant-Colonel Krieger had instructed his aides not to disturb him that afternoon for any reason. That he had a terrible headache and was going to try and sleep it away. That was partially true. The vulnax wraith surged as soon as the officer lay down on the bed. Possessing an additional servant across an ocean while she was awake was going to be very difficult. It would induce a deadly strain on the body of this host. It could stop his breathing. Maybe even stop his heart. But this was too important for caution.

Krieger lay paralyzed, overwhelmed by a profound seizure. His breathing stopped. His eyelids fluttered. His heart became arrhythmic.

The VanderMeer House

Molly had her back to the door and did not see a dark form silently entering the nursery, a knife extended in one hand. She had just finished feeding four-month-old Conor Gwyn Martyn II. She laid his sleeping body in the basinet of the nursery, cooing words of love and comfort to him. As she straightened and tied the laces of the dressing gown at her throat, she suddenly had an eerie feeling she was not alone.

Molly spun around. Seeing the hooded figure with pale white eyes, she threw her arms wide to guard the basinet and opened her mouth to scream.

"Quiet!" the awful voice growled. "Quiet, if you want your baby to live!"

Molly inhaled in absolute terror. "D-don't hurt my baby," Molly pleaded. "Please don't hurt my baby!"

"Do as I say!" The menacing figure extended a tin cup. "Take it!"

Molly felt paralyzed with fear.

"Now!"

Molly took the cup in a trembling hand. "P-please don't hurt my baby!" She glanced towards the pistol box on the wall next to the door, behind the intruder. *Too far away.*

"Do as I say!" The hooded figure withdrew a small bottle from a pocket. It poured a liquid into the cup. "Drink it," the unnatural voice demanded.

Molly hastened to do as she was bid, trembling as she did so, spilling some on the rug by accident. The cup was filled three more times. Molly choked the liquid down without argument. The intruder took back the cup and, along with the bottle, put them back into a pocket.

Molly heard a strange buzzing sound in her ears. She was confused and bewildered. *Who is this person?* Terrified as she was, Molly could feel herself become lethargic.

The rasping voice asked her a series of questions. Molly answered them truthfully but immediately forgot what was asked and what she had answered.

Finally, the figure demanded one last thing. "Do not leave this this room!"

Rachel shut the nursery door behind her as she left the room. The wraith withdrew. As if a heavy load was taken off her shoulders, Rachel fell to her knees at the top of the stairway, gasping for air, with only a foggy notion of what just occurred. Flashbacks. Her head was racked by an aching dizziness. She wanted to lie down but resisted the urge. She had but one thought. *Must get out of the house!*

Rachel saw the knife gripped in her right hand. She slipped it into the scabbard. It was too difficult to stand. Her legs had no strength. She went down the stairway a step at a time on her rump. At the bottom, she braced one hand against the wall. With slow steps, she lurched forward, going back down the hallway into the cuisine and to the mudroom. With each step, Rachel regained more control over her body.

On the back porch, the cold air hit her face, accentuating the urgent need to escape. Rachel looked out the back door and did not see anyone in the guard shack. She took a deep breath and moved on wobbly legs as fast as she could to the back fence. She pulled off her hood and replaced it with the scarf and knitted cap. Taking another deep breath, Rachel swung the board and slipped through the fence. For a few moments, she leaned against the wooden staves. Her breathing calmed but her heart still pounded with anxiety.

There are no screams, Rachel thought. *There should be screams. I would be screaming!*

She looked left and right on Common Street. No one was walking around in the cold. It seemed colder than before. The clouds above her were moving faster and starting to roil. A winter storm was coming. Rachel pulled on her gloves, tucked her hands under her armpits, and walked as fast as she could to the Cambridge ferry.

*

Lieutenant-Colonel Krieger broke from his trance gasping for breath. His chest ached. His head felt like something heavy rolled around inside of it. He heaved himself off the bed to the floor, crawled on his hands and knees, unlocked and opened the door.

"Guard!" he shouted.

A nervous corporal arrived. "Yes, sir!"

"Bring me the surgeon!"

"Yes, sir!"

When the surgeon arrived, Krieger demanded a strong opiate. He would remain in bed and sleep for several hours.

*

The last thing Molly would recall, when asked later by Dian, was the nursery door closing. She had the presence of mind to rush forward and lock it. She also locked the other door leading to the hallway. Then taking a pistol from the box, she dragged the rocking chair next to the basinet and sat with the pistol on her lap, staring at little Conor still sleeping peacefully. She did not move for a long time, not until she heard insistent knocks on the door.

"Molly? Are you there? Unlock the door." It was Dian, home from the market.

Molly rose from the chair and opened the door.

Dian was appalled by her friend's appearance. There were dark circles under Molly's eyes. She seemed feverish. Her hair was snarled. Something dark and red had left splotches on the front of her gown, Dian reacted with great concern.

"Molly! Are you all right? Why is the door locked? Is Conor all right?"

Without waiting for an answer, Dian rushed to check on the baby, who seemed to be sleeping peacefully.

Molly finally responded in a sluggish voice. "I-I am all right. I feel dizzy. I just woke up…a terrible dream. The baby is all right. I am weak… too weak to stand up."

"All right, but hand me that pistol," Dian said firmly. She helped Molly into the rocking chair again. "Now sit quietly. I will go down and bring us some tea to drink. Sentry is in the cuisine."

Dian hurried downstairs holding the pistol and quickly searched the house. She did not see anything amiss. She found Sentry sitting in a chair in the kitchen reading the Boston newspaper they had purchased while shopping.

He looked up and saw her alarmed expression. "Wha'?"

"Run fast! Bring Dr. Angove here! Molly is not well!"

Sentry stood up, gawking at the pistol Dian carried at her side, now pointed at the floor. "Wha' the hell is tha' for?"

"Molly was holding this pistol! She is terrified and on the verge of collapse. I am worried! Find the doctor!"

"Straight away!" Sentry grabbed his coat and ran out the front door.

*

Standing in the middle of Faneuil Hall that fateful Wednesday afternoon, Carter Trevathan did not hear any report of a disturbance occurring at the VanderMeer house. In that town, anything to do with the VanderMeers was big news. Yet hours had gone by.

If something had happened, certainly by now there should be some hint of gossip or a rumor.

Carter looked at his watch. It was already past the hour of three! The food carriages would be completing their business of the day. They would be cleaning up the coaches for the next morning, getting ready to divide up the profits. He should be meeting with them before they plundered the earnings.

What if she failed? Or was captured? Or arrested? And said something about me? Hell, she'd give up my name willingly if pressed. Shit! I should kill her!

Carter was desperate to learn what happened. He left Faneuil Hall. Weather had come in across the harbor. Another stinging ice rain was falling. He covered his mouth with a scarf and used another scarf under his hat pulled down over his head and under his chin. Only his eyes were visible as he took a long circuitous route on the Boston side streets, staying off the main thoroughfares so he would not be seen before he reversed direction. This permitted him to approach the VanderMeer house from the south while walking north on Marlborough Street, in case anyone at the house was observing pedestrians. But Marlborough Street was almost empty with the onset of this nasty winter storm. As he walked on the opposite side of the street from the house, he glanced towards the left at the guard shacks front and back. There were two guards at each station, lounging around on their chairs. No sign of any excitement. Like any other day.

How can that be! Did Rachel even do it? There must have been screams… The maid would have said something to the guards by now…Fuck!

Carter knew he would have an answer to that question soon enough. But he wanted to know now! If this plan was not successful, he would pay for it when he went to sleep that night. If he dared to sleep at all.

*

Molly's memory remained confused. She had no recollection of that entire Wednesday morning beyond breastfeeding her baby. Dr. Angove could not find anything physically wrong with her and presumed the trembling and forgetfulness was a just winter ague. He pronounced baby Conor fine and healthy.

That night, Molly was troubled by vivid nightmares. She awoke with no memory of what they were about.

The next morning in the nursery, after Molly fed Conor and laid him in the bassinet, she noticed small red stains on the rug. They looked almost like wine stains.

Wine stains? That's odd.

When she knelt to clean them with a pail of soapy water, her nose was assaulted by an odor so foul she recoiled violently, knocking over the pail. Panting with fear, she pushed herself backwards on the rug with the heels of her shoes. It took several minutes to bring her breathing back under control. But she did not clean the rug and she side-stepped to avoid the stains.

When Dian questioned her about the spots later that day in the cuisine, Molly was at the sink and did not turn to face her friend.

Molly's voice trembled. "I don't know what they are from."

Sensing Molly's fear, Dian went upstairs with a pail of soapy water and cleaned the stains herself. The red spots separated into individual blotches on the rag she used to daub it up. She thought that odd and saved the rag to show Sentry.

"What do these stains look like?" Dian asked him later, after relating Molly's reaction.

The veteran held the spots to his nose and frowned.

"Well, I know wha' this lighter spot is…my guess is wine. And this darker one is blood. I've smelled enough of tha' in my life to know for certain."

Dian could feel the hairs on her neck prickle. "Wine and blood? Mixed together? Why would something like that be spotting the rugs in the nursery? And why can't Molly remember anything about yesterday morning? Even to mention it frightens her."

Dian placed the rag into a wooden keepsake. She would take it to Dr. Angove later and ask him about it, too.

The Port of La Rochelle, France

Upon returning from Paris, Captain Beauregard LaTour of the ship *William's Queen* and Victorio, his first mate, arrived at midday at the hotel they usually stayed in when visiting La Rochelle, only to be confronted by a naval marine sergeant waiting for them in the lobby.

The marine sergeant had repeatedly checked with the hotel about the whereabouts of Captain LaTour and had been waiting impatiently day after day for the captain's arrival. He knew the captain on sight. Sighing with relief, he got up from his chair and saluted.

"*Bonjour*, Captain LaTour."

What's this about, LaTour thought, scowling. He glanced at Victorio before he returned the salute, a military courtesy he was still not comfortable performing.

"Yes, Sergeant?"

"Captain, I regret to inform you there has been trouble aboard your ship. The navy has stationed marine guards aboard it. I have a boat waiting to take you out into the anchorage."

"What kind of trouble?" LaTour demanded.

"I am not certain, Captain. I think it is better that you come with me to see for yourself."

"Is my ship undamaged?"

"Yes, sir. Your ship appears undamaged. *S'il vous plaît*, sir. Accompany me."

Captain LaTour and Victorio left their baggage for the hotelier to place in their rooms and followed the marine out to the wharves, where a naval launch was waiting with rowers. The sergeant ordered one of his men to signal a frigate in the harbor with flags to let them know the captain of *William's Queen* was arriving.

LaTour and Victorio were both tired from the coach ride from Rochefort, but their weariness evaporated, replaced by an adrenaline-fed expectation of bad news. LaTour decided he might as well press the sergeant for what he knew.

"When did the navy go aboard the *Queen*?"

"All I know is the port authorities boarded your ship three mornings ago and found it abandoned. Marines were posted as guards awaiting your return."

"Abandoned? What happened to my watches, my crewmen?"

"Apologies, Captain. I do not know."

In fact, the marine sergeant knew much more, but could not tell the captain anything as ordered by his lieutenant, who he could now see in another launch leaving the frigate for the merchant ship. The frigate was closer to the *Queen*, so they would arrive before the launch.

"Have any of my crewmen come aboard? There were several due to return to stand their watches."

"All I can tell you is there were orders given to detain anyone else who came aboard your ship after we posted guards. If anyone came aboard, they will still be there."

"How many?!"

"I do not know, Captain. *S'il vous plaît*, sir, I have orders not to discuss any of this with you. I've said too much already. But look there." He pointed. "My lieutenant just climbed the ladder to board your ship. He will be able to answer all your questions."

"This is bad business, Victorio," LaTour griped to the first mate.

Victorio nodded. "I count at least three of our crew standing along the rail."

As the naval launch came alongside the *Queen*, the three crewmen greeted them with expressions of relief and concern.

Captain LaTour climbed aboard. He was saluted by a marine lieutenant and two privates.

"Captain LaTour, I presume."

He did not salute back. "I am. What is this all about? This ship belongs to the Dutch Republic. You are standing on Dutch territory."

"And your ship is in a French harbor subject to French law, Captain," the officer snapped. "Three mornings ago, we boarded your ship when no one answered our hails. Screaming was reported coming from the ship the night before. We came aboard and found it abandoned with blood stains all over the deck, as you can plainly see." The lieutenant gestured.

LaTour was shocked. "What the hell happened here?" There were blood splatters on the deck house bulkhead and further down both sides of the main deck, as if something bleeding had been dragged over it.

"I trust you can tell us," said the lieutenant. "Obviously, someone was killed. Your watch could not be found when we searched the ship."

LaTour turned to his three crewmen. "What do you know?"

They all shook their heads. "I was to relieve the bosun and found the marines here when I came aboard. I searched the ship too. There's no sign of him. A step is broken off the forward ladder to the hold. Your quarters have been ransacked. I did not touch anything. Every place else seems unchanged."

LaTour examined the blood stains more closely. "This blood is everywhere. It looks like fighting took place."

"Look at these marks. Bleeding bodies were dragged along the deck," Victorio said. "At least two bodies...maybe even three."

Followed by Victorio and the marines, LaTour went below to his cabin. It had indeed been tossed, searched thoroughly, drawers pulled out and overturned, clothes thrown about. Even his hidden chart drawer had been broken into.

"Did your men do this?" he asked the marine accusingly.

"Certainly not, Captain. But it seems to me someone was looking for something you carried aboard this ship...and was willing to kill your watch to search for it. What would they find in here?"

"You can plainly see the gold coins lying on the deck right there. So, they did not come seeking money. The only other things of value are my logbooks and my charts, which I take with me when I leave the ship after a long sail. Maybe they were interested in that?"

"What could such things tell someone?"

"Where I sailed, for one. But that is a matter of state business for the House of Brunswick and the Dutch Republic," LaTour grumbled. "Let's search the rest of the ship."

He walked aft, stopped suddenly, and tilted his head intently, as if listening for something.

"What? What do you hear?" the officer demanded.

"I am listening for gurgling sounds...in case water is leaking into the bilges," LaTour lied.

They kept walking until they reached the forward ladder. LaTour saw the three-inch-thick oaken step torn out of the center of the ladder and tossed to one side. There were no signs any hammers or levering bars had been used to do this. It was simply ripped away.

"What does that mean to you?" the officer asked.

"I have no idea," LaTour replied truthfully, but he sensed it was a message of some kind. A threat!

They went back topside to the helm deck.

"Well, Lieutenant, you have seen my ship is empty of cargo, except for some food stores, as it was when I arrived here with Lord VanderMeer. As to what occurred three days ago, I am as bewildered as you."

"The French Navy and the port authorities of La Rochelle expect you to provide an explanation for this. The flagship of the House of Brunswick is boarded while at anchor in a French harbor and people are murdered. The French government and French Navy want to know why! It is not acceptable for the captain of said ship to claim ignorance of possible reasons."

"Lieutenant, I do not know the reason! I carried nothing valuable on this crossing except for Lord VanderMeer of the House of Brunswick. He is now back in Amsterdam with his father the Duke of Brunswick. I have been away in Rochefort to meet with Captain Pierre Trémoille, aide to Admiral de la Motte."

"Meeting about what?"

Captain LaTour had grown tired of the impertinence of this marine. "Lieutenant, I suggest you ride to Rochefort and ask Captain Trémoille yourself. Once again, I am not permitted to discuss matters of state business. What I can say is this—because the English Channel is too dangerous for any ship under any flag to sail without fear of being boarded, I sought safe harbor in La Rochelle in order to take Lord VanderMeer overland to Amsterdam. Lord VanderMeer visited Jean-Baptiste de Machault d'Arnouville. Perhaps you could direct your questions to the Minister of Marine?"

LaTour watched the presumptuous lieutenant's eyes dart left and right. The man was trying to think of something else to ask. LaTour pressed his advantage.

"What happened to the bodies of the men killed here?"

"We believe they were carried off on a boat," the marine officer replied.

"Why would somebody take the body of my bosun?"

The officer did not reply for a few seconds, then sputtered, "Once again, I expect *you* to give me a reason!"

"Lieutenant, I am tired of this. I am not your prisoner. It is windy and cold. I've nothing more to say to you."

At this, the marine pulled a writ from within his coat with great flourish.

"This is an order from the port authority. You are not to weigh anchor and depart La Rochelle without permission."

"Please tell the appropriate people I have no intention of leaving. My ship will be dry-docked here in La Rochelle for maintenance and upkeep, just as it did last year. Unless you have something else to tell me, I bid you *adieu*. And take your guards with you."

Once the French marines had left the ship, Captain LaTour met with his crewmen on the helm deck to have a deeper discussion about what happened. He did not learn anything new, except that at least another six members of the crew were waiting ashore. None of them wanted to board the *Queen* when they heard they would not be allowed to leave it again.

"I meant what I said. I intend to weigh anchor to sail over to the shipways of the yard and be pulled from the water to the dry dock. We will be here at least another month. That should make everyone happy."

The crewmen glanced nervously at one another.

"What?"

One of them spoke up. "Captain, the crew is consumed by dread. After three deaths in Amsterdam last year and now this, that makes four to replace. Many of them do not want to crew on the *Queen* anymore."

Now *that* was bad news! "How many men feel this way?"

"I'm not certain. But at least half."

"Half?! What about the three of you? Do you feel this way?"

Two of them raised their hands, their heads hanging in shame. LaTour noted they were both married men with families in Le Havre.

"I understand. It will pain me greatly to lose any of you. But I ask you to stay aboard until the work in the shipyard is complete. Can you do that for me?"

They offered relieved smiles and said yes, pleased to make this concession.

LaTour opened the arms locker and broke out muskets, pistols, and swords for the three crewmen. He asked they stay aboard to guard the ship while he and Victorio went ashore to find the rest of his crew.

"I don't think you'll be in any more danger. They did not find what they were looking for. Victorio and I will come back and stay aboard with you tonight."

After LaTour and Victorio rowed the ship's launch back to the wharf, they found the crew at one of the local waterfront taverns they frequented.

The entire crew was supposed to return this week. They were already there, twenty-three men. And they were all glad to see their captain.

After greetings, they all spoke at once with many questions. Captain LaTour calmed them down and told them what he knew. Confirmation of the bosun's death hit them hard. They grew quiet after hearing that. The bosun was regarded as a strict supervisor but he was respected and liked.

LaTour talked, telling them his short-term plans for the shipyard. He brought up the next subject before they did.

"I am told many of you have decided to leave the *Queen*. Is this true? Raise your hands if you are considering this."

Fourteen men raised their hands. Captain LaTour was devastated but did not show it. His continued success in surviving danger over the years was due to the collective camaraderie of these men; that is what he believed in his heart. But they agreed to stay with the ship until after the careening. And they all joined him when he paid for water carriages to go back aboard the *Queen* right away.

Sitting next to his captain on the ship's launch during the ride out to the anchorage, the ever-optimistic Victorio tilted his head and spoke into his captain's ear so as not to be overheard. "We've about eight weeks to change their minds. Money always worked before. And you are still the best captain they know…and the best one I know, for that matter."

At that moment, Beauregard LaTour felt far from being the best captain to these men. He was living with an evil he did not comprehend, and he could not control what it might do next. Four of his crew were dead because of the decisions he'd made, and not because of a storm nor the dangers of a foreign port of call. And he did not feel he could guarantee their safety in the future.

Colonel Gustave Dubonnet de Arras gathered his beautiful wife, Margaux-Lyneth, into his arms as they said good-bye. The Auvergne Regiment was marching southeast in the icy cold temperatures, ordered to join with the French army forming under Charles de Rohan, Prince of Soubise.

Later in the spring, planned for early April, this French army would march eastward into the German states to begin the invasion of Hanover. This small electorate state of the Holy Roman Empire was English territory, the only English territory on the continent. George II, King of England, was its absolute monarch. Like a feudal king, George II's will was law! Cut off a head. Issue a tax. No irreverent, sarcastic House of Commons here!

Hanover had no real strategic military value, except George II coveted this land as his ancestral home. That predilection of the current line of English kings had value. If the French invaded and retained control of Hanover after the war ended, England would bargain heavily to get it back. But first, the French army must engage the English Duke of Cumberland's Army of Observation, composed of English, Hanoverian, Hessian, and Prussian troops. The Duke of Cumberland was the son of George II. *Do not give up Hanover*, was his father's emphatic order. Once this fighting began, it was expected to continue until the end of the year…or to the end of the war.

A light snow was falling. Madame Dubonnet's stylish, wide-brimmed hat and heavy, dark blue long coat was covered in large crystalline snowflakes. The humidity was very low. Reflecting the early morning sunlight, the snowflakes sparkled like tiny jewels.

A fairy princess, Gustave mused.

Margaux's eyes were filled with tears, as they were the last time Gustave had marched off to war ten years earlier.

Gustave whispered, "Madame, you are more beautiful now than when we married."

"And you are still the handsome young lieutenant with whom I fell in love."

They kissed passionately for several seconds. The drumbeats of the march began.

Gustave accepted the reins of his horse from a corporal standing nearby and swung up into the saddle. Madame Dubonnet handed up a circular locket.

"What is this?"

"Open it," she replied.

Inside there was a lock of her blond hair. One half of the locket contained a small portrait of her face. It was meticulously painted by a skilled artist.

"To help you remember me."

"You are impossible to forget. I love you." Gustave leaned over and kissed her upturned face.

"I love you, too, Gustave. Come back to me."

The colonel spurred his horse and rode ahead to lead his regiment.

Crowds of cheering people lined the avenue in Amiens. Margaux was not cheering. She hated to watch this parade of doomed men. She knew many of them were marching to their deaths. The casualty rates among the line infantry regiments in war might rise as high as fifty percent. Some even higher. And half of those men would succumb to disease.

Once the last of the regiment marched out of sight, a frowning Madame Margaux Dubonnet was escorted back to her mansion by the six bodyguards who stayed by her side no matter where she went. These were men she trusted with her life. Upon arrival at the mansion, she went straight to her bedchamber, striping off her winter clothing as she walked, anxious to dress in something more comfortable. Her maids retrieved the clothes from the floor behind her.

In just her undergarments, she sat down at her writing desk and composed the first of the many letters she would write to her husband over the next ten months. *Gustave is a soldier, a virile man, and my husband*, Margaux would often assert to her loyal maids. He needs vivid diversions to read to help him forget the horrors of war.

I am lying in bed wearing only my undergarments, my fingers caressing my sex in a poor imitation of your lips, she began. The rest of the missive was increasingly graphic.

And she enjoyed writing such compositions.

When the letter was complete, the paper sprinkled with *parfum*, the pages covered with rouge kisses, it was wax sealed. Only then did she allow herself to be attended to by the maids. They removed Madame's white wig and jewelry, combed out her white-blond hair, unbuttoned her undergarments, which dropped to the floor, leaving her naked. They dressed her in a flowing, white, sleeveless chemise that hung to her ankles, made of fine linen. Margaux returned to her writing desk to compose the next missive while a hot bath was prepared for her.

This missive was confidential. It would be couriered to the ducal palace in Amsterdam to Colonel Rutger van Boekel. It concerned the arrangements for a meeting with the Duke of Brunswick-Wolfenbüttel. It was short and to the point. Margaux wrote she would be staying east of Antwerp at the fortified stone mansion of a retired general and his wife, Jacob and Louise de Witte. That she would remain at that mansion from the twentieth of February until the twenty eighth of February.

> *I expect you will provide a proper escort to and from Aanwas. I will be accompanied by my personal bodyguards, six men, skilled in fighting. These dates cannot be changed because of the complicated arrangements. I will travel to Antwerp without awaiting your reply, anticipating you will accommodate me. I look forward to meeting His Excellency.*

> *M. Dubonnet*

Margaux recognized the message to Rutger van Boekel was somewhat curt and demanding. It was meant to be. It was not her nature to be so, but it was necessary. The meeting had to take place *now*. For all the couriered messages from different French officials, military, and ambassadorial, each of whom insisted they must be present for this informal encounter with the Duke of Brunswick-Wolfenbüttel, an opportunity now existed to do this... alone...without interference.

First, Gustave was gone, not that she would have minded his presence. But in addition to the depressing deployment of the Auvergne Regiment, distressing news from Paris had arrived in Amiens by military courier from Paris just hours earlier. Unknown to Margaux, this news related back to an earlier event, the unsuccessful attempt to take the life of King Louis XV. On the fifth of January, a household servant in Versailles got past the guards and stabbed the king in the arm. The wound was superficial. The king survived. The servant's name was Robert-François Damiens. Two months later, Damiens would be drawn and quartered by horses for his crime. That would be the last time this type of horrific punishment was ever performed in France.

But that was not the only consequence of the attempt on the king's life. The king's mistress, Jeanne Antoinette Poisson, Marquise de Pompadour, had become so influential with the king, she was a de facto prime minister. She could affect the advancements of ministers and generals, have people dismissed from the Court of Versailles without explanation, and even intruded into domestic and foreign policies, making decisions that impacted the conduct of the war with England. Madame de Pompadour, a commoner, was effectively ruling France. This ambitious impudence earned her the enmity of the French political leadership of the day. She knew it. And she knew the names of her main detractors.

So it came to be that Madame de Pompadour successfully persuaded Louis XV that the capricious assassination attempt on his life by a mentally deranged nobody was part of a broader conspiracy by the aristocracy to challenge Louis' right to rule France. She gave the king a list of names.

"Start with these two," she whispered in his ear.

On the first of February, among the many people dismissed from further duty to the king, were two highly competent men, vital to the war effort, the leaders of the navy and the army.

Jean-Baptiste de Machault, Comte d'Arnouville, Minister of Marine.

Marc-Pierre de Voyer de Paulmy, Comte d'Argenson, Minister of War.

It was unlikely France would recover from the dismissal of these French patriots. But more disruptive, the ruling class of France was hierarchal. After the abrupt dismissal of these important ministers, it appeared no one would be appointed as their successors until August. This had the organizational effect of an oversized ball striking the ninepins of government on the manicured lawn of Versailles.

The news spread outward from Paris and reached every part of France within two days. In another two days, the news would reach the rest of Europe and all the warring powers. It reached Amiens just hours before the Auvergne Regiment marched off to war. The "competent" people who knew these men were shocked. Colonel Gustave Dubonnet de Arras still had his orders to follow. The logistics stabilized his thinking. But compounded with the earlier bad news? The man who tried to kill the king, Robert-François Damiens, also hailed from Arras! This suggested that Arras was a nest of rebellion.

Like everyone else, Madame Dubonnet was taken aback by the inexplicable dismissal of the Comte d'Arnouville. But Margaux seized on the opportunity created by this announcement from Versailles. The lessor ministers and ambassadors who chose to interfere and argue that they had a duty and the authority to impose their presence at this meeting with the Duke of Brunswick no longer had standing as far as she was concerned. She acted quickly, starting with the confidential missive to Colonel van Boekel.

Margaux had been fortunate as a child to have a family wealthy enough to afford tutors. She spoke five languages: French, English, German, Dutch, and Latin. She was an avid reader, with broad intellectual interests: poetry, history, philosophy, the natural sciences, and mathematics. By the time she was twenty, Margaux was erudite and intimidating. Her father had tried to arrange a marriage for her, but she had so many suitors pursuing her already, she refused any selection made by her father.

"I want to marry for love," she insisted.

"Love! A girl like you does not marry for love! You marry to advance your status and that of the family!"

"I intend to do that. But I want to love him as well."

Not a single man among all the men Margaux had encountered had that special attraction she was seeking. It was in Brest, at a military ball in 1745, where she had met Lieutenant Gustave Dubonnet, Comte de Arras. He was handsome, polite, and a graceful dancer. He could also quote Voltaire, her favorite philosopher. And the imaginative way he kissed her on a balcony that night gave her final proof that he was the one. They married two months later. They both had money. But for all their romantic love, after twelve years of marriage, they remained childless.

Margaux badly needed something to occupy her intellectual restlessness. She needed a challenge. Now she had one…a big one! She had not been idle.

Since learning of the existence of her sister Corrinne, Margaux-Lyneth became obsessed with reconciling the obscure details of her birth and infancy. There were things she already knew. She had once been in an orphanage operated by nuns in the small port town of Landerneau, in the Brittany region of France. The convent was part of a small Cistercian abbey that mysteriously burned down in 1727. All the orphaned children were rescued from the fire. Compassionate people from the farms and towns near to Landerneau, adopted many of them. Margaux was taken by a childless, wealthy family in the naval port of Brest. Her father was a successful shipwright for the French navy. Children not taken by anyone locally were moved somewhere else. But that was the extent of her knowledge. She'd never thought to learn more. But after hearing the name *Corrinne*, the idea of a sister surged so strongly in her memory, she could not sleep that first night.

Two days later, she went to her favorite bookseller in Amiens to see what she might find about the town of Landerneau. She moved slowly among the books. There was not much information to be found here. She found its location listed on the map of Brittany. It was near Brest, of course. *I could write father*, she thought. *No, he is too busy*. Her mother had passed away years earlier. It would take much time to learn what Margaux wanted to learn. And she did not yet know what questions to ask.

"*Bonjour*, Madame Dubonnet. Is there something I might help you find?"

Margaux turned and stared blankly at the clerk, considering the suitability of this young assistant of the bookseller. She had talked with him numerous times before. His name was William LaFont, a twenty-two-year-old, penniless Latin scholar, rejected by the Church after exhibiting effeminate qualities considered offensive in the sight of God. He'd found work at this bookseller in Amiens as a printer, a scribe, a book copier, and a researcher. He was polite and highly educated.

"William, how would you like to work for me?"

What? The young man hesitated. "Madame, I am already employed."

Margaux shook her head. "You do not understand, William. This work you do is beneath your dignity and intellect. I am talking about doing some important research, a genealogical and historical inquiry that might take you months, maybe even a year. I will double whatever you get paid here...no, I will triple that amount. And I will give you coinage for expenses covering your travel."

William LaFont was momentarily disoriented by the unexpected deluge of statements.

"Well?" Margaux pressed.

"What...where would I be traveling?" he replied, just to say something, anything.

"First to the town of Landerneau, in Brittany, near Brest."

"What will I do there?"

"You will research my history. I was an orphan once…in Landerneau… and I had a twin sister. We were separated at an early age. I want to know why we were separated. I want to learn where she was taken. I want to know how we came to be orphans in that place…and the names of our real parents. Do you think you can do that?"

William LaFont was bewildered. "Well…I presume I can. There should be written records…somewhere…maybe witnesses."

"Good, William! Good! You are hired. Tell your employer you are working for me now. Come to my residence this afternoon. You know where that is? Good. Bring writing materials to take notes. We will talk more then. And I want you to travel to Landerneau as soon as you can. Leave tomorrow, if possible. I will pay for all of this, of course."

It turned out their discussion would last two full days. He stayed in a room at the mansion. Margaux was pleased to see she had made the right choice. William was thorough and analytical.

"Your middle name, Lyneth, is not French," William had told her. "It is Welsh. If that is your given name before you were adopted, why is it Welsh?"

Welsh? Margaux did not know why. But it was the name she had before being adopted. Even something that simple was exciting to hear.

She mentioned the lullaby. Then hummed it to William while he recorded the notes he perceived on a blank sheet of music. William played the melody back to her on the harpsichord.

Margaux's eyes welled with tears at hearing the beautiful tones.

"Does that sound right to you?"

"Yes," she said softly. "My sister and I would hold hands and hum this melody to each other before we went to sleep at night. It is my oldest memory of her. I don't know the words or where the music comes from."

William LaFont realized the work he was about to do for her may not be the work of scholars, but witnessing Madame Dubonnet's poignant emotion at hearing a deep childhood memory played on the harpsichord, he thought it would be some of the most important work he would ever do.

"Do not worry, Madame. I will find answers to all your questions."

Louisbourg

For two days following the unexpected attack by an English blockade cruiser on the outer defensive works of Louisbourg, the dreary boring winter nights were repeatedly disrupted by sounds of fortress cannon fire. After the men of the Cap Noir battery were praised for their bravery in a cannon duel with an English warship, sentries in other batteries presumed such actions were now the new measure of their competency and the affirmation of how alert they were standing watch. This important news, more of a fast-moving rumor, was most welcome. *Imagine*, the gunners thought, *the firing of cannons at night is permissible if an enemy is detected.* Cannoneers had a distinctive penchant to seek any reason to fire their cannons. Like the men of the Cap Noir battery, the presumption was that gunners would decide if they saw the enemy. Once seen, the command to fire would be given by the battery officer. Even if the enemy later turned out to be wind-driven fog whorls. Which could momentarily resemble the billowing sails of a ship, if one stared at them hard enough in the blurry illumination of the lighthouse. The fog whorls also offered a natural bullseye to focus the gunner's aim.

It was akin to a celebration. The semi-circular Rochefort Point Battery was the most ardent participant. They had over half the compass to envision an enemy. There were two explosive instances the first night and one the second. A few cannoneers boasted a primitive knowledge of geometry when drunk. They used this pretention to describe their awe at the diameter and length of the cone-shaped, eerie hell hole that could be blasted in a fog whorl by a properly aimed twenty-eight-pound cannon ball. In the middle of the night, when added to the fiery tongues of flame, the shower of incendiary sparks, the cloud of acrid cannon *parfum*, and the window-rattling booms which accompanied such a blast, it was a spectacle to saturate all the senses.

The gunners were overcome with hoots and laughter.

Everyone else…not so much.

This phenomenon of noise and fiery light had the opposite effect on the common citizenry of the faubourgs. It made for a night of sleep disruption, screams of surprise, the ruination of one's digestion, unregulated flatulence into one's nightshirts, later described in more vulgar words. It basically turned everyone in the faubourg choleric and rude the next day.

But what a marvelous display of the Fortress of Louisbourg's cannon power.

Beginning with the first blast on the first night, Corrinne was forced to stay up with Marcus. He refused to go back to sleep so badly did he want to see the exciting cannon explosions. He pressed his face to the cold glass of the window and was not disappointed. With the next blast, he jumped and laughed at the sparkling display of fire and noise, then ran around the room with his arms in the air, whooping with happiness. Corrinne could not help smiling at his mania.

Corrinne described Marcus' joy the next morning to Marie-Louise, Madame Drucour, who remarked drolly in reply, "All men are like little boys when something goes *boom*." Over the winter months, they had become the very best of friends.

In the morning following the second night, Governor Drucour gave orders that battery commanders must draft a comprehensive report explaining why each cannon was fired. A separate report for each blast. If the reason was deemed ambiguous, the action was adjudged to be incompetence. And incompetence resulted in fines for the officers and demotions for the cannoneers.

Thus ended the winter celebration.

But Governor Drucour wanted to formally recognize Ensign Henri Gerrard and the men of the Cap Noir battery. There was no dispute they had single-handedly protected the arrival of Captain Vauquelin's courier ship *L'Valkyrie*. Despite being outgunned, they'd forced the withdrawal of a sixty-gun English man-o-war! *Sixty guns!*

With each telling of the story, the size and class of the British vessel became larger.

The governor waited another ten days before conducting a formal recognition of their valor in the great hall of the King's Bastion. This was to give the wounds, bruises, and broken bones of the cannon crew sufficient time to mend so they could stand at attention in a row. This presentation would include refreshments, dancing, and other festivities, announced the governor's proclamation affixed to kiosks throughout the faubourgs.

When the night came, Henri wore the formal marine uniform made by Major Péan's tailor back in Québec City. The white overcoat with a blue waistcoat beneath it had matching blue facings on the cuffs. He felt bad about the tattered and faded uniforms of his men. He mentioned this to Lady VanderMeer. On impulse, she paid a local tailor to fashion brand new uniforms for the bombardier sergeant and his five gunners. The New France colonial gunner's uniforms were blue coats with red facings on the cuffs, complemented with white gaiters on their legs and a tri-corner black hat with a gray metal trim. The men looked splendid to the people congregated in the hall of the King's Bastion for the ceremony. And more importantly, it brought admiring glances from the merchant daughters of the faubourgs to these humble soldiers whose existence was otherwise barely acknowledged. Feminine gazes of appreciation happened rarely, if ever. It was a memory they would never forget.

Lady Corrinne VanderMeer stood beside Madame Marie-Louise de Drucour. Anamosa was not there, remaining at the house to watch over Marcus and Calypso. Anamosa loved and was loved by Marcus and Callie. Corrinne had no worries in leaving Anna with this responsibility. It was a judgement Corrinne would come to regret one day.

Color Sergeant Gosse stood at one side of the room with the remaining ten volunteers from the Québécois Troupes de la Marine and the senior officers and staff of the other regiments in the Louisbourg garrison.

With the hall assembled, Governor Drucour called everyone to order. A single drummer signaled the march. Side by side, Ensign Gerrard and Bombardier Sergeant LaCorne preceded the five gunners, who marched in a line abreast to stand at attention behind them as best they could. Two of them had legs stiffened with splints, one man wore no hat, his head still heavily bandaged and another with a broken collarbone had an arm in a sling. All of them had hidden bandages wrapped tightly around their chest to support the broken and fractured ribs suffered after being tossed through the air by the explosive impact of heavy iron cannon balls. Henri had a stitched and partially healed gash in his scalp from a shard of granite blasted from the black rock. The blazing pink scar, with cross-stitched scars from the sutures, was an inch long from the hairline above his right eye, straight down on his forehead. His newest bandage was cut smaller to hide it beneath his hat. But the scar was visible.

"Attention!" Henri saluted for all of them.

The governor smiled and spoke with pride, some of the facts exaggerated for the entertainment of the audience. "We are gathered here tonight to honor and recognize Marine Ensign Henri Gerrard and six men of the Cannoniers-Bombardiers Regiment, for their brave defense of Louisbourg while manning the Cap Noir battery against a British blockade cruiser. The accuracy of the Cap Noir cannon fire inflicted heavy damage on this man-o-war, forcing it to withdraw. During the engagement, the Cap Noir battery was destroyed by repeated broadsides from the larger caliber guns of the cruiser. *Every single man* in the battery was wounded, as you can plainly see. But by God's grace, these soldiers survived to stand before you today."

The governor paused. One of his aides clapped, prompting broader applause and polite cheers from the people attending.

The governor continued.

"The battle skills demonstrated by the Cap Noir gunners provided the covering fire which permitted the courier ship, *L'Valkyrie,* to enter the harbor safely to deliver dispatches of intelligence vital to the defense of Louisbourg. Before we congratulate these men, I ask Ensign Henri Gerrard of the Troupes de la Marine, to read the battle report he submitted to me. Ensign Gerrard!"

Governor Drucour gestured for the ensign to step forward. Startled by the unanticipated request, Henri hesitated, then stepped to the appointed spot, received the report from the governor, and turned to face the audience. The report was concise and accurate except for some slight modifications. Henri gave all the credit to Bombardier Sergeant LaCorne and the other gunners for first observing the enemy lights and assessing the ship as an English cruiser; the evidence of their excellence in watch standing. Henri only took credit for ordering them to fire the cannons, as the officer in command was required to do.

He read the report loudly, mentioning each man by name, adding his own embellishments of their bravery under fire. He glimpsed the surprise on their faces. The gunners knew better. Henri hoped they possessed the common sense and intuition not to refute any of the details he'd asserted publicly.

"As every man in the battery was wounded under fire, and the Cap Noir battery position effectively destroyed, I ordered a withdrawal to the hospital."

Henri stopped talking and gave a short nod to the audience that he was finished. Stronger applause and cheers followed. Henri returned to his place beside Sergeant LaCorne.

The governor held up his palms to calm those gathered and continued. "Each man of the Cap Noir battery will be awarded an extra month's pay for their bravery. Bombardier Sergeant LaCorne is hereby promoted to First Sergeant."

More applause and smiles.

"As many of you are aware, this is the second-time Ensign Gerrard confronted an enemy of Louisbourg and was wounded. Therefore, by my authority as Governor of Île Royale and commander of the military regiments of this fortress, Ensign Henri Gerrard is promoted to the rank of lieutenant in the Troupes de la Marine, effective this date."

Bravos and cheers erupted in the hall.

Henri was stunned by the promotion. *For doing my duty?* He felt guilty and humbled.

Corrinne rushed forward from the crowd to hug Henri first. "Your father would be so proud of you, Henri. I am so proud of you, too!" She kissed his cheeks, intentionally leaving the mark of her rouge, knowing this would embarrass him.

Color Sergeant Gosse had clapped the loudest. "I think you've discovered the secret to advancement, Henri. Just like at Fort Bull! Find a way to get shrapnel blasted into your skull and you get a promotion," Gosse teased and slapped him on the back. "You only need to survive the wound!"

The musicians began playing. Laughter, drinking, and loud talking ensued. The Cap Noir gunners were congratulated by everyone. Even by the girls who talked with them!

Numerous other people crowded forward to meet the reclusive Lady Corrinne VanderMeer. Among them was Captain Jean Vauquelin, who edged his way closer and closer until he stood right beside her in an unobtrusive manner. When an interlude in conversation occurred, he turned, bowed, kissed her extended fingers, and introduced himself. Then he leaned close to her ear and mentioned beneath the background noise that he'd brought two sealed missives from France addressed to her.

Corrinne reacted instantly. "From who?"

"One from Jean-Baptiste de Machault, Minister of Marine. And the other from your husband, Lord Charles VanderMeer. These men *insisted* to me that no one else should ever become aware of these letters. I've delayed bringing them to you until I found a way to approach you that would not be conspicuous."

Corrinne's passion for letters had become her second most powerful craving.

"*Just ciel*! Give them to me!"

"*Pardon*, my lady, I do not carry them with me tonight. They are safely aboard my ship."

The captain's teeth were the whitest Corrinne had ever seen. And he was a very handsome man. Rumors claimed he was not married and was gaining fame as a resourceful captain.

And I am staring!

"Well then, Captain Vauquelin. I invite you to come to my home tomorrow night to dine with me. Lieutenant Gerrard will be there, too. We can celebrate his promotion and you can give me the letters at that time."

"My lady, I would be honored."

*

Lady VanderMeer's stone house was respectable by the cultural standards of Louisbourg. But it was very small. Dinner attendance was limited to the small gathering around the cuisine table. The table top was large enough for a meal set for four—Captain Vauquelin, Corrinne, Anamosa, and Henri—with room for the serving platters between them. Corrinne had secured the services of one of Madame Drucour's maids who had displayed a special affection for Marcus and Calypso, which they reciprocated. The twins were already asleep in their beds, and the maid sat with her needlework in the rocking chair in the nursery, watching over them. Corrinne had hired an excellent cook, also recommended by Madame Drucour, to prepare the meal. The cook had everything ready before Captain Vauquelin arrived. At the invited hour of eight, the night sky was clear and full of stars for once. It was dark and very cold outside. The house was warm and redolent of delicious foods.

Henri arrived first, wearing his new lieutenant's uniform of the Troupes de la Marine, a surprise gift by Corrinne. She had been alerted a week earlier by Marie-Louise of the governor's intention to promote the marine officer.

Anamosa was wearing a long, light-blue gown with white embroidered lace designs. Her black hair braided up and entwined with slender white-and-blue ribbons in a way that accentuated her high cheekbones. Upon seeing Anamosa's elegant appearance, Henri scooped her up off the floor and swung her in a circle.

"Anna! You are the most beautiful girl I have *ever* seen!"

Anamosa's eyes turned luminous. She giggled and kissed his cheeks.

Henri touched his cheek and inhaled with mock reverence. "I shall never wash them again."

Anna was beaming.

Corrinne wore a peach-colored gown of silk, draped with cream-colored lace, plus her favorite jewels, including the diamond pendant that hung between her bosom. Unconsciously, she wanted to draw similar appreciation from this naval officer.

Not much later, Captain Vauquelin knocked and entered in his naval uniform. He looked resplendent. With Captain Vauquelin's arrival, the cook moved to accept the officer's long coat to hang up. The captain delayed her for a moment to remove the two wax-sealed missives from an inside pocket. The captain turned to view the women with an expression of admiration. Exactly the reaction Corrinne had hoped to induce. Vauquelin touched his lips to her outstretched hand.

"Lady VanderMeer, your beauty is inspiring. You are even lovelier than you were last night. You must realize the captain of a ship is never supposed to get this close to a *Seirēn*. Louisbourg is surely a lonely, remote, and rocky shore. You've but to sing to make your allure irresistible."

Corrinne was warmed by his flattery. *You are very good!* The compliment was excessive, but his tone was heartfelt.

"So, I am a siren of Louisbourg?"

"Indeed!" Captain Vauquelin's eyes shifted to Anamosa.

"Captain Vauquelin, I present Mademoiselle Anamosa VanderMeer."

Like so many others, Vauquelin was captivated by Anamosa's blue eyes. He tilted his head with wonder, bowed at the waist, and gently lifted Anamosa's right hand to press his lips politely to her fingertips.

"Mademoiselle Anamosa, I have sailed the world's oceans and seas beneath the fairest of skies. But the blueness of your eyes is unmatched by any natural wonder I've seen save for one, the color of the ice in a glacier on the frozen lands of the northern latitudes. So rich and deep was that blue, it left me staring for a long time. Even so, the blue of your eyes is more magical. I think it could only be duplicated on the palette of a master artist."

Anamosa did not understand even half of what this man in uniform implied to her. But she appreciated his tone, his smile, and the length of the compliment he gave her. Her head dipped shyly to the left, but her eyes stayed fixed on Vauquelin, uncertain how to respond.

"*Merci, Monsieur?*"

Corrinne had never seen Anamosa react to any man like that, except to Henri.

Vauquelin straightened and addressed Corrinne. "I am charmed twice over, Lady VanderMeer. She is delightful."

Corrinne let her pleasure at this show. "Yes, Captain Vauquelin, Anamosa is indeed charming. She is also eleven!"

"*Mon Dieu.* Eleven! How extraordinary!"

Corrinne was about to add more but Vauquelin continued.

"Yet even more extraordinary—there is an English ship called the *Anamosa*. In fact, it was the *Anamosa* that Lieutenant Gerrard cannoned."

"The *Anamosa*!" Corrinne could not be more surprised. She looked at Henri. "The ship you fired upon was the *Anamosa*?!"

Henri was just as startled. "I had no idea…!"

Vauquelin was confused by their reaction. "My lady, the *Anamosa* is a blockade cruiser. I played a cat and mouse game with it in the fog for days but eluded engagement, and only because I was sailing *L'Valkyrie*. The *Anamosa* is almost its equal in speed. And its captain is the best I have encountered. And I have met many. He almost caught me once in the fog. He prefers to prowl the waters near the port entrance like a predator. But that night I trailed his darkened ship, close behind him, so I could turn into port after the *Anamosa* passed the entrance. When he finally realized I was there, it was too late. Of course, the exchange of cannon fire with the Cap Noir battery diverted the *Anamosa*'s attention. But I am curious, is Anamosa's name and that ship name more than just coincidence?"

Corrinne's mind was racing. It was safer not to trust this man she barely knew with too much information.

"Well, there is a rumor of an English ship with that name. But Anamosa is a tribal name. It means *white fawn*. A beautiful but rare name. I suspect it is more than a coincidence. Maybe someday we will know the whole story. Probably after the war is over." Corrinne decided to avoid any more discussion on this. "But *s'il vous plaît*, Captain. At this moment, all I think about are those letters you hold in your hand." She inclined her head. "I want to read them."

"But of course, my lady." Vauquelin handed the missives straight away. "I understand the power of unopened letters. It is strong enough to pull a compass needle."

"I ask your indulgence while I retire to my bedroom with Anamosa. Henri will remain with you. Give me fifteen minutes."

"Please, take your time. I have looked forward to conversing with Lieutenant Gerrard. I've learned from others he is an accomplished sailor."

Inside the bedroom, Anamosa talked in whispers with Madame Drucour's maid.

Corrinne moved over to the window. In the comfort of her favorite chair, she raised the wick on the lamp, broke the seal of the missive, and read Minister Jean-Baptiste de Machault's letter first. It was only a single page.

> *My Dearest Lady,*
>
> *I intentionally omit names and places. I am in contact with a certain lord of your acquaintance. He will write to you, so I will be brief. I am most pleased to learn you are safe inside thick walls of stone, somewhere strong, and out of danger. Indeed, so much has transpired since we first met, a lifetime has passed us by, yes? But even the walls of Rome fell to a determined enemy. So, I advise that you leave your place of safety as soon as it can be arranged. Some Celtic associates of mine intend to visit there very soon. It would not be wise for you to visit me. I suggest you go to the place where we first met. Do not delay for too long. Be certain you are gone by April's end.*
>
> *On another topic, from several people of high rank, I have received the most complimentary reports regarding the son of our common acquaintance. Please tell him how proud I was to hear his name mentioned with such praise from these esteemed people. Tell him that I pray for him every day. As I certainly pray for you and the new little people in your life! You must be overjoyed!*
>
> *The man delivering this missive to you is someone I trust implicitly. I miss you greatly. I am forever your friend.*
>
> *Until we meet again,*
> *JBM*

Charles' letter was many pages long. She read it fast and seized on the substantive phrases. He also did not mention names or places, and he, too, indicated she must leave, that an unnamed ship would soon come to get her and that their common fortune was now deposited in the Bank of Amsterdam. He attached a single sheet enumerating all their current assets, the account numbers, that an operational account to fund nautical expenses and property management was created but remained separate from the main one. He gave the name of a new shipping agent in Amsterdam, claiming the previous agent, Wittmann Bootz, was corrupted. And that he retained an agent they both knew to act on their behalf in America.

Corrinne knew he meant Thomas Hancock. With the beginning of the next sentence her reading slowed. She read every word with growing dread.

> *Our "ghostly" enemy has been desperate to find the châsse and is frustrated in that effort. I presume It is now trying to find you. My location is no secret. I am guarded always by my father's men. It will eventually learn your location. This is just another reason why you must leave. Even in a fortress, a man in a military disguise could assail you. My father persists in asking me to bring you to live with him. He wants to meet you and his "grandchildren." He has the best intentions. Please consider the advantages that his goodwill might offer you, Anamosa, and the twins. Regardless, you must never come to Amsterdam. Over here the enemies of this noble house are too numerous to name. And they all plot to eliminate me as an heir. You pose a greater threat to their deceits. It is better for you to return to your former life. More places to hide. More people you can trust to protect you.*
>
> *And me? I feel I must tell you that the prognosis for my future health is not good…according to the best physicians in Amsterdam…*

Corrinne stopped reading. She could not bear to learn what Charles might write next. Not now. She would wait until Captain Vauquelin left. Then she would read the letters all over again, when she could allow her emotions to break in private, as she knew they would.

*

Corrinne and Anamosa returned to the cuisine. Corrinne apologized for her absence.

Vauquelin shook his head. "No apology necessary. Henri and I had a most interesting conversation about the sea and other matters."

Henri's expression gave the impression he had things to tell Corrinne, but not now. For now, she concentrated on the dinner.

"Good! Let us delay no longer."

Corrinne pointed to their positions, took up a dish, and personally served Captain Vauquelin first. She was thankful the food was waiting atop the stove. Everything was still warm.

"Captain, I trust you do not mind that I do the serving. Living here in Louisbourg convinced me this simple gesture expresses respect for a guest. I learned this social grace from Madame Drucour. Marie has served me on occasions when I was privileged to dine privately with her and the governor. I have found it evokes a warm harmony among the people at the table."

"It only makes the food more enticing!" Captain Vauquelin was genuinely pleased. "My mouth waters."

The dish centered around fresh cod, with local sauces, vegetables, and hot bread. She filled each plate, before leaving the serving platters on the table and took her seat.

"*Voilà*! The wine I pour is from the governor's cellars with his compliments. It is very good. *Bon appétit*!"

Vauquelin raised his glass in toast. "To Lady VanderMeer, a woman of singular beauty and grace."

Corrinne did not mention the content of the letters she had received. And Henri did not disclose his private conversation with Captain Vauquelin. Instead, they discussed news from France and Vauquelin gave his interpretation of the events.

Vauquelin turned out to be entertaining and witty. He was brimming with humorous stories, many of them irreverent anecdotes concerning the French aristocracy. Lady VanderMeer responded with laughter, which encouraged the captain to continue. Henri's reaction was only slightly less effervescent. At a certain point, when relating the risqué rumors concerning the Court of Versailles, he switched to English out of respect for Anamosa's presence.

Anamosa had listened and watched the charismatic officer throughout dinner with a placid expression, taking small bites from her plate. From time to time, she had glanced at Henri to observe his reaction. Henri would wink and smile back at her. When the officer switched to English to relate how a woman of the court was caught by the Versailles palace guards running naked through the throne room, she looked at Corrinne with a questioning expression.

Corrinne interrupted the captain. "*S'il vous plaît*, Captain. Anamosa has a question."

"Why was the woman not wearing clothes?" Anamosa asked him in perfect English. "Had she been coupling with the king?"

Vauquelin's jaw dropped. "You speak English?! A thousand apologies, Mademoiselle. I did not mean to give offense."

Corrinne laughed again. "You did not offend her, Captain. But you should answer her question. And know that she speaks fluent Dutch and German, too."

"I am learning Latin now!" Anamosa added in the proud voice of a girl pleased to finally join the conversation. "But I also speak Ottawa, Seneca, Erigh, and various tongues used by the Iroquois…oh, and sign language. Lady Corrinne is teaching me algebraic mathematics, but I am not very good at it."

Corrinne patted Anamosa's hand. "You will be," Corrinne assured her.

"And Henri has taught me the names of all the important stars and constellations."

"Indeed?" Captain Vauquelin drained the remainder of the wine in his glass. "I suddenly feel like a peasant! No need for me to go to Versailles, I am sitting with royalty now. Bravo, Anamosa!"

Anamosa smiled. "*Merci*. So, was the naked woman coupling with the king?"

Vauquelin looked to Corrinne for help, who sipped her wine and nodded assent.

"I believe that was indeed what she'd been doing," he replied. "But she wanted to go home," he added quickly so this questioning went no further, "and the guards helped her do so."

Having Corrinne's approval, Anamosa continued asking the captain questions about every sort of subject: the names of the oceans and the islands he had been to, whether the sea storms were as bad as people said, what the people looked like around the world, how he had learned to sail a ship. Whether he had seen London or New York or China. If he was married.

They told each other amusing stories. The room filled with laughter. And with the laughter, the hidden pains, worries, and tensions dissipated. They relaxed even more. By the time the evening grew late, Vauquelin was utterly enamored with them all and slightly intoxicated. This was not typical behavior of aristocracy…or any aristocracy. *We even passed food to one another!*

Donning his coat and standing at the doorway, he bowed to Lady VanderMeer.

"Please forgive any bad manners I displayed, my lady. I believe…I believe I drank too much wine."

"Nonsense, Captain Vauquelin. You were a remarkable guest. You are most welcome to sit at my table on any day. Besides, you are a man of polished flattery! You must realize by now I yearn for flattery. It is more precious to me than new jewelry!"

"You make it easy for me." His tone became wistful. "This has been the most enjoyable evening I have spent with anyone since, well, since

I was a young boy. My lady you are a wonderful…" He stammered, searching for words. "Simply wonderful…a most generous and gracious host without compare." He turned and gently lifted Anamosa's hand. "And you, Mademoiselle, you are a prodigy of beauty and intellect. I envy the fortunate man in your future."

Fortunate man? Once again, Anamosa did not quite understand. *"Merci."*

Vauquelin opened his mouth to speak again, but he was now dizzy and out of words. *"Au revoir, mon amies."* He staggered out the door.

Henri put on his cloak. "I want to talk more but I'm tired from the day's events. My head aches. My ribs ache. I'll come tomorrow at the end of the day. The dinner was very good," he said. "And I am too full."

Corrinne did not argue. She had had too much wine as well. And she wanted to finish Charles' letter before she went to sleep…if she could sleep.

They hugged, and she whispered in his ear, so Anamosa would not hear, "The missives claim more change is coming." It was too big a burden for her not to mention. "I must leave Louisbourg."

When they stepped back, Henri's face had saddened.

"Let's discuss this tomorrow. Come in the morning if you like. I still have some coffee left to share."

"I will." Henri turned and picked Anamosa up off the floor again. This time his fractured ribs rippled with pain. *"Ooof!* You are almost too big to pick up."

She rubbed her nose under his chin as they hugged. "I love you," she whispered.

He set her down. They pressed foreheads together, then stared into each other's eyes.

"I love you too, Anna."

Corrinne felt humbled to witness this tenderness. She caught her breath as a distressing new thought occurred to her regarding leaving Louisbourg.

What about Anna?! Well, Henri and the other marines will just have to come with me.

Henri was dizzy as he walked into the dry, bitter cold night, clutching the cloak around his shoulders. The cold air on his face helped him focus. He must tell Corrinne about the missive Captain Vauquelin gave to him while she was upstairs. To Henri's surprise, it was from Captain LaTour! He was further surprised by Vauquelin's admission he'd been friends with Captain LaTour for nearly a decade. LaTour had never once mentioned this association. The missive was wax sealed and addressed with Henri's name. He'd not read it yet, deciding it would be rude to read it in front of the captain.

Henri plodded along the streets of the faubourg. Even the small amount of wine he drank had a lethargic effect on him. That, and the throbbing pain in his head and ribs.

I'll read it in the morning, he decided with a yawn.

La Rochelle, France

Captain LaTour was pleased with the work performed by his crew. It had taken several days, but they had successfully dragged and winched *William's Queen* out of the water and up on the shipway. In another day, they careened it to starboard. Now they could begin the important cleaning and preservation work of the hull.

The captain did the mental calculations.

A week to clean the starboard hull. Two days of rest. A day to careen it to port. Another week to clean the port hull. Two days of rest. Prop the ship upright on the ways...umm, a day, maybe two. Then all the interior hull work. Probably two full weeks for that. Another week to fix the things we don't know about.

It added up to the middle of March, maybe a week sooner.

"That's what I will tell Admiral de la Motte," he said aloud.

"Tell him what?" Victorio asked.

"That I'll be ready for sea by mid-March."

Victorio grinned. "Oh? You're certain we will have a full crew by then?"

Captain LaTour scowled. He'd forgotten about that.

"You need to feel them out, Victorio. We need to change their minds. What will it take to get them to stay? How much? And don't use this yet, but Admiral de la Motte considers the *Queen* a French warship."

"Warship!? We don't have any cannons!"

"All right, a transport ship. It does not matter to the admiral. He made me a French naval officer, he can do the same thing to the crew."

Victorio grimaced. "Let's just bribe them with money."

"Yes. But don't tell them where we are sailing after this. Not until they are all committed."

Chapter 11
Québec City
February 1757
The Letters

Captain Louis Antoine de Bougainville hurried from the officer quarters in Québec City after breaking his fast. He'd just heard a rumor Scout Captain Philippe Gerrard was seen somewhere in the city last night, purportedly walking the streets of upper town. But Bougainville hurried not to find Captain Gerrard. He wanted to confront Captain Russel Trieste, Governor-General Pierre de Vaudreuil's primary aide *before* Philippe arrived at the palace and caused a confrontation that would not be good for anyone. Trieste was searching for Captain Gerrard's missing letters. Philippe had been right. His mail had been intercepted.

When Bougainville entered the governor's mansion, the ensign on duty requested he wait in the anteroom outside Captain Trieste's office.

"Captain Trieste is already in a meeting with Governor Vaudreuil."

"If Captain Philippe Gerrard arrives here this morning, tell Captain Gerrard he is to meet with me *before* he sees anyone else. Is that clear?"

"Yes, sir!"

Bougainville took a chair in the anteroom and leaned his head back against the wall to collect his thoughts. He'd arrived in Québec only five days earlier and did not expect Philippe to follow him here so soon. The last he heard was that Philippe had gone south on Lake George to collect his scouting parties following the wilderness battle with the American rangers.

Just nine days earlier, Bougainville had been at Fort Saint-Frédéric, packing his baggage aboard a sled in the morning. He had stayed at the fort the night before, and was now anxious to start the next leg of his journey to Québec. Suddenly alarm spread around the marshalling yard about a ranger attack at Fort Carillon. Bougainville immediately ordered the sled driver to reverse direction. He arrived back at Fort Carillon in the early afternoon. By that time, the fort commandant, Captain Lusignan, explained that the battle with the rangers had moved inland some five miles to the west. Lusignan had ordered the remaining scouts in Fort Carillon and a platoon of grenadiers to go south to join up with Captain Gerrard, who was moving to cut off the ranger retreat. They had been gone for several hours.

The commandant was puffed up with pride and expectation that he would soon have the elite rangers encircled, forcing them to surrender. Bougainville was not so optimistic. Initial reports claimed Fort Carillon had already suffered over three dozen casualties: men either wounded, killed, or taken prisoner. Bougainville intended to join Philippe, but the commandant ordered him to stay at the fort to assist in its defense. During battle, it was the commandant's prerogative to give such an order to General Montcalm's aide.

Disgruntled and annoyed, Captain Bougainville had no choice but to do as the commandant ordered. To pass the time, he made copious notes of the engagement as reports of battle came back to the fort, none of them very good. He wanted something useful to carry back with him to General Montcalm. By afternoon the next day, the battle was over. The rangers had suffered heavy casualties, according to Captain Lusignan, and retreated south, with Captain Gerrard and his scouts in pursuit. Bougainville gave the commandant the rough draft of his report to read and edit.

"I must go to Québec City with my report. The governor and General Montcalm need this information, even if further amendments are forthcoming. And I must go *now*," he emphasized to Captain Lusignan. The commandant was disconcerted how the battle with the rangers would be perceived, since it had ended as a stalemate. Captain Bougainville was Montcalm's aide-de-camp. He could not be delayed now that the battle was over. All Lusignan could think to do was change the counts of French casualties, which he lowered. It was his prerogative.

Bougainville returned to Québec as fast as possible, traveling day and night by sleigh on the frozen rivers. He took time at the city barracks to purify his appearance before making his report to Governor Vaudreuil and General Montcalm together. The two men were in a meeting, maps spread out across the table in front of them, deep into an argument over the intended strategy and goal for the spring campaign. Bougainville's news and information were exciting. To learn the rangers had been defeated and forced to retreat! This was a major blow to the English! The senior officers gloated. That same day, Governor Vaudreuil drafted an amended report to send back to France.

He declared the battle a French victory. He lowered the number of French casualties even further and elevated the number of English casualties.

The two senior officers had met and argued every day since then. Sometimes Bougainville was called into the meeting, so he could describe what he'd learned previously from participating with Captain Gerrard's scouting raids on Fort William Henry.

Vaudreuil and Montcalm were now formulating an attack plan on Fort William Henry for March. Should it be a full siege or a raid?

"We must act now…lay siege while the English huddle inside their fort, licking their wounds, dying of the pox, and are without any support from Fort Edward," Vaudreuil stated with conviction.

Montcalm disputed Vaudreuil's notion that the attack should be attempted as a siege. "It's mid-winter! We cannot move the cannon or stage the proper lines of supply. The ground is still too frozen to dig any trenches."

"We don't need to dig trenches. We position our cannon in the trees and fire on them continuously. In their disease-weakened condition, they will surrender in days!"

"Trees do not matter! Our cannons would be exposed and in range of the guns from the fort!"

And the arguments continued.

Bougainville didn't care. While the generals argued, he confronted Captain Trieste about Captain Gerrard's missing mail. The two men had never liked one another. At first, Trieste denied knowing anything about it.

"I advise you to be careful what you assert to be the truth."

Captain Trieste sneered. "Or what? You will beat me over the head with one of your calculus books? Do not pretend to threaten me."

Bougainville analyzed the situation and then took charge. His voice calmed. "Captain Gerrard knows letters from his wife are being intercepted. He has received mail from other people in Louisbourg. He is coming to Québec City to find out why this is happening. I trust you respect this man's reputation. If he raises such an accusation with General Montcalm…you and I both know where that will lead. Governor Vaudreuil and General Montcalm must trust one another if we are to win this war. They do not need this distraction."

Trieste fumed. "What is it you want?"

"I want the letters! And I do not want Captain Gerrard's mail diverted again!"

For several seconds, Captain Trieste considered the difficulty of providing what Bougainville wanted. Governor Vaudreuil had indeed intercepted these letters. Trieste did not know what was contained in these letters, but he had interrupted the governor reading them more than once. To Trieste, this suggested Vaudreuil liked what he was reading. He presumed they were descriptions of sexual trysts. Captain Trieste did not care a whit about any of this. But Bougainville was right about Captain Gerrard's anger. From Trieste's observation, General Montcalm was straight-laced and moralistic, almost to a fault. The general would consider the governor's behavior of reading another officer's private mail highly offensive. It would provoke a confrontation. And General Montcalm would send a report back to D'Argenson, the Minister of War. *That would not be good.* And Captain Gerrard's aggressive nature was unpredictable. The man had almost drawn his sword on the governor in their last meeting! Trieste could not dare to ask for the letters; the governor would refuse. He would have to take them. But the biggest problem? Trieste was not sure where the governor kept the intercepted correspondence.

Probably in his desk…locked in a drawer. I'll have to find the key. He would not carry it on his person.

"All right. But I cannot promise anything." Trieste turned and walked away.

Bougainville sensed Trieste was going to help. He would have to wait and see.

That was where the impasse stood as Bougainville sat down to wait in Trieste's anteroom two days later. He did not have to wait very long.

Captain Trieste came into his office in a hurry, rummaging around his desk, when he noticed Captain Bougainville standing in the doorway.

Trieste paused and snapped, "I have no time for you today."

"He's here."

"Who is?"

"Scout Captain Gerrard arrived in Québec City last night, fresh from his battle with the American rangers. And his blood is up. That's how the *coureurs de bois* characterize war anger. I guarantee Captain Gerrard will protest the matter of his missing mail to Governor Vaudreuil and General Montcalm. A discussion about this between our generals will not end well. There is still time for me to dissuade Captain Gerrard from a confrontation."

Trieste stared at Bougainville with acrimony.

"Just give me the letters," Bougainville pressed, "and this will be over."

The governor's aide yanked open one of the drawers on his desk and withdrew a stack of letters tied with sail threads. He tossed them to Bougainville.

Bougainville noticed all the wax seals were broken. "Did you read these?"

"Don't be absurd," Trieste spat.

"Who broke the seals?"

"Don't goad me further, Captain Bougainville. You've got what you wanted. Now get out."

"Answer one question for me and I will. Did Intendant Bigôt read these letters?"

"Intendant Bigôt!? Certainly not."

"Give me your word on this, Captain. Don't frown. You can either give it to me or to Captain Gerrard himself. He will certainly come to ask you. Your choice."

"Intendant Bigôt doesn't know these letters even exist. You have my word. Now go!"

Bougainville turned to leave but hesitated. "Captain Trieste. With respect, sir. Please do what you can to ensure this does not happen again."

Before Trieste gave another curt reply, Bougainville left the office.

Beaupré, Saint Lawrence River

The marines had lost much body weight. Almost a pound a day since departing Louisbourg. When they reached Port Toulouse after marching the first three days, Major Péan found a missive waiting. It was from army headquarters in Québec City.

Do not go to Gaspé, the missive stated. *There are no sleds waiting at Gaspé. You must go further.*

"The sleighs are being staged at the Seigneurie de Rimouski on the Saint Lawrence River," he told his assembled officers and sergeants. It was just the first of many obstacles he expected. "All right…start hiring boats for passage across the Strait of Canceau to Pointe-à-Bouleau."

Major Péan had signed a voucher in Louisbourg and brought along a sack of silver for just these purposes. A courier schooner was available to carry thirty of the marines to Pointe-à-Bouleau, a place on the mainland a hundred miles to the south of Gaspé. The rest of the marines were carried by a small fleet of fishing chaloupes to the same place at a charge of two livres per man. That was robbery, as far as the major was concerned, but he had no choice. This transport took two days. They made it safely, except for two men who fell over the side during the night and could not be found in the dark. Even if they could swim, their packs would have dragged them under and the cold waters would have killed them in minutes. From Pointe-à-Bouleau, it was a snow shoe march overland for sixty miles to Pointe-à-la-Croix on Restigouche River. The rivers and streams of the Restigouche River watershed area were all frozen. The marines rested a day to prepare for the even longer wilderness march. They built wooden sledges and loaded their supplies. They shifted to ice skates.

Major Péan planned to go up the Restigouche River, take its northern tributary, and get across Lac-Matapédia. They marched a hundred twenty miles, up the frozen rivers, portaging overland to smaller lakes, up and down large and small hills, all of them heavily forested, ten nights of sleeping in the open when tenting was not practical, and more snowshoeing after crossing Lac Matapédia to reach the Seigneurie de Rimouski, on the Saint Lawrence River.

Once they reached this village, to Major Péan's pleasant surprise, there were indeed eighteen cargo sleds waiting for him.

"Transfer the supplies to these sleds. Two hundred more miles to go," Major Péan told his weary troops. "I know that is far, but the worst of the march is over."

The major had planned to travel on the frozen Saint Lawrence River, but the ice was groaning. The musket-shot sounds of cracking ice were heard continuously day and night. Péan and his officers inspected the ice all the way to the middle. It appeared strong enough, but the combined weight of the sleds and the men could be dangerous. Major Péan modified his line of march. He gave the men two full days of rest before continuing up the crude Saint Lawrence River road running along the southern bank.

They purchased horses, enough for five of the sleds. In these, they placed the sick and infirm. A few men skated ahead on the Saint Lawrence as scouts. The rest pulled the sleds in shifts. Horses pulled two wagons bearing the load of tents to lead the way. The major hoped they would not stumble into the hidden ruts. There was the snow on the ground which sloshed into mud during their passing. Despite the natural obstacles they faced, the marines moved along without much complaint. They were going home and were anxious to get there. They marched almost fifteen miles a day. When they reached the village of Montmagny, the major decided to cross the Saint

Lawrence to its north side and enter Beaupré. The riverside roads on the north bank were usually kept in much better repair. Once at Beaupré the exhausted marines became excited. Québec City was only two or three days further. Péan marched another day before he rested again.

At the village of Chateau-Richer on the northern bank of the Saint Lawrence River, Major Péan decided to stop. Sunset was still two hours away, but the men had marched all day from the village of Beaupré. They were cold and exhausted, like they were at the end of every day of this march. But now they were filthy from almost two hundred miles of continuous travel, covered in mud, half-starved from the physical exertion, and bent over from pulling the sleds.

"We are not marching into Québec City looking like this," he insisted to his officers and sergeants. "I want these marines to get decent food tonight and a long rest."

The major had been to Chateau-Richer before. This village had good food and wine to offer. Sometimes, even the women were friendly. They were close enough now to Québec City that Péan could sign an army voucher for any amount to pay for it. He wanted his marines to wake up feeling strong and rested in the morning.

"Sergeant Cabrelle! We camp here tonight. The food in this village is good. I want the men rested. Tomorrow, we finish the march to Québec City. It's only sixteen more miles."

As the order spread among the marines to camp, they gave a tired cheer. Many of them simply sat down at the place they were standing to rest a few minutes before starting the task of getting the tents up.

"Sergeant Cabrelle, pick a man who is a strong rider. Buy a horse if you have to, but I want the man to ride to army headquarters and deliver a missive from me regarding our arrival tomorrow."

Eleven marines volunteered. Sergeant Cabrelle selected the man, a corporal, who'd complained the least during the march.

The major gave him a sealed missive he had just penned. "Corporal, I will give you a Louis d'Or after we reach the city if you bring back six saddled horses for the officers to ride tomorrow morning. We will be marching at sunrise and will probably meet somewhere on the road."

"Yes, sir!"

The corporal saluted and jumped up on the saddle with the ease of a man who had been riding horses since his childhood. He galloped away.

"Color Sergeant Cabrelle!"

"Sir!"

"Send someone into the village and buy enough meat to feed these marines. In fact, you should go, and make sure we do this right. Buy anything else you want to eat! But not too much wine! Offer to pay the village women to prepare the food for them. And tell the headman, I will personally sign a voucher to pay for it all in the morning!"

Cabrelle grinned. "Yes, sir!"

That evening, Major Péan ate with his officers and senior sergeants at a round table in the Inn de Chateau-Richer.

"We marched four hundred and fifty miles in a month in the middle of winter," Major Péan reflected. "A hundred and thirty-seven marines left Québec City for Louisbourg. A hundred and twenty-two started the return march. A hundred and seventeen of us are still alive."

Major Péan drew his journal from a coat pocket and looked at daily entries. He read the dates and events aloud to them. Péan's humorous sarcasm caused them to laugh. They winced at the more painful memories.

"Add the eleven men that volunteered to stay behind in Louisbourg, and we lost only nine men in total. Five of them to disease. Four of them in accidents during the march. Of the four, two fell out of the boats and drowned in the Canceau Strait crossing from Île Royale. One fell from that high embankment near Lac-Matapédia and crushed his skull on a rock. Another broke his shin bone…which developed the rot. He lost too much blood from the clumsy amputation we attempted." Péan shook his head with regret. "That was no one's fault but mine. I should have brought a surgeon with us. I have a long list of other non-fatal injuries—fingers, toes, and the *tip of a nose*…I'm a poet, eh? All frostbite. I lost two fucking toes!"

Sergeant Cabrelle spoke up. "Don't worry, sir. You got them back in the soup we made for you that night."

Péan continued. "Eight men with *dissenterie* carried on litters when sledges or sleigh-wagons were not available." Major Péan noted in his journal. "Did you know they had all eaten from the same food pot? What does that tell us? In any case, if we hurry to Québec, they might still be saved. Armies expect losses of more than twenty percent during a winter march of a few weeks over mountainous terrain. If it's only twenty percent or less, they boast about it. Our Québécois marines suffered less than ten percent! Only nine men! God rest their souls."

Major Péan raised his glass in a toast. "This success was due to your leadership. I am proud of every one of you." They made complimentary remarks in reply. "Now, before we cross over the Saint Charles River bridge tomorrow, make certain the men clean up their appearance the best they can before we get there. If they carry any pieces of clean uniform, tell them to wear it! I want our marines to look smart and be marching in step, better than a regiment of grenadiers. The city will undoubtedly come out to cheer us. Remind them that all the young ladies of Québec will be there. And you never know," he addedly suggestively.

*

In early February 1757, Major Michel-Jean de Péan, commander of the Québécois Troupes de la Marines marched proudly into Québec City. His officers rode horses. The church bells were tolling. The cheering people of Québec City lined the road leading up from the Saint Charles River as the marines marched by, company by company.

Michelle and Madeleine stood arm in arm at the side of the road waiting to see Henri ride by on one of the horses. But he was not among them.

CHAPTER 12
LONDON
FEBRUARY 1757
Eccentric Allies

Colonel Wilhelm von Kleinfels' carriage crawled along Whitehall Street in London. The street was crowded with carriages moving in both directions. The smell of horse manure and urine was eye watering. There were vendors of every trade yelling out the prices of the goods they were selling. A few men stood upon short wooden stools shouting arguments to the passing people, most of whom ignored them, their eyes fixated on the ground to avoid the manure piles. The government personnel walking between the various buildings frowned at the noxious aroma, made worse after any rainfall, which was almost every day of the week in the winter. Other pedestrians, many of them in uniform, were forced to move peripatetically among the horses and carriages to cross the wide avenue.

Colonel von Kleinfels walked with a limp, the result of a stroke he'd suffered a year earlier. He could not walk very fast nor very far before he had to sit and rest. So, he'd left his hotel in a carriage two hours ago, leaving plenty of time to reach the recently completed Horse Guards Palladium where he would meet privately with the courier secretary of Lord William Pitt, 1st Earl of Chatham. Mr. Carlton North was trusted to open any of the wax-sealed missives addressed to Lord Pitt, many of which contained information of extreme confidentiality.

In December 1756, Lord Pitt had been appointed the Secretary of State for the Southern Depart. He was now responsible for Southern England, Wales, Ireland, and the strategically important American colonies. Colonel von Kleinfels had enjoyed dinner with this ambitious statesman two years earlier when Pitt was the Paymaster General in charge of contracting the German mercenaries. Kleinfels had not been the only person at that table, but the colonel knew he made an impression on Lord Pitt because they were seated right next to one another.

Two days earlier, Colonel von Kleinfels had couriered a sealed request to Mr. Carlton North, indicating he was in London and asked for a private meeting with him. He reminded Mr. North of his previous dinner with Lord Pitt, two years earlier. The missive also stated the Hessian colonel was carrying a confidential message from Frederick II of Prussia intended for Lord Pitt directly. He asked for a one-hour private audience at a place and time at Mr. North's convenience.

Frederick II had given no such orders to Colonel von Kleinfels, no direction to carry any message to Lord Pitt. If the colonel was exposed as a fraud, he would be subject to execution by either country. It was a gamble. But under the persuasions of the wraith, the colonel was not concerned.

A confidential reply was couriered back to Colonel von Kleinfels from Mr. North that very same day. His request for a meeting was granted.

The carriage stopped as close to the Horse Guards edifice as permitted. Once inside the palladium building, Colonel von Kleinfels maneuvered through the loud and crowded foyer to the appointments desk. He identified himself. The captain at the desk checked his logbook and determined the appointment was authentic. He stood and saluted a superior officer.

"Good morning, Colonel. Sergeant Carpenter will escort you to the proper meeting room."

Sergeant Carpenter accepted a slip of paper detailing instructions from the captain. He noted the colonel's left arm in a sling was pressing a valise to the side of his body. The officer's right hand used a walking stick. The sergeant came to attention and saluted the Hessian officer.

"Sir, please follow me. We will be going up the stairway. May I carry that valise for you?"

"That will not be necessary."

Using his walking stick, Kleinfels climbed the long marble stairway to the next floor while the sergeant followed a step behind him, but to the right, just in case there was a mishap on the stairway. At the top, the sergeant took the lead again and they walked to the end of a long hallway with meeting rooms on both sides. The hallway walls were covered with portraits of English nobility and military heroes. It echoed with the sounds of their footsteps. A few of the doors were open, most were closed. Kleinfels glimpsed inside the open doorways and saw round tables in some and long tables in others. At the end of the hallway, two stairways branched away to the left and right, going back down to the ground floor. The sergeant opened the door listed on the paper and peered cautiously into the last room to be certain it was empty. It was.

The sergeant stood aside and gestured for the colonel to enter. Colonel von Kleinfels walked towards a round table in the center of the room with four chairs. The room was beautifully appointed with historical paintings of military battles and personages on the wall. There were no windows. A portrait of King George II hung above a six-foot-long credenza, where a silver tray was placed. It was set with a silver pitcher of water and four crystal goblets.

"Mr. North will enter through this opposite door. I will wait outside in the hallway to escort you back down to the foyer. May I pour you some water?"

"No, Sergeant."

The sergeant saluted and left the room.

Kleinfels set his valise on the table and wandered around the room, examining the paintings to see if he recognized any of the battles depicted. He stopped at one of them and stared. The face of the commanding field marshal was remarkably accurate. The opposite doorway opened, and Carlton North entered.

Kleinfels turned instantly at the sound of the door. He snapped to attention, heels clicking.

"Such formalities are not necessary for me, Colonel," the courier secretary remarked politely.

Carlton North was thirty-seven years old, unmarried, and dedicated to serving Lord Pitt. The second oldest son from a family of merchant-traders that specialized in mining and shipping saltpeter for making gunpowder for the East India Company. He graduated with honors from Trinity College at Cambridge, majoring in Mathematics. His family purchased a commission for him in the army. North served with distinction in the 2nd King's Own Regiment of Horse for six years, rising to the rank of captain, seeing action at the Battle of Dettingen during the War of Austrian Succession. He was wounded twice, once by shrapnel in the left shoulder and once by a French cavalry lance that pierced his right thigh. He subsequently refused a permanent commission in the army and decided instead to pursue politics. With a letter of recommendation in hand from the commander of the 2nd King's Own Regiment of Horse, Carlton North received an introduction to Lord William Pitt, who was also a graduate of Trinity college and had also served in the 2nd King's Own Regiment of Horse.

Discovering the commonality in their backgrounds, the two men liked one another immediately.

North eschewed any overture from supporters to get a seat in Parliament, preferring instead to become Lord Pitt's missives secretary. Pitt considered the former cavalry officer to be his most valuable assistant. North was loyal to Lord Pitt alone. He was a man of complete discretion. He had shrewd instincts for accurately assessing the character of people he met after only one meeting. But he possessed one rare talent that made him perfect as Pitt's missives secretary. Carlton North could recall from memory, every word of anything he had ever read.

In this hurried meeting with Major van Kleinfels, North was dressed in a tailored suit of dark brown wool and velvet cloths, a cotton blouse with a white linen cravat around his neck. The requisite powdered wig of white curls was braided back into a short tail and covered the black hair beneath it, which was streaked with fine white hairs. A thick gold chain dangled across his chest bearing a large emblem in the middle certifying his service to Lord Pitt's office.

"Mr. North," the Hessian greeted the man. "Colonel Wilhelm von Kleinfels, at your service."

Carlton North was taller than the Hessian and stared at the man critically for a few moments.

"I *do* remember you, Colonel." North noted the officer's left arm in a sling with a prosthetic hand made of silver, protruding from the lace in the sleeve. The officer also used a walking stick. "Though you appear more battle weary than when we last met."

"Thank you, sir," he answered politely. "My sword hand is unaffected, and I can still shoot a pistol and ride a horse at the same time. Therefore, parts of me are still useful in battle...as my sovereign has assessed."

"But now you carry messages?"

"My sovereign honors and entrusts me with this privilege."

"I noticed you admiring that painting. Were you there?"

Kleinfels turned to the painting again, one of many paintings commissioned to commemorate the Battle of Fontenoy in May of 1745. It was a great French victory in the last war, fought near the city of Tournai in the Belgian low country.

"Yes, sir. I commanded a company of Hessian infantry fighting for the French."

North grunted. "Did you know Marshall de Saxe?"

"Not as well as I would have liked, but I was close enough to salute him on numerous occasions."

"And your opinion of him?"

"Being respectful to English generals, Marshall de Saxe was the most brilliant field marshal I have ever served, except for my sovereign."

"Indeed. He was a tactical genius. A ruthless and efficient enemy. A real bastard. We hang such paintings in Horse Guards to remind and humble our generals."

North closed the door and approached the table. "Do you have something for me?"

The colonel leaned his walking stick against a chair and opened his valise. He withdrew an ornate envelope sealed with a bright glob of red wax, chopped with the insignia of the King of Prussia. The outside was blank.

Colonel von Kleinfels, in fact, possessed two more such missives worded exactly like this one. They were intended for use, ostensibly, with the French government officials, where Kleinfels had served as a confidential messenger in the same role.

Carlton North broke the seal and opened it. It read:

Colonel von Kleinfels is my singular confidential emissary. Names and dates are omitted intentionally. This courier is authorized to carry messages to you directly from me.

Frederick II

King of Prussia

The king's signature was twice as large as the message in swaggering cursive script.

North nodded. "To the point, as expected. I anticipate King Frederick's message to Lord Pitt is verbal?"

"Yes, sir."

"Then speak."

"We have learned that Charles de Rohan, Prince of Soubise, has been given command of an army of twenty-four thousand men with orders to march on Hanover as soon as possible. This army is expected to become larger as more regiments are added to it. The French Minster of Marine, Jean-Baptiste de Machault d'Arnouville, speculates Charles de Rohan will not be ready to march until April. He has been ordered to rendezvous with other armies coming from Sweden and Russia. There is no decision on where they will meet or when."

"That is the message?"

"No, sir, there is more. If you please, I pause as a courtesy, that you might ask me questions."

"Continue without pause. I will interrupt with my questions."

"After the recent assassination attempt on King Louis, the French king was convinced by others in his court that the act was part of a broader conspiracy. He dismissed Minister Machault and the Minister of War, Marquis d'Argenson, with no replacements announced as I left Paris."

"By *others*, you mean Madame de Pompadour specifically?"

"Yes, sir."

"When were you last in Paris?"

"Ten days ago. I made this same report to my sovereign and he sent me here to see you."

"Why? Does he believe we English are uninformed of these events?"

"No, sir. He sees opportunity. My sovereign intends to invade Bohemia and seize Prague. He must do this early in the fighting season to be successful. He wishes to share this knowledge with Lord Pitt. Except for myself, you are the only person beyond his general staff who knows Frederick's intentions. He will leave three battalions of Prussian troops with the army of Hanover to help in its defense. My sovereign does not respect the marshal abilities of the Prince of Soubise. He anticipates the Duke of Cumberland should be able to resist and defeat the French invasion. However, should the French invasion somehow be successful, my sovereign promises he will return with his army and defeat the French before the year is complete. He wanted you to have that assurance from him personally."

The Hessian began another annoying pause.

What is it about him? Carlton North asked himself.

The missives secretary stared at the colonel intently, trying to comprehend something he sensed this man was hiding. Carlton North learned early in his life that he had a gift, an ability to *see* into the emotions and character of the people he met. He could discern their underlying passions as easily as the color of their eyes. Without any discussion, he could comprehend their ambitions and their credibility. This *sight* was strong enough to speculate on their future. It had saved his own life on the battlefield more than once.

But this Hessian colonel was opaque. It was like looking at a historical figure made of wax, like the ones at the museum on Fleet Street. He did not discern anything specific. It was more of a complete absence of character, a very sinister façade, a blackness. There was something lurking beyond this verbal message from King Frederick. Carlton North could not see it, and he was not used to being so confounded.

It was Carlton North's eyes and expression that provoked caution. The wraith suddenly became aware this man had a gift. He was the type of human that could perceive shadows in a darkened room.

North wanted the Hessian to speak with more candor. "Tell me plainly, Colonel. What does Frederick imply?"

"Sir, three battalions of Prussian troops alone cannot ensure Hanover's success against the French invasion. And if my sovereign encounters heavy resistance from the Austrians when he invades Bohemia, he will order those battalions to rejoin his army. Without them, the Duke of Cumberland will certainly be defeated, and Hanover must surely be occupied."

And there it was. It was well known that Lord Pitt and the Duke of Cumberland were bitter political enemies. Frederick was telling him in advance that the son of King George II, the Duke of Cumberland, would be *defeated* and Hanover would be *occupied* by the French. A great embarrassment for the crown and a disgrace for the Duke of Cumberland. Despite the treaty agreement to do so, Prussia would not come to the aid of Hanover against the French. Not immediately.

"You are saying that Frederick II is giving Lord Pitt his word that if Cumberland is defeated, Prussia will return, defeat the French, and will return Hanover to English rule before the year is complete."

Kleinfels nodded. "Yes, sir. That is his exact message. Lord Pitt has Frederick's word."

Enough had been said. Carlton North evaluated the quality of this information. He could validate the message, but not the messenger. It was vexing.

"Officially, you have come to confirm that Charles de Rohan will lead this army of invasion against Hanover."

"Yes, sir."

"What does Frederick want from Lord Pitt in return?"

"My sovereign wishes to demonstrate he will deliver on any promise he makes to his lordship. And if Lord Pitt has a reciprocal message for him, he will give it his full attention. A written confidential reply, simple, undated, an acknowledgment to my sovereign that we met."

"That is all?"

"Yes, sir. Except for an understanding that I am the only emissary from Prussia who can carry such private messages from Frederick, independent of ambassadors. My sovereign will accept your choice of a singular emissary in return, introduced in a similar manner."

Carlton North abruptly stood up and opened the hallway door.

"Sergeant, escort this officer down the outside stairway…not back to the foyer. Inform the appointments captain he has left."

The sergeant saluted.

Carlton North extended his hand. "Until we meet again, Colonel."

When their hands touched together, Carlton North sensed something ominous shy away from the light in the shadows. The Hessian was first to pull back his hand.

"It was an honor to see you again."

Carlton North spoke no further and watched Colonel von Kleinfels walk down the hall to the stairway.

*

Carlton North reported to Lord Pitt on his meeting with Colonel von Kleinfels. As usual, the minister relied on North's perceptions on the veracity of the messenger and the value of the message.

"Do you believe Cumberland will be defeated in Hanover?"

North nodded. "Yes, sir. The Prussian king will invade Bohemia and the Austrians will be taken by surprise. Frederick's message was a warning to you alone, that without his help, Cumberland will lose to the French. But he promises to regain Hanover for England by the end of the year."

"That is an extraordinary revelation for the Prussian sovereign to disclose to me. Why? What if the Austrian spies in London learn of this?"

"The message, of course, was verbal. We are the only ones who know. Militarily it is madness for Frederick to reveal his Austrian strategy to anyone, even his allies. I believe Frederick does this as evidence of the special trust he offers. This suggests that Frederick's message to you was entirely political in nature. Frederick II is going to invade Bohemia. Without Prussia's help, Cumberland will be defeated by the French and be disgraced. George II will be angry with his son, and Cumberland will no longer be eligible to command an English army. And if Frederick recovers Hanover before the year is over, England's only territory in Europe will therefore be reconstituted as an absolute monarchy. Our king, George II, will be happy again. Frederick II asks you for nothing in return. Does that help or hinder our global agenda for the war?"

Lord Pitt admired Carlton North's astute analysis.

"Frederick II is a very eccentric ally."

Berlin

After waiting all morning, Colonel Wilhelm von Kleinfels was finally admitted to see Frederick II, King of Prussia. Purportedly, Kleinfels had just returned from his final meeting with the French Minster of Marine, Jean-Baptiste de Machault d'Arnouville. A final meeting, not by choice, but because Jean-Baptiste de Machault had been dismissed by the king of France as the Minister of Marine.

But Kleinfels had not returned from Paris, but from London and his meeting with Carlton North. House Kleinfels required the continued patronage of the Prussian sovereign to obtain the money necessary to pursue the location of the châsse and hire the servants necessary to capture it, whether it was in French, English, or American territory. With the dismissal of Minister Machault, Colonel von Kleinfels' strategic usefulness to the king was diminished. His crippled condition made him unfit for any other service.

In Kleinfels' pocket he carried the undated missive with Lord Pitt's signature delivered to him personally by Carlton North. It was the acknowledgement that a meeting with Colonel von Kleinfels had taken place. It was a meeting King Frederick had not authorized.

The Hessian colonel entered the war chamber of the Prussian sovereign. It was a ballroom, made more useful, according to the king's wishes. He found Frederick huddled with three of his Prussian field marshals, over a round table that could comfortably seat twelve people. It was just one of a dozen others that filled this huge room. The tables were covered with miniature city models, select regional landscapes, plus heavy leather sheaves full of battle maps. All the models were still being modified. The information presented had been painstakingly collected, some of it purchased. But most of it was accumulated by German surveyors and cartographers of every nationality. It was an on-going project and had taken decades. When not occupied building such toys, the effort was performed by German model builders and sculptors who turned information into these table-top masterpieces. Most of the cities were part of the Austrian Empire. Each was reasonably accurate and highly detailed, a few completed with tiny soldiers, in the colors and uniforms of the country they represented, in fighting poses, firing muskets, swinging swords, charging on horseback with lances extended, some stabbing others with a bayonet. It included artillery pieces, mounted cavalry, and even ambulance wagons. The room itself was a closely guarded possession of Frederick II. Begun as a diversion to indulge an avid interest Frederick cultivated as a young prince, it was a sophisticated expansion of King Frederick's passion and fascination with war.

Rarely surprised, Colonel von Kleinfels stood in awe of this martial splendor. He had never seen anything like it. He'd heard rumors it existed but few outsiders below the rank of general were ever permitted entry. He was now one of those privileged few. He waited patiently at the edge of the room until the sovereign signaled him to approach.

Frederick was slapping his riding crop against his pant leg and arguing with his field marshals about the invasion plans for Bohemia, which he intended for the spring. He had absorbed Saxony into the Prussian state the previous September, just six months ago, but some of the regions there were already in rebellion.

"But, sire," one of them said, "there are barely enough troops in the army to maintain order in the lands we've occupied."

The other two generals nodded in agreement.

Frederick II made a sound of disgust. "I am *not* going to waste my precious Prussian infantry putting down rebellions! They are mobs, not soldiers. Let them organize. Let them concentrate and form ranks in one place and I will crush them! It is more efficient."

"A large Russian army approaches us from the east," a second general said. "It presents a greater threat to Prussia than the Austrians."

"And yet the Austrians do not move any troops to join with them? Do you not see their strategy? They expect the Russians to engage us first… to weaken us. That is what makes the Austrians vulnerable. They will not expect my attack."

The most senior field marshal spoke last. He was the oldest of them all. A thirty-year veteran of fighting battles, most of which he had won. He liked the young Prussian king. The man was aggressive and would take risks… but too many risks were dangerous.

"Your Majesty," he said respectfully, "our country is young. Our army has grown larger, but it does not match the might of the Russians. The Russians outnumber us three to one. It will take most of our forces to defeat this enemy before it overruns East Prussia. They will be here at the end of April. We must gain a position on the good ground to defeat them."

Frederick looked askance at his best general. "That is why you will never rise above the rank of field marshal," he replied.

This assertion confused all three field marshals. *But…there is no rank above a field marshal*, they thought collectively.

Irritated from arguing, Frederick reacted to their confused expressions. He spoke tersely. "Your king's goal is to expand Prussian territory! Not simply march around the decayed Holy Roman Empire defeating armies. I will beat the Austrians and occupy Bohemia in a matter of weeks! If I turn my attention and march to defeat the Russians, the Austrians will march on my rear. Besides, if I go now to defeat the Russians, what have I won? Prisoners? Regimental flags? Bah! I win nothing! I must march a thousand miles to capture anything Russian. And who wants that frozen-shit wasteland anyway? Most of the Russians coming here will see grass and trees for the first time! They will probably stop to picnic, or turn to farming! No! We invade Bohemia in April! The goal is to occupy Prague and force a surrender. Then, I will deal with the Russians. You have two weeks to construct a plan of march for me to approve and execute. Dismissed!"

After the generals saluted and left, Frederick's attention was drawn to the table model of the Hanover province. He brooded darkly any time he pondered this German province ruled by a foreign king. This was German territory populated by Germans! The English possessed it as the bizarre result of a marriage a hundred years earlier by the Electress of Hanover, a German woman named Sophia, who happened to be the granddaughter of King James of England. But worse, because of a law passed by the English Parliament in 1701, when Sophia died, her son George automatically became King of England! German Hanover became English territory because this foreign government passed a law! Not a shot had been fired by anyone!

Frederick detested this splotch of English territory on his map. It was a stain on historic German land. *I should have invaded and absorbed it in the last war, when I was allied with France.*

The current treaty between Prussia and England required Prussia's agreement to protect Hanover against invasion by France.

All right, he thought vindictively, *you say Hanover is English land. Then I will let you defend it alone when the time comes.* He would keep that acrimony a secret to himself.

"What is your opinion of Hanover?"

It was the signal for him to approach. Colonel von Kleinfels limped to the side of his sovereign and looked down upon the beautifully detailed model.

"Well?"

"Majesty, my memories of Hanover include excellent beer, scholarly genius in mathematics, mediocre production from its silver mines, and the odorous Leine riverfront."

"I mean from an invasion perspective!" Frederick snapped with annoyance.

"Apologies, Majesty. From an invasion perspective, a single brigade of your troops could rout Hanover's army in less than a week. Four days of marching to get there, plus an extra day to document their surrender."

Frederick grunted. "And if England deploys British redcoats?"

"A week and three days. The Hanoverian army will join with Prussia as soon as they are permitted to surrender. The redcoats will then be outnumbered, in fact, overwhelmed. If the English are foolish enough to engage you in battle, it would be settled in a matter of hours. This land is German, not English."

Another grunt. "Then why do I not invade them now?"

"I presume because of our treaty with England, and England's endless obsession with France as its historical enemy. Hanover is yours anytime you wish to take it. Now must not be the time."

"Hanover is an English boil on my ass!" Frederick slammed his riding crop for emphasis on the edge of the table, then used it to point at a nearby table set for four. "Let's sit there and drink brandy."

Boil on my ass! That comment only reinforced Frederick's weakness to Kleinfels. Hanover was a weakness of the eccentric kings of two countries: England and Prussia. A weakness he was now exploiting.

After the servant poured for them and removed the third and fourth place settings, Colonel von Kleinfels raised his glass in toast.

"To Prussia and its king."

Frederick took a sip and ignored the toast. "Did you bring Machault's answer to my question."

"Yes, sire. Charles de Rohan, Prince of Soubise, has been given command of an army of twenty-four thousand men with orders to march on Hanover as soon as possible. The Minster of Marine speculates he will not be ready to march until April. He's been ordered to rendezvous with the other armies coming west from Sweden and Russia."

Frederick fumed. "The man who poured this brandy has more marshal ability than Charles de Rohan." His eyes drifted toward the shaft of sunlight beaming through a tall window. "I could defeat him in a day. But it would require I delay my plans for Bohemia."

This validated another point in Kleinfels' plan.

"Minister Machault suggests that is precisely the intention of the Hanover invasion…to draw you away from any engagement with Austrian forces. To give time for Sweden, Russia, and a reconstituted Saxon army to gather for battle against you. Minister Machault also regards Hanover to be German territory. France only wants it because of its future bargaining value with England."

"And what of Minister Machault?"

"After the failed assassination attempt by a servant on King Louis in January, the French king became convinced Minister Machault was part of—"

Frederick snorted and interrupted. "The servant should have stabbed the whore mistress…Pompadour. She has a gifted mouth, good for many uses. No doubt it was she who convinced the king of this conspiracy."

"Indeed, sire. Minister Machault mimicked your exact words. The king has dismissed Machault and the Minister of War, Marquis d'Argenson. No replacements had been announced as I left Paris."

"The royal idiot dismisses the two men responsible for French success over the English during the last three years," Frederick groused. "I should be happy. My focus on Bohemia will work as long as I move quickly."

And another piece of Kleinfels' plan was confirmed.

Frederick raised a finger. A servant brought each of them a small plate of cheese, sausages, and hard biscuits, which had to be dipped in the brandy to be eaten. Colonel Kleinfels ate sparingly and only if the king ate something first. He waited for the sovereign to steer the discussion.

"So…with Machault dismissed, what usefulness can House Kleinfels offer me now?"

"The English have asked that I return to Boston to resume my liaison for mercenary support. My Hessian subordinate, Lieutenant-Colonel Krieger, is amassing a battalion at Rochefort to fight for the French in the Americas. He claims they will likely be deployed in May, either to Louisbourg or Québec City."

"You presume this is of interest to me? Have you forgotten Prussia has no navy?"

Unfazed, Kleinfels continued. "Sire, I must visit London and the Horse Guards Palladium on Whitehall to renew my contacts before crossing to Boston. But I also plan to see Lord Pitt. I can use a personal message from you as bait for a meeting."

Frederick II stopped nibbling his biscuit. He stared hard at Colonel von Kleinfels. He'd underestimated this Hessian before. He once challenged the colonel's assertion he could become a confidential messenger to and from the French Minister of Marine. Now, the French minister was almost a friend. They were enemies by treaty, but viewed their main enemies to be other countries. For France, it was England; for Prussia, it was Austria. So, they secretly agreed not to attack one another directly, if possible. The relationship with Machault had proven very valuable, as evidenced by this new information on Charles de Rohan.

But Lord William Pitt was a personage known to Frederick for over ten years. He was a man of consequence in English government. And without ever talking, they both agreed on something important—that Hanover was German! This meeting might be useful.

"You personally know Lord Pitt?"

The colonel nodded. "Yes, sir. I do."

Frederick's next challenge was sarcastic. "Next you will tell me you went to the same school together as boys!"

"No, sir. I dined with him in London two years ago when he was Paymaster-General, to discuss matters of financing for the Hessian mercenaries we provided."

"Indeed? And you were so charming—a characteristic I find hard to envision—and Lord Pitt was so moved by your erudite wit…that he will agree to see you again, two years later, for an encore?"

Under the persuasions of the wraith, Kleinfels was not intimidated.

"Majesty, I know Lord Pitt well enough to predict he will send a messenger to carry a note to decline to meet me, with an apology. But I realize I can only ask him once. And he will refuse to see me without a signal that I carry a confidential message from you."

Frederick gestured to the wine servant to pour them each more brandy.

"England is Prussia's ally," Frederick replied with indifference. "I have dozens of agents and ambassadors visiting London who meet with officials routinely. I can send a message to meet with Lord Pitt, or even the king, if I choose. What more could you offer?"

Colonel von Kleinfels only sipped his brandy when Frederick sipped, and only every other time. He had to convince him now, while the king was drinking brandy and listening.

"Sire, I would bring an offer of absolute confidentiality. A means to communicate that prohibits anyone else in English government or in Prussia from ever knowing what you say to each other. Lord Pitt is presently Secretary of the Southern Department, and leader of the lower House of Commons. But if the English suffer another major loss to the French, for example the loss of Hanover, a consensus exists that Lord Pitt could be elevated to Prime Minister. But if I wait until that happens, it will be too late for me to ask for this meeting."

Kleinfels stopped talking to let this point be assessed. He must wait for another invitation to speak.

Frederick II took his time considering this. For a Hessian to talk with the French did not take much finesse. But getting past the arrogance of the English was much more difficult, particularly for a German, who the English considered little more than barbarians. He stared at the colonel, desiring to test the man's composure.

"Tell me what you know of Lord Pitt."

Kleinfels took a deep breath and began. "As a young man, he was an officer in the 2nd King's Own Regiment of Horse, a dragoon cavalry unit. But he left the military and became a member of the House of Commons. He spoke out publicly against subsidizing the Hanoverian army. King George II detests him because of his consistent adversarial position on Hanover. Most of the royals detest him too. However, the common people of England celebrate him. He has compelling oratory skills. He does not believe England should be involved in land wars in Europe and declares in Parliament that England has nothing to gain by these land wars. Most of the king's ministers do not agree with him. But he is not dissuaded by this. And if England must fight, he prefers to use paid mercenaries. He prefers Germans, of course. He told me all of this at that dinner. But Lord Pitt is obsessed with defeating France, not in Europe, but defeating France's global ambitions. He wants to rout

France's ability to maintain or increase its global possessions. He believes France will be consumed in defending its borders in Europe during this war. That means New France will have to survive on its own. He is convinced the time is now for England to focus on invading France's territories in America to complete English dominance on the American continent."

Kleinfels paused, took a long sip of brandy, then waited.

Frederick noted the colonel had mentioned Hanover numerous times.

"Did Lord Pitt say all that to you or is this just your opinion?"

"Sire, Lord Pitt did not say the last few sentences to me directly. I inferred it from his other comments made at that dinner. He said England was too small a country with insufficient young men to field large armies of redcoats. That is why it conscripts so many of the Irish and Scots. That England needed more colonies like America, ones that England does not have to subsidize. His vision of empire is global and that England's future will be determined by its navy. Lord Pitt wants to build more ships, many more ships. As Prime Minister, that is what he will do. This is my opinion, of course."

Frederick had heard some of this before, but never presented as an opportunity. If the colonel could get such a meeting, then what?

"A compelling observation, Colonel. Except Prussia and England are allies by treaty. What more is there to say that cannot be said by my ambassadors?"

Colonel von Kleinfels nodded. "Sire, with your indulgence. I suggest you tell him something truthful, something useful, something he does not already know, and infer something significant for him to consider…something of impact with a longer view."

Frederick grunted with annoyance. "Speak clearly to me!"

Kleinfels glanced warily at the servants in the room.

Frederick looked over at the three men standing by the walls. He gestured for them to leave. The wine servant approached quickly to leave the brandy on the table and bowed before exiting. The king had known this man since he was a boy. The other two servants stood more than twenty paces away. They may have overheard everything said so far. But they would die a horrible death by torture should they utter a word of anything they overheard in any of his private chambers. And it would not stop there. Their families would suffer as well.

When the door closed, Frederick leaned forward. "I anticipate you have a suggestion drafted, yes?"

"Yes, Your Majesty." Colonel von Kleinfels stood and withdrew a draft from his pocket, outlining what he had already said to Carlton North about the Hanover invasion. Of course, Frederick had not seen this before. He handed it to the king. Then he sat down again in his chair.

Frederick read it. As suggested, something true, something useful, something unknown. But something significant was cleverly worded. Essentially a way to diminish and disgrace the Duke of Cumberland. The political implication was subtle!

"You expect me to sign this?!"

Kleinfels shook his head. "No, sire. This draft is written for your eyes only. For your convenience to modify and approve. All I need in writing is a short missive of introduction indicating that I am your confidential emissary, carrying an important message, much like we did for Minister Machault. What I have written in the draft I will only say in private to Lord Pitt."

"You could be executed for implying this to the English."

"Yes, sire. I understand. It is a risk for me personally. But Lord Pitt and the Duke of Cumberland are enemies. There is really nothing for Lord Pitt to do but wait to see if this all comes to pass. He doesn't even have to acknowledge the meeting. But the seed will still be planted."

"I will take no actions to defend Hanover."

"If that is your pleasure. The goal of this meeting is to create a special trust in communications between you and Lord Pitt. He will come to know, over the course of time, that whatever you decide to share with him will never be shared with anyone else. Sire, Lord Pitt admires you as the German leader. He will never say that publicly. Strength and honesty, even in an adversary, engenders trust between leaders. That can be very valuable…in certain situations…in my opinion."

*

Colonel von Kleinfels returned to London two days later. He did not meet with Carlton North this time. But he did renew his contacts at Horse Guards as the Prussian liaison in Boston. After establishing this connection again, he returned to Berlin and provided Frederick II with the undated missive with Lord Pitt's signature. A single sentence of acknowledgement that a meeting with Colonel Kleinfels had taken place.

Frederick II was stunned at this success. "I am impressed, Colonel. And I am not often impressed."

"Sire, I anticipate Lord Pitt will send his own confidential emissary to see you and validate this arrangement. As you have observed, the English do not trust Germans. He will want a messenger of his own."

"Then what will be your service to me?"

"With your approval, sire, I will return to Boston and resume my duties as liaison. I've learned from Minister Machault the English are amassing troops in the ports of New York and Halifax with intentions to invade the French port city of Louisbourg. I will obtain accurate counts of these English redcoats and send this information back to you. Their numbers are limited. If the redcoats are in the Americas, they cannot be used to support you in Europe. And I will return at once should you need me."

Colonel von Kleinfels would travel back to London and take passage on an English warship to Boston two days later.

The Strait of Canceau

The *ghost* knew the white eagle would not tolerate too long a journey. It was still winter, and the animal preferred to remain close to the breeding place. But too much time had passed since he communicated directly with the woman. The demon was across the great water. But the *ghost* observed a servant of the demon molest the innocent at the house in the water city. Now the demon knew where the woman had fled. The *ghost* must warn her. She must leave that place.

The channel of water was intimidating. He was flying along its southern shoreline and could easily see the other side. Still, this water channel was wide. This was not a river. And it was seawater. His power to persuade the eagle to do his bidding could be greatly diminished when crossing over salt-laden water this wide. He flew until the distance to the other side seemed less than some rivers he had crossed.

The eagle banked at that spot and they were across very quickly. On the other side, the *ghost* sensed the land of this place was limited. It was an island. But an island large enough that the land spirits would dominate. The eagle craved food and the ghost flew to a big lake at the center of the island before withdrawing its dominance. The animal started a glide and, within minutes, gripped a sizable fish in its powerful talons.

They had been flying all day long. The eagle was tired. After eating its fill, they found a tall conifer tree in which to roost for the night. The *ghost* withdrew all dominance, so the eagle could rest in peace. This also allowed the *ghost* to reach out more strongly.

In the distance, the *ghost* now sensed not only the presence of the woman, but also the boy become a man. And there was a new presence! A young female who exhibited a most potent aura. The ghost perceived she glowed with light, light as bright as the moon! Reaching out further with his thoughts, he hovered near her. She was wearing the amulet of the signs. The center jewel was glowing. She also possessed the dreaming gaze, that of one who could see animal spirits in her dreams. He could see her eyes brimming with wonder. She felt the experience to be just pleasant dreams. But they were much more than that. Much more. The *ghost* had never observed this in anyone else before. Finally! It was very exciting…and important.

With the glow of the girl so bright and clear, the *ghost* was compelled, drawn to her. And he knew the exact direction to fly when the sun rose again.

Louisbourg

Several days had elapsed since the dinner with Captain Vauquelin. Corrinne had read the letters again and again. But she had not yet talked about them with Henri as they had planned to do. The very next morning after their dinner, Lieutenant Gerrard and four other officers were called away to Gabarus Bay to inspect the fortifications and cannon emplacements completed over the past two years at great costs in labor and expense. They were to evaluate how the structures were holding up in the winter. With the threat of an English assault early this spring, the governor wanted to be certain the Gabarus Bay defenses were in good repair to support cannons of any caliber the commandant decided to place out there to defend against English landings.

Henri had taken Captain LaTour's missive with him and read it the first night by the light of a camp fire. It was disturbing.

> *Henri,*
>
> *Captain Vauquelin and I are old friends from my smuggling days. You can trust him.*
>
> *I am writing to you directly to share some painful information. Lord VanderMeer is not well. I expect he will write to tell Lady Corrinne of this in a missive. But maybe not the whole story.*

I made certain his lordship got safely to Amsterdam, to a ducal palace. We arrived in December. The Duke was away so I stayed on for a time just to be at his side if he needed me. Palace doctors visited Lord VanderMeer the first day to examine him. They discovered a bad rot in the bottom of his left foot. Since he feels nothing below his waist, he never complained about any pain. The rot had spread upward into the ankle. The doctors decided it necessary to amputate his left leg just below the knee without delay. His lordship also complained of sharp spasms of pain in his gut. At first, the doctors offered no diagnosis. But Lord VanderMeer insisted they speak the truth. They told him they cannot be sure, but that corrupting rot is believed to travel inside the body in the blood vessels. The doctors suspect his internal organs are likely diseased. They explained with candor that people paralyzed at the waist usually do not survive more than a year, and most of them die much sooner from various afflictions. His lordship pressed them, and they admitted he might not live even two more months!

It was three days before I was alone with his lordship. He confessed to me what the doctors had told him. He was relieved to hear there would be an end to this misery. The paralysis is very hard on him. He did not tell the doctors of a spreading numbness in his arms and hands that has stopped him from painting. He feared they would only try to "cure" him with treatments he considers primitive, that of forcing him to drink bitter liquids, bleeding him white, or cutting open the tips of his fingers to promote blood flow down his arms. He made me promise not to tell Lady Corrinne about any of this, that he would tell her what he wants her to know. I suspect he will not tell her everything. But he did not forbid me from telling you.

Lady Corrinne expects to be informed. Lord VanderMeer may not want to worry her, but Lady Corrinne must be told. I am sorry to burden you with this.

There is more. Word here in the palace is widespread that Lord VanderMeer has children. As direct heirs to him and the duchy, the children are in danger. Lord VanderMeer said the Duke intends to convince Lady Corrinne to come to Amsterdam so he can better protect her. His intentions are honorable, I think, but Amsterdam would be the worst place for Lady Corrinne to seek protection. I think she believes that already. If that is not enough, I was told by the captain of the palace guard that Lady Corrinne's present location at Louisbourg is common knowledge.

I am aware of a German mercenary regiment being formed in western France, in Rochefort. They've been contracted by France to augment the Louisbourg garrison.

Henri, these men are killers, without allegiance to anyone. You must assume that lurking among them will be assassins hired by those great houses which are enemies of Lord VanderMeer.

I am sorry, there is more.

Our company agent in Amsterdam was corrupted by our enemy in the châsse. I personally saw the effects of this. Lord VanderMeer intends to find another agent to replace him.

I have been warned that men are trying to locate where my ship is anchored. Some wear uniforms associated with this new mercenary regiment in Rochefort. Because this list of enemies is growing, I have no idea which enemy they work for. But from your point of view, it doesn't matter. These men are going to every port in France asking questions about my ship. By the time you get this missive, they will certainly have found it. But they will find it empty of cargo. I expect It will send its own creatures to learn the location of the châsse from Lady Corrinne. You must assume they will be mixed within this mercenary regiment.

Tell Lady Corrinne she cannot escape to France either. And I think it unwise she return to Boston again, not until this war is over…but who knows when that will be?

Try to influence her thinking. Convince her to go back to Québec City or Montréal and find a safe place to hide, among friends and people who will protect her, at least until we determine someplace better. Philippe is there!

As for me, as I am now a French naval officer. I take orders from an admiral. He will likely send me to do dangerous things.

As I read back over this missive, I can see that my cursive script is horrible, and I am rambling. I never was any good at writing letters. I will end it now.

Tell Lady Corrinne that having shared so many dangers with her, with Philippe, and with you…

A sentence was scratched out and blotched with ink to be unreadable. He held it up before the fire and could only make out two words: *my family*. The letter continued.

> *Now I am caught up in this war. I have no control when I will see any of you again. Please hug and kiss the little ones for me. You will all be in my thoughts and prayers.*

> *Adieu,*
> *Beauregard LaTour*

*

As directed by Colonel Louis Franquet, the Fortress of Louisbourg engineer, a camp set up in Anse de la Cormorandière, a particular cove on the Gabarus Bay furthest from the fort. The English would later refer to it as Kennington Cove. They placed tents amid the previously constructed battlements above the cove. A platoon of grenadiers from the Bourgogne Regiment had escorted them as guards.

Before the officers retired to their beds for the night, Colonel Franquet reviewed the strategy.

"If the English achieve a landing anywhere to the southeast of this cove, the French line will be flanked. We will be forced to fall back in a fighting retreat. To move their invading army into siege positions, the English will have to advance against our cannon-supported retreat. They will not find that easy to do. There are bogs and swamps to either side of the path of advance. This will cost the English time. Delay them. That is our objective for any retreat. Think about this tonight. We will discuss it again in the morning."

The night was cold, and the sky was devoid of clouds. Picking a spot among the grenadiers, Henri lay awake near the campfire away from his tent. He huddled beneath his blankets, his feet covered in double stockings pointed towards the fire to keep them warm and stared up at a night sky ablaze with stars. His thoughts stayed on Captain LaTour's letter before he finally fell to sleep.

Henri came awake with a lurch to see the first glimmer of an approaching dawn on the far horizon. Two of the grenadiers were warming their hands and feet near the fire. He pulled on his boots and moved over to them wearing his blankets over his head as a cloak.

"You're up early, Lieutenant."

"Thought I heard something," Henri said. He held out his hands to warm them.

The grenadiers waited for him to say more, until the silence became awkward.

"We're on guard, Lieutenant. You gonna tell us what you thought you heard?"

At that moment, they all heard a loud *screech* far above them in the air.

Henri smiled and pointed upward with a finger. "I suppose it was that eagle." Henri knew it was an eagle, but he never considered the underlying implication of his words.

*

Colonel Louis Franquet was a brigadier, who for two years had inspected all the forts along the Saint Lawrence River as the Director of Fortifications, making recommendations for improvements. In the spring of 1754, he was assigned to Louisbourg to prepare it for the expected assault by the English. It needed a lot of work and still needed much more. This winter, he was sixty years old and feeling his age. Nevertheless, Franquet was highly educated, experienced, and greatly respected. Henri enjoyed talking to this man who had something educated to say about almost any topic.

Colonel Franquet's tent was four times larger than any of the others, allowing enough room to meet with his officers around a map table. That first morning inside the tent, the officers gathered around a rough-hewn wooden table where a large fortification map was laid out. In addition to the chief engineer was Franquet's deputy engineer François Grillot de Poilly, Lieutenant-Colonel Michel Marin du Bourzt of the Bourgogne Regiment, and Lieutenant Henri Gerrard of the Troupes de la Marine. Lieutenant Gerrard of the marines had been added to the group, it was announced to the others, because he had previously blazed trails of retreat to the fortress from the various battlement positions.

Henri was grateful to be invited; it was another opportunity to learn. Engineer de Poilly tended to speak officiously and was critical of just about everyone and anything being said. Henri did not like this man, who substituted bluster to hide a flagging self-confidence, and maybe even incompetence, although he knew instinctively to never disagree with the senior officer out loud. Henri liked Colonel du Bourzt who was irreverent and cynical, a veteran given to making humorous remarks. Colonel du Bourzt had already decided the defense of Louisbourg was borderline hopeless. They had but one chance, which he'd already expressed to Henri privately.

"Pray the English start their assault late in the fighting season and perform their landing five miles further southeast of Gabarus Bay. Then we might have a chance to delay their march on the fort until September. If so, they will have to abandon the siege because of the winter weather."

"But wouldn't the English just try again next year?"

Of course, Colonel du Bourzt knew that only delayed the inevitable until the next year.

"Good analysis. But like I told you before, Lieutenant, think time...and money. *Money*," Bourzt repeated. "If England or France run out of money to fight this war, they will sue for peace and divide the spoils. That is the game we are playing."

Colonel Franquet began the meeting by reviewing the merits of each battlement position constructed over the past two years. He pointed out the places in the landing defenses he thought were weaknesses. The officers were encouraged to offer opinions of where and what type of new construction should be done. Colonel Bourzt pointed out that adding all these additional works to the defense would exceed the troop strength of the Louisbourg garrison required to man them.

"...even if we add sailors or marines to our lines from the naval squadron promised to us."

Engineer de Poilly intruded. "It's made worse by the present deplorable condition of these works, not to forget their design! If the defenses had been properly built to begin with, it would take less men to defend. The men could be spread out. One man can be as strong as three behind a properly made entrenchment."

Having helped cut, dig, saw, and place heavy logs to create the defenses, Henri did not accept this criticism, but remained silent.

Colonel du Bourzt, however, snorted in amusement. "I am confused, sir. Are you suggesting our lines will get *stronger* by spreading them out? While keeping the number of muskets the same? How does that happen?"

"You are obviously not educated on the science of battlements—"

"Really?!" The colonel's face flushed with anger. "And you cannot possibly appreciate the depth of my experience. So, when the time comes, you should position yourself at the farthest end of our line. Spread out so far, it should be the strongest point, yes? Just imagine...Engineer de Poilly, standing above the battlements swinging his battle sword in the air. With your ferocious courage on display, I am certain the English attack will falter—"

"How dare you, sir!"

"Enough!" Colonel Franquet ordered loudly. "We are all aware our troop deployment will be limited. More men are expected to arrive from France this spring. Even so, it will still not be enough, and we must also leave a regiment inside the fort for its defense. But, if we can delay a successful landing at any one place, the weather, the winds, the swells, the waves, and the rocks will all become our allies. Our strategy must include platoons placed strategically in reserve, which can be rushed in time to repulse any beachhead gap that is attained. Let's presume we add the new defense works suggested. Today, your task is to quantify a response to repulse a potential English landing at any of these gaps. Take notes, and take three grenadiers with you. They are not just your guards. The grenadiers have seen battle. Solicit their opinions. When darkness comes, we rendezvous back in this tent, take our meal together, and discuss our findings for the day. We will each take a section of the lines between here and the fort. I want this task completed in three days. Questions?"

*

Colonel Franquet's team of officers arrived back at the Louisbourg fortress after sundown three days later. They were to meet again early the next morning to brief Governor Drucour and the rest of the garrison officers.

Henri was exhausted. He was ready to sleep, but Captain LaTour's letter still weighed on his thoughts. Corrinne needed to know. He shed his filthy uniform, cleaned himself up in a washbasin, put on fresh clothes and headed to Corrinne's house.

Corrinne did not expect Henri as she opened the door. "Henri!" She beamed at him and lowered the hammer of the double-barreled pistol held in her other hand and set it aside.

As he came in, Anamosa ran to his arms for a long hug. Corrinne took her turn to embrace him.

"You look exhausted. Are you hungry? Can I warm something for you to eat?"

"Yes, please. And maybe a little wine."

They took seats at the table. It was after the hour of eight. The twins were asleep.

Henri took a swallow of wine first and then handed Captain LaTour's letter to Corrinne.

"You can read it later. I'll tell you what it said."

Corrinne's expression grew somber as Henri explained the severity of Lord VanderMeer's health, and she became alarmed when he spoke about the mercenary regiment.

"Charles was not so specific about how sick he was in his letter to me. I could tell it might be worse, but not as bad as what Captain LaTour described to you. He did not mention the mercenaries. But insisted I leave Louisbourg. There was not much else except for financial matters. Our fortune has been deposited in an Amsterdam bank."

Corrinne stopped, drank some wine, and stared blankly across the room. The prospect of Charles' impending death left her feeling numb and traumatized. Charles' companionship had become an important part of her life—different from her relationship with Philippe, of course—but very important nevertheless. She wanted it to continue.

Now a mercenary regiment riddled with assassins is coming.

Anamosa had been listening politely. During the long pause, she looked at Henri and spoke up.

"If we leave Louisbourg, will you be taking us?" Her tone sounded small and vulnerable.

Henri almost affirmed reflexively. The small detail of Québécois marines were ostensibly Lady Corrinne's bodyguards. But after the thorough assessment of Louisbourg's defenses and the possible roles he was intended to assume, he was certain Governor Drucour and Colonel Franquet would not permit him to leave. They would assign others to escort Corrinne.

But there was no other answer. "Of course," he replied. "But we must make plans first."

Corrinne shook her head. "I am bewildered." She looked at Anamosa and forced a smile to her lips. "Don't worry. We will go by ship. When the river is thawed. We will go to Québec City. Possibly overland to Montréal."

Having unburdened the news from Captain LaTour, Henri felt spent. "I should go. The governor has called for a war council in the morning."

Henri stood. Both women came to his arms. The hug good-bye was more poignant than usual. Danger was coming. The three of them embraced and rocked back and forth. Sharing comfort. They did not let go for a long time.

Corrinne's mind was already planning. *Full circle*, she thought, *we will return to where it all started. But Montréal will not be the end of this. Oh, Philippe…where are you?*

When they separated, Corrinne's eyes were wet. Henri touched his forehead to Anamosa's. Then he lifted the collar of his long coat and went out into the night.

The walk back to the barracks was cold and bracing. A sharp northern wind whistled around the eaves and roofs in the faubourg. The air smelled of snow.

Either tomorrow or the next day, he thought.

*

The next morning, Corrinne, Anamosa, and the twins were in the cuisine. Corrinne was preparing food for the children to break their fast. Corrinne had treated herself to a small pot of her dwindling supply of precious coffee. She savored each sip like a bee sipping nectar from a flower. With the new day, the plan for their departure had evolved to a list of potential problems to resolve. The ship of travel was an unknown. *Charles would be deciding this matter. Minister Machault as well. Even Captain LaTour would be worrying about this.* But a ship would come. Maybe in March. Certainly, by April. She must be ready. The first destination would be Québec City. *Michelle is there. We can live with her for a while.* Then maybe Montréal. To Corrinne's surprise, she felt herself longing for Boston. But until the war ended, she could not return there.

Philippe would advise me! If only he were here, she brooded.

Marcus sat on the floor to one side of the room, piling blocks of different shapes, one atop another to see how high a stack he could make. A few feet away from him, Calypso had a piece of charcoal and on a large sheet of drawing paper from the sheave left with them by Charles, she was making random pictures. Here a tree, there a house, stick figures of people and flowers all around.

Anamosa sat next to Calypso, pointing at an empty spot and encouraging her to add something new. When Marcus' pile of blocks fell over, he made an angry noise of frustration. Anamosa slid over next to him and helped begin a new stack, showing how to start with the bigger blocks. She watched and made suggestions.

"Anna, can you fetch me a few sticks from the back garden for the stove?"

Anamosa jumped to her feet and wrapped her woolen shawl around her shoulders before going out the back doorway. It was a little windy and cold, though not as bad as the day before. Only a few fast-moving clouds in the sky blocked the warm sunshine.

Ten paces away, at the edge of the garden-yard, by the stone wall that marked one edge of the property, there was a large dome-shaped baking oven with a rounded top. It was made of brick and stood about four feet high. It had a square iron door on hinges that, when opened, revealed a flat metal shelf on the inside. The oven was used most often to bake breads, but it could also smoke meat and fish, or slowly cook a pot of stewed meat and vegetables. It had not been used for two days, so it was cold that morning. To the left of the oven, a sheet of ragged sail canvas held down by rocks covered a pile of hardwood, already cut and split into the smaller staves suitable for this oven and the stove in the cuisine. Anamosa picked up several pieces and carried them back into the house.

As she started back into the yard for another load, she did not get four steps before she stopped in surprise. The white eagle was perched atop the oven. She stared at it intently, then went back inside. From the wall pegs next to the front door, she took down the smaller coats for Marcus and Calypso. She almost had them dressed before Corrinne noticed.

"Anna? What are you doing?"

Anamosa took the twins by their hands. "Come outside." Then she started towards the door.

"What? Why? Wait! Stop!"

Anamosa opened the door. "Look. On top of the oven." Anna went out the door.

"Wait!" Corrinne grabbed her shawl from a peg and hurried out to the back.

Anamosa walked several paces towards the creature. It had not moved. Its piercing gaze was fixed on them.

Corrinne was stunned. "Oh, my God," she said softly. "You found us again…" She moved to stand behind her children. The eagle's gaze shifted to stare at Corrinne. Her breathing increased with excitement.

The twins were fascinated with the beautiful creature. Marcus pointed and mumbled something.

Then the eagle hopped from its perch atop the oven and glided to the ground, landing less than two paces away from them. Even on the ground, the eagle stood taller than the twins. It hopped once more, cutting the space between them in half. It spread its wings wide and arched them forward, towards them all in an embracing gesture.

Anamosa let go of the twins' hands. Corrinne instantly took hold of them.

Corrinne's heart was pounding. Anamosa took a step closer and extended her right arm, palm down, fingers limp.

"Anna, what are you doing?" Corrinne's emotions spiked with apprehension. "Be careful!"

Despite their shared history with the raptor and the animal's indisputable mystical qualities, Corrinne could not dismiss the fact that this was an eagle, by nature a dangerous predator. She had no idea why it was here. But she did not want to frighten it and make it fly away.

"Anna, be careful! Do not go so close!"

But Anamosa got closer still, until her extended hand was only inches away from the eagle's sharp beak.

The eagle fixed its gaze on Anna for several long seconds. Then in one movement, it touched its beak to her fingers for a few seconds. Then it turned, took flight, and circled straight upward, higher and higher, until it could not be distinguished against the backdrop of the sky.

In that moment of connection, the *ghost* sensed the powerful curiosity and fearlessness of the young woman's aura. She was drawn to the spirit world as he'd been drawn to it as a child. She was compelled to touch it. In those few moments of time, the *ghost* communicated images to her that evoked empathy and comprehension, filling her with comfort and assurance.

She possesses the courage to reach out without hesitation. She hungers to learn more. I must teach her.

The ghost sensed the other woman's loneliness, but found her strong and as determined as before. Her little ones showed no fear whatsoever, just innocent wonder.

The eagle circled straight upward until its height in the sky was above the range of the muskets. Then it banked and flew back towards the southwest. The *ghost* would fly straight back to the breeding place and allow the female to rest again among its own kind until the spring sun warmed the land.

Servants of the demon were coming. The woman already planned to leave. There was still time.

*

Corrinne shaded her eyes with both hands. "I cannot see it anymore. Can you?"

Anamosa shook her head. "No."

"It's too cold out here. Let's go inside."

Marcus and Calypso had shifted to exploring the garden area while Anna and Corrinne had watched until the eagle was gone from sight. Marcus' hands were now covered in mud from turning over rocks. Calypso had found some broken shells near the oven. Corrinne gathered up Marcus in her arms and carried him into the house. Anamosa took Calypso's hand and followed.

Corrinne leaned back against the door once they were all inside. She felt as if they had survived an unexpected bolt of lightning. But the children seemed calm. Corrinne, however, did not feel calm. Her heart still raced. She decided not to discuss what happened with them. Not until she could explain it to herself. *If* she could explain it to herself.

"We'll not talk about this in front of the children."

"Yes." Anamosa nodded. "I understand."

Corrinne nervously cleaned the mud and grime from the twins' hands. When they returned to their play, she finished frying a pan of scrambled chicken eggs mixed with bits of beans, squash, and smoked fish. She buttered some warm bread and put cups and a pitcher of water on the table. All the while her rational mind was deluged by nervous questions.

Why did it come? Why was it here? To warn us? Of what? To help us? How? Something dangerous is coming when the eagle appears! What should we do? What is coming?!

Corrinne did not eat. She sat pensively, with one arm wrapped around her chest and gulped her soothing coffee with the other. She wondered if Anamosa had been changed by this. Corrinne certainly was! But Anna acted like Anna. She was attentive to the twins like any other normal morning. *Normal?!* Anamosa appeared unaffected. *Except she cannot be unaffected.* Anamosa had things to tell her. And Corrinne must know everything.

"Did it hurt you?" The question bubbled out. She could not help herself.

Marcus continued eating but Calypso was paying close attention.

Anna looked at Corrine quizzically, then she shook her head and smiled.

"No. I saw things. I felt things. It made me feel good."

Corrinne glanced at Calypso. "Well, it's important we talk about this," she said impatiently. "But maybe now is not the time. After the twins lie down to rest."

"Don't be worried. I will tell you everything. Like you've told me before, the white eagle is our friend."

Corrinne took a large sip of coffee, her expression still just short of grim.

Yes, the white eagle is our friend. But bizarre and very scary things tend to occur whenever it comes around. Something is going to happen...or it wouldn't be here.

CHAPTER 13
QUÉBEC CITY
FEBRUARY 1757
English Spy or French Spy?

Captain Philippe Gerrard arrived early in the evening at a residence in upper town Québec City. It was a city house formerly owned by Corrinne, who had graciously given it to Michelle when they departed the city for Boston years ago. He was filthy, grimy from months of scouting marches through the wilderness, and covered over with patches of more recent muds that carried the odor of the swamp that surrounded Fort William Henry. Ecstatic as Michelle was to see him, conversation would have to wait. Madeleine and Constance helped Michelle prepare a bath, more than one, so Philippe could clean himself. As the layers of grime sloughed from his face and skin, the punishment Philippe's body had endured became visible in a web of pink and brown scars atop a pale white skin that had not seen sunlight for six months.

Hours later, Philippe's aching muscles were relaxed from the prolonged soaking in the miraculous, soothing waters of two hot baths. His head and body draped with a blanket to hide his nakedness, he sat down on a wooden chair in this bathing and washing room of the house. The three women had also divided up the clothing he was wearing into piles, adding what was in his pack, to wash it all thoroughly. They stifled expressions of revulsion at what they found.

In his post-soaking euphoria, Philippe's weariness descended on him like a boulder. He was swaying back and forth in the chair as if drunk. Seeing this, Michelle took his arms, got him to stand, and led him into the guest room across the hallway. He was asleep as soon as his head touched the pillows in the darkened room. Michelle removed the damp blanket and covered him with a clean linen sheet and a fresh blanket. She was horrified by all the scars covering his body.

Oh, Philippe! How do you survive so many injuries?

241

*

Michelle knocked on the door to the guest room. There was no answer, so she entered. Philippe was sound asleep, lying naked in the bed, covered with the blanket up to his waist, leaving his upper body exposed. Michelle raised the wick on the lamp just enough to have some light. Again, she winced at seeing the crisscrossing scars all over his back, some were long streaks, others star-shaped. Her nurse's eye could tell many of the scars were the result of deeper wounds, piercings, the kind that could kill.

"And yet you are alive," she whispered with compassion and wonder.

Philippe turned his body towards the noise, blinking at the shadow in the doorway.

"Michelle?"

"Yes, Philippe. Good morning. I must go to work at the hospital. Constance has more water heating for a morning bath, if you like. Your clothes are washed and were drying all night. They might even be dry now. I washed the uniform in your pack because…well, it was mildewed…and smelled like offal."

While she talked, Philippe watched Michelle's eyes wandering over his body. She frowned at the continuation of scars across his chest, arms, and face.

Philippe was mortified.

"I know. I look bad. The Oneida forced me to run a gauntlet. It's a long story. Lost a couple teeth too." He hooked his cheek with a finger to show her.

Michelle inhaled with shock and turned her face away. More than fifteen years ago, they had been young lovers back in France. Henri was the result of that love. Now, a lifetime had passed. Michelle had taken and broken vows as a Benedictine nun. She had been raped and a child conceived from that encounter. He had loved and married another. But Michelle still cared for him deeply. Philippe had risked his own life to rescue her from a punishing captivity in the wilderness.

"I'm sorry," he said. "You didn't need to see my broken teeth."

"No, no," she said. "No apologies!" She stepped to him and ran her fingers through his thick, clean blond hair, feeling the lumps of scars and scabs beneath her fingertips. She held his face tenderly in her hands. "It's just…it's just that I don't know how you survived even half of these injuries… and I worry how many more lie in your future."

"The scars are permanent. There is not much I can do about it. It's a war." He shrugged. "My scouts consider them signs of honor. Some of the tribal women find them attractive," he added.

"But you are not married to a tribal woman, are you? I will pray that Corrinne recognizes you."

"I pray so, too," he replied in a voice that tried to be light. "I've not seen her in two years."

Michelle felt pained for them both but desired to cheer Philippe. "Then I will pray for you she keeps the lamplight low."

"Amen!"

"You are going to Louisbourg now?"

"Eventually. But not this trip. I must report to General Montcalm. And I will likely be called before Governor Vaudreuil. I need to dress in my uniform as soon as it's dry."

"Do you want this bath?"

"You're saying I need another one?"

"The bath is ready, Philippe," she replied indulgently. "Even the poorest Romans took baths every day, sometimes two. I will leave your uniform hanging on the door and put the rest of your things in the room. Constance will have food ready for you in the cuisine. Madeleine has already left for the hospital. You might see Crispin wandering around." Michelle's eyes lit up. "He is almost three. Be prepared for endless questions."

"I look forward to it."

Michelle opened the door and turned. "We are blessed and happy to see you again."

Once bathed and dressed in his clean uniform, Philippe left his hat, coat, sword, and pistol by the front door and went to the cuisine. The aromas made his stomach growl. He entered to find Constance working over the stove and saw young Crispin sitting in a high chair with a tray. Possessing the dark brown hair and poignant brown eyes of his mother, the child gazed at him fixedly.

"Crispin?! You are huge!" Philippe knelt before the chair and smiled at the boy who was gawking at him.

Crispin touched one of the scars on his face lightly. "Hurt?"

Philippe laughed. "Yes, more than you will ever know, I hope."

He took a chair next to the boy and nodded at Constance. "*Bonjour*, Constance. It sure smells good in here."

Constance smiled. "And you smell good too, Captain."

Crispin looked at Constance and pointed at Philippe. "Soldier." It was one of dozens of comments that followed.

Constance cooked whatever Philippe wanted. But he did not eat too much on purpose. His stomach had shrunk from the sparse wilderness diet he had endured for so long.

An hour later, Philippe knelt again by the front door after adding his shoulder pistol and sword to his uniform.

"Sword," Crispin said and pointed. "Pistol."

"You are very smart." Philippe hugged him. "I will see you tonight."

Donning his hat and cloak, Philippe went into the street, stopping for a moment to wave back and reply to Crispin's *au revoir*.

At the citadel headquarters, he was welcomed by the attending ensign. "Welcome back, Captain Gerrard. Captain Bougainville is expecting you."

"Where is he?"

The ensign led him down the hall to another small room with shelves full of books, a three-foot square desk, and a short stool holding his friend.

Captain Louis-Antoine de Bougainville held a quill and was inking a missive.

"Are you the resident scholar of this library?"

Bougainville smiled broadly. "Philippe! Good God! You look almost new!"

They embraced. Louis gestured for Philippe to sit on the bed.

"Before we talk about anything else." Bougainville reached down and pulled out a small iron box from beneath his desk. He unlocked the hasp and produced five letters tied with twine.

"As promised."

Philippe held the letters from Corrinne in his palms reverently. "Thank you for finding these."

"First, let me assure you, Intendant Bigôt does not know these letters even exist."

"*Merci*, Louis."

"It only took me a few days of badgering."

Philippe's tone turned curt. "Who broke the seals?"

Bougainville sighed with resignation. "All right, before you start contemplating a *vendetta*, please wait and consider my entire explanation."

Bougainville told him everything he knew and added his opinion. "You have nothing to gain by pressing this issue with General Montcalm or Governor Vaudreuil. In fact, you have something more valuable to lose."

Philippe's tone was skeptical. "I have lost a lot in my life. So, what would that be?"

"I have convinced General Montcalm to grant you leave to see your wife once the spring offensive against Fort William Henry is complete. That assault will begin before this month is over. We can talk more about that later. But when it is successful, he has agreed to permit you leave to take a full month to see your wife in Louisbourg. He is very interested about the defensibility of that fortress. He believes that the fate of New France hangs in the balance of its survival. It is one of the rare opinions that he and Governor Vaudreuil share. General Montcalm believes you will bring him the raw truth better than anyone else. But if you press the issue of your opened letters to the general, or to the governor, you will provoke a dispute between them at a point in time when it is vital to the future of New France that these two men trust one another. You have the letters. So, I am asking you to please let this matter rest. Can you do that for me?"

Philippe's jaw tightened. "How many people have read these?"

"Just one person."

"Who?"

Bougainville drew a line at that. Captain Trieste never admitted it was Governor Vaudreuil. But it had been obvious.

"I did not press for the name, Philippe. This is not Fort Carillon. It is the seat of government of New France. In certain situations, there are things better understood and left unsaid. I urge you to consider this tactic. Be assured, I've taken steps to make certain this never happens again."

Philippe seethed.

Bougainville spoke with compassion. "I understand how offended you are. I would be, too. But you have a choice. You can make this much worse in many contexts, or you can take advantage of the general's promise and go to Louisbourg after this new campaign."

Philippe's eyes glowed with anger. "I want to know why he did this!"

Bougainville was frustrated, too, for other reasons. "I promise you, someday you will get an answer to this question."

"How do you know that?"

Bougainville stated firmly. "Because I expect this person will tell you the reason himself."

"And how do you know that?!"

"Because when this person learned of your arrival, he also learned you now possess the letters, even though by then I had them in my possession. Philippe, he expects you to challenge him publicly! And it will not go well if you do. I say again, this happened only to you! Therefore, I speculate his action was not performed perversely. I speculate he felt justified in reading them."

"Justified!?"

"Yes, justified! Think about a possible reason, Philippe! *Think*. What if he accuses you of something?"

Or accuses someone else, Bougainville did not say. He paused, hoping Philippe might come to this idea on his own.

"Accuse me of what?"

"That's my point! You do not know what he might say! But if you wait… in fact, if you betray no emotion about how you feel, he will tell you. His ego will demand it! Then you will know the truth. Please wait until then. In military parlance, your silence will give you the high ground, yes?"

Philippe was thinking.

Bougainville stood. It was always a good sign when Philippe started thinking.

"Oh, and I personally placed your letter to Lady Corrinne in the dispatch pouch to Louisbourg seven days ago. And I watched as courier sleds moved down the river. She will have it soon. Think of her joy! I am going to give you use of my quarters. Stay here and read the letters! I have not broken my fast today. I will be back in an hour. And then we will go together to see General Montcalm. After that, we will attend the afternoon council of war devising the strategy of attack on Fort William Henry with Governor Vaudreuil. I anticipate you will be questioned about your actions in the latest conflict with the rangers. Enjoy your time reading the words from your wife. I've not had mail in over two months. I cannot even imagine not getting any for two years!"

Bougainville turned to leave.

"Wait." Philippe reached inside his coat, took out his final report signed by the commandant of Fort Carillon, and gave it to Bougainville.

"A copy of my full report for you to read while you eat. I have two wax-sealed copies for General Montcalm and Governor-General Vaudreuil in my pocket."

Philippe had read four of the five letters from Corrinne, which stirred strong emotions in him, when there came a soft knock on the open door to Bougainville's quarters.

"Apologies for my intrusion, Captain."

"Major Péan!" Philippe was shocked.

Michel Péan doffed his hat and bowed. "At your service, Captain Gerrard."

The two men had known one another for over a decade. Péan usually commanded Intendant Bigôt's gendarmeries, the police of Montréal and Québec City. The Dunemoore Company routinely had confrontations with Bigôt's Grande Société. Philippe and Michel Péan had never been exactly friends, but they respected each other as men of their word…an honor of a sort. Years had passed since they had seen each other last.

"I thought you'd be dead by now, Major," Philippe admitted.

"And your scars suggest you have risen from the dead recently!"

They found themselves laughing and embracing one another.

"I bring you greetings from Lady Corrinne and your son."

Philippe sank back onto Captain Bougainville's chair. Major Péan shut the door and took a seat on the bed.

Péan talked for thirty minutes, telling Philippe of the extraordinary bravery of his son at the Battle of Lake George and the attack on Fort Bull, and his promotion to ensign and deployment to Louisbourg. Péan shared the words of endearment from Corrinne.

"She misses you terribly, I was told to say. Unfortunately, I find it impossible to express the deep emotion of her words. Lady Corrinne suspected someone has been intercepting her mail to you. She asked me to find out who it was. But Captain Bougainville has obviously solved that mystery, I am pleased to see."

"Henri volunteered to stay?"

"He did, along with eleven other marine volunteers. I could have ordered him to leave or replaced him with another officer. But I've learned long ago, Henri makes important decisions first with his heart. I will not overrule him for that, unless it is a military necessity to do so. Minister Machault ordered Governor Drucour to protect Lady VanderMeer. Drucour ordered the Québécois marines to fulfill this duty. Captain Gerrard, with sincerity, your son is one of the finest marine officers I have ever known, except maybe for you," he added. "Did you come all this way just to get your mail?"

"No, although I would not hesitate had I known. I am here to attend the war council on attacking Fort William Henry. What about you?"

"Oh, I've been ordered to attend as well."

"I mean what will you do next? Will you be part of the attack?"

Major Péan grimaced. "Me? No, no, no. I will return to my policing duties, of course. Québec City and Montréal are reported to be overrun by miscreant *coureurs de bois* and rogue tribal warriors. There is a serious need for proper policing," he said, a small smirk on his face. "Besides, I've come to recognize that I am an incompetent field officer. I simply do not have the heart for it."

Philippe laughed at this. "That's not what I've heard, Major."

"Regardless, Captain, know that I am a much better policeman than a soldier."

"Major Péan!" Bougainville had returned.

Philippe and Péan stood. "Apologies for entering your quarters uninvited. I saw Captain Gerrard and had some messages from his wife to deliver. That is done, so I will withdraw."

"You will be at the war council?"

"Unfortunately, yes. The governor must believe I have something to add to the strategy. He will be so disappointed."

Bougainville knew better.

After Péan left, Bougainville asked, "Did you finish the letters?"

"All but the most recent one. I will save that for tonight."

*

The night before, instead of looking for Philippe, Captain Bougainville had dinner with General Montcalm at the general's request. They dined alone in the general's quarters. Bougainville had dined with his general many times, but never alone in his quarters. He felt privileged, but this request had also made him anxious. As soon as they were served, and the door was closed, the general divulged the reason in his very first statement.

"I heard from the captain of the guard that Marine Scout Captain Gerrard is back in Québec City?"

Bougainville was surprised. "Yes, sir. I heard that, too, but I've not seen him. I expect he is staying with someone he knows in the city to rest and purify himself before he reports to you tomorrow morning."

Montcalm was quiet as he chewed mouthfuls of food. And then he asked, "What is your opinion of Captain Gerrard?"

An even more surprising question. "He is one of the finest wilderness officers under your command—if not *the* finest." Bougainville went on to relate details from the scouting patrols where he accompanied Captain Gerrard.

"Do you trust him?"

The most surprising question of all. Bougainville was taken aback.

"Trust Captain Gerrard? I trust him with my life. In truth, he has saved my life...more than once. *Mon général*, is there something I should know?"

"I dined with the governor last night. He believes Captain Gerrard's wife...Lady Corrinne de Chanaye, is it? He believes Lady de Chanaye might be an English spy. He believes Captain Gerrard should not be trusted."

The general's tone was not harsh or accusatory, but Bougainville stopped eating. "How did the governor arrive at this suspicion?"

Now the general's voice turned to one of disapproval. "The governor has been reading Lady Corrinne's letters to Captain Gerrard. Sanctioned in times of war, he presumed to tell me. Mind you, they contained nothing that could be construed as treasonous, except that she has been residing in Boston for almost two years. Purportedly, she is married to Lord Charles VanderMeer, the son of the Duke of Brunswick of the Dutch Republic. I was surprised by this revelation, too. What is even more surprising is that she wedded Captain Gerrard in Québec City in 1754. The marriage consecrated by Archbishop André Nicolet himself, may he rest in peace. Lady *VanderMeer,* I should properly say, has taken sanctuary in Louisbourg. She is reputed to have escaped from Boston because she is a French spy. That is what the governor attests. English spy or French spy? This is all convoluted and very confusing. Can you imagine my surprise when Governor Vaudreuil asked me if I trusted Captain Gerrard?"

Bougainville took a large gulp of wine. Montcalm continued.

"Naturally, I told the governor Captain Gerrard is my best wilderness tactician."

Captain Bougainville spoke with sincerity. "I strongly endorse your opinion, General."

"Good! Someday I hope to learn more about Lady Corrinne from Captain Gerrard himself. She sounds remarkably resourceful…and purportedly possessed of extraordinary beauty."

"Everyone who claims to have met Lady Corrinne shares those opinions, General."

"*Çest vrai*! Now I am very intrigued."

Bougainville decided he must confess something more.

"General, you should know that Captain Gerrard recently learned his mail was being intercepted by someone in Québec City. He has not received any mail from his wife in over two years. Then to learn someone has been reading his personal mail! He is very provoked. I managed to coerce those letters from Captain Trieste. I will see Captain Gerrard tomorrow morning. I plan to give him these letters to mollify his anger."

Montcalm sat back in his chair. "It is most fortunate we dined together tonight and shared this information. It would not do to have this *coureur de bois* officer confront the governor, not on the eve of an attack on an English fort. What do you recommend?"

"That you meet with him first."

*

Captain Gerrard accompanied Captain Bougainville to make a report to General Montcalm at army headquarters. The general had the map of the Fort Carillon and the surrounding lakes and rivers spread out on a table in front of them. At the general's invitation, Captain Gerrard pointed and explained in detail the attack route of the rangers as they came up Lake George, where the first ambush took place, the ranger retreat, and the actions of the French troops to try and surround them.

"Late in the day, I set up a line, here, atop a ridge the rangers would have to cross to get back to the lake. It was either cross here or go further inland. The snow was deep and heavy, wet from drizzle. It packs on your snowshoes. You must stop and clean them every ten steps. Your muskets get wet. Your powder gets wet. Your hands and feet are numbed from the cold. The rangers were not going inland, and neither would I, given that position of march.

"By this time, everyone on both sides was cold and exhausted. But we could not light any fires that night if we wanted the ambush to work. They could not light fires if they wanted to break through us by surprise. As soon as they were ready, the rangers made a probing advance at what happened to be my center, to see if anyone was on the ridgetop. Volleys of musket fire ensued. People were wounded. The rangers fell back and took a position on the ridgetop across from mine. A hundred paces of valley floor lay between us. It got darker.

"There was a force of three hundred troops, militia, and Indian warriors pursuing the rangers from behind. They would close upon them by morning. The rangers knew this, too. Our numbers were evenly matched at less than a hundred men each. I knew the enemy would try to escape during the night. They had no choice but to try and break through. I just had to hold my position. Near midnight, they made a concentrated attack on my right flank. There were repeated sorties. More men killed and wounded. My right almost collapsed. It forced me to shift men to reinforce. But in the dark, many of the rangers silently flanked me on my left and moved past the end of my line without engaging. The attacks on my right continued without stopping during this time. The ranger attacks ceased abruptly, there was silence. I counter attacked at the middle and overran their main encampment. We managed to kill or capture some of their rearguard before I realized they had flanked us on the other side. We gave chase in the dark. They could move as fast as we could. Once the rangers reached the frozen lake, they switched to skates."

General Montcalm nodded thoughtfully. *That's why we do not fight battles in a dense forest wilderness in the middle of winter, in the middle of the night.* But he did not say this out loud.

"Your force was too small, Captain. You needed two to three times the men. You should have attacked from both your center and left instead of reinforcing your right. You would have drawn them back."

Philippe replied with regret. "Yes, sir. One of many lessons I learned that night. The Fort Carillon commandant sent troops to the initial ambush site. He also worried another attack of Fort Carillon was imminent. He sent a platoon of grenadiers to reinforce my position. It was not enough. I do not blame the commandant. I failed to recognize the diversion. And I should have presumed this. The rangers were not attacking, they were escaping. I've learned afterwards that the ranger commander, Major Rogers, was wounded severely in this battle. Some of his senior officers were also killed or wounded. This will forestall their ability to conduct further operations against us this winter."

General Montcalm straightened. "Do you agree with Governor Vaudreuil's plan to attack Fort William Henry without delay?"

"General, I am not informed of the details of this attack. But I can say Fort William Henry is on a strict defensive footing. There are no routine daily patrols moving about. The fort is plagued with sickness. The few enemy captured by my scouts claim it is smallpox. The redcoat foot battalion in the fort will not move until the weather improves. We can attack, burn, and destroy anything outside the walls. But we can do little more than that. Certainly, we cannot get into the fort without suffering substantial losses. It is worthwhile to destroy all the boats they've constructed. That will frustrate and permanently delay any English attacks planned for this fighting season."

"What is your count of regular troops?"

"Minimal, General. Much reduced from what they were last year. Only three hundred fifty to four hundred men of the 44th Foot. Less than half their original strength. Fort Edward is little better at four hundred fifty to five hundred men of the 48th Foot. These are the same foot regiments nearly destroyed when attacking Fort Duquesne two years ago. More than half of them are inexperienced replacements. I don't feel they have recovered from that initial defeat. There are about four ranger companies assigned to the fort, but they've been bloodied by us in this latest battle. I'm not certain how fit they are. Most of the other regular regiments in the area were sent to Halifax or will be soon, according to the prisoners. The latest scout intelligence from this month revealed that the redcoat presence in the city of Albany is greatly reduced."

"So, the port of Halifax? Does this suggest Louisbourg is the next target? Or Québec City?"

"If it was Québec City they would be amassing troops in Albany. Louisbourg must be first. It controls access to the Saint Lawrence River. To lay siege to Québec City, the English must first invest Louisbourg. And they've invested Louisbourg before in 1745, with irregular militia from the colonies. They know how to accomplish this."

General Montcalm knew all this history. He'd concluded this was the goal of the English from other reports. What he was contemplating now was a full-scale siege and investment of Fort William Henry in the coming summer, to give the English another Fort Oswego to lament. But this attack could not begin until any threat to Québec City was refuted.

"Very well, Captain. You will join us when we meet with Governor Vaudreuil to discuss the winter raid being planned."

"Yes, sir."

"Captain Gerrard, one more question. Did we win this latest battle against the American rangers?"

The general had just heard his account. Philippe did not expect this question.

"Win? Sir, this was just a raid to destroy supplies and capture prisoners. We tried to capture the rangers, but they escaped. Neither side won anything. I guess, the best we could say is we did not lose…and we forced them to retreat."

"I value your candor, Captain, and I always expect candor from you. But if Governor Vaudreuil claims in this war council that we French won this engagement, and insists that the rangers attempted to attack Fort Carillon but were repulsed…how will you respond to that assertion?"

Philippe's eyes shifted to Captain Bougainville for only an instant.

"I'd answer that the rangers attacked, and we did indeed repulse them, and that my scout companies pursued them back down Lake George as they retreated."

"Good. I think that interpretation sounds better."

"Yes, sir."

"Captain Gerrard, it is no secret that my relationship with the governor is normally contentious. It is important, as you support my position in this war council, that you avoid any pointed disputes with the governor or his staff officers, particularly with the governor's brother, Captain Rigaud de Vaudreuil, who will command this assault on Fort William Henry. Even if you find his comments outrageous. Even if his words are insulting. If there is to be a counter argument advanced in this meeting, about anything, I will make it."

"Yes, sir."

CHAPTER 14
ANTWERP
FEBRUARY 1757
Destiny, Both Wonderful and Tragic

They were sitting in the spacious de Witte library, drinking tea together. Margaux was enjoying the second day of her visit with Madame Louise de Witte. Louise had been her most trusted friend for over ten years. Margaux had already told Louise the whole story about the Duke of Brunswick, and the portrait, to permit Louise to ask questions that Margaux may not have thought to ask herself. General Jacob de Witte was away for two weeks, somewhere south of Antwerp, meeting with the French army.

"He is not really retired then?"

Louise scoffed. "Jacob will never retire. It's enough for me to know that he no longer takes part in the battles."

The chamberlain came into the library.

"Madame, there is a gentleman at the door. He is not wearing a uniform but claims to be Colonel Rutger van Boekel of the Dutch Republic. He asks to see Madame Dubonnet."

Madame de Witte nodded. "Permit him entry. We will come to the foyer to meet him."

After the chamberlain left, Margaux said lightly, "So, it begins."

"You must be very excited," Louise suggested. "How long will you be gone?"

"I am not sure. If the portrait is genuine, which I believe it is, then I will ask the Duke if I can meet Charles VanderMeer. If he says yes, I am off to Amsterdam."

"Lord VanderMeer is dying?"

"That's what they tell me. Lord VanderMeer is married to my sister. I hope to meet him before anything happens."

Louise smiled sadly. "You are rejoined with a long-lost sister because her husband is dying. This is destiny, Margaux. Both wonderful and tragic at the same time."

Margaux's expression fell. "It is, isn't it? And I would not be going were it not for her portrait." Margaux abruptly stood. "Forgive me, Louise. I am anxious to go."

They walked arm in arm to the foyer. Introductions were made to Colonel Rutger van Boekel.

"Madame Dubonnet, it is a great pleasure to see you again. I have brought a carriage for you, and a small escort of Dutch cavalry. Are you ready to meet the Duke?"

Margaux was quiet for a moment before answering. "I am ready to see my sister."

Rutger smiled warmly. "She is with us, too, my lady."

Louise sent the chamberlain to pack and bring down Madame Dubonnet's baggage.

*

The coach ride to Aanwas took about four hours. The countryside was mostly flat farmland. There were wetlands and small streams to ford. Rutger rode with Madame Dubonnet to converse and answer her questions. Dutch and Austrian cavalry preceded and followed the coach. Her six civilian bodyguards rode directly behind the coach. At the border crossing of the Dutch Republic, the Austrian cavalry held back, and the Dutch took the lead.

It was cold and windy. The mud flaps over the windows were pulled shut, except for a tiny square that allowed Madame Dubonnet to gaze out occasionally, lest she become nauseous.

"I intend to ask the Duke if I might visit Charles."

"You do not have to ask. The Duke already decided to invite you to his palace in Amsterdam," Rutger told her. "Lord VanderMeer is gravely ill. He is not expected to live much longer."

They arrived at a travelers' inn on the edge of a sparsely populated town. Lifting the mud flaps, Margaux saw about a dozen armed Dutch soldiers posted around the inn. A person ran out when the coach stopped, opened the carriage door, and dropped the step case. Margaux was assisted to the ground.

"Your bodyguards will have to remain outside. I trust that is acceptable to you?" Rutger inquired.

"Yes, of course." Margaux gave orders to the men.

Allowing her to take his arm, Rutger escorted her inside.

The entry to the inn was nothing special, just a front desk where the hotelier smiled and bowed to her before gesturing towards a hallway. Rutger continued to a room that appeared to be the restaurant. It was not very large at ten by six paces. There were many tall windows, four on each side. The curtains had been pulled back to permit the afternoon light. Because of the overcast skies, the wall lanterns had been lit. All the chairs and tables had been pushed to one side of the room, except for three uneven tables that were pushed together to make one long table down the middle. The cloth covering these tables was a thick dark blue felt, with William's tri-color flag embroidered at the center.

"I am nervous," Margaux confided to Rutger.

"You needn't be," he assured her. "I've known the Duke a long time. He is a gentleman and unassuming. He is very excited to meet you."

Just as Rutger said this, Louis Ernest, Duke of Brunswick-Wolfenbüttel, made an entry. Margaux turned, bowed her head, and curtsied low.

"Your Grace," she addressed him.

He was not very tall, a little obese from age, and a rosiness lay upon his cheeks. She noticed his warm brown eyes.

"No need for that," the Duke replied. He was smiling. He took her hand, lifted her up, then politely touched his lips to her fingertips. "Madame Margaux Dubonnet, I am honored you came."

"The honor is mine." Margaux was at a loss for more words.

The Duke hesitated. "Forgive me for staring, Madame. Your likeness to Lady Corrinne is quite astonishing."

Behind the Duke, two men brought in a sheet-covered easel, the bulky outline of a framed painting could be seen beneath the canvas.

Margaux's eyes followed them. They set it at one end of the table. Without asking permission, Margaux was drawn a few steps closer to the easel. She began to tremble. The Duke slipped his palm under her elbow.

"Remove the drape," he told the men.

They carefully lifted the sheet. The portrait had been mounted in a simple wooden square, just enough to keep the oil painting from curling at the edges. It had been transported in a very protective leather valise. Because of the powdered glass mixed in with the oil paints, the portrait captured every bit of light coming through the windows. The colors came alive and were almost radiant.

In addition to her braided hair, the circlet, the beautiful dress, it was the woman's compelling green eyes, a gaze brimming with love, that captured Margaux's heart. She knew the truth in an instant. Her eyes widened. Her fingertips covered her lips.

"Oh…oh, Corrinne," she gasped.

The Duke steadied her at the elbow.

Margaux's breathing quickened. She stepped closer and reached out a trembling hand to touch Corrinne's face, but at the last moment pulled back her fingers. One of the Duke's valets brought a chair up behind her. The Duke gently urged her to sit and gave her a clean linen kerchief from his pocket.

No one spoke. The room remained silent out of respect for Madame Dubonnet's wrenching display of strong emotion.

"I have missed you so much," Margaux said loudly, unheeding of the others present in the room. It was the first outburst in a series of heavy sobs. "I convinced myself…the face I saw in my dreams…was just that…a dream… something from my imagination. *But I remembered your name!* And I still remember our lullaby!" More heavy sobbing.

Recognizing Madame Dubonnet was confessing, the Duke gestured with both hands for everyone to leave the room. And he followed them to wait out in the hallway. The sobbing continued from inside the room.

"She asked to see Charles," Rutger whispered while they waited.

"Good. We will take her to the palace. She will ride with me, so I can prepare her."

𝕐

Amsterdam
The Ducal Palace

The carriage ride to Amsterdam took two days with an overnight stay at a fortress in the port of Rotterdam. Upon arrival at the ducal palace, with a hand on Margaux's arm, Louis Ernest walked her up the stairs to a bedchamber prepared just for her arrival. Three maidservants were waiting to attend to her needs. They curtsied.

"I need to check on Charles. Maybe you would like to refresh yourself. Take your time. Send one of these maids to find me when you are ready."

*

Unbeknownst to the Duke, Rutger had taken the portrait of Lady VanderMeer back to the palace artist.

"Put her back in the gilded frame and hang it on the wall immediately." He gave the man a slip of paper. "Have this inscription made on a nameplate. Dedicate all your people to this! Get this done as fast as you can! You have an hour, no more than two. Get it done!"

With that task complete, Rutger went to wait outside Madame Dubonnet's room.

*

Margaux undressed to take the hot bath they had prepared for her. The candid conversation with the Duke during the carriage ride had been beyond her expectations. He was charming, forthcoming, honest, indulgent, empathetic, and had answered every one of her questions regarding her sister's history to the best of his ability, telling her when something was still unknown to him. She was overjoyed to learn Corrinne had twins! It gave Margaux hope she might still conceive a child, too.

*

Louis Ernest sat in a cushioned chair next to his son's custom-built wheeled chair and told the servants to open the curtains and the windows. When they did this, fresh spring air spilled into the room, dispersing the stuffy, foul odors that permeated the massive bedchamber. The afternoon sunlight reflected warmly on his son's face. He knew in a few minutes, Charles would awaken. The Duke waited patiently.

They'd had a lifetime's worth of good conversation during the last two months. Because of Charles' illness, the Duke had minimized his official traveling and withdrew from his public obligations where he could. He was overcome with angst at the thought of his son's impending death and visited Charles for a few hours every day, with few exceptions. They often took meals together, laughed, and told stories to one another. The Duke loved hearing about Charles' adventures in the American continent.

When Charles came of age to be the legitimate heir to the duchy, by then Louis Ernest was indeed the Duke of Brunswick-Wolfenbüttel. Louis had his son sign a confidential letter of abdication to any title, so if Charles' relationship to the Duke ever did become known, Louis Ernest could offer proof of abdication to the crown, and persuade any menacing aspirants that Charles was not a rival.

With regular monthly stipends of money coming to him, Charles attended university at Leiden, southwest of Amsterdam. He became highly educated, a man of science, economics, philosophy. But Leiden was also a college of skilled artists, Rembrandt and Huygens, whose accomplishments drew Charles' interest. He learned the techniques for cutting gems and making jewelry and became an accomplished artist, eventually combining these skills into a business. Charles had long ago discovered the reason why the Duke was his benefactor; that he was his father. Louis Ernest finally revealed the story of Charles' beloved mother, Mariel, on the day Charles graduated from university, explaining why his birth and relationship was kept a secret, that there were multiple claimants to the Duchy of Brunswick. Charles had observed the corrupt and deceitful behavior of the aristocratic class. He preferred no part in it, but Louis wanted to keep Charles around, and made him a de facto member of the palace staff, ostensibly for the creation of royal portraiture. This permitted the Duke to continue an informal relationship with his son. He repeatedly warned Charles never to assert he was an heir. Charles VanderMeer was very happy to assume the identity of a commoner.

Soon Charles VanderMeer's renown as a portrait artist and a purveyor of unique jewelry pieces spread. His fame led to a commission by King Louis XV of France, which required Charles to journey to New France, where another fate awaited him.

Two years earlier, Louis Ernest was ecstatic to learn he had grandchildren! Now he was consumed with grief. His son was dying. It was a miracle Charles was still alive. Both of Charles' legs were amputated above the knee to forestall the gangrenous rot, and he had no feeling below his waist.

Louis Ernest reached over and laid the back of his hand on his son's brow. He winced and grimaced. The fever was very high! Tears came to his eyes.

"Bring the physicians," he growled to a servant standing by the door.

For some time, Charles had stopped sleeping in his bed. He'd soiled it so often, it left his skin scalded raw. Inspired by the carpenters aboard *William's Queen*, Charles designed a wheeled chair for the palace carpenter to create. It had a commode-like seat and a shelf beneath it a few inches off the floor. The shelf held a chamber pot. Charles could sit—well, not comfortably—but he could sit with some semblance of dignity, as he described it. The chair could recline for sleeping or adjust straight up. It had a fold-over reading table, allowing him to read, write, or take his meals. The design of the chair allowed the servants easy access to wash and keep Charles' body clean and the sores minimized. It may have prolonged his life, albeit for only an extra few months. The infections were constant and accompanied by high fevers. His body fought them off, but he was weakening.

It was only a matter of time.

Charles' eyes fluttered open. The Duke wiped his eyes and forced himself to contain his emotions. Charles smiled wearily at seeing his father sitting nearby.

"Good morning, Charles. Look, I've brought you the Amsterdam shipping news. And this…this satchel of some very old personal journals…three of them." He held the book sack up by one hand. "Did you hire someone to find the writings of a bishop? Someone named Brevelaer?"

Charles was almost delirious. He licked his cracked lips. "What? Water… please!"

"I am such a fool," Louis mumbled. He rose, got the pitcher, and poured his son a glass.

Charles gulped down the water and held out the glass. "More," he gasped.

Louis refilled the glass a second and a third time before setting the pitcher down atop a nearby serving table.

After drinking the third glass, Charles' breathing became labored. "What…what did you ask me?"

The Duke held up the satchel of journals again. "These journals were written by…a Bishop Brevelaer? Did you hire someone to find this man's writings?"

Charles' attention intensified. "Yes! How did you come to have these?"

"The scholar you hired is downstairs, sitting outside the foyer. He brought these journals…three of them," he repeated. "He claimed they once belonged to a Bishop Brevelaer. Are they important to you?"

Charles held out a trembling hand. The Duke withdrew one of the journals from the satchel.

"This is written in Roman Latin," Charles said to himself as he feebly opened the tome. "Corrinne is so much better at reading this." He turned the pages randomly. Then he pointed at something on one page. "My God! That says *Vaelblez*! This is it! These journals discuss Lord Vaelblez!"

Just then, Charles' bowels abruptly evacuated into the chamber pot. The noise and odors were hard to ignore.

"Oh…forgive me!" Mortified and embarrassed, Charles felt drained of energy. He exhaled and handed the journal back to his father.

"It's all right, Charles," the Duke replied, wishing there was something he could do. "It's all right." His son was dying right before his eyes. The Duke had never felt so helpless in his life.

Louis barked at the servants to bring the people necessary to clean this up.

"Father...I have no control over myself," Charles slurred with anguish.

"Don't worry, Charles. Things like this happen in battlefield hospitals all the time."

But Charles no longer seemed to be listening. His chin had drooped to his chest.

"Charles!?"

With tears streaming down his cheeks, Louis stood and touched his hand to Charles' forehead. The fever was fierce. He'd seen this before in field hospitals. Fevers like this could kill! Louis twisted out cloths from the basin of cold water. He laid one on his son's brow. With the other, he wiped the drops of perspiration off Charles' face and neck.

"Bring me towels," he shouted.

The chamberlain and more servants arrived to attend to Charles.

"Where are the goddamn physicians?!" Louis Ernest began shouting orders. "Fan the miasma out of this room again...do it continuously! Clean and bathe him! Change the bedding on his chair!"

"Yes, Your Grace!"

The doctors entered and saw the excrement in the chamber pot. It was surrounded by blood. The army physician spoke with alarm. "He's failing, Your Grace. He's bleeding from his bowels. I am afraid the end is near."

"NO!" Louis Ernest's voice was strained and desperate. "*No!* Fill that tub with cold water from the river. HURRY! We must bring down the fever. He must live! DO IT NOW!"

Servants carrying buckets scurried to do his bidding.

The Duke continued to wipe his son's face, neck, and chest with cold, wet cloths. One doctor offered to do this for him, but the Duke waved him away. For half an hour, the Duke tenderly ministered to his son. Charles finally responded and lifted his head again. His father's unexpected touch was very comforting.

"Thank you," Charles whispered. "I feel terrible. I am so hot."

The cold-water bath was now ready.

"We'll remedy that now, Charles. Don't worry."

The Duke picked up the satchel and stepped back out of the way to allow the doctors and the servants to attend to his son. Louis Ernest suddenly remembered Madame Dubonnet was waiting. He left the room and walked swiftly down the palace hallways to her bedchamber on the opposite wing. He found Rutger van Boekel waiting outside the door.

"Rutger, is she in there?"

"Yes, sir. The maids say she will be ready at any moment. What is that?"

The Duke looked down. He was still gripping the satchel of journals in his left hand.

"Umm…journals, from some arcane bishop. They are important to my son for some reason."

The door opened and Madame Margaux-Lyneth Dubonnet swept into the hallway. She looked beautiful in the decorative dress they had selected for her. She was smiling, until she saw the Duke's miserable expression.

"What's wrong?"

"We must hurry," the Duke replied in a choked voice. "My son will not live much longer."

They talked as they walked. The Duke disclosed what she was about to see, how the air was foul, that Charles was delirious. When they neared the bedchamber, the Duke stopped ten paces short of the door.

"Rutger, go in and ensure Charles is presentable…or at least not naked."

The Duke looked down at what he carried in his hands. "I don't know why I am still carrying these…except that they are very important to Charles. He's not explained why. He can barely talk…I don't know…"

Margaux saw the Duke's extreme distress. Acting on instinct, she hugged the man. The Duke began to sob in her arms.

"*Shhhh*, my lord. Shhhh. I am here. I will talk to Charles for you."

The Duke slowly regained his composure and dignity. He looked at her through reddened, anguished eyes.

"Madame, your sudden appearance is going to surprise him. You must prepare yourself. He slurs his words sometimes. I don't know what he will say or do."

Margaux suppressed her own anxiousness.

"Don't worry. I will do the right thing…whatever that must be."

Rutger came out of the room. "Charles is clean. The cold bath did indeed bring down his fever. But he is shivering now. They've dressed him in a clean shirt and combed his hair. He is covered with a blanket at the waist.

The bedding in the chair is fresh, but the smell in the room is only slightly improved. They are fanning the stench out. There is a chair to sit upon next to him."

"Thank you, Rutger." The Duke wiped his eyes with a sleeve and took a deep breath. "I will go first. The two of you follow behind me. I will make Charles aware he has a visitor."

"Don't tell him my name," Margaux suggested. "It may confuse him. Let him ask me questions."

That sounded sensible. The Duke nodded. "As you wish, Madame."

They went into the room. Margaux saw the very pale, skeletal face of Lord Charles VanderMeer, sitting in a reclining chair with wheels, surrounded by a dozen other men and servants, all of them looking very grim. The room had a stench, but it was not overpowering.

The Duke approached and laid his hand on Charles' forehead. The fever was down, for now.

"Charles," he called softly. "Charles…someone is here to see you."

Charles VanderMeer blinked. His head lolled to the right. Louis stepped aside, and Margaux moved forward. Her legs were trembling so hard, she immediately sat down on the chair.

"Hello, Charles."

His expression expanded with utter surprise. He spoke in croaks. "Corrinne? Corrinne! Is it you?"

"Yes, Charles," she said, intuitively reacting to what Charles hoped to hear. "I'm here. I'm so sorry you're sick, my darling." She reached out and took his right hand in both of hers. She could feel the fever heat radiating from his palm.

"What…how did…are the children here?"

"No. They are in Louisbourg. They are safe."

"You are in danger," he gasped. His breathing was rapid.

"I wanted to see you," she said truthfully. "I do not care about the danger."

"Corrinne…I have found…Brevelaer's journals!"

The Duke held up the satchel.

"Yes. There!" He pointed with a trembling finger. "He writes of…of Vaelblez…of *Lord Vaelblez*! You must read them…the Latin is Roman. The secret to the vulnax is written there…we…we can defeat the wraith!"

At this inexplicable rambling, tears spilled down Margaux's cheeks. "Yes, my love. I will read them. I promise you."

Upon hearing those words, Charles became less agitated. His breathing slowed. Each shallow breath a strain.

"You must kiss the children…kiss the children for me. Tell them I love them."

"I will, Charles. I promise."

"Corrinne!" He paused and took a deep breath. "I am dying!" His voice was weakening.

Margaux sobbed and steadied herself. "Don't worry, my love. God's angels will sweep you up in their arms, my love."

He took another deep breath. "Corrinne…you are…the most…beautiful… remarkable woman…I have ever known. My life was a joy. A joy. A joy. Corrinne, I love you…love…you…"

Charles' voice trailed off. His expression abruptly went blank. His breathing stopped. A long exhale emitted from his mouth. Margaux watched the light leave his eyes.

"Oh, Charles," she moaned loudly and reached out to embrace him.

Men in the room coughed to hide their emotion.

The Duke stepped forward to lay a hand on Charles' head. "Good-bye, my son." He slipped his fingers down to close the eyes and gently took hold of Margaux's shoulders to help her stand. She turned, and the Duke held her in his arms as she sobbed and sobbed.

Even the stoic Rutger van Boekel was moved, finding it hard to swallow.

The Duke slowly led Madame Dubonnet back into the hallway so the chamberlain could take charge of the servants and workmen and do what must be done. He escorted her downstairs to his library and mouthed for brandy to be served. He steered her into a chair and took one beside her.

Margaux had no idea that the death of a man she'd never seen before today would affect her so intensely, so dramatically.

"I-I am sorry for my outburst…"

"Nonsense, Madame. It was as if Lady Corrinne were here. Charles certainly thought so. You were…*wonderful*."

They sat quietly and sipped the brandy. It was fortifying. Louis Ernest pushed back his grief.

"You honored Charles and you honored me. I am forever grateful."

"I intend to write my sister and tell her of my experience and my role in all of this. I want her to know Charles was not alone. May I do this in your name as well?"

"You have my blessing, Madame. I doubt I could do this better than you. I only hope I can meet her and the children someday…"

"I will make certain she knows that."

Rutger entered the library. "Your Grace, Charles has been removed from the room and was taken by the doctors to the mortuary. And one of Madame Dubonnet's bodyguards would like to see her, to check on her well-being."

The Duke nodded and Rutger opened the door wide to allow the man entry.

"Apologies, Madame. Will we be staying here tonight?"

"Yes, Róbert." After he left, she looked at the Duke. "What will happen now?"

"I will bury my son in the palace cemetery, next to his mother, my wife, Mariel."

"Should I walk with you?"

Rutger interrupted before the Duke could reply. "Forgive me, Your Grace. I do not think it is wise for Madame Dubonnet to remain here in the palace. Charles addressed her repeatedly as Lady Corrinne. Many people heard this. The rumor will spread that Lady Corrinne is here. And whomever it was that harmed your son might attempt to harm her."

Louis Ernest scoffed and shook his head. "I think my palace guards can protect her."

An idea came to Margaux. "Your Grace, those journals?"

The satchel was lying at his feet. "Yes?"

"Your Grace, I promised your son. Corrinne must read them. She is my sister. Allow me to take them to her."

The Duke and Rutger traded glances of surprise. "But she is in Louisbourg," the Duke reminded her.

"I will find a ship sailing there."

"Madame, English cruisers blockade that port."

Rutger replied to this with a suggestion. "Your Grace, Captain LaTour's ship flies a Dutch flag. He is very loyal to Charles and Lady Corrinne. He will find a way to get there."

"Who is Captain LaTour?" Margaux asked.

They explained who he was and his relationship with Lord and Lady VanderMeer.

"His ship was in La Rochelle," the Duke told her. "It may be there still. He is an honorable man. But he also knows the dangers of entering that port. He will not take you."

Margaux was undeterred. "But Captain LaTour will take my letters to Corrinne, yes? Then he will take these journals to her, too, as Charles was promised. That is what you intended to do, yes? Let me do this, Your Grace, for you and for Charles."

The Duke reflected on this. He reached a decision and moved the satchel closer to her chair.

"If that is your wish, Madame. Then I will arrange for a proper escort to take you to La Rochelle and have a Dutch ambassador accompany you."

"I will leave for La Rochelle in the morning," Margaux avowed. She was exhilarated with the thought of performing something so important for the sister she hoped to meet. She recalled Louise's words: *Destiny. Both wonderful and tragic at the same time.*

There was another knock at the door. The chamberlain entered with the palace artist who looked at Rutger and nodded.

Rutger stood and spoke. "I ordered Lady Corrine's portrait to be mounted again in the state dining room hallway. I arranged this without your permission, my lord. I hope I've not overstepped."

"Rutger, you do things all the time without my permission."

Louis Ernest stood and held out his elbow to Madame Dubonnet. "Madame, I invite you to join me in seeing Lady Corrinne's portrait hanging on the wall. You will be the first person outside of the palace to see her. I cannot think of anyone more deserving."

When they stood before the painting, its colors eclipsed the portraits of all the others along the hallway.

Beneath it was an engraved brass nameplate.

Lady Corrinne VanderMeer
Wife of
Lord Charles VanderMeer
Son of
Louis Ernest, Duke of Brunswick-Wolfenbüttel
1757

CHAPTER 15
LOUISBOURG
FEBRUARY 1757
A Day for Anamosa

Two weeks after the startling visit by the white eagle, Corrinne left the twins with Anamosa and walked alone to the market area between the faubourgs. A drenching rain the day before melted much of the snow packed on the ground. This created streams of runoff towards the harbor, cutting ruts in the streets. She avoided those and the standing, muddy puddles, which were unpredictably deep. Walking close to the houses and buildings, she did not step anywhere near these watery places. It was not too windy, but the air was still moist and chilly as the most recent storm moved out to sea. She had a scarf muffled around her face and neck. The collar of her coat was lifted behind her head. Her gloved hands shared the inside of a muff to keep them warm and a deep cloth bag hung over her left arm.

Corrinne could have waited another day. The market would be open tomorrow as well. But she needed the fresh air to clear her mind. Henri had left Captain LaTour's letter with her. That gave her three letters to read, which she did, every day, obsessing over every word and sentence, trying to deduce hidden messages she imagined were there. Corrinne's world was small, and she had no one to talk with about her anxious feelings. She could not confide too much with Marie-Louise de Drucour. This woman was a good friend, but she was also the governor's wife. Henri would listen, but she only saw him two or three times a week and not for very long. Sometimes he would even nod off to sleep at the table from exhaustion.

Her every morning began with three thoughts.

Charles was dying.

All the letters urged her to leave.

And mercenary assassins were coming to kill her, or worse.

If that were not enough, Anamosa told her of having dreams where she became an animal: a fox or a hare, a seagull, a hawk, or a raccoon. They did innocent things, but her descriptions were so elaborate, so vivid, she made it all sound real. Corrinne suspected it was because the eagle touched the girl with its beak. Except for the ones of lovemaking with Philippe, Corrinne could not recall her own dreams with so much vivid detail. Those dreams only left her frustrated. Her own excitement would make her awaken from them too soon, usually ending with Anamosa standing beside her bed, shaking her gently, and asking if she was all right.

"You were moaning."

The people at the faubourg market were always cheerful—"*Bonjour*, Lady VanderMeer! *Bonjour*! Fresh rolls today! The cod is fresh, caught just hours ago. Where is Anamosa? When will we see your twins again?"— and very talkative. The range of topics was limited, dominated first by the weather, rumors of the war, what ships arrived and left, low-voiced risqué comments about her anatomy from the few men who dared, which she did not mind. The women's gossip was usually the best. They would whisper about who was sleeping illicitly with who and why. Sometimes three or four of them would collect in a small gaggle and then the rumors became a ferocious competition of salaciousness. Corrinne was never judgmental and never participated, swearing she was becoming a spinster, with no stories to share. This was her only recreation. The women made her laugh. But if they asked more than one question about Lord VanderMeer, she would politely move on to the next stall.

She bought three loaves of hot bread, a chicken to slaughter, paying extra to have it drained of blood and the feathers removed, and a small canvas sack of fresh oysters from Île Saint-Jean. They were expensive, but not for her, and for a few livres extra, they added two island lemons to her bag! *Where did you get lemons?* They smiled and didn't say. There followed the usual vegetables and three fresh cod, deboned to filets with the scales scraped. And the pastry baker had somehow found the means to make a chocolate torte sprinkled with island sugar, rock milled into a fine powder. That made her smile. But to her disappointment, not a single stall had any coffee beans left. In total, she had bought more food than they could consume in three days. Fortunately, the icy winter days allowed her to keep it fresh in the cold outdoors, wrapped and placed in a large clay bowl inside the dome-shaped oven, protected from scavenging animals.

When the bag became heavy, she turned for home, but extended her walk down to the harbor quay wall and took the long way back, so she could view the ships. Among the merchant vessels, there were two French frigates in the harbor that were not there yesterday. She stopped and admired them. Curiosity about them made her walk uphill to the King's Bastion to see Marie.

They sat down to drink some tea together. Corrinne offered to share some of the oysters and other foods she bought. Marie gave her fresh cheeses and butter she purchased the day before.

"I saw two frigates in the harbor. Where are they from?"

"They are from the naval base at Rochefort. They are leaving again tomorrow. They stopped long enough to unload a small company of Swiss mercenaries, about seventy soldiers, who will join the garrison. They are billeted inside the Queen's Bastion barracks."

Corrinne choked on her tea.

As the days went by, rumors concerning the Swiss mercenaries were popular and dreaded by Corrinne. They did not appear menacing, but Corrinne heard the Swiss were always complaining about the barracks, the food, and having to work on the battlements with other soldiers, which they claimed was not part of their contracted services. They looked down their noses on the Troupes de la Marine, considering themselves superior. Marie had told Corrinne the governor had to intervene in disputes among the commanders when the Swiss refused to take orders from any senior officer other than their own. Henri claimed they were mostly arrogant whiners, but he was watching them carefully, too. When enough time passed, Corrinne became less anxious about possible assassins in their ranks.

Two beautiful days arrived back-to-back three weeks after the Swiss arrived. This was the first time in months that the weather boasted sun and blue skies. On the first day, Henri came to Corrinne's house to eat supper with them near sunset. After Henri answered her usual questions about the Swiss, he talked about the weather.

"I am certain tomorrow will be beautiful and sunny like today. Good weather is like good storms. When it happens, the ship captains will tell you it lasts at least two days and sometimes three until this 'good' storm passes over you. Because it's so pleasant, Colonel Franquet announced work on the Gabarus Bay battlements is suspended for tomorrow. So, I was thinking"—he reached over the table and took Anamosa's hand—"that maybe Anna and I could shop at the market together. What say you?"

Anamosa almost swooned. Her eyes widening at this thought. She trembled with excitement.

"Oh, yes! Yes! May I go, Corrinne?"

Corrinne's heart glowed to see the love in this young girl's face so exposed and vulnerable.

"Of course, you can."

Anamosa loved Henri. Anyone could see this. Any *woman*, that is. Henri didn't. Henri only saw that Anna was very happy. Henri was unable to perceive the depth and strength of Anna's emotions.

Someday, he will see it and will react with complete surprise, Corrinne mused. *As if he had had no idea! As if it had just happened!* But Henri was in love with Anamosa, too. He simply did not realize how much he loved her yet. *Men are so flawed!*

Henri noticed Corrinne's warm, knowing smile. She was looking at him.

"Oh, do you want to come, too? You could bring the twins."

"No, no. You take Anna tomorrow and enjoy the day together. If it is this sunny the day after, come back at noon and you can be my escort with the twins. You'll make the hens of the faubourg markets burst with gossip."

"Agreed! And I will pray for another sunny day." He looked at Anna. "I will be coming from the Dauphin barracks tomorrow. Wait for me near the Frédéric Gate arch at noon."

*

The next day was even better than the first. There was not a cloud in the sky and the temperature had risen. It was glorious. The marines rejoiced at having the day off to themselves. In the condensed barracks beneath the Dauphin Bastion, Henri had made a conscious decision to live side by side with his Québécois marines. It alienated him a little from many of the Louisbourg garrison officers, but a few of the senior, veteran officers nodded with admiration. They understood the intense loyalty this would evoke in the marines.

"We are at war. The marines only take orders from you. There will be deadly consequences in every decision you make," Major Péan had warned Henri, the morning he left Louisbourg forever.

In this instance, positive consequences. Indeed, it facilitated an unbreakable bond among the small group of marines. So much so, some of them started to mimic Henri's dress, wearing a cutlass worn over the shoulder. And Henri had started to teach them how to fight with the cutlass as well as hand-to-hand, using the lessons he received from Sentry Cheever. Before long, all the Québécois marines would be dressing like Lieutenant

Gerrard, even the veteran grenadier, Color Sergeant Gosse, who was the first to adopt the cutlass.

"You're dressing in a formal uniform just to go for a walk?" Color Sergeant Gosse asked quizzically from his bunk.

Henri was combing back his hair. "Yes. I'm shopping in the faubourg market. There is a new stall set up. One of the merchant captains brought gold and silver trinkets ashore yesterday." Henri did not want to mention Anamosa. "I am going to pick out some things to use as gifts in the future."

Color Sergeant Gosse had a new thought. "You mean jewelry…gems?"

"Well, I don't know if you call it jewelry. The items are colored stones and things of shiny metal."

"Girls will like it, I'd wager. Is there a girl in your plans?"

"If there was, Color Sergeant, it would be ungentlemanly to discuss it in a barracks."

There is *a girl!* Gosse concluded. The grenadier got up and started putting on a clean uniform, too.

"This is a good idea, Lieutenant. Every maiden in Louisbourg will show up at that stall today. I can just station myself by it, and pick out the ones I like."

Henri rolled his eyes. "And do what? They are not apples on a tree! It's the middle of the day. They'll have their mothers with them."

"Not all of them, Lieutenant," Sergeant Gosse replied with optimism. "You just don't understand how this works. You don't study these faubourg women like I do. All you do is stain your linen every other night."

"I do *not!*"

"Yes, you do, Lieutenant. These quarters are very quiet."

"You just have a lewd imagination!"

"You should try and approach some of these maidens. Spring is almost here. It is a known fact, just like the weather, they get a lot wetter…"

"Stop it! These are young girls!"

"Young? Bah! They are becoming women. And that means they are highly curious and willing to listen and learn from a master tutor." He stopped dressing for a moment and smiled. "Like me. I have lain with women of every color, nationality, and size from all over the world."

"So you are an expert?"

"I am!"

Henri was dubious.

"You see, Lieutenant, convincing young maidens to surrender their virginity is much like the formal siege of a fort. Penetration is inevitable. But you begin with the parallel trenches of polite conversation, getting closer and closer until you can hold hands. Then you mortar them with compliments, watch their expressions carefully and correct your aim. Concentrate on identifying their weaknesses. You must find an isolated place to sit next to them, a place where they cannot be seen by other people, a comfortable place, a place where they don't feel the need to defend their virtue so strongly. Then you gently infiltrate one hand up the back of their dress"—he pantomimed this part—"moving closer and closer, undoing a button or two, like any competent sapper. If you hear their breathing become faster, they are ready. You attempt a sortie, sneak a kiss on their neck like a sniper. Apologize immediately, of course. Claim their beauty was overwhelming, even if it's a lie. But ask quickly if you can do it again. If they say yes, you have created the breech you have been waiting for. It's time for—"

"Time? Stop!" Henri shook his head to clear it of Gosse's nonsense. "Color Sergeant, I cannot believe you even took the *time* to compose that." He positioned his saber over his shoulder and put on his hat.

Color Sergeant Gosse balked. "Wait! I'm almost ready. And I'm not done. Let me tell you about the frontal assault. That is the best part!"

Henri opened the door. "I'm going to Frédéric Gate, Sergeant."

Henri went outside and started walking along the quay wall that angled to the left about thirty degrees after a few minutes of walking and lead straight on towards its center, crowned by the archway of Frédéric Gate. There were a lot of people congregating at the bottom of Rue Toulouse, which ended across from the gate. Most people were gawking as the world visited them. All the merchant shipping traffic, people, and goods usually passed through and beneath this arch. It was the heart of a curious city, starved for news and gossip about what transpired at the gate that day, because something usually happened there every day. Although one could not be sure today's entertainment. That was the fun of it.

The sun was high in the sky. The day felt warm for once. Henri squinted carefully towards the gate but did not spot Anamosa. There was a large crowd of people mingling there. He hurried to get closer.

*

Corrinne had helped Anamosa get ready, braiding up her hair, adding a small butterfly pin to one braid. Its wings were dotted with a mix of red and green stones. She applied a dash of rouge to the girl's high cheekbones, enhancing their healthy glow with just a suggestion of a blush.

"God, you have beautiful skin," she complimented.

Anamosa picked out her favorite blue dress to wear. The one she often wore to church. It hung almost to her ankles. But it would be hidden beneath her long darker blue winter coat. The sun was out, but it was still very chilly, just a few degrees above freezing, and it would be windy down by the harbor.

"Here's something you will like. Captain LaTour said it comes from a land called Russia."

Corrinne circled a slender sable wrap around Anna's neck. Captain LaTour had brought this back from Europe as a surprise present for Corrinne years ago. She secured the thin leather lacings in the eyelets of the collar. This touch of dark, lustrous fur added an elegance to Anna's appearance that Corrinne did not anticipate. Corrinne quickly positioned Anamosa in front of the standing mirror to admire the look.

"Look at you! My goodness, Anamosa! You look two years older! You are simply stunning. Henri will be so pleased and proud to walk with you!"

Anamosa's smile gleamed.

Corrinne led her to the door. "Now, be sure to walk near the houses. Don't step in any of the puddles. Some of them are very deep. If you stop to eat, take small bites…"

"I know, Corrinne. I know. I've been watching you."

Corrinne grinned. "Of course, you have." She kissed the girl's cheeks and sniffed back tears of envy. "I only wish Philippe were here, so we could walk with you. Have a good time! Make Henri spend money on you," she shouted as Anamosa walked away.

Spend money? Corrinne clucked a sound of disgust and frowned at herself. *I should not have said that.*

*

Anamosa walked quickly to Rue Toulouse and turned right to walk downhill towards the gate. For the first time, she perceived the eyes of men and older boys gazing at her as she walked by. Some of them smiled. One boy waved. She found their unexpected interest curious. She liked it. As she neared Frédéric Gate, it was thronged on all sides by townspeople. Many of them were watching, inspecting everyone or anything carried through the gate and watching the goods coming off the cargo launches from the ships in the harbor. They were interested in catching the first glimpse of specific items they desired. Bolts of new dress cloth were very popular. When the waiting women saw it, they would trail the conveyor along the streets to whatever shop, stall, or government warehouse the cloth was taken.

Anamosa decided not to mingle with the crowd. She moved further to the right of the gate and stayed back towards the center of Rue Le Quai Mur, the road running alongside the wall, to remain in the open, to be seen more easily. She craned her head and looked towards the Dauphin Bastion in the distance, watching for Henri. She noticed a few women lingering conspicuously nearby. They wore gaudy clothing, their faces painted with facial rouge. Anamosa recognized who they were. These women were watching the gate, too, looking for those lonely seamen who sought a certain kind of companionship.

But the sunny day drew people of every class and distinction to this commercial crossroad in Louisbourg. Among the onlookers were a few of the new Swiss mercenaries recently arrived and added to the garrison, including Captain Bergen Stoecklin and two of his subordinate officers.

Captain Stoecklin was a veteran mercenary, familiar with assignments to foreign armies and cities all over the world. He considered Louisbourg the most dismal place yet. Despite the port's consistent commercial shipping and its impressive size, it was still wet, cold, and foggy. Quite possibly the most forgotten outpost he'd ever visited, and for its size, remarkably isolated. Bastions bristling with cannon were the predominant architectural feature. Men outnumbered the women three to one. There was nothing outside the walls except for a remote fishing village on the other side of the harbor bay, inhabited by Basques. He visited the village in his first week to reconnoiter. He found a suspicious people who made it clear with their eyes, be they men or women, that soldiers of any variety were not welcome there, ever! He asked a few of them the same question.

"Do any foreigners live in your village?" They shrugged.

Louisbourg had few redeeming qualities. *At least the wine is decent.* But the Swiss captain and his friends quickly learned the best place to encounter females who might be friendly to them was at Frédéric Gate. There were not many, but there were a few, if you were patient. They stopped at the end of Rue Toulouse directly across from the arched stone gateway and calmly surveyed the crowd.

The bright sunshine had brought people out of their homes that day. Captain Stoecklin was looking for a whore, a clean one, not one of the wet, soggy ones, smelling of cheap perfume, which barely disguised their real smell. That day there were a lot of town women, too. They would do. They were possible. Harder to approach, of course. But with a handful of silver coins that would catch a glint of the sunlight, sometimes you could draw a look. No success yet.

"I told you! It's like fishing," he teased his lieutenants. "Be patient."

It was still winter, but in a very rare event, three new merchant vessels had arrived in the harbor the previous day. The ships attracted a larger crowd than usual.

Captain Stoecklin watched the jostling crowd roll, ebb and divide, as the cargo was carried in through the gate.

"They are like gulls! Look at them! Inspecting everything to see if it might be edible. They even squawk like gulls."

His friends laughed. "What's that make us?" one of them asked.

Stoecklin regarded the lieutenant with a smirk. "It makes us *desperate!*"

At that moment, the crowd to Stoecklin's right thinned out. That's when he saw her...just standing there...all alone!

"My God! Look at that beauty! She's mine!" He left his friends and walked toward a girl with dark hair and bright eyes.

"*Excusez moi, Mademoiselle.* Are you available?"

Anamosa had been staring straight ahead, watching for Henri. Startled by the low voice, she flinched and turned towards the uniformed man. He rattled some coins in his left hand. But it was the ugly, leering smile that told her everything she needed to know. She reached into her right coat pocket. She'd previously removed its lining for this purpose. Her hand insinuated further into the unthreaded seam on the side of her dress. She gripped the slender haft of the eight-inch boning knife hanging in a thin, leather belt scabbard around her waist. Under the bulk of the coat, her movements were not detected.

She's a native girl, thought Captain Stoecklin as he studied the impassive expression and stunning blue eyes of this young girl who did not reply.

"More then," he suggested. He made a show of adding a small gold coin to his palm.

Anamosa did not look at the money, her face remained expressionless.

"Come, come. That's more than you would make in four months in this shithole." His voice had an edge of impatience.

Anamosa had decided if he reached a hand towards her, she would slice open his palm and run. It would not be necessary.

"Step away from her!"

Anamosa knew that wonderful voice. She turned and smiled. Henri gently pressed Anna behind him with his left hand while keeping his eyes on the captain.

Stoecklin grinned sardonically. "Well, I guess that was inevitable. Something this beautiful? She's yours, right? Is that it, Lieutenant? You have some personal arrangement with her, yes? Your private Indian whore?"

Henri saw two other Swiss officers walk to the captain's sides. Henri reached up and slowly withdrew his cutlass. He stepped sideways to his left to draw their attention away from Anamosa. She instinctively backed into the crowd, which had suddenly become very quiet, watching this drama unfold.

Captain Stoecklin looked at the cutlass and smirked. "Is this a jest? Does this mean you are challenging me?"

Henri stared at the captain, saying nothing. He studied how the other two officers were standing, knowing they would move first in the way their bodies leaned. They were all right-handed.

The captain smiled at his two friends. "Well, this will certainly break our boredom. Do not interfere, gentlemen. But bear witness, the marine drew first." Stoecklin's sword hissed from its scabbard. He unlimbered it in the air, cutting arches from side to side.

"Put away your sword, Captain."

Henri's eyes shifted to his right. It was Color Sergeant Gosse and another marine private.

"Oh? So, is this to become a skirmish with the peasant marines of Louisbourg? Over a *whore*?"

A dark scowl on his face and with surprising speed, Henri lunged in a fleche. Captain Stoecklin was prepared for this and easily parried the cutlass slash to his left. But Henri anticipated that movement, too. He stepped into the captain and, with his left hand, gripped the pommel of the captain's sword, twisted it clockwise and up, taking the rapier from the surprised officer's hand. Gently, he laid the captain's sword on the ground.

It was over in a second. The crowd was murmuring loudly.

Henri now stepped sideways to his right, permitting the captain access to the sword, while holding his cutlass before him, pointing the tip towards the ground. Growling, Captain Stoecklin retrieved his sword. The other two Swiss officers half-drew their swords.

"Put away your swords! Come to attention!"

That was the voice of grenadier Colonel du Bourzt, who had a woman on his arm. He'd been taking a happy promenade on the quay street on this beautiful sunny afternoon…until now.

Henri put his weapon away and came to attention, along with Color Sergeant Gosse and the other marine private. Captain Stoecklin faced the colonel with a sullen expression as he casually slipped his sword into its scabbard. The Swiss officers came to a relaxed posture of attention.

"What goes on here! Public brawling with swords?!"

"It was my fault, Colonel," Henri said quickly. "I drew first. It was an argument about the speed of a cutlass versus a rapier. I was showing Captain Stoecklin disarming moves we use aboard ship."

"Is this true, Captain?"

Captain Stoecklin barely concealed his glare at Henri, but gave a curt nod to Colonel du Bourzt.

Colonel du Bourzt knew this wasn't true. And it certainly wasn't over. But he wanted to defuse this situation before it drew any larger crowds or attention, though it looked like more than half the faubourg was already here. And more people were streaming out of the nearby shops to witness this.

"All of you, Color Sergeant Gosse as well, will stand before the governor tomorrow morning at the hour of nine. Make certain your stories are the same and believable. Captain Stoecklin, withdraw with your officers"— he pointed—"back up Rue Toulouse. You, marines, withdraw that way to the Dauphin bastion! I don't want to see any of you out here again today. Dismissed!"

As the Swiss officers turned up Rue Toulouse, the gate crowd erupted with noise, laughter, and conversation about the excitement they just witnessed. By the end of the day, every citizen of Louisbourg would claim they were there at the scene of the scuffle.

"I think this lovely day has turned out exceedingly well, don't you, Lieutenant?" Color Sergeant Gosse said sarcastically. "To think I got into my dress uniform just to go on a *fucking* stroll along the quay wall to Frédéric Gate and back again. And I get placed on report with the governor as a bonus! How exciting! I feel so rejuvenated!"

"Apologies, Color Sergeant," Henri responded stiffly, "but he called Lady Anamosa a whore."

Henri went into the crowd, many of them nodding with approval and smiling at him. A few men patted him on the back. The Swiss mercenaries were very unpopular with French civilians. Henri found Anamosa. Her expression was radiant. He took her hand.

"Anna, I apologize that happened to you. Now come on, we don't have much time."

Henri led her by the hand and walked one street over to the right of Rue Toulouse where the market stalls began. He went directly to the stall he knew displayed the trinkets. There were all sorts of other objects made of shiny metal, sparkling gem stones, carvings in wood, ivory, and jade.

"Pick out something you want," he told her.

Anna smiled up at him. "You pick something for me."

Henri cast a bewildered look at the merchant. The merchant, noticing the hopeful blue eyes of the girl, winked and nodded.

"Lieutenant, I think these *jewels* over here are appropriate." The man gestured toward a display of necklaces. One necklace, in particular, stood out—a thin-braided strand of blue and white linen yarn, holding a small gold cross. The cross had a tiny purple stone at its center. "This comes from the islands. It once had a gold chain, but that was melted down. One of the island women made the braid. The gold cross has some value, but I am not the type of man who would melt down a cross." He laughed, then said flatly, "Ten livres."

"Ten?!"

The merchant's tone was cajoling. "You offer silver. This is gold."

"That is not a gold bar, sir! Five."

"Eight."

Anamosa's smile had disappeared.

"Seven...and I'll buy something else." Henri had picked up the necklace and now looped it around Anna's neck. "This looks beautiful on you." The smile returned. She kissed the cross and let it dangle.

The merchant spread his hands over the other items. "What else?"

"Um, something for a boy and girl, the age of two. And something for their mother!"

They haggled over prices until the merchant was certain the officer was leaving the stall without any money. Henri knew he had been fleeced, but

Anamosa was giggling and heady with happiness. He had not heard Anamosa giggle like this before. As they returned to the stone house, she had her arm curled within his elbow. People were looking at them, smiling with admiration at the attractive couple. *She liked those stares even more!* It was the most memorable day of Anamosa's life.

"You are back so early," Corrinne said with surprise and looked at Anamosa. "Did you enjoy yourself?"

"Oh, yes!" Anamosa replied with passion. "A man called me a whore! Henri had a sword fight! He bought me this necklace!"

"What!?" Corrinne choked. She looked at Henri with alarm.

Henri awkwardly explained what took place at Frédéric Gate. "No one was hurt."

"The entire population of Louisbourg looked on while you had a sword fight with a Swiss officer? And *no one was hurt* is all you can say?!"

Henri straightened and replied tersely, "Captain Stoecklin called Anamosa a whore. He's lucky I did not cut him." Henri handed a cloth bag to Anamosa and opened the door. "I've been ordered to remain in my quarters until tomorrow." He left without turning or saying good-bye.

Corrinne had never seen such an expression of resentment on Henri's face, nor had Henri's tone to her ever been so brusque.

But Anamosa was still smiling. Nothing could ruin this day for her.

"He bought you all presents," she declared happily.

She reached into the cloth bag and withdrew them one by one. Each one came with a colored ribbon as a bow. Calypso got a beautiful tiny ivory doll with black hair, no bigger than a person's hand. It was dressed in strange, colored clothes made of silk. Calypso gasped with awe.

"It's a China doll," Anna explained. "She is a China woman."

Marcus got a small wheeled cannon made of tin and four wooden soldiers in blue uniforms. He immediately sat on the floor of the cuisine and started making cannon noises.

"He bought you something, too."

"He did?"

Anamosa placed a sculpture on the table depicting two hands beginning at the wrists. Each made from contrasting shades of ivory.

Corrinne was speechless. The life-sized hands were upright and entwined at the tips of the fingers, almost in prayer. *Or in love.* One hand was feminine, slender and smooth, made from creamy white ivory. The other hand was a reddish tinged ivory. Its texture appeared coarse and in some places callused, obviously the hand of a man. What drew Corrinne's greatest admiration was the detail of the skin, the vasculature, the suggestion of tiny hairs, the even tinier pores, the fingernails, and even the wrinkles at the joints, all of it carved so delicately. It had to be done without making a single mistake. The hands looked real!

This is the work of a master artist. Corrinne gently caressed the exquisite piece, immediately regretting her impulsive admonishment of Henri.

"Charles would be impressed," she whispered with sadness. She became emotional.

Anamosa talked on without stopping, repeating all the events of the day, step by step. How Henri appeared so suddenly to protect her. How the crowd reacted with low *ohs*, *eeks*, and *ahs* when Henri took the sword away from the Swiss officer. How another officer arrived and made the others stand at attention. How the crowd spoke of Henri with pride.

"Some of them applauded."

How Henri took her hand and led them to the merchant. How the merchant and Henri argued about every item, the things the merchant said, and how Henri answered. How they walked arm in arm on the way back.

"Henri was so good to me." Anamosa recalled everything exactly, as if seeing it for the first time in her mind's eye. "Henri gave the merchant all the money he had left for your present."

"Yes…Henri would do that." Corrinne looked searchingly at Anamosa. "Did it hurt you…when the man called you a whore?"

Anamosa was unaffected. "No. I am not a whore. There were other women standing there alone. I think they were whores. He just made a mistake with me."

"That officer should not be making such mistakes," Corrinne replied shortly, her anger rising again. "Were you frightened?"

"No." Anamosa did not mention the boning knife she had inside her dress. She would have cut the man if he'd dared to touch her.

The more Corrinne thought about the scene, the more her anger increased. She stood up.

"Anna, watch the children. I am going out. I won't be gone long."

Corrinne took her gray cloak from the peg and left the house. She was going to talk with the governor's wife, Madame Marie-Louise de Drucour.

*

Three Swiss mercenary officers and two Québécois Troupes de la Marines stood at attention before Governor Augustin de Drucour the next morning at the hour of nine, as ordered. Henri explained what happened, repeating the same story he told Colonel du Bourzt. Captain Stoecklin confirmed this explanation without challenge.

"I've been informed a young faubourg woman was treated with disrespect and called a whore! Can anyone tell me about that?"

The governor did not expect any of them to answer and they didn't. But he wanted the Swiss to know that he knew about it. They'd been here less than a month and had fomented much dissension.

"Good. Because if I ever hear that one of my officers has called any woman of Louisbourg a whore, they will be placed in stocks in a bastion cell for a week to marinate in their own urine and *merde*. Captain Stoecklin, for this public display of brawling with swords, you and your lieutenants are fined two weeks' pay."

Captain Stoecklin opened his mouth to protest but thought better and remained silent.

"Lieutenant Gerrard, for drawing your sword first, you are fined two months' pay. Color Sergeant Gosse, as a veteran grenadier, I find your participation particularly unacceptable. You are fined three months' pay."

Henri almost protested that the sergeant had done nothing wrong, but at a stern look from Gosse, he snapped his mouth shut.

The governor waited to see if any of them would protest, in which case he would double the fine. They did not.

"You are dismissed!"

Lieutenant Gerrard and Color Sergeant Gosse left the King's Bastion immediately. But Colonel du Bourzt detained the Swiss officers once they were outside. He pointed at the captain and gestured for the two lieutenants to keep walking.

"Captain Stoecklin."

The captain came to attention and saluted.

"At ease, Captain. I don't require false honors from you. Do you know the identity of that young girl you called a whore?"

Stoecklin shrugged. "She was an Indian."

"She is Lady Anamosa VanderMeer. The daughter of Lord Charles VanderMeer of the House of Brunswick."

"With respect, Colonel, am I to be impressed?"

Colonel du Bourzt squinted and took a half step closer. "What you should be is wary of crossing swords with Lieutenant Gerrard again."

Stoecklin made a scoffing noise. "Why, because he disarmed me? I've met and—"

"If he could disarm you, Captain, then you are dead! That marine is Lady Anamosa VanderMeer's personal bodyguard. And he could cut through you and your two friends at the same time, like wheat!"

Stoecklin smirked. "Is that all, Colonel?"

Colonel du Bourzt sensed he was wasting his breath. He could see the contempt in the other man's eyes. He despised these mercenaries. There would indeed be another time.

He replied with certainty. "For now. You are dismissed, Captain."

Without saluting, Captain Stoecklin turned and walked slowly back to the Queen's Bastion. He had just learned the valuable piece of information he was seeking. He presumed Lady VanderMeer would be hiding somewhere remote outside the fort.

Lady VanderMeer is inside the fortress after all.

Now he just had to find out exactly where. But he could not ask anyone where Lady VanderMeer lived, to prevent anyone from recalling his interest after she was dead. And he had to wait for his departure ship to arrive before he acted.

*

Color Sergeant Gosse waited until they'd walked out of earshot.

"Lieutenant, you do understand, this thing is not over between you and that Swiss captain."

"I do, Sergeant. I will pay you back...for your fine."

"Fine? Don't worry about my fine. I don't spend any money anyway. What's more important for you to know is that mercenary plans to kill you. He will come at you with others, but he will act alone. If you kill him, the others will act against you."

Henri's banked anger now simmered again after being reminded by the governor that the captain had called Anamosa a whore.

"Unless they plan to use pistols, the captain better bring more than two men with him."

"Well, as long as you're not surprised," Color Sergeant Gosse said, snorting with amusement.

The grenadier sergeant had sparred with this marine lieutenant using a wooden cutlass and dirk numerous times. He had never bested this officer. Not once.

"And I'm thinking four extra men might give them a chance."

CHAPTER 16
BOSTON
MARCH 1757
Carpet Stains

The shriek from upstairs was filled with panic. Captain Martyn and Sentry Cheever bolted from the cuisine where they had been breaking their fast together. They ran up the stairs and entered the nursery room to find Molly sitting on the floor against a wall across from the baby's crib, her arms wrapped around upraised knees, tears streaming down her face, a crazed look in her eyes.

Frightened by his mother's wrenching scream of terror, little Conor was wailing in his crib.

With the twelve-inch dirk pulled from his belt, Sentry began a search of all the upstairs rooms and closets to check for an intruder.

Captain Martyn sat down next to his trembling wife and gathered her up in his arms.

"Molly! Molly, I'm here! I've got you! Are you hurt? What's wrong? What happened?"

"It was here again," she said in a low, choking voice.

"What was here? Who?"

"IT! *The hooded thing!* It speaks a foul tongue!"

Dianamora, entering the room and seeing Molly incapacitated, picked up little Conor from the crib, cooed to him, and retreated to the rocking chair to comfort the baby in her arms.

With others in the room, Molly's adrenal urgency began to drain. She became confused and befuddled. "I don't understand," she mumbled as she leaned her head against Conor's shoulder and sobbed softly. "I don't…why?"

Sentry returned. "There is no'one else in the house," he announced firmly and slipped the dirk back in its scabbard. "Wha' happened?"

Conor shook his head in bewilderment. "She said that someone or some *thing* was in the room…a 'hooded thing' speaking 'foul words.'"

This was the fourth time in two months Molly had had such outbursts of terror and panic. It was the second time Captain Martyn had seen her act this way.

Sentry and Dian traded glances of concern. *She's getting worse*, they thought.

Conor Martyn was captain of an English warship, a man routinely away at sea for long periods of time. He could not conceive of a more worrisome situation than leaving his beautiful young wife and baby behind, with his wife going hysterically mad. So far, she had not harmed the baby. But the baby was bawling and Molly did not try to comfort him. Who could say what might happen the next time?

Conor lifted Molly up in his arms and carried her to the bedroom. He placed her in bed and pulled a coverlet up to her chin. Her eyes were closed. He watched them roiling back and forth beneath the eyelids.

"I'm right here, Molly. I'm here," he whispered and hugged her tightly.

Back in the nursery, Sentry was standing with his hands on his hips as he scanned the room, his mood was dark. Dian was gently rocking the baby in her arms.

Sentry stabbed a finger at the floor. "You say this only happens in this room?" he asked Dian. "It started back in January...but it only happens in *this* room."

"Yes," Dian answered in hushed voice. "And speak more quietly."

Conor returned. "She's asleep, but her sleep is not restful."

"Molly imagined an intruder."

"There was no intruder," Conor replied. He wanted something more substantial, not just imagination. "You said so yourself."

"I knoo'. But I did find tha' loose board on the back fence. Tha' was the same board loosened the first time, when Dian killed tha' assassin. Maybe these same people tried again."

"But Molly doesn't remember seeing anything!" said Conor with exasperation. "Not anything real! Just this imaginary hooded man! She didn't hear anything! Except foul words. And she cannot even recall the words. She cannot even repeat the sounds!"

The captain was distraught. Sentry had seen men in war reach this type of breaking point. They were simply scared. But his instincts told him the cause of Molly's torment was *in this room*.

It may still be in here now! That was the most disturbing thought!

The veteran marine's tone became low and practical. "Back in January, when Dian and I returned from the market tha' day, Molly was terrified. She could not explain why she was terrified and was just as confused as she is now."

"All right," Conor replied reluctantly, "her hysteria is not getting better… it's getting worse. So, what can I do about that? Hire an exorcist?" he asked, exasperated.

"Shhhh!" Dian whispered harshly. "Don't speak about such things! And talk more quietly! The baby is finally asleep."

Conor dropped his voice. "Sorry. I—I don't…Molly's fear is not imaginary. She is scared. You say it's *this* room? So, what is it about *this* room?"

Sentry focused on what they knew. "Back in January, Molly was nah' harmed. Nothing was taken. And the guards ootside' the house, front and back, did nah' see anyone either. There was no' sign of anyone being in the house, no'one in this room. No' sign of an intruder back in January and no' sign today!"

Dianamora was an island woman. Her childhood culture was more accepting of the notion of otherworldly spirits, including ones of a dark and evil nature. The relentless march of Molly's madness reminded her of people possessed—cursed. Dian's suspicions had latched on to that notion almost from the beginning. She'd kept it to herself. Until now.

"No sign…except that spot on the rug." Dian pointed the toe of her shoe towards the hand-sized reddish blemish on the carpet.

Sentry and Conor turned and bent to look more closely at the spot. It looked like something had been spilled.

"Is tha' new?"

"No," Dian replied. "It appeared in January. I asked Molly about it. She could not explain it."

"In January?" Conor squinted at the faded stain. "What is that? Wine?"

"That's what I thought at first," Dian whispered. "Molly won't talk about it. But whatever it is, it's not wine. I've tried to scrub it out with a brush three or four times. The stains cling to the weave and keep coming back. Molly has never tried to clean it. She steps around it. That's why I scrubbed it so many times."

Sentry frowned. He recalled the rag Dian had showed him in January. Now, he got down on his hands and knees to smell the stain. There was no odor. But it did look to have a sticky, flaky appearance...like something dried...but not wine...more like... *Blood?* He thought about wetting his finger and tasting it, but only for an instant as his brain recoiled in horror at the thought. Sentry was not that brave. He looked up at Conor, an idea forming.

"What?" Conor demanded, seeing the thoughtful expression on Sentry's face.

"I've seen soldiers with a type of mania. Sometimes what a soldier experiences in battle scars their memories. They seem all right, until some minor thing provokes a memory so terrible they fall into a craze aboot' it. They rant as if they were right back in that battle again. We kin' usually calm them down. But these memories can be so bad they can last for years. I'm just sayin'."

Conor shook his head. "I don't understand. What are you saying?"

"That maybe...maybe this stain in the rug somehow provokes bad memories for Molly. It sounds foolish, I knoo'. And I dinnah' knoo' how a hooded man connects to a rug stain. But, if we kinnah' come up with anything else, I say, let's roll up this rug and burn it. Get it to hell and gone and out of the house."

Conor was desperate to do something! Anything! Burning this stained carpet was doing something. He started moving furniture.

*

Later that afternoon, after they had burned the rug to ashes in Boston's common dump, Conor and Sentry sat in the library and sipped some brandy together. Conor stared into the fireplace, still deeply troubled by Molly's breakdown.

"Well...tha' stained carpet was too ugly for a nursery anyway," Sentry said to thaw the silence. "I thin' Molly will be cheered with something new. Dian and I will shop for a replacement tomorrow."

More silence.

After a long pause, Conor spoke. "What if something happens when I'm at sea?"

Sentry felt the captain's torment. He gripped Conor's knee for a moment to reassure him.

"Dian and I will be here, Captain. We'll look after Molly and little Conor."

"I'll be patrolling off the coast of Cape Breton Island," the captain said, as if he had not heard the words of comfort. "I don't know when I will be back. And if they decide to lay siege, it could be months!"

"Dinnah' worry, Captain. We'll take care of them both." Sentry tried to change the subject. "So, they're goin' tah' try a landing?"

Conor exhaled, resignation in his voice as he said, "That's the plan. But that's been the plan every year, unless something stops them. There are a lot of redcoats in Halifax now. Ten thousand at least, maybe more. It looks serious this time. But the navy must get them there first…and make a landing on that rocky, stormy coast. That means they need a lot more ships-of-the-line. A lot of transport ships. A lot of landing boats. They'll be landing under fire by the French who have entrenchments and artillery batteries built everywhere. Who can say for certain if we're ready for that? But I cannot delay my return much longer. The commodore sent orders to me by courier this week. Now that the repairs to the *Anamosa* are complete, I've been ordered to put back to sea, to sail to Halifax for resupply and probably sail to patrol the seas near Louisbourg again."

Sentry spoke glumly. "Then it's goin' tah' be years before it's over."

"Yeah. So, what about you?" Conor asked. "I could use a marine first sergeant aboard the *Anamosa*. You ready to join the marines again?"

Sentry coughed amid a sip of brandy and shook his head. "Nah' likely, Captain. I did my part and more in the last war." He pointed at his eye patch.

Sentry wore a black leather eye patch over his left eye to cover its opaque white cornea. The telling scar left by the Spanish rapier that caused the blindness lay straight down the left side of his face, starting above the brow, through it, over the eye, and ended outside his mouth at the chin. If he smiled, which Sentry labored never to do, it revealed his two upper front teeth were also missing. When Sentry did smile, his visage was a mix of horror for some and clown-like amusement to others. He was very aware of the effect his face could have on people and took pains to keep his expression placid and his lips closed. His smiles were more of a close-lipped grin.

"Noo', I'm a married man now, Captain, haven't yah' heard? Dian could get with child sometime soon. She waits for me tah' come to bed every night! Tis true. Maybe even tonight?" he added lightly. "Yah' jist' never noo'!" Sentry smiled broadly with fake cheer, attempting to lighten Conor's mood. Sentry's "war face" was terrifying. Picturing Dian's reaction when that face came to her bedside, Conor barked out a laugh, spitting some of his brandy on the floor.

Sentry grinned, pleased he'd provoked the captain's laughter.

At that moment, Dian came through the door with a tray of cheese, hard biscuits, and sweet breads. "Finally, something is funny on this difficult day." She placed the tray on the low table between them and took a seat. "Sentry, you may pour me a dram of that brandy, if you please. And will you share your amusement with me?"

"How is Molly?" Sentry asked quickly.

Dian sighed. "Molly is still asleep. Soundly asleep. No bad dreams. A good sign."

Another pressing topic to discuss came to Sentry's mind. Lord VanderMeer had sent him a letter with distressing news. The letter was in his pocket. But after the traumatic events of this day, he wondered if he should wait. Then again, they were in this peaceful library, relaxed by the warmth of the fire, and sipping brandy together. The baby was fed and asleep. Molly was resting peacefully. Who knew what tomorrow might bring? How many times in his life had Sentry thought like this, or heard those words spoken by another.

"Since we are together…yah' should know I received this letter from Lord VanderMeer a few days ago." He withdrew the letter from his pocket and held it up. "This is addressed to me, directly, wax-sealed, and all. It's several pages long, with some directions concerning this house and the house in Saybrook. But his lordship also wrote tha' his health had turned…for the worse. It's like what he told Thomas Hancock."

Conor set down his glass. "Something more?"

"No, much of the same. This letter is dated six weeks ago. Tha' means he lived two months more. The doctors were wrong."

"Why is Lord VanderMeer dying?" Dian asked softly in disbelief. "He is not that old. His wound is crippling but not fatal. That's what Dr. Angove said."

"I've seen sailors and marines wounded in the neck or the back suffer a similar paralysis," Sentry replied grimly. "To ignorant marines like myself, we tend tah' create explanations for such bad fortune. Usually, we invent a fiction we can agree tah' accept. Paralysis is nah' just being wounded. You are wounded again each time you wake up. It's worse than being killed. It becomes an endless punishment. You must rely on everyone else as if you were a child. And it does nah' get better. It only gets worse. A numbness of the body tha' seems tah' spread like a disease, almost like the black rot. Since doctors kinnah' cure it, the numbness spreads outward like poison, until it finally reaches the heart and it just stops beating. But before tha' happens, it robs the man of all his dignity. The royal doctors told his lordship tha' paralyzed people rarely live more than three months…and usually much less. I can tell yah' from my experience, there is truth tah' this."

"Does Lady VanderMeer know?" Dian asked.

"He's written Lady Corrinne, so by now, I assume she knows. His lordship says the arrangements concerning this house and the one in Saybrook will remain the same, like Mr. Hancock told us. If he passes, Lady Corrinne will assume the responsibilities. He tells us nah' tah' worry. He affirmed it was Lady Corrinne's idea in the first place."

"Everything is her idea," Conor complained. "What possesses her to stay in Louisbourg anyway…with her children? We cannot help her while she stays there."

Possesses her? Sentry knew exactly why Lady Corrinne chose Louisbourg. But he was not going to talk about this.

The conversation soon became muted. Since Molly was purportedly asleep, Conor excused himself to go to bed.

*

Conor undressed and slipped naked into bed beside Molly. He drew up next to her body. Of late, she would tense and draw away from him. Not this time. She was wearing a thin nightdress. It was not very warm. She had her knees pulled up to her chest to trap her body heat. She was sleeping soundly as Dian had reported.

Conor had tried to make love to Molly on several occasions only to be rebuffed. He'd seen the mania in her eyes and understood her mind was not right for anything intimate. But burning that carpet seemed to make a big difference. Conor was pressed to put to sea again. When he did, he could be gone for months. He desired Molly's touch and desired to touch her in return. He had to try. He carefully pulled on the thin nightdress, easing it up over her knees, then above her waist. Now it was loose enough to allow his hands to roam over her warm, naked skin.

Molly moaned, rolled onto her back, and straightened her legs. Conor was not certain what that moan suggested. Was it the beginning of a seizure or another rant of nonsensical words? He stopped. He did not want to frighten her. Instead, he pressed his face into her neck beneath the chin and gently nuzzled, kissed, and licked the skin.

Molly blinked in the darkness. She could feel Conor's hardness against her thigh.

He wants me, she thought.

She felt his hand moving down over her sex. His probing fingers searched and found the little bud of pleasure.

Molly gasped. She wanted him, too. She moved her hand down to grip his erection. He groaned.

Conor was very encouraged. She was aroused and so was he. But he wanted to be certain she would not suddenly start screaming for him to get away from her, like she had not too long ago. Conor took a chance and threw back the covers. He kissed his way down her stomach, slid his body over her legs, and placed his mouth over her sex, using his tongue and lips in a way he knew she liked, sucking at the little bud of sensitivity. Molly's pelvis pitched upward from the expanding pleasure. She gasped.

There you are. Conor allowed himself a burst of hope. *There's the Molly I love.* He wanted to enter her but decided to bring her to orgasm first with his mouth. Following that, Molly would often become completely wanton, at least she had before. The room was dark, except for a few wavering slivers of light from the hearth. He could not see her face, but he could feel and hear her reactions. She pulled on his hair now and pressed his face deeper between her legs. He rotated his lips and tongue around that special spot, flicking it repeatedly.

Molly gasped his name. "Oh, Conor!"

It was her voice. This was the Molly he knew.

Her pelvis arched again as the orgasm began. "Yes! Yes!" She pulled his hair harder.

That hurt, but he wasn't stopping now. She bucked as the pleasure peaked two, three, even four times before it began to subside. He slowed the movement of his lips and tongue. Her hands guided his movements to slow even further. She pressed her fingers on his cheek. A signal to stop.

Conor rolled off her to his back. He reached over and pulled the night dress further up until he could caress her nipples and breasts with his fingers. He decided not to say anything. He was hard as a marlinspike, but he wanted her to say something first. After several seconds of awkward silence, he spoke. "Molly, are you all right? Do you want something?"

"Do I want something?" her voice sounded confused, almost angry.

Conor exhaled glumly.

Molly rolled onto him and straddled one of his legs. She had been driven near to madness by something evil, something that robbed her of sanity. Nothing in her Puritan upbringing prepared her for an experience this horrifying and so threatening. She would never allow Puritan sensibilities to dictate her life going forward.

"What do I want? I want you inside of me, Conor. I love you. I've missed you. It's been too long. I want to stay awake all night and be sinful. That's what I want. Let me show you."

She moved up to her knees and lowered her sex onto Conor's hardness.

It would not be all night. But it was certainly several hours. Molly suggested everything they did. Conor felt certain whatever dark spirit had been bothering her had burned up in that carpet.

*

Dian was cooking up a skillet of eggs mixed with bits of bacon and vegetables. She'd sprinkled it with island spices.

"Tha' smells bloody marvelous," Sentry said as he sipped his tea. "Yah' were marvelous, too, last night, Dianamora."

Abandoning the eggs, Dian sat astride his lap and kissed him. "No more than you."

Molly entered carrying little Conor in a day bassinet. Dian and Sentry stared at Molly. She seemed happy. Molly smiled.

"Good morning."

They replied in kind. Dian got up and helped with the bassinet.

"Did yah' sleep well?" Sentry asked cautiously.

"My sleep was wonderful. Though I did not get much sleep," Molly added cheerfully.

Sentry and Dian's eyebrows shot up and they traded looks. Conor entered the cuisine, wearing his uniform. He looked sleepy, but he was smiling and relaxed.

"How aboot' you?" Sentry jested. "Are yah' rested, too?"

"Every part of me is rested, I think."

They laughed.

"Damn! Maybe we should burn all the carpets," Sentry suggested. "Did we discover a secret from Arabia?"

They sat around the table to eat. It was the first decent conversation in months that was not tense and worrisome. Molly was animated, her tone optimistic, which made them all feel hopeful.

Sentry gestured at Conor's uniform. "You goin' somewhere today, Captain?"

"No, not today. But soon, I think. Like I said, naval headquarters has standing orders for me to put back to sea to Halifax. Commander Rous will order me to patrol off Louisbourg again, I'm sure."

Molly leaned over and pressed her head to Conor's in sympathy. She voiced no complaint. This simple gesture of affection was one he'd not experienced in months.

"And you'll be going back to Saybrook?" Conor asked. "Because of the letter...from Lord VanderMeer?"

"Oh tha'. Yes, I've some repairs and other things to dah' at Winter House. No hurry though. I'll wait until the weather improves."

*

Sentry Cheever had indeed received new instructions from Lord VanderMeer. But he could not share this with Conor nor even Dian. He was entrusted with another letter, wax sealed, with instructions to hand deliver this missive to a Boston silversmith, whose name was written outside the folded pages.

> *This man is a trusted business associate of mine, an artist, a man skilled in gravestone engraving and silversmithing. Thomas Hancock will commission him to make a carving in stone, the details of which are included in the letter to him. When complete, it will resemble the drawing I've included for you to see on a separate page. The writing is Latin. At a future date, once the châsse is inserted into its new tomb, this stone carving is to be laid at the very top of the vault before it is hidden beneath the earth and sodded over. If the vault is ever discovered again, the inscription will serve as a warning to others not to disturb what lays inside. If they choose to ignore the warning, they do so at their own peril. You have witnessed the evil of which I speak.*

Sentry Cheever had studied the separate page of symbols and the inscriptions written in Latin. He could not read Latin, but he could guess at the meaning of the symbols. The skull and crossbones were ominous. The odd-shaped cross did not seem proper. This second slab of stone carved with symbols, and much less thick, would be laid atop the heavier capstone slab, designed to seal the vault. The symbol stone was not a gravestone per se, it was meant as a sign, a warning to anyone who might open the tomb by accident. When the vault construction was completed, as it was designed and intended, the tomb would be difficult to discern to a casual observer. It was beneath ground level, buried in a manner to reinforce the perception the gentle mound was unremarkable and a natural feature of the surrounding terrain. Thus, a long time might pass before the tomb was discovered, and maybe never. That was the hope, anyway.

After reading Lord VanderMeer's words regarding the tomb's potential discovery, Sentry studied the icons and words of Latin on the separate page.

MALO MORTUUM
FUGE CITO NUMQUAM REVERTETUR

Evil Death
Flee Quickly Never Return

Sentry had visited Winter House numerous times. He'd been the foreman during the construction of the vault. The stone masons hailed from New Haven. They'd brought the stone linings with them, designed from the plans sent to them by Lady VanderMeer. The vault was excavated to a depth of fifteen feet, but the stones were only a height of twelve feet. The stone slabs were so cumbersome, it required a heavy custom-made winch, a davit, and special triangular rigging just to lower them into place. The width was six feet. That left plenty of room for the anticipated reliquary when it was delivered. It did not matter when. Sentry just had to have the vault ready to receive the coffin when it arrived. As soon as the light of day lengthened and the weather warmed, Sentry planned to load up the symbol-covered stone panels on a wagon and go back to Winter House.

He began making a list of tasks to do.

Need to contact the stone masons in New Haven again. Have them do this work. They have the special winch and rigging. Probably need to buy the equipment from them this time. And C. Bernard Conway, Esquire. The lawyer. He will be involved. They will all have to be paid. Thomas Hancock will be involved. And where is the châsse now? Captain LaTour will know, he thought, then wondered if he would ever see that man again.

The vault was sophisticated. When finished, there would be three feet of earth covering the capstone and warning slab. In a short time, it would be overgrown with wild grasses, shrubs, and trees. *Or maybe I should have these planted right away,* he mulled. Even so, Sentry was not convinced this tomb would remain undisturbed, that it would stay hidden.

This thing haunts the VanderMeers. It has servants who stalk them. And the thing cannot be killed...Can it?

Sentry would never forget the experience inside the carriage hangar. Images of the creamy smoke, the smells of burnt flesh, the unnatural growls, and the shaking châsse suddenly flared up from his memories.

Some curious fool will break into it...eventually. He grimaced at the thought. *Hopefully, long after I'm dead.*

Québec City

The large round table was covered with a map depicting Fort William Henry's location on the south shore of Lac du Saint-Sacrament. The map could be considered a cartographic work of art. It was enhanced with detailed relief lines and other features of the surrounding topography, along with box notations of significant information gleaned from years of scouting reports.

Governor Vaudreuil began the war council with his objectives and expectations. The twenty-eight senior officers attending the war council each had a role to play in this campaign. He intended to hear from each one of them. Four, six-foot long, polished oak pointers were available to draw everyone's attention to specific locations on the map. Vaudreuil had one. Montcalm had one. Two others were available for use by the attendees.

"We have successfully repulsed the attack on Fort Carillon by the American rangers. The English now expect us to retire for the rest of the winter. We will not. Instead, we will press our advantage from the previous victory with a surprise attack on Fort William Henry. All the outlying buildings will be destroyed, the boat building yards burned and made unusable. If the opportunity presents itself, we will invest this English fort. If it becomes apparent we cannot hold this investment, we will spike its cannons, and burn this fort to the ground before we withdraw. As you are aware, the men and supplies to do this are already assembled. They need only your leadership. I want to review the command structure and the intended order of march. The march will begin tomorrow."

Most of this, everyone knew. Governor Vaudreuil gazed around the table, looking for frowns. He did not see any.

"Good! Today, I have the pleasant duty of honoring one of our officers with special recognition for his years of service. Major Michel Péan, come forward."

Captain Gerrard was standing across the table from Major Péan. Philippe saw the restrained expression of utter surprise on the major's face at the mention of his name. He could almost read Péan's panicked thoughts. Philippe suppressed a smile.

The other officers were almost as surprised as the marine major.

Struggling to keep his reactions under control, Major Péan plodded forward. The other officers stepped aside to let him pass. His mind raced to deduce what was happening...and why. Everything happening in the governor's headquarters that morning was being orchestrated. And *everything* had planned consequences. The major did not want any recognition! He preferred criticism to this! Michel Péan could not conceive what he had done to merit recognition. True, he boasted a little too much about his successful winter march from Louisbourg. It couldn't be that...could it?

Standing in front of Governor Vaudreuil, Major Péan came to attention and saluted. It was then he noticed the weaselly little eyes and devious smile of Intendant Bigôt standing behind and further back from the other officers.

You little turd pile! What have you done?

"You may stand at ease, Major."

The governor turned and accepted a written proclamation from Captain Trieste. He cleared his voice and read it aloud.

"Major Michel Jean Hugues de Péan, it is my honor to recognize your distinguished career of service to his majesty King Louis XV and to the people of New France."

Distinguished career? This is worse than I thought!

"And your outstanding achievements, beginning with leading Troupes de la Marine in establishing two forts on the Rivière aux Boeuf under deplorable conditions."

Worse than deplorable.

"Defending these same forts from hostile attack!"

Yes, the lice, gnats, and fucking mosquitoes were especially bad!

"Your commendation for leadership at the Battle of Lac du Saint-Sacrament."

Uh-oh!

"Your commendation for leadership exhibited beneath the wall and guns of the enemy during the Battle of Fort Bull. The outstanding commendation you just received from Governor Drucour of the fortress at Louisbourg. And your leadership in bringing back the Québécois marine battalion after a harsh winter march, with minimal casualties."

As planned, Captain Trieste initiated a polite applause from the assembled officers.

Oh, God...Where are you sending me now?

Governor Vaudreuil turned and accepted a flat box of polished black leather from Captain Trieste.

"Major Péan, in consideration of this list of commendations and your exemplary performance as the commander of the gendarmerie, by the order of King Louis XV, I am most pleased to announce your elevation as a chevalier of the Ordre Royal et Militaire de Saint-Louis."

From the flat box, Governor Vaudreuil lifted an ornate medallion badge suspended from a broad ribbon of bright red satin. He turned to hang it around the neck of Major Péan and found the major's head already bowed with gratitude and humility.

Péan's head hung with depression. He'd just been made a Knight in the Order of Saint Louis. An old and prestigious honor, normally presented near the end of an officer's career.

"King Louis the Great instituted this order in 1693," the governor reminded everyone. "The back of the medallion is inscribed with the words, *Bellicae Virtutis Praemium,* reward for wartime valor. Join me in congratulations to Major Michel de Péan. Tomorrow, he will no doubt add to this military reputation by proudly leading the militias in support of the attack on Fort William Henry."

For a few minutes, the officers thronged around Major Péan and congratulated him. The major smiled with modesty and accepted their polite compliments, while at the same time wondering why this had happened.

This? To get me to lead the militia against Fort William Henry? The governor already ordered me to lead them. I do not require cajoling. No, there is another reason...Bigôt? He did this. Why?

After a few minutes, Governor Vaudreuil called the council back to order. "When asked, each officer is to briefly explain their specific responsibilities."

He pointed at each man and invited them to speak, moving clockwise around the table, intentionally skipping over Captain Gerrard. He wanted the scout captain to speak last. There were a few questions but not many. When it was Captain Gerrard's turn, Vaudreuil interjected, "And finally Scout Captain Gerrard. But I want Captain Gerrard to first present his report on the recent attack on Fort Carillon. Captain?"

Philippe presented his summary report on what was now called the Battle of Snowshoes to the war council. He obeyed General Montcalm's order that if challenged by the governor, to defer to the general for reply.

Briefed by Captain Trieste, Governor Vaudreuil was now aware Captain Gerrard knew about the intercepted letters. The governor anticipated the scout captain's venom would spill out in front of them all. Vaudreuil awaited this confrontation with alacrity. He welcomed the opportunity to accuse the captain's wife publicly of being an English spy and have the scribes make a record of it. He slowly angered when he perceived he could not accuse Lady Corrinne VanderMeer of being a spy without admitting he had read Captain Gerrard's letters. He did not want anything like *that* recorded by the scribes.

Philippe noticed the intensity in the governor's gaze as he related the events of the battle that occurred atop the snow and ice ridges in the forests west of Fort Carillon. He presented valuable intelligence collected on Fort Edward and Fort William Henry in southern Lac du Saint-Sacrament from the scouts he led in the battle's aftermath. He only made one slip. It was at the end of his report. It was impulsive. He regretted it as soon as he had said it.

"Is that all you want to say, Captain?" the governor goaded acerbically.

Captain Bougainville could see a spark of anger appear in Philippe's eyes.

"Yes, Governor. That is the end of my report. Is there something you think I missed?"

Philippe saw General Montcalm's expression turn stony and Captain Bougainville's eyes widen in warning.

"No, Captain Gerrard. Not today," the governor replied. "At another time."

There was a tone of promise in his voice. The attending officers glanced at one another in puzzlement. They could tell something between the governor and Captain Gerrard had been left unsaid. The governor looked around the council room. He returned to the topic at hand.

"We know the enemy position at Fort William Henry is weak and rife with disease. After our success at the Battle of Snowshoes, I assess the English will not expect this winter assault. Therefore, unless there is a contrary opinion, I authorize a full attack on Fort William Henry without delay. The commander for this campaign will be Captain François-Pierre de Rigaud de Vaudreuil."

Everyone present knew this already. Governor Vaudreuil wanted the scribes to record this order, to ensure his Canadian troops received all the credit for any success. And he expected success!

General Montcalm, who disagreed with a winter campaign, replied with a question. "So, you would characterize this campaign as a siege?"

The governor considered the question a trap. No matter how he answered, it would be circulated back to Paris with sour opinions. Depending on the results, of course.

"It is winter. As you have so often reminded me, General Montcalm, a siege in winter is not practical. The Canadians of New France will attack this fort as an opportunity…an attack the English will not expect."

Montcalm pressed his point by repeating what Captain Gerrard had just reported. "Because, as Captain Gerrard presented, the grounds around Fort William Henry are too frozen to dig siege trenches."

Governor Vaudreuil's momentary glance at Captain Gerrard was not friendly. The governor wanted his words to be the last ones recorded by the scribes.

"As I said, General, this attack is not intended as a siege. This council is adjourned to follow my given orders."

Away from the council, the governor spoke privately with his brother, Rigaud.

"You heard Captain Gerrard's confirmation. Fort William Henry has only three hundred troops fit to fight. You will command five times that number. But you cannot take siege cannon. Despite this deficiency, the bottom of the cannon embrasures at that fort are only ten feet above the ground. They are within arms' reach of your tallest men. Take sufficient scaling ladders. Your numbers are large enough to sustain the losses necessary to storm the walls and invest this fort. This is what I expect of you."

Once free of the exploitive politics of the governor's council of war, General Montcalm walked towards his headquarters with his aide-de-camp Captain Bougainville and Scout Captain Philippe Gerrard. He asked his captain of scouts for an opinion on the likelihood of success in this attack on Fort William Henry.

"You presented the council with information that the garrison of Fort William Henry is infested with smallpox, and those not sick are almost too weak to stand their posts. That the fort will capitulate quickly. Do you feel the same way out here on the street?"

"Yes, General. If we lay formal siege to this fort, it will capitulate within days. But it will not capitulate in this winter assault."

Montcalm abruptly stopped walking towards army headquarters. "Why do you say that?"

"As I reported to you earlier, General, the garrison of this fort is the 44th Foot Regiment. About a hundred of them are survivors of the massacre by the native tribes at the Battle of Monongahela two years ago. The soldiers captured after that battle were tortured and slaughtered in gruesome ways. We witnessed this sort of brutality at Fort Oswego. At Fort Duquesne, the butchery was worse—much, much worse. I was there. When Rigaud attacks with his tribal allies, the men inside the fort, sick or not, will fight to their deaths before they are taken captive. And that fort has a lot of cannons! The fort's commander, Major Eyre, is a veteran English officer. He is an engineer and an artillery specialist. Two years ago, with only four cannons, he repulsed the grenadier attack led by General von Dieskau at the first battle on the south shore of that lake. That was before Fort William Henry even existed. And Major Eyre built Fort William Henry! This commandant will not surrender it easily, if at all. I'm not saying the fort cannot be taken by a ladder assault with the number of men Rigaud brings with him. But this victory is not certain. It will be a bloody affair for both sides. Even if we win, we cannot hold this fort. We can raise a flag or set it afire, but then we must retreat. If we stay, we lose men to disease whom we can ill afford to lose. I think a direct assault is unnecessary…sir."

Philippe paused to allow the general to consider this information.

"You believe the governor's order to attack Fort William Henry is unnecessary?! The governor asked for opinions. You gave no such opinion at the governor's council."

"Governor Vaudreuil will order his brother Rigaud to do this. If I gave my opinion at the council, it would have provoked an open argument."

"Captain Gerrard, I give you permission to speak bluntly. If I gave you the order to attack Fort William Henry, how would you do it?"

"General, I do not want to presume—"

"Tell me your plan of attack, Captain," Montcalm said tersely, "without caveats!"

"Yes, sir. In the winter, doing anything in this dense wilderness is all about logistics. The more men you take, the more problems you have just to feed them. I would take less than half the men Rigaud intends. You can move faster. But I would select men who are familiar with how to survive out there, my scouts, most of the marines, some of the militia, maybe fifty of the warriors, and any of the grenadiers and piquets who would volunteer to go with us, as those veterans are always welcome. In total, no more than... six hundred men.

"I would also take a battery of three field howitzers, dismantled and dragged on ice sledges, plus two mortars. But this artillery would be used only to provide cover for the raiders, because that's what we would be, just raiders. There would be no assault on the walls. We would burn and destroy everything of value outside the walls. All the supply sheds, all the boats, the construction of the new entrenchments being built east of the fort, plus all the boat building tools, the ways, the winches, ropes, tackle, the whip-saw stands and equipment. I would position a hundred men to guard the road coming up from Fort Edward in case the English attempt to reinforce Fort William Henry in the middle of the raid, though that is unlikely. Capture anyone foolish enough to come outside the walls. Maybe use the mortars to toss hot rounds into the fort to start some fires. Then after two or three days, unless we find other exposed targets, we withdraw. My goal would be to destroy any capability that allows the English to launch an attack on Fort Carillon this summer. Because that is certainly the English intention, sir."

Montcalm nodded in agreement. "Very good, Captain Gerrard. I agree with you. This is my confidential order to you. Except for taking cannon with you, I order you to convince Rigaud de Vaudreuil to execute *your* plan."

Philippe squinted. "The governor expects Rigaud to assault the walls!"

Montcalm's smile was sanguine. "What the governor expects is success! Success of his military genius in contrast to mine, which he will describe in his report to the Minister of Marine. Therefore, I order you to bring him this success! Convince Rigaud! That should not be too difficult. That man seems obsessed with only his reputation." Montcalm's expression and tone changed to that of a commander who expected results. "But conduct *your* raid, Captain, in a way that minimizes casualties, so I can conduct a proper siege and invest that fort when summer comes."

*

After leaving the war council, Major Michel Péan pocketed the ribbon and medallion. He brooded about his surprise elevation to chevalier as he walked to his lavish Québec City mansion.

There is simply no reason to elevate my status…and no reason to do this so publicly. What do they gain from my elevation?

But another battle to fight lay ahead of him. He would spend this last night with his beautiful wife, Angélique des Méloizes.

At least, I had three glorious weeks with her, he groused.

Angélique had a whispered reputation in Québec City that was not very kind. Michel Péan did not care, and he would challenge any man to a duel who dared to say something insulting about her within his hearing. They had been married almost ten years. She was from an aristocratic family, a descendent of René-Louis Chartier de Lotbinière, judge of the Provost and Admiralty Courts.

Angélique was an ambitious woman, who avidly desired to become a member of the Court of Versailles. For that she needed money—lots of money—sponsors, and influence. She appreciated the power of her beauty and used sex for influence with abandon. Intendant Bigôt showed her a way to get the monies she needed by marrying Major Michel Péan, who had become a high percentage partner in Intendant Bigôt's Grand Company. Then, while the major was away on military missions, all the money earned from his shares in the Grand Company flowed directly to her. In return, she shared Bigôt's bed.

More recently, Angélique shared Governor Vaudreuil's bed. It was a much more lucrative dalliance. He was very forthcoming with suggestions on how to receive a proper introduction at the Court of Versailles.

"You need to own landed estates back in France," Vaudreuil told her. "And use that to leverage a titled marquisate from the king. A simple enough task, if you are properly supported by persons of influence in the Court."

Angélique was already deep in her plans for that, and Michel Péan—although he did not know this—had a role to play. He was important to her, and she did not neglect him.

On the day Michel Péan returned to Québec City, Angélique left the bed of her current patron and lavished affections on her husband, who she considered the best lover she ever had. In her way, she really did love the major. And there was no doubt he loved her, to the point of distraction. Michel Péan was a shrewd man, but he had a blind eye where she was concerned. She spent his money, much of it back in France, and on what Michel did not know. But he did not care, so long as she was happy. Angélique des Méloizes was the most extraordinary woman he'd ever known. And for some reason, she loved him. Probably the money had something to do with it. Even so, she was a gift from God. When he got home from Louisbourg, she proved it again.

Major Péan entered the foyer of his mansion. Angélique had been waiting. She flew to his arms and kissed him amorously. She was already dressed for bed.

"Come with me," she whispered seductively. "My body aches for you."

Though it was early in the afternoon, Angélique led her husband up the stairs where the bed had been turned down for them by the servants. Mesmerized by just her scent, all of Michel Péan's stress and worries melted away. They shed clothing in a frenzy as they walked into the bedchamber. When naked, Angélique took him in her mouth to increase his excitement, then stood up to press him onto his back in the bed. Angélique guided Michel's hands, encouraging him to fondle and touch her nakedness before straddling his waist.

"God, I love you," Michel whispered reverently.

"Show me," she challenged.

They both exhaled groans of pleasure as she slowly lowered her hips over his hardness.

Michel Péan was submerged in wonderfulness. If only he could live this moment forever, like an immortal being…like her.

"I think you are an angel."

"I am." She moaned the words, orgasm already affecting her speech. "I will show you."

Michel felt the miraculous gripping sensation, as something in her sex took intimate hold of him. Then Angélique undulated her hips in that delicious way. No other woman he'd ever known had ever been able to do this. She continued slowly, controlling his reaction, increasing his desperate need for release in tiny steps. And when it peaked, his body thrust upward in an arch. Michel Péan cried out from the shattering intensity of the orgasm that spiraled over him in waves.

It was the first of many.

CHAPTER 17
LA ROCHELLE, FRANCE
MARCH 1757
Linard the Lanyard

Madame Margaux-Lyneth Dubonnet was exhausted. It took ten days to reach Amiens, with only brief stops at night, and only when the steering lamps on the coach could not project enough light to permit the driver to rein the horses through the darkness.

During the daylight hours, she did her best to study the journals along the way. It was difficult. Reading even a few sentences while the coach was rocking and swaying made her nauseous. But the chronicle quilled by this tenth century Normandie bishop was both disturbing and mesmerizing—because it might be truthful.

Bishop Brevelaer began by inking his sworn oath and testimony before God that what he put down in this journal was true. Margaux understood enough of the Roman Latin to realize the priest who set down this script was terrified. He was afflicted by a loathsome creature from the darkness, a *vulnax wraith*, an unnatural spirit, a demon that attacked people in their sleep, and devoured small portions of their life essence to sustain its own ability to endure.

> *Licking life from living flesh, leaving necroses, bruises invisible and painful every place touched that never heal. Night after night, the vulnax returns and gnaws towards the soul, pulping muscle, grinding bone, until its victims go mad with pain. Some take their own life hoping to escape, only to fall into the dominion of absolute evil for embracing this choice: eternal damnation.*

Margaux closed the journal after reading that. What a hideous fate! She raised the mud flap to gaze outside the window, paying homage to beauty ordained by the Creator, a tree, birds in flight, a clear stream running alongside the road, animals grazing, spring crops in the field, anything she could dwell upon that helped dispel the foul images the words had evoked.

How did Corrinne and Lord VanderMeer ever come to be ensnared in this web of evil?

Margaux paused in her impulsive deliberation. She was not certain what she should do. It must be written in the other journals. And Bishop Brevelaer warned, a malevolent spirit awaits those who dare to confront this wraith.

After several days and nights by candlelight, Margaux finished studying the first journal. It described a long war and the joining of four Great Houses, former enemies that put aside differences of less importance to defeat an evil conqueror named Lord Vaelblez. He was a man possessed by the vulnax wraith. His troops were cannibalistic and would consume the flesh from the fallen on a battlefield.

How lovely.

Upon reaching Amiens, Margaux took a full day of rest at her home. She purified herself, then filled a few trunks of baggage to support the rest of the journey to La Rochelle. She added six letters to the regimental dispatch pouch. She had managed to write to Gustave, apologizing for not writing every single day. She added more pages than usual to each of them, describing truthfully the events associated with her visit to the ducal palace of Louis Ernest, how she met Lord VanderMeer, if only briefly, and witnessed his heart-wrenching death. The joy at seeing the portrait of her sister, Corrinne. That she hired William LaFont from the Amiens bookseller to research and discover the lineage and history of her infancy and childhood.

I am now obsessed with communicating with my sister, Corrinne, who yet has no idea I even exist. I have three journals written in Roman Latin by a Normandie bishop, inked over seven hundred years ago. I promised Lord VanderMeer I would ensure Lady Corrinne receives these journals. To do this, I begin traveling tomorrow morning to the port of La Rochelle, where a Dutch ship sits anchored in the harbor. It flies Dutch colors and the Dutch Republic is neutral. I'm assured by the Duke of Brunswick that this ship can pass by the guns of the English blockade cruisers and enter Louisbourg harbor. This is presumptuous, of course, but...

In addition to six bodyguards, Madame Dubonnet was now accompanied by a small troop of French cavalrymen. She left the Dutch ambassador behind. His presence allowed her to pass through the Austrian Netherlands without delay. But he was highly inquisitive of her reasons for going to La Rochelle in such a hurry. Now that she was back in France, he saw no value for what she intended to do. Charles' paralysis and death was due to an assassination attempt. Margaux was suspicious of the motives behind the ambassador's incessant questions. She thanked him, said to thank the Duke, and told him to take the Dutch coach back to Amsterdam.

Because she was the wife of the Auvergne Regimental commander, she arranged her transport from Amiens to La Rochelle using military courier coaches. Not as fast as single-rider horse couriers. These coaches, nevertheless, were still organized for speed. She ordered fresh horses at each relay station. Every two days, she permitted herself three hours of rest outside the coach and a bath. She reached La Rochelle by the third week of March and hired a local coach for travel. She visited the harbormaster first and was relieved to learn *William's Queen* was still at anchor.

"It came down the maintenance shipways almost two weeks ago. It should have sailed by now, but I hear the captain is having problems with his crew."

"Where can I find the captain without having to go out to the ship?"

"The Harbor Hotel," the man replied.

Madame Dubonnet was taken to the Palais de Aquitaine, an old hotel dating back centuries. She secured a suite of rooms for a week, ordered a bath for herself and her maidservants, and paid all her bodyguards for their long service in silver and gold coin.

"I may not return to Amiens for a month, maybe more."

She dismissed four of them, indicating if they returned to Amiens she would employ them again when she returned. Róbert and Marcel, the most expert of the men, agreed to stay with her.

After saying good-bye to the others, she went to the room's writing desk and quickly inked a message to Captain LaTour. She pressed a wax seal on it and handed it to Róbert.

"Go out to *William's Queen* and give this to the captain. The message states that a courier awaits him at this hotel with a message from the ducal palace in Amsterdam and Lord Charles VanderMeer. It is vital the captain comes to this hotel to receive this message. Nothing more. Do not mention my name or anything about me. Bring him back with you, if possible. In the meantime, I am going to bathe and rest until you return."

"Yes, Madame."

"And you should both get rooms here. Tell them I will pay for it."

"Yes, Madame."

"Marcel, go to the Harbor Hotel and see if Captain LaTour is staying there. If he is there, tell him you are escorting a courier from the Duke of Brunswick with a message from Lord Charles VanderMeer. Do not mention my name or anything about me. If he is available, we will meet later today. If he is not there, don't leave a message. Just come back and tell me."

"Yes, Madame."

Tired as she was, Margaux could not sleep. She was bathed and dressed before Marcel returned. The captain was indeed staying at the Harbor Hotel, but he was out on his ship.

"Good. Get something to eat. Then wait outside my door until Róbert returns."

At that moment, Róbert was on the helm deck of *William's Queen*, standing before a frowning Captain LaTour and Victorio, as the captain broke the seal and read the message. He exchanged looks of surprise with Victorio.

"You are a courier? For Lord VanderMeer? Is he still alive?"

"Captain, I am just the messenger to you. The courier is waiting for you at the hotel. That is all I know. Except, I was asked to bring you back with me, if possible. It's my understanding the information for you is vital."

They turned their backs to confer in whispers. "Should I go alone?"

"No," Victorio replied instantly. "Tell the crew we are going ashore to retrieve a message from Lord VanderMeer. They still have cargo to load. They won't go anywhere."

"Very well," he told the messenger. "Wait down on the raft. Both of us will come with you."

LaTour called the crewmen on deck and told them he was going ashore to retrieve a message from Lord VanderMeer. He put the acting bosun, a dependable seaman named Linard, in charge while he was gone.

"Send our cargo launch over to the normal place to wait for me. I won't be gone long."

Captain LaTour and Victorio joined Róbert in the hired harbor launch. It took almost an hour to get ashore and over to the Palais de Aquitaine. Róbert left them in the splendor of the atrium.

"I will inform the courier you are here."

Margaux listened to Róbert's report.

"I want to meet with the captain, here, in my room, alone. Marcel, you stay with the other man for now."

They went down and Róbert explained the courier's preference. "This is Marcel. He will wait with…your name is, Victorio? Marcel will wait with you, for now. It may be that you will be invited to see the courier later, but for now this meeting will be private."

Captain LaTour ogled the antique opulence he passed along the hallways: the chandeliers, the paintings, the gilded furniture. Róbert knocked on the door and stepped halfway through.

"Madame, Captain LaTour is here."

"Let him in."

Madame? LaTour was surprised to hear a female voice answer. The next surprise left him standing immobile just inside the door, his mouth hanging open in astonishment.

"Please come in, Captain LaTour." Margaux gestured at a chair for him.

"What! My lady! What are you doing here? How did you get here?!"

She stepped closer to the captain. His uniform was sweat-stained. He smelled of it. Gustave often had this working odor when he came home from field exercises with his regiment. It instantly told her a lot about this man. It was pungent, familiar, and comfortable to her.

"Prepare yourself for another surprise, Captain. I am not Lady Corrinne. My name is Margaux-Lyneth Dubonnet. I am Lady Corrinne's sister."

Captain LaTour felt as if someone had hit him on the head with a belaying pin.

"*Sister!*"

"Yes, Captain. I am Corrinne's sister."

"Lady Corrinne's sister?!"

"Yes, Captain." She smiled. "Sister."

"B-but she has never mentioned a sister to me. And you look identical to her! You even speak like her."

"That's because we are *twins*."

"*Twins*! Her babies are twins!"

"I know, Captain. I hope to see them someday."

LaTour had never felt so bewildered. "Forgive me, Madame. What is your name again?"

"Margaux-Lyneth Dubonnet," she said, enunciating slowly. "I have traveled here from Amiens…actually, I traveled here from Amsterdam."

"Amsterdam! That's where I left Lord VanderMeer. Did you see him?"

"Captain, please sit down with me, and I will explain."

LaTour stepped tentatively to a cushioned chair and sat down, his eyes affixed to her face.

Margaux took another chair at the same parlor table, which was covered with a pristine white cloth.

"Would you like some wine, Captain?"

"Um…yes. *Merci.*"

She poured them each a half goblet of red.

LaTour took a large gulp.

"You asked about Lord VanderMeer." Margaux's expression turned solemn. "Yes, I saw him. I am sorry to tell you, Lord VanderMeer has passed away."

"Oh, no!" LaTour groaned. His face wrinkled in pain.

Margaux saw tears in his eyes, which, of course, made her eyes fill as well.

"Apologies, Madame," LaTour said in a grief-laden voice, "I knew his death was coming, but Charles was my dear friend."

"I understand."

"You were there? When he passed?"

"Yes." She told him the startling story of how she came to be at Charles' bedside at the moment of his death. "Charles was delirious. He thought I was Corrinne. I let him believe that to comfort him. So he would not die alone."

LaTour slowly regained his composure. "You came all this way just to tell me about Lord VanderMeer?"

"Well, yes. But not just about his passing."

Margaux lifted the satchel and placed it to one side on top of the table. "These leather-bound journals are centuries old. They were inked by a Normandie priest. His name was Bishop Brevelaer. Before he died, Lord VanderMeer paid a scholar to locate and obtain these journals for him. These were very important to Charles. Believing I was Corrinne, Charles gave them to me, insisting that I read them. Which means it is important for Corrinne to read them. I've read the first journal and perused the last two. They are inked in Roman Latin. Very difficult to interpret." She frowned. "The words describe unnatural things, evil things, about something called a *vulnax*."

Margaux saw the captain's eyes widen. She paused before continuing. "Then you know of what I speak?"

He took a hasty swallow of wine. "I know a little about this. Lord and Lady VanderMeer knew everything."

She refilled his glass. "Charles ranted about the dangers contained in these journals before he died."

LaTour felt a terrible unease come over him, as it did each time he thought about the wraith.

"Madame, I know enough to tell you, whatever those journals claim, it is real. I have witnessed this…*thing*. It disturbs me greatly to even speak of it."

She saw profound fear in the eyes of the sea captain and suddenly felt nervous.

"Very well. We will not speak any more about the journals. Instead, I will speak about Louis Ernest, the Duke of Brunswick. He told me that Charles' paralysis and death was caused by an assassination attempt when he was in the American city of Boston?"

"Yes. That is true. It is the reason why I took Lady Corrine and her children to Louisbourg. So they would be protected while Charles came further with me to Amsterdam."

"The Duke believes that Lady Corrinne and her children are still in danger, even in Louisbourg. That assassins may already be there. He claims my sister and her children need to be transported away from that place. And since your vessel is owned by Lord and Lady VanderMeer, the Dukes expects you to do this. That is the other message I bring to you."

"It is true," LaTour said slowly, measuring out his words, "I fly a Dutch flag. But *William's Queen* is a conscripted French naval vessel. I am a French naval officer. I must do what the French navy tells me to do. As it happens, Admiral de la Motte has already ordered me to sail to Louisbourg, but on a military mission. I should have sailed two weeks ago. But there is a problem. Most of my crew has sailed with me for nine years. Now, half of them have decided not to sail with me anymore. There have been some unexplained deaths, and with the war…many of these seamen have families. I've managed to keep them around long enough to careen the hull and cajoled them to remain until the cargo was loaded, all the while trying to change their minds. Unsuccessfully, I might add. The last of the cargo loads tomorrow. But without this crew, I can sail nowhere. It will take me weeks to find enough men to fill out my crew. Months, even! The French navy has press-ganged any experienced seamen within miles of this port."

"If they change their minds and decide to crew with you, when could you sail?"

"With tomorrow's tide. And I would do it before they changed their minds back again."

"Of course. You've offered them money?"

"I have."

This cannot be allowed to continue, she decided.

"What did your crew think of my sister?"

"Lady Corrinne? She knew all their names. They revered her. We all did."

She knew all their names. Margaux focused on that attribute. *Memory*. Margaux had a talent for remembering names as well. People liked being remembered. It made people feel valued and appreciated. It inspired loyalty. *They are loyal to Corrinne*, Margaux thought. *She probably talked with them, too. Complimented them. Noticed things about them.*

"What if I ask your crew to sail with you…*for her?* This is something Corrinne would do, yes?"

Captain LaTour stared.

"What?"

"Madame Dubonnet, I am sorry to stare. You look, talk, act, and now it appears you even think like Lady Corrinne. I am trying to get used to the idea that there are now two of you in my life. I am twice blessed," he added.

Margaux sensed the compliment was genuine. Everything Captain LaTour said, his expressions, his honesty, his terrible sadness to learn of Charles' death, the fact his crew had remained with him for nine years, all of this spoke to the strong empathetic leadership of the captain. *Corrinne must really like you*, she thought. *I do already.*

When the pause became prolonged, LaTour spoke again.

"Madame, my first mate, Victorio, is waiting in the atrium. If you plan to come aboard my ship, he can help with the crew…after he meets you first… and after he swoons, of course."

She stood and went to door. "Róbert, please bring up the captain's first mate." She returned to her chair. "You will have to tell me what to say."

"The crew talks with Victorio more than with me. They trust him. They trust me, too, but as a captain. They seek counsel from Victorio."

She poured some more wine. The captain was finally starting to relax.

Róbert opened the door again and gestured for Victorio to enter. Margaux stood and smiled. Captain LaTour stood too. He enjoyed Victorio's open-mouthed surprise.

Victorio came a few steps closer and dropped to one knee. "My Lady Corrinne, I am speechless at seeing you again."

Margaux touched him on a shoulder, so he would rise, then embraced and kissed his cheeks.

"As I told your captain, I am not Lady Corrinne. I am her sister, Margaux-Lyneth Dubonnet, from Amiens."

Victorio looked at Captain LaTour, who nodded in affirmation. "Now I really don't know what to say. I did not know she had a sister."

"We were orphaned and separated in our infancy. Lady Corrinne doesn't know I exist…as I did not know she existed until a few months ago. I will let Captain LaTour explain all the details of this to you. But as the captain and I have discussed and agreed, I will come out to the ship and convince the crew to sail with you, to rescue and transport Lady Corrinne and her children away from Louisbourg. We need your help on what I might say."

"This is remarkable." Victorio rubbed at his eyes. "If I close my eyes… your voice…I mean…you are remarkable."

Captain LaTour handed Victorio his glass of wine. "Here, drink some of this. It helps."

Victorio became increasingly helpful as the minutes passed.

"How many men are in your crew? And how many admitted they will be leaving?"

"My normal complement is thirty seamen. And my crew are all veterans. Four of them died over the last year…all of them grotesquely murdered. We have not discovered who did this or why. That is the main source of their angst. Out of the twenty-six men remaining, sixteen have told me they are leaving. That leaves me with ten. I could barely weigh anchor and cross the harbor with that many men…let alone an ocean."

Margaux nodded. "I understand. If Corrinne knew all their names, I want to greet each one of them, by name, before I ask them to change their minds. I have an idea. We need to make a list for me to use."

It took two hours of discussion, Margaux's questions, their answers. In the end, they reached a consensus. Then they tested Madame Dubonnet's memory. It was as remarkable as Lady Corrinne's.

"So…I will come aboard your ship in the morning, and together we will convince the crew to sail to Louisbourg. These men are frightened by unexplainable deaths. But frightened men march into battle all the time if they believe in what they are doing. My husband's regiment does this all the time. Rescuing my sister, Lady Corrinne, who knows them all by their first name, gives real meaning to why they are doing something so dangerous."

Victorio was nervous. He did not wish for her endeavor to end in an embarrassing failure. "Madame, I've tried to convince them for almost two months. These are men who trust me. But I could not turn even one of them. Their minds are made up," Victorio said. "I just wanted you to know that. And I also want you to know, if anyone could persuade them, it would be Lady Corrinne. They would do anything for her. So, why not her sister?"

"Your visit alone, they will consider a miracle," Captain LaTour added.

"Good, let's use that, too. You know why? It is almost a miracle that I am here. It is certainly fate and a destiny. And they have a part to play in it."

Yet Margaux discerned the lingering doubt behind their hopeful expressions. Margaux stood, and the men followed suit. She embraced and kissed them both.

"Now, I want you both to be at ease. Captain LaTour? Victorio?" They nodded. "Good! Don't worry! Everything will turn out all right."

After they were gone, Margaux asked Róbert and Marcel to dine with her, something she had not done before. But out of all her bodyguards, these two men were veteran Auvergne Regimental sergeants, personally selected by her husband. They had been with her the longest and were the most devoted.

"This dinner is overdue. You have served me well, for a long time, and never with more excellence than during these last two months. I want to tell you a story about my family history. You deserve to know everything, and there is nothing I want to hide. You will be with me when I go aboard *William's Queen* in the morning. You will be with me when we leave La Rochelle to go north to Brest and Landerneau. And you will be with me wherever I go from there…and I am uncertain where that will be. It is fair for you to ask why."

Margaux bathed again after dinner. Relaxed and wrapped in several towels, she sat down at the escritoire to compose *the* letter to Corrinne.

There was so much to tell her. It would end up being twelve rambling pages. Almost every page had some type of extraordinary revelation to explain. The page describing her account of Charles VanderMeer's death was the most difficult to pen.

Charles' delirium was so overwhelming, he immediately believed it was you he saw standing at his bedside. It made him so happy you had come. So, I allowed him to believe this. He said you were the most beautiful and the most remarkable woman he had ever known. And that you brought him great joy. So, I told him I loved him, and that I would kiss the children for him. And I hugged him. I knew him for mere minutes, but I sobbed as if I had known him all my life. I held his gaze in mine and watched him pass on. I hoped to give him comfort he was not alone. I am crying now even as I write this. Forgive me if I have trespassed.

On the last page, she described how she would speak to the crew. That most of them were reluctant to sail because of the inexplicable murders. She wrote out what she planned to say the next morning to change their minds.

If you are now reading this, then I obviously said something convincing.

When I leave La Rochelle, I plan to travel to Brest to see my father, Lucais de Clermont. He designs and builds ships for the French navy. I will probably stay there for a long while, as my husband Gustave de Dubonnet is the commander of the Auvergne Regiment and has already marched to fight yet another war. I have also hired a young scholar, skilled in historical research, to learn the history of our birth. Having found you by destiny, I feel an obligation to that destiny to learn our birthing history. The scholar's name is William La Mont. I gave him a bag of silver and gold coinage and sent him on his way. Hopefully, I will write to you in the future with more welcome news.

I have often stared into a mirror and talked to the reflection, to get advice from my subconscious—at least that is what I would tell myself. I always felt better after doing this, eerie as it seemed. Now I know the reflection was not me...it was you that I saw. So, in a way, you have shared in my happiest and saddest moments. I cannot wait to see you,

Corrinne. May God's angels sit at your side always to keep you and your
children safe and bless you as you awaken and before you go to sleep.

With all my love,
Margaux

When Margaux was finished, she wiped away the tears and read the
entire letter over, scratching out so many words, she had to replace five of
the pages completely with new ones.

"This is possibly the poorest, most splotched correspondence I have ever
inked," she grumbled to herself.

Margaux made that a postscript line, along with an apology. Instead of
folding up the twelve pages, she left the pages fully open and enclosed them
in order within a small square of sketching canvas she found available in the
escritoire. On impulse, she also took a special sheet of paper from the valise
she carried. This one already contained a special writing, but she added to
the top of the page a title, *My Earliest Memory of You*. She placed that page
in the back of all the others. Then she pulled the corners of the sketching
canvas to the center and dripped a heavy amount of wax over the juncture of
the corners to seal it and impressed it with the military signet of the Auvergne
Regiment. In an afterthought, she inscribed Corrinne's name on the front of
the missive, using the special florid script she had learned from her religious
tutors, to give it the appearance of a special present.

With that finished, Margaux perused the last two Brevelaer journals for a
while until she fell asleep. Roman Latin required careful concentration. There
was not enough time to study them more thoroughly. But she understood
enough to appreciate the last few warnings from Bishop Brevelaer.

> *A person possessed by a vulnax wraith must be buried alive, to trap*
> *the evil spirit within the body. The body must decompose back into the*
> *dust from whence it came, for the possession to end. Even the bones.*

Burying people alive? It gave her nightmares.

*

The next morning, she broke her fast with her bodyguards. The day was
going to be sunny. But it was still March and the sea breezes from the ocean
lowered the air temperatures over the harbor to January levels. She carried

the letter to Corrinne inside the satchel of journals and hugged the satchel to her chest, not entrusting this small but precious cargo to anyone else.

Margaux went to the harbormaster first and asked if he could supply her with a boat for the day. He was already enchanted with her beauty and agreed immediately.

The harbor boat was rowed by four men with a *le barreur*, a helmsman at the stern. The boat was painted, with distinctive colors of red, white, and blue stripes, to indicate someone important was aboard, which was normally used for senior navy or city officials.

As they neared, Margaux marveled at the beauty of *William's Queen*. Even reefed, the new sails of white canvas bunched on the different masts gleamed in the morning sunlight. There was a long rectangular wooden raft lashed to the ship's port side. Eight paces wide and ten paces long, she would learn this was used as a platform to transfer cargo on and off. There were two crewmen waiting on the raft to secure the harbor boat lines to the cleats. A stepping ladder with stiffened-rope guides was extended down to the raft from the helm deck.

Many of the crew were standing along the main deck rail, watching the approach of the harbor launch. They had been told Madame Margaux Dubonnet was coming, and her relationship to Lady Corrinne? They were *sisters*! The crew was curious about this exciting new circumstance. But Captain LaTour had reinforced the need to be cautious about what they might say. He reminded them that morning, "While Madame Dubonnet is Lady Corrinne's sister, Madame Dubonnet believes Lady Corrinne is married to Lord Charles VanderMeer. Not Philippe Gerrard! That perception must not be changed."

This was a smuggling ship. A smuggling ship had secrets to keep. The crew naturally understood this. They may not feel predisposed to sacrifice their lives for Lord VanderMeer, but confronting dangers to protect Lady Corrinne was another matter. She was very important to them.

Captain LaTour watched Madame Dubonnet's approach through his telescope.

"Victorio, if this works, it will be for one reason alone. Lady Corrinne was one of us long before Philippe Gerrard. She is a member of this crew, just like you or me."

LaTour handed the telescope to Victorio. His second-in-command looked at her face. There was no mistaking that smile. She had her hair braided up, much like Lady Corrinne would wear her hair on occasion.

"My God! She looks exactly like Lady Corrinne!"

"At least we now know we were not dreaming yesterday," Captain LaTour said. "*All hands on deck!*" he ordered loudly.

Captain LaTour went down the ladder and over the raft to where the harbormaster's boat was being tied off. He extended a hand to help Madame Dubonnet step onto the gently bobbing platform. They spoke to one another for a minute.

The two line-handlers from *William's Queen* looked back at Victorio. They waved their hands and pointed with excitement.

Aboard the ship, Victorio smiled and returned the wave. He and the rest of the crew could not hear what was being said. Victorio turned to the crew standing along the trail.

"All right, form two lines abreast, right here. Take off your hats. Be respectful. Remember what the captain told you. And be prepared to hear some bad news. But seeing her is good news, yes? Make her feel welcome."

Margaux was not certain how long she would be on the ship. *However long it takes*. She turned to the boat captain and handed him some silver and asked that he return an hour before sunset. The lines were cast off and the boat rowed away.

Captain LaTour slipped her arm to his elbow and escorted her to the ladder. He followed her up until they stood together, along with her bodyguards, on the main deck.

Margaux could see some smiles and deferential movements by the crewmen. It was obvious they saw the likeness to Lady Corrinne, and what they saw, they liked...a lot.

"*Bonjour!*"

"*Bonjour*, Madame!" the crew replied in one voice.

She began slowly, and the crew hung on each word. "My name is Margaux-Lyneth Dubonnet. I am from Amiens in eastern France. By now, Captain LaTour and Victorio have explained to you that I am Lady Corrinne's sister. Lord Charles VanderMeer is the son of Louis Ernest, Duke of Brunswick-Wolfenbüttel. All of you know about the attempted assassination on Lord VanderMeer that left him paralyzed." The crew nodded. "The Duke contacted me because his son's life was failing. He asked me to visit with Charles in

Amsterdam, which I was happy to do. The Duke also sent me here to see all of you for a reason. Before I tell you about that, I want to become properly acquainted with each of you."

The day before, with the help of Captain LaTour and Victorio, they had made a list of the crew members' names and added something distinguishing about each man's appearance so she could distinguish each. They placed a star to the left of the name of any man who chose not to sail again. Then Margaux memorized the list. And to the captain's and Victorio's amazement, she recited the list of names and the distinguishing characteristics twice, without error. Doing a third variation, she had them describe a characteristic at random, and she replied with the man's name. She was ready.

Margaux stepped forward to the first man on her left. She noticed he was wearing a white lanyard cord to which a bosun's pipe whistle was attached. *Linard the Lanyard*, she recalled.

"You must be Bosun Linard, I presume."

"*Oui*, Madame," he replied in a tone of wonder.

She smiled and pointed at his chest. "The bosun's pipe."

"Ah, *oui*, of course." Margaux embraced him and kissed his cheeks.

Then she addressed the man standing behind the bosun. He had only one ear, the other one had been torn away long ago in a sail rigging accident. *Etienne One Ear*.

"*C'est un plaisir de vous rencontrer*, Etienne," she greeted before embracing the man.

And the next. He had a rope burn across his face and over his nose. *Gilles of the Rope Burn*.

"*Mon plaisir*, Gilles."

Then came Geron the Toothless. His front teeth were knocked out when the swinging boom of the mizzen mast had smashed into his mouth. Victorio said he had pulled six broken teeth from Geron's mouth…with *pliers*. "*You will know him the moment he smiles*."

Margaux knew him instantly. His smile was terrifying. "*Bonjour*, Geron. I find your curly black hair very handsome."

"You do?" Geron touched his hair and smiled more broadly.

Even more terrifying. She embraced him and moved on to the next. *Remy of the One Crossed Eye*.

"*Bonjour*, Remy. You arrange the cargo lines and tackle, yes?"

"*Oui*, Madame."

"And you reefed the new sails, I've been told. The ship looks beautiful when you see it from afar."

"*Merci*, Madame."

Next stood Tinidor the Unwashed. *"You will know him when you are within a few feet."*

Margaux did not breathe through her nose when she embraced him, but she kissed both his cheeks as the unspoken reward. *That probably does not happen to him very often*, she thought.

And so, it went on. She addressed the men individually. The last man in the line had white hair. He was obviously the oldest man. His skin was permanently weathered and wrinkled. But she perceived a brightness in his blue eyes.

"They call you Turiau, yes?"

"They call me a lot of things, Madame. Grand-père, mostly. I allow it. I probably knew all of their grandmothers, anyway…maybe even a few of their mothers."

Whistles rose from the crewmen.

"They should honor you, I think."

He grinned. "See, you smelly slugs. She knows a real man when she sees one."

Margaux embraced and kissed his cheeks.

Madame Dubonnet had said something unique to each one of them as she moved down the line. By the time she was done, she had addressed every man by his name. She'd complimented them, embraced or kissed their cheeks. And to her surprise, something delightful happened she'd never expected; a connection occurred. It was easy to see this in hindsight. She saw it in their eyes. They had been noticed. It was personal. *Corrinne had made it personal, too*, she thought.

She moved back to the helm deck to stand in front of Captain LaTour. As she began saying more to the crew, Captain LaTour was close enough to notice the four birthmarks on her neck just above where the hair began.

Those marks are the same as Lady Corrinne's!

Margaux was beaming. "I am so grateful to all of you. You've made me feel welcome. I expect Lady Corrinne enjoys seeing you too." She paused and gathered her breath. "For the last two weeks, I have traveled with little rest from Amsterdam to La Rochelle and finally to your ship this morning to fulfill a promise I made to Lord Charles VanderMeer as I sat at his bedside and watched the light go out of his eyes."

Madame Dubonnet did not have to pretend emotion as she recalled this scene. She found it hard for her to continue. Not a sound could be heard coming from the crew on the main deck. She breathed deeply and recovered.

"I am aware that several members of this crew have been murdered without explanation. And that some of you suspect a curse follows this ship."

Ohhh, don't talk about that! Captain LaTour thought with alarm.

"Lady Corrinne and I were separated at the age of two. So long ago, we'd forgotten one another, except for a lingering childhood memory of someone else in our lives. I only learned about Lady Corrinne two months ago. That knowledge brought me to Amsterdam to sit by Lord VanderMeer's bedside, to hold his hand, to comfort him while he died. And because of the promises I made, it has brought me here, to this ship. And now I know all of you. Think about the tragedy and the miracle in all of this. That is called *destiny*," she pronounced the word forcefully. "If there is a curse haunting this ship...then it ends today." She pointed at the deck with emphasis. "There are two of us who worry about you now. Lady Corrinne has not yet learned of me. Think about that. You will carry a letter to her from me. She will learn of me... from you! Imagine her joy! And after that, this wonderful ship will carry Lady Corrinne and her children to safety. You will do this! That is your role in this destiny! And in doing this, you will see evidence that if there ever was a curse, it has been broken."

Captain LaTour's head was spinning. *Madame, you do not know of what you speak! You are standing right above it! And they know it is there!*

"The Duke of Brunswick informed me that the people who killed his son now intend to kill Lady Corrinne. But worse, they intend to kill her children!"

She paused. The crew cast worried glances at one another.

"Unlike you, I've not had the privilege to meet Anamosa, Calypso, and Marcus. Captain LaTour tells me they are a joy to behold, like all little children. Some of you have little children, yes? Lady Corrinne fled to Louisbourg to be safe, surrounded by all those French soldiers. The Duke of Brunswick believes her assassins are already there, lurking among the mercenaries, waiting for the opportunity to commit this heinous murder."

Margaux did not know if this presumption was true, but she could tell this had the same effect on the crew as it had on her when she first heard it.

"I am told that no other ship can sail to Louisbourg faster than this one." A few of the crewmen nodded. "Captain LaTour told me yesterday that some of you have decided to leave the ship. But if that happens, *William's Queen* cannot sail!"

Margaux's voice was filled with emotion as she continued. "It will take weeks for Captain LaTour to find your replacements, if they can be found at all. By then it may be too late! For Lady Corrinne's sake, please do not abandon her and her children. *Please!*"

The crew was not certain what to do. Victorio was standing behind the captain. He saw the crew's hesitation. He raised his hand. "Give us a show of hands. Raise your hand if you will make this voyage."

Almost half immediately raised their hands. Then one by one the others followed. Until only one man remained: *Turiau*.

Madame Dubonnet's expression was one of surprise. She stepped over to Turiau.

"Why, Turiau? Why would you not go?"

"I am too old, Madame. If there is going to be trouble, I would be a burden to the crew. I cannot fight like they can. Better that I stay behind."

The protests started instantly. The men honored Turiau, told him how important he was, that his age did not matter. Turiau was humbled by their unexpected praise. He had unwittingly provoked the crew to act as one.

"You see!" Margaux emphasized to all the seamen. "This is your strength! Every man has value. You are not just one man. You are one crew! You come to the aid of one another. You leave no one behind! I see this in you. Lady Corrinne sees this in you. She knows you will come back for her. And Turiau, your age and wisdom, the experience you bring to this crew, this inspires them! If you do this, you do it together!"

Captain LaTour decided now was the time. "And know that your wages for this trip will be doubled. But only if you all agree to go. We are already short-handed."

This was something LaTour planned to offer as a last resort when the final transfer of cargo came aboard the next day. But now seemed a better time.

"Turiau?"

Turiau slowly raised his hand. The crew broke out in a loud cheer.

"Then it is settled!" Captain LaTour announced. "Once we bring this last load of cargo on board, we sail on the next ebbing tide."

Victorio got the men back to work before they had a chance to rethink their decision. A flag signal was sent to the shore to have the remaining cargo brought out to the raft. It was something else LaTour had purposely delayed, to gain more time to convince the crew not to leave.

The captain took Madame Dubonnet below to the dining cabin. Victorio took the bodyguards to the crew's mess and had food and drink brought to them. He wanted to sit and learn all he could about Madame Dubonnet.

The steward served captain and Margaux coffee and sweetbreads before closing both doors to give them privacy.

"Goodness, this is good coffee."

"Madame, what you just did with my crew, it was something only Lady Corrinne has done. And it seemed as if she were saying the words. Is it true? About the assassins? They are already there? Among the mercenaries?"

"That's what I've been told, Captain." In so many words, but no reason to change the story now.

"Well, at least Henri is there to protect her."

She blinked. "Who is Henri?"

She doesn't know? Captain LaTour thought fast. "Ensign Henri Gerrard is a marine officer of the Troupes de la Marine. He is very devoted to protecting Lady Corrinne and her children. And he is deadly good at what he does."

"That is comforting to know." Margaux lifted the satchel and placed it on the table.

"We've already talked about these journals. You must deliver this priceless cargo to her."

"I will personally place it in her hands," he assured.

"Good. There is also a missive." She showed him the wax-sealed sketching canvass inside the satchel as well. "It's a very long letter to my sister. It is priceless to me. When I saw her portrait, the one Charles painted, there is no denying we are sisters. The portrait now hangs in the ducal palace with a brass plate beneath it describing who she is. There is no dispute about it now."

She has no knowledge of Philippe either, the captain concluded.

"I hired a scholar to research our common birth and infancy. What little I know, I include in my letter. I hope to learn the identity of our mother and father...and our lineage, if possible. You can tell her that. I told her how to write to me. But if you take her away from Louisbourg, she will have to write me, so I know where she is."

"I will make certain she knows this. Lady Corrinne will be overjoyed when she learns about you. If I am a judge of her reaction, she will write the same day she receives this letter."

Captain LaTour reached over and knocked on the serving window. The steward, Pierrik, entered. He whispered something in the captain's ear before leaving again.

"What?"

"Do you like coffee?"

"I do. Coffee is hard to get in Amiens."

"Lady Corrinne loves coffee."

The steward returned with a five-pound canvas sack of roasted coffee beans. LaTour untied the throat lacing and let her smell the contents. Her eyes widened.

"This comes from the Antilles. Smells good, yes? Consider this a gift from your sister."

They talked for some time. Captain LaTour told her about his sea experience, being careful not to say too much. She talked about her husband. How they met. That he was marching again in this new war. LaTour told her about the twins and the home Lord and Lady VanderMeer had in Boston.

There was a knock at the door. "Enter."

It was Róbert. "Madame, the harbormaster's boat has returned. It is needed by someone else."

"I will come up shortly. Take this sack of coffee with you."

As Róbert left, Victorio entered. "*Pardon*, Madame. Captain, the rest of the cargo is here, but the harbormaster's boat is blocking the loading platform."

Madame Dubonnet handed the satchel of journals to the captain. "I guess I must leave now!"

LaTour placed the satchel in his cabin.

Together they went to the helm deck. Madame Dubonnet said good-bye to a few of the crew members she saw. There were a dozen more down on the loading raft, standing by to receive the cargo. Once she neared the harbormaster's boat, the crewmen took off their sock-caps in farewell.

"Many of you live in Le Havre, yes? Well, when you come back to Le Havre, send a message to me in Amiens. It's only a hundred miles away. It would take me but two or three days by carriage to come and visit you.

I would consider it an honor. I will help celebrate your return with your families, and maybe you can bring a letter to me from my sister."

She embraced Captain LaTour last.

"You are a very honorable man, Captain. It's easy to see why Corrinne thinks so highly of you. Go with God. Bring her to safety."

"You have my word, Madame."

CHAPTER 18
LAKE GEORGE WILDERNESS
MARCH 1757
Fort William Henry

The French began the winter campaign to attack Fort William Henry in early March. The various detachments making up the French assault force had already been marshaled at Fort Saint-Jean on the Richelieu River in preparation for this, a hundred twenty miles north of Fort Carillon. They totaled more than fifteen hundred men. Two hundred fifty French regulars, grenadiers drawn from the four metropolitan regiments of regulars, plus fifty piquets, selected from each of those same metropolitan regiments. To these were added three hundred Troupes de la Marines, including all the marines recently returned from Louisbourg, one hundred thirty-two of Captain Philippe Gerrard's scouts, and six hundred men of the Québec City and Montréal militias, called up expressly for this purpose. Added to this was a hundred officers to command these companies, most of whom were Canadian. This included Major Michel Péan.

As was his practice, Governor Vaudreuil invited over three hundred tribal warriors to join the campaign by giving them the usual promises of plunder and trophies. Joining the French with enthusiasm were Abenaki and Caughnawaga Mohawk warriors, collectively referred to as the "Praying Indians" because of their hundred-year association with the Jesuits and subsequent conversion to Catholic Christianity. But this conversion to a religion of love and peace did not dissuade them from plundering forts after winning a battle and scalping the survivors before suspending them over fires, until their skin blistered, peeled, blackened, and sloughed away from the bones to sizzle in the coals. The hideous screams of the victims were indescribable.

It is their traditional right, the pious Jesuits rationalized.

*

With the French forces organized into columns, Captain Philippe Gerrard led his six companies of *coureur de bois* scouts as the vanguard of the assault force. The weather remained bitterly cold, but it had stopped snowing following five straight days of winter storms. The scouts were spread out and moved south, down the Richelieu River on ice skates. They were on guard against a ranger ambush somewhere along their intended line of march, first to Fort Saint-Frédéric on Lake Champlain. Philippe did not anticipate a skirmish after the bloodying the rangers received the previous month, but the rangers had a nasty tendency of launching surprise attacks when least expected.

On this first leg of the journey, they were still deep within French territory. Philippe's usually cautious concentration was not at its best. His mind kept wandering back to Corrinne's letters. He had read Corrinne's letters so many times he had them memorized. They carried her scent, that delicate bouquet from the *parfum* she favored. And she had pressed rouge-colored kisses liberally throughout the pages. Of course, they were now all smudged and smeared by Philippe's reciprocation. Corrinne had written, asking if he remembered certain days, nights, and other intimate situations that needed no details to recall. Having been starved of any physical contact with his wife for over two years, Philippe's imagination was enhanced by her suggestive hints. Before he left Québec City, he wrote another letter to her and personally placed it in the Louisbourg dispatch pouch aboard the courier sled at the Québec City wharves. He stayed until the sled was pulled by a horse team away from the wharf and down the Saint Lawrence River.

Philippe's letter was short: *My love. I've read all your letters and read them still. My body trembles from the memories. I will see you soon. P.* He dared not say much more, expecting his letter might still be intercepted by someone. Corrinne made mention of her suspicion at the beginning of all her letters, saying she withheld greater detail for this reason. *I presume my letters will be opened and read. As you know well, many of the men in the government of New France embody corrupt, vile, and perverse personalities.* Philippe took a degree of satisfaction in what she wrote. It meant Governor Vaudreuil read this repeated declaration, too.

Philippe believed Louisbourg was going to be invaded by the English, maybe as soon as the summer. He decided Corrinne and the children must come to Québec City. He was going to retrieve them. Philippe told Michelle of his intentions. She was overjoyed at the prospect of seeing Corrinne and

Anamosa again, and the new babies! He asked Michelle to locate a safe place for Corrinne to stay somewhere west of Québec City. He also asked her to find out, with discretion, if Corrinne's old city house in Montréal could be purchased. Michelle was not certain how to do this.

"Ask Monseigneur Eric Nicolet to help you. Say it is my request...as a favor to me. He will do it. Tell him if the church can buy that house, I will buy it back from them with a profit for the Jesuits."

*

By the ninth day of the month of March, they had reached Fort Carillon. The assault force congregated and remained at Fort Carillon for several days, concentrating its supplies and finalizing the attacking order of march on Fort William Henry. During this time, Philippe began his confidential persuasion to convince Rigaud not to scale the walls of Fort William Henry; to conduct the attack, instead, as a raid.

"The fort commandant, Major Eyre, is aware the walls of his fort are scalable even without ladders. I assure you he is ready for this. Your casualties could be fifty percent in just trying and failing. However, if we concentrate on destroying their boats, we destroy their ability to make any attacks during the coming summer months. It doesn't matter how many troops they amass for this. If they cannot transport these troops, you will effectively stall the English army. That is a victory! I can guarantee this success for you, Rigaud," he emphasized. "And I will validate whatever assertion you want to make to the governor regarding this victory."

Rigaud remained undecided. And he was highly suspicious of Captain Gerrard's motives in being so supportive.

"Captain Gerrard, I do not recall this passionate argument during your presentation to the governor. It makes me skeptical...but your reasoning is clear. I will consider your recommendations...after we control the lands around the fort."

*

Captain Gerrard led one company of *coureur de bois* scouts halfway down Lake George on ice skates before exiting onto the western shore and switching to snow shoes. In less than two days, they reached the hills to the west of the fort. Accompanying him was Major Michel Péan and about a hundred of the most experienced militia. The objective was to secure the western approaches to the fort, establish points of ambush, and assess the readiness of Fort William Henry in anticipating a surprise attack. To their surprise, they did not encounter foot signs of any patrols in the recent snowfall.

The bulk of Commander Rigaud de Vaudreuil's forces were now advancing down the eastern shore. He ordered three advance *coureur de bois* scouts sent ahead on the ice, this time all the way to the shoreline in front of the fort. They carried axes to chop at the ice to determine its strength.

From his position on the western hills, Philippe used a nautical watch glass to scan the activity inside the fort. He saw the sentries moving around, smoke rising from a few heating stoves, muddy ruts and tracks on the road leading to the fort's only gate on its eastern side, no boat building in progress, in fact no activity outside the walls at all. There were also a handful of sentries posted along the lakeshore, all of them huddled around a sentry stove to keep warm.

Péan was at Philippe's side. "What do you see?"

Philippe handed him the watch glass. "Only the sentries seemed to be moving. The ones in the fort pay little attention or even look over the walls. I don't think they realize we are here."

Major Péan swept his scan towards the eastern shore. "No sight of Rigaud yet. I expect he is a half day behind us. But I see three skaters coming down the ice."

"What? Let me see." Philippe took back the glass. "Those are my scouts! Fuck! What are they doing out in the open?"

Péan snorted. "Probably following one of Rigaud's orders."

"Well, I don't see any targets of value on this western side. Major, can you deploy the majority of your militia in ambush positions here? Leave behind someone you trust in charge. Bring the best of the rest along with my scouts. We can circle the fort to the south. I want to get a closer look at those isolated breastworks they are building in the east. They were empty the last time I was here. They will not stay empty for very much longer, I suspect."

*

The advance scouts in the east reported back to Commander Rigaud de Vaudreuil. The fort displayed no activity that it was expecting an attack. They described no one moving about outside the walls expect for a few sentries by the shoreline huddled around a fire. They seemed more interested with staying warm in the chill winds coursing down the lake.

"We have an opportunity!" Rigaud said softly. Using surprise as an advantage, he decided to chance storming the fort in these early morning hours with ladders.

*

The *coureurs de bois* and veteran militia huddled around a dozen fire pits in a small ravine a mile south of Fort William Henry. In the depth of the ravine, the fires would be hidden from the eyes of the fort sentries. They were near enough to the road leading north from Fort Edward that if any reinforcements came up that road, they could quickly establish an ambush. Captain Gerrard and Major Péan decided they would invest the isolated breastworks in the morning and destroy as much of it as possible.

The two marine officers could not sleep, both preoccupied with the *what ifs* of the coming battle the next day. Instead, they talked in whispers through most of the night.

Major Péan told Philippe about Henri and the battles they had fought together side by side against Sir William Johnson and later again at Fort Bull. And the recent deployment to Louisbourg.

"He volunteered for a spy mission in Boston! He was taken there by that pirate captain, LaTour!"

"You fucking know Captain LaTour is not a pirate, Major."

"Of course, I know." He laughed. "But it irritates LaTour when I call him that. In any case, Henri returns from Boston with ciphered intelligence about the English build-up of troops in Halifax, and he brings your wife, Lady Corrinne, with him, who announces herself as Lady Corrinne *VanderMeer*! I trust you already know all this."

"I do. It was the fiction we created to stay in Boston. But I didn't stay very long, obviously. The twins are mine. I didn't even know Henri had left Boston and later arrived in Montreal, let alone that he went to Louisbourg and then back to Boston as a spy. He is very lucky."

"Considering all the scars I see covering you, luck runs in your blood."

"These? Compliments of an Oneida gauntlet."

"Like I said. It's in your blood. Your son is very brave and almost foolish in the chances he takes. But the militia and the marines admire him. Even the grenadiers consider him one of their own."

Péan described the sequence of promotions Henri had received and why.

"So, he's an ensign." Philippe remarked with surprise and pride. "Took me what? Over a decade to become a captain."

"Henri deserved it," Péan said. "You can be proud of that."

"And you, Major? An authentic chevalier...who would have guessed?"

"Fuck! Certainly, not me," Péan replied. "Let me ask you. What do you think provoked my abrupt elevation to the Order of Saint Louis?"

"I could say your corruption...but even that has limits. You happen to be a competent field officer. I saw you construct those forts on the Rivière aux Boeuf. That was not easy. You took command after General von Dieskau was captured. Lieutenant de Léry commended you for valor at Fort Bull. Are you averse to such recognition?"

"No more than my aversion to chiggers. But a chevalier! It's undeserved! No matter what you think of me, Governor Vaudreuil and Intendant Bigôt are much worse. And when the two of them collaborate to publicly award me with this type of recognition, I must ask...for what? It's like they gave me a new suit of shiny armor...with intentions to invite me to go swimming in the river."

"So, they made you a knight...and ordered you to lead the militia... that's the reason?"

"No. They could just order me to do this. They've done that before."

"Well, I'm out of suggestions. I am going to try and sleep a few hours."

Major Péan did not sleep.

*

Fort William Henry's commanding officer was Major William Eyre. He was thirty-eight, a veteran of the War of Austrian Succession and the Jacobite Rebellion. He was first and foremost an engineer, and early in his career he served as a member of the Royal Engineers. Any task requiring the expert eye, design, and measurement skills of an engineer drew his passion. But he possessed a practical nature. He took pride in being an officer of the English army and was a consummate professional. When not building bridges or roads or breastworks in some remote wilderness, William Eyre could proudly command a regiment of line infantry in battle or command an artillery battery in defense. Or build a fort. He could do any of these things with distinction. William Eyre had supervised the breastworks and the placement of the artillery that defeated French General von Dieskau at the first Battle of Lake George. He was, subsequently, ordered by Sir William Johnson to build the new fort he now commanded: Fort William-Henry. He had never built a fort before this one. There was a particular log inside the walls upon which a plaque was nailed. It had his name on it. Major William

Eyre, Engineer. In his opinion, that plaque established this construction as *his* fort. The fort may be named for the grandson of George II, but that plaque commemorated Major Eyre as the owner. It was the deed…in his opinion.

"And I will be damned before I ever surrender this fort to the French!"

The men of the 44th Foot defending the fort admired and respected their stalwart commanding officer. He was highly educated, constantly quoting engineering formulas and facts about how to reduce stress in bastion overhangs with the proper placements of buttresses. Or how water expanded when frozen. Or that the steam that lifted the lid on their teapots would one day be used to turn a mill wheel. Things none of the common soldiers cared about. The major was a little stiff, very droll in humor, but he had proven himself fearless in the face of the enemy—more than once. And that was what was important. Major Eyre also checked on the well-being of the sick men every day. Ordered what he could to minimize their discomfort. Insisted that everyone rinse off their hands after using the latrines. He cared about his men. Only three hundred and fifty were fit to fight, including the seventy American rangers. About a hundred and thirty of the fort's men were seriously sick with scurvy and smallpox. The fort was severely debilitated by these sicknesses. Even those men who could stand guard were weakened by the psychological miasma that hung over the garrison. But because of the major, they'd found strength to endure the winter. And it had been a long, cold, miserable winter. Now, it was March. The warmer days were almost here. He'd been promised relief by a new regiment of foot in the spring. He just had to hold on until then.

William Eyre knew how to defend his fort. His men knew this, and they had confidence in him. The one thing the major liked more than resolving engineering challenges was aiming and firing cannons. The opportunity to fire a cannon at something did not come along very often. And Major Eyre had plenty of cannons inside his fort.

On Saturday, the nineteenth of March, in the early morning hours before sunrise, one of his sentries on the wall shouted out that he had heard a noise coming from the direction of the lake. Major Eyre ran up the ladder to the top of the wall and listened. At first, he suspected the ice was thawing, but the sound was even and repetitive. The noise was a chopping sound. But not of wood. Someone was chopping out on the ice. The major usually recalled his shoreline sentries back into the fort at night. An hour earlier, it was still dark when he ordered only two sentries back out. It seemed even colder in the morning twilight. The sentries had lit a small fire to stay warm. But he certainly had not ordered anyone to go out on the ice. The noise meant only one thing.

*

On the southeast side of the fort, in the early morning twilight, Captain Gerrard, Major Péan, and their combined forces had overrun the new battlements, only to find them empty. They searched for plunder and found a small cache of gunpowder—three casks. Instead of polluting this store of powder, Major Péan ordered the casks to be fused. Philippe picked spots to blow holes in some of the more sophisticated portions of the breastworks, the diamond-shaped bastions; the obvious work of the fort's engineer.

Major Péan sent a messenger back to the militia force in the west, telling them to hold their position, even when they heard cannon or musket fire from the attacks that would soon take place. Good thing too. Unbeknownst to them, Major Eyre would soon deploy the officers inside the fort with orders to prepare to defend a frontal assault on every wall with cannons.

*

"The French are here!" Major Eyre declared. He ordered the ramparts manned. "No drums! Do this quietly! Gunnery Sergeant! Load the thirty-two-pound cannon facing north with grapeshot, if you please."

The troops responded and filled gaps along the walls on every side. The other fort cannons were loaded sequentially, a ball in one and grapeshot in the next.

When the thirty-two-pound cannon was loaded, the major directed the aim more to the northeast and personally turned the elevation screw for range.

The cannoneer sergeant frowned. "With respect, sir. At that turn of elevation, will not the fire load go over the heads of the attackers?"

"Very observant, Sergeant Hennessey. Indeed, it will. But I am not preparing to fire at the attackers. I am aiming for the French commander. And he is hiding among those trees out there."

"He is?" the sergeant asked, surprised. He scanned where the major was looking. He didn't see any movement, only darkness and shadows.

"Yes, Sergeant, he is. You must understand your enemy. The Canadian French and their savage allies love their trees. They use them as shields. That is where they like to hide. And those trees right out there"—he pointed—"are out of musket range. Do you agree?"

The sergeant nodded.

"If you know this, that means the French commander knows this, too. The range of a musket is an easy range to predict. Cannons, however," the major said, smiling sardonically at the sergeant, "like this thirty-two-pound iron beauty, have a long reach." He patted the iron snout affectionately. "Yes, indeed. This black bitch has a very long reach."

*

Commander Rigaud de Vaudreuil understood he had only one chance for a surprise attack. If he was going to do it, it had to be now. He ordered a full company of grenadiers to advance on the run with scaling ladders. Other regulars were sent forward on a different path to begin destroying the boat building works.

After running two thirds of the way to the eastern wall, the attackers were still unopposed. In the few minutes that took, Rigaud concluded this initial sortie just might be successful. He quickly ordered three more companies to make ready to reinforce this assault. If anyone from the first sortie got into the fort, he would order a full-scale attack.

Just then, the thirty-two-pound cannon loaded with grapeshot erupted with flame. The distance to the forest was just far enough that Rigaud and his men saw the flash and fire before they heard the sound of the blast. Rigaud and his men acted instinctively and threw themselves on the ground. If they had not done that, the death toll might have been horrendous. A dense cloud of one-inch lead balls and nails buzzed and whistled angrily through the air, ripping the limbs off the trees, smashing over the smaller ones, peppering the ground with explosions of earth. Miraculously, no one was hurt. But the French attack was immediately abandoned by the elite troops, who retreated back to the safety of the trees, leaving the field in front of the fort littered with scaling ladders.

*

Just before Captain Gerrard lit the fuse on the powder casks in the breastworks south of the fort, the thirty-two-pound cannon on the north side wall of the fort belched out its fiery load. Even from this distance, it was easy to observe the impressive destructive effect it unleashed on the forest where the main body of French forces were probably located.

Philippe looked through his scope. The troops in the fort had manned the walls.

"I guess Major Eyre knows we are here."

"No more surprises," Péan remarked. "Commander Rigaud, meet Major Eyre. I would wager, Major Eyre himself aimed that cannon."

*

Major Eyre ordered one cannon fired into the surrounding trees, from each side of the fort. He succeeded where Captain Gerrard's persuasion did not. He had just convinced Commander Rigaud de Vaudreuil that a frontal assault on Fort William Henry was out of the question.

The soldiers in the fort kept up random fire with musketry all day long to discourage any attacks on the outlying works. With the western perimeter held by the militia, the southern lands now occupied by the *coureur de bois* scouts and more militia, and the main force of French pinned down in the eastern forests, Rigaud de Vaudreuil called war council once the sun set. A new strategy was determined.

Commander Vaudreuil sent two hundred regulars to block the road leading up from Fort Edward in case they sent reinforcements. The rest of the forces now concentrated on destroying everything of value outside the fort. They would raid at night, to avoid the musket fire.

But just to be sure the English could not be tempted into surrendering, Vaudreuil sent an officer to the fort under a red flag of parley, offering honors of war, to avoid being massacred by the savages, like Fort Oswego. The French officer had been blindfolded when he came inside and blindfolded again before he left the command quarters of the fort. Major Eyre sent back the reply Fort William Henry would be defended to the last man.

It was a stand-off between the opposing forces. For the next three nights, the French raided and burned, until there was nothing left to burn or hack into useless pieces outside the fort. During the day, the fort came under sporadic musket fire from all sides. Major Eyre would respond with occasional blasts of grapeshot. The morale of the 44th Foot had never been so high. Even the sick came up on the ramparts to fight alongside their brothers. Outside the walls, the plunder, destruction and burning of the works, boats, and out buildings was total.

At the end of the fourth night of heavy raiding and with the advent of another heavy snowstorm, Commander de Vaudreuil announced his decision to withdraw.

Casualties on both sides had been minimal during this time. The French suffered seven men killed and nine wounded. Major Eyre later reported no one killed and seven men wounded.

Fort William Henry was virtually untouched by anything other than musket balls. But the strategic capability and value of this fort had been obliterated. For all practical purposes, and considering the multitude of sick soldiers, it was no more than a well-defended hospital. Any type of supplies stocked external to the fort, the food, gunpowder, tools, the kegs of whiskey for certain, all of it not carried off was burned up inside the buildings, none of which were left standing. The damage to the substantial fleet of lake vessels was even worse. Four sloops—one of which was still on the way to being built, all of them intended or already carrying ten to fourteen guns apiece—were torched. Over three hundred sixty bateaux, the entire transport capability of the army, were burned or chopped into unusable pieces. The sawmill, the whip-saw stands, the stock pile of timber, the sheds, sentry huts, magazines, and any type of tool, any special device or machine, anything having to do with building boats, even the custom shipways erected to stage the brigantine vessels, and half the whaleboats the rangers preferred to use, all of this was destroyed. The outer breastworks to the east were heavily damaged but were the easiest to repair. But the entire capability that made the Fort William Henry a strategic fortification would have to be rebuilt.

The French raiders had performed their mission well.

The army's ability to conduct a formal campaign up Lake George would be delayed at least a year. It would take months just to resupply the fort from Albany.

But Major Eyre still held his position. The 44th Foot held their heads high for once. They had finally achieved a victory against superior forces that outnumbered them five to one. The day the French withdrew, Major Eyre reflected to his officers about the outcome.

"Like the first Battle of Lake George, the French did not bring any cannons with them. Even one siege mortar could have made a difference."

*

Only a day's march away, Lieutenant-Colonel George Monro was advancing the 35th Regiment of Foot to relieve Major Eyre and the weary men of the 44th Regiment of Foot. When Monro heard Fort William Henry was under attack, he ordered the 35th to abandon everything they could not carry on their backs and did the best he could to advance to the fort with the greatest speed.

On the twenty-seventh of March, they arrived to find the battle over and Major Eyre victorious in the defense of his fort, even though the surrounding support works and boats were utterly destroyed. But the fort had survived, and Major Eyre proudly led his men south to receive the praise and rest they well-deserved.

Lieutenant-Colonel George Monro took command and settled in the fresh troops of the 35th, expecting the French attack and subsequent withdrawal had exhausted the enemy, giving them leave to think there would be no additional fighting for the rest of the fighting season.

*

Commander Rigaud de Vaudreuil withdrew his forces to Fort Carillon to rest for a night. Major Péan did not stop there with his militia. These men were mostly farmers and were anxious to get home. They had spring planting to worry about. He continued to Fort Saint-Frédéric before resting. Over half the militia did not even stop there and continued further, breaking into smaller and smaller groups as they made their way home.

Captain Philippe Gerrard gathered his scouts in Fort Carillon, which was their main base. He transferred command to his able lieutenants, informing them he would be gone for two months. Panther Claw asked to go with him to Louisbourg.

"I've never been there," was his simple reason for going.

By now they were close friends. "I am honored."

Philippe informed Commandant Lusignan of Fort Carillon of his upcoming absence. He also informed Rigaud de Vaudreuil that the *coureur de bois* scouts would resume their patrols from Fort Carillon. The two men shook hands.

Philippe congratulated the commander. "You have a great victory, sir. The threat of English attack up the lakes is gone for at least a year."

Rigaud de Vaudreuil replied in a reluctant tone. "And you were right. If I had tried a full-scale attack of the walls, we would have been repulsed with great losses."

Philippe grinned. "The way I will retell it, Rigaud, was that you did try to scale the walls, and you found the forts' thirty-two-pound cannons too formidable. Observing that, you commanded we destroy everything outside the fort instead. Which we did! And all of that is the truth! And that is exactly what General Montcalm and Governor Vaudreuil will hear from me, if I am asked."

*

Captain Gerrard and Malsum continued north the next morning on skates. But already the lake ice was groaning. The spring thaw was proceeding rapidly. At the Richelieu River, the ice was only safe if one skated close to the banks. There was flow down the center. Still, skating was much faster than canoeing. At the Saint Lawrence, they found the river flowing and carrying dead trees and other spring debris. They shifted to an army bateau for transport to Québec City. Disorganized elements of Rigaud de Vaudreuil's forces were already on the river, the grenadiers among them, every soldier anxious to get back to the city.

When they finally arrived in Québec City, Philippe spent one night at Michelle's house to clean himself. Malsum was given a servant's room in which to sleep, to the dismay of Constance and Madeleine. Michelle had seen tattooed warriors before at Fort Niagara. She welcomed the fierce death mask visage of the warrior with traditional hugs and kisses.

"Welcome to my home."

Malsum was surprised. That did not often happen to him.

The next morning, Philippe felt rested, and his appearance was purified. At the front door to the house, he took Michelle by both hands to say good-bye.

"If I do not return today, then I've gone downriver heading for Louisbourg. I will not be back until sometime in May. But I will be bringing Corrinne, the twins, and Anamosa back with me."

"Are you coming back by ship?"

"Hopefully…if I can find one to take us…that is my intention."

This was a very dangerous journey with the English cruisers prowling the mouth of the river.

Michelle hugged Philippe tightly, then kissed his cheeks. *"Dieu soit avec vous."*

"God be with you, too, Michelle."

Malsum was surprised when the white woman hugged him for a second time and gave him the same blessing.

As they walked down the hilly streets of Québec City, citizens gazed upon Malsum with a look of revulsion. He was used to that. Some walked to the other side of the street.

Captain Philippe Gerrard reported to General Montcalm at headquarters. Captain Bougainville was in attendance.

"Welcome, Captain. Reports of victory at Fort William Henry have preceded you. It appears you were successful in persuading Rigaud de Vaudreuil to use raiding tactics."

"Thank you, General, but I think the grapeshot from the cannons fired by the Fort William Henry's commandant was far more convincing than anything I said to him. Rigaud could see his forces would have been shredded."

It was impossible to ignore the hulking, frightening person standing behind Captain Gerrard. General Montcalm shot glances at Malsum's death mask tattoos until it became awkward.

"*Pardon*, General, let me introduce Mkuigen Malsum. He is an Abenaki warrior and is my most valuable scout."

Montcalm cautiously held out a hand.

Malsum gripped it politely. "I am very honored to meet the commander of the French soldiers. Word of your victories resounds among the tribes across the rivers and lakes."

General Montcalm and Captain Bougainville were stunned by this greeting. This was a fierce-looking savage. His head was shaved, leaving only a black shrub of hair at the top, which was adorned with a few feathers. Bones dangled from his ears and nose. Any skin not hidden by clothing was covered with tattoos. They had expected patois and the usual grunts. But this man spoke *perfect* French, almost without any Canadian accent!

"Monsieur Malsum, I believe your diction may be better than mine," Montcalm replied with sincerity. "You are educated, then?"

Though his expression was impassive, Malsum was thoroughly enjoying their astonishment.

"I have no formal schooling. My mother was Abenaki. She was very skilled in medicines and healing. She was taught by the Jesuits to speak French and taught me in my childhood. My father was Scottish. They insisted I speak both languages and corrected me every day for any mispronunciations. I am told my English is a Scottish variation. I can also speak numerous tribal tongues."

General Montcalm had never met anyone like this man. His eyes took in his attire, and he noticed something disturbing hanging from Malsum's belt. "What is that?"

Philippe interjected quickly. "Malsum's *nom de guerre* is Panther Claw. He is so named for the knife he carries."

Malsum withdrew the gruesome hooked-shaped blade to show them.

With that revelation, General Montcalm could venture a guess at the black shriveled thing dangling from the belt. He suddenly remembered etiquette and gestured with one hand towards a table set with dishes of steaming food.

"Captain Bougainville and I were about to break our fast together. Please join us."

"Thank you, sir." Philippe accepted for both. "Malsum and I would be honored."

While they ate, Philippe described the attack and raid and his conclusions.

Montcalm had already heard much of this from messengers sent by Rigaud de Vaudreuil each day for the duration of the attack. Rigaud wanted his version of what was happening to be reported first. The general glanced repeatedly at Malsum. The man's table manners were like any French officer, except the frightening death mask tattoos suggested he would be just as comfortable eating someone's hand cooked above a fire on a spit as he would be enjoying the plate of eggs, bacon, and warm bread.

"Malsum is my best advisor. He possesses extraordinary knowledge of tribal culture, lore, and politics, if you permit me to call it that. Feel free to ask him any questions to satisfy your curiosity."

Montcalm did not hesitate. The general's questions were polite, and his enthusiasm grew with the candor and honesty of the answers he received. Montcalm was apologetic when asking something that might be considered indelicate. Captain Bougainville asked a few questions about their creation mythologies. The frank discussion lasted nearly an hour. Montcalm realized he had only scratched at the surface of what this man might teach him.

"The depth and richness of your knowledge is profound, Monsieur. You have taught me more about tribal people and customs in one morning than I have learned in a year. I am grateful for your honesty and patience with my shameful ignorance."

"General, I am grateful and honored you invited me to dine at your table. An invitation like this…well, it has never happened to me before in my life."

"Indeed? Then allow me to apologize for our disgraceful behavior. And I promise you, Monsieur Malsum, this will not be the last time you dine with me. Captain Gerrard, from now on, when you attend my war councils, be certain Monsieur Malsum attends with you. His counsel and expertise are far too valuable to ignore."

"Thank you, sir," Malsum responded.

General Montcalm stood and they all followed suit.

"I would prefer to spend more time talking with you, but I must go to the governor's palace for the first of what will surely be many contentious and tedious discussions regarding the results at Fort William Henry."

"General, if I might ask an indulgence," Philippe interjected politely. "I would like to leave immediately for Louisbourg…to conclude another assignment by the governor."

"But of course, Captain Gerrard. That is what I promised. Return by the end of May…or sooner, if possible. Monsieur Malsum, it has been an honor to meet you."

*

They walked down to the wharves of Québec City. With the temperature stabilizing at warmer levels, the thawing of the river had accelerated. The ice flows were smaller and drifting apart. If the captains were careful, the river was navigable once again.

"That one." Philippe pointed at a vessel. "I know the captain."

It was a schooner, recently lowered into the water from its high stocks. The new sails were already being adjusted to the rigging.

"Snow Hair!" the captain greeted loudly. "Obviously, you lived through all the recent fighting."

"*Bonjour*, Captain Fleurant. We need passage to Île-Royale."

"But of course. Do you have money?"

"But of course," Philippe mimicked in jest.

Fleurant threw open his arms. "Then welcome aboard. You, too, Malsum."

The cargo schooner was called *Proud Recluse.* It plied its trade between Port Toulouse, Gaspé, and Québec City. It had been up out of the water all winter long, propped high on stocks to keep its keel clear of the crushing ice. Now caulked, tarred, and in good repair, it was ready to find goods of any kind to bring back to the deprived populace of Québec City. And carrying passengers when the ship was empty would help defer losses.

To stay out of the way of the crew, Philippe and Malsum stood far aft of the helm. It was a good place to stand and watch the lands to either side of the river glide by. April was almost here. The trees were budding with new greenery. It could still turn cold, but not for very long if it did.

The superstitious crew knew Malsum by sight and reputation. They did not want to stand anywhere near him.

"I am glad we are on our way. The governor would have found a reason to delay my journey. General Montcalm will validate my leave of absence. He is a great leader."

Malsum spoke up. "Your General Montcalm was the first white officer of his rank ever to treat me with such respect."

"Montcalm is a fine officer, better than any I have met before. He is also an honorable man. The respect he showed you was genuine."

"I will not forget it."

The winds were blowing from the west, favorable to downriver transit. Once the schooner navigated to sail a long stretch of shoal-free waters at the center of the channel, Captain Fleurant came aft to talk with them. He politely nodded to Captain Gerrard.

"Apologies for not talking with you sooner. I needed to get my ship's course steadied in the middle of the river." He addressed Malsum next. "Monsieur Malsum! I've not seen your pleasant face in this part of the river in many seasons. And I can see you are just as popular with my crew as ever. Are you hunting for a new soul to devour?"

Philippe's eyes widened at the captain's irreverent words.

Malsum was unperturbed. "That depends, Captain. Are you feeling sick?"

The captain laughed and slapped himself on the chest with both hands. "Not me! I'm fat and healthy after a long winter respite in Québec City."

"Have the English or Americans been raiding anywhere on the river?" Philippe asked.

"No. But Malsum's Malécite brothers war constantly…most of the time as allies for us…but the English have started to offer them large bounties for French scalps. Never certain who they are allied with these days. Probably depends on their mood. I don't trust the Malécite, never did, but they do not challenge anyone on the river, so I'll trade with them. I intend to harbor for half a day at the port of Rimouski. Because of the war, the Malécite have expanded their lands to the north and have a small village on that part of the river. They are trading furs at Rimouski. I want to find something I can sell in Port Toulouse."

"Do you expect trouble?" Philippe asked.

Captain Fleurant shook his head. "No. But if you want your passage to remain a secret, it would be better for you to stay aboard the ship when the Malécite come around. The Malécite sell information to both sides. We will not be bothered going to the mouth of the river on the way out. But coming back, the English cruisers will be patrolling. They've seen me often enough and usually do not stop me. But you never know when that courtesy will turn."

When the helmsman shouted a turn in the river was coming, the captain moved out of conversing range to stand by his steersman.

"Do you have enemies among the Malécite?"

Malsum nodded. "I have enemies among most of the tribes. It was a Malécite war chief who killed my wife a long time ago. I wear his face."

Philippe regarded him with confusion. "You wear his face?"

"He was the first. I tracked him down. He was alive when I cut away his face. I boiled his skull, removed all the flesh, and brought the skull to my mother. She cast a spell on it. Then she tattooed the image of his skull on my face. She told me that way all the men I kill in the future will remember this Malécite war chief as their enemy in the afterlife."

They were now sitting side by side as the schooner moved downriver. Malsum's revelation about his wife and mother was unexpected.

"Your mother could cast spells?"

"Yes. The white villagers we lived among called her *Chanter*."

Provoked by Malsum's words, Philippe shared his story about Chittaqua, the Erigh medicine man, who could cast spells and had tattoos covering his body. He talked about how Chittaqua had saved his life more than once. And that Philippe now believed him to be the spirit of a white eagle.

"A *ghost eagle*?" Malsum was impressed. "So, this Erigh healer became a ghost eagle. My mother told me about such shaman spirits, those who inhabit the bodies of animals after their deaths. I thought this to be only legend. That is what my father told me. Just tribal legends. But you are *white*, Snow Hair. Do you believe this?"

"Yes," Philippe replied. "I do not speak of it often. I do not just *believe* this to be true. I *know* this to be true. I have seen the ghost eagle. It has come to my aid more than once. It is Chittaqua. Do not be surprised if he appears during this journey as well. And for your sake, I hope he does. I think it will be good for you to…well, meet him."

Malsum considered this remarkable. That Snow Hair confided this secret to him was a great honor. Because he had come to trust Snow Hair more than any other white man, he decided to tell more of his story.

"My mother was Abenaki…and half French." Malsum began without preamble. "She began tattooing my body at an early age. She explained the symbols would give me spiritual strength. She claimed they would keep evil away. My face tattoos, my death mask, was the last one she did. And she did this while singing words I did not understand. Maybe my mother was a sorceress, like many people claimed, be they white or tribal. Even so, she was also kind to people she met…unless they made an enemy of her. Then those people would get sick and die."

Philippe was fascinated by what this intensely private man was telling him. He did not dare interrupt or ask a question for fear he might stop. And Malsum talked on and on.

"My mother killed my first father, an Abenaki clan chief, using spells of sorcery, or so the Abenaki claimed. She never told me why she killed him. But as a result, she was driven away by her own people. They cursed her. She cursed them back. They denied her any future association with the tribe. She cursed them as a people. Cursed their ancestors. Cursed all their names. I was only a boy of five summers at that time. But I could see that even the bravest of the Abenaki were frightened by these curses. She was no longer welcomed among the Abenaki. And they would have killed us both. But my mother went far to the south to live among the white settlers, who are usually enemies of the Abenaki. She dressed like the white settlers and lived near them peacefully. They finally accepted her. She gave me the name Malsum, but never explained the reason for this name."

"Your mother was a healer?" he probed to keep Malsum talking, realizing he might never again have this opportunity.

"As I said, the white villagers called her *Chanter*, because she sang songs with words no one understood, including me. She was a skilled healer, possessed a knowledge of medicines, and sang over people when healing them. The white villagers liked her for this. She could mix potions and powerful healing poultices. This had value. They would pay her. That is how we survived. And for more money, she would toss bones and tell people of their future, be it good or bad. They say she had the sight. And that I inherited her sight, too. She married a Scotsman from Vermont after telling his fortune. He was a good man, who treated her kindly, and me too. He had a love of books, especially poetry. For years, he taught me to read and write, made me read books of poetry…to be certain I was properly educated, he told me. He especially liked the Scottish poet, James Thomson, and his poem *The Seasons*."

And then, to Philippe's astonishment, Panther Claw began to recite aloud.

"Lend me your Song, ye Nightingales! oh pour
The mazy-running Soul of Melody
Into my varied Verse! while I deduce,
From the first Note the hollow Cuckoo sings,
The Symphony of Spring, and touch a Theme
Unknown to Fame, the Passion of the Groves.
When first the Soul of Love is sent abroad,
Warm thro the vital Air, and on the Heart
Harmonious seizes, the gay Troops begin,
In gallant Thought, to plume the painted Wing;
And try again the long-forgotten Strain,
At first faint-warbled. But no sooner grows
The soft Infusion prevalent, and wide,
Than, all alive, at once their Joy o'erflows
In Musick unconfin'd. Up-springs the Lark,
Shrill-voic'd, and loud, the Messenger of Morn;
Ere yet the Shadows fly, he mounted sings
Amid the dawning Clouds, and from their Haunts
Calls up the tuneful Nations."

"I presume, Thomson liked bird songs. That is from the poem, 'Spring Season.' There are four poems in all. Summer, Autumn, and Winter, too. At one time, I could almost recite them all. Poetry is useful for the white man's world, but a fool's talent here in the wilderness. Did you ever feel the need to quote poetry to an attacking bear?"

They both laughed. And Malsum continued. "The Malécite people often came to trade with the white villagers in the spring. When I had lived sixteen summers, I saw a girl among them. She was staring at me, but not in fear. No girl had ever looked at me in that way. After they finished trading with the white men, the Malécite left to return to their village. I followed them for three days. On the third night, I crept into their camp. I woke this girl with a hand over her mouth. She nodded and did not scream. She came away with me willingly and became my wife. No one saw me enter the camp and no one saw us leave together. My mother chanted good spells over this girl. For six moons, we lived in a small log cabin near the white man's village fort. She grew large with child. I loved her. She loved me. When I was away hunting one day, the Malécite returned wearing war paint. She was the daughter of the chief. He tried to take her back with them. The white villagers told me she fought to stay and stabbed her father in the arm with her knife. In anger, he struck her in the head with a tomahawk. She died. They left. When I returned, I saw her lying on the ground. Her head was smashed open. I think I started howling in sadness. I was confused and do not remember this clearly. But the white village women came to my side. They knelt and tried to comfort me. My father, who was considered a great warrior by the other whites, told me to go after the Malécite and avenge my wife's death. So, I did. And as I was leaving, my mother told me to bring back his skull. So, I did."

The reflection on his dead wife provoked Malsum to fall silent.

"Where is your mother and father now?"

"My mother's good and bad predictions too often came true. Because of this, some of the white villagers accused her of being a witch. A few of the men came one night to murder her and succeeded. My father died defending her. They would have killed me, too, but I escaped in the dark and went north. I had lived seventeen summers by then. I knew how to survive. Yet because of my tattoos, I was not welcomed by any other tribe. Some hunted me and tried to kill me. I took their faces with my knife. Soon they were all too scared and stopped looking for me. I've been alone ever since. Like you, I began trapping and trading furs. The French did not reject me. They welcomed me. Some have even died for me."

They were both quiet for a while.

"Everyone but the French are my enemies," Malsum added abruptly.

For Malsum to share something like this was extraordinary. Philippe would not betray this trust.

The *ghost* flew for two days until it reached the water channel again, and one more day to get to the narrowest place to fly across. But it would wait and fly across tomorrow. The white eagle was weary. It withdrew to permit the female to hunt. She easily clawed a large fish from the water and took it to a high perch in a tree. It ate quickly and hunted once more before it perched to rest for the night.

The path to this place had not been the straightest. The female was driven to mate. It would veer suddenly for no apparent reason. But the *ghost* knew the tingling feeling associated with this action; a male eagle approached. The *ghost* would surge with all its dominance to persuade the female to fly away in a different direction. After each occurrence, her strength to resist his dominance increased. Mating was a powerful, natural urge. But the ghost was close enough now to see servants of the demon near the woman. She had to be warned. The girl was with her, and she glowed brightly. The brightness of the boy become man was near her, too. He also should be warned. And it could see the brightness of the man coming down the great river. There was still time. But who should he visit first?

The girl, the *ghost* decided, while it still controlled the white eagle.

During the night, the *ghost* reached out with its thoughts to visit the dreams of the young girl. It guided her to the body of a winter owl. This bird had a smooth rounded head without the distinctive ear tufts most other owls had. Almost as large as the female white eagle, the owl was also white, its body speckled with black-and-brown feathers. The *ghost* whispered to the girl. *Dwell calmly with this animal spirit. See through its eyes. Watch how it looks for prey.*

The owl circled high above the fortress, gazing down at the surrounding lands outside the walls that had been cleared decades ago to create a field of fire for muskets and cannons. Altered by man, the natural landscape was now irregular, without aesthetic. In some places, there were wetlands, other places had small mounds. Dominated by sparse grasses and weedy plants with succulent roots extending into the watery earth, the ground was tunneled and inhabited by voles. Their small size made them almost invisible.

The owl's night vision was acute. It could easily see the small rodents moving about on the ground. Its glide was silent, graceful, and deadly. The girl was exhilarated by the bird's physical strength, the fierceness of its spirit and the profound sense of freeness it embodied. Suddenly, she noticed a warm brightness. It seemed familiar to her. The *ghost* gently drew attention to another, larger brightness, which also seemed familiar.

The woman, the ghost whispered. And when the girl's attention returned to the less prominent brightness. *The boy become man*, the ghost whispered. The girl was drawn more strongly to this light. It filled her with great joy and harmony. She was reluctant to move away. But the owl glided silently towards another mound-covered field. As it passed over the eastern battlements, the girl noticed three concentrated points of light, not so bright and which glowed with a dull, reddish tinge. It made her fearful.

These are your enemies, the ghost whispered.

The girl sensed the hate and evil emanating from that light. She recoiled so strongly, the owl reacted, too. The girl drew away from the bird and awakened in her bed as if leaving a nightmare.

*

Anamosa sat up in her bed panting heavily. Moments later, she was comforted in the warm embrace of Corrinne's arms.

"What's wrong, little love? A bad dream?"

"Yes! And a good dream, too!"

Corrinne knew that talking about bad dreams helped to dispel lingering fear. They moved to the chair by the window. Anamosa whispered about what she had just experienced.

"I was flying with an owl. It was hunting and feeding."

And what she had perceived. The eerie illumination of the surrounding landscape, the outlines of buildings, the ocean, and small animals scampering across the ground.

"Then I saw you," she whispered. "You were like a bright light. And I saw Henri, too! It was wonderful. But then I saw the glow of three evil things. And they stared back at me. It scared me. That's when I woke up."

"Evil things?" This sent a shiver up Corrinne's spine.

"Yes. I sensed they were evil. I think."

"Three of them? Here? Inside the fort?"

"Yes, I think so," Anamosa answered. "But it is night. I could not tell where. But they were close together."

*

It was the girl's first time to be guided on how to *see* beyond what the owl saw. The *ghost* expected the girl to fear the evil things she saw. But it was necessary. He would guide her again tomorrow. Help her learn how to influence where the owl would fly, so she could do this again on her own. This was very soon for one so young and inexperienced. But there was not enough time left.

In the morning, when the glow of sunrise appeared on the horizon, the *ghost* surged to dominance and forced the white eagle to cross the narrows. The animal screeched with fear the entire way across. The *ghost* suppressed the eagle's instinct and kept flying hard towards the rising sun. Before the sun had reached its highest point in the sky, the *ghost* could see the high towers of the water city in the distance. It withdrew again to allow the bird time to hunt, feed, and rest before flying the rest of the way.

When the animal was rested and fed, the *ghost* flew directly at the distant spire, veering towards the water. At the last possible moment, it circled outside the walls to avoid any attempts by soldiers to shoot at the eagle. The female didn't like nearing the seawater at all. And it became very difficult to control her. The most the animal would tolerate was flying over the shoreline but higher in the sky. When the woman's house was directly on the left, the *ghost* banked inland and started a gentle spiral downward over the yard. It landed atop the dome-shaped small structure. No one was outside. The eagle was stepping back and forth, foot to foot, panting with nervousness. It did not want to linger here for very long.

Corrinne and Anamosa were drinking tea together in the cuisine. The twins were sitting on the floor playing with their toys. They all heard the distinctive loud *screech* at the same time. They glanced at one another with recognition and hurried to the back door. Since they saw their mother and Anamosa move to the back door, Calypso and Marcus followed them.

Corrinne touched one hand to her lips. "My God! It's come back again!"

Anamosa went outside immediately and walked directly towards the eagle, stopping ten paces away, like before. The twins followed her. The sun was shining. It was a warmer day in April, but not that much warmer than the last time the eagle had visited.

Corrinne managed to scoop up a wriggling Marcus in her arms and shouted. "Anna! Pick up Calypso!"

Anna turned and took the little girl's hand who only wanted to stand beside her.

"*Bird*," Calypso said loudly and pointed. "*White bird*."

"Yes, it is. Don't move, Calypso."

"*Down*," Marcus insisted and squirmed even more.

Corrinne set him down but gripped one of his hands strongly. He pulled.

"No, Marcus! Do you want to go back inside?"

Marcus stopped pulling. "*Bird*," he said.

"Yes, it's a bird. An eagle."

"*Eagle*," Marcus repeated. "Big *eagle*!"

Corrinne tried not to smile. "Yes, a very big eagle!"

Anamosa extended her hand, like before, palm down and limp.

"A-Anna! Be careful!"

The eagle hopped and easily glided down till it was only a step away. Anamosa stretched out her fingers further. This time, the eagle touched its beak to her fingers for several more seconds. Calypso mimicked Anna's movement and extended her hand too.

"Nooo!" Corrinne shouted.

The eagle gently touched the smaller girl's fingers for a moment, before it turned and hopped back up atop the dome. Marcus came running up and Anamosa grabbed hold of his hand too. Corrinne was standing by them all in the next second.

"Wh-what do you want?" Corrinne asked nervously. "Are we in danger?"

The *ghost* stared at Corrinne patiently.

"Big eagle!" Marcus said loudly with a smile.

"White eagle," Calypso added, as if it were a game.

"Is it about what Anna saw in her dreams?" Corrinne pressed.

The white eagle turned its head to the left, to stare at a large building further in the distance and higher up in the fort.

Corrinne looked to where the eagle was staring. "The Queen's Bastion? Something in the Queen's Bastion?"

The white eagle took flight. It began spiraling upward, higher and higher, until it turned to fly west. It was out of sight in another minute.

"Back in the house," Corrinne said sternly. "All of you."

Corrinne penned a message for Henri, tied it with a ribbon, and handed it to the guard standing outside the front door.

"Please deliver this to Lieutenant Gerrard."

"Yes, my lady."

Corrinne thanked God and blessed her good fortune there was no guard posted in the back. The message to Henri was simple. *Important. Come to dinner tonight.*

The Strait of Canceau

Captain Fleurant of the *Proud Recluse* saw the sails of a ship emerging from the Strait of Canceau through his telescope. It was an English cruiser, a frigate, a big one, fully sailed and on patrol. It was bow on, heading straight for him. He reversed course and began tacking against the wind. It was less than an hour to reach the Canceau Point, before he could turn due west. It was a race against the wind for now. The *Proud Recluse* had a slight advantage. It was faster and more maneuverable. But the frigate had cannons.

Philippe Gerrard and the Abenaki warrior called Panther Claw were down below. They felt the vessel list in a sharp turn and climbed topside.

"What's happening?" Philippe asked the captain.

The captain jerked his thumb behind him. Philippe looked back and saw the sails.

"That's a frigate," Fleurant replied. "I'm guessing an English one. It's coming after me."

"How do you know?"

There came the muffled sound of a cannon blast. A ball splashed in the water, back of the stern, a hundred paces distant, but close enough.

Oh, Philippe thought.

"That was just a ranging shot." The captain came left a few degrees, enough to foul the aim of the gunner on the frigate if they fired another shot without delay. They did. A second ball splashed down, still back of the stern but much closer.

Captain Fleurant started counting silently. He could imagine a gunner on the frigate turning the elevation screw on the first cannon. They usually had two cannons at the bow. He steered back to the right. Another blast.

"Thirty-three!" he shouted. "Second cannon! Start your count, Bosun!" Fleurant added five seconds to his count for the first cannon. It was crude, but it told him how fast they reloaded the first cannon.

The third shot fell short of the stern again about twenty paces and on the port side.

Philippe did not interrupt the captain. He found himself counting the time interval, too.

Malsum already decided this was futile. The other ship was bigger and had cannons! But there was nothing he could do.

The English frigate struggled with its tacking to close the distance against the wind. For almost an hour, they matched the tacking course changes of the smuggler. The balls eventually started falling to port or starboard. They had the range. The warship slowed its rate of fire, to conserve ammunition.

They're closing the distance. Philippe considered what he should do if the frigate did get close enough to seize the ship. The water was freezing. There weren't many options other than fighting.

"The rate of fire has slowed," he observed to the captain.

"They don't want to sink us," Fleurant said. "They want my ship as a prize."

The captain saw the land to port start to fall away. They were at the point. He waited an extra few minutes to be certain, then counterrotated the helm to change course to the west. Once the sails were properly set, their speed increased.

It wasn't long before the frigate came into view, and it was closer now. But the English warship did not make a dramatic course change. They did not fire any cannons. The distance slowly started to open.

Captain Fleurant glanced back and smiled with satisfaction. "That's it. Keep going."

"What's he doing?" Philippe asked.

"He has charts. Just like me. He can see me hugging the coastline and knows the land will soon tack back to the north. He intends to get by me and to the north, before he turns. That way he will have the weather gage, the wind behind him, as he closes."

The silence between them became prolonged. Fleurant knew Philippe wanted to ask the question.

"You want to ask what I plan to do, yes?"

"You will have to turn around at some point."

"True enough. But I know these coastal waters better than that English captain. Soon you will see a break in the land on the left. It looks like a river mouth, but it's an opening to a smaller bay full of coves. Lots of places to hide. The water's deep enough for me, but not deep enough for that frigate, and there are uncharted shoals. We go in there and wait. The English captain is hunting for prizes to capture. He won't wait very long. He will go further west towards the Saint Lawrence."

They stayed in the isolated bay overnight and continued into the Strait of Canceau the next morning. All seemed well until they sailed a third of the way through the narrow strait. Suddenly, the frigate reappeared coming around a bend in the strait barely two miles ahead of them. Again, straight at them, bow on. The English ship did not go to the Saint Lawrence as the captain had predicted. It went back into the strait instead, then anchored halfway through in the middle to wait for them.

Captain Fleurant knew the English had trapped him this time. He shouted orders to his crew and steered hard to the right. There was an extremely small cove there. The entrance was narrow, and the cove was shallow. Fleurant knew he could not turn around once he was inside. But that was not his plan.

Philippe and Malsum were already wearing their packs.

"I am going to drive hard aground," he shouted to Philippe. "Get ready to step off on the bow. The water will not be too deep."

The frigate dropped anchor outside the cove and immediately lowered a boat full of red-coated marines.

The *Proud Recluse* slid with a hiss upon the sand and mud shoal inside the cove. The bow lifted before it stopped.

"Good luck, Captain," Philippe shouted. Fleurant waved in reply.

Carrying their pack and weapons over their heads, Philippe and Malsum stepped off the bow and waded through the chest-deep freezing cold water. As they advanced onto the shore and into the trees, Philippe glanced back to see the English marines board and storm over the length of the *Proud Recluse*. Fleurant and his seamen stood still with their arms raised above their heads. One of the marines slammed the butt of his musket into Fleurant's head.

After putting more distance behind them, Philippe stopped. He withdrew the small telescope from his pack and counted the warship's guns. Two on the bow, two on the stern, and fifteen on the starboard side, meaning the same number to port, thirty-four guns in all. The frigate was powerful enough to stop and board any French trade vessel coming through the strait and powerful enough to engage another French warship. Something to remember.

"What now?" Malsum asked.

"We follow this coastal path. Watch for a fisherman to take us across."

They walked all day to let their clothes dry out. They did not see any fishing chaloupes. Near sundown, they camped inland a short distance, down in a ravine, and slept around a small fire pit to stay warm that night. At sunrise, they began walking again. It wasn't long before they came to a place where the strait was very narrow.

Philippe triangulated the distance. "It's half a mile or less, I think. I don't think the strait gets much narrower than this. We cross here," Philippe said. "The frigate has chased out all the fishing chaloupes."

"A raft then?"

Philippe nodded. "Yes."

It took them a few hours to lash one together, scavenging fallen trunks and sapling vines from the surrounding forest. They shaped two paddles out of some animal skins and tree branches. Neither the raft nor the paddles would take much abuse without falling apart. But it was good enough for this short distance. Philippe threw some sticks into the channel and with his telescope watched to see if there was a current. The pull was slightly to the right.

They decided to eat before they tried to cross. As they ate, Philippe thought he saw something white flying in front of the green forest background on the other side. *White! Probably a gull.* He viewed it through his telescope. *Too big for a gull.* Then it banked around and flew back in the other direction. It was hard to mistake the six-foot wingspan of this creature.

"That's no gull," Philippe said, excited. "That's the white eagle. I've not seen it in more than a year. Just there." He handed the telescope to Malsum and pointed. "There."

"It landed…perched high on a tree," Malsum said. He handed back the scope. "There…right at the top."

"I see it. It's waiting for us."

"Waiting for us?"

"Yes. Let's go."

The *ghost* saw the man coming closer. The man would have to cross the water. It made the eagle fly back and forth until it was certain it was seen. Then it perched and waited.

The night before, the *ghost* had reached out to the girl as she dreamed. He had guided her with images and thoughts to the owl again and helped her to direct the owl's flying with gentle dominance of one wing over the other. She learned quickly. He stayed with her and, through images, told her when she must withdraw from the owl completely. The *ghost* withdrew from the girl's dreams.

In the morning, the female eagle hunted and fed itself. But the eagle's urgency to mate had grown stronger still. The *ghost* used this fear to induce the eagle to fly towards the man. The mating would require the eagle to cross the saltwater channel, something the animal resisted doing. So, the *ghost* perched in a tree. Even at rest, the female eagle's urgency to mate was getting stronger. It was lifting one talon and then the other, over and over. The animal's growing anxiety was made worse by the *ghost*'s oppressive aura, which the eagle sensed. It knew the female's panic would increase enough to overcome the fear of the water channel. But the *ghost* wanted to wait for the man.

Philippe and Malsum slowly made their way across the narrows and grounded the raft directly in front of the tree where the white eagle was perched. Philippe stepped up on the shore a few paces away, dropped to one knee, and waited. Malsum followed his lead and did the same thing.

The eagle immediately glided to the ground right in front of them.

"I've never seen anything like this," Malsum whispered in awe.

Philippe stretched out his hand. "Oho, old friend," he greeted gently.

The eagle craned its neck and touched its beak to Philippe's hand. This close to men, the eagle's urgent needs to fly away spiked to the brink of panic. The *ghost* withdrew its dominance completely. The raptor flapped up into the air and flew directly across the channel. On the other side, it banked northwest on a path leading straight towards the breeding grounds.

"Where does it go?" Malsum asked in wonder.

"I don't know. Usually when the white eagle appears, it is a warning. Something will happen. We'll see it again...I hope. Let's find the coastal trail. It will lead us to Port Toulouse. I'll buy some horses once we're there, and we can ride the rest of the way."

Louisbourg

Henri did not come to dinner that first night after Corrinne sent the message. She learned he was away at Gabarus Bay. But he came over the second night, after riding back. It was dark. He was exhausted. His uniform was still wet from the morning fogs and sweat-stained from working the battlements in the afternoon sun. After reading the note, he had come directly here, not stopping to purify himself. *Important?*

At Corrinne's house, they embraced in greeting. His expression turned serious.

"What's wrong?"

"Nothing is wrong, exactly," Corrinne said tentatively. "Let's sit down. We've some things to talk about."

The twins were already in bed. Corrinne put a warm plate of food and a glass of wine on the table in front of Henri. He was more tired than hungry. He picked at the food while they talked.

"The white eagle came again," Anamosa announced with a proud smile.

Henri looked at Corrinne with surprise. "Came where? Here?!"

"Yes. It landed atop the oven in the back garden. We all went outside to see it."

"It touched my hand with its beak again," Anamosa added. "It touched Marcus' and Calypso's hands, too."

"What!"

"Nothing bad happened," Corrinne said quickly. "Not that I can tell, anyway. But Anamosa is having dreams again. Tell him."

Anamosa related her two experiences with the owl, how it hunted, and how the white eagle's spirit guided her.

"Guided you? How?"

"It shows me…images…and I…I sense, feelings. About things I should think or do. Nothing frightening. It's like a signing language, but without using hands. The spirit taught me how to see things that are invisible to us. I was looking down from high in the sky and I saw Corrinne!" Anamosa's voice became excited. "She was a bright light. And I saw you, too, Henri! You were another bright light. But then I saw three smaller, reddish lights.

They were close together. They scared me," she admitted, her voice losing her earlier excitement.

"I asked the eagle if we were in danger." Corrinne interjected. "It looked towards the Queen's Bastion. Then it flew away."

"The mercenary barracks," Henri said.

"Yes. Imagine how happy I am to know that," Corrinne replied evenly.

"Did you feel this evilness in Captain Stoecklin and the other Swiss officers?" Henri asked Anamosa.

"No. Those men did not scare me. They were unkind, cruel maybe. I would not fear to cut them. But they are not *evil*, not like this. Not like what I saw in my dream. *That* scared me."

"In your dream, you didn't see their faces?" The question was rhetorical. Anamosa shook her head.

"I will have guards posted on the back door, too," Henri said. He ate a few mouthfuls of food. In his exhaustion, the food was tasteless.

Corrinne had grown pensive from the discussion and now sat with her arms folded across her chest.

"It's already mid-April, and I have no idea when, or how, I am ever going to leave this place. I feel trapped. And the eagle's visit to us was a warning...it's always a warning. Minister Machault has been dismissed. I've not received any letters from Charles. And still no letters from Philippe! I do not understand this! I am nervous about even leaving the house!"

Henri reached out a hand to her. "I am here, Corrinne...for you and Anamosa, Marcus, and Calypso. I will protect you."

Henri's tone was sincere and brave. Corrinne was comfortable with the assumption Henri could confront the Swiss danger. But protecting her from the possessed servants of the wraith? Corrinne was not convinced that Henri could do this by himself.

"I will protect the twins," Anamosa asserted in a voice that sounded so innocent and young and brave.

That's all it took. Tears spilled from Corrinne's eyes. She held out her arms to Anamosa, who rushed to embrace her.

"Of course, you will, my little love."

Henri got up and placed the heavy crossbar over the back door. They normally did not use this because they were constantly going outside to the wood pile.

"Just until I get a guard posted in the back," Henri assured them. He bent down and embraced them both. "I must to go back to the barracks. I will come by again in the morning."

*

For several weeks, Captain Bergen Stoecklin and both of his trusted lieutenants walked casually around the faubourgs east and west, learning more and more about the fortress-city with each passing day. They noted and memorized the names of the streets, counted the number of paces between the corners, what types of buildings they passed, learned who lived where and what business, if any, they conducted. Upon return to their quarters inside the Queen's Bastion barracks, they transferred the memorized information to a special map they were making, which grew richer with added detail and information. By the third week of such reconnaissance, the map had outlined multiple approaches to a specific target: the stone house residence of Lady Corrinne VanderMeer.

Stoecklin expected the exhaustive details to expose weaknesses in their planning; to reveal obstacles to a quick, efficient kill.

It was all far too elaborate. But he was bored.

The kill was the easier part of his plan. The sun would set around half past the hour of six. He still had to pick the day. He could not do it until the ship arrived. There were marine guards posted on her doors. Consistently on the front door, less frequently at the back door. The stone walls of the garden yard were six feet tall. They provided cover in two directions, and the half-wall of the remaining side, where the dome-shaped oven was located, overlooked a wide rectangular space of land, fifty paces wide and seventy paces long. This land was the vegetable garden of an adjoining house. The mix of beans, squash, and corn crops had just begun to sprout. The tall back and side wall had six-foot swinging doors on hinges, set at the middle. They were three-foot-wide, quarter-inch steel plates, with slide-bolts that only opened from inside the wall to permit access as approved by the owner.

Captain Stoecklin decided he would scale the half wall and go in through the back door. If there was a marine guard posted on the night he chose, the guard would be killed. The guard at the front door would be distracted by one of his lieutenants, clubbed by the other, and carried into the back yard after Stoecklin unbolted the metal door. Stoecklin would enter though the back door and slay everyone inside the house.

They would all return to the Queen's Bastion for the night. That was the hard part. The waiting afterwards. But there really was no choice. They would rendezvous with the Dutch ship before it sailed with the tide the next day.

The escape must be pre-planned with the captain of the ship. Stoecklin decided a delay of two days from the time the ship arrived until they sailed should allow enough time for any final changes. This captain must remain unaware of the assassination.

Louisbourg

The morning after Henri's dinner with Corrinne and Anamosa, events in Louisbourg began to change dramatically. The first squadron of French warships promised to Governor Drucour by Minister Machault arrived in Louisbourg: four heavily armed ships-of-the-line and three frigates from the naval port in Brest. They had sailed in January, going first to the French island colonies in the Antilles, to patrol and show the flag, before turning back north to Louisbourg, their ultimate destination.

Then in February, the French king dismissed the two ministers responsible for directing the war effort, which the French had been winning until their dismissal. Few if any within the French government agreed with this decision.

French Admiral Dubois de le Motte, the most highly decorated naval officer in the French navy, was certainly not one of them. Despite Minister Machault's appalling dismissal by King Louis XV, the seventy-four year old was resolved to fulfill Minister Machault's last order to him.

"Defend Louisbourg from English invasion. That is what we shall do!" Admiral de la Motte knew if Louisbourg was invested by the English, all New France would fall soon after. "Only the next Minister of Marine, who has not yet been named, can rescind that order. Unless, of course, the king himself intervenes. But he has neither the balls…he has given those away… nor does he possess the requisite vision of the world."

*

Henri stood at the quay wall and watched the magnificent warships enter the harbor and drop anchor. Saluting cannon from the various bastions and batteries boomed repeatedly in welcome. Henri swelled with pride at seeing them. He wondered if Commodore Beaussier de Lisle might be in command of the squadron. Unfortunately, he was not.

The crowd of people thronging the wall near Frédéric Gate was the largest Henri had ever seen. And more people continued to stream down from the faubourgs. The whole city was turning out for this welcome. The reinforcing presence of the French squadron of warships filled the fortress city with renewed optimism. The threat of an English invasion was no longer a certainty.

Caught up in the citizens' excitement, Henri suddenly realized he'd been watching for too long. He hurried to Corrinne's house, knowing she would want to come out to see this, too. He was right. They were all dressed and waiting. Henri and the marine guard posted at the front door escorted them down to the quay wall. Henri carried Marcus on his shoulders, so the boy could see over the crowd. The marine guard joyously carried Calypso high on his chest. Anamosa hooked her hand in Henri's uniform pocket.

"What a beautiful sight!" Corrinne exclaimed with a tinge of relief.

Another saluting cannon fired.

"*Boom*!" Marcus said loudly.

"Boom, indeed!" Henri responded with a laugh.

Calypso's head swiveled back and forth. She smiled at every person she saw, most of whom rewarded her by smiling back.

The sun was shining that morning, though it was still cold. Corrinne closed her eyes and raised her face to the sun's warmth. "What a perfect day." Her mood lifted.

Suddenly, the crowd at Frédéric Gate spread out to either side. Governor Drucour was approaching the gate on Rue Toulouse with Marie-Louise de Drucour on his arm. They arrived amid two columns of grenadiers and were preceded by six rat-a-tat drummers. Boats had been lowered from the arriving ships as the captains came ashore to pay their respects. In the first boat was the squadron commander Commodore Joseph du Bauffremont.

Henri and Corrinne were too far back in the crowd to hear what was being said. But it was easy to guess. They saw much saluting and bowing. And after all the captains and other civilian dignitaries had come through the gate and received the perfunctory welcome, the governor and the column of soldiers turned around. To the sound of a victorious drum beat, the naval officers were escorted ceremoniously to the King's Bastion where the governor would conduct a more proper welcome and begin the two-day celebration.

Merchants and vendors sped to their shops and stalls to prepare for the sailors and other visitors who would come ashore to buy and trade goods. With that, the crowds around the gate began to thin, except for those people still curious to see who else might come ashore. As the larger landing boats approached the gate, rumors spread they were bringing more troops to reinforce the garrison. Most people welcomed this news.

Corrinne frowned at seeing the approach of these troop carriers. There could be more mercenaries among them. Henri saw her frown. He was also interested to learn who else was coming on the warships. Henri did not care if they were French. Any of them could be hired assassins. Henri gestured to Corrinne they should leave. They returned to the house where Corrinne prepared hot food to break their fast, inviting the marine front-door guard to join Henri at the table.

They were in the middle of eating when a knock came to the front door. Henri got up and opened the door cautiously. It was two of his marines, arriving to stand their guard at the front and back doors. They were all familiar with these men. Henri allowed them to enter so they could greet everyone before taking their posts. One of them handed a letter to Lady Corrinne that he retrieved from the mail orderly at the King's Bastion.

"I told him I would see you, my lady, so he gave it to me."

"A missive for me! *Merci*, Corporal. This day is getting better and better."

The marines left by opposite doors to continue their watch outside. The front-door guard returned to the barracks. Only Henri and the children remained in the cuisine. Corrinne broke the seal on the missive. What she saw made her stagger into a chair.

"*Mon Dieu*!" She broke into a smile. Her heart was pounding with excitement. "It's from Philippe! He is on his way here! What's today's date?" She remembered it. "It's already been two weeks. *Mon Dieu*! He could arrive at any time!"

CHAPTER 20
LOUISBOURG
APRIL 1757
Hail the Falcon Queen

The unexpected appearance of a French squadron of heavy ships-of-the-line and its escort frigates forced the lighter English frigates patrolling the waters east of Louisbourg harbor to retreat to Halifax and report the new enemy strength. The agreed-upon plan for the invasion of Louisbourg specified a fleet of English ships that was ten times the number of the French. Nevertheless, English courier ships were dispatched without delay to report the build-up to London.

Halifax responded by sending more powerful warships to patrol the entrance. It would prove not to be enough.

North Atlantic

For once, Captain LaTour's crossing of the Atlantic encountered almost no inclement weather. Storms in the northern waters of the Atlantic happened suddenly and were always violent. Consequently, when he did see the black storm clouds gathering in the northwest, he rigged the ship for a heavy storm, reefing most of his sails and taking down the flags and pennants. But driven by strong westerly winds, the storm passed by him to the north, smattering the ship with less violent winds and stinging rains.

LaTour counted his lucky stars and was properly grateful.

Then, a few sailing days away from Louisbourg, he saw the sails of, not one, but two warships coming up from the south. A sense of foreboding descended on him like bad weather.

"French or English?" Victorio asked while looking through a watch glass.

"They are not flying their colors. I cannot tell from the sails…but they are both frigates. The English cruisers near Louisbourg are usually frigates," LaTour replied.

"We have to show them something," Victorio asserted. "Or they will board us."

"I know that!" LaTour replied with irritation.

LaTour wrestled to make this decision…which flag to fly? French or Dutch? If the frigates were English, they would board him no matter what he was flying. And if he flew French colors, they may first open fire. *So then, Dutch,* he decided.

"Do you think the frigates might be French?" Victorio asked. "They are both set with four jib sails. That's the usual rigging for French frigates."

It is? LaTour frowned. *If the frigates are French…do I fly French or Dutch colors? Either way, I am still boarded.*

"Raise the Dutch flag," he decided impulsively. "We are going to be boarded no matter what we do. But we will not be fired upon if we are flying Dutch colors…at least, I don't think so."

Victorio supervised the crew and got the tri-color orange-white-blue flag raised on the stern and slipped in the *William's Queen*'s placard in the slot across the rail. "And the House of Brunswick pennant?"

God's balls! Captain LaTour considered this. "No. No pennant."

LaTour was carrying three sets of credentials. He had orders from the former Minister of Marine, Jean-Baptiste de Machault to retrieve the Swiss officer from Louisbourg. But Minister Machault had been dismissed. *If the frigates are French, better not use that one.* His ownership papers from Lord Charles VanderMeer? *He's dead. But he is still the owner. Probably better to not use that one either, not at first.* His orders from Admiral Dubois de la Motte only confirmed what Machault had ordered him to do. *But not if they are English! Only if they are French. If English, then maybe use Lord VanderMeer's papers?*

Victorio shouted from the main deck. "Captain, they've raised *French* signal flags, telling us to heave to and prepare to be boarded."

French? New questions arose. LaTour was north of the Louisbourg latitude on purpose to avoid the blockade cruisers if possible. *French? Out here?*

LaTour took over the helm and shouted. "Heaving to!" He turned to tack through the wind. "Do not free the jib sheet!" When the jib sheets were held back, LaTour rotated the helm the opposite way, as if to tack in the other direction. But without the jibs to steer to bow, the speed was slowed almost to a stop.

LaTour settled on using Admiral de la Motte's written orders. Leaving Victorio in charge topside, he hurried to his quarters to get those, and at the last moment thought to bring Lord VanderMeer's ownership papers...*I might as well bring Machault's orders, too.*

One of the two escort frigates came close aboard to inspect him. It moored to the port side and pushed over a boarding brow. The other circled nearby. *William's Queen* was flying the flag of the Dutch Republic, a neutral country.

The French captain of the thirty-two gun *La Comète* came over the brow and sent one of his ensigns and two marines to inspect belowdecks without asking for permission.

"Bosun Linard! Go with the ensign and answer his questions!"

The frigate commander saluted Captain LaTour out of respect.

"I am Captain Severyn Peltier of *La Comète*. Your name, Captain? Your ship's name, and from where you sailed?" The officer spoke with a bored tone, suggesting he'd asked these same questions hundreds of times before.

LaTour answered his questions. When he was done, LaTour suddenly found it difficult to believe what he had just told the French officer.

The French captain squinted skeptically. "You wear the uniform of a French naval officer!"

Merde! LaTour had forgotten about that.

"You are flying Dutch colors. You claim to be sailing from La Rochelle and you are going to Louisbourg? Which is under an English blockade... not to forget, we are at war!"

"Yes, Captain."

"What? That's how you respond? 'Yes, Captain.' And if I say you are a smuggler?"

"*Smuggler*? No, Captain. I am not a smuggler! I sail under French orders!"

"From who? You are flying *Dutch* colors!"

"Yes. The owner of my ship is Dutch. In peacetime, I am occasionally a smuggler."

"What?"

LaTour noticed Victorio's eyes widen in panic.

"I mean, because of the war, my ship was conscripted by Admiral de la Motte," LaTour quickly added. "Um...here are my papers."

The French captain read the admiral's orders.

During that interval, the ensign came up from inspecting below. "I see only normal cargo down below, Captain."

"Why are you going to Louisbourg?"

"My orders are to rendezvous with a Swiss army officer…a Captain Bergen Stoecklin. He is a mercenary there…to bring him back with me to France."

"These alleged orders do not say this."

"That is correct. But these do." LaTour handed him the written orders from Minister Machault.

"You do realize Jean-Baptiste de Machault is no longer the Minister of Marine."

"Yes, sir. I know that. But he was the minister when these orders were given to me. Admiral de la Motte has since confirmed I should still follow those orders."

"You are French! How comes this ship to be Dutch?"

LaTour handed over the ownership papers signed by Lord Charles VanderMeer and the Governor-General of New France, the Marquis Duquesne. Then he explained when the purchase was completed.

"I had been trading in the Antilles until Admiral de la Motte gave me these firm orders."

Captain Peltier looked over all three seemingly official documents and shook his head in bewilderment.

"Captain LaTour, either you are the cleverest smuggler I have ever encountered, or you are telling me the truth."

"Maybe I am both!" LaTour jested with an embarrassed laugh, only to see Captain Peltier scowl in response. "*Pardon*, Captain."

The captain of the frigate handed the documents back to LaTour.

"Captain LaTour, you are free to go. But if I do not see this ship in Louisbourg harbor within the week, I will report your ship and warrant you as a smuggler."

"Oh, I will be sailing right behind you!"

"I advise you not to do that. There are four French ships-of-the-line just over the horizon. If we encounter the English blockade vessels, there will be a battle. Better you wait out here a day before you continue your sail."

"Yes, sir. I will."

The frigate pulled back its brow and sailed west with its companion vessel.

The crew of the *William's Queen* had, once again, seen demonstrated evidence of their captain's extraordinary good luck.

Once the frigates were hull-down and moving west, LaTour decided what to do.

"We'll reef most of the sail today and keep going slowly west," he told Victorio and Bosun Linard. "Tomorrow morning, we will raise full sail and finish this crossing."

Louisbourg

It was the morning of the third day marking the navy's arrival. Madame Marie-Louise de Drucour had bills posted on kiosks throughout the faubourgs. It announced a celebratory ball at the King's Bastion that night, in honor of the naval officers in Commodore du Bauffroment's squadron. Senior officers of the Louisbourg garrison were also invited, along with senior administrators of government and local merchants. Of course, any of the women in the faubourgs who desired to be present were invited.

The women of Louisbourg knew the men would outnumber the women at least three to one. And most of these young naval officers were unmarried.

Captain LaTour and *William's Queen* entered port the same day the postings went up for the ball. The arrival was barely noticed among the massive warships dominating the harbor. No cheering crowds this time. The ship was assigned an anchorage circle much further out from Frédéric Gate than usual. There was a long line of cargo boats and rafts near the wharves and quay wall docks either unloading or waiting to unload. The wharves and docks were overflowing with food, ammunition, and other supplies transported to Louisbourg by the naval squadron. This included sugar, coffee, pineapples, and other luxury commodities from Haiti.

LaTour, Victorio, and Bosun Linard gathered in the captain's dining cabin.

"Well, you've seen it. The cargo docks are backed up. I don't know when we'll get our cargo offloaded, let alone sold to the government or merchants. And the navy is not here for profits. They will simply give it all to the fortress. Prices will be quashed. Victorio, you and I will go to the harbormaster, report our arrival, and learn what he wants us to do. Then you come back and take charge of the ship while I go on to the King's Bastion and report our arrival to the governor. After that, I will find this Swiss army captain, Bergen Stoecklin, as per my orders from Admiral de la Motte. Then I will call upon Lady Corrinne."

They were silent for a few moments.

"Do you plan to tell her about Lord VanderMeer and Madame Dubonnet?" Victorio finally asked.

LaTour winced at the thought. "First, I need to find out if Lady Corrinne knows about Lord VanderMeer. She will be happy to see me. I don't want to make her day worse. But if I do not do it today, I will certainly do it tomorrow. I have the old bishop's journals to deliver and the missive from Madame Dubonnet. She'll want to discuss her departure from Louisbourg. My orders regarding Captain Stoecklin's transport back to France conflicts with taking her to Québec City. Let me get some questions answered. I know the crew is anxious to go ashore, but our cargo position is not scheduled. This could change at any time." He looked at Bosun Linard. "Make a list and let half the crew go ashore today. Make certain they do not boast about who we are."

The captain and Victorio were rowed by two crewmen to a spot along the quay wall cargo docks that had a tiny open space, just wide enough to allow them to step off at the bow. LaTour carried a large satchel of gifts over his shoulder for Lady Corrinne and the children.

"Back away from the dock," he told the crewmen. "Wait somewhere close by and watch for Victorio's return."

When they reached the harbormaster's building, they found a large crowd of people thronged around the entry doors: sailors, merchants, buyers, and naval officers. That had never happened before.

"It will take us an hour, if not longer, to get a turn at the counter," Victorio said.

"I cannot wait that long. You know what to say. I am going to the governor's office."

LaTour turned to head up Rue Toulouse only to come face-to-face with the frigate captain escorted by a marine private.

"Captain Peltier! *Bonjour*!"

"*Bonjour*, Captain LaTour. So, you told me the truth after all. You only smuggle during times of peace."

"No, no, Captain. I am strictly a *trading* vessel now. I smuggled things a decade ago…as did everyone else."

"You *admit* to smuggling?"

LaTour's expression turned remorseful. "Captain Peltier, we must all have a past we are not proud of…but now I am a naval officer, like you."

"You are certainly *not* like me. But do not be concerned, Captain. Go about your business."

Captain Peltier pushed by LaTour and on through the crowd with his guard to enter the harbormaster building.

Captain LaTour hurried up the hill as fast as he could walk and returned the salute from the guards at the entrance to the King's Bastion. Just several steps inside, he faced the ballroom's double-doors, already wide open. The room was noisy and congested with workmen hanging decorations, setting up chairs and tables, and other preparations for the festivities scheduled that night. He recalled the governor's recording aide was down a hallway to the right and found the man unoccupied.

"*Bonjour*, Lieutenant." He could not remember the officer's name.

The lieutenant looked up with surprise. "Captain LaTour! Back so soon?"

"Yes. With orders from Admiral de la Motte." LaTour showed the orders to the lieutenant who recorded them in a logbook, before he frowned.

"You're here for Captain Stoecklin?"

"Yes. Will Governor Drucour want to see me today?"

The lieutenant shook his head. "Not today. No time. But come to the celebration ball tonight. You will see him there."

"Do you know where I can find this man, Captain Bergen Stoecklin?"

The lieutenant's frown returned. "He is probably lying about in his barracks at the Queen's Bastion. The Swiss mercenaries are not very popular. A lot of people will be pleased to learn Captain Stoecklin is leaving Louisbourg."

LaTour immediately was put on guard. "Is there something I should know about the captain?"

"This is my opinion, but Captain Stoecklin is rude and acts superior to everyone else. He called a faubourg woman a whore in public! Provoked a sword duel with a marine. He is a very unpleasant person."

"I see. Thank you for your candor, Lieutenant."

LaTour went back outside and turned right, heading further uphill towards the equally large Queen's Bastion. There was a two-story barracks built in the bastion marshalling yards. It had been constructed by the English to garrison its soldiers after their successful siege of Louisbourg in 1745. He saluted more guards standing outside the barracks and went to the guard captain's desk. A corporal stood and saluted him. LaTour introduced himself and asked for Captain Stoecklin.

"I will send someone to find him, sir. *S'il vous plaît,* you may wait over there." The corporal pointed towards some chairs against the wall. He printed

Captain LaTour's name on a slip of paper for the messenger. "Find Captain Stoecklin and tell him this man is here to see him."

Captain Bergen Stoecklin was playing cards with three other Swiss soldiers when the messenger came to the table.

"Captain, you have a visitor waiting downstairs."

"A visitor? For me?" Stoecklin raised his eyebrows and glanced around the table with amusement. "A female one, I trust?"

"No, sir." The messenger gave him the slip of paper. "A French naval officer, a Captain LaTour?"

Stoecklin's eyes widened. "Tell Captain LaTour I will be coming down to see him without delay."

"Yes, sir."

A trio of other mercenaries sitting nearby had overheard the name of the visitor to see Captain Stoecklin. They looked at one another. The senior man among them, a sergeant, gestured for the others to follow him. They went down to the guard captain's desk and asked the corporal about Captain LaTour. The corporal pointed towards the naval officer sitting across the room by himself. They approached him.

LaTour got to his feet before the three mercenaries reached him. "Captain Stoecklin?"

"No, sir. I overheard your name being spoken. You are Captain LaTour?"

"I am."

"Your ship is *William's Queen*?"

LaTour was on guard again. "And who are you?"

Just then Captain Stoecklin arrived. The soldiers snapped to attention.

"You men are dismissed! Withdraw," he ordered tersely. "Captain LaTour, yes? What did those soldiers want with you?"

LaTour shook his head. "I don't know. They confirmed my name and asked about my ship. Then you came."

"Let's talk outside. It's a beautiful day."

After further introductions and polite conversation, Captain Stoecklin got to the point.

"Your order states you will transport me back to France, yes?"

"Yes."

"How long will the crossing take?"

"Two weeks, perhaps three weeks if there are delays due to the weather."

"Good. I have two other Swiss officers who accompany me. Is that a problem?"

"Not as long as someone pays me for their passage."

Stoecklin laughed. "Yes, of course. How soon can we leave?"

"I have to offload my cargo first. The wharves are jammed with supplies coming off the warships. That may not happen until tomorrow, and it may even be a day later."

LaTour decided not to mention Lady Corrinne.

"I would like to see your ship. Today? Is this possible?"

"When my cargo is offloaded, I will send someone to come and get you."

"I want to visit today."

The contemptuous expression and imperious tone rankled, and LaTour would accept none of this.

"Captain Stoecklin, I just anchored in the harbor well beyond the warships. I have not been assigned a cargo raft nor a position on the docks to move my cargo. You will wait until I am ready."

Stoecklin sensed this was a battle he could not win. "Very well. Tomorrow then. *Bonne journée, Capitaine.*" He turned his back and walked away before Captain LaTour could refuse or protest further.

Captain LaTour stared as the man walked away. Showing his back was an intentional slight. LaTour fumed.

*

Corrinne began making plans to attend the celebration ball as soon as the front-door guard brought her one of the kiosk flyers. Like everyone else in Louisbourg, she was starved for news. For herself personally, she was starved for attention. And a room full of naval officers would certainly provide a lot of that. Besides, the letter she received from Philippe, she interpreted it as a sign, a turning point event. Her life was in motion again, and she could take the next step. Her mood was positive, and she wanted to elevate it further. The celebration ball would do that.

With Anamosa's assistance, she went through the trunk of clothes that held the gowns reserved for just such occasions. She had brought six of them to Louisbourg and used only one so far. She lifted them carefully, and laid them all out. Then she tried them on, one at a time, and inspected her look in the standing mirror.

"Do you like this one, Callie?"

To Corrinne's pleasant surprise, Calypso took an interest in admiring the garish dresses, smiling, even saying yes. Callie never said *no. Mommy looked beautiful in everything.*

Marcus watched, too, chewing on a sugar biscuit, a serious expression on his face, trying to puzzle out what was so exciting about any of this.

After trying on all six gowns, they had narrowed the selection down to two when Corrinne heard a loud knock at the front door.

Corrinne slipped on her day dress and went downstairs followed by everyone else. The knock on the door sounded again.

"Lady Corrinne? Are you there?"

The voice was slightly familiar, but to be safe, she gestured the children to get behind her, withdrew the double-barrel pistol from the holster on the wall, and cracked opened the viewing port. Upon seeing Captain Beauregard LaTour's smiling face, she screamed with joy, put away the pistol, and threw open the door.

"Beauregard! Beauregard!" She threw her arms around him in greeting.

Captain LaTour entered, laughing. And with equal joy, allowed himself to be surrounded by Corrinne and the children. He sat down in a chair to give the twins better access to climb up on his lap. Anamosa had her arms wrapped around the captain's neck.

Corrinne pulled another chair directly in front of him and grasped both his hands. Tears of happiness rolled down her cheeks. LaTour's arrival was another good sign. She could not speak fast enough.

"It is so good to see you! I am so happy you are here! I got a letter from Philippe! He is coming to Louisbourg. Right now! He could arrive any day! Even today! Won't that be wonderful?"

"Philippe will be here, too? This must be fate."

"That's what I think, too. Do you bring letters or news?"

"Both. But I am anchored beyond the warships. It's hard just getting to the docks. I've brought presents for you. But I see Marcus has found them."

Marcus was already searching through the satchel beside the chair. He was emptying it and found many packages wrapped with bows. Marcus was quickly joined by Anamosa and Calypso. They began opening all the gifts.

While the children were preoccupied, Corrinne spoke quietly. "What about Charles? How does he fare? I've not had mail from him in almost two months."

LaTour shook his head and cleared his throat. "I'm so sorry."

"Oh, no," Corrinne lamented. She sat back in her chair. Her tears of happiness had changed to ones of sadness. "Were you there?"

"I was at the beginning. But not at the end. Word came to me the day before I sailed. From what I was told, his infirmities turned severe. His passing was a blessing."

"I wish I had been there," she said in a voice filled with guilt and regret. "He should not have died alone…someone who loved him should have been with him."

LaTour replied quickly. "I am certain Lord VanderMeer was not alone. I'm told his father personally took charge of his care."

Corrinne had been dreading news of Charles' death for some time. Now that it had come, it did not lessen the pain of being told. He'd written her four letters, warning it was only a matter of time. The last one spoke of the gruesome amputations he'd endured, but he also wrote of the enjoyable conversations with his father. Charles had shared important years of her life, including the birth of Calypso and Marcus, who both now carried Charles' last name, *VanderMeer*. She thought about that, too. What else might that bring?

When LaTour saw her sad, far away expression become prolonged, he gave her better news.

"I have some missives and other things for you still on the ship. I will bring them to you tomorrow."

Corrinne sniffed back her tears. Her resolve strengthened.

"I am ready to leave this place, Captain. Are you ready to take me?"

"My Lady Corrinne, it is my great privilege to take you anywhere in the world you want to go. But if you will permit me, I would like to change my ship's name back to the *Falcon Queen*."

Depressed from the news of Charles' death, she was cheered by this request. It was another sign. Destiny was intervening, in a good way.

"Hail the *Falcon Queen*," she declared softly. "I will so christen it again, with champagne, as soon as I step on board. Does the crew miss me?"

Captain LaTour expression brightened. He chuckled softly. "My lady, you have no idea how happy the crew will be to see you. They have personally brought you a great surprise. It only awaits your presence."

"The crew brought me a surprise? I love surprises! Now that you've told me of its existence, I feel denied. Well, tomorrow then, for certain. But we cannot leave Louisbourg until Philippe gets here. He is going with me this time. To Québec City…or maybe all the way to Montréal? What say you?"

"Speaking for the crew, we would be delighted to see those cities again. It will be like old times, yes?"

"Yes, it will," she said wistfully. "Now I am excited that sailing with you also lies in my future. But I am going to the ball tonight, in celebration of the navy's arrival, to be doted upon by all the handsome young officers. Henri will be there, too. He's to be my escort. I insist you come as well."

"I would be honored. I will have to go back to the ship and purify my appearance."

"We are not certain," Anamosa suddenly interrupted, "which presents go to whom."

All the packages had now been unwrapped and were spread around on the floor, amid a messy pile of colored linen-paper and ribbons. Marcus had what looked to be a hundred painted wooden soldiers gathered in front of him. He was uninterested in anything else. There were at least a dozen silver or gold necklaces, rings, and bracelets, all of which Calypso had claimed, either around her neck, on her fingers, or circling her wrists.

"Callie, you look like a gypsy princess!" Corrinne said, laughing.

LaTour saw Anamosa's disappointment.

"Anamosa, those were all for Calypso and Marcus. I brought something *special* for you," LaTour said. He reached into his pocket and withdrew a small piece of black linen tied with a red ribbon. "Here."

Anamosa smiled brightly and carefully untied the package. Inside the linen wrapper was a beautiful three carat emerald ring, set on a gold band engraved with a Celtic filigree. Anamosa's mouth dropped open in wonder.

"This comes from a land in France called Brittany." Captain LaTour slipped it on her largest finger. It was still a little big, but he knew Corrinne could get a jeweler to fix that.

"*Merci! Merci!*" Anamosa bubbled with joy and hugged him tightly around the neck.

Corrinne was impressed. "Well, Captain…that is a most exquisite gift for a young maiden. It makes me wonder about mine…" She could tell by the look on his face that had been her gift.

"I've saved yours for tomorrow, my lady," he explained with haste.

"Just come to the ball tonight," she repeated, "and dance with me. That's gift enough."

"Then, if you please, I will take my leave. The *Falcon Queen* requires my attention." He stood up and hugged them all. "And I promise to come back to see your little ones every single day!"

Captain LaTour encountered Henri near Frédéric Gate, when Henri ran up and embraced him.

"It is so great to see you! I was just told your ship arrived! Did you see Lady Corrinne?"

"Just left her house! But look at you, Henri. You must have grown another foot! And you are a marine lieutenant now?"

"Yes. It's nothing." Henri tried to shrug away the compliment. "Major Péan and most of the marines were recalled to Québec City. I volunteered to stay behind with half a platoon to act as guards for Lady Corrinne. So, I was promoted. There is a ball tonight!"

"I know. Lady Corrinne made me promise to go."

Henri smiled. "You dance?"

"Not in twenty years, maybe longer. You?"

Henri grimaced. "No. I got my color sergeant to teach me a few steps at the barracks."

"Your color sergeant!" LaTour laughed. "Won't we be a pair! Don't worry, Henri. The women know what to do. And I will probably flap around like a torn jib sheet and soak up all the embarrassment."

"I'm escorting Lady Corrinne."

"There, you see, no one will be looking at you anyway. I must get back to the ship. I'm having trouble getting cargo offloaded because of them." He pointed toward the harbor with annoyance.

"Yes!" Henri spread his arms wide towards the harbor. "Don't these huge man-o-wars look grand?"

"They do, indeed. I will see you tonight then."

Back aboard the *Queen*, LaTour learned that none of the crew had gone ashore.

"The cargo master keeps saying we will have a slot on the docks this afternoon," Victorio complained. "We stand second in the line of waiting merchant ships. So I kept the crew aboard."

"Well, let's keep them aboard until this unloading snarl is resolved. If we do get a chance, we will need to move fast. That will take all hands."

"What about you? Did you find Captain Stoecklin? And see Lady Corrinne? The crew is asking about her."

LaTour could feel the crew's eyes and knew they were listening intently. "Let's talk in my cabin."

*

Captain Bergen Stoecklin sat down with his two lieutenants to finalize the details.

"My luck still holds. The day has come. We will act on this tonight. The celebration ball will mask all our activities. It's perfect. First, we must make an appearance at the festivities in a manner not too obtrusive, yet noticeable so that people will be able to witness seeing each one of us. I will choose the appropriate time to leave by the side door to the east. It is unguarded. Once our work is done, we will return to the ball as if we had never left. Tomorrow, we will be going out to the ship waiting for us at anchor. A Dutch ship. *William's Queen*. The captain and I met this morning. He has only to unload his cargo before he puts back to sea. It is all arranged. Good fortune and our true home awaits us."

The *ghost* was back at the breeding grounds. It had managed to dominate the female, changing her direction of flight to avoid the flurry of male eagles flying nearer to the fertile female the closer they got to their destination. Her urge to mate was so strong she was submissive to the approach of the males; any one of them was acceptable. But when a white-feathered eagle approached, she reacted differently, aggressively, turning towards the white eagle. It was unfortunate, but the mating was inevitable.

With resignation, the *ghost* withdrew and gave into the euphoric joining of the talons, the falling, lazy circular tumbles through the air, the sudden flash and burst of pleasure, and the exhilaration at separating just short of crashing into the sharp, protruding limbs of the treetops.

Before the sun set that day, the *ghost* perceived new life germinating within the female. The *ghost* did not try to dominate the female after sensing this life, except to help her on occasion. It was better to allow the female's instincts to drive the preparation of a nest, high in a tree, near the lake of the breeding grounds. For the next five moons, the *ghost* would have to wait for the eggs to be laid, to hatch, and the fledgling eagles become mature enough to fly and feed themselves.

The night before, the *ghost* had reached out to join with the dreams of the girl, who had reached out on her own to join with the spirit of the great owl. The *ghost*'s connection with the girl was much stronger after the last visit. As before, the girl thrilled as the owl glided silently over the dark fields below and snatched an unsuspecting vole in its talons. It did this repeatedly.

The *ghost* conjured images in the girl's dreaming, showing the owl and its prey, side by side, with the face of the girl away to the side of both creatures. The girl's dreaming was interrupted as a question took form in her thinking.

Are you the owl or the mouse? Then the owl's sight moved over the lands until the three reddish lights came into view.

Anamosa awoke panting with fear, but not loud enough to awaken Corrinne. She lay there in the dark of the bedroom, searching for meaning in the dream vision. *We are in danger*, she decided. But from who? Or what?

The *ghost* and the demon gazed at one another across the endless void of the dream world. Neither of them faltered. The demon's servants would attack soon. This effort took concentration and exhausted the strength of the female eagle even as it slept. The *ghost* was forced to withdraw from the girl's dreams to allow the eagle to rest peacefully for the remainder of the night. It could not do more. The girl had been warned. She must learn to trust her instincts and prepare.

Rochefort Citadel, France

Lieutenant-Colonel Karl Krieger rolled restlessly in the bed as his nightmarish possessor forced him to invade the dreams of the servants far away, across the great salty sea. Three of the newest servants were its primary interest that night. They had important information for the vulnax. The ship was in the water city, near the woman. The vulnax's rage and desire surged. This presented another chance to question the crew, to learn the location of the châsse. Question the woman, too! The time was now. The châsse must be found. The wraith was determined not to be disappointed again.

Isolate them somewhere secret, where we will not be disturbed.

The wraith decided quickly. It sensed the servants' confusion. The servants would attempt to obey. But they were not clever. The wraith had to be specific. The stone house of the woman? That was a good place. Isolated and out of sight. *Use the stone house of the woman*, It told them.

But capturing and taking captives in the water city would not be easy to do. Too many others might see and interfere. *Do this in the dark*, It told them.

The new spirit was already at that house. A young female. His enemy was teaching her to use the sight. This female must be slain before she gets stronger. *The girl at the house must be slain*, It told them.

The woman was at the house. She would know the châsse's location. She had made this decision. The woman was guarded. The guards must be eliminated. Getting servants to this water city had been difficult. Replacing them would take too long. If anything goes wrong, they would be revealed. They could only be used once. There was no place for the servants to retreat. But the ship was there now! The opportunity to learn the location of the châsse made the risk to the servants unimportant. The vulnax gave more specific commands.

Capture the captain from the ship. Take him to the stone house, alive, to be questioned. Kill any guards and everyone inside the house, but not the captain and not the woman.

*

Lieutenant Henri Gerrard stood before his marine platoon inside the Dauphin barracks and asked how he looked. He'd worn his cleanest, pressed gray-white marine dress uniform. The outer waistcoat hung almost to his knees. The long sleeves were folded back at the wrist, with six-inch royal-blue cuffs adorned with gold buttons. The inner waistcoat was shorter, also royal blue but trimmed with gold ribbon on its edges. Royal-blue pants, covered up over the knees with white stockings. White gaiters slipped over the shoes, over the stockings, and side-buttoned up the legs almost to the knees. A white lace cravat hung around his neck and draped in a frill outside the inner waistcoat at the top. No ceremonial sword. No white wig. His blond hair was tied back in a tail. He wore his cutlass belted over his back, as usual. His head was topped off with a dark navy-blue tri-corner hat with gold trim.

The marines stared.

"Well?" He prodded.

"Um…if I were a maiden, I'd hump you, sir."

"Corporal!"

"I'm just sayin'…no offense, sir."

Color Sergeant Gosse squinted at him. "Lieutenant…are you expecting a duel tonight? I mean, the battle cutlass over your shoulder seems a touch out of place at a formal ball."

"I *am* still guarding Lady Corrinne," Henri asserted firmly.

"Of course you are, sir. And if you are attacked, during one of the baroque dances, then I am confident your choice of weapons will prove helpful. Don't forget, like we practiced, the *allemande courante* has three steps and then a hop, not a balance."

Three steps and a hop. Henri nodded and repeated the dance pattern to himself. He was nervous about the dancing.

"Who is on guard at the house tonight?"

Two marines raised their hands.

"Good. Let's go."

They left the barracks and strolled into the dark, which soon merged with the cold harbor air. A moist, light breeze was blowing inland. The waning quarter moon looked elegant in the night sky…at least Henri thought so. The skies were clear of clouds and bright with stars.

As they walked together to the stone house, the marines asked him endless questions about the ball. What kind of dresses would the fancy ladies be wearing? Did they really show their teats? What kind of food would be served? Could he stuff some in his pockets and bring back some wine for them? Would there be a lot of women there?

"I don't know. I am certain, I do not know. Again, I don't know. I'll try. Not as many women as men."

They turned right at Rue Toulouse and joined the rambling, disorganized line of naval officers streaming up from Frédéric Gate, all of them headed to the King's Bastion. They turned left after two streets and walked another two blocks before they reached the stone house. A single-horse carriage waited in front of the house.

"A carriage? I've never seen a carriage here," one of the marines said.

The marine guards relieved the two men posted front and back.

"You look as sharp as a bayonet point, sir!" one of the marines complimented before he walked away.

Henri took a breath, adjusted his hat, and knocked on the door.

Anamosa opened it. Since Corrinne wore a ballgown, Anna wore her favorite blue dress. She beamed. Her hair was braided up and accented with white ribbons.

"Anna! You look beautiful!" Henri embraced her and detected the scent of Corrinne's *parfum*.

His sincere tone was flattering. Anamosa did a tiny pirouette, and then swayed to show off the flounce in her dress.

"My little Anamosa is gone. You are simply lovely…a charming young maiden."

Anamosa blushed under his praise.

Corrinne came down the stairs, Calypso and Marcus following her like little ducklings. Corrinne decided to wear the verdant green velvet gown with a low-cut bodice that draped over the stylishly slender panniers on the hips. As usual, she did not wear a white wig. One of Madame Drucour's dressers helped arrange her hair up in waves and braids, all secured in place by gem-studded combs. Her favorite tear-drop diamond pendant hung down to the center of her bosom. Any light fortunate enough to fall upon it reflected with ecstatic brilliance.

"My lady, you look better now than the day I first saw you," Henri said with awe.

"Lieutenant Gerrard! You look splendid, too. My very handsome escort for the evening. Are the guards posted?"

"Yes. New ones. And there seems to be a carriage waiting out front?"

"Good. There are only three carriages in the entire fortress. This one belongs to Madame Drucour, who loaned it to me for the evening. I was lucky to get it."

Henri went to the back door and opened it. The marine came to attention and saluted.

"Do you need anything before we leave?"

"No, sir. Uh, maybe some hot tea when you come back?"

"You can depend on it. This door will not be barred, so you can come in if there are any…well, just in case you're needed."

"Yes, sir."

Corrinne took her light gray wool shawl off the hook. It did not accent her gown, but it would help to keep away the chill while they rode in the carriage. Henri held out an elbow and they went out the front door. The marine guard in front came to attention and presented arms.

"Take care of my children," Corrinne said lightly.

"With my life, my lady."

The carriage pulled away. It would not be a long ride. Corrinne leaned back and looked up at the starry sky. "All the beautiful stars," she remarked. *Now, if only Philippe were here*, she thought.

In the distance, Henri heard the mournful howl of a wolf. He became alert and sat up in the carriage. "Did you hear that?"

Corrinne looked puzzled. "Hear what?"

"A wolf's howl."

"A wolf? No."

They listened carefully to the sounds of the night the rest of the way to the King's Bastion. The howl did not recur. It had been loud enough for Henri to know he did not imagine this. And if Corrinne did not hear it, the howl was meant for him. He could not interpret this any other way.

Henri was now on guard.

The carriage pulled up to the bridging walk crossing over to the bastion above its shallow moat. Corrinne asked the military driver from the Bourgogne Regiment to take care of her shawl until she returned. Henri held out his hand. She took it and stepped down the two steps to the ground. Lanterns atop poles illuminated the walk. She could hear admiring murmurs, a few of them vulgar, from the men who stepped aside to let her pass. Vulgar or not, she gloried in this attention.

"Henri, if you insist on giving the men menacing glances, you'll permanently crease your forehead before this night is over. I am used to this… or at least I used to be used to this…it does not bother me. I rather like it."

"Like it? It's disrespectful," he whispered harshly.

"Maybe so, but it's also flattering. Now smile, or you will tarnish my entrance."

Corrinne's nose wrinkled from the odors of decaying vegetation rising from the stagnant waters of the moat. Together, they entered the double doors and on into the ballroom already half-full of people.

The number of lamps had been doubled, the room was suffused with warm amber light. Corrinne's pendant sparkled, casting light everywhere, like reflections of the morning sunrise on the harbor waters. The noise in the room quieted and heads turned towards her. Corrinne walked straight to Governor Drucour first, who lifted her fingertips to his lips. She hugged Marie-Louise who extolled how handsome Henri looked to embarrass him. Then the governor gestured to the musicians arranged by his wife; two violins, a viola, and a cello, with a harpsichord at the center.

The dance lines formed. Corrinne wanted to dance but waited to allow introductions to the senior naval officers and others who edged near to the governor just to meet her. Henri was uncomfortable and stayed at her side. He tried not to frown when the men stared shamelessly at her bosom.

After a respectable amount of time, Corrinne whispered to Henri, she wanted to dance. They went down the room and took a place at the end of the line where the women and men were circling after going up the floor to the music.

Corrinne made certain to pair off with Henri for her first pass. Henri's heart was racing but he managed the three steps and the hop, twice, to the other end. Henri did not follow the rotation in the same order. There were too many men. But Corrinne continued to circle, each time dancing with someone different. There was no lack of willing partners.

*

They were Swiss mercenaries and servants of the wraith. They were focused on capturing the captain of the ship. They expected the captain would be going to the celebration ball. One of them lingered near Frédéric Gate, near the stream of French naval officers from the warships coming through the gate before heading up Rue Toulouse. Of the three servants, he was the only one who had seen Captain LaTour's face when the captain visited the harbormaster's office. He was confident he would recognize the man again. The other two servants waited at the head of Rue Toulouse near the King's Bastion. The plan was to abduct the captain during his walk from the gate to the bastion. They would use their numbers and the threat of their daggers to usher him off to a side street, and in the darkness, force him to walk to the stone house.

The man by the gate had a telescope and watched the captain's ship for signs he was coming ashore. But when the sun went down, the telescope became useless. The standing lanterns near and around the gate would illuminate the faces of the officers coming through it. He stood close by, a few paces to one side, and inspected the face of every single person.

After a time, the stream of officers coming from the warships dwindled. He had decided the captain might not be coming after all when Captain LaTour abruptly came through the gate. He was walking rapidly, in a hurry, and fell in amongst the crowd of officers moving up Rue Toulouse. There were too many others around him. The servant joined in the stream and followed the captain up the street. No one paid any attention to the servant amid all the talking and the jostling.

Near the bridge walk to the bastion, Captain LaTour was still pressed close to the other officers. The servant fell out of line and went over to his abettors.

"There's no chance to do this now. We'll wait here until he comes out… when everyone is drunk from wine and brandy. It will be easier."

*

"Lady Corrinne looks like a flagship cruising among the rowboats!"
Henri turned towards the voice. "Captain LaTour! You came!"
"I wouldn't miss this."
"Get in line. She'll want to dance with you the next time around."

LaTour grimaced. "*Nooo.* No. I am many things, but a dancer is not one of them. I am too clumsy. Besides, I must ingratiate myself with Governor Drucour first."

"She will make you dance with her!" Henri replied, grinning with certainty.

"We'll see." LaTour moved away through the crowd of people.

But on the next circuit around the floor, Corrinne's ninth, another officer in military dress paired up with her. The man was tall, with a battle-hardened face and a confident expression. *A little too confident,* she thought. His uniform was different from any she'd seen in the garrison. *A foreigner, maybe. From one of the ships?*

At the turn of the line, she saw Henri's scowl and came over to him. "I've been neglecting you. Let's get something to drink." As they moved towards the serving tables, many people greeted her, mostly men, but a few of the faubourg women she knew. Corrinne stopped to speak with three acquaintances. After commenting on her beauty, they all wanted to meet her escort.

"This handsome officer? Why this is the famous Lieutenant Henri Gerrard of the Troupes de la Marine."

"Lieutenant Gerrard!" one of the women exclaimed. "It is *you*!"

"He is the gallant officer who confronted the Swiss," another explained to Corrinne.

"I know," Corrinne replied, glancing at Henri with admiration. "I heard all about it."

"I'm surprised you danced with Captain Stoecklin," said the third.

Corrinne's smile tightened at hearing that. "Yes," she replied tersely. She looked again at Henri for confirmation. He gave a curt nod.

When the ladies took their leave, she turned to Henri. "So that's why you were scowling. I did not know it was him. It makes me want to leave."

"Captain LaTour is here," Henri offered.

She brightened again. "Where?"

"He is pushing his way to the front towards the governor."

"I want him to dance with me!"

"He claims he is too clumsy to dance."

Corrinne scoffed. "Nonsense! He can do a ballet on the helm deck of his ship in the middle of a storm. Of course, he can dance. And he *will* dance with me. Let's have something to drink and find him."

Henri was anxious to see this, too.

*

Captain Bergen Stoecklin left the King's Bastion by exiting through the unguarded eastern door. He left it unbolted behind him to permit reentry later. He rendezvoused with his two lieutenants, Mettler and Roos, and they marched away from the illuminating bastion lights into the darkness of the streets of the eastern faubourg. All the noisy activity was occurring at or outside the King's Bastion, leaving most of the other faubourg streets deserted. It took only minutes to reach the back wall of the stone house. They moved quietly down its western wall to the metal side gate.

They had planned this carefully. No speaking was necessary. Stoecklin went further down to the end where the wall joined with the house. Lieutenant Mettler knocked on the gate, drawing the marine guard's attention. The guard picked up his musket, left the back door, and cautiously approached the gate.

"Maurice," the Swiss lieutenant said quietly, "I've brought the wine for you."

"I am not Maurice," the guard replied harshly. "Get away from this gate or you get a bayonet in your chest."

Under the cover of darkness, Stoecklin hoisted himself up and stealthily slipped over the six-foot wall. The verbal exchanged provided the necessary diversion.

"But this is where I was told to deliver this wine," Lieutenant Mettler replied, faking puzzlement.

"I told you—"

Coming up from behind, Stoecklin slipped his hand over the guard's mouth and slit his throat. He allowed the man to slowly slump to the ground. The he unbolted and opened the gate. They dragged the marine's body over to the other side of the yard and laid it in the corner. As planned, Lieutenant Roos climbed over the shorter wall and sidled down to the front of the house and waited out of sight just beyond its corner, ready to charge in ambush. Lieutenant Mettler went back out the side gate and walked down the street, staggering a little, pretending to be drunk.

As soon as the marine guard in the front saw the man, he pointed his bayonetted musket at the soldier who was now staggering around the street intersection in confusion.

"It mush be thish way," Mettler slurred and started walking towards the marine.

The marine spoke loudly in warning. "Stop right there, or I will stick you!"

Lieutenant Roos moved swiftly. The marine had his throat cut from behind just like his companion. The two lieutenants dragged the body around to the back gate and placed it next to the other one in the back yard.

"Good," Stoecklin whispered. "Now change out of those bloody coats and return to the ball. I will follow you in a little while."

Stoecklin went to the small window at the back of the cuisine and briefly glanced inside. He did not see anyone except for the native girl with her ear pressed against the front door. She was alone.

The twins were asleep upstairs. Anamosa thought she'd heard a noise coming from the front of the house. She listened with her ear against the door for several seconds before she opened the viewing portal. Standing on her toes, she looked left then right as best she could, trying to see the guard. Was he not there? She lifted the bar and was reaching to pull the pistol and open the door when she felt a rush of cold air draft into the room behind her. She turned and saw the face of the man from the Frédéric Gate fiasco. He was leering at her. He had a dagger in one hand and his sword extended in the other. She stepped sideways towards the stairway, but the man stepped forward and blocked her path with his sword.

"No, no! Don't move. Where are the children?"

"They are not here," Anamosa answered calmly. She could pull her fishing knife from the scabbard beneath her dress, but it was no match for his sword and dagger. He must come closer.

Stoecklin knew she was lying. They were upstairs. He could not believe his good fortune at seeing this girl again. *There's time for this*, he decided.

"Take off your dress," he said in a cruel voice.

Anamosa did not move. This man was here to kill her no matter what she did.

"Take off your dress," he repeated angrily, "and do exactly as I say. If you scream or make any noise, the children die. If they wake up, they die. Now take off your dress and lie down on the floor."

Anamosa was alone. No one was going to help her. She had witnessed instances of violent death all her life, seen people killed in vicious ways, seen people tortured. If she was going to live, if the twins were going to live, she must find a way to kill this man. She started unbuttoning her blue dress from the top. He avidly watched her nakedness appear. Taking a cautious step closer to him, Anamosa could smell his rancid sweat and the wine on his breath. She focused on his gaze. His eyes were following her fingers as they moved down the dress from one button to the next. When the dress was completely unbuttoned, she did not take it off but let it hang open. She was not wearing anything beneath it. The one-inch-wide embroidered linen belt around her waist was visible now. It looked like a decorative belt, but it was attached to the scabbard of the boning knife. The hang of the dress still covered the scabbard, so long as she did not take it off. *Do not take it off*, she said to herself. *He must not see the knife.* The left side of the dress had flapped back, exposing a small breast. His eyes were drawn to the breast. She did nothing to cover it.

Stoecklin licked his lips at seeing such unspoiled beauty, such virginal nakedness. He put away his sword and transferred the dagger to his right hand. He waved the point of the knife and gestured at her to lie down.

Keeping her expression placid, Anamosa dropped to her knees and slowly laid back on the floor. She used her hands subtly, to keep the right side of her dress concealing the scabbard.

With the girl lying on the floor and vulnerable, Stoecklin took off his coat, opened his trousers with his free hand, pulling up his blouse-shirt, exposing his erection. The trousers dropped to the floor around his ankles.

"Don't move," he warned in a low, ugly voice.

She expected he would also drop to his knees, to lie atop of her. That was the moment she intended to act. As he lay upon her, she would draw her knife and stab him.

But he pounced, like a fox would upon a rabbit. Anamosa was unprepared for how fast he moved. The next few minutes lasted an eternity, full of searing pain, choking, more pain. She could not move. Her screams were muffled by his hand. She pounded her fists on his sides, but he was too heavy, too strong. The tearing pain numbed her thinking. At some point in her agonizing struggles, her hand brushed against the hilt of the boning knife. She seized it frantically, pulled it from the scabbard, and plunged it into his side. The slender, pointed knife cut through the shirt and skin. Eight inches of sharpened steel slid between the man's ribs without any resistance.

"*Oooooof!*" Stoecklin yowled. A bloody spray of air gushed from his lungs amidst his cry of torment.

Desperate to stop the pain, Anamosa pushed and pulled the hilt of the knife back and forth. The blade had two razor-sharp edges. It cut everything it encountered and easily sliced the muscle of Stoecklin's heart in two. The man went limp atop of her. She thrust the blade to the hilt. Once more! Again!

Anamosa fainted.

*

Anamosa's senses sluggishly returned. The room was strangely quiet. The pulsating pain was constant and pressing down on her. She lay there, gasping for each breath, barely conscious. From somewhere far away, she heard a child's voice calling her name. Concern for the children spurred her attention. But everything hurt. It hurt to move. Her throat was sore. It was hard to swallow. Her vision blurred, her eyes could not focus.

"Anamosa!" A tiny voice brimming with fear.

She had to do something! Anamosa slowly removed the choking hands from around her bruised and swollen throat. The blood throbbed in her head. With all her strength, Anamosa groaned and tilted him up enough to slide out from under the heavy body. In the wave of excruciating pain created by that small effort, she passed out again.

Calypso called out. Louder this time. Anamosa's eyes opened wide. She raised herself up on one elbow.

"It's all right, Calypso," Anamosa rasped. "Stay there!"

Panting rapidly, Anamosa rolled over onto her stomach. Pulsing, stabbing pain was the result. But with great effort, she pushed again with both arms, and hauled herself up to her hands and knees. She vomited. More pain. She took a few deep breaths. Her vision cleared. Blood pooled on the floor everywhere. Her blue dress was torn and soaked. She was dripping blood! She grabbed hold of a nearby chair. Groaning loudly, she pulled herself upright. Her legs began shaking violently.

"*Anna?!*"

"I'm coming, Callie!" Anamosa began sobbing uncontrollably. "I'm coming, babies! I'm coming! Stay there! Don't come down!"

She had to stop the bleeding! Leaning on whatever she could grasp for support, Anamosa staggered to the stove and grabbed both towels they used for the dishes. She pressed hard at the place where the blood dripped from between her legs. The pressure felt like a knife. Overcome with dizziness, she bent over and vomited again. More pain. The vomit was bloody, too. Her mouth was bleeding. She buttoned her dress near the top. Holding one towel against her genitals to stem the blood flow, she dipped the other towel in the water basin and wiped off her face. It came back bloody. She put this damp towel over her shoulder. With a trembling hand, she pulled the pistol from the holster by the door. Then step by painful step, she climbed the stairs, babbling words of comfort to the terrified twins.

"Here I come. Don't cry, babies. It's all right."

When she got close enough to them, she sat down on the next lower step. She placed the pistol at her side and hugged the littles ones to comfort them while they cried. She felt cold. Her heart was pounding.

"Anna, *hurt*?" Calypso asked with concern.

"*Blood*?" Marcus touched her dress.

"Don't worry, babies. Don't worry. Mommy's coming soon." Anamosa's dizziness suddenly worsened. She wanted to lie down. "Mommy's coming," she managed to say once more. Then she laid her head back on the upper step and lapsed into unconsciousness.

*

Captain LaTour was jostling among the senior officers and civilian intendants of government to get some time with the governor.

Henri took hold of his elbow. "Lady Corrinne is waiting to dance with you."

LaTour turned. She was right there.

"Take my arm, Beauregard." It was akin to an order.

"But…"

She led him to the beginning of the line and took a place across from him. The music barely paused between melodies before the dancing began again. Most of the celebrators were now deep into their cups. The music strains had changed and tended towards the livelier Spanish compositions. The harpsichord notes became predominant and playful.

Corrinne smiled and extended her left hand. LaTour extended his right. She led him forward and suppressed her laughter as he attempted to match the steps of the man in front of him. He gave up trying to discern a pattern and simply hopped from one foot to the other all the way down the floor, shooting Corrinne anxious glances every few steps. She beamed at him with pleasure in return.

As they rotated back to the beginning of the line, he begged not to go around again.

"My lady, I need to speak to the governor," he said over the sound of the music. "He's made it clear through messengers he wants to speak with me, too. And I think it concerns you."

Corrinne blinked. "Me?"

"Yes. I'm certain Minister Machault...before he was dismissed...the minister ordered Governor Drucour to protect you. Machault also indicated he would arrange for a ship to transport you away from Louisbourg. The governor will presume that is me. And, of course, it is me. But he could be waiting to tell me a dozen other things I can only speculate about. I won't be long. I just want to arrange a time to meet with him tomorrow."

"All right. I understand." Corrinne looked at Henri. "What about you? Are you ready for another *allemande*?"

Henri stammered. "W-well...if..."

"Oh!" Corrinne said, her tone held mild disappointment. "Then let's leave. I've had my fill of leering young officers for the evening. And with Captain Stoecklin in this crowd, I do not want to be anywhere near him."

Captain LaTour suddenly felt guilty. "My lady, I will try once more... if you like."

Corrinne laughed. "You're a gentleman, Beauregard. Go. Go speak with the governor. But I am curious to hear what more he has to say about me. Come to my house after this, and we will sip some brandy and visit further."

Henri extended his elbow and they turned to leave the ballroom. Departing was not easy. Many of the faubourg merchants and their wives used the appearance of this departure as an excuse to approach Lady VanderMeer, to expand upon their acquaintance, and compliment her beauty. Corrinne was gracious to them all, as was her nature. It took a few minutes, but eventually they got through the crowd.

As soon as Henri was outdoors again, he listened for the wolf howl. But the night was full of the loud voices of partially drunk naval officers, boisterous groups of young men gathered out in the plaza at the end of the walking bridge. Henri waved at their carriage driver waiting patiently with two other carriage drivers.

Henri helped Corrinne up into the open carriage and a few hoots and whistles followed her. Corrinne made a show of wrapping her shawl around her shoulders.

More whistles sang out.

"*Bonne nuit*, gentlemen! Thank you for the dancing!"

More cheers and comments followed, most of them complimentary. Some referred to parts of her anatomy, preceded by words like *great, magnificent,* and *glorious*.

"Why do you encourage them?"

"They are like you, Henri. They fight to protect me. It doesn't hurt my feelings."

They pulled away. The carriage had only one post lantern to illuminate the way. It dangled off a pole next to the driver's seat. The ride was slow.

"Well, the ball was nice. Thank you for being my escort. *Brrr*! It's gotten colder. Just look at those stars!"

In the distance came the howl of a wolf.

"There it is again! Tell me you heard it this time!"

"Heard what? A wolf howl? No. I did not hear a wolf howl."

Henri no longer cared if she didn't hear it. He did! He was supposed to hear it!

"Something is wrong!"

"What's wrong?"

"I don't know. Something."

As the carriage neared the house, in the light of the post lantern, they saw no sign of the guard posted to the front door.

"See! The guard is missing," Henri said tensely. As he stepped out of the coach, he pulled out his cutlass.

"Stay by Lady VanderMeer," he told the driver.

The driver set the brake and jumped down from his seat to help Lady VanderMeer down the steps.

Henri opened the door and saw a scene of horror.

He charged into the house. A man was lying on the floor in a pool of blood. "Anamosa!" he shouted. The sound of children crying erupted from the stairway.

Corrinne rushed into the house and screamed.

"NO! NO! NO!" Henri reached the upper steps to find Anamosa covered in blood and unresponsive. "*No*! Please! No!" He checked for a heartbeat. She was alive!

Corrinne came up the stairs behind him. "My babies! Marcus! Calypso?" They reached out to her and she gathered them up in her arms. "My God! What has happened?"

"She was attacked!" Henri said, sounding frantic. "We need to take her to the hospital." He put his cutlass back in the scabbard and carried her limp body in his arms. He saw blood all over her, particularly on her lower body. "Oh, God! Please! Anna, don't die! Please! God help her," he prayed in an anguished voice.

The carriage driver was shocked at seeing the young girl in a dress covered with blood, "What can I do?" he asked.

"The hospital!"

Corrinne came out the front door carrying both children. "Wait! I am coming with you!"

Henri climbed up into the carriage cradling Anamosa tenderly in his arms. He reached out with a free hand to help Corrinne and the twins get in. The carriage driver went straight until he could turn left and steered down the street directly to the hospital facing the harbor. Once inside, two of the nurses came running up.

"My God! What happened?! Who is she?"

"Lady Anamosa! I think she was raped!" he responded angrily. "She's lost a lot of blood."

The senior nurse pressed her fingers to the side of Anamosa's throat. The pulse was rapid and weak. But she could feel it.

"She lives," the white-haired nurse stated. "Carry her to that room. Place her in the bed."

Two more nurses joined the first two. They tucked thick bandages into her genitals to staunch the bleeding. They cut away her dress and washed the blood from her body with lukewarm wet towels. Anamosa remained inert and unmoving during this care. Henri saw the extensive bruising of her body, neck, and face. He averted his eyes. They elevated her feet with pillows and covered her with several blankets.

Corrinne had taken a chair in the room still holding the distraught twins. She turned her tortured eyes to Henri. His expression matched the way she felt.

"Who did this?" she asked tersely.

"The dead man on the floor was Captain Stoecklin. My guards are missing. I don't know why. They would not abandon their posts. Stoecklin did not act alone."

Corrinne didn't hesitate. "Find them, Henri. Find them and kill them! I will stay with Anna."

The nurses heard Lady VanderMeer and glanced at one another.

Henri went to the bed. The nurses moved back a step. He bent over Anamosa and kissed her lips and then her forehead. "I love you, Anna," he whispered. "Don't leave me." He turned to the nurses. "Where are your doctors?!"

"At the ball."

Henri's expression hardened. "At the ball!? Then one of you go to the King's Bastion, find a doctor, and bring him back here!" He turned to the traumatized twins who were still whimpering and kissed each one of them on the head. Then back to the senior nurse again. "Lady VanderMeer requires shelter and comfort for her children."

"Don't worry, Lieutenant," the senior nurse replied, nodding. "I will take care of them all. Go find these foul men! Do what you must!"

Henri went out to the carriage. "Take me back to the house." When they got there, he gave the driver new orders. "Go to the marine barracks at the Dauphin Bastion. Find Color Sergeant Gosse. Tell him that Lady VanderMeer's house has been attacked. Bring them all here!"

"Yes, sir!" The private slapped the reins on the horse's rump and the carriage lurched down the street in a gallop.

Henri pulled his cutlass and went back inside. The night was cold, but the room was hot and stifling with the smell of blood, excrement, and the stench of death. It was a potent mix of disgusting odors that reminded him of the Battle of Lake George. He stooped by Stoecklin's dead body and saw a dagger lying to the right of his head. He also saw the hilt of a knife protruding from the Swiss captain's side. He recognized the hilt. It was Anamosa's boning knife. He withdrew it and tossed it over into the washbasin. That she had managed to kill this murderous bastard, despite his greater size and strength, was a miracle.

Where are my guards?

*

It took a while longer, but Captain LaTour waited patiently and finally got his short audience with Governor Drucour.

"Captain LaTour! Welcome back to Louisbourg."

LaTour saw the governor swaying a little. It was obvious that he had imbibed too much. He leaned closer and talked over the music.

"Governor, I know this is not a good time. I just wanted to pay my respects and ask if you might have time tomorrow for me to see you. I bring some missives addressed to you…private ones."

"Certainly, Captain. I am anxious to speak with you as well. Stop and see Lieutenant Christophe in the morning. Tell him to clear some time for you and that I want to meet with you as soon as possible."

With that comment, the baroque music began a new song. LaTour saluted the governor and took his leave. He suddenly felt self-conscious for saluting the man amidst a public celebration. People stared at him. He was embarrassed and left the ballroom quickly.

Once outside and across the bridge, LaTour turned right instead of going straight down Rue Toulouse. It was an angular but shorter route to Lady Corrinne's house this way. When he reached the darkness of the adjoining streets, he was abruptly gripped by three men. One of them put a knife to his throat.

"Just keep walking, Captain. Do not cry out if you want to live."

"What do you want from me?!"

Someone punched him hard in the lower back near the kidney. The explosion of pain was enormous.

"Keep silent and keep walking!"

This voice was menacing and familiar. The last time he'd heard it was in Amsterdam. Lord VanderMeer's former agent, Wittman Bootz, had threatened him with this same voice. With terrifying realization, he knew.

The wraith!

*

After the carriage arrived at the Dauphin Bastion to retrieve the marines, word spread quickly that Lady VanderMeer's house had been attacked. The captain of the guard at the Dauphin Bastion personally brought word to the governor inside the ballroom.

"The marines charged off to her defense!"

"She was attacked? But Lady VanderMeer was just here! Attacked where? By whom?"

The governor would have asked more questions, but he ran out of words. Fortunately, Grenadier Colonel du Bourzt was standing right next to the governor and heard the same report.

"Colonel du Bourzt. Take your men to Lady VanderMeer's house and learn the truth of this. Send a messenger back to me as soon as you confirm what has happened."

Colonel du Bourzt clicked his heels together. "Yes, sir!"

The colonel had imbibed as well. His walk was unsteady, but he reached the grenadier barracks inside the King's Bastion in only a few minutes and ordered up two platoons of men. They fell into ranks in the marshalling yard, as if the fortress was under attack. Carrying torches, they started marching to Lady VanderMeer's house.

*

Henri's rage was barely restrained. He wanted to kill. But who?

Think, Henri! Think!

He stepped cautiously into the back yard and stopped in the darkness for a few moments to allow his eyes to adjust. There was no sign of the guards. *They would not abandon their posts.* He kept telling himself this. He moved to the center of the yard and turned in a circle, looking in every direction.

The gate? He went over to the gate and found it unlocked. *That's how they came in.*

When he turned around, his night vision had improved and in the dim quarter moonlight he noticed the shadowy lumps on the ground in a far corner of the yard. He went to investigate. It was the guards. Their throats had been cut from behind. The bodies dragged there. Henri seethed.

Stoecklin did not do this alone.

Grim-faced and ready to kill, Henri went back into the house and was greeted by a fist pounding loudly on the front door. Henri had not been wearing his dirk that night. He bent and picked up Stoecklin's twelve-inch dagger from the floor. Holding the dagger in his left hand and his cutlass in the right, Henri went to the door and cautiously opened the viewing port.

"Captain LaTour?" The frightened, contorted face of the captain filled the window.

"The châsse," La Tour whispered hoarsely.

Henri understood the danger instantly. Staying behind the door, he slowly pulled it open with his left hand. Captain LaTour was forcefully shoved into the house by the bottom of a boot in the center of his back. The captain stumbled across the floor head first, slipped on the blood-covered floor, and fell atop Stoecklin's dead body.

Sentry Cheever's words came to Henri in a rush. *Wait for it. You are not fencing. The cutlass is a slashing weapon. This is shipboard fighting. Your goal is to kill, to kill quickly, and be ready for the next man. Parry, then thrust, while choosing the spot for the kill.*

The first man into the doorway had his blade blocked down by the dagger. The cutting edge of Henri's cutlass slashed across the man's neck, cleanly separating the head from the body. The head rolled outside, the body collapsed in the doorway. The next man made a stabbing thrust at Henri. This rapier blade was lifted sharply upward by the dagger before the cutlass was run through the center of the man's chest. He dropped where he stood. The last man backed away into the street. Henri followed, his eyes maniacal with rage, his cutlass dripping with blood. They faced each other, illuminated by the light spilling out through the open front doorway.

A galloping sound approached, which both men ignored.

Henri walked forward slowly, his weapons pointing at the ground, purposely showing an unguarded chest, waiting for the man to make the first move. Captain LaTour staggered back to the door. He had heard something he wished had never reached his ears. The *wraith* was here!

"Do you think this is over, Adaelric?"

"It is for you," Henri replied in a voice full of certainty and rage.

"It is never *over. Everyone you care about will die."*

"Not this night."

To the marines and Captain LaTour watching and listening, the voices they heard spoke in nonsensical sounds. One of them guttural and evil. The other in low growls of anger. The sounds were unnerving. The veteran marines glanced at one another with uncertainty. Should they help? They looked to the lead of Color Sergeant Gosse, who looked and listened with an expression of disbelief on his face.

When Henri's adversary decided the marine was close enough for the kill, he thrust his sword straight ahead with extraordinary speed. But anticipating this move, Henri turned sideways and stepped closer at the same time. As the blade slid across the front of his uniform slicing the lapels, causing minor cuts on his chest, Henri slashed down with his cutlass and cleaved the man's sword arm halfway between the wrist and elbow. The man screamed loudly, lifting and gripping the bloody arm stump with his other arm. Henri slammed the twelve-inch dagger blade into the man's armpit, piercing through the lungs to enter the heart. He collapsed to the ground and quivered a few seconds before dying.

Rochefort Citadel, France

Lieutenant-Colonel Krieger sat up in bed as the last servant's life expired. His head pounded with ache from the strain. He laid back down and closed his eyes. It almost hurt to breathe.

The vulnax could barely restrain its dominance. Its rage surged chaotically, back and forth, like waves in the center of a storm. Once again, *It* was defeated. All the servants on the island were dead, killed by a scion of *Adaelric*. The whore queen! The ship! They were all there. The châsse was there, too, somewhere, although it could not be seen. It had to be on the water. On the ship! But the ship had been searched! No matter. The châsse had to be on it! Made opaque to the sight by the seals. Even with the seals, if it was on the ground, or in the earth, it would be visible. But not over water. Yes, the châsse was hidden on the ship! Cleverly disguised in a place where it could not be seen. The ship! The ship! The ship! The servants should have gone out to the ship. Seized control of it. With the death of all the servants, the opportunity was missed. But the girl with the sight had almost been killed. Another opportunity missed. *The whore queen knows she is discovered again. She must flee. But to where? No matter.* The vulnax could no longer rely on servants. It was determined to be present for the next attack.

It was early in the morning. Lieutenant-Colonel Krieger had ignored the constant knocks on the door of his quarters that occurred every hour as per his orders. Now, as he sat on the side of his bed, rubbing his aching temples, there was another knock.

"What?" he demanded.

"Sir. Just checking on your well-being. It will be midday in another hour."

"I will be there soon. No more knocking."

Krieger got up and went over to the washbasin. He filled a mug from the ewer and drank several glasses of water. Then wiped his face with a damp towel. He felt the stubble of the two-day-old beard. He decided to have his barber shave his head and face before he went to see the fort commander. Major Sauer should already be drilling the mercenary regiment. They totaled seven hundred and two men. He'd been informed they would have to march to Brest for transport to New France. He'd not been told the name of the port of final destination, but even if it was to be Québec City, the ship would stop in Louisbourg on the way.

We will start the march to Brest tomorrow morning, he decided.

*

In the quiet aftermath of the carnage, Color Sergeant Gosse and eight other marines who managed to hang onto every part of the carriage for the ride to Lady Corrinne's house, now stood gaping in awe at a severed head, an arm, and four dead bodies. There were pools of blood all over the cobblestones. Lieutenant Gerrard's face and dress uniform was covered with blood. Illuminated by only the minimal light streaming out the open doorway, the lieutenant exhibited a very forbidding visage to his men.

As blood dripped from the blade of his cutlass, Henri spoke in a calm but grim voice. "Lady Corrinne's house was invaded tonight while everyone was busy with the celebration at the King's Bastion. *Including me!* I failed her! The dead man lying on the floor inside the house is Captain Bergen Stoecklin. A Swiss mercenary. This is the same man who verbally assaulted Lady Anamosa at Frédéric Gate. This time, he managed to *rape* her!"

The last two words were spoken with wrenching anger and guilt. The marines remained silent.

"Two of our fellow marines lie dead behind the house. Their throats were cut. They gave their lives in defense. Unfortunately, it was not enough." Henri pointed his sword at the man standing in the doorway. "This is Captain LaTour, the master of the *Falcon Queen*. He was pursued by three more Swiss mercenaries but managed to give warning in time for me to deal with their attack. I believe there may be two more Swiss murderers *au large* inside the fort."

Henri turned to the carriage driver. "Private, I require the use of your carriage for the night."

"I am at your service, sir."

"Color Sergeant, I am going back to the hospital. I want four men to go with me. They will stand guard over Lady Corrinne, Lady Anamosa, and the twins for the rest of the night until they are relieved."

"At once, sir!" Color Sergeant Gosse called out the names.

Henri waved with the tip of the blood-covered cutlass. "Leave all of this mess untouched. I want others in the fort to see it to send a message. I will send the carriage back to you, Sergeant. Take the bodies of our brothers lying behind the house to the Dauphin Bastion. I do not want these brave marines to lie outside uncovered. Tomorrow, we will give them an honor-filled burial."

"Sir!" Color Sergeant Gosse began barking orders to prepare the dead marines for transport.

Henri moved over to Captain LaTour and spoke quietly. "Captain, these men I just killed had nothing to do with Captain Stoecklin, except for being part of his mercenary company."

"Lord VanderMeer warned me that enemies of the House of Brunswick would send assassins to Louisbourg," LaTour replied. "Captain Stoecklin must have been one of them. But the last man you just killed spoke to you with that voice of evil. You know of what I speak. I thank God you were here tonight, or I would not be alive."

"I was not here for Anamosa," Henri said, his gaze stony. "She lies unconscious at the edge of death at the hospital."

LaTour grimaced. "I am going with you to the hospital."

Henri paused. He suddenly realized Anamosa was not wearing her amulet. He pushed past Captain LaTour and went back into the house. He searched the floor area. It wasn't there. He went upstairs into the bedchamber and found it lying on the small table next to her bed. For some reason, Anamosa had chosen not to wear the amulet under her blue dress that night. The same blue dress that was now a bloody rag. Henri slipped the amulet into one of his deep uniform pockets and went back outside. The thought of the bloody blue dress made him think of his own appearance.

"Color Sergeant, have someone bring me the cleaner uniform from my bunk. This one is unseemly. Also bring my dirk. I will be at the hospital for the rest of the night."

"Yes, sir."

Captain LaTour was already in the carriage with four marines. Henri climbed up on the carriage's front seat with the driver. He stood up in the boot well and spoke loudly for the marines to hear.

"You men should also know that Captain Stoecklin has two lieutenants, two accomplices, Lieutenants Mettler and Roos. They are still free. I know their faces. This business with Lieutenants Mettler and Roos is mine alone, *not yours*. I will deal with them…" He looked down at his bloody appearance and left the words unsaid. "But not tonight."

The carriage pulled away and had only just turned the corner when Colonel du Bourzt arrived, accompanied by a lieutenant leading thirty grenadiers.

The colonel found Color Sergeant Gosse and four marines standing in the middle of what looked like the aftermath of a battlefield.

Color Sergeant Gosse and the other marines came to attention. Gosse saluted.

"Sir!"

The grenadiers spread out across the front of the house. Colonel du Bourzt looked inside the open doorway. Another bloody body lay dead on the floor. He did not see Lady VanderMeer.

"Color Sergeant, what the hell happened here?!"

Gosse did his best to explain what he knew about the attack and the dead marines.

Colonel du Bourzt was aghast. "He raped Lady Anamosa? *She is a child!* Is that Captain Stoecklin's body lying on the floor?"

"Yes, sir."

"Good!" The colonel's headache from the wine had already begun. He gestured at the severed head and the other dead bodies.

"Lieutenant Gerrard did *all of this*?" he asked with surprise.

"He had no help from me, Colonel. He didn't need any. I saw him do it with my own eyes, sir."

The colonel saw the nods of agreement from the other marines. *Like cutting wheat*, the colonel recalled his own words, which he'd said, partially in jest at the time.

"Where is he now?"

"Lieutenant Gerrard left in a carriage."

"Jesus! Does he intend to kill more mercenaries?!"

"Not tonight, Colonel," Gosse said in a tone that suggested Henri's vengeance was not over yet. "Lieutenant Gerrard went to the hospital. Lady VanderMeer is there, too, with her children. Lady Anamosa is there and… well, she has lost a lot of blood."

"*Christ*," the colonel said with angry disgust.

A crowd of citizens from the faubourgs had started to gather nearby, attracted by all the torchlights and the soldiers. More people arrived as the rumor of the attack on Lady VanderMeer's house spread further. A rape was rumored as well. Many of them were cursing the Swiss mercenaries and shouting with outrage.

The carriage returned. Color Sergeant Gosse gave orders to his men to load the dead marines into the carriage.

"With your permission, Colonel, I want to take the bodies of our dead brothers back to our barracks and prepare them for burial."

"Permission granted."

"Colonel, Lieutenant Gerrard asked that this"—he gestured toward the carnage–"remain untouched. He wants the governor to see it...sir."

"I hear you, Sergeant."

The marines left. Colonel du Bourzt ordered half of his grenadiers to positions around the house as guards. He gave his lieutenant orders.

"Keep the people away. Do not touch anything! Post a guard outside the back door. Allow no one to enter this house without my permission! And send back to the barracks for another platoon. Make a camp in the back yard. This will be a long night."

Colonel du Bourzt and the rest of his grenadiers marched off to the hospital.

CHAPTER 22
LOUISBOURG
APRIL 1757
A Kiss from Calypso

W hen Henri entered the hospital again, all three hospital doctors were present along with more nurses. Two of the doctors were swaying from drinking too much wine at the naval ball. They came to the hospital only because Governor Drucour ordered them all to go. The senior physician, Dr. Pernell Michaux, was a veteran army surgeon of twenty-two years and in charge of the hospital. Seeing Lieutenant Gerrard, he dismissed his two subordinates. He had been waiting for the marine lieutenant to appear. After introductions, Henri spoke first.

"How is she?"

"Lady Anamosa is resting quietly. I've given her a small amount of opium tincture for the pain. She is severely bruised, but suffered no broken bones. She was choked in the attack. Her vaginal canal suffered serious trauma. She is unconscious, so I stitched some of the larger tears in a few places and swabbed it all with astringents to staunch the bleeding. She has lost much blood, which I am sure you already know. At every opportunity, the nurses give her spoonfuls of water, which is all she can tolerate without gagging. They will continue to do this until she regains consciousness. She needs plenty of water now, but her throat is very swollen. When she can drink larger amounts of water, I will give her medicinal broths and other tonics that will be restorative."

"Will she live?" Henri asked in an emotional voice.

"Lieutenant, I have done all I can…for now. She has a high fever. Water is most important. And rest. A nurse will sit at her bedside constantly. I will be here all night long, able to come to her aid if I am needed. You are a military officer, so you know that the first two days after someone is severely injured are the most important for survival. Lady Anamosa is young and strong. But she is in God's hands, for now."

Henri moved to enter the room.

"Lieutenant!"

"Yes?"

"I must insist you remove your bloody clothing."

"I've nothing else to wear. My sergeant is bringing me another uniform."

"If you want to sit by her, you may do so wearing a blanket or a linen sheet. The nurse will take you to a room where you can clean your hands and face, at a minimum. I prefer that you fully bathe and purify yourself as soon as possible. We have a room for that purpose."

"I will bathe when my clean uniform arrives."

Henri went to the bathing room and stripped off his uniform down to his undergarments, stockings, and shoes. Around his neck, he still wore his amulet and a small leather pouch, carrying the hairs of Roland, his wolf friend. The cutlass belt and scabbard he draped over a chair, along with Anamosa's amulet. The uniform was in a pile when the senior nurse came into the room holding a blanket and a linen sheet.

"Wash your hands, arms, and face in that basin, if you please, Lieutenant."

While Henri complied, she glanced at the pile of bloody clothes on the floor. She had seen Lady Anamosa walking arm in arm with this lieutenant one sunny afternoon in the faubourg marketplace. The girl was young but there had been no mistaking the expression of love on her face. That a grown man had savagely raped away her innocence was unforgiveable. The nurse had been the victim of such an assault when her village was invaded by Danish mercenaries. And it was not just one man who raped her. She was seventeen at the time and barely survived the inflammatory infection. It ruined her ability to ever have children. She never married. She emigrated to Louisbourg before the last war and had been there ever since, even during the two-year English occupation after the previous invasion.

"Wash the blood from your hair, too." She emptied the basin of blood-tinged water into the drain and refilled the basin from a pitcher.

Henri took off the amulet and the leather pouch until he finished.

When he was done, she gave him a towel to dry his hair. "What should I do with your clothes?"

"Can you burn them for me?"

She nodded with approval. "Of course. Did you get them?"

Henri stopped. "Get who?" He looked at her face and saw the anger sparking in her eyes. Then he understood. "Yes. Four of them are dead. Lady Anamosa killed her rapist with a knife, while he was raping her," he said, restraining his anger. "I killed three more accomplices an hour ago. There are two more. I will get them, too. But not tonight. I know who they are. And they aren't going anywhere. For now, I want to stay by Anna's side until she wakes up."

"You smell very bad, Lieutenant. That means your body is filthy. Wrap yourself in this sheet and blanket. I'll have a bath prepared for you. Don't wait too long. It's not good for Lady Anamosa."

"Lady VanderMeer?"

"Her children are sleeping further down the ward. One of my nurses watches over them constantly. Two of your marines stand guard outside their door. Lady VanderMeer sits with Anamosa. Two more marines stand guard there as well. She will be happy to see you. I will be available all night long and into tomorrow."

"*Merci.* What is your name?"

"I am Nurse Cardon. Desiree Cardon."

"*Merci beaucoup*, Nurse Cardon."

Henri wrapped himself in the sheet and blanket, took hold of his cutlass, the pouch, and the amulet and went down the hall to Anamosa's room. His two marines snapped to attention as he approached.

"Any problems?"

"No, sir."

"I'll be staying here the rest of the night. I need only one of you to man this post. Take turns sleeping every two hours."

Henri found Corrinne sitting by the bed, her head resting against the high back of the chair, her eyes closed. He touched her shoulder lightly.

Corrinne awoke. Her eyes were bloodshot from crying. "Henri! Where are your clothes?"

"Probably burned by now. They were covered in blood," he explained. "I will sit with her. Go sleep with the twins."

Corrinne stood and exhaled wearily. "I don't know if I can sleep."

"Where is Captain LaTour?"

"He is asleep…somewhere."

"How is Anamosa?"

Corrinne reached out to Anamosa and caressed her hair and forehead. "She has a bad fever. That worries me the most. She takes spoonfuls of water, dreams, and talks gibberish. Otherwise, she hardly moves at all."

"I will stay with her now."

They embraced. Corrinne went off down the hall, still wearing the beautiful green ballgown, now splotched with blood stains.

Henri hung his cutlass, belt, and scabbard over the head of a nearby chair. He introduced himself to the nurse sitting with a book across the room and then held up the amulet.

"I need your help. She must be wearing this at all times. It contains powers of protection and will help her."

To make his point, Henri showed the nurse the one he was wearing. They gently lifted her head and slipped the amulet around her neck. For a moment, Henri thought he saw the center stone glow. He took the chair where Corrinne had been sitting. He leaned close to Anamosa's ear and whispered.

"Anna. It's Henri. I'm right next to you. *Je t'aime*, Anna."

She did not respond. With his eyes welling up, Henri took hold of her right hand and laid his head on the bed next to her waist.

*

While the female eagle slept, the *ghost* reached out to the young girl whose dreams were violent and frightening. She had been attacked, not by servants of the demon, but by another enemy. An enemy she had killed, but not before being injured severely. The girl now stood at the very edge of the abyss. She was lonely, full of despair, and pain-weary of life to the point of letting go.

The *ghost* was tempted constantly by the seduction of the abyss. The abyss was comforting. It was a place without pain, without sadness, without loneliness. And far away, in its yawning depths and distance, there was a warm inviting light. The *ghost* was no longer part of a living body. It was a spirit unattached to a life of its own. It survived by encroaching on the spirit of another living creature. This was not a natural existence. It would be easy for the *ghost* to let go and float towards the light. It is what the *ghost* wanted most to do, except for the demon it would have done so long ago. The demon was the evil spirit whose bonds the *ghost* had broken in its ignorance. One day the *ghost* would let go and float into the light of the abyss. But not until the demon was confined again for eternity.

For now, he must protect the girl from herself.

The girl had already reached out to the abyss, sensing its soothing reassurance. She could almost touch it to embrace its temptation. She simply had to let go of this life. So much of that life was already gone, she could let go of the little that was left with just a thought. Because to stay alive, she had to struggle, to endure the pain, the sadness, the loneliness. For what purpose?

The healing spirit of the *ghost* rushed to surround her with images of the boy become man. *Oh!* The girl was filled with great joy at seeing those images. She felt warmth in her hand. She looked down and saw an image. Her hand held a glowing orb, a bright silvery light, as if it held the full moon. It was wondrous. A new thought came to her.

Open your eyes.

*

Anamosa blinked once. There was brightness all around her. Everything was blurry. She blinked again. Her vision cleared. She was instantly aware of the pain. It was right there. More subdued than usual, but close by. Waiting. Like a sleeping animal. Ready to strike. A powerful lion of the mountains, with sharp teeth and claws. *Be careful. Don't move.* She must not disturb the beast. Her eyes danced over towards the windows. She saw bright daylight, full of the sun. There was a woman sitting in a chair by the window. She did not know this woman. She did not know this place. She was in a bed, covered with a blanket, her head on a pillow. She was so *thirsty*! It was hard to swallow. *Why is it hard to swallow?*

Her memory began to conjure the terrible images. The beast with claws began to stir.

"No! No! No!" Her voice sounded tiny and desperate to her ears.

Anamosa's hands moved in defense and her right hand brushed against something... She looked. It was someone's head...with blond hair? The head lifted. She saw the face that gave her joy.

Henri smiled. "Thank God!" he breathed with relief. "Anna," he whispered. He kissed her hand. "*Je t'aime!*"

Anamosa licked her cracked and dry lips. "*Je t'aime, Ahhree.*" Her voice came out as a tiny, vulnerable, rasping whisper.

She had a beautiful child-like voice. He pulled the chair closer to the bedside, so he could lean forward to kiss her. He kissed her forehead and then her lips.

Anamosa experienced a wave of pure bliss. She reached out with her fingers to lightly touch his face and magic hair.

"I've been so worried." He sniffed back the tears. "You've been asleep for over a day!"

"*Thirsty*," she whispered.

"Yes! Thirsty!"

He gestured to the nurse, who was already hovering nearby, smiling at the wonderful scene of tenderness she'd been privileged to witness.

Together, they slipped another pillow underneath Anamosa's head and shoulders. Anna winced as they did this. The nurse gave her a large cup of water. The cup had two handles, so it could be gripped with both hands. She drank four full cups before she stopped, panting afterwards from the effort. Although the cup was empty, she did not let it go.

"I must tell Dr. Michaux she is awake," the nurse said. "I'll be right back."

"Tell Lady Corrinne, too!"

*

The morning after the ball, the governor came to see the result of the carnage at Lady VanderMeer's house.

"Lieutenant Gerrard did all this?"

The exhausted Colonel du Bourzt nodded. "According to witnesses... all this in less than a minute."

The governor was outraged that a rape could occur in the very heart of his fortress city.

"Remove the bodies. Burn them. Scatter the ashes in the ocean. Have the house cleaned and scrubbed thoroughly inside and out. The back yard, too. Even the street in front."

When the army was finished, the inside was scrubbed clean. It was freshened further by Marie-Louise de Drucour's servants, until there was no trace of any stains or offending odors. Only then did Madame Drucour convince Corrinne to go home. The nurses at the hospital looked after the twins. Henri was there and Captain LaTour came around to play with them and bring them presents.

The carriage came to get her. Corrinne's gray shawl was wrapped around her shoulders, under which she was still wearing the sad-looking ballgown from two nights' earlier. The diamond pendant was tucked away in a hidden pocket inside the dress. The grenadier soldiers guarding the house allowed three faubourg women claiming a familiarity with Lady VanderMeer to greet her as she stepped down from the carriage. The other citizens who had crowded to welcome her, politely held back. They could see the exhaustion, her haunted expression, the dishevelment of her hair. There was no cheering, just sympathetic smiles and waves. Corrinne smiled weakly and returned the waves. The three faubourg women waiting to greet her were the gossipy friends from the market. They offered hugs in consolation and, in turn, gave her over to Marie-Louise who waited inside the door.

The house was filled with a few vases of spring wildflowers, hot breads and pastries, and fresh coffee offered by other citizens of the faubourg. Marie-Louise also had a hot bath prepared for her upstairs. Corrinne was humbled by the empathy and generosity of these people, and those she encountered everywhere else she'd lived. It always left her with a sense of awe over the inherent goodness in people when tragedy strikes others.

Corrinne wasn't sure if it was the luxurious hot bath, that her hair was shampooed and combed, the fresh clothing or the miraculous hot coffee. Each one a giant step, lifting her spirits to near normal. She invited the servants with Marie-Louise to sit with her and share the sweet breads and coffee. She let them ask all the questions they wanted and did her best to answer truthfully… well, almost. She learned that the Swiss volunteers had been disarmed and were now restricted to their barracks, under guard, where they would remain until arrangements were finalized to ship them back to France. The marines buried their two dead brothers-in-arms at the small military cemetery in the eastern part of the fortress. Henri in attendance, along with small elements from every unit in the garrison and naval representatives from the ships.

Corrinne returned to the hospital a couple hours later with changes of clothing for the twins. She entered the front door and a nurse hurried up to her with the exciting news about Anamosa. Corrinne went directly to the room and found Dr. Michaux already there, examining Anamosa's condition. He paused and waited long enough for Corrinne to gently hug the young girl and drip tears of joy on Anna's swollen face as she kissed her.

Henri moved back to another chair and gave room to Corrinne to enjoy some of Anamosa's first words.

"I'm hungry," Anna said hoarsely. She'd been awake long enough to realize that craving.

"Of course, you are, little love!"

Dr. Michaux, had already stipulated a special menu for her, starting with brothy soups full of bits of beef and vegetables to which he added spoonfuls of various tonics. One of the nurses went to get a bed tray.

"Lady VanderMeer, *s'il vous plaît*, may I have a moment with you?"

The doctor took Lady VanderMeer into an empty room to confer with her privately, away from Anamosa and Lieutenant Gerrard.

"Lady Anamosa's consciousness is most welcome. She has passed the first critical obstacle in her recovery. Waking up! Eating food is very important. But more difficulty lies ahead of us. Like any wound, the trauma to her genitals, the severe tearing. The tissues are inflamed. The inflammation is now the greatest danger. Now that she is conscious, I can administer stronger medicines and some herbal poultices."

Corrinne nodded. She already understood this. "How long till she recovers?"

"That's why I wanted to talk with you privately. Anamosa's body does the healing. I heard a rumor that you plan to leave Louisbourg. But Anamosa must not be moved from the hospital until her strength improves and the inflammation is *completely* gone. Or it will likely get worse, maybe even fatal. I must visit and examine her several times every day to ensure she recovers. To answer your question, without relapses, presuming her recovery proceeds at the current pace, then it will take a few more weeks. No more than a month."

A month? Corrinne had hoped to leave Louisbourg much sooner than that. *So be it. Anamosa comes first, before anything else.*

Île Royale

Philippe and Malsum rode horses on the army road leading north from Port Toulouse. They had been delayed for three days because Malsum had been sick. They had eaten a stew of oysters and mussels from Île Saint-Jean after arriving at Port Toulouse. Philippe was unaffected. Malsum suffered painful vomiting and diarrhea.

"The white man's poisonous food," Malsum grumbled.

Louisbourg was a little over seventy miles north of Port Toulouse as a bird flies. It was a four-day journey by horseback, if the horse trotted. Philippe could sit-to-trot and ride comfortably at a trotting pace on a horse. Malsum had very little experience on horseback. After being so sick, he could tolerate no more than a slow walk. Impatient as Philippe was to get to the fortress, it would take them time. After the first day, they changed to the existing Mi'kmaq trails to the northeast. It was a shorter path. But this path had more obstacles. It wended through marshlands and required fording rivers and streams. Malsum improved as each day went by, and their speed of advance accelerated.

On the morning of the sixth day, they had reached the eastern coastline of Île Royale. Malsum gazed upon the vast emptiness of the Atlantic Ocean.

"How long does it take to cross this water?"

"One or two moons," Philippe replied.

Malsum now understood why the oldest legends never spoke of the white man for uncounted seasons before they appeared suddenly and in great numbers. The white man had to learn how to build the great sailing ships first.

They broke their fast with some dried beef and root vegetables he'd purchased at Port Toulouse. Philippe expected to reach the outer breastworks in a few hours.

"It won't be long until we see the breastworks along the shoreline of a bay south of the fort. We need to approach this place cautiously. It will be guarded by sentries who are expecting the English to invade. We will be challenged."

"And when we enter the fort?"

Philippe had not thought about that. "We are marine scouts. We will stay at the barracks with the other marines. My son commands them. And they are Québécois marines. They are familiar with the Abenaki. They probably know of you. They are friends."

Before they broke their camp, Philippe pulled his officer sash and other articles of uniform dress from his pack, and dressed until he had some resemblance to an officer of Troupes de la Marines. The uniform was threadbare in places, stained, and splotched with blood and dirt. It reeked of rancid sweat after months of wear in the field, not that any of this bothered him.

"How do I look?"

Malsum stood with his arms folded in front of his chest and surveyed him. "You look like the poorest officer in the French army."

Philippe smiled wryly. "Thank you. I am not ashamed. This uniform has earned its wear and dirt. When we encounter the French sentries, they will be regular troops from France. Speak your best French to them."

"So, you can dress like a peasant…but the ignorant savage must show scholarship? *Very well, I will speak English*," he said, switching to English.

"Malsum, please do not speak English…even in jest. They are on the alert for spies. Your English has a Scottish accent anyway."

"Latin then? *Aut cum scuto aut in scuto.* Either with the shield or on it."

Philippe did not argue with him further.

At the southernmost redoubt of the breastworks on Gabarus Bay, a French ensign and three regulars did indeed challenge them with raised muskets and bayonets.

"And who is this?" the ensign asked, eyeing the frightening visage of the warrior.

The warrior answered in perfect French. "I am Mkuigen Malsum. A shaman of the Abenaki tribe. A healer and a sorcerer. A healer like your healers, only much better. A deadly sorcerer when I choose to be."

The ensign nodded. "I believe you."

"We are going to Louisbourg."

They were escorted the rest of the way to the Dauphin Gate.

Once inside the fortress, the enormity of the natural harbor was accentuated by the surrounding quay walls and enceintes of the fortress. Cannon snouts could be seen everywhere. It was easy to appreciate the strength of this city. Philippe saw huge warships at anchor. They were anchored close, and there were a lot of them.

The sergeant of the guard approached.

"Halt right there. And dismount."

Seven armed French soldiers stood with their arms at the ready. They were glancing nervously at Malsum.

"I am Captain Philippe Gerrard, commander of scout companies for General Montcalm. This is my chief scout, Mkuigen Malsum of the Abenaki."

The Bourgogne Regiment sergeant reacted at once. "Are you Lieutenant Gerrard's father?"

"The same."

"Captain, I am required to escort you to the King's Bastion to see the governor."

"Why?"

"Anyone with your rank, or anyone coming from Québec City, is required to see the governor."

"Very well. Where are the marine barracks?"

"Right behind you, Captain."

"I want to see the person in charge of the barracks."

The sergeant went into a doorway beneath the Dauphin Bastion and returned seconds later with a giant marine wearing color sergeant stripes. Five other curious marines appeared outside the doorway.

The man came to attention and saluted like a grenadier. "Color Sergeant Gosse, at your service, sir. And may I say, I am honored to meet the father of Lieutenant Gerrard."

Philippe returned the salute and shook Gosse's hand. He introduced Malsum.

Color Sergeant Gosse smiled. "*Mon Dieu! Impressionnant!* Monsieur Malsum, I am certainly pleased to know you are fighting on our side!"

Malsum nodded in greeting.

"I would like Malsum to share your quarters."

"It would be an honor to have you with us, sir."

"Where is Lieutenant Gerrard?"

The color sergeant's expression changed. "Your son is at the hospital. He is all right, but he is visiting with someone there."

"I must report to the governor first. I will rendezvous with my son at the hospital after that."

"Captain, allow me to accompany you to the governor's bastion," Color Sergeant Gosse said. "There are some things you should learn about before you see your son."

*

Upon hearing the name *Scout Captain Philippe Gerrard* whispered in his ear, Governor Drucour sat up straight.

"He's here? Now?"

Lieutenant Christophe nodded. "Yes, sir."

Governor Drucour stood. His military council followed his actions. "Gentlemen, I have another matter that needs immediate attention." He dismissed the council and spoke quietly to Lieutenant Christophe. "Escort the captain to my private quarters."

Philippe's expression was hard and preoccupied as he saluted and shook the governor's hand.

Drucour gestured for him to take a chair. "Welcome to Louisbourg. Your reputation precedes you."

Philippe's anger simmered to the fore. "Excuse my rudeness, Governor, but how does it happen that my daughter is attacked in my wife's house at the center of your fortress?"

"All of us are outraged by this terrible crime. The men that did it were posted here for two months before they acted. We were all surprised. They killed the guards that were posted around Lady Corrinne's house."

"Governor, as you might presume, my attention for any discussion with you will not be productive. Permit me to go to the hospital immediately."

Drucour stood. "Of course, Captain. I understand. I have much information to share with you and many questions to ask. But nothing is more important than your family."

Color Sergeant Gosse was waiting on the street side of the bridgewalk when Philippe emerged from the King's Bastion.

"With permission, Captain, allow me to escort you to the hospital. We can go by the house, so you can see it. Lady Corrinne and the twins are staying at the hospital now, to be near Lady Anamosa. Lieutenant Gerrard stays there all the time when he is not on duty."

They walked quickly. Color Sergeant Gosse spoke of the structure and layout of the fortress and the unit make-up of the garrison. He went down the side street to the house, pointed out the side gate to the back yard, and explained how the attack took place.

"There was a second assault on the front of the house less than an hour later. Three more Swiss mercenaries. Lieutenant Gerrard dispatched them all in less than a minute. I was approaching the house with my marines and saw it all. He is an extraordinary officer, I am proud to tell you. The remaining Swiss mercenaries are restricted to their barracks. They've been disarmed and are under constant guard. I've heard they will be transported back to France."

Philippe's expression remained grim. When they reached the hospital, they entered the front door and immediately saw doctors and nurses. There were two marines standing guard in the foyer. They came to attention and saluted him.

"I am Scout Captain Gerrard. I am here to see…well, Lady Anamosa first."

Gosse saluted. "I must take your leave, Captain. I will see to the accommodation of Monsieur Malsum."

"Thank you, Color Sergeant."

The marine guard led Philippe down the hallway, passing by people who gawked at the unshaven, rugged appearance of the wilderness officer. They met another marine guard and exchanged salutes. Philippe went into Anamosa's room during one of the rare times she was alone, except for the nurse watching over her. She seemed to be resting, her eyes were closed.

Philippe hardly recognized her. The bruising on Anamosa's face had suffused throughout her skin. It had turned more purplish and brown as the days went by. The bloat and swelling to the face and neck was so ballooned it concealed her delicate beauty. She looked taller, too, from the little girl he last saw in Boston.

The nurse in the room looked up with surprise at this huge, bearded fierce-looking marine officer striding to the girl's bedside. She stood and quickly approached the man. The officer's teeth were bared as he stared down at Lady Anamosa. She heard an angry sound, the hiss of air being sucked between his teeth. There was a feral odor about him.

"May I help you, sir?"

The man took several calming breaths before replying. "I am Captain Philippe Gerrard." He sat in the chair next to the bed and carefully took hold of Anamosa's hand.

Anamosa's eyes moved from the touch, blinked once, and opened. She did not smile. Her eyes widened at the sight of the bearded man with scars all over his face sitting in the chair. It was another face she loved. It was the face her mother, Okeanneh, had loved so long ago.

"Fleep!" It was all she could manage. Her throat was raw and dry that day, still difficult to swallow or talk.

Calloused as Philippe was from years of brutal wilderness fighting, his eyes filled to see her so injured.

"Oho, Anamosa," he whispered.

"Oho, Fleep," she replied.

He wanted to hug her but worried that doing so might aggravate her injuries. Anamosa's eyes were bloodshot. "Your eyes are…"

"It's from the choking," a man's voice said from behind him. "The rapist choked her."

Philippe stood and turned.

It was Henri. He was fully grown, over six feet tall, as tall as he was. Philippe could see the hardened, determined face behind the smile. Henri looked ten years older than the boy he remembered from Boston. He was missing part of an ear, and his face already showed other scars of war. He carried a cutlass belted across his back.

Philippe smiled with pride. "Oho, Henri!"

"Oho, Papa!"

They came together in a hard and fast hug and slapped their hands hard on each other's backs and did not let go for several seconds. Corrinne entered the room at this moment. She'd run down the hall after learning Philippe was in the hospital. With fingers over her mouth, tears streamed down her face and over her fingers. But she waited until the two men she loved most in the world broke their embrace.

Philippe saw Corrinne to his right…standing just a few paces away. He took off his hat and let it drop to the floor. He glanced down at his filthy uniform and held his arms out to each side.

"Corrinne…I am…"

"I don't care!" she cried. Corrinne threw herself at him, grasping him tightly in both arms, kissing his lips, his face, his beard, his lips again. He was her favorite food and she was starving. They sank to their knees during the embrace. "I love you! I love you! I love you!"

"I've missed you so," Philippe said. "I wasn't sure I'd ever see you again."

"Those are my words! I say them every day." Corrinne kissed him again and again. "And I prayed for you every day. I got your letter," Corrinne said and laughed a little. "All three sentences! I've read it a lot!"

"I'm sorry, my love. They secreted the mail from me. I got the letters from you, finally, all at the same time. I have them all memorized. Certain pages, more than others," he added.

"Well, you shall have to point out all your favorite sentences. And I'll show you what I was thinking when I wrote them."

Philippe grinned, as his imagination sparked.

Corrinne examined his face further. "Oh, my precious, what they have done to you?"

"Nothing good." Philippe glanced back at Anamosa, who was watching them all, her face impassive. "What have they done to her?"

"Oh, yes. My Anamosa!" Corrinne stood. "Hello, little love."

They moved back to the chairs. Philippe sat down. Corrinne sat on his lap with an arm around his neck. Every place on his body she touched felt raw-boned and hard-muscled. Henri pulled up the second chair. Together, all three touched Anamosa's hands.

"I-I love you," Anamosa managed weakly for the first time.

They all replied, cooing over her. Philippe doted on Anamosa. He spoke of how much he missed her. How much he loved her. How important she was to him.

"Callie…Marcus," Anamosa rasped.

"Oh, yes! Thank you, Anna! Come with me, Philippe. Come meet your two beautiful children. They are playing in a room down the hall."

He frowned. "Looking like this?"

"Stop saying that! Marcus will be mesmerized. And Callie will pull on your beard, so she can kiss you."

"I will stay with Anna," Henri said.

Beaming with pride and joy, Corrinne took Philippe by an arm and led him from the room. After they walked away, Henri told the marine private at the door to leave the hospital and retrieve something for him.

Corrinne and Philippe came to a larger room of the hospital with three beds, dedicated to her and the twins. Two more marines guarded that door. They came to attention.

"It's an honor, sir," one of them said.

Philippe stopped in the doorway and gazed at the twins.

"They will be two years in June," Corrinne whispered proudly. "Come, come meet your children."

They stepped quietly into the room together. A nurse was holding Calypso in her lap, showing her a wide book full of colored sketches of Louisbourg, painted by a soldier-artist. Calypso pointed at different objects in the picture and said their names aloud: *tree, cannon, cow, soldier, ship*. Marcus had been carefully piling various-sized wooden blocks into a column, a tower of sorts in his mind. The column now stood as tall as he was, which was his goal. He'd been trying to solve this all morning. They'd kept falling over until he learned to put the wider blocks on the bottom. Now that it was standing alone, Marcus moved back a step and raised his arms in victory.

"Aha!"

Seeing them for the first time, Philippe was overcome with emotion. *My God!* He sagged to a sitting position on the floor. *How could I have missed... so much of their lives?* Corrinne sat next to him.

Hearing them enter, the twins stopped what they were doing. They stared and blinked at the bearded man sitting on the floor.

Corrinne held out her arms. "Come, Marcus. Come, Calypso. Come see your *Papah!*" It was the first time Corrinne had ever said that word to them. She'd been careful never to say it in relation to Charles.

Encouraged by his mother, Marcus walked over and peered closely at Philippe, as if trying to see around the man's beard. Philippe smiled. Corrinne did not speak, totally enthralled by every magical moment of this first meeting.

"Oho, Marcus."

Marcus looked him up and down and suddenly brightened with surprise. "*Sword!*" He stooped down to touch it.

"Yes! It is a sword," Philippe said.

Calypso came over and perched high inside her mother's arms. She gazed intently at Philippe. The little girl's expression was haughty, as if she was granting Philippe a rare indulgence, that he should be grateful she was even looking at him. Philippe felt properly humbled.

"Oho, Calypso," he greeted gently. To Corrinne, he whispered, "My God, Corrinne! Look at her hair and those green eyes! She looks just like you! My God."

Corrinne leaned over and kissed Philippe.

Seeing her mother's action, Calypso leaned closer to Philippe's face. "Papah?"

Philippe's eyes widened. "Yes, Calypso. I am your Papah."

Calypso hesitated. Then she leaned closer and kissed his lips briefly. Her nose wrinkled. She leaned back. "Stink!"

Philippe laughed. "Yes, Calypso. I do smell. *Pardon.* You are just like your Mamah!" He looked at Corrinne. "At least she kissed me first."

"Just like her Mamah," Corrinne said.

"*Knife,*" Marcus said as he tried to tug the eighteen-inch skinning knife from its scabbard.

"Oh!" Philippe guarded his son's hand. "Careful, Marcus! Sharp."

As the twins played on the floor in front of them, Corrinne told Philippe stories of what happened since the twins were born. Of Winter House. Of the repeated attacks on Charles. She focused on the children. There was not enough time to tell him everything.

Philippe lightly touched the pink scar across her throat. "And this?"

"Yes," Corrinne replied soberly. "Let's talk about that later."

*

Captain LaTour heeded Governor Drucour's message sent out to the *Falcon Queen* at noontime to come to his headquarters immediately. He wondered if it was about his decision *not* to unload his cargo. He'd decided if he was going to Québec City or Montréal, he would bring those people some luxury goods. He had heard the Québécois citizens were suffering from famine and war. He permitted his crew to go ashore now, half of them one day, the other half the next, and would continue to do so.

Captain LaTour stood before Lieutenant Christophe's desk and waited patiently.

"Yes! Captain LaTour! Follow me."

Upon entering the governor's office, LaTour again waited while the governor finished talking with two of the faubourg merchants.

LaTour saluted as they exited.

"*Bonjour*, Captain LaTour. Sit. How do Lady VanderMeer and Lady Anamosa fare on this first day of May?"

"I've not yet seen them today, but yesterday Lady Anamosa seemed a little better. It's going slow. I am told it may be another few weeks, unless…"

"Captain, how soon can you be ready to sail?"

The unexpected question left Captain LaTour confounded. "How soon? Within a week, or less…after I am provisioned for the intended journey."

The governor leaned back in his chair and bridged his fingers.

"Captain, I have a difficult decision to make, one that affects you. When you brought Lord VanderMeer here, you knew Lady Corrinne was not Lord VanderMeer's wife, yes?"

LaTour's expression fell. "Governor, I…"

"It's all right, Captain. I am just stating the obvious. They both confessed this charade to me on the first day of their arrival in Louisbourg. Minister Machault approved Lady Corrinne's sanctuary. The minister alleged that Lord and Lady VanderMeer were spies for France, when they resided in Boston. But I am not certain that was the entire truth either."

"Governor…"

He held up a palm. "The Swiss mercenaries were here for almost *two months*, before they acted. Were they waiting for a perfect time? No. You recorded your sailing orders with Lieutenant Christophe. 'Transport Captain Stoecklin back to France.' They were waiting for you. Your ship, Captain LaTour, was to be their escape vessel."

Captain LaTour sputtered. "Governor, I was not aware of any of this! I had written orders to transport him. That's all I knew!"

Drucour held up a palm again. "It is all right, Captain. I believe you. If I thought you were a willing accomplice in this monstrous act, you would already be hanging in front of Frédéric Gate!"

Hanging! LaTour's hand instinctively touched his throat. He swallowed hard. It was LaTour's least favorite word. Uttered, yet again…by another minister…of another government.

"There is no need to dispute or defend the veracity of anything I just said, not anymore. Minister Machault has been dismissed and Lord VanderMeer is dead. God rest his soul. Lady Corrinne, nevertheless, remains a guest of Louisbourg."

Captain LaTour was very nervous where this one-way discussion was going. He interjected, "Lady Corrinne does not intend to remain in Louisbourg."

"I am aware of her intentions, Captain. I like Lady Corrinne. I admire her. She is charming and intelligent. She has also become close friends with my wife, which can be awkward at times. But with Lord and Lady VanderMeer's admission that they were not married, it follows that Lady Corrinne's children are not Lord VanderMeer's children. They are the children of the marine Captain Philippe Gerrard. And yet, the Dutch government insists they are Lord VanderMeer's progeny. I must presume the Dutch government is *not* aware of Scout Captain Gerrard, although Lord VanderMeer was certainly aware of him. The Dutch also claim the House of Brunswick has many political enemies, suggesting more assassins may be en route to Louisbourg. That is a problem for me. Mercenaries are not very popular in Louisbourg. I am hoping Lady VanderMeer can leave Louisbourg at the first opportunity. Which brings me to you. Now that her real husband is here…"

"What? Captain Gerrard is here?!"

"Oh? You did not know? Yes, Scout Captain Philippe Gerrard arrived in Louisbourg on horseback from Port Toulouse earlier this morning. He may be at the hospital. I suspect he is here to escort Lady Corrinne to Québec City, but beyond introductions, we've not taken time to talk about his intentions. Lady Corrinne and her marine captain are overdue for a reunion, I think."

Captain LaTour was excited. "Governor, with your permission, I would like to go to the hospital and see Captain Gerrard."

"Good. Then you can carry a message to them for me. But first, Captain LaTour, as your senior naval commander, I order you to transport Lady Corrinne and her children somewhere else. I planned to tell you this when your ship arrived…but then the attack occurred. Also, please inform Lady Corrinne and Captain Gerrard, I want to meet with them both tomorrow

morning at the hour of ten. It will be a private meeting, except I want you
there, too. That is all. You are dismissed."

Captain LaTour stood and saluted. "Yes, sir."

*

Marie-Louise de Drucour delayed Captain LaTour as he left the governor's
quarters. She handed him a wax-sealed message.

"Please give this to Lady Corrinne for me."

LaTour looked at the small folded note. "Yes, Madame."

The captain went straight down Rue Toulouse directly to the gate and
found his crewman waiting at the Frédéric Gate loading docks with the ship's
harbor launch, where he'd left him.

"Row out to the ship. Tell Victorio to begin provisioning the ship to sail.
We will likely go to Québec City, but after that…" LaTour didn't know. All
he knew, was someone else would tell him. "And possibly back to France.
No one else is to know of these orders."

"Yes, Captain."

*

Marie-Louise entered the governor's chambers. "Augustin, I am going
to prepare Lady Corrinne's house for tonight. I will have a meal cooked for
Corrinne and Captain Gerrard. And I will have some of my maids stay with
her children at the hospital, so Corrinne and Captain Gerrard can have a
night together alone."

Augustin de Drucour chuckled. "And thus, Marie-Louise de Drucour
becomes the public advocate in the scandal that is about to break over our
city."

"Yes, Augustin, I will. But you are the governor. I will leave it up to you
to explain my good intentions to everyone. And at the same time remind
them that Lord VanderMeer *died* months ago." She turned to leave and
hesitated. "Oh, and please let those few citizens that feel sanctimonious
know, especially the *priests,* that I do not care what they think. Thank you,"
she added in a lyrical tone.

Governor Drucour did not care if Lady Corrinne and Captain Gerrard
enjoyed a night filled with the most shameless and wanton acts of their own
invention. By the next morning, a scandal of lust would be the least of their
problems.

*

Commodore Chevalier Joseph du Bauffremont approached the governor after the egregious attack on Lady VanderMeer's house and the rape of Lady Anamosa to offer his sympathies. But having watched Lady VanderMeer's celebrated dancing the night before, the commodore had an observation to share.

Drucour met with the obese, pompous naval officer but did not bother to ask the man to sit. He did not intend to tolerate him for very long.

"I must say, she is a most exuberant dancer. Did you know Lady VanderMeer bears a remarkable resemblance to Lady Corrinne de Chanaye of Québec City? I met Lady de Chanaye on several occasions when my ship visited Québec City several years ago. The last time was when my frigate provided escort to a Dutch trading ship, *William's Queen,* as it left port. It was carrying Lady de Chanaye and her new husband, Captain Philippe Gerrard of the Troupes de la Marine."

"I am not familiar with the woman of whom you speak," Governor Drucour responded. "I personally met Lord and Lady VanderMeer for the first time when they arrived in Louisbourg late last year." Drucour declined to mention the ship's name. "Lord VanderMeer's identity was validated to me in writing by the Minister of Marine, who further directed that Lady Corrinne VanderMeer be given sanctuary. What you refer to is probably a coincidence."

Commodore du Bauffremont nodded thoughtfully. "By this you mean Minister of Marine Jean-Baptiste de Machault, who was dismissed in February for conspiracy against the king? Of course, the resemblance could be a coincidence, as you say, albeit a very beautiful one. But they do have the same first name. Interesting, yes?"

Drucour bristled. "Commodore, do you imply this interesting coincidence should demand my full attention? I am much more concerned about the attack on a woman in her home, in the faubourg, in the middle of this fortress! An attack by foreign mercenaries who raped an innocent young girl, who now fights for her life in the hospital. Would you agree that horrific act demands more of my attention?"

"Oh, but of course," Bauffremont replied apologetically.

Chapter 23
Louisbourg
May 1, 1757
Surprises

Captain LaTour hurried to the hospital. It would be so good to see them both together. He was undecided when to tell Corrinne his important news about the journals and the missive from Madame Dubonnet. But after the tragedy occurred, he told his crew they would have the honor of presenting it all to Lady Corrinne once she finally came aboard to cheer her mood. It would be their surprise to her. This would also induce the crew to keep it all a secret until that time came.

He reached the hospital and found two marine guards posted in the foyer as usual. They came to attention and presented arms. It made him uncomfortable doing so, but LaTour saluted them.

"Where is Captain Gerrard?"

"In the children's room."

Halfway down the hallway, he stopped in to see Anamosa. Henri sat in a bedside chair as usual. He took the other one.

"*Bonjour, mon amour petite*," he said cheerily. "Oh, my goodness! Was that a smile?"

"Yes," Henri answered for her. "She started smiling this morning, when my father arrived. Her throat is sore. It hurts her to talk."

"She does not need to speak. Your smile is reward enough!"

She smiled again.

LaTour took her hand in his. She scratched his palm lightly with one finger. He noticed the jeweled silver amulet peeking out by the neck from beneath the hospital chemise she was wearing.

"You're wearing Chittaqua's talisman! Who brought that to you?"

Anamosa's eyes shifted to Henri. Another tiny smile.

"Oh, of course he did. Now I'm jealous. I must bring you something, too. I'm going to see Marcus and Calypso. Do you want me to hug them for you?"

Anamosa smiled and nodded. LaTour stood, bent, and kissed her forehead. "God be with you always, my little love."

He went to the door and felt a hand on his shoulder. It was Henri. He spoke in a whisper.

"If you want to bring her a *big* surprise, there is a small gold cross necklace with a purple jewel she likes. She probably keeps it in an etui bag by her bed. Knock on the door to the house. Some of Madame Drucour's servants are in there cleaning. They will let you in."

LaTour went down the hall to the room dedicated to the twins. Seeing Captain Gerrard, his heart swelled from the good memories they shared… except for the ones about the storms…and the ones concerning cannons… like Le Havre…and the threats of hanging from Intendant Bigôt…and Queen Charlotte's prison in Halifax. *Well, most of them are good.*

They embraced and hugged each other tightly. "I see your face wears one or two more scars, Philippe." In truth, LaTour was stunned by the tangle of scars Philippe had collected. The beard barely covered them up. He turned his attention to the twins. After many hugs, he gave them each a sugar cookie fresh from his shipboard galley.

"My lady, I also bring you a note from Madame Drucour."

"Oh?" She took it, broke the seal, and read the generous offer. "What an *interesting* surprise," she said and handed the note to Philippe.

"What about the twins?" he asked.

"Marie will send two of her maids to come and watch them. Marcus and Callie know them well. They've helped me with them before. That will give us the house together…all alone."

The way her green eyes glowed at him made Philippe's heartbeat elevate.

"I also bring a verbal message from Governor Drucour. He asks you both to attend his offices in the morning at the hour of ten. I am ordered to attend with you."

"For what purpose?" Philippe asked.

Since they were alone in the room with the twins, LaTour summarized the discussion he just had with the governor in one sentence. "The *Falcon Queen* is now dedicated to your departure from Louisbourg. Just like old times, yes?"

Philippe was jubilant. He had planned to petition the governor for a ship to carry them to Québec City.

"This is very good news." Philippe looked at Corrinne. "Travel overland is exceedingly dangerous."

Corrinne was convinced it was Captain LaTour's destiny to be here, once again, to take her away. But for the governor to offer this without petition?

"The governor is not unkind, but he was never pleased to give me sanctuary. He is anxious for me to be gone," she said. "More so now, after what happened."

Philippe shrugged. "Fate brings us a boon. It provides us a ship for travel. I am not curious about the reason for his generosity."

But Corrinne was curious to learn his reason.

"I must prepare the house before you arrive," she told Philippe. "Captain LaTour, will you escort me back?"

"Of course."

Corrinne kissed Philippe in a manner that hinted of things to come. She stopped in to see Anamosa and told Henri of her plans. "Your father will stay with me tonight."

Henri's expression brightened. "Of course, he will."

After Corrinne left, Henri went to speak with Nurse Cardon, then went to his father. Two other nurses were already occupying the twins' interest.

"Father, I have a surprise for you."

"Another surprise?"

"Follow me."

Henri escorted Philippe to the hospital bathing room. He pointed to a clean marine uniform hanging from a hook on the wall. It was worn in places, but all the pieces were there, including a sash, undergarments, and stockings.

"I thought you could use this."

"How did you...?"

"It's one of mine. But I think it should fit. We are about the same size. Just transfer over your epaulets."

Philippe touched the clean and pressed material of the uniform with appreciation. "I've not worn anything this clean...well, in a long time." He laughed softly. "I can wear this when I see the governor in the morning. That way he can stand being in the same room with me."

Without thinking, Philippe started to rub the beard on his face. Like all his other scouts, he'd been crudely shearing his whisker growth for months using his skinning knife, so the face hair would not foul the firing hammer on his musket. But how would he shave this off?

"This is Nurse Desiree Cardon," Henri said, as if reading his mind.

Philippe turned to see a woman in a dark gray uniform with a white bib and apron. She was a tall, slender woman with brown hair and eyes. Strands of white hair intermixed with the brown. Her dignified posture and expression suggested she was experienced.

"Nurse Cardon, my father, Scout Captain Philippe Gerrard."

"Captain Gerrard." Her smile was brief and polite.

"Nurse Cardon is the senior nurse in the hospital. She has been very kind to Anamosa…and to me. She will see to…"

Nurse Cardon spoke for herself. "I will assist you in purifying your appearance. Take off your uniform and undergarments, stockings, all of it, until you are naked. Place them in that basket. We will wash what is possible to wash and burn the rest."

There was an implicit certainty in her tone that Captain Gerrard was expected to do exactly as he was told. She reminded Philippe of one of his scout company sergeants.

Philippe bowed slightly. "I am pleased to meet you, Mademoiselle…"

"I am *not* a mademoiselle. I am a *nurse*. You may address me as Nurse Cardon."

She said *nurse* as if saying the word *general*. Philippe felt a sudden compulsion to salute. He concealed his smile.

"I am pleased to meet you…*Nurse* Cardon."

"We shall soon see," she promised.

As she said these words, a line of four nurses entered, each carrying two buckets of steaming hot water, which they poured into the deep porcelain tub. They were all dressed alike. Three of the four had hair tied back in a bun and were matronly. The fourth nurse was younger. Her black hair was braided up and out of the way.

"If you will cooperate, Captain, we will scrub you down like we do the sick and wounded men. We will thoroughly shampoo your hair, too. It is the only way to ensure you are clean of the lice and the other vermin foulness you've collected in the wilderness. Otherwise you will infest all our other patients, including your children! How long has it been since you bathed? One month? Two?" She saw his look of embarrassment. "Don't be embarrassed, Captain. I've seen much worse. I am a competent barber and can shave your face, if you will allow me. And given its appearance, you should take advantage of this. I've been taking care of the sick and wounded soldiers and sailors for over twenty-five years. Just do as we tell you—first by undressing. Then you will stand at attention, over the drain, arms extended straight out from your side. We will wash as much of the caked grime as we can off you before you step into the cleaner bathwater."

Henri restrained his smile. "Captain, if it makes any difference, I also submitted to this...purification ceremony."

"Can't be worse than a gauntlet?" Philippe jested.

Henri's expression suggested that Philippe would soon find out. "I leave you in the expert hands of Nurse Cardon. I will be with Anamosa when you are done."

Four nurses worked together to get this bathing conducted quickly and efficiently. Buckets of hot water arrived constantly. The water in the tub was changed as often as they thought necessary. Philippe felt like a cavalry horse being scrub-brushed and rinsed in a stable. His body was riddled with bruising, which he tolerated and tended to ignore. The nurses found all the tender spots as they scrubbed him down, making him wince and flinch.

They are like an artillery crew, Philippe mused. *Reloading and firing a cannon.*

In the end, there was no doubt in his mind he was clean. The washing of his hair was wonderful. They massaged the scalp, washed, and rinsed it three times to get it clean, and then brushed it straight.

"Now move over to that stool."

After he was out of the way, the nurses began soap mopping and brooming the dirty water down a center drain that led out to the harbor. They covered him with long towels. Nurse Cardon scissor-cut his hair evenly at shoulder length, and tied it back in a que. She scissor-clipped his beard to the point where she could shave him with a straight razor and soap. She did this without cutting him—not one nick.

She held a mirror before his face. "I expect you will not recognize yourself."

Indeed, it was always like seeing the face of a stranger after Phillipe shaved. He accepted the hand mirror from her. Even more revealing now were the crisscrossing web of lumpy pink scars, the result of days of being tortured by the Seneca and the skin piercings and lashes he incurred from running the Oneida gauntlet.

Philippe was aware of this coarse evidence, marks of the brutality his body had endured. Tarnished by the grime that settled in and around the contours of the ropey scars, after months of fighting, sleeping, eating, and surviving on the open ground of the forests, his skin faintly resembled the grainy appearance of tree bark. At least that is what one of the *coureur de bois* scouts jested on a day when Philippe tried to wash off some of the dirt in the icy cold waters of a stream. Covered beneath his uniform clothes, in the wilderness, he didn't think about it very much. All the *coureurs de bois*, militia, and soldiers had scars of their own to boast with pride about when around a campfire. Nothing remotely close to Philippe's, of course, but he never participated in these pointless comparisons anyway.

Now exposed in the harsh sunlight coming through the hospital window, the cleanliness of his appearance revealed shocking contrasts.

"My God," he said softly, examining his face. "I should not have shaved."

With no beard to cover it up, he saw the pitted, star-shaped scar that had healed over the hole in his cheek. It blazed with redness. It rivaled an older scar that ran above it, from over his ear, across the cheek and down to his chin beneath his lips. He stood and moved the mirror up and around, at different angles, to see other parts of his body. His torso, back, and legs were scarred…everywhere. The pale white skin showed it all.

"I've become a monster," he whispered with regret.

"You are *not* a monster. You are a fighting man, Captain. A man of great courage. I measure this alone by the scars," Nurse Cardon responded compassionately. "Captain, I think it wise if you permit Dr. Michaux to examine you."

Without waiting for an answer, she gestured for another nurse to get the doctor.

"I admit, I've never seen a body so scarred from battle before…at least, not one that still lived. If you permit me to be impolite, how did you come by so much punishment?"

"Running a gauntlet," he replied glumly. He was depressed. *What will Corrinne think?*

Dr. Michaux came into the room carrying a twelve-pound cannon ball in one hand. He shut the door behind him. He had Philippe move over to the window to stand in the brighter sunlight. Certain scars were much deeper than superficial wounds. He pressed and prodded with his fingers until Philippe winced or made a noise. "This one should have killed you," he said more than once. Questions followed.

"Do you find it difficult to shit?" *Only when I've not eaten in two days.*

"Is the flow of your urine strong?" *Enough to fill my boots as I march when I cannot stop.*

"Do you vomit after eating?" *I ate some skunk once. It was cold, and I was that hungry. Tasted as bad as it smelled. Tasted worse after I puked.*

Dr. Michaux handed him the cannon ball. "Without bending your arm, lift it slowly out from your side, all the way up to above your head and then slowly lower it." On the way back down, the doctor stopped him. "Now hold it out straight at your side."

Philippe's arm was trembling. "How fucking long do I hold it out?"

"That's good enough. Now repeat this exercise with the other arm."

Without being told, Nurse Cardon laid a towel on the floor.

"Now lay down on that towel. I am going to lift and bend your legs. Tell me when you feel pain."

I feel pain everywhere, he thought.

The doctor eventually got around to pressing on the side of Philippe's left knee to see if it would straighten.

"Fuck!"

"Captain, this leg is permanently damaged."

"You think I don't know that? You do see that it is fucking bent, yes?!"

The doctor did not care about his complaints.

"Please sit on the stool and open your mouth, Captain." He examined the inside and whispered to Nurse Cardon. She left to retrieve something.

"To answer your question, the bent leg was obviously not set correctly, or you started walking on it too soon. Sometimes, these injuries can be straightened with surgery. That is what I was trying to determine. In your case, too much time has passed. I can feel the lumpiness of healing on other bones, in places where they were broken. All your ribs in the front and back seemed to have been fractured at some time in the past. You're also missing a toe."

"Frostbite."

"But only one of your fingers is bent. That's good! Remarkably, your spine is still straight."

"I am so pleased."

"Captain, for what you have endured...you appear in good...*no*, not good, *acceptable* health. When you get old, the pain of these injuries will worsen."

"Old? I hope to live so long." Philippe brooded. "Are you aware there is a fucking war going on?"

Nurse Cardon returned with a small canvass sack of mineral salts and another one of ground cloves. Another nurse carried in a large steaming tea kettle. She poured a sailor's mug full of hot water and set it aside to cool.

The doctor continued. "Captain, as often as you can, you need to rinse your mouth and gargle with water mixed with these mineral salts. Preferably hot water. It will help purify the tissues in your throat and around your teeth. At the spot where the large molar is missing, your jawbone is nearly exposed. The tissues there are very thin. If the jaw becomes diseased, it will poison your blood. You could die within a week. I have seen this happen before. The ground cloves have additional purifying properties and will help with the odor. I expect the tribal peoples you encounter have other herbal remedies. You should ask their healers for medicines as well."

The doctor paused. Philippe presumed it was his turn to talk.

"So, am I healthy enough to fight and die for my country?"

"You have certainly done a lot of fighting. We owe you a debt of thanks. Do you have any other questions?"

"Tell me about Anamosa."

Dr. Michaux explained everything he knew about Anamosa's condition, from the night she arrived, what he did to suture the wounds, the tonics and poultices he'd administered since then to encourage faster healing.

"She is recovering slowly. The inflammation of the tissues in her genital area is still the most concerning. While it is not getting worse, it's not getting much better, not as fast as I would like. If not for this hospital, I do not think she would have survived. That is *not* a boast. But so far, I see no reason to be too pessimistic. She is young, strong. She is making progress. If there's no relapse, she'll recover fully…in another month."

"Thank you, Doctor. Apologies for my rudeness."

"Captain, it has been an honor to meet you."

The doctor left. Nurse Cardon poured two spoonfuls of salts in the mug of warm water, stirred it, and told Philippe to gargle, rinse, and spit it into the drain. She added some of the ground cloves to a second cup and stirred.

"Don't gargle with this mixture, just rinse your mouth. Chew on the clove lumps. You may dress, when you're ready."

Nurse Cardon left the room.

Philippe's whole body ached. He remained low spirited from the images he saw in the hand mirror. He dressed and went to see Henri sitting beside Anamosa's bed. He took the other chair. Even in her weakened condition,

Anamosa gawked and made a noise of surprise at seeing Philippe's clean face and appearance.

"What do you think, little love?" He leaned forward so Anna could touch it with her fingers as she was wont to do. She smiled with approval.

"Well, that's a good sign," Philippe said, feeling better. He addressed Henri next. "What do you think?"

"That you look younger?" was all Henri could think to say. "I'd almost forgotten your face without a beard. Corrinne will be pleased."

"I hope so," Philippe replied with less certainty.

"She loves you," Henri reminded him. "You're all she talked about from the time you left. A few scars will make no difference."

"I hope so. I'll be down the hall with the twins, so they can get used to seeing me. Later, I'll be going to the house. Oh, the governor ordered Captain LaTour to transport all of us to Québec City. That was welcome news."

Henri nodded with mild enthusiasm. "Yes, that is good news."

Philippe left the room.

Anamosa stared at Henri. Her eyes were brimming with tears.

"*Ahree?*"

Old Saybrook, Connecticut

As soon as the weather took a turn for the better, Sentry Cheever rented a wagon for six weeks and hired two retired soldiers he knew. Together, they loaded the granite and oak wood panels that Lord VanderMeer had so laboriously crafted for the crypt. He sent the younger of the two soldiers, Ben Thomas, on ahead to New Haven to contact the masons and C. Bernard Conway, Esquire, to let them know when Sentry expected to arrive at the house in Old Saybrook; that he would be waiting for their assistance.

The older soldier, Kip Sealy, rode with Sentry in the wagon. Kip was forty-eight, originally from Cardiff in Wales, and a three-time wounded veteran. He'd joined the redcoats when he was sixteen and fought in wars and uprisings all over the empire. After twenty-three years of service, he'd risen to the rank of a simple sergeant, primarily because he had not been killed. But his third wound was a ball through the palm of his right hand, leaving it partially paralyzed, which made aiming and pointing a musket impossible. Forced to retire, he returned to Cardiff after being absent since he'd joined the army and found no surviving family. He took what little money he'd had to buy working passage on a cargo ship to Boston. In just his first week after arriving in Boston, by good fortune, he met a widowed seamstress, who also hailed from Wales. They decided it would be of benefit for them both to marry. Kip had worked as a day laborer on the docks ever since. Other than his crippled hand, he was strong from hauling cargo on and off the ships.

Sentry had met the man at the pub. They'd been friends since that first day. When Sentry offered Kip steady work for six weeks, the veteran considered it a chance for a new adventure. The only drawback to Kip was that he talked incessantly. The good news? Since marrying a Welsh woman, Kip's Welsh-accented English was rejuvenated. Unfortunately, Sentry could barely understand anything Kip babbled on about during the journey to Connecticut. Sentry's part in the conversation was limited to *huh?* and *what?* But if Kip laughed at something unintelligible, Sentry politely laughed, too. Kip did not seem to mind.

Sentry Cheever had waited for two days at Winter House before the stonemasons arrived from New Haven. They did not sleep inside the house. There was something about the place that made Sentry nervous. They camped outside in a soldier's tent.

Only four stonemasons came this time: two journeymen and two apprentices. The first time there were eight, as much more construction was involved. They brought a wagon full of their tools. Ben Thomas rode in the wagon with them, his horse tied to the back.

After some good-natured greetings and introductions, Sentry explained what he wanted to do. The masons went into the house to get the davit and rigging stored in the basement.

"Where's the lawyer?" Sentry asked Ben Thomas.

"Mr. Conway says he will be along in another day and would be pleased if you will wait for him."

Sentry frowned. "He must want money."

As the pieces of rigging came up, Sentry set Ben and Kip at work clearing away the dirt at the top of the vault, telling them to preserve the grassy sod to use later. The masons made sure the capstone was completely clear before they used levers to get the custom metal strapping slipped underneath it at both ends.

Sentry assisted and studied every step in this procedure, as the next time they opened the vault, they would be depositing the châsse inside of it. *When does that happen?* Sentry had no idea. But it was likely he would supervise the work. To that end, he got Kip and Ben involved so they could assist him again when the time came.

There were detailed drawings how the rigging, pulleys, and lines connected and how the davit itself should be mounted in the custom hole created for this purpose. But Sentry learned best by doing. The masons allowed him to do most of the rigging work himself while they supervised and answered questions. At the end of the first day, they were ready to set the panel pieces and decided they would start that effort the next morning.

The masons had brought their own food. Sentry sent Ben off on his horse to the roadside inn where he purchased two full-sized rib cuts they could spit and roast. The inn also sent back a wagon with a keg of ale. The night was cool and beautiful. They ate together on the long table in the back yard and shared jokes and discussed the war, politics, and the future. Again, *huh?* and *what?* were both liberally peppered throughout the conversation.

The next morning, Sentry brought his wagonload of granite inserts alongside the crypt. They were all custom cut to fit. This would be the first time the masons had ever seen these inserts. They worried that the sides of the crypt may have settled too much, that there would be problems getting the panels to drop into place. But they also brought along some jacking-screw mechanisms, a type of spreading device to temporarily force the stone vault walls apart if necessary. Turned out, it was not necessary. The slotted design of the original stone pieces had not budged. It was a tribute to the expert workmanship of the stonemason. Even so, the humble masons were impressed with their own handiwork.

When Sentry threw back the canvass coverings lying atop the pieces, the men stared at the beautiful display: six oak-framed panels with enigmatic designs carved into the granite sections. Four rectangular pieces were the same. One of those rectangular sections, the top panel, had the symbols carved on both sides. Two more, the end pieces, were square versions with the same four symbols.

"This is the work of a master artist," the senior mason complimented.

"Lord VanderMeer was indeed a master artist," Sentry agreed.

"What do the symbols mean?" another man asked.

"I was told the symbols stand for the moon, the sun, the stars, and the seas," Sentry answered.

There were several *ahs* of acknowledgement as they guessed which symbols meant what.

Châsse Panel

The master mason was squinting. "What is their purpose? Decorative? Religious? Spiritual?"

Sentry shook his head. "I really dinnah' know," he lied. "I was never told the reason."

"Do we seal the edges against moisture?" the master mason asked.

Sentry shrugged. "I suppooz' so. Whatever yah' think is best. I mean, the top panel will need to come off later when the casket is finally placed to rest. So, don't affix that."

"The joints of all the outer stones were well-cemented," the mason commented. "I did not see evidence of any moisture in the vault whatsoever. So, these wood and granite panels should already be protected. Nevertheless, we'll seal the edges of the rest with wood resin as an extra precaution… except for the top panel, of course."

When the pieces were carried to the edge of the vault, Sentry cautioned them before the work began.

"Lord VanderMeer, the man who made these pieces, passed on a few months ago. They cannot be replaced if they are damaged. We must be careful how we handle them."

They began with the bottom panel, symbol side up. They used three straps made of multiple canvass strips, each of them stitched together as one strap. Six men lowered the panel into place, including Sentry, with the master mason supervising. The mason exhaled with relief when the panel was in place. It not only validated the length, the width, but the squareness of the corners.

"Perfectly square with a fraction of an inch to spare. If the other panels are cut with this precision, this whole edifice will be a tribute to Lord VanderMeer."

The mason had the feet of the ladder wrapped in canvass and rags to prevent scuffing the bottom panel. He personally climbed into the bottom of the vault wearing only his stockings as the next four panels were lowered. Again, the fit was perfect, as intended. The master mason accepted the bucket of wood resin and hand brushed the edge-joints to seal them before he climbed out.

"We'll let the sealing resin set overnight before closing it with the top panel and completing the work."

They covered the open hole with a large tarp and anchored it with rocks. It was mid-afternoon, so the masons rode off in the wagon to buy more food for the evening supper, even though there was still half a roast leftover from the night before. Ben and Kip went with them.

While they were gone, C. Bernard Conway, Esq. rode up to the house to find Sentry alone.

"Color Sergeant Cheever, a pleasure to see you again. Are the masons finished already?"

"They've gone to town to buy some food. There is more to do, but we'll be finished tomorrow."

"Good. Serendipitous. I hoped to speak with you privately, anyway. May we sit?"

"Of course." Sentry took him out back and showed him the rigging, the davit still holding the capstone aloft but swung out of the way. They took a seat at the outdoor table. Sentry gave him a mug of ale to drink.

"It's a bit warm, but tastes good."

After some pleasantries, the lawyer got to work.

"Thomas Hancock corresponded with me about Lord VanderMeer's passing. Very unfortunate, of course, but his lordship's demise makes Lady Corrinne VanderMeer the sole owner of this property. You and your wife, Dianamora, are the permanent leaseholders, sans rent, until Lady VanderMeer deems otherwise. However, my fiducial obligation requires that I oversee and safeguard the property's value. In consideration..."

Sentry frowned slightly. "Mr. Conway, if you please sir, can yah' explain this to me in English."

"Apologies, Color Sergeant, I meant no disrespect. Essentially, I am your landlord and the designated agent of Thomas Hancock or Lady VanderMeer, unless they dismiss me. As the landlord, I am retained to ensure the property does not fall into disrepair. You have been absent from living here the whole time, except for this short visit." He gestured with both hands. "As you can see from the vines growing up and over the house, and the grounds overrun with wild grasses, bushes, and weedy plants, nature is trying to reclaim this building. If left untended, tree branches, roots, and vines will break it apart at the joints, not to forget the potential for damage by the winter frost heaves."

Sentry's frown deepened. "Are yah' about to ask me for money?" His voice carried an edge, a warning to beware.

"No, no. What I want to propose is that I retain someone locally to take care of the property, the outside only. Just to preserve its appearance. It would require a small maintenance fee, but that would be billed to Thomas Hancock. But you, as the permanent leaseholder, you must approve this as well. That's all."

"So, you want my signature then?"

"Yes."

"All right," Sentry complied. "If tha' is all yah' want. I'll give yah' that."

"And since I am here, may I also intrude on you to conduct a tour inside the house, together, as an inspection. I am *required* to do this periodically, but I can only do this when you are present. Now seems to be a good time, yes?"

Sentry was suspicious of the lawyer's motives, but they went inside and went through all the rooms and the basement overrun with cobwebs. There were dust covers on all the furniture, which was good, but there was thick dust everywhere. The structure of the house appeared to be unaffected by pestilence, which had been the biggest concern.

"There. That was not difficult! I must prepare a statement of inspection to send to Thomas Hancock. One that we must both sign. I will go somewhere to write this document and bring it back to you to read. Will that be satisfactory?"

"Yes."

With that business out of the way, Sentry invited the lawyer to join him later in the day for supper with the stone masons.

"Thank you, Color Sergeant. I will get a room at the inn for the night and come back in about three hours with the inspection documents."

"Three hours sounds like the right time."

This occasion with the New Haven stonemasons turned out to be a pleasant repast with plenty of food. The masons had found a vendor of wine in the village, and more beer, of course. Those men who were veterans of the wars ended up telling stories, most of them funny, a way of celebrating a time of tragedy. The evening ended well. Sentry signed the inspection document and invited C. Bernard Conway, Esq. to be present when the masons dropped the capstone on the vault the next morning. The lawyer was curious to peer down into this enigmatic vault. He accepted.

The surprises of the next day would be remembered by everyone. Some would recall them in their nightmares.

Brest, France

The 1st Battalion Volontaires-Étrangers Regiment was assembled and camped to the northeast, just outside the walls of the mighty fortress seaport of Brest in Brittany, France. They numbered over seven hundred soldiers and officers. Lieutenant-Colonel Karl Krieger now waited impatiently for two ships-of-the-line to have a deck cleared of cannons to make room for the mercenaries to be transported. There was no official word of the destination port after the crossing, but unofficially, it was to be Louisbourg. He did not think they would get there in time for him to sequester and question Captain LaTour and search the ship, *William's Queen*. He was certain the châsse was aboard that ship, cleverly hidden somewhere. But even if that ship sailed, getting to Louisbourg would bring him closer to the location of the châsse. Once there, he would convert more servants.

The regiments' daily training was restricted to just marching and formation drills in ranks, musket firing, and reload drills performed on a firing range. The men were now proficient at three rounds per minute. The goal was four. After ordering Major Sauer to oversee that training, Colonel Krieger retired to his tent with orders not to be disturbed. He laid down on the cot inside the tent and closed his eyes. With one hand, he grasped the gold-threaded pouch hanging around his neck and submitted to the night visitor's complete possession.

The vulnax surged to dominance and visited its various servants. It was most interested in the three men at Louisbourg. But all three of the men were dead, slain by Adaelric's scion. The ones in the water city of Boston were of little use. The wraith wanted to locate *William's Queen*, the ship holding the châsse. All its intensity was focused on this. The ship was not in Boston. It should be in Louisbourg, unless it sailed elsewhere. Chances were that it had sailed. But to where? The châsse must be found, smashed to pieces, the seals broken permanently. Until new servants were converted in Louisbourg, there would not be any progress.

It visited Colonel von Kleinfels, who was now in Boston, giving him the task to learn what the English naval ships blockading Louisbourg reported. Maybe they had seen the ship? It visited servants in London and Amsterdam. Every servant was devoted to thinking and searching for *William's Queen*. The vulnax did not expect to learn very much.

Then something completely unexpected happened.

Old Saybrook, Connecticut

Just before midday, the masons were ready to set the top panel in place. This panel was unique from the others in one way, the inlaid granite stones had the sun, moon, stars, and sea symbols cut on both sides, facing into the vault chamber and out. Sentry presumed this was intentional, maybe as a warning to anyone in the future happening upon the crypt, maybe to give them pause. Of course, Sentry had already commissioned the stone carving on the new slab, which had very specific warnings of the plague. But that slab would not be added to the crypt until the reliquary itself was lowered into it and sealed permanently.

As soon as the top panel was set in place and the straps removed, to the ears of everyone standing around the vault, there arose a faint buzzing sound. The air around them turned warmer. The hairs on their arms and neck prickled. The men looked at one another to confirm others heard and felt this, too, that it was not their imagination playing tricks.

Sentry blinked with surprise. The master mason turned to him. "Color Sergeant. You do hear this buzzing noise? Did we do something to cause this?"

Sentry had last heard the sinister buzzing at the VanderMeer house in Boston inside the carriage hangar, during the sealing ritual. He was not certain what to do…except to finish what they'd started.

Fast!

"No, you did nothing wrong," he affirmed without further explanation. "Position the capstone to lower it in place."

As the mason slowly swung the heavy stone towards the vault, the buzzing was replaced by a low rumble, reverberating up through the top panel. Bits of dirt on its top bounced from vibrations coming from…?

Conway found the whole evolution mildly interesting. Now, he moved several steps back from the vault's edge.

The master mason reacted to the vibrating rumble. "What the…?" He stopped swinging the davit.

Sentry could see fear rise in the expressions of the men. It was like the fear of soldiers reacting to the drum command to march forward as a battle commenced. The sergeant in Sentry instinctively took charge. He spoke loudly, and in a commanding voice. "All right! Steady everyone. Dinnah' worry! I expected this! These granite symbols have a wee touch of *magic* in them. I will need to recite an invocation before we finish lowering the capstone. I will say this *prayer*." Sentry emphasized the word *prayer* and hoped what he had just said was not blasphemous. "Then we lower the stone and everything will be fine."

I hope!

Before anyone could ask questions, Sentry recalled the ceremony in the carriage hangar. It had been frightening and unforgettable. But he only remembered what each person said, and the last verse Lord VanderMeer recited to finish the *sealing*, as he later referred to it. Having no better idea, he went with that.

"*I am the Sun*," Sentry asserted loudly. After he said the words, he felt invisible eyes staring at him.

"*I am the Moon*." Whatever it was, *It* moved perceptibly closer to him. This only stiffened Sentry's resolve he was doing the right thing.

"*I am the Stars*," Sentry continued.

"*I am the Seas*." The rumbling strengthened. Sentry looked each man in the face, held up his palms before his chest, nodded with a confidence he did not really feel, and gestured them to remain calm.

"*And cast into the pit,*
He will rot beneath these signs.
Until the Sun, the Moon, and the Stars fall from the skies,
And all the Seas evaporate."

Sentry gestured to the master mason. The capstone dropped the last few inches into place. Its heavy weight resounded with a defining *thonk!* The rumbling stopped instantly. The air around them was no longer warm and tingly.

"There!" Sentry announced with a grin. "Cover it with dirt, replace the grass sod, and we are done."

The men moved to finish this task. They wanted to bury whatever was in this vault as quickly as possible, then get away from this place.

While those actions were occurring, Conway and the master mason took Sentry aside.

"Can you explain what just happened?" the master mason asked pointedly.

The lawyer vigorously nodded in agreement. "Yes, please do!"

"First, I was told this might happen," Sentry lied. "But like I said, there seems to be a bit of magic involved…"

The master mason scoffed and then demanded, "What *kind* of magic?"

"Nothing harmful, obviously. I was told to say the prayer. I intended to do it after the capstone was lowered…with no one the wiser. But, it turned out differently."

"Those words have violent meanings," Conway added. "That's not like any prayer I've heard before. Not even at a funeral."

"Me either," affirmed the master mason. He did not like Sergeant Cheever's enigmatic answers. "I am suspicious, Color Sergeant, about what we did here. I feel we have unwittingly participated in something…unnatural. And when we are done today, the masons are *finished* with this place. Do not bother us to come back here again."

The master mason stalked off. He gave the apprentices orders to take down the davit and rigging and store it away again in the basement.

"Here is my inspection report of the house," the lawyer said and handed the two-page document to Sentry. "This copy is yours to keep. I will mail the original to Thomas Hancock. I will need your signature."

He took out a pocket inkwell and a quill.

Sentry signed the document.

"You should know, I feel obliged to describe what I witnessed today to Mr. Hancock, but I'm not going to do that. Only because I worry it would impact the valuable relationship I've cultivated with this man. I advise you to tell him yourself. If Mr. Hancock somehow hears rumors and confronts me with questions about any of this, I will present him with my frank opinion and relate this conversation as well. I don't know what happened here today, Color Sergeant, but Mr. Hancock should be made aware."

Sentry Cheever knew a threat when he heard one. His expression tightened.

"I appreciate this forewarning, Mr. Conway. Mr. Hancock is very much aware of my instructions from Lord VanderMeer. If you plan to impugn me, do what you must. I am prepared for the consequences of my actions. You should be too," he warned.

Within an hour, everyone had left, except for Kip Sealy and Ben Thomas. Sentry loaded their baggage into the wagon. He locked up Winter House and left the property. There was still daylight remaining. He pushed the horse team at a fast gait to the ferry crossing. He planned to be on the other side of the river before nightfall.

"I know of another inn along the way. We can get a good night's rest and press on in the morning right at sunrise. Is tha' agreeable to you?"

"Whatever you say, Color Sergeant," Kip replied.

Both veterans had plenty of questions to ask and things to say. But they had a long wagon ride ahead of them back to Boston. Sentry was the kind of man who would tell them in due course…if he decided it needed further explanation.

Sentry did not care what C. Bernard Conway, Esq. might say to Thomas Hancock. But he was very concerned what the buzzing, the rumbling, and the visible vibration of the top panel portended. Lord VanderMeer was dead. Lady Corrinne was still in Louisbourg…so no way to ask them. The task they asked him to do was complete. He tried not to speculate what might come next. It was difficult. He decided to write down everything he saw and heard when he got to the inn for the night; add to it as necessary with more memories, when he got back to Boston. Then figure out a means to get this information to Lady Corrinne. She must be informed.

Rare was a day going forward when Sentry Cheever did not think back on what was in the stone sepulcher.

Brest, France

It was like searching for a certain fish in a sea full of fish. Impossible to do, even for the vulnax. But when the four sealings symbols covered the vault, even partially, it was like a powerful bright beacon had been lit. The wraith could not perceive the place, or conjure why these symbols were used. The vulnax bones were not there! But when the words of the sealing incantation had been pronounced, the wraith shook and upset the closest surroundings to make an impression on the man evoking the words, to make him think about it. If the man's thoughts dwelled on the sealing ritual, the wraith could clearly see his brightness and even follow his movements across the land. Eventually, he would stop thinking and become invisible again. But the man had performed a *sealing*. It made an indelible mark on the man's spirit. He would wear the scar forever. And every time the man recalled images of this ritual, the vulnax could see him…if it was watching. There was an advantage to glean from this type of *sight*. But what? It must be determined. The wraith intruded on the dreams of Colonel von Kleinfels. There was now something specific for this servant to do. The vulnax shared the sounds and the images of the sealing, over and over, and accentuated the identifying nature of the man's brightness.

This man is bonded to the whore queen. Learn his identity.

CHAPTER 24
LOUISBOURG
MAY 1757
The Mending

As soon as the sun went down, Corrinne directed Marie Drucour's two maidservants to the hospital to look after the twins and sent Philippe to the house. These kind and caring women would watch Callie and Marcus overnight. They'd done this before and loved the twins. The table was set for a meal of roasted beef, simmering in a wine sauce with roots and vegetables. It had been set on the side of the wood stove to keep it warm.

Corrinne pressed a few drops of her precious perfume to her neck and between her thighs. There was only a little remaining. She used very little rouge on her lips, but did apply some skin paste over the scar on her throat. It would easily rub off. But she did not want that to be the first thing Philippe asked about. She was dressed in a white silk chemise, the only one she owned. She was naked beneath it. Over the chemise, she wore a long dark green house coat. She could shrug off the coat and allow the chemise to glide off her shoulders in almost the same movement.

Philippe approached the house with a nervousness he'd not experienced before...not with Corrinne. She'd not been alone with him since Boston, over two years ago. Using Nurse Cardon's hand mirror, he'd thoroughly examined the scars on his body in the glare of sunlight beaming through the hospital window. Among men in the wilderness, warriors and *coureurs de bois* alike, scars were marks of honor, symbols of strength, the ability to endure pain, a visible measure of fighting prowess. He had run the Oneida gauntlet, twice in the same day, and lived. It was a legendary feat. He had the scars to prove it. Snow Hair's reputation and prestige was widespread among the tribal peoples in the northeast.

But among the cultured white citizens of Louisbourg and Québec City, scars would also be viewed with a perspective on their attractiveness. None of Philippe's scars were attractive in any way. They were given birth in great pain, the issuance ugly, misshapen. At least, Philippe thought so.

When Corrinne heard the knock, she took one last quick look around the room, then opened the door. She stared for a few seconds at the clean-shaven face of her husband, illuminated from the inside light.

Philippe saw her stare of surprise and interpreted it as shock. His mood plummeted.

Corrinne saw his hesitation. "Come inside, my love!" She took both of his hands. "Look at you! Shaved and clean. You are so handsome!"

She smiled warmly and brought him into the room. The facial scars were more prominent after shaving. She didn't care but saw something in his eyes she'd not seen before. *Anxiety? Shame?*

"What is wrong? Is Anamosa all right?"

Philippe took off his hat. "Yes…yes, Anna is fine. Henri sits with her."

The food aromas were redolent from the wines and spices and the smell of freshly baked bread.

"Do you smell all that cooking? Yes? And this?" Corrinne spun in a circle. "How do I look? Do you like what you see? Want to see more?"

Emotions filled Philippe's chest, making it hard for him to breathe. "You look…you look like an angel." His eyes were luminous.

She pressed her body against him and kissed him long and hard. He seemed preoccupied.

"What's wrong?"

He touched the star-shaped scar on his cheek. "I'd not seen how many scars…"

Corrinne shook her head vigorously. "No! No talking about things that trouble you. I don't care about your scars! I will kiss them all! I love *you*, Philippe Gerrard! I love you! To me you are handsome and beautiful and strong. We've not been together in over two years! You've been wounded, tortured, and shot. I had my throat cut…"

"That pink scar? Your throat was cut!?"

"I lived in exile! We were attacked numerous times. Poisoned. Mathilde is dead. Charles was shot and paralyzed! Now Charles is dead! I had two babies! Your babies! Who knows what will happen tomorrow! But tonight… tonight…Philippe…tonight is our night! And I want to live it with abandon! Like the Romans! Like there is no tomorrow! I want to live it in shameless debauchery…all of it with you! We deserve this, Philippe. This time is for us…you and me…just us! Our love has earned this! No sadness, no tears! At this moment, I am overwhelmed with desire for you! My body aches for you! Pretend it is our wedding night! Do you remember that night? The wondrous aurorae and the stars? No one else in the world mattered that night! No one else in the world matters this night! I want to feel your hands on me and have you deep inside of me…as many times as it is possible before the sun rises!"

Before he could say something, Corrinne threw her arms around his neck, leaned into him, pressed and rolled her mons against his trousers. They kissed for a long time. Philippe's breathing became heavy.

"Good! Now I have your attention."

One of his hands slipped inside the house coat and gently caressed her breasts, rubbing his thumb over the silk to excite her nipples.

Corrinne gasped. "Ohhh! God! Yes! So good. That's what I want." She slipped her hand inside his trousers and gently held his hardness. It was Philippe's turn to gasp.

She smiled and jested. "Smell the food? Are you still hungry?"

"Not for food."

"Good! That's good," she said softly. "Come with me." Her tone was urgent. Insistent! Like there was a fire in the house and they must race to save themselves.

Corrinne led him upstairs into the bedroom. The room was illuminated with only a few candles, just enough to see. She began to undress Philippe with haste. He let her. First, his sword belt, his knife, his outer uniform coat, then the inner coat, his blouse. She tossed each piece on the nearby bed. She kissed the scars on his chest and pressed him backwards to an armless cushioned chair she'd placed purposely in the middle of the room.

"Sit."

She removed his boots, gaiters, stockings, pulled off his trousers, then his small pants.

Philippe was naked, excited, and erect. In the dim warm candlelight, the scarring on his body was muted.

"Now it's my turn." Corrinne shrugged and the housecoat flopped to the floor. She slipped the laces of the chemise over her shoulders. It dropped to the floor soundlessly.

"What do you think?"

In the golden candlelight, the beauty of her nakedness was beyond his wilderness dreams. She was perfect. Her eyes were veiled and seductive. He watched as she licked her lips and stepped to the chair.

"Perfect," he whispered.

Philippe reached up and took hold of her breasts. They were warm and heavy. He plunged his face into the soft fur of her mons and licked.

"Oh, God! Yes! More!" She moaned. She ached for this. She ran her fingers through his hair, lifted his chin, and spoke with urgency.

"Now let me. Let me!"

Philippe was throbbing and at the brink of an orgasm at just seeing her. "I won't last very long."

"You are not supposed to," Corrinne told him. "Two years! Remember? We have the entire night ahead of us! The first one is for you."

With that statement, she straddled him and slowly lowered her sex on him. "Oh, God!"

Philippe's head lolled back for a moment as the exquisite liquid warmth enveloped him. He eagerly pressed his face into her breasts, licking and kissing.

She groaned with pleasure. "Oh, yes!"

Philippe groaned, too. Corrinne held his shoulders and began rolling her hips tenderly back and forth. Corrinne moved slowly, on purpose, trying to extend the pleasure for him. Philippe was bubbling with need. He gripped her hips strongly and groaned long and loud as the overdue orgasm streamed from him in powerful pulses. He shuddered repeatedly. "I love you. I love you."

She continued her movements on his lingering hardness and seconds later experienced her own shattering, as wave after wave of pleasurable contractions foamed upward.

They held onto one another tightly. The overdue pleasure was so strong they dissolved against one another in a satiated exhaustion, panting with relief.

"Oh, God, Corrinne. I've missed you so much," he whispered. "I am so blessed. I've dreamt about this moment…for years! It was better than any imagination from my dreams."

"It better be," she whispered in jest.

They began kissing and rubbing against one another again, both luxuriating in the feel of each other's naked skin. It was not long before his hardness inside her stiffened. Then Philippe did something he knew Corrinne loved. She'd done this with him before. He slipped his hands under her hips.

She wrapped her legs around the back of the chair for balance. She lay her head down on his shoulder, her lips pressed to his neck. He lifted her a few inches. This produced in her a perception of having no weight. With just the strength of his hands, Philippe held her up and moved her back and forth on his hardness. She closed her eyes and just *floated*, concentrating on the sensation that started to build. And build it did! After a few seconds, the sensations became more palpable, more needful. Philippe did everything. Finally, when she was so close, her lips trembled, and she began uttering words in a babble. Hearing that, Philippe held her still and started thrusting upward. The sliding touch on that special spot was so moist and light, the orgasm approached in tiny steps. He listened to her reactions and slowed, delaying everything just enough, so not a tingle was wasted. He held it all back until she could not hold it back any longer. Corrinne dug her fingers into his shoulders and lifted her face towards the ceiling. Philippe thrust more quickly. The orgasm burst forth in blossoming, repeated pulsations, each larger than the one before. It went on and on for a blessedly long time. It left her gasping.

Philippe held her tenderly, kissing her face and neck, her shoulders, inhaling the heady scent of her *parfum*, rocking her back and forth in his arms, repeating the words, "I love you," over and over.

Corrinne recovered and looked at his face. "I don't remember another time between us when my pleasure was that strong, or lasted so long. It was that good. Now I'm hungry."

"What? I made you hungry?!"

"I told you. I plan to do this all night," Corrinne assured him. "The food will get cold. We will need our strength. Come. Let's go to the cuisine and eat naked, and see what mischief we can invent with the food."

They went downstairs. Giggling, she led the way.

"Sit in this chair." Corrinne served the beef and vegetables in a wine sauce in bowls. It had cooled a little.

Philippe took a mouthful. After months of eating burnt animal carcass and wild onions, this was ambrosia.

"It tastes wonderful," he told her.

"Good." She kissed him. One of her hands groped around in his lap. "We need to keep this hard for dessert."

"What?"

"Just eat!"

The food was lukewarm, but it was excellent. And thinking about the *dessert*, they both ate very fast.

"This is a berry pie." She brought the dessert dish over and scooped some onto his plate. "The berry plants have just started to bear fruit. It's fresh. I love the sweet tartness of the flavor. Keep eating," she said.

Philippe took a bite. He immediately ate two more mouthfuls. "I've not tasted a dessert this good…in my life, I think."

"Really? Now for the best part!" Corrinne took hold of the arms of the chair and turned it sideways. With both hands, she cupped a large amount of the warm berries mash out of the pie, dropped to her knees and coated Philippe's erection with the sticky, sweet berry mash.

A coy look crossed Corrinne's face. "I've always wanted to do this to you." Then she fellated him, making sounds to indicate how much she loved the taste…of everything.

It was erotic. Philippe was speechless. Grunts and groans his only language. It was not long before his legs stiffened, and he exhaled loudly in a throaty moan of pleasure.

Once they washed away the stickiness of the berries with a hot wet towel, Corrine led him back up the stairs with one hand.

"That will be my special dessert for you from now on. We'll try different pie fillings and see which one you like best."

"I want to do something for you. Tell me what to do."

Corrinne thought. "All right." She walked over to the window. "The stars are out." She cracked open the window just a little, to allow some cold harbor air to stream inside the room. "This is my very favorite chair," she told him. "I sat here on many winter nights thinking about you, wondering about you, *lusting after you*. I touched myself," she confessed.

"Good! Sit down," he said.

"Oh? I was going to sit on you."

"You first."

She sat down. Philippe knelt before her and lifted and placed her legs up over his shoulders. "Now, stare up at the stars," he told her. He put his mouth, lips, and tongue on that special spot.

"*Uhhhh!*" Corrinne's body jerked, and she moaned in a husky tone of pleasure. "*Ohhh, yesss!*"

She ran the fingers of one hand gently though his hair and with the other caressed her breasts and excited her nipples. She gloried in the star-filled sky and yielded all her thoughts to the drenching sensuality drawn out by his tongue and lips. Her abdomen arched as the orgasm began. Philippe held on, supported her hips with his hands. He did not stop, but licked more slowly, stretching out her pleasure. As she started to relax, he kept kissing her lightly until she placed a hand on his head.

"Oh, please! A moment! Enough," she urged breathlessly.

Philippe stopped and looked at her with a grin. "Apologies. My skills lack proficiency."

"Oh, don't worry. I intend to give you *plenty of opportunity* to improve. Oh God…I am drained. I'm uncertain which to do next?! More of this or maybe fantasy."

Philippe's eyes brightened. "Fantasy sounds good."

She smiled. "Good. Get up. Switch places."

Corrinne ran over to her bed and got a few pillows and a blanket. She came back and slipped one pillow low in the chair, to support the small of Philippe's back so he could lie back more comfortably. She put the other one on the floor before the chair.

She draped the blanket over one arm. "I hope to be here awhile," she explained. "It may get cold."

Corrinne knelt and began fellating him again. Her hands were cold.

Philippe inhaled loudly.

When he was erect, she rose and turned around. The seat of the chair was made wide enough that she could back onto him, and wrap both of her legs back around either side of his waist. Taking hold of him with one hand, she guided him inside of her, exhaling a sound of pleasure as he entered. She carefully slipped her legs forward, not to lose the connection, until she laid flat on top of his body. He was lounging now and fully inside of her. She laid her head back upon his left shoulder. She licked his neck and whispered into his ear, "Now touch me everywhere."

Philippe decided she was far more imaginative than he was. He would just obey Corrinne the rest of night. With his left hand, he caressed her breasts and nipples. With his right, he licked his fingers and lightly stroked and touched that very special spot. He felt her body tremble.

Corrinne groaned and rocked her hips to the left and right, slowly, to keep him hard and excited. It lifted them both to a plateau of constant pleasure that was sublime and went on and on. She climaxed three times before she sat up. He was still deep inside of her. She touched and caressed Philippe between her legs until he finally shuddered.

Dreamily exhausted, Corrinne lounged back and pulled the blanket over them. They were silent, savoring the sensuality of so much warm naked skin still tingling from the contact. Philippe's left arm was across her chest. His hand cupped a breast. His right palm and fingers lay over her mons. Not to excite her necessarily, though his fingers did move, more to hold her intimately. Corrinne had never felt so safe. The anxieties of yesterday and tomorrow were gone. There was the now. It was just them. Two people profoundly in love, deeply loyal, fiercely protective. Mesmerized by the soft, cooing whistle of the gentle breeze passing over the wing of the window pane left ajar, Corrinne fell asleep in Philippe's embrace.

In the middle of the night, three low gongs of the Julien Le Roy standing clock woke them up. They were both drunk with sleep. Only one candle still burned. They got up. They took a pillow each and Philippe took the blanket. Corrinne led Philippe by the arm to her bed. He got in first. Without speaking Corrinne massaged him until he was hard and lowered her sex atop of him. This lovemaking was sleepy and slow, with Philippe kissing her breasts. They orgasmed together and fell back to sleep, this time with her lying face down on top of him.

Philippe slept soundly. He reacted to the gong of the clock at the hour of six. He was alone in the bed. Corrinne was already awake; an hour earlier, he would learn. She had been heating water and filling the bathing tub in the other room. He got up and stood in the connecting doorway, squinting from the light and scratching his head. Corrinne was pouring scented bathing salts in the water and stirring it with a long brush, making bubbles, when she noticed him.

"Oh, good! Come! Take a bath with me. Then I will cook for us and we will break our fast before we go to the hospital and see Callie and Marcus and Anna. Oh, and later to see the governor."

There was steam rising from the water when Philippe put a leg into the thin layer of soap bubbles. "Uh...hot!"

"Oh, it's not that hot," Corrinne chided her big, tough *coureur de bois* with amusement. She stepped into the bubble-coated water and sat down, pulling her knees to her chest to make room for him. "See?"

"I usually bathe in icy streams and lakes. We don't do that for very long." Philippe eased into it. Once the water was up to his chest, he had to admit, "It does feel good."

"Oh?" Corrinne smiled. "So, you agree?" She stretched her legs in between his and started to massage him with her feet and toes. "How about this? Does this feel good too?"

"Yes. It does," Philippe replied in a low voice and smiled. "I worry about my...my vitality."

"Vitality?! Now that's a curious name for it. Not '*petit* Phillipe'?" Corrinne smiled and crawled up and over his lap. The water sloshed around them to new levels. "Well, you let me worry about *petit* Philippe. I've all sorts of remedies for a shrunken vitality." She kissed him deeply with her tongue, then guided him inside of her with a groan. "*Oh yes!* There it is! Does this help you? It helps me. Let's do this for a while. Like you, the sun will soon be up."

Brest, France

After leaving Captain LaTour and his ship in La Rochelle, Margaux-Lyneth Dubonnet decided she was close enough to the port city of Brest to visit her father, La Chevalier Lucais de Clermont. She'd not seen him in over five years. They had grown apart after her mother died. The chevalier had slumped into a deep depression. To overcome the dark thoughts of joining her in death, Lucais immersed himself in building warships for the French navy. He was a premier naval architect and a shipwright. It was his passion and the source of his wealth. But he withdrew from all other social life, except as it related to his ship designs. He became aloof and disinterested in Margaux's life. He stopped writing to her beyond half a page. She forgave him for this. She understood the reason. And she had Gustave.

But Margaux came to Brest this time with many questions to ask her father, now that she knew about Corrinne. When she arrived with her two bodyguards, Róbert and Marcel, she found him looking very unwell. He had lost a great deal of weight. The jowls of his face hung loosely. His skin had a yellowish tinge. But he welcomed her unexpected arrival with great enthusiasm—that was certainly a longed-for surprise.

"Margaux! Margaux! Margaux!" The chevalier hugged his daughter tightly and rocked her back and forth in his arms. "I am so happy you've come to see me! Do you plan to stay a long while? I hope so."

Margaux beamed. "Yes Papah, for a few weeks at least. These are my… protectors, Róbert and Marcel."

"*Bonjour*, gentlemen! You are all welcome to stay at my home. This house is big and empty. I live alone, you know? Plenty of room. And Gustave?"

"The Auvergne Regiment has marched to the east."

"Yes, of course. Another war. This time we fight Prussia! The world is mad! When will these endless wars stop? But, it is good for my business! The shipways are filled with four new ships-of-the-line. My newest design. They carry more than seventy cannons. Two new frigates. These frigates are very fast, probably the fastest in the world. Tomorrow morning, we will go down to the shipways and you can see and admire these new queens of the sea."

Marshall Debarge, the Clermont house chamberlain, was standing nearby. Margaux stopped to hug this cherished gentleman. He was older than seventy years, white-haired, always dressed perfectly in his livery as the chamberlain, and extremely polite. He was like a second father to her. Yet she found his expression muted for someone who should be celebrating her arrival like her father did. Her suspicions spiked. *Something is wrong.*

The chevalier gave orders to his chamberlain to prepare the necessary accommodations for his daughter and her men. The large staff of household servants included a valet, two maids, and two cooks who seemed only too happy to have more people to serve. Exhausted from her journey from La Rochelle, she enjoyed the dinner with her father. He did all the talking, more talking than ever before, jumping uncharacteristically from subject to subject. After a while, he began slurring his words. Which was odd. She had not seen him drink that much wine. She attempted to ask him a few questions about her childhood adoption. But as if noticing her surprise at the way he was talking, he became evasive, his answers became short. He waved off the questions as irrelevant now. *Maybe he just doesn't remember anymore?* Then he abruptly excused himself.

"I am tired."

Margaux was tired, too. They said good night.

The next morning, a small, open top, day carriage was brought around. She joined her father on a tour of the Brest Arsenal. Róbert and Marcel followed on horseback. As they approached the great drawbridge over the river, Róbert brought his horse up next to Margaux. He had a familiar look in his expression.

"With your permission, Madame, I'd like to cross to the other side and reconnoiter the faubourg…to understand the city better."

He would wink at me if it were not impolite. She had decided long ago the experienced regimental color sergeants were truly the best bodyguards. *Like cautious generals.* Be it a trip to the market or a hundred-league overland journey, there was always a strategy in how they guarded her. A strategy that varied with the mission and the surroundings.

"Of course, Róbert."

The carriage continued up the same side of the river with Marcel in trail. Not too much had changed since she was a girl, except that the scale and speed of shipbuilding in Brest was greatly increased. Her father had the carriage driver turn around at the top of the arsenal, where the wall ended, far up the winding La Penfeld River that divided the city. The main city of Brest was triangular-shaped, as defined by its walls, a mile and a half across at the base where the river emptied into the bay. Inside the walls, the city faubourgs ran along either side of the river. It was almost two miles in length. Most of the shops and heavy works dominated the riverbanks, all dedicated to the building of warships.

When Margaux was small, her father used to hold her hand and they would walk this route. He would proudly point out the important places as if it were her first time. He said the same things each time. She was familiar with everything. She was pleased to do this now by carriage. She did not have the right shoes for a walk, and her father seemed too old and weak for prolonged exertion. They were on the river's western side, heading south. As usual, Lucais expounded on the port's history, telling her more of what she already knew. She let him prattle on without interruption, instead observing his face. And his speech—it was full of slurs.

"Bresht is the largest and mote important navall pot in France. It is divided by La Penfeld River. The fortifications were designed in 1689 by the Marquis de Booban to protect the docks, yardsh, and shipways. The English attocked this monstruction in 1694. The attack was soundly depleted. I live in the foobourg on the right. It is called the Recouvrance."

Margaux knew where he lived. She knew all the rest of it, too. She did not correct his numerous mispronunciations. Like the night before at dinner, the slurring worsened the longer he talked. The horse plodded along at a walking gait. They passed by the new ships-of-the-line being built. Lucais began describing their length, number, and types of masts and spars, displacement, draft, material selection for wood, the interior quarters for the crew and officers, the size and placement of cannons, the number of decks, the design of the rudder, the maximum speed over water, and a myriad of other facts and numbers.

The descriptions soon became almost a babble. But Margaux had heard it so many times before, she knew it by heart.

As far as Lucais de Clermont was concerned, overseeing ship design was the best part of this effort. Another engineer in Brest was the Director of Works. That man managed building everything and was certainly under the most pressure during wartime. Together, the two of them reported to Amédée-François Frézier, the Director of Fortifications in Brittany.

Eventually, they reached the building where Lucais managed the designers of the warships. It was three stories tall, full of draftsmen, former naval officers, men of science, and experienced shipwrights. They were met by a man who ran out of the building to greet them carrying rolls of plans under one arm. His name was René Hilaire, Lucais' primary design assistant, another man Margaux had known since she was a young girl.

"*Bonjour*, Margaux! *Bonjour*, Monsieur Clermont!"

After an embrace, Monsieur Hilaire gave a quick explanation of some problems, put to them by the navy, they had encountered in the latest design. Lucais de Clermont disagreed with those conclusions. Grumbling, he took the plans and started inside the building. Margaux caught Monsieur Hilaire's sleeve and asked him bluntly.

"What is wrong with my father? He is slurring his words."

René Hilaire's eyes shifted evasively. He did not want to say anything, but Margaux pressed him further.

"Madame, I am uncomfortable talking about this. Your father is sick, I think. The slurring started over a month ago. A doctor came to see him, but he dismissed the man after only one examination."

"What was the doctor's conclusion?"

"I don't know, Madame." His tone was evasive. He did not want to say.

"All right. I will talk with the doctor directly. Tell me his name. Don't worry, Monsieur Hilaire, I will not tell my father you told me."

Once she had the name of the physician, a doctor she was acquainted with, Margaux gave the carriage driver directions and was in front of the doctor's home soon thereafter. A maid answered.

Margaux introduced herself. "I would like to speak with Dr. Legrande."

The maid took her to a waiting room. The doctor arrived without delay and greeted her warmly.

"Madame Dubonnet! It is good to see you again."

After the usual greetings and discussions of journey, the doctor inquired, "What may I do for you?"

"I require your candor, Dr. Legrande. My father is slurring his words. He has become forgetful. I am told you examined him. What is wrong with him?"

"I should not be telling you this," he replied in more formal tones.

"Nevertheless, I am confident you *will* tell me everything. What is his ailment?"

The doctor considered her words and came to a conclusion. "He has developed a hard, internal growth in his abdomen. I felt it beneath my fingers. It is large. I suspect it will grow larger. It was already painful a month ago, according to your father. I expect the pain is worse now."

"A *growth*! What is that?" She was alarmed.

"It is a condition that occurs sometimes in older people. Our knowledge of the cause is limited. The body contains two fluids that maintain health and balance among the flesh, bone, and muscle. The blood and the lymph. Blood flows in vessels carrying nourishment to the body. Lymph flows among the different tissues of the body. These flows are balanced. As people advance in years, we believe this balance is lost. We do not know why. Probably due to the matter of aging. We contend the body reacts to the imbalance as it would to a cut, a wound, or a broken bone. Depending on the severity of the injury, the body heals in different ways. If it is a cut, it forms a scab. If it is a deep wound, it grows a tough scar tissue cap over the wound. If a bone is fractured or broken, it grows a type of healing bone. Such scars and healing bone, do not appear normal, but they work. With an imbalance in the vital fluids, the imbalance is everywhere. There is no specific place to heal. So, the body forms a type of scar in those places where the imbalance is greatest. At least, this is what we postulate. The body creates a type of *cyst*, a hard tissue sac. It does not have a function that we can determine and continues to grow unless the imbalance is corrected. Except, unlike a wound or a broken bone, the imbalance is rarely corrected. We call this growth a *tumeur*. Your father has a *tumeur*. It is growing. It is pressing against other organs in his abdomen and debilitating their function."

Margaux's mood had fallen with each word of explanation. "Is there a remedy, a treatment?"

The doctor glanced down and shook his head. "Other healers and doctors have tried various medicines, substances, tonics. Sometimes they appear to work. Most times they do not. Sometimes they work for only one person. Too often, the remedies poison the patient. In truth, we don't have a cure." Dr. Legrande's expression was sympathetic. "I have seen these hard growths grow in more than one part of the body at the same time. Sometimes they spread to the outside of the body, erupting up through the skin. *Sometimes*... the body finds a way to cure the imbalance. The person simply gets better. Some people claim healing through prayer. Who am I to say that is not true? But in my experience, that happens rarely, and we have not discovered why. The rapid loss of weight is a symptom. I expect your father is not eating well because he is constantly nauseous. The yellowing pallor of his skin and eyes is another indication of the degree of imbalance in the fluids. The slurring of his words that you are hearing? And the flaws appearing in his logic? That is a new symptom. I did not observe this when I examined him several weeks ago. Since you are observing that now, it suggests the imbalance has spread into his thinking, his mind. I am sorry, Madame...Margaux, your father is dying."

Margaux winced at the bluntness of his last words. She looked out a window for several seconds before responding to Dr. Legrande's statement.

"How long will he endure?"

"That is also uncertain. I told him he needed to take to his bed, to rest all the time. This might give the body time to reestablish its balance. He refused to accept my diagnosis or my recommendations for rest. He reminded me of the war and his need to build warships for France. But I think he knows it is getting worse. To answer your question, he could live for a few months, maybe even a year. Or something worse might happen as his *tumeur* gets bigger."

"Is there something I can do?"

"Yes, make him rest. Resting and prayer will give him the best chance for a miracle. But sadly, these *tumeurs* usually do not stop growing. Eventually, they interfere with the blood flow to other organs in the body. I was a military surgeon for twelve years. I've seen bodies torn open by cannon ball. I've examined the abdominal organs and viscera of the dead. We continue to learn how the body is connected. Some things are easy to discern. We breathe air in and out of the lungs. The stomach is for food. The heart is for pumping blood. The purpose and functions of the organs in the lower abdomen are less understood. But we know if they are damaged or become necrotic, the person will die quickly. This *tumeur* appears to be in the center of those. I wish I could be more optimistic."

Margaux looked out the window again. Dr. Legrande politely remained silent.

She took a deep breath. "*Merci*, Doctor. I may call on you to visit him again."

"As you wish, Madame."

Depressed in her thoughts, Margaux rode back to the house and sent the carriage back to the design building with instructions to await her father.

"When Róbert returns," she told Marcel, "bring him with you to my father's office."

The chamberlain met her inside the door.

"I just met with Dr. Legrande. He told me everything. I am sure you have much to add to my knowledge. But I am too depressed to hear more of it right now. I will wait for my men in my father's office," she told the chamberlain. "One of them went on an errand for me."

While Margaux waited in the office, she browsed the shelves of books stacked from floor to ceiling on all the walls. There was one shelf full of leather-bound journals covering a thirty-six-year time span. She picked one at random and paged through it. The entries were chronologically dated. It was full of artistic sketches of ship designs, calculations, self-notes to the author, records of on-going arguments with people whose names she did not recognize, a lifetime of history of a man passionate about building ships.

The only empty spot on the wall contained a curtained, five by seven-foot window behind the ornate desk. The desktop was littered with scrolls of paper, sheets of draft plans, more sketches, memorabilia, a pile of open missives, the wax seals broken, dishes of half-eaten and moldy food, and other detritus.

Margaux rang for a servant and started to straighten up the desk. It took several trips. She had cleaned and sorted the top until it was at least usable to write letters when Róbert and Marcel entered. She gestured for them to sit in the two black leather chairs in front of the desk.

"My stay here will be longer than I planned," she began. Margaux told them about her father's slurred speech and what she had learned about the illness from the doctor. "Of course, I will try to get him to stay home and rest. He will likely ignore me, too. But I cannot leave him if he is dying. I do not know how long this will be. You are welcome to stay here with me, or I will release you from my service. I give you this choice."

The bodyguards looked at one another briefly. "Colonel Dubonnet asked us to protect you, Madame," Marcel answered. "If it is truly our choice, we prefer to stay by your side until the colonel feels it is no longer necessary." Róbert nodded his agreement.

Margaux smiled affectionately at these two loyal men. "I am so fortunate to have you by my side. Know that I am privileged with great protection here inside this fortress. So, I would need only one of you on most days. You are welcome to remain in the rooms you were provided. Take all your meals here. Tomorrow, I will give you each a purse of money for your wages to date. Feel free to explore the city. In fact, information like this may prove helpful to me."

Róbert raised a hand. "To that suggestion, Madame, I did a quick exploration of the eastern faubourg. The land area inside the walls is larger than this side, but the civilian faubourg is smaller. Most of the land nearest the river is taken up by works dedicated to shipbuilding. There are also several naval and military barracks over there. At the entry gate furthest to the northeast, I received permission from the sentry to ride out and explore. There is more faubourg outside the walls. But I saw a broad empty space, too. A troop marshalling yard of sorts. A large encampment of tents occupied about a third of this. I walked my horse to the guards standing on the perimeter of the camp and asked about them. Their uniforms were not those of French metropolitan troops. The guards were unfriendly and refused to answer even simple questions. They ordered me to leave the area. They spoke French with a strong German accent. So, German mercenaries, I assume."

"Mercenaries?"

"Yes, Madame. A full battalion. The encampment is temporary. A bivouac of tents. I think they await ship transport for a crossing."

Just as Captain LaTour predicted, she thought.

"It's such mercenaries who threaten my sister. My father will know who they are and where they are going. He will tell me."

After they were gone, Margaux wrote to Gustave first, explaining where she was, her father's illness, and her plans to stay in Brest until he passed or got better. She wrote a confidential missive to Colonel Rutger van Boekel, informing him of the success in reaching Captain LaTour, that *William's Queen* had sailed for Louisbourg carrying the journals, and ostensibly would transport Lady VanderMeer to Québec City. She again mentioned the illness of her father and her intention to remain in Brest. She wrote one more letter to her chamberlain at her home in Amiens, giving him the abbreviated information that she would remain in Brest for an indeterminate time because of her father's illness. That any letters from her husband should be sent to her father's house. She added that if William LaFont came to see her in Amiens, he should be sent to Brest.

She sealed the letters and gave them to Róbert. "Have these added to the military courier dispatch pouches to my home in Amiens. They will relay it to my husband's regiment, wherever that is now. And this one to Colonel van Boekel…find a trustworthy, private courier service for this one. Give them half of their fee in advance, the other half will be paid by Colonel van Boekel when the missive is received."

"Yes, Madame."

Margaux went to her room to lie down. Two hours later, the chamberlain, Marshall Debarge, touched her shoulder gently. She saw a look of concern on his face.

"Yes?"

"Madame, your father has returned. But once inside the house, he collapsed in the foyer. We assisted him to bed."

Margaux got up instantly. "I will be there directly."

So it begins, she thought.

A ugustin de Drucour, Governor of Île Royale, sat at his desk, holding his aching head and rubbed the temples with his thumbs. The headaches were getting more frequent. He did not know the cause, only that they started with the new year. *Probably from the threat of invasion*, he had surmised. He knew many others who suffered from them. He did not sleep well the night before. This headache started shortly after he got out of bed. He went into his office. In the brighter sunlight coming through the larger windows of that room, he noticed the faint wavering vision at the edges of his eyes. The throbbing started immediately. He called out to his wife, "Marie! It's starting again!"

"All right." Marie hurried to the cuisine. "Bring a full pot of coffee to the governor," she told the cooks. She turned to the valet. "The governor has one of his bad headaches. Tell Lieutenant Christophe."

She returned to the office and closed all the curtains. This blocked much of the light coming into the room, but not all of it. She steered Augustin to sit in the large cushioned chair he used to relax. Only because she could never get him to lie down in bed once he was dressed. She retrieved a pillow from the bed and propped it behind him.

The cooks brought in the coffee with six teacups, as they'd been told to do when this happened before. They placed a small table by the chair, and filled all six teacups. This was so the governor could drink the coffee quickly, as soon as it was cool. Tea alone did not work. There was something about coffee. Neither of them understood why coffee mitigated the pain. They just knew it worked.

Marie filled a washbasin with cold water and drenched a few towels in it. She wrung one of the towels and draped it over his eyes and covered this with a square piece of black linen. The cold helped with the pain and the black linen blocked the wavering light. Marie took a seat and waited. She read some poetry and glanced at the clock. After a quarter hour, she went over and sipped the coffee from one cup.

"Augustin, the coffee has cooled." She held the cup to his lips.

He swallowed all of it in one gulp. He drank the other five cups in the next few minutes. Then he laid back his head, situated the cold towel and black linen, and waited. Usually, the pain and the wavy blurriness would subside after a few hours. Marie stayed in the room. She refilled the cups again, then read or napped in the other chair to be certain the governor was not disturbed.

As Drucour lay quiet and meditative, he sorted through the possible reasons for these crippling headaches. Stress was certainly high on his list, created first by the threat of imminent invasion. There was the lack of sufficient troops. Another source of stress. No navy for defense. Then the order to give sanctuary to protect Lady VanderMeer. Which, after a few months, had diminished to no more than an annoyance, then to nothing at all. He had more important matters to worry about. The arrival of the squadron of warships was the first visible good news. It was an indication that Versailles intended to fulfill the promises they made to him regarding sending more men and ships. It was news good enough to proclaim a celebration ball. Then the terrible, horrible turn for the worse. The attack on Lady VanderMeer's house. The rape of Lady Anamosa. The death of three Swiss mercenaries, courtesy of Lieutenant Gerrard's deadly cutlass. The sequestering of the remaining mercenaries, effectively eliminating them from working on the battlements, plus having them disarmed, and guarded day and night, taking these additional guards from the work force. Then Commodore Bauffremont's startling revelation that he suspected Lady VanderMeer was an impostor. That she was Lady de Chanaye of Québec City, forcing Drucour to defend her identity to the commodore, an identity Drucour already knew was a deceit. *That rumor will spread all over this gossipy faubourg in less than a day*, he groused silently. *At least he did not accuse her of being a spy.*

Next, the coureur de bois *Scout Captain Philippe Gerrard suddenly appears, ready to spirit away his wife and spends a very public night alone with her, while her children are watched over in the hospital by Marie's maidservants! The faubourgs were always watching and listening.* So, whose children are they? *That will be the next logical question.* The Dutch Republic insisted these children were fathered by Lord Charles VanderMeer and were the heirs to the Duchy of Brunswick. They demanded the French government have them protected. Versailles reminded the governor the Dutch Republic was neutral in this war. They wanted the Dutch Republic to remain neutral. They ordered Drucour to continue providing sanctuary.

Now, as the headache was nearly gone, Drucour mumbled in the quiet darkness. "Lady Corrinne needs to leave with Captain Gerrard. Captain LaTour can take them all," he told Marie-Louise.

"She will not leave until Lady Anamosa is healed. And I don't blame her."

"She needs to leave…as soon as possible."

"Not. Until. Anamosa. Is. Healed," Marie replied in a terse but gentle avowal.

*

Captain LaTour was waiting outside the governor's private offices at the King's Bastion when Captain Gerrard and Lady Corrinne arrived. He was taken aback by Philippe's clean-shaven face.

"Yes, Captain LaTour, it is I, Philippe Gerrard."

The governor's appointment secretary, Lieutenant Christophe, appeared from another door. "The governor will see you now."

They went in. Governor Drucour gestured them over to the long table he used to hold his military councils. He sat at the top in his usual chair. Captain Gerrard and Lady Corrinne took seats on his right, Captain LaTour to his left. Within a minute, servants brought in two trays of sweetbreads, tea, and coffee.

"Captain Gerrard, your appearance is greatly improved from yesterday," the governor remarked pleasantly.

"The nurses at the hospital were very helpful."

"We are fortunate to have such an experienced staff. And how is Lady Anamosa today?" He directed this question to Corrinne.

"Dr. Michaux believes it might be several weeks before she is fully healed."

"But she *is* healing? Good. Well, to business. Captain Gerrard, before I speak on other topics, I would like you to remain behind afterwards, to brief my war council on General Montcalm's war progress."

"It would be an honor, sir."

"Good. The purpose today is to discuss your departure from Louisbourg on Captain LaTour's ship. There is another problem looming. Before we discuss that, Lady Corrinne, I promise that you are welcome to remain in Louisbourg, as long as you want. I mean that."

From numerous dinner discussions over the winter, Governor Drucour was aware of Lady Corrinne's remarkable intellect. He had only to make the slightest suggestion to stimulate her thinking.

She detected his sincerity. "Thank you." But she also detected the unspoken word...*but*.

"But, if Louisbourg harbor was a stage, the curtain here is about to drop. And I do not control when that will happen." Drucour wanted them to leave. He could not order them to leave. Versailles saw to that. However, if they decided to leave, he would not stop them. "If you are anxious to leave right now, you have both the means and the opportunity."

"My intention is to depart Louisbourg as soon as Lady Anamosa is healthy enough for this travel," Corrinne said calmly, her voice carrying an edge of curtness. She had already made this intention clear more than once. She started extrapolating his reasons.

"*Bien*. I think this is wise. Captain Gerrard?"

"Arranging for Corrinne's departure is the reason why I came to Louisbourg. Captain LaTour's presence here at the same time seems like a gift from our collective stars."

"*Indeed*. I just received a new piece of information. In the recent dispatch pouch delivered by Commodore du Bauffremont, there is mention of a missive from the Dutch Republic to the government in Versailles. After Lord VanderMeer's unfortunate passing, God rest his soul, the Dutch claim that Lady Corrinne VanderMeer's twin children are now direct heirs to Louis Ernest, Duke of Brunswick-Wolfenbüttel. The Dutch have requested the port of Louisbourg continue as a sanctuary for Lady Corrinne and her children. The government of France has agreed. Not that any of this matters, since you are leaving, but I thought you should know."

"Were there any other missives mentioning me?" Corrinne asked. Her instincts were alert.

"No. Just the one. I found it commendable that the Dutch government would act so quickly to protect you."

This duplicity in identity was so obtusely presented, it elevated the tension in the room.

Why tell us this? Corrinne wondered.

Philippe was puzzled. *He's not telling us something.*

Captain LaTour had only one thought. *God's balls!*

The pause became prolonged. Corrinne prodded. "Was this the looming problem you mentioned earlier?"

"No. *Pardon*. Another squadron of ships-of-the-line is anticipated to arrive at Louisbourg harbor at any time. I expect the number of English cruisers patrolling the entrance will match our strength in proportion. Captain LaTour may have told you that I have assigned a frigate to escort his ship? Good. But here is the looming problem. If the English patrols increase to blockade strength, a frigate as escort will not be enough to run the English blockade. Captain LaTour's ship risks becoming ensnared here, in Louisbourg, until the threat of invasion is thwarted. Once in place, the English will blockade the entrance until the winter months. Apologies for rambling on. I drank too much coffee this morning."

"Is there more?" Philippe asked.

"No. That's the extent of it. Except my military council is waiting. Captain Gerrard, can you present to them now? Or would you prefer to delay for another day?"

Philippe looked at Corrinne. She seemed lost in thought, but only for a moment.

"Please, do as the governor requests. Captain LaTour will escort me to the hospital. I will wait for you there."

Everyone stood.

"Thank you, Governor," Corrinne said politely.

"As always, my lady, the pleasure was mine."

Philippe walked with them across the bridge until they could not be overheard.

Corrinne frowned as she said, "I deduced the governor wants us to leave, and leave quickly, using the threat of an English blockade as the reason. That is all I have. But he already knows I won't leave without Anamosa. There must be something else. Well, I will think about it more. Maybe you will learn something after meeting with the military council."

Corrinne embraced and kissed him and whispered in his ear, "Last night was wonderful, my darling. I've already thought of new things for us to do. Don't be too long."

"I will do this as fast as possible," Philippe assured her with a smile.

Corrinne took Captain LaTour's arm and they went off down the street. She asked him dozens of questions while they walked.

*

The officers of the military council were seated at the table and along the walls. In addition to the fort's senior garrison officers, which included Lieutenant Henri Gerrard, the senior officers from the naval warships were present, along with the governor's main civilian assistants. Philippe noticed the beautifully detailed military map hanging on the wall at the top of the table. It would make his explanations easier to understand.

"Gentlemen, I am pleased to introduce Scout Captain Philippe Gerrard of General Montcalm's staff. He is visiting here for a short time only. Captain Gerrard has been involved with most of the major battles we have won in the west. I've asked him to share his observations, counsel, and advice gained from those experiences. He will answer those questions from you he is comfortable answering. Captain Gerrard?"

There was polite applause. "Thank you, Governor Drucour. Thank you, Commodore du Bauffremont, ship captains, and all the officers senior to me, which is just about everyone else in the room, except for my son"—he pointed—"sitting among you, there, in the back."

They turned and looked. Henri raised his hand. The room resounded with polite laughter and a few friendly comments.

"I was not prepared for anything formal, but I will do my best to give an account of the battles in the west. There are some questions I will politely decline to answer, but I trust they will not be asked. With that, I'll start with a list of the major engagements where I participated and the month and year they occurred. Then I will accept your questions."

Captain Gerrard began with the capture of the three-river junction to establish Fort Duquesne, followed with the English ambush of Jumonville de Villiers. It was a very long list of engagements. It ended with the recent winter attack on Fort William Henry. When he was done, one of the garrison officers raised a hand.

"Yes, Colonel?"

"Lieutenant-Colonel du Bourzt of the Bourgogne Regiment. Very impressive, Captain. So the only battles where you did not participate were the attacks on Fort Beauséjour and Fort Gaspareaux, the first battle on Lac du Saint-Sacrament, and the destruction of Fort Bull?"

"There were *many battles* where I did not directly participate, Colonel. Fort Beauséjour and Fort Gaspareaux were two of those. They were lost to the English in 1755. Should any of you have questions about the last two battles you mentioned, Lac du Saint-Sacrament and the destruction of Fort Bull, Lieutenant Henri Gerrard was present at both of those."

They all turned and looked at Henri again. He nodded humbly.

"Before I take questions, understand that my personal opinions may not be shared by other officers in the field during those engagements. I certainly do not speak for any of the commanders. Nor will I share any future strategies being contemplated by General Montcalm and Governor Vaudreuil."

The questions began. Philippe answered them with candor. He used the large map hanging behind him. The room was captivated by Captain Gerrard's knowledge of the wilderness, the difficulty of the terrain, the native tribes and customs, his frankness, the details of the fighting, and his summary opinions. The council went on for nearly three hours.

Commodore du Bauffremont did not raise his hand until the end.

"Yes, Commodore."

"Captain Gerrard, with all these glorious victories behind us, would you assert that France is winning this war?"

"Commodore, I only command the *coureur de bois* scouts for General Montcalm. I do not feel comfortable answering your question with the level of credibility a flag officer like you should expect. I will say this, if France declares victory at the end of this war, Louisbourg will still be French."

There were loud murmurs of approval, some table knocking, and applause.

Governor Drucour interceded to thank Captain Gerrard for his generous presentation.

"I think we have occupied enough of his time for today."

More applause. Philippe shook a lot of hands as he moved through the room to leave. He was anxious to get outside. Henri reached his side just as Commodore du Bauffremont captured Philippe's right hand and full attention near the door.

"Captain Gerrard, one more question I'd hoped to ask you. Are you the same Captain Gerrard that married Lady Corrinne de Chanaye in Québec City in November 1754? I only ask this because I commanded the *Champion Mer*, the ship that escorted the Dutch ship, *William's Queen,* down the river."

Philippe noticed an unfriendly glint in the naval officer's eyes. He replied politely, "I am afraid I do not recall your ship, Commodore. If you were there, then you must also know I was unconscious from a head wound at the time. If you will excuse me, sir."

Philippe left the King's Bastion with Henri at his side. Once they walked down Rue Toulouse and turned the corner to move down a side street, he stopped and checked to be certain no one was following them.

"What was the reason for that question?" Henri asked.

"The commodore knows I married Corrinne. He wanted to make it a point to tell me."

"Why?"

"I don't know. The commodore has certainly told Governor Drucour by now. Corrinne's identity here in Louisbourg is as the wife of Lord Charles VanderMeer. Governor Drucour knows the truth, that Corrinne and I are married, but until today there was no one else around to dispute this. Not officially, anyway. Maybe he told me so I cannot deny it if someone else publicly asks me?" He paused as an afterthought occurred to him. "That explains why Governor Drucour is so anxious for us to leave. Drucour's support of Corrinne makes him complicit in our deceit. When we are gone, that problem goes with us."

They walked faster when they reached the street that led straight down to the hospital. Upon reaching the hospital, Henri stopped.

"I have to go back to the barracks and talk with my men. Do you need me right now?"

"No, I will stay here with Corrinne. Come join us when you can. You are part of this discussion concerning our departure."

Henri walked towards the Dauphin Bastion. Philippe entered the hospital and was told by the marine guard that Lady Corrinne had taken her children back to her house along with Captain LaTour.

Philippe checked in on Anamosa, but found her asleep. He did not want to wake her up, but noticed her face was covered with sweat. *A fever?* He mentioned that to Nurse Cardon as he left for Corrinne's house.

*

After Lieutenant Henri Gerrard returned to the marine barracks in the Dauphin Bastion, he told Color Sergeant Gosse to call the men together.

"The ones on guard, too?"

"Yes, Sergeant. Captain Gerrard is at the hospital. I think he is capable of assuming the guard for a while."

"That's for certain," the color sergeant replied. Gosse sent a runner to the hospital to collect the guards.

While Henri waited for all the marines to assemble, he decided to talk with Mkuigen Malsum. He found a quiet place away from the other bunks and asked Color Sergeant Gosse to join with him.

"Monsieur Malsum. First, my apologies, I've not had time to talk with you before. The attack on Lady Corrinne and things associated with my father's arrival has occupied much of my thoughts and time...when I am not sitting at Lady Anamosa's bedside."

"I understand, Lieutenant."

It was the first time Henri had heard the Abenaki warrior speak to him directly. The French had a Québécois accent. The longer they talked, the more impressed Henri would become with this man.

"Have you been treated fairly? The bunk? The food?"

"I have, indeed. The weevils in the bread were properly baked."

Malsum did not smile, but Henri could read humor in the man's eyes.

"He is very good at dice," Gosse offered. "The men claim he's cast a spell on the dice, so they fall in his favor."

Henri was appalled. "What? Who said that?"

Gosse replied quickly. "They said it in jest, Lieutenant. They all like Malsum. He is just very lucky."

Malsum nodded. "It is probably just a rare run of luck."

"As you say. When the marines assemble, I will speak with them about some forthcoming changes."

"Do you want me to leave?"

"No, Monsieur..."

"Just call me Malsum."

"Of course...Malsum. On the contrary, Malsum. You are a marine brother, too. I invite you to stay and listen. My father spoke highly of you. Maybe you will have counsel to offer me afterwards."

Malsum saw a lot of the father in this son. "Lieutenant, I am honored by this consideration."

"Good."

"Um, sir, do you want to tell me anything, in advance...so I can be supportive," Gosse hinted heavily.

"Nice try, Color Sergeant," Henri said. "It will not be a long speech. But I prefer everyone to hear it at the same time...even you."

"Something bad then?" Gosse asked, still fishing for information.

"He is the cleverest of all the dice players," Malsum stated impassively.

"Oh? Then why do you have all my money?" Gosse asked.

"You were the last one left in the game."

"Wait. Did we get paid?" Henri asked.

Just then, the runner and the marine guards from the hospital started coming through the door. They were out of breath from trotting the entire way. Henri moved up to the front of the barracks by the washbasins.

"Gather up close. Sit and share bunks, if you like."

"Are we in trouble?" one of the men asked.

"Just you," another man replied.

"No one is in trouble," Henri said. "Just the opposite. I have news for all of you. Let me tell you everything first, before you shout your questions. This information is confidential. I order you not to share it with anyone outside this room. Do you hear me?" He looked and pointed at each face until he saw them nod. "All of you are aware that my father, Scout Captain Philippe Gerrard, arrived in Louisbourg yesterday. He has come to escort Lady Corrinne and her children as she leaves Louisbourg on the trading ship *Falcon Queen*. Captain LaTour is the master of that ship. You've already met him. The day of departure will be decided soon, but it is safe to say it will be some time in the next ten days, maybe less. You volunteered to stay behind in Louisbourg to guard Lady Corrinne and her children when the rest of the battalion made a difficult overland winter march back to Québec City. Two of our brothers lost their lives in Lady Corrinne's defense. That is what our brothers did. That is what all of us were prepared to do. You have accomplished your mission with honor. I consider it a great privilege to be your commander. Now the time has come, with the departure of Lady Corrinne, when this marine unit has completed its voluntary assignment. You've earned a journey home like heroes. Captain LaTour has room aboard his ship to transport all of you back to Québec City."

The marines began hooting and cheering.

Henri held up a hand. "I'm not finished. The ship is shorthanded for crew, so like any good naval marine, you will demonstrate your sailing skills as a courtesy for your passage."

They were so elated, the marines made jokes about how easy that would be as compared to standing a winter post outside in the drizzly cold rain.

"Given what I see and hear, I presume everyone is willing to stand watch to sail back home?"

A resounding chorus of *Yesses* and *Yes sirs* filled the air.

Henri left the meeting to return to the hospital. During the walk along the quay wall, he brooded over Lieutenants Meckler and Roos, the two officers who abetted Captain Stoecklin in the rape of Anamosa and the murder of her marine guards. Lieutenant-Colonel Du Bourzt had pulled him aside at the hospital that first night and warned him not to take his own revenge against these Swiss mercenaries.

"It's one thing to kill them *during* their crimes. But if you plan to kill them *now*, without receiving sanction by the governor, you will be brought up on charges."

"They are guilty! I will not let them get away from Louisbourg alive," Henri replied with resolve.

"I understand. But they are isolated and guarded right now. If you are incarcerated for an act of revenge, what good will that do for Lady Corrinne and Lady Anamosa? Let me find a way to charge them for the murder of your guards."

Henri was temporarily mollified. But nothing had happened regarding the Swiss officers in over a week. There were warships in the harbor. He worried the governor may have already arranged to have the mercenaries board one of them for transport back to France. If this was true, he might be able to get the marines aboard such a warship to throw these officers overboard once they sailed. But that would take much cajoling on his part. Much risk for the marines. Other people might get involved who would foil this plan. There were too many unknowns. Henri preferred to just do this himself. Yet the words of Colonel du Bourzt rang true.

Nevertheless, Henri vowed to find a way to get justice. Maybe the other mercenaries themselves could be induced to kill them? How could he make them do that?

Henri decided to mention this idea to Lieutenant-Colonel du Bourzt.

*

Before sailing to Louisbourg, Commodore Chevalier Antoine du Bauffremont had been approached by a direct representative of the king, who gave the commodore confidential orders.

"The King is concerned this malaise of disloyalty, encouraged by Minister Machault and Minister d'Argenson, has spread to our American colonies. Augustin de Drucour was personally selected by Minister Machault to govern Île Royale and the port of Louisbourg. Now all we hear is that Louisbourg is in danger of falling to the English, along with complaints Versailles does not authorize enough troops or ships to protect its territories. These were the same complaints expressed by Ministers d'Argenson and Machault. Yet Louisbourg remains the strongest fortress in New France. Who can the King believe? The King has expressed confidence that you might be a worthy successor to this failing governorship. Additionally, the Dutch government has demanded our cooperation to safeguard Lady Corrinne VanderMeer, wife of Lord Charles VanderMeer, heir to the Duchy of Brunswick. This sanctuary was arranged by Minister Machault. The King was unaware of this foreign person's presence in Louisbourg. Where did she come from? And why is she there? You are ordered to answer these questions and conduct a full inspection assessing Louisbourg's defenses. Send a sealed report back to the King."

Bauffremont recognized the messenger as one of Madame de Pompadour's smarmy puppets, of course. But this whore had become influential enough to displace the two most powerful ministers in France. Everyone in contact with Versailles needed to be very careful what they said concerning her.

Implicit in the verbal order to send back a report was the expectation it would contain information to support Governor Drucour's dismissal. This would later be followed with an announcement by the King that Commodore du Bauffremont was the new governor of Louisbourg.

"This report must be done with haste to support your appointment as Governor of Île Royale by the end of summer."

"I am honored to serve my King and country," Bauffremont had replied.

It was a very fortuitous order. Inspecting Louisbourg was an opportunity for increased status, promotion, and great wealth. As for the defenses, from what he'd already learned, the complaints by Governor Drucour were valid. Indeed, there were not enough troops to repel a determined English invasion. The mercenaries sent to reinforce the garrison had already caused serious problems. Even greater numbers of mercenaries were anticipated to arrive, suggesting more problems.

Versailles' unexpected interest in Lady VanderMeer was a surprise. But after arriving in Louisbourg, the commodore recognized Lady VanderMeer for who she was: Lady Corrinne de Chanaye. There was unexplained mystery in this. Bauffremont decided to be careful what he said about her.

The commodore would be joined by two more squadrons of French ships-of-the-line scheduled to arrive in Louisbourg over the next few months. If they remained in the harbor until the winter months, any plan by the English to land and invest Louisbourg would be effectively scuttled. At least until next year's fighting season.

Then what? Would Versailles anchor another fleet in the harbor again next year? Who could say? Certainly not the new temporary ministers. They were weak, ill-informed individuals, mere puppets. Becoming governor of a colony destined to be captured by the enemy was not an attractive proposition. But Bauffremont must provide the report as ordered. Versailles had requested it without delay. He had to report something. *The fact that Lady VanderMeer was an impostor?* That seemed sufficient to report. He could add the sudden presence and admission by Captain Philippe Gerrard that Lady VanderMeer was his wedded wife. Bauffremont had personally seen them married in Québec City. It was all true. *Yet the Dutch government inexplicably insists she be given sanctuary and protected?* Versailles wanted to know why. *What is her purpose there?* they asked. *Just sanctuary? From what…or who?*

These were intriguing questions. Very confident he now had good reasons to confront Drucour despite the turmoil caused by the Swiss mercenaries, Bauffremont did not delay in approaching the governor after the military council. He was stalled by Lieutenant Christophe, the appointments secretary.

"The governor is in another long meeting with his garrison commanders. I will schedule you next, sir. Please feel free to wait over there."

Unknown to Bauffremont, he was about to wait for hours. The idle time gave him space to think, something he'd not planned to do. So, he thought about himself…his favorite topic. Instead of pondering the answers to the questions posed by Versailles, he abruptly asked himself the most important question of all.

Why pick me *for this?* He pondered this question with introspection for the first time since being tasked with this mission. *My career is not exactly distinguished. There are many other military men senior to me. Many more qualified and more deserving of a governorship. Louisbourg requires an able commander. Everyone realizes Louisbourg is vulnerable to invasion.*

That thought was a hard slap across the face.

Yes! Everyone realizes this! It's all they talk about. Our spies have confirmed the English will invade. It's only a question of when. So, why me?

"Because no one else wants this!?" Bauffremont whispered this aloud, as if permitting his subconscious greater volume. "Everyone else is too smart to accept this. Versailles must consider me a fool!"

Commodore du Bauffremont stared at the shaded window and discerned his dim reflection on the glass. He gazed at himself, seeing a fifty-six-year-old, overweight naval officer sitting so proudly on the couch. A man confident enough to confront a sitting governor.

Confront a sitting governor? Confront Drucour? Is that what I am contemplating?

Commodore du Bauffremont had participated in the military councils of war since arriving. He found Governor Drucour to be not only competent, but also highly respected by his garrison officers. Drucour's preparations for the defense of Gabarus Bay consisted of interlocking battlements with pre-sighted artillery positions and fallback points. It seemed a good plan, except for one major flaw. There were simply not enough troops to defend both the battlements and the fort. It was the singular weakness of the plan. And it had been reported back to France repeatedly.

Versailles expects *Louisbourg to fall! They will let it. They will spare no more troops for Louisbourg. France fights another land war on its borders in Europe. And when the crown jewel of its American colonies falls to the English? Then what?*

Versailles could no longer blame Ministers Machault and d'Argenson. They had dismissed these brilliant ministers without reason.

They will want to blame the military. Versailles wants a new governor, someone with military gravitas, a flag officer. Not a purported incompetent, like Drucour. Award it to a veteran commodore for instance, someone who would not hesitate to accept the dubious privilege of governing Île Royale, he deduced. *That way Versailles will not be criticized by their internal enemies for doing nothing. And if Louisbourg falls under my command? What does that say about me? That I am expendable...and stupid?!*

This was another slap across the face.

Military influence in state affairs became stronger during a war. *Strong enough to challenge a king? What if France is invaded by Prussia and England? Will the King fall? Is Versailles that weak? The threat of revolution must be greater than anyone realizes.*

Considering these conclusions, the commodore abruptly changed his mind about everything. He decided not to report that Louisbourg's defenses were poorly constructed. He would report just the opposite, because the opposite was true. In fact, maybe his report should include the signatures of all the garrison and squadron commanders?

And at the end, make a new request for troops? Bauffremont liked that idea. He would think about that. *And this sudden obsession with Lady VanderMeer? Why is she so important? They must think she is a spy? Is she a spy? English or French? Maybe both? The Dutch Republic is neutral, but they insist on protecting her. And insist she be given sanctuary in Louisbourg. She is a nobody. What is Versailles so worried about?*

Commodore had a sudden flash of insight so strong he stood up. *Of course.*

The delay had ended up being a productive, if not disturbing, two hours of the commodore's *quiet* time, during which he felt he had done some of the best thinking of his life.

*

After leaving his marines in a state of euphoria, Lieutenant Henri Gerrard hurried back to the hospital and found Dr. Michaux and Nurse Cardon hovering near Anamosa. The doctor was bent over her waist, examining her genitals. Without asking permission, Henri went straight to Anna's bedside, leaned over, and kissed her forehead. He could feel the heat of a raging fever on his lips.

"Anna," he said tenderly. He sat in the chair and held her hand. Her eyes showed the painful signs of the fever, but she managed a smile. He kissed the back of her hand and could feel the heat in the skin there, too.

It was bad.

Dr. Michaux proceeded as if Henri was not there. The doctor picked up a specially prepared tubular-shaped roll of wet linen wrapped around a thickened paste-like mixture. It was an inch in diameter and three inches long. He very slowly and very gently inserted it inside the vagina, watching Anamosa's expression carefully trying to minimize the invasive pain. When he was done, he gave instructions to Nurse Cardon.

"Have her drink what we discussed. A teaspoon an hour for the next four hours. I want cold compresses around her neck and in her groin area. Change them constantly. We may need a cold-water bath. Get the tub ready. Draw the water from the deep well."

"Yes, Doctor."

Michaux turned his attention to Lieutenant Gerrard.

"The damaged tissues in Anamosa's vaginal canal have inflamed again, much more than before. I'd hoped this would not happen, but I am not surprised. We must bring down her fever. We'll try cold compresses for a while. Failing in that, we'll lower her into a cold bath. I inserted a doughy mix of Apiaceae powder, wrapped in a wet piece of linen, inside of her. I learned this remedy from a Turkish physician I met in Egypt, who learned of it from a Persian healer. Armies crossing over those lands for tens of centuries left a brutal legacy of raped women. The powder was collected from the roots of local weedy plants with tiny wild flowers. There are related varieties of these weeds all over the world, and it would seem, right under our noses. You dry the roots and mill them into a powder. The paste it makes appears to contain several curative properties specific to this type of injury, though no one knows why. It's an ancient herbal remedy. Some of the medicinal genius lost in the arrogant prejudice of our Christian enlightenment. It doesn't always work. But it has produced good results for me for the majority of the dozen or so times I've tried it."

"Does Lady Corrinne know about Anamosa's fever?"

"She and Captain LaTour were here earlier, but only briefly. Her twins were crying and very upset, so they took them home. I know she stopped in to see Anamosa long enough to tell her where she was going. She mentioned you were coming."

Henri stroked Anna's hair.

"Well, I'll stay here. I want to help somehow."

Dr. Michaux laid a reassuring palm on Henri's shoulder. "Just your presence does wonders for her, Lieutenant. But I think you know that."

When the doctor left, Nurse Cardon arrived with two other nurses. Henri got up and out of the way while they began banking rolls of damp, cold towels on Anna's body as the doctor instructed. Henri slipped off his cutlass, took off his outer uniform coat, and laid both items on the other chair. He went into the bathing room, rolled back his cuffs, and washed his hands.

"My hands are clean," he told Nurse Cardon when he returned.

Two marines showed up at that time to resume their guard in the foyer. Henri explained what he knew, the presumed location of Corrinne and the twins, Captain Gerrard and Captain LaTour. And Anamosa's condition.

"I will be staying by her bedside."

The nurses gave Anna the first of several teaspoons of a white powder mixed with mint tea. Ten minutes later, the pain fell away, and Anna went to sleep. Holding her hand, Henri laid his head beside her waist and went to sleep, too.

During the next few hours, the nurses continued to bank Anamosa's neck and groin with more cold towels and give her teaspoons of medicine at the appropriate times without disturbing Lieutenant Gerrard's sleep.

The Nesting Grounds

The female white eagle flew back to the nesting grounds near the lake, and after a few short circles, landed directly in the nest from the previous year. It was undisturbed by other creatures. Female eagles created a unique aerie and would use it over and over. Other eagles usually avoided it. The scent of the previous occupant acted as a repellant. In less than one moon, the female laid three eggs in the nest. In another moon, they hatched.

This time, her white-feathered mate stayed with her to assist in bringing food and sitting on the eggs. The *ghost* pondered the thought that it might join with her mate. But not for long. It was used to the female eagle now. The female was far more intelligent than the male. The *ghost* understood the creature's tendencies, its moods, what it would do without much urging and what it would not do. She tolerated the invading spirit's presence, begrudgingly. The eagle had a strong will. If forced to do something it did not like, it would stop in mid-flight and drop straight towards the ground, willing to die, if necessary. The *ghost* understood what those limits were. The *ghost* decided to remain with her.

There were three new chicks this time. The *ghost* could not abandon them. They would all have white feathers. There was a danger that one or more of the fledglings would be forced out of the nest. The *ghost* must prevent this. With her mate available to hunt and bring back food, the female's strength did not wane as it had the last time.

The *ghost* attempted night flying, to reach out to the dreams of the young girl. It was something the female eagle did not want to do. It was dangerous to fly at night and more dangerous to land among the pointed branches of the trees. If the female's life was endangered, the fledglings were endangered. The eagle felt this instinctively and reacted to this instinct. After an exhilarating plummet straight down, the *ghost* added more to its knowledge of what the female would not do.

However, the female would tolerate twilight flying before sunset.

Like now.

The sun was still brimming with colors when the *ghost* gently surged to dominance. It flew straight up to a great height before starting a downward glide, banking in gentle circles. Gliding downward this way might mitigate the female's tendency to suddenly plunge with anger. That's what the *ghost* thought. This would be a good test. The *ghost* peered across the void and perceived the new light that flashed so brightly into its perception when a sealing ritual was conducted unexpectedly. This was not a servant. The light was bright and pure, but not so bright as the first time. The *ghost* decided it would visit this one after the fledglings took flight.

For now, the ghost gave all its attention to the young girl. Although her light was still the brightest, her thoughts were troubled. She had been severely injured. Fortunately, she had reached out in her sleep to the owl and had joined with it, hoping for comfort amid the ethereal sensation of flying. The *ghost* drew close to her, sensing her distress, the great heat she felt, the dull pervasive pain. She had thoughts of joining with the owl permanently. The girl did not realize this would cause her death. With alarm, the ghost showed her images of the boy become man.

Nurse Cardon and three other nurses surrounded Anamosa's bed along with Lieutenant Gerrard. The girl's fever had spiked dangerously high. She had stopped responding to any questions. Dr. Michaux checked on her and changed his mind about the bath because of the poultice he inserted hours ago. He did not want to chance having it dissolve too quickly. The fever may be indication it was working. They left Anamosa in the bed. The nurses removed Anamosa's chemise, leaving only the amulet and covered her entire body with towels drenched in the icy cold water drawn from the deep well. Henri volunteered to help. They took turns with the handle fans. While the others changed the towels, two of them would continuously fan the girl to speed the evaporation of the water from the towels, thus carrying away the heat.

They had been doing this for hours when Dr. Michaux came around again to check on her progress. He felt her skin. Inspected the poultice. This time, he did not speak, a grim frown on his face.

Henri saw the doctor's resignation. *We are losing her*, he thought.

"Nooo! Please no!"

Nurse Cardon noticed the purple jewel in the amulet shimmering brightly with an eerie glow. Earlier, she had presumed it to be just a reflection of the daylight coming through the window. Now it was night. With the lieutenant's plea, the glow grew even stronger. It was obvious something spiritual was at work here, something good.

"Call to her, Lieutenant!"

Henri looked at the nurse, his face marred with agony. "What?"

"Look at the jewel! She hears you! Call to her!"

"Anna, don't leave me. Come back. I promise to protect you forever! Come back. I love you."

In the strengthening darkness, the eagle abruptly stopped its glide and tucked its wings. It dropped towards the ground.

The *ghost* crowded many images of the boy become man into the girl's thoughts.

Call to him!

Anamosa inhaled deeply. "*Ahhree!*"

It was the first word she had spoken in hours. Anamosa's voice was weak, but she'd called to him.

"Yes! Anna!" Henri answered with anguish. "I'm right here! Don't leave me, Anna! *Je t'aime!*"

The girl heard the faint echo of a voice. It sounded familiar. The voice became louder.

Look at him!

The *ghost* dared not delay any longer. It withdrew its dominance from the female in the middle of its dive towards the ground. The female extended its six-foot wings in the darkness and began flapping them. In seconds, it hovered and landed at the aerie to the urgent, hungry screeching of the fledglings. Her mate took off to hunt small animals in the nearby open fields.

Henri's tears dripped on Anamosa's fingers. She opened her eyes and blinked.

"Ahhree?" Her voice was soft but clear.

His throat was choked, thick with emotion. "Yes, Anna! It's me! It's *Ahhree!*"

"Oho, Ahhree!"

"Oho, Anna!" He laughed with relief.

Dr. Michaux heard the excited voices and rushed back into the room. He laid a palm on her forehead. He smiled and shook his head with amazement. It was hard to believe. "This fever has broken!"

The nurses gasped and clapped their hands. Henri coughed and inhaled deeply to suppress his tears.

"You scared me again," Henri told Anamosa. "You scared me again!"

"I was flying with the owl," she explained. "The eagle was there, too."

Henri thanked Chittaqua in his thoughts.

The nurses interpreted Anamosa's words as delirious nonsense. But Nurse Cardon's eyes were luminous. She did not think the girl spoke nonsense. She had witnessed so much suffering and death in decades of nursing, it was rare she was so affected by a patient. But this girl was different. The girl's fever was the hottest she had ever touched…and the patient lived. The fever had gone on for many hours. This girl should not have survived. Yet she did.

His love called to her, she thought. *Love compelled her to return.*

"Lieutenant," Nurse Cardon interrupted. "We need to dress Anna again and change the wet bedding. Go lie down across the hall for a while. I'll come get you if anything changes."

Henri was drained, emotionally and physically. It was the second time that Anamosa had come so close to death. But this was much worse than the last time. He nodded his assent.

"Anna, I am going to lie down for a while. Is that all right with you?"

She nodded.

It was almost a week since the attack. The swelling in her face and neck had decreased considerably. But there was still a lot of purple, brown, and yellowish bruising visible. Her smile, however, was almost normal.

He kissed her forehead. It felt cool.

"I'll be right across the hall," he assured her.

Henri took his coat and cutlass with him. The guard outside the door came to attention. He went into the room across the hall, laid his things on a chair, flopped backward on the bed, and closed his eyes.

"Thank you, God," he whispered. "Thank you."

Fatigue battled with awareness. He wondered about his father and Corrinne. *Where have they gone? They've not been here in hours.* And then he slipped into a dreamless sleep.

Nurse Cardon came into the room and gently pulled off Henri's boots and moved his legs up on the bed. He was sleeping soundly with the exhaustion of a solider after a battle.

*

Several hours earlier, Corrinne, Philippe, and Captain LaTour had eaten together at the house. The twins were bathed and changed and were now playing with their toys. They had just finished eating when a messenger arrived from Governor Drucour asking them all to attend the governor's private offices. And not just any messenger, but Lieutenant Christophe himself.

"The reason?" Corrinne asked.

"The governor at present sits with Commodore du Bauffremont and Lieutenant-Colonel du Bourzt. He requires your collective attendance… all of you."

"All of us? And the reason?" Philippe repeated for her. "The topic?"

"Captain, I believe it relates to your previous discussion. The governor explained he wants to complete that discussion today. He also said to tell you this is *not* an order. He asks your indulgence to his request and fervently hopes you will come." Lieutenant Christophe added his own opinion. "You should come. It is that important."

Corrinne rolled her eyes. "Dare we say no?" Corrinne glanced at Calypso and Marcus, wondering who she trusted to watch them while they were away.

Lieutenant Christophe saw her glance. "The governor said to bring your children with you. Madame Drucour looks forward to sitting with them. She will also be in this meeting. Everyone can be in the same room."

"Well, that's different," Corrinne said. "Tell the governor we will come right away."

He bowed his head. "*Merci*, my lady. Captain Gerrard. Captain LaTour."

Lieutenant Christophe left. The three gathered up some personal items. The two marines guarding the house accompanied them.

Corrinne carried Calypso, and Philippe carried Marcus. They speculated back and forth where this discussion would lead to next.

"What could the governor possibly want to know that he doesn't already know?" Corrinne wondered.

"It's the commodore," Philippe replied in even tones. "He interferes in this. The question is *why*."

"He will accuse me of being a spy," LaTour offered glumly. "Or a smuggler. Probably both."

Corrinne shook her head. "Oh, Beauregard, he won't! We are beyond all that business now."

Once inside the King's Bastion, they were escorted to the governor's private quarters. Marie-Louise took the twins to the side. Introductions were made. In the center of the room, there was a square arrangement of couches, each wide enough for three people, with a low, square, polished oak table in the middle. This was a place reserved for informal discussions with important visitors. This congregation of people was anything but important. The governor and his wife sat on one couch. She was on the side where she could watch the twins playing nearby on the square rug. Corrinne and Philippe sat to the governor's right. Corrinne could also see the twins at play. Colonel du Bourzt and Commodore du Bauffremont sat at Philippe's right. And Captain LaTour was on the last couch, alone, sitting in the middle, feeling very conspicuous, thinking this seating arrangement was intentional. Hence, this discussion was about him.

Refreshments were served on the center table. Plenty of coffee, tea, and assorted sweetbreads. The servants left the room. Corrinne could not resist the coffee and poured herself a cup to sip. No one else partook.

"Lady Corrinne, Captain Gerrard, Captain LaTour, thank you for coming on such impromptu notice. Since I've already had numerous cups of coffee, I will get right to it. This meeting concerns confessions. Commodore du Bauffremont has confessed to me he's been given special orders by Versailles to assess the defenses of Louisbourg…and to provide his opinion in a report that will go on to document reasons for my dismissal. He confessed his reward for doing this will be the governorship of Île Royale, replacing me. A startling revelation, yes? But refreshing candor. I see your surprise. Lieutenant-Colonel du Bourzt is here as an unbiased witness to these discussions, because I trust his integrity for discretion.

"This gathering also concerns Lady VanderMeer. I confessed to the commodore everything I know about Lord and Lady VanderMeer and the business reasons for their pretense in identity. I explained your residency in Boston, and the reason why you came to Louisbourg, which was to escape further assassination attempts on Lord VanderMeer's life. The commodore confessed, he already knew about your marriage to Captain Gerrard in Québec City, so there was nothing to reveal in that regard. However, Versailles has expressed great interest in knowing the commodore's opinion about Lord and Lady VanderMeer. Versailles does not know why you are here. Your purpose? Versailles is unaware of your marriage to Captain Gerrard. I told the commodore of your intentions to leave Louisbourg. In this context, I considered the best resolution to this situation is for us to come to a collective agreement about what the commodore will report back to Versailles... particularly as it relates to your identity."

Corrinne put down her coffee cup. "So then, should I presume Versailles will now consider me an English spy?"

"Not exactly, my lady," Commodore du Bauffremont interjected in a logical tone. "I believe Versailles has concluded you are a *Dutch* spy. After all, you arrived here on a Dutch ship."

Captain LaTour's gaze was glued to the floor. *God's balls.*

"A Dutch spy!" Corrinne glanced at Philippe. "What possible information of any value about France could I provide to the Dutch Republic that they do not already possess?"

"A good question. That is probably at the root of their curiosity. Versailles may be thinking why the Dutch would send one of their spies to Louisbourg." Commodore Bauffremont shook his head. "Unfortunately, my lady, Versailles rarely provides their reasons. I was ordered to learn everything I can learn about you, and report. And whether you are a spy for the Dutch...or the English, if you are a spy, I am directed to arrest you. Um, not Captain Gerrard, however. Versailles knows nothing about Captain Gerrard."

Corrinne could not believe what she was hearing. The commodore could not possibly be so stupid. *You fat, pompous ass! You have the insolence to threaten me with arrest in front of my husband!* She looked at Philippe and saw *that* face. She last saw this face during their first year together in New France, just before he killed an assassin sent by someone in France to kill her. *One of the many reasons why I love you so much.*

"For you to threaten me like this is absurd! I freely admitted to my false identity as the wife of Lord VanderMeer when I arrived in Louisbourg."

"Yes, I know. Governor Drucour has explained this to me. And I told him, Versailles' interest in 'Lady VanderMeer' came as the result of the Dutch Republic's request and insistence that you be provided sanctuary. Up until now, they knew nothing about you. And still don't, except that you exist. I speculate Versailles simply presumes you are a spy."

Corrinne nodded. "All right. Lord VanderMeer and I were spies for France while we lived in Boston."

Drucour spoke in a loud agitated voice. "We cannot talk about that!"

The commodore ignored the governor's rant and replied to Lady Corrinne. "You spied for France? Well, this could solve everything!"

Corrinne ignored the governor's protests and directed her reply to the commodore. "We brought intelligence to Louisbourg regarding the English build-up of troops in Halifax. They are destined to be the invasion force of Louisbourg. Captain LaTour's ship, flying under the colors of the Dutch Republic, had access to Boston as a neutral trading partner. And still does, unless someone compromises him! He can fly the colors of the Dutch Republic or France as he chooses to do so. In fact, he carried the messages about Halifax and provided us transport from Boston. The French navy knows all this. Double flags have great value for France!"

Captain LaTour expected the commodore would simply arrest him at that point. *He will hang me later...above the quarterdeck of his flagship.*

"No, no, no!" Drucour declared emphatically. "Commodore, none of this information can leave this room. Colonel du Bourzt, I order you to witness I have told Commodore du Bauffremont that what I am about to disclose is a state secret. It cannot be repeated."

"So noted, sir." Colonel du Bourzt presumed this restriction included him. He found this entire conversation fascinating. Add Lieutenant Gerrard to this mix? What a family!

Drucour's tone had an edge. "Commodore, I am revealing this to you now to put an end to this inquiry, or investigation, or discussion, or whatever you want to call it. Six months ago, the original reason provided to me by Minister of Marine, Jean-Baptiste de Machault...*the reason why* I gave sanctuary to Lady VanderMeer, was to safeguard her identity as Lady VanderMeer, thus preserving her ability to return to Boston sometime in the future, as a Dutch citizen of a neutral country. Ostensibly, so Lady VanderMeer could continue in her role as a French spy."

"But why can I not tell Versailles this?"

"Because of other spies," Corrinne said. This was obvious.

"Do you not see?" Drucour asked with astonishment. He added more. "Commodore, I am the direct recipient of routine intelligence communications from Boston regarding the intentions of the English and the Americans. This intelligence is vital to the war interests here in New France. If the English hear through their spies in Versailles—you do acknowledge the English have spies in Versailles? Yes? Good—if the English learn that a person named Lady VanderMeer, formerly of Boston, now living in Louisbourg, is a spy for France..."

Corrinne finished this argument with reluctance. "If my identity as Lady VanderMeer is compromised, I can never return to Boston. But worse to me than that, many people in Boston who were associated with Lord and Lady VanderMeer…people I hold dear…these innocent people will be arrested. And if the English ever capture me…you can guess what happens next."

Commodore du Bauffremont suddenly realized he was grossly mischaracterized.

"I am not trying to play the part of a villain in this."

"Too late," Philippe said. To Corrinne, he whispered, "Although *stupid* villain might be more accurate."

Corrinne squeezed Philippe's hand to keep him quiet.

The commodore saw it in their expressions. "You do not believe me? Why would I speak with such candor? I am trying to weave a way through this, to come up with something that complies with the orders Versailles has given me. I must reply to them, right away. I want to say something that supports Governor Drucour and does no harm to you, my Lady VanderMeer. They simply don't know why you are in Louisbourg. So, they will presume the worst. And no matter what that is, it ends with you being arrested and executed. I am trying to find a *solution*."

Drucour held up a hand to mitigate the tension that was mounting among those present. "I will validate that Lady VanderMeer's Dutch identity is authentic as it stands. That she is here because of assassination attempts on Lord VanderMeer's life. That is what everyone believes anyway. At least for now."

"We need to agree on the exact words of my missive." The commodore looked at Drucour. "That is our purpose here, yes?"

"Do not mention the attack on Lady Anamosa," the governor said.

Philippe was losing patience. "All right. We are leaving Louisbourg," Philippe stated tersely to everyone. "She will no longer be here. Put that in your report. Lady VanderMeer returned to, where? Amsterdam! Say that."

"She is a member of the House of Brunswick. It is an insufficient explanation."

"She may be considered a member of a Dutch royal house, but she is French! And she is most certainly my wife!"

Drucour replied calmly, "No offense, Captain Gerrard. But that degree of honesty is not beneficial for either of you. You intend to remain in New France, in Québec City, yes? Lady Corrinne is a popular person. She is a topic of gossip in Louisbourg. Her departure, with you, will be noticed. Other people in Louisbourg will make reports to Versailles, or to the ministries for various reasons. They might mention her. No, they *will* mention her. It is gossip! If Versailles is unsatisfied with the information in the commodore's missive, they will make further inquiries…maybe another one to Governor Vaudreuil."

Corrinne exhaled. There was little choice. "What do you suggest, Governor? My husband is right. Commodore, just report Lady VanderMeer indicated she was sailing for Amsterdam on *William's Queen*. That is what we will tell people when we leave this room. Some may believe that, some will not, but as soon as we sail, the speculation will diminish within a week, or when another dramatic event occurs, like the arrival of more warships, yes? Governor Drucour will not have to deal with any more tedious meetings like this, hopefully. He has an invasion to worry about. But in truth, we are going to Québec City. If more inquiries pursue us in six months, my husband and I accept that risk. I predict no one will care."

Philippe knew the last statement was more of a hope than a prediction, but it didn't matter.

"Anamosa!" Corrinne said suddenly. She'd forgotten about her. She stood. "I will send one of the marines to bring Henri here."

Marie stood. "I'll do it."

Philippe pressed the commodore one more time. "Commodore, you have enough information. Just say what we suggest. I think no matter what you say, it will not be the end of this. But it is enough for this fighting season, yes?"

The commodore nodded reluctantly. "As you say."

Drucour asked a question he'd wanted to ask for a long time. "Lady Corrinne, will you ever go back to Boston?"

She glanced at Philippe. "I would go back. Obviously, I cannot until the war is over. That is years away. But only if the Americans do not consider me a spy. I like Boston," she admitted. "I like the people of Boston. They openly accuse the English of oppression. They talk about freedom. The Americans do not like English rule. Are we not sympathetic to this idea?"

CHAPTER 26
LOUISBOURG
MAY 1757
You Are What You Leave Behind

Henri Gerrard awoke in the dark. He felt someone's hand on his shoulder. He sat up in an instant, grabbed the hand by the wrist, and twisted it. The person cried out and fell to his knees.

"Lieutenant! It's me, Private Vallier!"

Henri let go of the wrist. The marine stood. Henri saw Nurse Cardon standing in the shadowed doorway.

"Is Anamosa all right?"

"Yes, Lieutenant. She is sleeping peacefully. There is no fever."

Henri rubbed the sleep from his eyes and stood. "I'm sorry, Private."

Nurse Cardon brought him a basin of hot water with a towel. Henri wrung out the towel and wiped his face vigorously to help banish grogginess.

"Wait! You're supposed to be guarding Lady Corrinne!"

"Yes, sir. Lady Corrinne sent me to get you. She is with Captain Gerrard at the King's Bastion."

"King's Bastion? How long was I asleep?"

"Just for an hour," Nurse Cardon told him calmly.

A little sleep drunk, Henri staggered across the hall to check on Anamosa. She was asleep. He felt her forehead. There was no fever. He kissed her cheek and breathed easier. Through the window, he could see it was very dark outside.

Private Vallier carried the officer's coat, hat, and cutlass scabbard.

Henri dressed as he talked. "Lady Corrinne sent for me? Why?"

"I don't know, sir. But I think she wants to hear about Lady Anamosa."

Henri nodded. "Thank you. Nurse Cardon, please tell Anna when she wakes up that I will be coming back."

The two marines left the hospital and walked quickly to the King's Bastion. The private answered all the lieutenant's questions, as much as he could answer. By the end of the up-hill walk, Henri was fully awake. The torches were lit at the bridgewalk over the moat. The other guard was waiting inside.

Lieutenant Christophe saw Henri and came over to him.

"Is everything all right?" Henri asked.

"Yes, Lieutenant. Follow me."

They left the guards behind and went through two doors and down a long hallway. Christophe stopped at a third door and knocked softly. It opened.

"Shhhh," cautioned Madame Drucour. She pointed at some blankets on the floor. The twins were asleep. One of the maidservants sat in a chair nearby, watching over them. "Follow me," she whispered.

They went through an adjoining door that opened to a larger room. Henri saw Corrinne, his father, the governor, Captain LaTour, Commodore du Bauffremont, and Lieutenant-Colonel du Bourzt, all gathered on couches around a table. Henri came to attention and saluted.

"At ease, Lieutenant," the governor said. "Come, join us. Take a seat."

Henri sat next to Captain LaTour. The captain said, "You're just in time."

What does that mean? Henri wondered.

"Anamosa?" Corrinne asked.

Henri gave a long explanation about what had occurred over the last seven hours.

"The fever finally subsided," he added at the end. "She was sleeping when I left."

"As I said, she should not be moved," Corrinne said pointedly to the governor, as if repeating an earlier assertion. "But I will move her if I have to."

"Lieutenant, help yourself to the coffee and whatever else you want." The governor gestured and then provided a summary of the recent discussion.

Henri did not eat. He just listened. Twice, Corrinne added something to the explanation. Three times Commodore du Bauffremont spoke.

"So, that's where we are, Lieutenant," the governor summarized. "Anamosa should not be moved, yet Lady Corrinne must leave."

Henri had nothing to add to that argument, but another idea came to mind. Colonel du Bourzt was there. There may not be another opportunity like this.

"Governor, may I discuss something related to the attack on Lady Anamosa?"

Everyone was interested.

"Of course."

"Two of the Swiss officers, Lieutenants Meckler and Roos, assisted Captain Stoecklin in this attack."

Drucour was tentative. He had not expected something so far afield from what they were discussing.

"And you know this, how?"

As Henri hoped, Colonel du Bourzt spoke up. "I sent two of my grenadier sergeants to mingle with the mercenaries to ask about the night in question. They brought back the report the Swiss volunteers are very angry to be sent back to France without any payment. They blame these two lieutenants. The soldiers volunteered that Lieutenants Meckler and Roos came back to the barracks that night with the front of their uniforms covered in blood. My conclusion? They were the ones who murdered the two marine sentries."

Henri did not hesitate. "Governor, I request a military tribunal to be seated and to charge these two officers with that crime. I request we do this before my marines depart from Louisbourg…so they can see justice done if the officers are found guilty."

The colonel spoke up again. "Governor, I was told by my sergeants that many of the Swiss mercenaries stand ready to testify. They want to absolve themselves from any participation in this attack. They hope to stay here and complete their service. This tribunal could make the entire matter go away, except for the foul history, of course. And it will return these men to garrison duty—both for work and watches. They are badly needed for defense."

Drucour absorbed this new information. "Did the two of you rehearse this proposal together?"

"No, sir," Henri replied. "But I was aware of Colonel du Bourzt's investigative efforts and the results. Since he was sitting here, it seemed a good time to bring it up."

"Of course, it did," the governor replied with soft sarcasm.

Corrinne and Philippe thought so, too. They looked at the governor with expectation.

Governor Drucour could tell it was time to make a quick decision, something the entire faubourg would applaud.

"Very well. Lieutenant-Colonel du Bourzt, I order to you to organize this tribunal."

"Yes, sir."

*

Over the next three days, activities shifted towards getting Corrine ready to move aboard the *Queen*. Other than clothing and personal baggage, she only wanted to take her bathing tub and the Julien Le Roy standing clock. She also had two flat chests of gold and silver coinage concealed inside her favorite chair. Four inches deep, eighteen inches long, and twelve inches wide, they were mounted on the four-inch side. Victorio and Stefan had made the chests an integral part of the chair's side support. When the chair was tipped forward, you could see the slots for the chests to insert or extract them.

Captain LaTour was elated. He informed the crew they would be leaving soon. They could finally present Lady Corrinne with their surprise.

"I never meant the delay to be this long," he told Victorio. "I'm worried she will be angry with me when she learns of her sister and the missive."

Victorio was not so sure. "Angry or not, I think it is a blessing for her, after everything she's been through in Louisbourg. Aboard ship, it will allow her to celebrate without inhibition."

At Corrinne's insistence and assurance, Philippe stayed at the house and shared her bed. "The twins must get used to seeing us together like this," she told him.

Even on the first night, Marcus and Calypso climbed into the bed between them, and each night after that. The twins were overjoyed to sleep like this. It was natural. Of course, Corrinne and Philippe had to sacrifice their prurient lifestyle, temporarily, they hoped, but Philippe confessed to Corrinne he had never been so happy.

After surviving the last fever, Anamosa's health improved rapidly, to the point she even started to walk up and down the hallways of the hospital unaided. Dr. Michaux assessed she was out of danger but should stay in the hospital for another two weeks just to be certain the inflammation did not recur.

Anamosa had other plans.

Five days after the fever, the military tribunal sat in the King's Bastion. The two Swiss lieutenants were found guilty when twenty-six of the mercenaries testified the officers had returned to the barracks with uniforms bloodied as evidence of their crime. Others testified they overheard them discussing plans for the murder. The Swiss officers' explanation for the bloody uniforms was rejected by the tribunal. On the next day, Lieutenants Meckler and Roos were summarily executed in the Queen's Bastion marshalling yard by a firing squad of eight Québécois marines, at the command of Lieutenant Henri Gerrard.

Two days after that, Corrinne was breaking her morning fast with Anamosa at a table in the hospital.

"You look so much better, little love. Are you ready to leave this place?" she asked with excitement. "We plan to leave tomorrow afternoon when the tide goes out."

"I'm not going with you," Anamosa announced. Her expression was placid and certain, like always. Like this should not be a surprise to anyone.

Corrinne was shocked to silence for a few seconds. "What do you mean? Of course, you are going with me. You cannot stay here! Why would you *want* to stay here?"

"Henri is staying here," Anamosa replied.

Another shock for Corrinne. "What? Henri is not…? Who told you this?"

"Henri told me."

"Henri! Well…well, Henri is mistaken. He is going…" Corrinne stood as her agitation flared into action. "I will talk to Henri," she asserted firmly. "He is going, too! He should not have said otherwise to you!"

Corrinne walked rapidly back to the house.

"Find Lieutenant Gerrard!" she said to the guard standing near the front door. "Tell him I must talk with him right away."

Inside the house, Corrinne found Philippe sitting in a chair with Calypso. Marcus was playing on the floor with his tin soldiers and cannons as usual. Calypso seemed enamored with the scars on Philippe's face. She kept touching them, saying the word *hurt*, before kissing them. Philippe was overjoyed with her simple ministrations until he saw Corrinne's angry expression.

"What's wrong?"

She told him of her conversation with Anamosa. "I sent the front guard to find and bring Henri here."

"Why would he tell her that?"

*

Henri was standing before Governor Drucour inside the King's Bastion explaining his decision to remain with the garrison.

"It is my decision, if you will permit me, Governor."

"Have you told Captain Gerrard and Lady Corrinne of your decision?"

"Not yet, sir. I wanted to tell you first…well, I told Lady Anamosa this morning. I've thought about this a long time. My marines have completed their mission to guard Lady Corrinne. They can go home on Captain LaTour's ship."

"Lieutenant Gerrard"—the governor leaned forward in his seat—"as valuable an officer as you have demonstrated yourself to be on so many occasions, I formally release you from your decision to volunteer. You can go home with your men."

"Sir! Unless you order me to go to Québec City, I want to stay and defend Louisbourg."

"But why? Québec City needs to be defended, too."

"Governor, I can fight battles in the west, or I can fight this battle. Louisbourg is where the war for New France will be won…or lost. If Louisbourg falls, Québec City and Montréal will be next. I've been assigned duties for defending the Gabarus Bay battlements against the anticipated landings. I blazed the trails of retreat. I know the artillery positions and the fallback points. Lieutenant-Colonel du Bourzt depends on me in my assignments for these tactics."

Governor Drucour nodded slowly. "Have you told your men of your intentions?"

"If you permit me to stay, Governor, I will tell them now."

The governor exhaled with resignation and stood. "Permission granted, Lieutenant. Don't delay in doing this. Your discussion with me will not be the last of it."

Henri saluted and left the bastion. On the way down Rue Toulouse, he encountered one of the house guards coming back from the Dauphin Barracks. The marine explained Lady Corrinne desired to speak with him.

Anamosa must have told her, Henri thought. "I've something to tell you, Private."

Standing there on the main street of Louisbourg, Henri informed the marine of his decision.

"I see your look of surprise. I know you have questions. I will answer them later. Right now, you are the only marine that knows of my decision. Keep it to yourself."

"Yes, sir."

"Go back to the house and send the guard in the back to the barracks. Then go down to the hospital and send those guards to the barracks, too. You stay at the hospital and guard Lady Anamosa until relieved. Don't reveal anything I've said to anyone."

"Yes, sir!"

*

Marie-Louise de Drucour came into the governor's office with a pitcher of water. "How does your head feel?"

"Better."

"Was that Lieutenant Gerrard meeting with you this morning?"

"Yes." The governor told her the rest of the story.

"Corrinne is going to be very upset. Does she know of his plans?"

"I don't think he's told her yet. Maybe I should double the bastion guard?"

Marie had a new realization. "Oh, no! What about Anamosa?"

"Lieutenant Gerrard claims he told her this morning, just before he told me."

"Oh, the poor girl. She adores him with her heart and soul. What did she say?"

"I don't know." The governor looked at his wife. "But consider the circumstances. If I were Lieutenant Gerrard, and you were Anamosa, and the man you loved told you he was staying, what would you say?"

Marie smiled. "That I'm staying, too. That I would never leave you."

"You have your answer."

*

Once again, Lieutenant Gerrard gathered his marines in a cloistered section of the Dauphin Bastion barracks. Color Sergeant Gosse and Mkuigen Malsum were there, too. They all saw the cheerless expression on his face and glanced at each other pensively. It was going to be something they would not like hearing.

"So, tomorrow's the big day," Henri began. "I expect you are all ready for the journey?"

The marines nodded and smiled and relaxed a little.

"I have something to tell you. This morning I met with Governor Drucour and petitioned him that I might join the Louisbourg garrison permanently."

There were exclamations, expletives, and other sounds of surprise.

"Knowing this day was coming, this is a decision I've been contemplating for a long time—for weeks anyway. This is a personal decision for me. But I expect you have questions. Ask."

"*Why?*"

Henri nodded. "Good question. I told the governor that I can fight battles everywhere in this war, and like any of us, I just follow orders. When you get back to Québec City, you will probably fight alongside my father in the rivers and forest lands surrounding Lake Champlain. You do not escape this war by going back. You are elite marines. Years of war lie ahead of you. But in my opinion, Louisbourg is where the war for New France will be won… or lost. Right here. If Louisbourg falls, Québec City and Montréal will be attacked next. Maybe not right away, but within a year, certainly within two, the English will come in strength with their navy and their redcoat troops. But if Louisbourg survives, they cannot go up the river and lay siege. New France will survive. I told the governor this. He believes this, too. So, I choose to stay here. Your mission here was voluntary, like mine. This mission will be over tomorrow."

Grumbling erupted throughout the room.

"I want to stay with you," someone said.

"Me too," a different voice declared.

Henri shook his head. "Don't say this impulsively! Don't decide to do this because of me. I'm doing this because I believe this is the right thing to do. Louisbourg is the primary objective of the English. If they achieve a landing in Gabarus Bay, we can only win by stiff defense and counterattacks. Chances are very high you will lose your life defending this city fortress. Chances are also very high you will lose your life defending Québec City and Montréal. But Louisbourg will be first. Some of you have families back in the river cities or the farms and villages. Think about them. You are not being ordered to stay here and fight. You have a way home. I want you to think about this. I have not told Lady Corrinne or my father of my decision. I am going to do that now. If some of you decide to stay, I will be honored to command and lead you. And I will fight at your side whenever the war comes to us."

A few hands went up with questions.

"No more questions for now. Rumor of my decision is already spreading. I need to explain myself to Lady Corrinne and my father. Talk it over among yourselves. I will come back later to answer questions."

Henri left the barracks. The voices of his men in heated debate were loud as he shut the door behind him. He walked quickly to Corrinne's house and knocked on the door. Captain LaTour opened it.

"There you are!"

Corrinne and his father were sitting at the cuisine table, sipping coffee. Corrinne looked upset. His father's face was somber.

"When were you going to tell me?" Corrinne immediately challenged in a bitter tone.

"Today. After I told the governor and got his permission, and after I told my men, which I just finished doing."

"But you told Anamosa!"

"Yes. I told her first. She decided on her own to stay."

"Because of you!" Corrinne accused.

Philippe Gerrard did not challenge him. Henri was a man and a soldier. If he was determined to stay in Louisbourg, that was his decision. But Corrinne deserved a better explanation.

Henri interpreted his father's silence and the serious expression on his face. He responded to Corrinne in a calm, respectful voice. "You cannot force her to go with you."

"Oh yes I can! She is my *ward*! I am not leaving her behind!"

"It is better for Anamosa to stay."

"Here?! She was raped here! She is in danger here!"

"These assassins came here to kill *you*, to kill Marcus and Calypso. Not to kill Anamosa. She just happened to be there. This danger will follow *you*, when you leave here. Like it always has before."

It hurt to hear Henri assert this.

Henri glanced at his father. "I am staying in Louisbourg to fight the English. It is the right thing for me to do."

Corrinne's tone elevated. "Fight the English?! She's a young girl! What will you do with her while you are fighting the English? Leave her alone in this house?!"

"No. I will check on her well-being every day. She will live with Madame Drucour."

"What?!" Corrinne was stunned. "Madame Drucour?! Do not tell me you've asked her to do this!"

"No, I did not ask her. You will ask her. Madame Drucour will do this for you."

Corrinne was not going to dignify this ridiculous presumption. "Don't do this, Henri," she pleaded. "Come to Québec City. You can still protect Anamosa there."

"My contribution to this garrison is valuable. I am needed here."

"You are one man! Don't overthink this."

Henri stared. The condescending words hurt, but he did not show it. *She's upset,* he told himself.

"You've been attacked *three* times! Anamosa is in danger *because* she is with you. You need to worry about Marcus and Calypso. Anamosa almost lost her life to protect them. Keeping Anamosa here with me will protect her more than if she goes with you."

Corrinne could not accept this. "You don't you understand. I cannot leave Anamosa behind!"

"But you are *not* leaving Anamosa behind. You are leaving Anamosa *with me!*"

The truth of this assertion was profound. A silence came over them.

Corrinne felt betrayed. Philippe was not completely in agreement with Henri, but his son was right about one thing. The danger was following Corrinne. And Henri was not going to change his mind. Philippe was not going to try.

"I am going back to the hospital," Henri announced as the painful silence became prolonged.

*

Henri went to tell Anamosa everything that had taken place that day.

"Corrinne has not yet agreed, but she will ask Madame Drucour to take care of you. Madame Drucour will say yes. You will live in the King's Bastion. And you will see me every day. Corrinne is terribly unhappy that you are staying."

"I know," Anamosa replied. "But I do not want to be apart from you again."

"Corrinne is leaving on Captain LaTour's ship tomorrow. Dr. Michaux thinks you will be ready to leave the hospital in another week. If you feel strong enough to walk, we will eat with Corrinne at the house tonight. Then tomorrow morning you can walk beside me to Frédéric Gate to say good-bye, if you feel strong enough."

Anamosa was determined to show everyone she was better. "I am strong enough."

*

Henri went back to his barracks to see how his marines were fairing with his decision. Five of the marines had chosen to stay and join the garrison with him.

Color Sergeant Gosse, formerly of the Guyenne Regiment Grenadiers.

Corporal Luc Chapelle.

Private Nicolas Vallier.

Private Pieter l'Alcyon.

Private Costin Méchins.

And to Henri's surprise, Mkuigen Malsum announced in front of them all that he would join with the garrison marines, too.

Lieutenant Gerrard wasn't sure what to say. "I am…we are honored that you would join with us. But what will my father say?"

"He will probably say words of good luck. Captain Gerrard and I will see each other again. If this is to be the most important battle of this war, I should be remembered for fighting in it."

"Then you've not told him?"

"I will tell him in the morning, when we bid one another farewell."

Henri suddenly recalled Major Péan's words…*This is war. You are an officer. There will be deadly consequences in every decision you make.* Two of his marine brothers had been murdered because of Henri's decision to volunteer to protect Lady VanderMeer. Now five more Québécois marines put themselves at greater risk because of his decision to stay…as did this extraordinary Abenaki warrior, Mkuigen Malsum.

*

Corrinne approached Marie-Louise about caring for Anamosa. Marie could see the teary redness of her friend's eyes.

"Anamosa is as dear to me as anyone else in my life," Corrinne choked out the words.

"Don't worry. I will care for her and love her," Marie promised, in tears herself, "just as you would. Anamosa will live with Augustin and me. We will treat her as if she were our own daughter. I will see her tutoring continues."

Corrinne sniffed and enumerated the practical details. "I have her clothes and baggage ready. Send a carriage or someone around to pick them up."

Marie nodded. "Of course."

"Oh…and this will sound strange. You should know Anamosa often experiences, well, mystical dreams, visons about flying with an owl, or talking to an eagle. Her descriptions are very vivid and beautiful to hear. I will miss hearing them," Corrinne added, nearly bursting into tears again. "It's part of her culture and spiritual beliefs."

"I am privileged to do this for you, Corrinne," Marie replied solemnly. "You honor me with such trust."

"Promise me, Marie! Promise me! If ever this fort is forced to surrender to the English, God forbid, promise me that Augustin will order Henri to take charge of Anamosa's escape. I don't want her captured. I don't want her going to France. Henri must bring her to me in Québec City or Montréal."

"I promise you," Marie said sincerely.

Corrinne winced at the thought of saying good-bye to this dear friend. So she didn't.

"I should go. I have more things to do at the house. I will see you in the morning…at Frédéric Gate when the tide is high."

*

Henri brought Anamosa to the house that evening. Together with his father, Corrinne, the twins, and Captain LaTour, they ate a quiet dinner together. Not much was said. Anamosa was dressed in a hospital chemise and nursing coat. Captain LaTour helped lift their spirits by talking about the sailing route, explaining to Calypso and Marcus they might see some siren mermaids on the way.

"And the sea will probably kiss you," the captain said with a sparkle in his eyes.

"*Kiss?*" Calypso wondered aloud, her eyes as big as tea saucers.

"When you feel the sea spray on your face, that's how the sea kisses you. It means she likes you a lot!"

"*Kisses!*" Marcus giggled.

Henri smiled. He wondered if the look of surprise in the faces of the twins was the same as his own when he was first told of sea kisses.

After dinner, Corrinne took Anamosa upstairs. She had left a dress out of the baggage that was to be sent to the governor's residence for Anna to wear the next day. A long, light yellow one, embroidered with many small colorful flowers. Included were a pair of high-top supple brown shoes and white stockings.

"For tomorrow," Corrinne told her. "I will add your boning knife and scabbard to the satchel."

They sat on the big chair together and gazed at the waning sunset. The lighthouse beam was already piercing the shadows with its comforting light. Anna rested her head on Corrinne's shoulder while she caressed her hair, as she had done so many times before.

"Are you taking this chair with you?" Anamosa asked.

"Maybe. We'll see if there is room in the morning."

"I like sitting in this chair with you."

"Ohh." Corrinne felt another stab of pain to her heart. She hugged Anna closer. "So do I, little love."

"The clock is gone?"

"Yes. It is already aboard the *Queen*. My bathtub, too!" They both fell silent, and then Corrinne said, "You must take good care of Henri for me, Anna. He is very brave, but sometimes…sometimes he is too brave."

Anna lifted her deep blue eyes to Corrinne's. "Don't worry. I will watch over Henri through the eyes of an owl. And the eagle spirit looks after him, too. And he can hear the howl of his wolf spirit, when no one else can hear it."

They talked about the days when they first met and other memories, so such memories would not be forgotten because of absence, time, and distance. When the darkness became complete, they went back downstairs. The men had been entertaining the twins. Corrinne put the shoes, stockings, the dress, and boning knife and scabbard in a small satchel and gave it to Henri to carry for her.

Terribly depressed, Corrinne turned her attention to Captain LaTour. "What time does the tide turn?"

"At twenty-two minutes after the hour of one. We should all be aboard by noon. Shall we meet at Frédéric Gate at the eleventh hour then?"

There was agreement. Everyone said good night. No one wanted to start saying anything even suggestive of good-bye. Not yet. Captain LaTour walked with Henri and Anamosa to the hospital. Once in Anamosa's room, he took out the gold cross with the purple center stone and presented it to her.

"I believe this belongs to you, little love."

Her eyes widened with joy. "I thought it was lost!"

LaTour was pleased she was happy. "What else can I do for you?"

Anna replied without hesitation. "Corrinne wants her chair to go with her, too. The one Victorio made."

LaTour thought that a strange request. "I'll send Victorio to come and get it in the morning."

"Don't tell her I asked you to do this. Let it be a surprise."

*

Corrinne could not fall to sleep. Her mind swirled with *maybes* and *what-ifs* from her subconscious. After checking on the twins, she went over to the chair. The night sky was clear again and full of stars.

Philippe felt a draft of cold air from her absence and got up too. He joined her in the chair, drawing her legs up over his lap and snuggled her into his arms. He could sense her pensiveness. She rested her head on his shoulder, placed a hand on his chest, and watched the lighthouse beam in the darkness. The beam of light had always been there, in good weather or bad, its strong lenses reaching out through the heaviest fog and rain.

All she had wanted since arriving in Louisbourg was to leave this place as soon as she could. Now the last night had come. She doubted she would ever see this lighthouse beam again…and that made her melancholy.

"It's just a lighthouse," she whispered.

"What?" Philippe nuzzled and kissed her ear.

She turned her face to Philippe and they kissed for a long time. Just having her chemise-covered body pressed against him was enough. She felt his hardness react like a spring.

"Well, that didn't take long," she whispered. "We have to be quiet, so we do not to wake the children."

In unhurried movements, she stood. Philippe slipped off his small pants. She lifted the chemise above her waist. He positioned himself in the middle of the chair. She placed her knees to either side of his hips and took hold of him with one hand. They kissed as she lowered herself and their bodies joined. The soft moaning of their intimate embrace echoed back and forth inside their mouths as they muffled the deeper sounds of pleasure.

Corrinne held his shoulders and moved very gently, rolling her hips forward and back almost leisurely. If they allowed the passion to build slowly, the resulting flood of pleasure would be magnified. Philippe covered her breasts with kisses. They paced themselves, feeding off the mutual sounds and intensity of their breathing. Corrinne controlled the peak, pressing down harder with her mons to increase the delicious friction, to accentuate the spiral beginning of her pleasure. Philippe sensed his climax beginning. Like a glowing ember deep inside him, it gathered to a fiery strength. When it burst forth, he buried his face in her breasts and groaned. She ground her mons in a circle to trigger her own climax with his. All they had to do now was hold on to one another. The slightest thrust or rocking movement created uncontrollable convulsions of intimacy, just enough to spur the orgasm still higher. Corrinne pressed her face and lips into his neck and hummed a moan that went on and on.

An equally slow relaxation followed, all breathing and whispers. Philippe pulled her hips closer so the connection would remain. She reached behind her hips and touched him to keep his excitement elevated above that first embrace. So, they would not have to start all over when the urgency returned.

"Oh my God," she whispered. "My blood still swirls around my sex like a river in flood. Just think, soon we can do this every single night!"

"Where did you get this chair?" Philippe asked in quiet amazement.

"I designed it," she whispered proudly. "Just for this purpose. Do you like it? Victorio built it for me."

"We must take this with us."

"Mama!" It was Marcus' voice. "Water."

"Coming, baby," Corrinne replied. "Oh well…we have to go back to bed," she told him. "They will get in between us now. No stopping them."

*

The cuisine was filled with the happy noise of children and the smells of cooking food when there was a knock at the door. Philippe opened the viewing window and saw Victorio's smiling face. He opened the door. Stefan was with him and they had a cargo wagon.

"We're here for the chair and anything else you want to send with us. The baggage, too?"

"My chair?" Corrine asked with surprise.

"Captain LaTour told us to fetch it."

"I did not ask him to do that…"

They came in, went upstairs, and a few minutes later were tilting and maneuvering the bulky shape out the front door.

"What a surprise!" she said. "It's like he read our minds." After a pause of a few seconds, she said, "Wait! A surprise. I'd completely forgotten amid all the other turmoil."

Victorio came back in. "Anything else?"

She pointed at a few trunks. "And Captain LaTour told me two weeks ago he had a surprise for me. That I had to wait until I came aboard. Has he said anything to you about what it is?"

"I think so," Victorio answered vaguely. "Something about a gift from the crew…"

"Yes! He said that exactly."

"I'm sure you will get it when you are aboard. Captain Gerrard, will Monsieur Malsum stay in a cabin or with the crew?"

"I think he'd prefer a cabin," Philippe answered in careful words. "I expect the crew would prefer Malsum stay inside a cabin, too. Yes?"

Victorio nodded with certainty. "And it will be interesting."

*

They walked down to Frédéric Gate early, getting there before eleven. Philippe carried three large satchels full of children's clothes. When they reached the head of the gate, other citizens of the faubourg had gathered to say good-bye. Corrinne stood among them with the twins, answering questions. Her friends brought send-off gifts for the children: a necklace and hair barrettes for Calypso, a miniature pistol carved out of wood for Marcus. Philippe turned over the last of the bags to the crewmen sent ashore to assist them.

Color Sergeant Gosse arrived, leading his marines in a marching column of twos, muskets slung over their shoulders, some of them carrying baggage. Malsum followed a few steps behind the column. The people of the faubourg moved aside to let them pass, saying words of praise to the men.

"Good luck to you, boys. Godspeed."

Marcus saluted.

"Present...arms!" Color Sergeant Gosse shouted in response to Marcus' salute. The muskets were unslung and rattled to the present-arms position.

Marcus laughed with glee. Gosse ordered the marines to attention and dismissed them from formation. Gosse and four marines stood idly by. The other four picked up their bags. They joked and said good-bye to their brothers and went down to the ten-passenger harbor launch supplied by one of the warships by order of Commodore du Bauffremont. This larger launch would be used to take the entire party out to Captain LaTour's ship.

Philippe noticed LaTour's ship was flying its Dutch tri-color flag. To prolong the illusion, he surmised. Just as he thought that, Captain LaTour stepped off the *Queen*'s cargo launch as it bumped against the loading dock.

"*Bonjour*," Henri called from the other direction. Anamosa had her hand hooked in his left arm.

Anna looked radiant in that yellow dress with the embroidered flowers. She beamed with the biggest smile Corrine had ever seen on the girl.

Arriving in a carriage coming down Rue Toulouse was Governor Augustin and Marie-Louise de Drucour. Colonel du Bourzt marched up behind the governor's carriage leading a full platoon of his grenadiers.

The convergence of people provoked the conversation none of them looked forward to having.

Henri announced to his father that Color Sergeant Gosse and four marines had decided, like him, to remain with the garrison. Malsum stepped forward next.

Corrinne looked at this big warrior with the fearsome death face. She embraced and kissed both his cheeks. "Monsieur Malsum, thank you for protecting Philippe. I feel much safer with your presence," she said.

"*Merci*, my lady. But I hardly protect Captain Gerrard. He does not need it. And I have chosen to remain with Lieutenant Gerrard and the Québécois marines in the Louisbourg garrison."

His French is perfect, Corrinne thought.

Philippe and Malsum had a short but polite discussion about his decision.

"As I told Lieutenant Gerrard. If Louisbourg is to be the most important battle of this war, Panther Claw should be remembered for fighting in it alongside his French friends."

Philippe was surprised and impressed. "General Montcalm will be disappointed to hear this. But I wish you good fortune and good luck." They embraced. "I will wait for you in the west."

Unexpectedly, Malsum turned to Corrinne again. "My lady, not to be alarming, but I inherited a gift of sight, from my mother. Captain Gerrard knows this story. He can explain it to you sometime. But seeing you now, and the brightness of your spirit, I also perceive there is something dark pursuing you. I will recognize it if ever it stands before me. And should I have this opportunity, I intend to slay it and take its face."

Corrinne was wide-eyed. The warrior's voice was emotionless. He said this with such conviction, she did not know how to reply.

"Malsum means what he says," Philippe added. "And he means no disrespect."

The governor and his wife were shocked and confused. Henri, Anamosa, and Captain LaTour were also startled by the Abenaki's ominous words. But they understood the import of *something dark*.

Corrine handed the twins over to Philippe. She took hold of Malsum's hands and spoke in a low, serious tone. "I am honored…*honored* by your generous offer, Monsieur Malsum. And if it is possible, please make this dark thing *suffer* before it dies."

Everyone standing within earshot was startled further at the vehemence in Corrinne's voice.

Malsum was not done. He gently lifted Lady Corrinne's hands, touched his lips briefly to her fingers, and replied as a knight would an order from his queen, "As you command, my lady."

Awkward silence ensued.

How does anyone follow that? Governor Drucour asked himself.

"Well, this conversation has been...very reassuring," the governor interjected. He was happy to promote some civil discourse into this event. "Lady VanderMeer," he said loudly. "Scout Captain Gerrard. Marie and I would like to bid you both farewell and safe journey."

"Thank you, Governor," Corrinne answered for the crowd to hear. "Thank you for providing me a haven as requested by the Dutch Republic...and more importantly, for your cherished friendship."

With great reluctance, Corrinne turned to Anamosa. She took her aside to talk with her more privately. "Listen to me, precious. Never forget that Henri loves you. He loved you from the moment he saw you at Fort Niagara. Remember that. Even if another woman comes into his life. No matter what happens in the future, Henri loves you above all others! And you must help him, too. He is too much like his father. He is reckless and takes chances that threaten his life. You must remind him of your love."

They both tried hard not to sob, but it was not possible. Corrinne hugged and rocked the girl in her arms.

"Oh, little love. I worry I will never see you again. I love you so."

"You will see me again," Anamosa sniffed and replied calmly. "And you will see Henri, too. I promise."

"We should board," Captain LaTour said.

Corrinne frowned. She hugged Henri and looked him closely in the face.

"You. Take. Care. Of. Anamosa!"

"I will."

"And take care of yourself."

"I will."

Corrinne pressed a small sack of coinage into Henri's hand. It was heavy.

"What's this?" Henri asked.

"You know what it is," Corrinne replied. "Anamosa may need things. Shoes, clothing. And you should buy her presents from time to time. Do this for me, Henri. Keep her smiling. Don't frown at me. Just accept this like a gentleman and use it wisely. And when the fighting starts, don't do impulsive things. You have Anamosa to worry about now."

"I will miss you too," Henri replied with a smile.

They hugged each other tightly again.

"All right. That's enough." Corrinne turned one last time to the crowd of people and waved farewell.

"*Adieu, mon amies. Adieu.*"

She accepted Calypso from Philippe and walked down the stone steps to the naval launch waiting alongside the dock. The waiting sailors assisted her into the boat and to a seat. When everyone was aboard, they pushed off. Six rowers easily maneuvered the boat towards the *Queen*.

Everyone was surprised when Lieutenant Colonel du Bourzt's grenadiers fired a musket salute in the air. Marcus whooped at the sound and smoke. Corrinne continued to wave with one hand as the distance to the dock widened. By the time they reached the ship, the people by the gate were hard to identify.

All except for Henri and Anamosa, standing alone together, to one side. They looked out towards the ship with an arm raised in farewell until they saw Corrinne step onto the *Queen*'s helm deck.

The next time Corrinne looked back, they were gone. She winced in pain.

CHAPTER 27
LOUISBOURG
MAY 1757
I Have Missed You

The crew of *William's Queen* was ready to weigh anchor and make sail. But for now, they were lined across deck in two rows, waiting for Lady Corrinne. She greeted them each with affection, by name, and spoke as if it had only been yesterday when she saw them last. She asked about La Rochelle and their families. She introduced each man as her "very good friend" to Calypso, who smiled and began her enchantment of them all. Marcus watched with puzzlement from Philippe's arms. He was more interested in the nearby warships and the big cannons. When the greetings were complete, Corrinne stepped back and spoke to them collectively, telling them how brave and wonderful they were to make the dangerous crossing just to come back for her.

"I've long considered you as adventurous heroes in my heart. Now I am certain of it."

At the captain's signal, one of the crew stepped forward. It was Knute, the seaman renowned for his mastery of lines, knots, and the intricate creations of beauty he made from them. The crew had drawn to see who would present the wax-sealed missive from Madame Margaux-Lyneth Dubonnet. Knute had won. He first presented his newest creation to Calypso. He'd made it completely from a single strand of white sailor-twine, thirty-six feet in length. It was a necklace, an intricate design that laid upon the chest like a crescent-shaped doily. It was a pattern of repeated designs, a dozen different sizes and shapes, four rows of them in all.

"Twelve different snowflakes, but in different sizes," Knute explained. He presented it as a gift to Calypso. The little girl's mouth opened with wonder, even at her young age, she recognized it as something very special. Callie took it carefully into her hands.

"Pretty," she said.

Knute smiled and addressed Lady Corrinne. "And we brought you this."

It was a very large wax-sealed missive. It was much heavier than a normal letter and wrapped with sketching paper, so the interior sheets would not be folded. Corrinne's name, written on the front, was inked in a florid calligraphic script, the kind a person might see in old historical texts.

Corrinne wondered who would write to her in this baroque fashion. Perhaps it was becoming popular. She glanced at Philippe, who shrugged. And at Captain LaTour, who smiled and nodded towards the missive.

"So, this is my surprise?"

Maybe it's from Charles? Her heart beat faster with this thought. But for what purpose? The calligraphy? To draw my attention this was something special? Maybe I should not open it right now?

"The writing is beautiful. Thank you, Knute."

"Do you want to know who it is from?"

Knute was never very talkative. He was not known for speaking in sentences longer than four words. This statement was nine words long and had ended as a cryptic question—a veritable speech for him.

Corrinne smiled. "Well, of course, I do. Do you know who wrote it?"

"Yes! Madame Margaux-Lyneth Dubonnet!" Knute announced the name as if it were royalty. He had practiced saying it for hours.

"Margaux-Lyneth Dubonnet? And who is Madame Margaux-Lyneth Dubonnet?"

"She is your *sister!*" Knute said it loudly and proudly.

"My sister? B-but I don't have a sister…" Corrinne was momentarily confused. *Margaux.* The name surged forth from her earliest memories. She was staggered and spoke softly. "*Mon Dieu!*" Her hand trembled so hard she almost dropped the missive.

Captain LaTour and Philippe moved to either side of her. Philippe accepted Calypso in his other arm and LaTour took the missive from her, so she would not drop it.

Corrinne stared blankly, unable to speak.

The crew wondered if they'd done something wrong.

Victorio noticed signal flags being raised on *La Comète,* the thirty-two-gun frigate that was to be their escort. He went up behind the captain and talked into his ear. "Captain, *La Comète* is signaling us to weigh anchor."

LaTour nodded. He addressed the crew.

"We all appreciate how overwhelming this is for Lady Corrinne to learn for the first time she has a sister. Let's permit Lady Corrinne to go below and give her time to absorb this wonderful news. I am sure she will be thanking all of you personally. We've just received a signal from *La Comète* to weigh anchor. Prepare to sail!"

With Captain LaTour going first, carrying Calypso, a bewildered and speechless Corrinne followed next. Philippe followed last, carrying Marcus. They went straight to the dining cabin. Pierrik, the steward, had set the table with a wide variety of cakes, pastries, and sweet biscuits, plus hot tea and coffee, wine, and a pitcher of cold water mixed with freshly picked seasonal berries to make a delicious drink for the children. Marcus and Calypso were giggling, their mouths circled with powdered sugar within minutes.

The ship rolled gently as the anchor was heaved up.

"Please excuse me," Captain LaTour announced. "I am needed on deck."

Corrinne was still not talking.

Philippe touched her hand. "Are you all right?"

She licked her lips and nodded. "Yes."

Philippe slid the missive in front of her. "Then you should read this, I think." He gestured to the steward to pour them cups of coffee.

Her heart pounding with anticipation, Corrinne carefully broke the wax seal. She noticed it was impressed with a military insignia, a regiment of some sort, *Auvergne*.

Just that little bit of knowledge caused her stunned brain to start turning. She took a sip of coffee.

"Captain LaTour had this for weeks and didn't tell me?" she murmured. "Why would he do that?"

"I don't know," Philippe replied. "Maybe because of the attack…and the aftermath. He will explain why. I'm sure his reasons will be sincere."

Pierrik set a linen napkin next to Corrinne's coffee mug. She would use it shortly to dry her tears. Corrinne sipped her coffee and started reading.

> *Dearest Corrinne,*
>
> *Hello, my love. My other half. My long-lost heart and soul. I was consumed with joy to learn you existed several months ago. Memories of you lay dormant in me. Then I saw your portrait painted by your husband, Charles. To learn you were alive and I could write to you is a miracle. If you are reading this for the first time, you are feeling what I felt, the moment I saw your face. Random memories sprang to life instantly.*

Philippe watched Corrinne's expression change through every emotion, as she read page after page of Madame Dubonnet's letter. Like the weather, a few passing storms, separated by periods of sunlight, followed by an occasional rainbow, and accompanied by sounds of muted laughter, tears of anguish, smiles of happiness. All Philippe knew was the letter came from a sister Corrinne was unaware of until that morning.

Corrinne paused, she looked up, but her stare remained unfocused. Philippe decided to chance a question.

"So, you do remember her name...Margaux?"

"Yes. I remember her name. Margaux-Lyneth. She was...is my twin."

"Twin!?"

Corrinne did not respond to his surprise and continued reading.

Twins? Philippe tried to conceive the import of *two* Corrinnes in the world.

Soon the ship's speed increased. They heard water rushing and splashing down the sides. They were in full sail. There came a muffled cannon boom from the Island Battery, guarding the harbor entrance, to salute the ship's passage. The *Queen* leaned gently as it began its turn to the north.

They had left Louisbourg.

Brest, France

Margaux-Lyneth Dubonnet walked down to the ship design building on the La Penfeld riverfront. Marcel followed five steps behind her. Her father had taken to his bed because of his *tumeur*. He was in pain and had almost stopped eating, as Dr. Legrande predicted. So, she carried messages back and forth to René Hilaire, Lucais' primary design assistant. Her father would answer the questions for her to deliver back to Hilaire, or referred her to one of the decade's worth of design journals on the shelf in his office library. Either way, Margaux began to understand her father's functional role in the designing of these warships as more of an organizer of when certain design commitments were completed to support the actual building requirement. After a week of back and forth, she anticipated and made the decisions her father might make. But she never admitted this to René Hilaire, who mentioned he was pleased with the speed of her father's participation now that he was managing from his bed. Margaux wanted no credit for this, just that the business continued as planned...until the inevitable occurred.

That morning she was present to see a new seventy-four-gun ship-of-the-line, *Minotaure*, slide down its construction ways and into the river. Saluting cannons boomed. It would be another month while it was outfitted with its cannons, white sails and rigging, plus captain and crew, before it went to sea. But it was an inspirational moment of French pride to see it float gracefully on the river. The long mooring lines attached to its port side were tightened using manual capstans on the riverbank to bring the ship snugly to a finishing dock. The *seventy-fours*, as her father referred to them with affection, were the premier warships of the French navy. But two new eighty-gun versions were on the shipways. Lucais de Clermont made it known he was against adding the extra cannons and offered his opinion, sketches with engineering calculations, to the French navy, stating, "The extra guns offer no tactical advantage in battle, just extra weight, lower speed, and a weather imbalance above the center of mass." That did not stop the admirals, however. On both sides of the English-channel, senior naval officers in France and England demanded more and more cannons of even greater caliber added to the hulls, attaining one-hundred and twenty-gun behemoths within another ten years.

When Margaux returned to the house, she told Róbert and Marcel she wanted to go riding.

"I want to do something different. I helped launch a powerful warship for France today. I like to think it would not have happened ahead of schedule if I had not made some timely decisions for my father. I deserve a reward, yes?"

Róbert and Marcel smiled in agreement. "You'll get no argument from us, Madame. How would you like your horse saddled?"

"I will ride astride, with a dress specially made for this. Gustave only permits me wear something so immodest, or scandalous as he labels it, when we visit his family vineyards in Amiens. Evidently, his *crétin* relatives drink so much wine they mistake me for a man."

"Um…with respect Madame, I think it would take an extraordinary amount of wine not to appreciate your femininity," Marcel replied. "Then we will meet you out at the stables in an hour?"

"An hour is perfect. And I want to go exploring outside the walls…to the northeast, as you did Róbert. Maybe we can visit those mercenaries again. It they are bound for Louisbourg, as my father confirmed, I intend to send my sister a letter of warning. I need to know more about them. The regiment's name, their numbers, the nationality, and their commander's name."

Brest

William LaFont's coach horses were spent, panting heavily, their sides covered in a lathery sweat as the military overland coach approached the northeast gate of the fortress port of Brest. He was also exhausted after having traveled several hundreds of miles in pursuit of the natal lineage of Margaux-Lyneth Dubonnet and her twin sister, Corrinne de Chanaye. He had it all written down in two journals he'd kept. One was a detailed collection of his raw notes, his theories, conclusions, questions, clues, and chance discoveries. The second journal was a polished editing, a concise summary of the first one. Something he could present and leave with Madame Dubonnet. He'd traveled nearly a thousand miles by his estimate, crisscrossing France, visiting multiple cities and villages. Mostly by horse, as it was faster that way. On the longer destination legs, he traveled by overland coach. He had a good story to tell, but it was far from complete.

To complete this history, William LaFont must leave France and travel to Wales. Difficult to do with France and England engaged in war. He needed the guidance and help from his employer and benefactor, Madame Margaux Dubonnet. But when he plodded into Amiens on a very tired horse and went to her residence, he was depressed to learn she was not there. The chamberlain gave him instructions to go to Brest, that he would find Madame at her father's home.

"Madame is waiting for you there."

William LaFont purified himself and rested overnight at the residence. The chamberlain had a new pouch of coinage to give him too. *She thinks of everything.* The next morning, he secured transport on the daily military coach leaving for Paris and carrying dispatches. In Paris, he would obtain passage on another military coach destined for Brest, this one filled with senior army and navy officers. They brought wine with them and were boisterous. He tried to sleep.

The coach passed through the northeast gate and traveled along the La Penfeld River road in its eastern faubourg, arriving at the military headquarters. He knew this city from his previous visit to interview Madame Dubonnet's father. It did not take long to learn Lucais de Clermont's memories of his daughter's adoption. There were not very many. Most of the detailed facts were lost with the death of Margaux's mother. But it gave him enough information to travel further to Landerneau.

He found transport on a local carriage and went across the drawbridge to the western faubourg and on to the house of Chevalier Lucais de Clermont. He was met at the door by the chamberlain, Marshall Debarge, who encouraged his entry with a smile.

"Welcome Monsieur LaFont! Madame Dubonnet will be so pleased you have returned. Madame is not at home, but she will be back later. Please follow me. We have a room prepared for you. I will send the maidservants with hot water for your bath. Just make any request of them you like related to your comfort, food, clothing, and they will see to it."

For the next hour, William LaFont luxuriated in his bath and afterwards he dressed in the clean clothes they provided. Most everything else in his baggage was taken away for a thorough cleaning. He declined to eat, deciding instead to wait until Madame Dubonnet returned. He took a seat at the small writing desk and reviewed his notes, knowing Margaux would have many questions.

*

Margaux Dubonnet sat patiently on her horse while Róbert had another testy interaction with the sentry. When the mercenary sergeant said something threatening, she moved her horse forward, and introduced herself in an officious tone of voice.

"I am Madame Margaux-Lyneth Dubonnet, daughter of Chevalier Lucais de Clermont, chief designer for the naval shipyard of Brest. What is your name, Sergeant?" Silence. "So, you refuse to tell me your name? Very well. I will have the military adjutant to Admiral de la Motte informed of your insubordination. Your regimental commander will be called to the admiral's offices to explain your behavior."

The sergeant of the guard's expression turned sullen. "Sergeant Hegler," he offered tersely.

"What is the name of your commander, Sergeant Hegler?"

"Lieutenant-Colonel Karl Krieger, of the 1st Battalion Volontaires-Étrangers Regiment."

"Good. That was not too difficult, was it, Sergeant? I would like to speak with Colonel Krieger."

"Colonel Krieger is away from the encampment. I will provide a message to him that you visited…once he returns."

During this discussion three other sentries appeared and joined with the two already standing to either side of Sergeant Hegler.

It was now an impasse.

Margaux Dubonnet decided there was little more to learn, and she was tired of being insulted. She turned her horse and spurred its gait. Róbert and Marcel followed. She went back through the gate, slowed, and walked along the eastern river road of La Penfeld River. The day was beautiful, but the rudeness of the mercenary sergeant had ruined her mood. That and the foul odors that occasionally fumed up from the river made her reluctant to explore further east in the faubourg. She decided to cross over the great river drawbridge.

"We could go to the outdoor café in the market," Marcel suggested.

"Thank you, Marcel, but no. I am still vexed by the attitude of that sergeant. And my stylish rump is aching," she added with a smile. "It's been a long time since I rode astride a horse. Let's go back to the house."

When she entered the house through the backdoor leading up from the stables, the chamberlain met her with good news.

"Monsieur LaFont arrived a few hours ago!"

"He did? That is wonderful! Where is he?"

"He is in a guest room."

"Good. Show him to the office while I purify my appearance. Róbert, Marcel, please join Monsieur LaFont in the office. I want you to share in what he will be telling me. This is so exciting!"

After William LaFont was escorted to the office, he was confronted by two large, stern-looking men, armed with swords and shoulder pistols. They introduced themselves and seemed friendly enough. They continued to ask him several questions, also in a friendly manner, but LaFont could tell they were assessing him. Fortunately, Madame Dubonnet swept into the office and embraced the young scholar.

"It is so good to see you, William! I can hardly wait to hear what you have learned! Everyone sit. Marshall, please bring us some refreshments. You look tired, William."

"I confess that I am. It's been many long days jostled on a saddle or bouncing around inside of coaches. But I have learned quite a lot. And I've penned a summary for you to read." He presented the custom journal to her. "My research is incomplete, however, as I will relate to you."

"Then begin at once," she said with enthusiasm.

It would be a captivating discussion, with William LaFont doing most of the talking while the others in the room remained gripped by his exciting presentation style. He made this personal history sound important, tragic, romantic, and even heroic at certain points. The story began with his first interview with Lucais de Clermont.

"You father provided me with very little recall, other than the name of the Cistercian Abbey in Landerneau. I went to Landerneau. This congregation also supported the convent with its adjoining orphanage, which, as you know, burned down in 1727. There was very little that was not burned to ashes in this fire. The entire abbey was a complete ruin. And after thirty years, much of that was washed away, absorbed into the earth, or scattered by the wind. Very few records remained and the ones that did were not useful to my examination.

"However, I was directed to an elderly sister from this convent, a Sister Angelina. She was being cared for in the new church they built. This old woman was reputed to be eighty-three years of age. Angelina might not be her given name. And she could not recall her surname, or what day of the week it was, or what year it was, but anything to do with her younger years prior to the fire, those memories were vivid and intact as if it had all happened yesterday. She could recall *everything.* I spent several days talking with her, asking her the same questions over and over, just to be sure of what she claimed. She enjoyed every moment of sharing her memories with me. She was delighted and proud to hear about your success in life, Madame. She said to say she loved you from the moment you and your sister were born. I hope you don't mind that I shared details of your personal life with her."

"Not at all, William." Sister Angelina's words warmed Margaux's heart. She only wished she'd known about her sooner.

"I've made many notes of what she said in my journal. She recalled details about your mother from the day she arrived in Landerneau until the day you were born. Your mother's name was Seirian l'Aigle. *Seirian* is a Welsh name. *L'Aigle* is French. There is even a town by that name eighty miles west of Paris in the Normandie lands. But your mother did not come from l'Aigle. She was from Wales. Her native tongue was Welsh, but she also spoke some French and English. She came to the Landerneau convent to give birth. *Because I dare not give birth in Wales.* According to Sister Angelina, those were Seirian's exact words."

William paused. It was an emotional moment for Margaux. A tear dripped down her cheek.

"*Seirian*," she repeated reverently. "My mother's name was Seirian l'Aigle." As far as Margaux was concerned, that singular piece of information alone was worth all of William LaFont's expenses for what he had accomplished so far. And he was just getting started. "Please continue."

"Sister Angelina did not know what provoked your mother to flee from Wales to give birth. She did not know from what port in Wales she departed. However, the reason your mother came to this specific nunnery, in Landerneau, was because Seirian had a sister who had taken vows in this nunnery years earlier. Her name was Carys…Sister Carys."

William paused again.

"Sister Carys," Margaux repeated. "She would be my aunt…Corrinne's aunt, too! Is Sister Carys still alive?"

"Sister Angelina did not know. But I learned much more about her. Twins were a welcome surprise and celebrated by everyone in the convent." William looked at his notes. "*Beautiful they were to behold. Blond hair and green eyes. Blessed by God.* Those were Angelina's words. She said more. *Their eyes were already open, and they stared at everyone and everything that moved near to them.* This next part is difficult. According to Sister Angelina, your mother hemorrhaged after you and Corrinne were born. Seirian had lost too much blood giving birth. She weakened and passed on. But not before giving her babies names. Margaux-Lyneth and Corrinne-Eirian. She said you both slept with your arms around one another."

Margaux's voice, choked with emotion, pronounced the name with reverence. "*Corrinne-Eirian.* I doubt my sister Corrinne knows her middle name."

"After the fire, there was chaos. You became separated in the confusion. There was very little food. The weather was bad. A lot of cold rain. The survivors were scattered. Some given shelter in smaller churches and spread out across the countryside. The children were destitute, half of them infants. A call went out from Landerneau, begging families to adopt the orphans. Sister Angelina remembered your mother and father coming to adopt you. But they only wanted one child. Sister Angelina searched frantically for Corrinne, hoping to convince your parents to take you both, but did not find her in time."

William could see the effect that troubling information had on Madame Dubonnet. "Shall I continue?"

"Yes."

"According to an elderly priest of the abbey, who also still lives in Landerneau, a week following the fire, a group of six sisters, using two donated farm wagons, left the town with eleven children of various ages, some of them infants. Their goal was to go east to find another Cistercian Abbey that would give them shelter and permanent succor. I learned the locations of the abbeys in that direction and went to them, starting with the nearest. I found nothing in the first four. In the fifth one, Pontigny Abbey, southeast of Paris, in the city of Pontigny on the River Serein, they had a record of the six sisters arriving from Landerneau in May of 1728. But there were only eight children. Somewhere along the way, three of the children had disappeared. I prayed they were adopted, as no names were recorded. I assumed your sister, Corrinne, was among those that arrived safely, because she is still alive today, yes? There was another entry that three of these Landerneau sisters departed again with only three children the same year, 1728, no month recorded, but their intended destination was Saint-Vincent Abbey in Mâcon. That was a hundred forty miles south of Pontigny. Why that abbey? I do not know. It was larger. That might be the reason. I was at the end of this trail, so I followed that possibility. And good fortune awaited me. There was a record of three sisters arriving from Pontigny in July of 1728 with three children. There was another entry, *No room in the abbey for anyone other than for monks.* However, it said, *the sisters were given monies to establish a small orphan convent on Rue de la Chanaye in Mâcon.*"

Margaux reacted instantly. "Chanaye!?"

"Yes, Madame! Chanaye! That's exactly what I thought. That was the first time I saw that name. I went to the street, Rue de la Chanaye, and found no evidence of an orphanage or a convent on either side of that street. Of course, that was almost thirty years ago. A lot can happen in thirty years. After three days of knocking on doors and asking residents, I found a woman who remembered the convent. She said it was very poor and eventually ran out of donations. She recalled that was in 1729, the same year her husband had died. A rumor, she recalled, was that the sisters left to take the children to a large Cistercian orphanage in Paris. Without a name to go on, I went back to Saint-Vincent and learned the names of every Cistercian congregation between Mâcon and Paris. Then I got on my horse and stopped at each one.

There were nine of them. I thought they might give these sisters and children a place to sleep, if only for a night, but if they did, not one of them made any record of their passage. When I reached the southern edge of Paris, I tried the last Cistercian name on the list. And by God's grace, low and behold, there was an entry, not for three holy sisters, but a solitary woman. Her name was Carys Chanaye. She had a two-year-old daughter with her. The little girl's name was Corrinne. There were several sisters in this convent who still remembered Corrinne Chanaye's arrival, and described her beauty to me, which was already apparent, even at her young age. What they described to me was your features exactly, Madame."

With that revelation, Margaux-Lyneth broke down sobbing. The burly veteran sergeants and the scholar in her employment all wanted to console Madame Dubonnet, but went only so far as to stand near her and offer words of comfort. Hearing her sobs, Marshall DeBarge, the chamberlain, entered the office, and seeing Margaux's distress, knelt by her chair and took her into his arms as would a father. The chamberlain spoke soft words, which he had evidently used many times before, in a way that brought the heavy sobbing under control.

When her sobbing subsided, William LaFont added something more to help her recover.

"Madame, when I heard these sisters describe Corrinne, I realized that my journey and what I had learned might be the most important work of scholarship I had ever undertaken in my life. And it is not over."

"Thank you, William." Margaux stood and excused herself for a time.

"Let us take a walk outside, William," said Marcel after she was gone.

They went into the garden between the house and the stables and took seats on some rusted chairs among the flowers.

"That is quite a story," Róbert complimented him. "I am amazed you learned so much. You were very determined."

William nodded his thanks. "I am a Latin scholar. Don't ask me why, but most of my time is spent searching through old Latin tomes that sit decaying in libraries for centuries, creating dust that clogs my nose. At least doing this search for Madame Dubonnet, I was talking to real people with real memories. These people were so excited they might help me. The lady in Mâcon that recalled the three sisters who went north to Paris? She believed she had validated her entire life by telling me this. That somehow, this was her purpose. To help me find this long-lost sister." William shrugged. "Who knows? But I like to think there is truth in her assertion."

The backdoor opened. "Madame awaits you in the office," the chamberlain announced.

They went back and took their seats again.

"Thank you, William," Margaux greeted them. "I am much recovered now. Please continue."

"Um…here…Carys Chanaye identified herself as a maidservant of a French nobleman in Paris. She did not admit to his name. But asserted Corrinne was this nobleman's bastard daughter. The sisters told me this was not an uncommon occurrence in Paris. They accepted Corrinne Chanaye into their care. There are more records at this orphanage, particularly entries in a journal kept by an abbot who apparently took a personal interest in Corrinne's education. He writes of her in his journal, that he believed her to be a genius. I read through it. There were *years* of entries about Corrinne made by the abbot. They would not release the journal to me. But I think it is worthwhile for you and your sister to read it someday. Unfortunately, the abbot died. There is an entry Corrinne Chanaye leaves the orphanage at the age of thirteen. To where? No entry. She just disappears. All the possible suggestions given to me by those sisters turned up false. But, I thought, she is married to Lord VanderMeer. Madame, you told me Lord and Lady VanderMeer were married in the Rouen Cathedral?"

"You went to Rouen!"

"Yes. I had no other trail to follow. I thought I might learn more about Lady Corrinne's origin if the marriage was recorded in the Rouen Cathedral. There are indeed documents of marriage certified by the Archbishop of Rouen, Nicolas II de Saulx-Tavannes who is also deceased. There is no record of Corrinne de Chanaye's place of origin, except a carefully appended notation to the marriage record that she was from somewhere in Belgium."

William LaFont decided to stop here. He had learned more than that. He had located another document, not included with the marriage certificate, indicating Corrinne de Chanaye was recorded as the bastard daughter of Pascal Nicolet of Paris, also deceased, brother of Archbishop André Nicolet of Québec City, recently deceased, by murder. Both records were vaulted in the same library of the Rouen Cathedral, yet filed separately. Not difficult to find for a scholar more used to paging through the dusty shelves of decayed books, piles of flaking parchments, and the worm-eaten remnants of ancient

Latin texts. But examining the marriage certificate and the random document of her connection to Pascal Nicolet, side by side, William LaFont's trained eye discerned these documents to be identical, written at the same time, cut from the same ream of paper, easily related by natural and identical watermarks.

Forgeries, or at least fictions crafted at the same time, he'd concluded. Corrinne de Chanaye was established by the Church as a commoner from Belgium.

William LaFont did not try to solve this mystery. His instincts told him this was done more recently and intentionally. But why? He was averse to presenting that information and his speculation to Madame Dubonnet. Not without knowing why. In any case, the answers to that question were immaterial to the history of the birth of Margaux-Lyneth and Corrinne-Eirian.

Margaux was perplexed. "Somewhere in Belgium? Her years after Paris were spent in Belgium?"

"Madame, I don't know. Since all trace of her whereabouts since the age of thirteen have vanished until her marriage. I will presume, or conjecture, that Lord VanderMeer may have wanted to present his wife as Belgian and not French, for reasons only Lady Corrinne can tell you, that is if my conjecture has any veracity."

He waited for Madame Dubonnet to say something.

"What you have done for me is remarkable, William. You said your research is not over?"

"That is true. There is more to learn about your birth story, but that history lies in Wales. I have questions to answer concerning your French surname's origin. Who were your grandparents? How did Seirian l'Aigle come to be from Wales? Where did she live? What was the name of your *father*? And why did Seirian come to Brittany to give birth? Why did she say she dared not give birth in Wales? To learn the answers to these questions, I must go to Wales. And because of the war, that is not possible."

Margaux did not like people to characterize things she wanted as not possible.

"How natural is your English?"

"I spent two years studying Latin at Cambridge when I was fourteen and fifteen," he replied in English. "I could speak English fairly well before I went there. But speaking it every day has softened my French accent...I trust."

"It sounds almost perfect to me. Do you speak Dutch?"

"I do. I can converse. It is not as good as English," he answered in Dutch.

"If I offer you the means to go to England, safely, more importantly to Wales, do you want to go?"

William LaFont straightened in his chair. He was very interested. "I've never been to Wales."

"Good. I know of a safe arrangement."

The chamberlain interrupted them. "Madame, there is a German officer waiting in the foyer. His name is Lieutenant-Colonel Karl Krieger. He claims you wanted to see him."

Marcel and Róbert stood up as if to form battle ranks.

"Well, this should be interesting. Follow me, gentlemen."

They walked into the hallway leading to the front door. When Madame Dubonnet stopped short of the visitor by five paces, Marcel and Róbert positioned themselves in front of her, a pace further and to either side. William LaFont stayed a pace behind her to the right, observing the meeting with curiosity.

Margaux-Lyneth Dubonnet had never seen such a menacing glare before, although the man's features held no expression. He had large, dull, black eyes. *Spider eyes*, she thought with a chill.

The chamberlain continued to the door behind the visitor and stood with his hand on the handle, ready to open it when gestured to do so by Madame Dubonnet. To either side of the door, there were three-foot-tall decorative Chinese vases covered in a dark blue lacquer, with red kanji symbols painted vertically on the outside. One of them held a silver knobbed walking stick that Lucais de Clermont used on occasion. The chamberlain knew the walking stick disguised a rapier blade. He could draw it in an instant if necessary.

"Madame Dubonnet. My guards informed me you were upset I did not receive you when you visited. I thought I would save you the trouble of coming back to my encampment. How might I help you?"

His voice had an edge of disgust she found offensive.

"I wanted to learn if you are scheduled for transport to Louisbourg on Île Royale?"

Not only does she look like the whore queen, she has the same voice, he thought. The vulnax surged to dominance.

"*It is remarkable. We have met before, Maeve. I have missed you.*"

Maeve? Madame Dubonnet was puzzled by the enigmatic words. The man's voice had changed to a rasping sound. And the way he said *I have missed you?* It was evil and suggestive.

The chamberlain reacted without being told. He opened the door wide and yanked the rapier from its walking-stick scabbard.

"Your tone offends me. Leave my house," Margaux demanded.

"*As you wish. But we will meet again.*"

He turned his back, walked out the door, and down the stone steps. A mercenary corporal waited at the bottom of the steps on the street, holding the reins of two saddled horses.

"He threatened you, Madame," Marcel asserted, expecting a further command.

Both Marcel and Róbert looked for a signal to defend her honor. Knowing her protectors would kill the colonel or worse, get hurt trying, she shook her head.

"No. Do not accost him. Not now. Not here. Like he said, we will meet again. For now, I want to know everything we can find out about him. Go to the military headquarters and make inquiries in my father's name."

Róbert and Marcel left to do her bidding.

"What now, Madame?"

"What now, indeed, William. Are you ready for another journey into my history?"

"To Wales?"

"Eventually, Wales. But first to Amsterdam. I will ink a letter of introduction to a confidante of Louis Ernest, Duke of Brunswick-Wolfenbüttel. His name is Colonel Rutger van Boekel. He will provide you identity papers as a Dutch Ambassador to England and help you craft a legitimate reason to go to Wales. I'm not certain where you should go in Wales. But rest here a few days. We will find some maps of Wales, and together, identify a place for you to start."

✹

Gulf of Saint-Lawrence

It had been almost a week. The weather had been very fair. Captain LaTour was pleased. He stood beside the helm, his face raised to the sun. With his frigate escort, *La Comète,* in the lead, they were making good time to Québec City. Though he had to reef some sail to slow the *Queen*'s speed. The hold of his ship was full of luxury goods for the people of Québec City. LaTour wasn't sure what would fill the hold afterwards, or where he would sail to next, and by whose order? But traveling with the Gerrards was always a bit of a dice throw.

At least the frigate is not lobbing cannon balls at me, he mused.

Philippe brought the twins on deck every day, so they could hold the bottom of the helm and enjoy the feel of the sea. Philippe held the top of the wheel and steered the course. Every day, some random wave would slap the starboard side. The saltwater spray rushed across the deck to mildly drench the young visitors. Their screams of joy and giggles in response to each occurrence was like a choir of angels singing to the crew.

"Kiss! Kiss!" Marcus would shout.

Captain LaTour could not have orchestrated this better.

Lady Corrinne visited the main deck multiple times each day, brooding and staring at the sea. She talked with individual crewmembers, thanked them for their courage, repeatedly. Then she'd go below to read the missive from her sister over and over.

She had composed a long letter of reply to Margaux, adding a new page to it every day, describing her joy at learning of her existence, her reactions to Charles' excruciating death, how pleased she was that Margaux was at Charles' bedside.

That you were present and did something so compassionate, personal, and poignant is extraordinary. We must rejoin our lives. There is a greater purpose in this now. It is a fate that will not be denied.

Captain LaTour saw how absorbed and emotionally moved Lady Corrinne became reading the words of her sister. He decided to withhold the journals for a few more days. Now it had been over a week. He sensed he may have waited too long. With the morning sun's warmth lingering on his face, and the encouraging wind at his back, he went below to present the journals.

LaTour laid the satchel on the table in front of her. Corrinne pulled out a volume.

"What is this?"

"My lady, I fear my sense of timing is flawed."

Corrinne opened the front cover. She was stunned to see a volume of Bishop Brevelaer's personal journals. There were three! The dates showed they covered the time before, during, and after Lord Vaelblez' death and burial.

She looked at LaTour with breathless wonder. "How long have you had these?"

"Madame Dubonnet brought them to me in LaRochelle." LaTour realized he had indeed waited way, way too long.

"La Rochelle? My sister mentions these journals in her letter to me! I've already written a page in reply and asked her to send them."

"My lady," LaTour said with remorse, "I made a bad decision with good intentions. I knew these journals contained words that describe evil and occult things. I did not want to overwhelm you…after all that happened. And you were reading your sister's letter over and over. It is a pathetic excuse… unforgiveable, really."

Corrinne read the first few pages in the first volume and shook her head in wonder.

"Is this all, Captain? Do you intend any more surprises for me?"

"No, my lady," he replied crestfallen. "No more surprises."

"This is written in Roman Latin. It will take me *days* to interpret it accurately. Oh, don't look so glum, Captain. I am not angry with you. You were probably right to hold them back from me until now." She spoke to appease him, even though she wished she had known of them sooner. She paged to the back of the first journal and a little into the beginning of the second.

"Lord VanderMeer hired a scholar to find them," LaTour offered.

"Yes. Charles would do this…even as he was dying. They are remarkable…these journals may hold all the answers on how to rid ourselves of the wraith."

Captain LaTour started to feel a little better. Philippe entered the dining cabin with the twins.

"Hello, my angels," Corrinne greeted loudly, holding out her arms.

They immediately crawled to their places at the table. LaTour knocked on the steward's window. Pierrik looked out, saw the twins, smiled and nodded. All sorts of good things to eat and drink appeared in minutes.

Philippe turned one of the journals with a finger. It was an old leather-covered text.

LaTour cleared his throat. "I've a course change to plot," he said and excused himself before Philippe could react.

"What are these?" Philippe gestured.

Corrinne told him.

"Why did he wait? Is he hiding anything else?"

"He said there is nothing more."

"What does it say?"

"It will take me days of study to interpret." She explained the import.

"Victorio says we will turn into the river before the day is over. So, it's three days before we anchor in Québec City, maybe less."

Pierrik entered with a tray full of sweetbreads, pastries, and a pitcher of the berry-flavored water. He started serving the twins.

With the arrival in Québec City imminent, Corrinne felt uncertain. "Before I lose myself to interpreting Roman Latin, what happens after we arrive?"

"We get you and the twins to Michelle's house. Then I must report to headquarters. Another campaign will begin soon."

"So, you will be gone," she noted sadly.

"Yes. But not for a few weeks. We'll have a little more time together."

Corrinne's pensiveness was growing. The near future was upon them.

"Where will we live? I mean, eventually?"

"Before I went to Louisbourg, I asked Monsignor Eric Nicolet to assist Michelle with this. They've probably found something by now. And if you decide that won't work, we'll find something else. Eric was also going to have the Church purchase your city house in Montréal, to sell back to us later. Not that Montréal is our destination. Just to have alternatives."

Corrinne felt her life sliding backwards—fast. Philippe would become preoccupied by the war and would get orders to fight somewhere in the wilderness, probably for months. After all their travels, trials of character, and tragedies, the thought of ending up where they started was depressing. It was also full of danger and unknowns they could not control. It suddenly did not seem wise. Coming to Québec City was a decision of safety. But only temporary safety. Was it not? Shouldn't they be making decisions about a new future? With a plan to reach that goal? What was the goal?

Corrinne wore an expression Philippe knew too well. "What's wrong?"

She looked wistful. "Philippe, we struggled so hard to leave Louisbourg and get to Québec City, now I'm asking myself, why? For safety, yes. But is this where we are going to end up? At the same place we started? With the war closing in on us? That was never our intention! Then I wonder, where would we go if we could go anyplace we wanted?"

Philippe reached across the table and took her hand. "The war has stalled everything, made the future unpredictable. But we have each other and the twins. The future brought us these blessings. The future will present us with a new horizon. We'll recognize it when we see it."

"Of course, we will." She rose from her seat and leaned over the table and kissed him. "You're right."

But Corrinne was filled with uncertainty. The content of the journals would only add to her unease.

CHAPTER 28
QUÉBEC CITY
JUNE 1757
A Plan for Armistice

Captain LaTour saw the flag signal from the frigate, *La Comète*. It was coming alongside before they started up the river. LaTour turned into the wind, ordered *heave to*, and the jibs were not freed. The ship's speed slowed to a stop and drifted. He lashed his helm and hung three fenders of heavy fishing net over the starboard side. The frigate came around and matched his course, heaving to the same way. They threw over lines to hold position and put over a cross-deck brow.

Captain Severyn Peltier did not plan to be aboard for very long.

"I've no chart for this river," he told LaTour.

"I have several." LaTour sent Victorio down to his cabin to get one of them. "You've not been to Québec City before?"

"Not as a captain."

"You don't have to escort me any longer. I am in familiar waters. I can go the rest of the way alone."

"I have to go there. Commodore du Bauffremont gave me the Versailles dispatch pouch for Québec City. I must hand deliver this to Governor Vaudreuil."

After what they'd discussed in Governor Drucour's private rooms, that information made Captain LaTour a little uneasy. *Dispatch pouches arrive all the time*, he reminded himself.

Victorio returned with a rolled chart of the river channel all the way to Montréal. They unrolled it between them. Captain LaTour indicated the route he would take, the locations of the permanent sandbars, shipwrecks, and other water hazards. There was a course line already marked out on the chart.

"Just follow me," LaTour offered.

Captain Peltier gave his thanks and went back aboard the frigate. LaTour waited for the warship to break away before he resumed sailing. Philippe Gerrard stood next to LaTour, who explained why they heaved to.

"I offered to go the rest of the way unescorted. But Captain Peltier explained he's delivering a Versailles dispatch pouch to Governor Vaudreuil, a pouch that he received from Commodore du Bauffremont in Louisbourg." LaTour saw a frown appear on Philippe's face. "Yes, I feel the same way. But dispatches arrive all the time."

"This time it's different." Philippe went below.

Captain LaTour raised his French flag. Today this ship was the *Falcon Queen*. And as word of the popular ship's arrival in the harbor spread, the church bells in Québec City began to toll. The Québécois were ready for good news and the *Falcon Queen* always brought good news. Cheering people began running down to the waterfront.

Corrinne and Philippe stood on deck together; Philippe holding Marcus, Corrinne holding Calypso. The twins were smiling with excitement.

"I'd forgotten how beautiful the bells sound," Corrinne said to Philippe.

"It's all for you, and the *Falcon Queen*," Philippe replied. "They know your ship."

Corrinne's mood had sagged after Philippe revealed what Captain LaTour said about the dispatch pouch. But under the cloudless blue skies and seeing the banners waving above the walls of the citadel atop the Cap Diamant promontory, Corrinne forgot her trepidation about the future and enjoyed the homecoming to Québec City as it was meant to be enjoyed. The city and people celebrated her arrival.

*

From his balcony, Governor-General Pierre de Rigaud, Marquis de Vaudreuil, watched the *Falcon Queen* and the escort frigate drop anchor in the river harbor. He was looking forward to finally meeting the infamous Lady Corrinne de Chanaye, the object of obsession for Intendant-General François Bigôt. But other business first. He turned to Captain Trieste.

"Send a messenger to Scout Captain Gerrard right away. I want to see him tomorrow morning. Coordinate a time so General Montcalm can attend as well. Just the three of us. Do you have the documents prepared?"

"Yes, sir."

*

Intendant François Bigôt walked out of his offices across from the governor's palace and up the stairs to the rampart overlooking the river. He could see the ships. He ignored the push of other citizens rushing by him to get a position on the walls to view the waterfront. A raft would be pushed against the *Falcon Queen* to facilitate the offloading of its cargo. The *Falcon Queen* always brought quality goods.

Messengers had already run to the governor's palace. Purportedly, Lady de Chanaye was returning to the city along with her woodsman. François Bigôt had waited years for this…for years! Hoping this whore would make the mistake of returning. Only the pen-stroke of the governor could stop her arrest. Maybe he could arrest her before the governor had a chance to act. His secretary had followed and stood behind him.

"Inform Captain LaTour I want to see him immediately with his cargo and passenger manifests."

*

Harbormaster Jesper Gossard came aboard the *Falcon Queen*. "Welcome home, Beauregard! What have you brought us this time?"

"Very good things, Jesper, as always. And"—he gestured to his right—"Lady Corrinne de Chanaye with her twin children."

"*Bonjour*, littles ones!" He bowed respectfully to Lady de Chanaye. "Your beauty has been absent from our city for too long, my lady. You look radiant."

"*Merci*, Jesper. Always the gentleman."

"You make it easy for me."

With his long glass, Captain LaTour scanned the riverside wharves. "I see a carriage waiting at the head of the dock. That must be for you. Why don't you go on ahead to the city house? I'll have your personal baggage delivered in a few hours."

"Are you ready, Corrinne?" Philippe asked.

"Yes," she replied with resignation. "Do I have a choice?"

Corrinne carried Calypso and stepped down the ladder to the cargo raft. Philippe followed with Marcus. The ship's launch awaited them. Once aboard, they were rowed to the passenger landing. As soon as Corrinne stepped onto the wharf, many of the citizens, mostly the women, crowded around her to express welcomes and make a fuss over the twins. Corrinne was gracious as always, addressing some of the women she recalled by name.

The carriage ride up the hillside to upper town Québec twisted and turned. Corrinne gazed at her former residence with nostalgia as it came into view.

Neighbors came out of nearby houses to welcome her. Corrinne took time to greet them all and answer what questions she could.

The crowd on the street drew Michelle outside with Crispin holding her hand. She made a squeak of joy when she saw Corrinne. They embraced.

"My goodness, Corrinne! Look at you! You never age! And your beautiful twins. *Bonjour*, Calypso. *Bonjour*, Marcus. This is my son, Crispin! Come inside. Come inside. This is Constance. She is my housekeeper. We have a room all prepared for you."

"*Bonjour*, Michelle," Philippe said drolly.

Michelle turned, seeing him properly for the first time. "Oh! Yes. Philippe!" She embraced him. "You shaved! Good to see you again."

Crispin was very intrigued to see the return of the tall soldier with all the scars, this time without a beard. Philippe took a chair in the cuisine and patiently answered the boy's endless questions while the women conversed in a separate chirp of voices.

The frigate, *La Comète,* delivered the dispatch pouch that originated in Brest. Among the other correspondence from Versailles there was a sealed missive to Governor-General Pierre de Vaudreuil. It was a letter like the one given to Commodore du Bauffremont concerning the identity of Lady Corrinne VanderMeer, expressing the same questions about her identity. Ostensibly, it was from the king himself. The letter explained it had been sent to the governors in Québec City and Louisbourg in case Lady VanderMeer's location had changed.

The Breeding Grounds

The fledging chicks were six weeks old. They all had white feathers now, short ones, still not long enough to fly. Full growth was weeks away. One of them was a little smaller than the other two. The *ghost* did its best to influence how they were fed. He wanted them all to survive. He could influence how the female distributed any kill, but he did not control the male.

The day before, the female circled above the aerie in the late afternoon twilight. The *ghost* reached out and perceived the glow of the woman and the man. They were much closer now. It also perceived the glow of the man in the water city, and the extremely bright glow of the girl. The boy become man stayed near to her. The girl had survived the attack. The boy become man had slain the three servants of the demon that threatened her.

For now, they were safe.

A familiar servant of the demon had returned to the water city. That servant would recruit others and would be searching for the woman and the châsse. They might attempt to harm the new person in the water city that the *ghost* could now see. If the *ghost* could see him, the demon could see him, too. It must visit this new person as soon as the female could tolerate a long journey.

The *ghost* withdrew its spirit from the body of the eagle as far as it dared, so it could extend its perception even further. It gazed outward across the dark abyss and saw the faint red glow of the demon. It was far. The *ghost* could not sense how far away it was…but it was coming.

The *ghost* withdrew its dominance, and the female eagle hunted for fish one more time before returning to the nest for the night. It would be another moon before the fledglings would take flight. The *ghost* would journey to the water city first. The person there had performed a sealing ritual. It was important to understand the reason why.

Brest

Róbert and Marcel learned that Lieutenant-Colonel Karl Krieger was a Hessian officer. Evidently, one skilled in assembling mercenary regiments. His orders were to command the 1st Battalion Volontaires-Étrangers Regiment, which would report to Governor-General Augustin de Drucour in Louisbourg, Île Royale, there to be assigned to the garrison in the defense of the fortress port. The regiment was scheduled to board two transport ships-of-the-line in Brest over the next four days.

"The transport ships are tied to the outfitting docks on the east side of the river. A cannon deck on each ship is being cleared of its armament to make room for these troops."

Margaux Dubonnet concluded there was little more to learn about this mercenary regiment beyond the menace of its sinister commander. But the man's odd assertion that they had met before and his referring to her as *Maeve* was still very disturbing. The night before, she had a frightening nightmare, one in which she had participated in some arcane funeral of this person named Lord Vaelblez. There was a Druid priest present in this strange dream who also addressed her as Maeve, although this priest seemed respectful.

As the day wore on, the memory of her night terrors faded and Margaux composed another long letter to Corrinne, sharing the startling, joyous, and often tragic revelations discovered by William LaFont concerning their natal heritage. She abbreviated the major points of his findings; there was simply too much to put in one letter. She added the news that William LaFont had just embarked on yet another journey, this time to investigate their Welsh beginnings. *Raised in France, yet we are Welsh!*

In the last page and a half, she provided a description of her confrontation with Colonel Krieger and the subsequent nightmare.

> *Before I sent them to you, I had read Bishop Brevelaer's first journal, where Lord Vaelblez' name was mentioned prominently, along with the names of Maeve and her husband Adaelric. I must assume the vividness of the horrible events described in these journals inflamed my imagination and caused my nightmarish dreams. I am curious why Charles thought them so important for you to read. Nevertheless, Colonel Krieger uttered his threatening words to me while standing in the foyer of my house! He had a malignant glare. He addressed me as Maeve. This did not seem coincidental. But you have these journals now. Your husband Charles made me promise to read them, believing I was you. Maybe there is a history you know that I do not. Charles was certain more assassins would be sent to harm you. I judge that Lieutenant-Colonel Karl Krieger embodies the evil of an individual capable of such heinous crimes, and much worse. Beware.*

Madame Dubonnet decided to go a step further. She carried this sealed missive over to naval headquarters and personally handed it to Admiral Dubois de la Motte, asking if he would carry it in the dispatch pouch for Louisbourg. She also mentioned Lieutenant-Colonel Krieger's rude behavior in the foyer of her home, without going into the details. The admiral knew her father, Chevalier Lucais de Clermont and asked about his health. At the end of the conversation, the admiral gave her his word, Governor Augustin de Drucour would be made aware of the mercenary colonel's penchant for insolence to women. That had been Margaux's goal. She hoped her new letter to Corrinne arrived in time.

The next day, she again went over the river bridge by carriage, this time to the boarding dock where the mercenary regiment would begin marching aboard. She took a position to one side of the loading brow. As per tradition, the common soldiers were the first to board. The officers of the regiment would board last. Margaux waited for them. Lieutenant-Colonel Krieger was leading his staff of officers. As he approached the spot where Madame Dubonnet was standing, she purposely stepped in front of the colonel, impeding his progress. Róbert and Marcel were not forewarned of her actions and were not pleased.

"You are right!" She scowled at the officer. "We have met before. I know who you are. You have been marked," she asserted tersely to the man's face. "That mark will follow you. And we will meet again."

The malevolent glare appeared. *"Sooner than you think, Maeve."* Krieger stepped around her.

Marcel had a hand on his partially drawn sword as the mercenary walked away.

"Madame, may I presume there was reason for you to provoke this dangerous man?"

"I want to give him nightmares, too."

"I don't believe that man has nightmares, Madame," Róbert added. "He is the nightmare!"

"You stood too close to him!" Marcel said with mild reproach. "What if he attempted to harm you?"

"Then he would undoubtedly be lying on the ground right now, in a pool of his own blood, with your sword through his chest. I should be so lucky."

"Madame, I believe Colonel Dubonnet would not be happy with you… or with Róbert and me."

Margaux Dubonnet faced Róbert and Marcel. She smiled indulgently and patted their strong chests with affectionate approval.

"My gallant, handsome protectors, you can be assured, when your colonel gets angry with me, he also finds it impossible to stay angry for very long."

Québec City

Governor-General Pierre de Vaudreuil stared at the portrait of his father hanging on the wall in his private office. These offices were much more opulent than the ones in Montréal, though the palace in Montréal felt more like home. He was Canadian-born with allegiances to his people and the lands. His father was a former governor-general of New France. He often talked to the portrait, as if his father were in the room with him. Not out loud, of course. But in whispers. His aides were too close. He sometimes imagined answers from the portrait. His father had been very intimidating.

Every part of New France is under siege, he declared to his father silently. *The English have nearly emptied Acadia of our citizens. Acadia supplies more than half of Québec City's food, in addition to supplying Louisbourg's food. We face famine before this year is over, made worse because I've called up the provincial farmers for duty in the militia. The limited regiments of metropolitan regulars sent by Versailles, I am forced to send everywhere. I dole them out a company at a time, to support the local militias. France and England declared war last year.*

The King is distracted because of his whore mistress. It is accepted that Madame de Pompadour now speaks for the government. France sends armies by the tens of thousands to fight all over Europe. It sends me single regiments to defend New France, a territory holding lands on this continent three times larger than all the European countries combined. Our entire population, by the last count, has us with little more than fifty-five thousand citizens, including the children! The American colonies number a million people and more. Our claim to territorial sovereignty is questionable simply by our number of residents. We might as well be a village! And the challenges to our borders is also a test by numbers. We can barely marshal five thousand fighting men to face an enemy who comes with three times that number. The tribal warriors are my army in the wilderness. They know how to fight out there. The English do not. At least not yet. And we must find a way to negotiate a peace before the English appreciate how weak we are and overwhelm us.

Versailles will never allow you to make peace, his father's portrait told him. *New France is expendable. The monarchy's survival is paramount. France's borders in Europe must be defended first.*

Governor Vaudreuil knew this already. He had gambled in 1755. He had planned to force the English to run out of money, time, patience, and political support. He'd estimated it would take two years until the costs became unbearable to the British Parliament. His plan would work if the English could not declare any further victories after those early ones in Nova Scotia. Since losing the two lightly defended forts in Nova Scotia, New France consistently delivered major defeats to all of England's attacking forces. But the loss of Acadia severely damaged the food supply. The English were dominant in the Acadian lands just by the presence of their troops in the port of Halifax. Acadia would never be retaken. England would never give it back, even if peace was negotiated today. Vaudreuil had insufficient forces to take it back. He had not pressed this point too sharply with Versailles. Instead he argued that had he been made governor a decade earlier, he would have placed a Louisbourg-like fortress city in Baie Verte and another at Gaspé. Either of those forts could have better guarded the mouth of the Saint Lawrence River.

Louisbourg, Québec's single lifeline guarding the Saint Lawrence, was in constant jeopardy. It was too isolated, essentially landlocked walls within an island. It would run out of food without constant resupply by ships. It was too far away to receive effective military support from Québec City, even if Governor Vaudreuil could provide them.

Vaudreuil ranted silently at the portrait again. *Louisbourg is the tiny plug in the huge bottle of French wine labeled New France. And the English navy is a very big corkscrew.*

Yes, Governor Vaudreuil had gambled in 1755. He had won all the big battles: Monongahela, Fort Bull, Fort Oswego. The English settlers were driven out of all their territory in the Ohio River valley, anywhere north of the Allegheny River or anywhere around the great lakes. All the smaller English forts had been captured and razed. But the English had not given up. His two-year plan had not brought the English to their knees as it should have. They persisted. Lord Pitt, the new English prime minister, was building more ships, a lot more ships. Lord Pitt was not concerned with marching English armies around Europe. His focus was on the greater prize: capturing all North America. French spies in Parliament learned the English intended to have *thirty thousand* redcoat regulars deployed to the American colonies for the fighting season next year. Thirty thousand soldiers! Numbers equaling more than half the entire population of New France!

Vaudreuil was running out of time. He planned to capture Fort William Henry during the summer. This victory would become a symbol of French power and dominance in the Iroquois lands. The Iroquois was England's primary tribal ally. They had declared itself neutral as long as they were not attacked by the French. He decided to use this victory and fashion an armistice. An agreement to cease hostilities based upon certain conditions along a line of fixed boundaries. Governor Pierre de Vaudreuil planned to conduct affairs like a sovereign and negotiate a truce with the English without approval from Versailles. His actions must be discreet, so they were not interpreted as an act of treason in France.

Without revealing his sense of desperation, he called General Louis-Antoine de Montcalm to his headquarters to review military strategy in a private meeting. Vaudreuil introduced his plan to Montcalm the same day the *Falcon Queen* arrived in Québec City. Vaudreuil had already selected Scout Captain Philippe Gerrard to be his instrument, his emissary in this plan. Now that the elite wilderness fighter was back from Louisbourg, he first wanted to get agreement from Montcalm.

General Montcalm did not trust the governor. But he followed orders. He came to the meeting and listened with skepticism.

"We have both lost our primary ministers of support. I no longer have Minister Machault and you have lost Minister d'Argenson. My confidantes in France tell me they were both summarily dismissed, accused of some type of conspiracy. Have you heard anything different since then?"

Montcalm did not reply.

"No? Very well. Then you do not disagree with me. The dismissal of these ministers suggests that we are on our own in defending New France. I expect someone will take pity on us and send us a regiment of troops. But I assert we need an army of metropolitan troops of about fifteen to twenty thousand to win. Do you disagree?"

Montcalm did not reply. As far as he was concerned, Vaudreuil was not above hiding two scribes inside a closet or under the table, one taking notes of what was said and the other to act as a witness.

"No? Very well. Let us presume there is no change in the numbers of our regular fighting forces. And further, let us presume Louisbourg will fall to invasion, if not this year, then next year. And presume the English will double the size of its redcoat troops deployed to America—say half of them staged in Halifax and the other half in Albany. Now, my military question for you. If it comes to saving New France as a territory, what do you consider defensible boundaries based on our current forces?"

Montcalm rose from his chair and walked up to the map. Using the wooden pointer, he easily explained his thoughts. It was obvious to Governor Vaudreuil that his military commander had already been thinking about this possibility.

"I agree with you." Vaudreuil stood and accepted the pointer from Montcalm. "France has no settlements in any of these wilderness areas." He pointed them out. "Here, here, or here. Other than Fort Duquesne, it is just empty land. Land we cannot defend or even populate. We've not enough people even if we sent them on a migration! I intend to send someone to speak with the Americans to suggest a truce, a cessation of hostilities along the boundaries you just pointed out. I see your expression. This meeting today was not a ruse. The decision to do this," he said loudly, "will be mine alone! There you see. No hidden witnesses. I intend to use Scout Captain Gerrard to deliver my proposal after we invest Fort William Henry."

*

It was day two after his arrival in Québec City when Scout Captain Philippe Gerrard was escorted to the war council room in Governor Vaudreuil's chambers. The room was familiar, Philippe had been there many times before. The walls were covered with detailed maps of the various territories comprising New France. One of them was a beautiful work of art. It hung on the front wall and presented a variegated topography of the lakes and forests surrounding Fort Carillon. The long table was occupied by Governor-General Pierre de Vaudreuil at the head and General Louis-Joseph de Montcalm opposite to where Philippe was invited to sit.

Philippe came to attention and saluted the senior officers.

Vaudreuil reacted informally. "At ease, Captain Gerrard. Please take a seat."

There were servants in the room. Philippe refused the offer of refreshments. The servants were dismissed, leaving the three of them alone.

"I trust your journey to and from Louisbourg was safe and uneventful? *Bien*. And your wife and children are well?"

"Yes, sir. They are here in Québec City."

"Good. I asked General Montcalm to join me in meeting with you because we share an intense interest in several topics." Vaudreuil gestured to Montcalm. "General, why don't you begin."

"Captain, I am most curious about the military preparedness of Louisbourg to defend against English invasion. Give us your frank opinion."

"Yes, sir. I was there for two weeks. A few days prior to my arrival, a squadron of ships-of-the-line under the command of Commodore Joseph du Bauffremont arrived from Brest with orders to remain and defend the port. Governor Drucour expects two more squadrons of ships to arrive by the end of this month. I'm not sure how many, but they anticipate a total of more than fifteen ships-of-the-line, accompanied by escort frigates. These ships will remain until the fighting season ends."

"And the garrison?" Vaudreuil asked.

"Five thousand. The majority regulars. They anticipate reinforcement with more mercenaries. They've asked for more regulars, but metropolitan troops are uncertain because of the land war on the continent. In the meantime, they've constructed formidable battlement and artillery positions on Gabarus Bay. I have seen them. If properly manned, it will repel a landing. But there are just not enough troops to defend the fort and reinforce the battlements at the same time to repel the various landing strategies. It's a matter of numbers."

"So, strong naval forces based within the harbor would be the best defense?" Montcalm inquired.

"Yes, sir. That is my opinion. That is the intention. If they remain, Louisbourg should survive this season."

"And the number of troops in Halifax?"

"Five thousand confirmed, and maybe as high as twelve thousand redcoat regulars, according to recent intelligence delivered to Governor Drucour. Maybe even more. There are also American rangers and other supporting American regiments. They are staged for the invasion of Louisbourg. Everyone knows this."

"If they do not successfully invade this year, what will the troops in Halifax do?" Vaudreuil asked.

"Now I speculate. The English want to invest Louisbourg and Fort Carillon. They do not have enough troops to do both. If they do not invade Louisbourg this year, they will leave the troops in Halifax in place for next year."

"So, you think Louisbourg first and then Fort Carillon?" Montcalm asked the question as if this was already a topic of debate.

"Yes, sir. But the English know the strength of our military in both places. Fifteen thousand redcoat regulars are enough to lay siege to Louisbourg or Fort Carillon…and win, if it's conducted properly."

Montcalm squinted. "Your point, Captain?"

"If I were the English commander, I'd request another fifteen thousand regulars and attack both objectives at the same time, next year. Of course, the English must decide militarily to send these additional troops."

Vaudreuil and Montcalm glanced at one another.

They've already discussed this, Philippe realized.

"As you know, we have formulated plans to attack and invest Fort William Henry," Vaudreuil said. "Your scout battalion will play a key role in this attack. I will have a war council this week with a full review of our plans. Our native allies have grown in numbers with many coming from lands, rivers, and lakes as far away as Fort Detroit. They will number in the thousands. The numbers of our forces available to conduct this siege is not of concern.

General Montcalm and I disagree with the use of native forces, but let's set that disagreement aside for right now. Presuming we invest Fort William Henry by the end of this fighting season, we will threaten Fort Edward… and could invest it before the winter if we choose to do so. Do you agree?"

"Based on my previous scouts, it would not take much of a push to do it within days of investing Fort William Henry. Holding these forts, however, would not be wise. Better to just destroy them."

"Your opinion is noted. However, our forces could threaten Albany. General, I prefer you continue with our strategy from this point."

Philippe knew something was coming. What was the point of telling him this with no one else in the room?

"As you wish, Governor. Scout Captain, when we invest Fort William Henry, whether we continue our campaign and invest Fort Edward or not, our forces, augmented by thousands of our native warriors, will threaten Albany. I anticipate the English will immediately reinforce the west to forestall any expanded invasion, probably by moving troops from Halifax back to Albany. That will take time and the fighting season will end for this year. Our victory over Fort William Henry, by itself, may induce the English to send more troops in the spring. The likelihood of an attack on Fort Carillon and Louisbourg at the same time, as you conjecture, will become a real possibility."

Montcalm stopped talking. Philippe felt the pressure to reply, so he agreed.

"As you say, sir."

"At the same time, a victory over Fort William Henry presents an opportunity for a negotiation with the Americans," Vaudreuil said.

"You mean the English?" Philippe asked, then regretted speaking too quickly.

"No," Vaudreuil replied pointedly. "I mean the Americans. What is your opinion on the sustainability of Fort Duquesne?"

Philippe blinked at the sudden change of topic. "Fort Duquesne? I've heard rumor of a new road being cut through the wilderness from the city of Philadelphia, directly west, with the intention of attacking Fort Duquesne again."

"And?"

"And…I do not know how long this will take. But the English will not make the mistakes they did the first time. Fort Duquesne can be shelled into submission from the other side of the Onondaga River. I think we will be forced to abandon and burn it…then retreat all the way to Fort Niagara, abandoning Forts Machault, Le Boeuf, and possibly Fort Presque Isle. That is, if the English march with enough strength."

"If the English double the number of regular troops in America, General Montcalm and I must consider the possibility that New France cannot win this war militarily. After our victory at Fort William Henry, I intend to propose an armistice to the Americans. Not a surrender. A truce. We want to submit this to a senior American officer who will carry it forward to the English for consideration. You have a relationship with Sir William Johnson. We want you to carry this proposal to him."

Philippe looked from Vaudreuil to Montcalm and back to Vaudreuil. They were serious!

"With respect, Governor. I am not an ambassador. I lack negotiation skills, as it has been pointed out to me more than once by both of you."

"But you have a *relationship* with Sir William Johnson," Vaudreuil said, emphasizing the key to the mission. "He will accept the veracity of our proposal if *you* bring it to him. You have earned his respect. You will have to defend our position, of course, and convince Sir William the proposal is genuine. That it will bring an end to the fighting in America."

"If the English plan to bring more troops in the spring, it's because they are determined to win. Why would they agree to an armistice?"

"General, what would be our fallback position if Fort Carillon falls?"

"The same as I have already described."

Philippe realized it was General Montcalm who designed the military strategy of this proposal and the effect it would have on the boundaries of New France.

Philippe did not think the English military would consider this at all. But after learning what General Montcalm proposed, the *Americans* might think about it. The independent traders on both sides had suggested similar tribal treaties.

Would Sir William consider himself English or American? Philippe wondered.

"Governor, I don't have the gravitas to represent you effectively. You should send a general, or a civilian emissary with the proper credentials."

"Nonsense! You lived with Sir William at his fort for a few weeks. Getting through Mohawk lands alive to see Sir William Johnson requires your wilderness skills. You are a member of the Oneida tribe, the son of a chief, yes? That's gravitas among the tribes. And effective immediately, I promote you to the rank of Colonel in the Troupes de la Marine. That is senior enough. The enemy knows who you are, *Snow Hair*. They know your name. You can revert to a lower rank afterwards, if you are uncomfortable with this promotion. We will do this, Captain Gerrard…um, Colonel. You are *ordered* to do this. I leave the details on how you do this to General Montcalm. I have documents prepared for you to take. And our discussion this morning cannot be repeated to anyone outside this room. It must remain secret. Talk privately with me or with General Montcalm. But no one else. Is that understood?"

"Yes, sir." Philippe submitted. He looked to General Montcalm for validation.

General Montcalm nodded solemnly.

*

After the meeting with Captain Gerrard ended, Governor Vaudreuil went back to his office to finish reading the dispatches brought to him on the frigate *La Comète*. He had already read the one concerning Versailles' interest in Lady Corrinne VanderMeer, ending with the extraordinary direction, delegated by the King no less, to arrest her. *Ridiculous*, he thought. *The King has no idea who she is!* This confirmed the missive was from Madame de Pompadour. Vaudreuil was undecided what to do with this royal command, considering the dangerous mission Lady Corrinne's husband would undertake for New France. If a similar message was delivered to Governor Drucour, as the missive stated, maybe the matter had been resolved. He was in no hurry. He finished going through the rest of the mail in this pouch, sorting them into three piles. He found another missive, this one addressed to Intendant François Bigôt. The outside handwriting was the same. Vaudreuil opened it. The letter was identical to the one addressed to him and concerned Lady Corrinne VanderMeer. In Vaudreuil's hands, the letter was a political nuisance at worst. In François Bigôt's hands, and the hostility the administrator harbored for this woman, the letter was a weapon. It authorized Bigôt, by direct authority from the King of France, to arrest Lady Corrinne VanderMeer. Intendant Bigôt did not need Vaudreuil's approval!

He does not even have to tell me he is doing it! Now the King's whore mistress subverts my authority!

With contempt, he tossed the letter in a pile of others slated to be burned. The governor fumed. No missives from Versailles in the future must ever reach Intendant Bigôt…*or* Captain Trieste.

*

Major Michel Péan, chevalier of the Order of Saint Louis, decorated war veteran, had waited patiently to see Governor Vaudreuil as ordered, sitting outside the private offices. He was here to finish the discussion on why, he, Major Michel Péan, personally, was being sent back to Paris, and maybe to Versailles, to answer charges of corruption levied against him alone. He had already spoken about it twice with Intendant Bigôt.

Major Péan was directly accused. If the charges were corroborated, he would indeed be blamed…for all of it. All the other corrupt administrators in New France, government ministers at every level, and the nobility, stretching all the way back to Versailles, all of them were the recipients of shares in the continuous dividends paid by the Grand Société, the company Intendant Bigôt had set up years earlier. A company that gave it a monopoly on the sale of supplies to and from the king's stores. It allowed them to corner all trade in the colony. It had been methodically pilfering the treasury of France, buying and selling goods on both sides of every transaction, fixing prices, declaring goods spoiled that were not spoiled, reselling them through a third party back to the government and paying for them again with treasury money, to be resold later for mark-ups sometimes as high as fifty percent. The war had created enormous opportunities for profit. As far as Péan could tell, there were more people in the government circles involved with this corruption than not involved. And these people wanted this money flow to continue, which it would if Major Péan was exonerated.

Michel Péan's five percent was paid directly to his wife, Angélique-Genevieve d'Avène Des Méloizes. Buying and selling goods in Michel's name, using agents in France, Angélique managed to carve out almost two million livres safeguarded by these agents. Now she wanted her husband to purchase estates with this money when he went to France to face these charges of corruption. If he managed to stay out of prison, of course.

"This is for our future beyond New France," she confided lying naked atop of him one night.

Michel Péan loved his wife. He would do anything for her.

"Why me?" he later asked Bigôt. "I was not even here! I was getting shot in my ass at Fort Bull, or freezing to death in Louisbourg."

"Because you are named by everyone else as the man who ran the business. You are the only one who can explain how it works. This is a good thing," Intendant Bigôt explained.

"A good thing?"

"Yes. The people who will be doing the investigation are shareholders, well, almost all of them. They have an interest in accepting your explanations as valid and honest. You just answer questions in a certain way that everyone can validate as the truth. Here is a list of questions for you to memorize and the answers. You will be given more questions by our agents after you arrive in France."

"What if they ask me about *you*?"

"Don't forget, Angélique has been the recipient of the dividends you received. We have receipts with her name on them. If you do not convince the investigators, she may also be charged with conspiracy."

Intendant Bigôt understood Michel's weaknesses. Bigôt was sleeping with Angélique when Michel was away in the war. That is, when Governor Vaudreuil was not sleeping with her.

"Why was I made a chevalier?"

"To give you stature as a war hero. Think of it as a type of armor. If you say something is true, then it must be true, because the King would never celebrate an immoral person, or induct such a person as a Knight in the Order of Saint Louis. The King is the Grand Master of the order! Condemn you, and the investigators condemn the King!"

Now, as Michel waited to see the governor, he realized this meeting may be simple. The governor wanted his name never mentioned. He could imagine it. *Mention my name, Major, and you've earned a permanent assignment at the most northern outpost of Hudson Bay.*

Michel reflected glumly on his predicament. He recalled a drowning deer caught in the flood waters of the Allegheny River in the middle of the winter. It got thrashed and crushed by the giant ice flows. Its only hope was to climb out of the river…if it did not freeze to death first. The ill-fated animal disappeared around a river bend before he could learn its fate.

The door to the governor's office opened. The governor stormed out without a sideways glance at him. He told Captain Trieste he was going to the dining room and gestured for the captain to accompany him. Trieste followed, but pointed at Major Péan and mouthed he should wait there.

The governor's office door was left open. Major Péan was dressed in an impeccably tailored uniform with the Order of Saint Louis ribbon and badge dangling on the left chest. Péan stood, stretched his legs, and wandered near the open door. He glanced inside. A dispatch pouch lay open on the governor's desk. Missives were sorted into three piles.

Michel Péan had frequented these offices for over a decade. He knew every doorway, every secret hiding place, the location of the keys to all the locked drawers. He knew the peculiar habits of the occupants. Captain Trieste, for instance, hoarded discarded missives for his own use. He sold the information. Governor-General Vaudreuil read any official mail to Québec City, whether addressed to him or not. The leather carrier pouch had the insignia of *La Comète* emblazoned in gold letters on the outside. This news from Versailles was brand new. Péan was curious. He went into the office to the desk. He read the missive atop the center pile. It was addressed to Vaudreuil from Versailles. It regarded Lady Corrinne VanderMeer.

Lady Corrinne VanderMeer? What the hell? He read it. *A spy? Lady Corrinne?*

Péan put it down and picked the top missive of another pile. The exact same handwriting. The same missive. He flipped it over. Addressed to Intendant François Bigôt? He read it to the end this time. It delegated the vengeful administrator with authority from the king.

"*Merde!*" he whispered.

Péan dropped the document and retreated to his chair in the waiting room. He'd dared too much. Learned too much. Governor Vaudreuil could order him executed for this. The transgression might be discovered. He wondered if he'd disturbed anything else. Or had a servant seen him through a peephole? There were several of those, too.

I should leave, he debated. *No, I should stay. Trieste told me to stay. Leaving would be suspicious. Or would it?* A bigger question intruded. What should he do with this information? Forget what he read? *Yes. Forget it. It does not concern me.*

Ten minutes later, the governor returned with Captain Trieste. The governor waved Major Péan into his office. After they sat down, the governor stared at him in question.

"You look nervous."

Péan affected his most innocent look. "No, sir. I'm just hungry."

*

Captain Beauregard LaTour stood before Intendant François Bigôt's desk as the snide administrator reviewed the cargo and passenger manifests.

"After your cargo is sold to the Grand Société agent on the river wharf, you will itemize the total sales revenues in a document. Bring it back to me and be prepared to pay a thirty-two percent tax."

"A tax? Even though I am selling my cargo directly to you?"

"You are selling your goods to another company," Bigôt corrected him with contempt. "The lower your sales price, the lower your taxes will be. But you will make a profit. Your profit will be taxed at thirty-two percent. By law. Where are your passengers?"

"Scout Captain Gerrard is at military headquarters, I presume. Lady Corrinne and her two small children are residing at her former city house."

"What are her intentions? Where does she plan to reside?"

"She has not told me this. Maybe you can ask Scout Captain Gerrard?"

François Bigôt smirked. "You think that is funny?" He regarded the captain with acrimony. "You believe nothing has changed? That it is just like before? That there is not a war in progress? That you are free to smuggle?"

"Monsieur Bigôt—"

"*Intendant* Bigôt!"

"Intendant Bigôt. I know there is a war. I have participated in this war. The *Falcon Queen* carries cargo, but it is also a French warship, albeit a small one. I carry four swivel cannons. And I take my orders from Admiral Dubois de la Motte."

"You think so? You are in New France, Captain LaTour. Admiral de la Motte has no authority here. You will take your orders from the *vice-roi*, Governor-General Pierre de Vaudreuil, or his designated representative. That would be me, if you are confused."

"Very well, Monsieur Designated Representative, what are my orders?"

"You still find humor in this? After you unload your cargo and pay the tax, barges will be brought out to your ship from the Grand Société warehouse. You will purchase a full load of furs for transport back to France."

"You cannot force me to buy your decayed company furs."

"Oh, yes I can, Captain. And I will. Either follow your orders, or be relieved of command. Your ship will be impounded by the government, a new captain appointed, and it will still purchase a load of furs for transport to France."

Captain LaTour did not reply.

"Do you understand?"

"Yes. Anything else?"

"I will give you the name of the company agent in France who will purchase your cargo. Oh, and you will be taking back a passenger with you… possibly more than one."

"Who?"

"You will be told the name just before you weigh anchor. You are dismissed, Captain. You know, I find it very pleasing to dismiss you. *Dismissed*, Captain LaTour. Leave my office!"

LaTour left the intendant's building. He was so angry, he walked the wrong way and ended up entering the governor's palace. He turned around and headed towards the citadel's main gate.

"I should hire someone to knife that little shit," he grumbled to himself. "There must be blackguards for hire somewhere in the city. Give them double the usual price, if they do it slowly. But only if they describe his death to me afterwards."

Then he wondered who his passenger might be. To *where* would he be sailing? That was the more important question.

Chapter 29
London
June 1757
Convergence of Fates

L ord Pitt seethed in anger after reading the latest dispatches from Halifax. In January, he had assigned thirty ships, eighteen of them ships-of-the-line, and seventeen thousand troops to be staged in Halifax, all intended for the invasion of Louisbourg by April. Now it was May and he received the news that the French port sat unprotected and uninvaded! Inexplicably, his troops had not moved out of Halifax to take advantage of this strategic lapse by the French.

"Lord Loudon is not even present in Halifax! Do something!" He raged back in writing to the army and navy commanders in multiple heated dispatches.

After learning Commodore Joseph du Bauffremont was commanding a small squadron of ships sailing towards Louisbourg, the always dependable Rear-Admiral Charles Hardy took his own initiative to load eleven thousand troops in New York aboard ships destined for Halifax.

Prague

In May, Frederick II defeated the Austrians in the Battle for Prague as he predicted. But he'd lost nearly fifteen thousand troops in the effort. The remainder of this Austrian army retreated into the city of Prague. Together, the Austrian army and city population numbered over a hundred thousand. The Prussian army was so weakened from the previous battle, it could not afford the casualties in troops it would cost to finish taking the fortified city. The Prussian sovereign decided instead to surround the city in a siege and starve the Austrian army and Prague's citizenry into submission.

A second Austrian army started closing on the Prussian rear. Frederick was forced to split his army in half to engage this new threat. The Austrians outnumbered the smaller Prussian force. Frederick lost this battle and was

543

forced to retreat after losing more men. Worse yet, he was forced to abandon the siege of Prague and withdraw from Bohemia altogether to regroup his scattered corps.

Given the losses he sustained in June, Frederick II recalled his six infantry battalions from the Hanoverian "Army of Observation," commanded by King George II's son, Prince William, Duke of Cumberland. Frederick had only provided these battalions to meet his treaty obligations with England to help defend the borders of Hanover.

"Let the English send over some of their redcoats," he fumed. Frederick II was not going to waste his elite Prussian infantry on this lost cause. He considered an Army of Observation to be doomed just by the name it espoused.

"Armies are not meant for *observing* anything." He scoffed to his general staff. "They are meant for attacking!"

Québec City

Scout Captain Gerrard met with his officers and senior sergeants at the military headquarters inside the citadel atop Cap Diamant, but only half of them were present. The other half remained at Fort Carillon and some of those were visiting families in Montréal. They'd become too scattered and Philippe immediately gave orders for the nascent scout battalion to begin a rendezvous march to Fort Carillon. He was told nothing much had changed on Lake George. The reduced French scout companies still performed routine patrols down Lake George, and observed no counter-scouting activities from Fort William Henry. Not even by the enemy rangers. That was curious. But the English were intimidated by the appearance of nearly a thousand tribal warriors from dozens of different tribes collecting to the north of Fort Carillon. It was obvious the French intended some type of campaign. More arrived each day. So, they stayed inside Fort William Henry.

"When will you leave for Fort Carillon?" one of the sergeants asked.

"Soon. Another war council is scheduled for later next week. Probably right after that."

"Where is Malsum?"

"Malsum chose to join the marines still at Louisbourg. Only half of those that were left wanted to return to Québec City. My son was among those who volunteered to serve in that garrison."

Philippe sought out his friend, Captain Louis-Antoine de Bougainville. He found the man reading a mathematical text in his small quarters.

"*Bonjour*, Archimedes!"

Their reunion was filled with laughter and congratulations. Philippe explained everything that had happened, ending with Malsum's decision to stay in Louisbourg.

"My wife asked me to invite you to dinner tonight at her former city house."

"I would be honored and thrilled to meet her and your little twins!"

"Good. She will be pleased to hear you are coming. Louis de Bougainville, the famous mathematician!"

"Famous? Not yet. Maybe someday. You met with the governor and the general this morning?"

"Yes. They wanted to know about the defensive preparations at Louisbourg."

"And?"

"And? That word seems to be a popular question. The French navy will anchor three squadrons of warships in the harbor until the fighting season is ended. One of them is there already. Two others were expected and might have arrived there even now. With that battle fleet present in Louisbourg, the fortress will not be invaded this year."

"Will you be staying in the barracks? Of course not, forgive me. Stupid question."

"I need to see someone else today. We will plan to see you tonight, then, after sunset?"

Philippe walked to the Terrain des Jésuits to see Monsignor Eric Nicolet. The monsignor told him Corrinne's former city house in Montréal had indeed been up for sale and the Church bought it.

"It was sold to the Church at a very reduced price. People do not value property in Montréal with the threat of siege a possibility."

"I am ready to buy it back from you. Name your price. But the Church should retain the title. I do not want to identify myself as the owner, not until I am ready to occupy the house."

"Of course. As you wish."

"How are Joshua and Leah?"

"They are healthy and living safely with Denis and Mary, who are taking good care of them both. They miss you, of course."

"Please tell them we talked. That I will come to see them, maybe in late September. In Montréal."

"They will be overjoyed to hear this."

"I see you are wearing your father's cross. That's good."

"Yes. The stone glows eerily every so often. I don't know why. I am curious to hear the whole story from your perspective someday."

"The stone glowing is a good thing. After the next campaign is over and I return to Québec City, I promise to tell you. Or, I can tell you when I come to Montréal. It is a very long story…much of it you will find difficult to believe. Your father was deeply involved, God rest his soul. But let's talk instead about Lady Corrinne and her twins…my twins too! They are all here in Michelle de Propei's city house. Maybe you can come by to visit them tomorrow? It would help."

"I will."

Philippe went back to the house to sit with the twins and Crispin. Corrinne smiled with relief when he showed up.

"Problems?"

"Not really. You just missed seeing Major Péan."

"Major Péan? What did he want?"

"Said he just wanted to welcome us to Québec. And to ask about Henri and news from Louisbourg."

"Did you tell him everything? About Anamosa?"

"Yes. He appeared genuinely heartbroken to hear about the attack. He was not surprised Henri elected to stay, or that Anamosa wanted to stay with him. But he also wants to meet with the two of us, privately. He did not say why. Just that he wants to tell us both at the same time. Of course, I am at my best when someone tells me they have a secret for me and then decides not to tell me. So, I've been imagining various unpleasant secrets."

"To meet with us privately? He used that word?"

"That word? Privately? Yes! He used that exact word! Don't become paranoid, Philippe. I am only one thought away from paranoid conclusions. I told the major to come see us tomorrow. Is that all right? Should we wait that long? Maybe you can go find him right now."

"I'm sorry. I wish I'd been here with you." Philippe explained what he had done that day. He did not tell her about his future mission to see Sir William Johnson, not yet. There were so many unanswered questions about this exceedingly dangerous journey, he did not want to complicate the uncertainty of it any further, not until he had some answers…and a plan to discuss.

"I spent time speaking with Madeleine this morning," Corrinne continued with restrained irritation. "She had a lot of questions about Henri. I told her of Henri's decision to stay in Louisbourg, and that I was unhappy with it. So was Madeleine...tearfully unhappy. I was polite, sensitive, and understanding about her feelings for Henri. I did not mention Anamosa, but my loyalties rest with Anamosa should it ever come to choosing one over the other."

They paused.

Philippe began to brood over what the governor asked him to do. Corrinne was reflecting about the ambiguity of their life now that they were in Québec City. *We are not supposed to be here.* She'd concluded this much at least, even as the *Falcon Queen* anchored. But the next question was far more difficult. *If not Québec City, where are we supposed to be?*

They were in the library of the city house. Constance was watching the children in the cuisine. Marcus was not feeling well.

When the pause grew awkward, Philippe took a deep breath. "Tell me what you are thinking."

Corrinne shook her head as if clearing the litter in her brain. "Constance could not find any bread today. There is no bread to buy. There is no harvesting being done since the farmers were called up by the militia."

"The farmers were released a month ago. They should be harvesting by now."

"The neighbors claim they've been called up again. For the new campaign. The one that will take you away." Her voice had an edge to it. "Of course, there is no more food coming from the Acadian farms. The people expect famine this winter. They are already talking about it. Montréal's condition is expected to be even worse. And Marcus woke up with a bad cough this morning after you left. He's got something. No fever yet, but... Michelle said she would ask a doctor to come from the hospital. No one's come so far. According to Michelle, the hospital is full of the sick, twice as many of the citizens as the soldiers. And half of them are children. So, no, I am not taking him to a hospital full of sick children. And I do not expect a doctor to visit. When I am not worrying about that, I sip mint tea and interpret the Roman Latin in Bishop Brevelaer's journals...just to cheer me up," she added drolly.

"Did you discover anything?"

"Yes. No. Just some interesting things Bishop Brevelaer learned." She winced. "I don't want to talk about that now." She stood and moved to sit on Philippe's lap. "Tell me some happy news."

"Well, my lap suddenly feels much better," Philippe teased.

"Oh, it does, does it?" Corrinne rocked her hips back and forth. She leaned into his face and licked his lips playfully. "At least we have that to look forward to."

"Captain Louis de Bougainville is coming to have dinner with us tonight."

Corrinne brightened. "Bougainville! The mathematician? The writer?"

"The very same man. And he is very anxious to meet the extraordinarily beautiful woman the citizens of Québec City are boasting about, claiming her as one of their own, who is also married to the very lucky, deeply fortunate and appreciative Scout Captain Gerrard. He wants to meet our twins, too."

"Well, that should make for good conversation." Corrinne was thinking what to prepare for this distinguished man of science. "He really said *extraordinarily beautiful*?"

"He claimed there are artists hoping to capture you in oils."

Corrinne suddenly remembered there were some oil paintings she foolishly permitted an artist to paint a decade ago in Québec City. Ones she preferred remain undiscovered.

"What time?"

"The custom is the sunset hour."

Louisbourg

Lieutenant Henri Gerrard stood upon the quay wall by Frédéric Gate. He cheered and waved his hat in the air, joining the other citizens of the faubourg in celebration as another squadron of warships entered Louisbourg harbor. Just the day before, a second squadron from Toulon had arrived, four ships-of-the-line and two frigates commanded by Commodore Joseph-François de Noble Du Revest, which purportedly had fought its way unscathed past an equally large English squadron at Gibraltar. That day, the famous Admiral Dubois de la Motte himself arrived leading nine ships-of-the-line and two frigates!

Louisbourg harbor now hosted a total of eighteen ships-of-the-line, ranging in armament from sixty-four to eighty guns, and five frigates. They would later learn that Admiral de la Motte arranged for two other ships to transport two battalions of metropolitan regulars from the Régiment de Berry to Québec City, intended for assignment to Fort Carillon under General Montcalm's command. But the admiral brought other reinforcements for Louisbourg.

Mercenaries.

With subdued celebration, the citizens watched a seven-hundred-man battalion of German mercenaries disembark to reinforce the Louisbourg garrison. The 1st Battalion Volontaires-Étrangers Regiment would reside in the Queen's Bastion barracks with Lieutenant-Colonel Karl Krieger commanding.

Lieutenant Gerrard and his handful of marines watched company after company of the mercenaries march up Rue Toulouse with smart precision on their way to their new barracks. None of the citizens were cheering, but some of them smiled politely.

Henri took his six marines back to the Dauphin barracks to give them the result of his meeting with the governor that morning.

"The good news is, you will all be promoted to sergeant. Before you ask, I don't know when any of us will be paid. You will be fed, clothed, and provided with a place to sleep. It is unlikely the English will attempt a landing to invade, with this battle fleet in the harbor. So, you will all live another year."

"That is good news," cheered Color Sergeant Gosse. "Let's get drunk."

"You may be asking yourselves, why am I being promoted to sergeant? Because you volunteered to stay. And because the governor is expanding this squad of marines to a full battalion of Troupes de la Marine...or one as large as it can get. The Dauphin barracks will hold these marines as they arrive from...well, I don't know where. I've been given command of this battalion."

Gosse smiled. "Excellent, sir! Congratulations! May I suggest you buy the first bottle of brandy."

The other marines smiled.

"We have brandy?" Henri asked skeptically.

"Lieutenant, we are marines. That is a big fucking navy in our harbor. The marines are part of the navy. The navy always has brandy," Gosse reminded him with assurance.

Henri nodded. "Yes. You're right. I will get us some brandy."

The other marines smiled.

"What if I don't want to be a sergeant?" asked Private Pieter l'Alcyon.

"Oh? Don't worry," said Gosse. "A battalion of marines, what, three hundred of them at a minimum? Three hundred will make a lot of shit. The marine privates will be carrying a lot of shit buckets from the barracks to the latrines every day. You will still have that honorable work to do...

Private l'Alcyon. Or, as a sergeant, you can *order* the privates to carry the shit buckets. I will let you think about how this works."

"If I command these marines, I intend to train them for night-raids and counter-attacks," Henri continued. "We will start getting expert with the cutlass beyond what you may know right now because, as sergeants, we will be training the new marines when they arrive. Color Sergeant Gosse will train us in defense, because in between the English cannons shelling us, the redcoats might assault a position of weakness with fixed bayonets."

"You can be certain they will," Gosse affirmed. "Ten feet of pig sticker, with the last two feet, a razor sharp triangular spear with three sharpened edges. This will be line infantry, hand-to-hand fighting. No hiding behind trees."

Henri smiled. He was going to love working with Color Sergeant Gosse.

"Never forget, you are marines," Henri said in a somber voice. "You are elite fighting men. Nearly as good as the regular grenadiers. But you will be trained to fight with a cutlass hung over your shoulder in a scabbard. And you will train the privates in your platoon to be as good as you or better. You will dress proudly and walk proudly. That exhibition of pride starts right now. Clean out these barracks. No garbage. No rotting food remains on the floor. No dirt! Sweep it out. Keep it swept. Make it ready for inspection at any time. If no one is in a bed, I expect the bed to be made up." Henri stopped. A new idea taking shape. "Color Sergeant Gosse, is it possible for us to train to become something akin to *marine-grenadiers*? Something new? Not seen before?"

"Marine-grenadiers?" Gosse nodded with an expression of grim promise. "Yes indeed, Lieutenant, sir! My cock is already hard with the thought of this."

"Very well. Then it begins with the six of us. Marine-grenadiers. We will establish the disciplines this elite troop will represent. Color Sergeant, make a list. When it's ready, I want a plaque of these disciplines posted on the wall. I want the marines to memorize these disciplines. Let us do this right."

Québec City

Marcus was sick and coughing constantly from the afternoon on into the night. He complained that his sides were aching, so Corrinne could only spend an hour with Captain Louis Antoine de Bougainville. She found the man charming to the extreme and probably one of the most intelligent people she had ever met. They discussed topics during dinner that ranged over the sciences like they were dishes on the menu. Astronomy, mathematics, of course, botany, earth history, alchemy, and some current scientific theories.

"Some night gazers think stars twinkle because of temperature."

"Temperature?" Corrinne had never heard that before. "How? Why? What are the stars?"

"Well, they make light, like our sun. One theory is they are just like our sun, only much farther away."

"Really? And temperature?"

"Well, remember, this is a theory. A Dutch noble lord, a man of science, placed a tall candle burning in the corner of his palace on a winter's night. Then he stood across the dark room in the opposite corner. The room was totally dark, except for the candle. The room was actually a ballroom, so diagonally, it was maybe fifty paces. Then, at a distance of…well, I'm not certain, but let's say three to four paces in front of the candle, he had a servant pull a cord attached to a small wagon that was carrying a square heating stove, which stood lower in height than the candle stood by three or four feet. The servant pulled the wagon very slowly perpendicular to this candle, until it was between his lordship and the candle. This Dutch lord told him to stop. He claims, in the heat rising from that stove, the flame of the candle appeared to waver. To him the candle appeared to be guttering. But to the servant looking directly at the candle from an angle, that is, no stove in between, the flame on the candle was not moving at all. Pure heat is invisible. You cannot see evidence of it unless it contains something solid, like wax, oil or ash particles, or smoke. His lordship and the servant could both see the candle at the same time, but his lordship was looking at it through the heat rising straight up from the stove. So, in a sense, in his eyes, the candle *twinkled*."

Corrinne was fascinated. "So, what makes the stars twinkle?"

"Good question. The theory says it is caused by the different temperature of air currents in our sky, as warm air turns to cold air and back to warm air, *ad infinitum*. Seamen experience this all the time. The air is invisible like the heat it holds, of course. We feel hot or cold in a breeze. A cold breeze turns to a warm breeze. But the heat of the air roils like eddies in a river. It blurs the light from the stars back and forth. Just like air in that ballroom, going from cold winter air to the hot air rising from that stove. Ergo, the stars twinkle. But another observer miles away may not see the same thing."

"That is genius."

"Oh, hardly my lady. And in any case, I wasn't the one who performed this experiment. The mathematics his lordship used to explain this was terribly flawed. That didn't help. But we'll work out the math on this someday. The observed phenomenon, however, could be duplicated. It was real. That was enough for me."

Corrinne looked at Philippe. "This is extraordinary. Captain Louis is extraordinary."

Philippe nodded. "Yes, he is. And Louis is *my* friend. I see him every day."

Constance came into the dining room and said Marcus was coughing again. Corrinne excused herself and did not return.

"My compliments, Philippe. Lady Corrinne is exceptional. Not only in her singular beauty, but she might be the smartest woman I've ever encountered."

Philippe nodded. "Yes, she is. And Corrinne is *my* wife. I sleep with her every night."

They both laughed.

Philippe's tone grew serious. "Is this coughing malady widespread? My men don't complain of it."

"It seems to be a child's disease. There are a lot of children coughing like that at the hospital," Bougainville added somberly.

"How bad does it get?"

"Not to frighten you, and the majority of the children do survive. However, a third of them do not. According to the doctors, Michelle de Propei is considered on par with the best healers in Québec City. Your son will receive the best care by staying in a bed right here."

After Bougainville left, Philippe went into the room where Marcus lay sweating, and sat on the bed opposite to Corrinne. His son's breathing was labored and had a bubbling wheeze to it. Marcus' head felt warm. Though not a blazing fever, it was hot enough. Corrinne was worried and kept placing cold cloths on his brow.

"Michelle said she'd bring home a poultice to place on his chest, one that should help with his breathing. She said to give him water only, or weak tea. Don't feed him anything that requires him to chew to eat. He might vomit and that will irritate his throat worse than it is."

Constance came into the small servants' room they'd set aside to care for Marcus. It was one of three in this house.

"How is he?"

Corrinne wiped Marcus' sweaty face with a cold cloth. He smiled at her. "He's fighting it. My little man is fighting it," she replied with a quavering voice.

"Michelle is here. She is mixing two poultices in the cuisine. She'll come in a few minutes."

"Constance, I cannot express my appreciation enough for the love you've given to my children."

"They are easy to love, my lady. They are wonderful little people. Calypso has charmed Crispin. They are playing together in my room."

Philippe decided he and Corrinne were staying the night in this room. "I'll get us some chairs."

Philippe brought in a cushioned one for Corrinne along with a foot stool. He got a rocker for himself. And an extra table chair for Michelle if she needed one.

Michelle came into the room holding a tray of folded flannel towels, plus a tall bottle of olive oil. She'd made up two poultices. One was made of stewed wild onions, the other was a crushed paste of water and mustard seeds.

"These will make the room a little pungent, but the Mohawk healer and the Chinese herbalist at the hospital cannot agree which one is better. We will try them both. Rub some olive oil on his chest and we will place the onion one on him first. No longer than an hour, I'm told. Besides, the smell is strong. It will be good to get it out of the room."

Philippe's eyes were watering.

"*Stink*!" Marcus protested weakly.

"I know, my angel," Corrinne said tenderly. "Just for a little while."

"Now we wait," Michelle said.

Philippe gave Michelle the rocker. "I will get us some small glasses of brandy to sip."

Y

Québec City Waterfront

The next morning, Captain LaTour transferred half of his cargo to the docks and was forced to accept an abysmal price from the smirking Grand Société company man.

"Don't worry, Captain. Lower profits mean your tax bill will be less," said the buyer.

"So, I've heard. I point out to you, sir, that a higher sales price means my net profits would be greater after taxes. That's my last load for today. It will take two more days to unload the rest. I want to see the furs I'm to carry."

"Certainly. Those three warehouses over there are full of furs."

"I'll have my cargo launch take me there directly."

The buyer handed him a list of the goods he had just purchased showing the prices. Then he left the barge.

LaTour gave the pricing manifest to Victorio. "Don't lose this! Make us copies. Let the braver merchants from the city come along our starboard side to make purchases out of sight of the wharf. Sell it to them at prices lower than any of these. That will give them an edge on the Grand Société. Don't sell too much. Save enough to unload more tomorrow and the balance the day after."

Captain LaTour took old Turiau with him to look at the furs. He was once a *coureur de bois* and had an eye for quality. When they got to the warehouses, he found them packed almost to the roof. The stench was appalling.

He pulled a neck scarf over his nose. "These are rotting!" he shouted with disgust at the warehouse supervisor.

The man shrugged. "They've been sitting here for months. Trade ships find it difficult to get here because of the English cruisers patrolling the river mouth. I'm used to the smell. But not all of them are putrid. Not yet. Choose the pallets you want. I'll have my men move them to the front so you can sort through the furs."

"Get started with this, Turiau. I will send you two more men. Who do you want?"

Turiau paused. "Send me Tinidor. He smells worse than the furs. And Audrik. He's tall enough to reach some of the higher stacks."

"Whatever you pick, place them on a separate pallet. Have it covered and tied down under clean canvas. When full, move the pallet immediately to our barge." LaTour did some quick calculations. "We'll load them two high by nine long, thirty-six per hold, two holds. Aye, seventy-two of these pallets, a respectable haul indeed. It will be nice to trade some furs back in France again, eh, Turiau? Good profits to share among the crew."

"Is that where we're going, Captain? France?"

"Well, there's a war. They've not told me the port yet. But where else can we go to sell our furs? The islanders certainly don't clamor for beaver skins. Profits will be huge if we can get this load back to La Rochelle, or

Brest for that matter. Pick only the cured ones. We won't begin loading them up from the barge for another three days. Keep a list of the different types for me to see as you go. Keep them sorted by type on the pallets, too. Tie a colored ribbon or something to identify what they are under the canvass. I'll have someone bring you the colored ribbons."

"Aye, sir."

*

It had been a long night for Corrinne, Michelle, and Philippe. Marcus continued to wheeze and cry from the pain of coughing. But around half past three in the morning, he finally fell to sleep. His fever had broken, too.

Michelle got a few hours of sleep before she went back to the hospital. She visited the room to check on Marcus before she left.

"I'm going to the hospital now," Michelle whispered. "The coughing could start again as soon as he is awake. Madeleine will be coming home to sleep soon. She had night duty. I will send two more poultices with her to prepare for you. Let Marcus sleep, but as soon as he wakes up, apply the poultices as before. The onion one first and the mustard pack on his back two hours later. We will probably have to do it again tonight, so I will bring more poultices with me when I come back home."

Corrinne hugged her tightly. "Thank you. I don't know what I would have done without you."

After she was gone, Philippe told Corrinne to go lie down.

"Get some sleep. I'll watch him."

"What about you?"

"Me? I'm used to being awake for two days at a time in the bush. I'll just nap in the chair. I'll be fine."

It seemed to Philippe he only nodded off a few minutes when something gripped his shoulder. Philippe awoke with a start and grabbed the wrist to throw the attacker off balance. Constance suppressed her cry of surprise at seeing the angry face of this giant *coureur de bois* glaring down at her. The man's expression softened. He let go of her hand.

Philippe looked quickly at Marcus. He was still asleep.

"I'm so sorry, Constance," he whispered. "Terrible things happen quickly in the wilderness. The enemy usually attacks at night. I am truly sorry. Did I hurt you?"

Constance rubbed her wrist. She saw the knife in his right hand. "No, Philippe," she whispered. "It's all right. It's just that the officer that was here yesterday has returned. He is outside the front door."

Philippe shook his head wearily. "What time is it?"

"Nine thirty."

"Do we have any coffee brewed?"

"Yes. Tea, too."

"Please bring some of each to the library for us. I'll meet the major there. Then awaken Corrinne. Tell her we will wait for her before we talk. I'll leave this door ajar, so I can hear if Marcus calls out."

Philippe went to the front door and welcomed Major Péan.

"Follow me," he whispered, holding a finger to his lips. He gestured at the doorway left ajar as they went by it.

The major was dressed in a uniform that looked newly purchased. Philippe was wearing the uniform that Henri had given him. And he could not recall when it was last washed.

"Nice medal," Philippe teased.

"Yes. Did you know it permits me to go to the occasional meetings of the Order of Saint Louis back in Paris, the ones attended by the King?"

"No, I did not. I guess that's some time away for you."

Constance entered with a tray of tea, coffee, and sweet biscuits.

"Thank you. We'll pour it ourselves."

Philippe arranged three of the cushioned chairs to place Major Péan in the middle.

"I'm interested to know why you wanted to meet with us. But we must wait until Corrinne is here. So, what have you done since I went to Louisbourg?"

"I have been studying the last three years of commercial books for the Grand Société company."

"No more soldiering then?"

Major Péan smiled indulgently. "It would seem so, yes? Oddly enough, I miss it."

"Where do you study ledgers?"

"Either at Intendant Bigôt's offices, or some office in the governor's palace."

Philippe squinted. "Did you want to do this?"

"No. I was ordered to do this."

"Ordered to read commercial documents? Why?"

"Bigôt and Governor Vaudreuil want me to become familiar, no, not just familiar, an expert actually, on how the Grand Société embezzled the colonial treasury of New France."

Philippe thought he jested and laughed a little. "That's blunt. Even for you."

"What's blunt?" Corrinne said as she entered.

They stood. Major Péan bowed slightly, lifted her hand, and kissed her fingertips.

"I am impressed, Michel. Twice in two days."

"You deserve it. And I am practicing for when I get to Paris, possibly even Versailles."

"You're going to Versailles?!"

"Possibly, but Paris for certain."

"Why?" Corrinne asked.

"As I was explaining to your rugged scout captain, for the last three months, I have studied and become expert at explaining and defending the commercial transactions of the Grand Société. This company has a monopoly on all things shipped, imported, exported, traded, and sold anywhere in New France. I was surprised to learn, I am a five percent shareholder in this company, with the dividend awards given to Angélique when I am absent from the city, away in the field. Of course, the governor, Intendant Bigôt, and it appears twenty-eight other shareholders between New France and Versailles, also receive various amounts of money from the profits of this company. However, it appears there are a few honest people left in the French government who believe this company is gratuitously corrupt. I know that surprises you. The bigger surprise I found was that Major Michel Péan, that's me, was singled out to be the person behind it all, and furthermore is pointed to, by all involved, as the only person who can answer the questions. So, I am going back to France to answer such questions before a tribunal of three judges."

Corrinne stopped sipping her coffee. "Do you think we'll ever see you again?" she asked sincerely.

"My lady, you obviously think my chances of escaping this sophisticated entrapment are not so good."

"What do you think?" Philippe challenged.

"Well, as Intendant Bigôt pointed out to me, the people involved in this fleecing do not want their flow of money to stop. They all have an interest in seeing me exonerated of all charges. So, there's that. And I was made a chevalier in the Order of Saint Louis. The King is the Grand Master of this order. If you condemn a knight of this order, you are condemning the King, logic implies. Thus, it becomes a risk to accuse me of something without tarnishing the King. And I have indeed studied the books of the Grand Société. I see the manipulations. I understand the ambiguities. Maybe I can talk my way out of it. Otherwise, it is the bastille for me, and everybody loses. *Everybody* does not want that."

Corrinne was now confused. "Apologies for saying this major, but was this the private topic you wanted to discuss with the two of us?"

"I apologize back to you both. No, it was not. It has just been on my mind a lot, as you can imagine. You are two of the few people I trust enough to share any knowledge of this. But I came here for another reason altogether. I came here to alert you to something I inadvertently discovered in the governor's office."

Péan shared how intimate he was with the governor's office and Bigôt's offices after a decade of constant visitation.

"So, while he was dining, I read this confidential missive from Versailles to Governor Vaudreuil about Lady Corrinne VanderMeer."

"We are familiar with this." Philippe related the discussion they had with Governor Drucour in Louisbourg about the same thing, and the decision made by Commodore du Bauffremont.

"That's good to know. But what I came to tell you, *privately*, is that the same letter with the same language was sent independently to Intendant François Bigôt, who is authorized by the king to arrest Lady Corrinne VanderMeer if he deems her to be a spy."

Corrinne's jaw sagged a little. "I hope you are jesting."

"No, my lady, unfortunately I am not. Governor Vaudreuil reads all the official mail coming to Québec City, no matter who sends it or whose name it addresses. You can be certain, he has read the letter to Intendant Bigôt, because it was laid open on his desk when I saw it. Vaudreuil is aware of Bigôt's vindictiveness. The governor keeps three piles of missives on his desk. One of them is the "burn" pile. The missives in that pile will be destroyed. I think that is what will happen to the missive to Bigôt. However, Captain

Trieste is responsible for burning such confidential documents. And Captain Trieste is not always discreet."

Philippe's jaw tightened. "What are you saying?"

"Captain, I recommend that you bring up the conversation you had with Governor Drucour and the decision resulting from that discussion. The missive mentions that both governors received the same instructions from Versailles. It is fair to say you presumed Governor Vaudreuil already knew about this. But then ask him for some assurance, in writing, these instructions from Versailles will not be used against Lady Corrinne."

"That won't make any difference," Corrinne said tersely. "Even if the governor gives my husband a written assurance, if Bigôt gets his hand on this missive, he then has direct authorization from the King of France, which supersedes any order from the governor."

Michel Péan knew that Intendant Bigôt secretly and routinely communicated with Madame de Pompadour. She was also a shareholder in the Grande Société. A missive like this originated from her, of that Péan had no doubt. The question was why? But her reason was not important.

The major tried to mitigate the revelation. "During times of war, the governor has the powers of a viceroy."

"Bigôt won't ask for permission from the governor!" Corrinne almost shouted. "He will act on this authority! Tell him, Philippe."

Philippe shook his head with disgust. *We've not been back a week and we are in it again!*

"Corrinne is right. If Bigôt has the chance, he will act. He will cite the missive as his authority to arrest her."

The library grew quiet.

"I deeply apologize," Major Péan finally said. "My purpose was to preempt something unexpected happening to you."

Corrinne was aggravated. "Don't apologize, Major. I am not happy about this…but if you had not told us, when Bigôt decides to act on this missive, we would have been caught completely by surprise."

They all heard a cough from the other room.

Corrinne exhaled wearily and stood. "I must go. My son is sick."

Philippe was frustrated and angry at being boxed in again.

"Is there something I can do to help?" Michel Péan asked.

"I don't know, Major. *Is* there some way you can help?"

"The governor does not intend for Intendant Bigôt to get this missive. I guarantee it. It gives the intendant authority to act on his own. Vaudreuil will never accept this. He will order the missive destroyed and probably has already given that order. Intendant Bigôt will not get this missive unless Captain Trieste, acting on his own, gives it to Bigôt for some type of recompense. The chances of that happening are very low in my opinion. But it is a way for this to happen. I will confront Captain Trieste, unless you disagree."

CHAPTER 30
LAKE GEORGE WILDERNESS
JULY 1757
She Always has a Plan

Lieutenant-Colonel George Monroe, commanding officer of the 35th Regiment of Foot, at Fort William Henry, received constant reports from his Mohawk scout allies that a great *herd* of warriors were gathering north of Fort Carillon. It was purportedly so large the natives did not have a way to describe how many. Monro did not expect the French regulars would attack his fort again so soon. The strategic value of Fort William Henry lay in its boat-building capabilities, which was effectively destroyed by the French raiders only three months earlier. He was slowly rebuilding it with supplies and craftsmen sent up from Albany. But the fleet of boats necessary to make an assault up Lake George would not be ready until next spring. He assessed, therefore, that the French would encourage their native allies to conduct sporadic raids throughout the summer to slow or damage the efforts to reconstitute the boat-building works, but nothing more.

"That's what I would do," he told his officers.

George Monro was born in 1700. He'd spent his entire military career as a member of the 35th Regiment of Foot, which was originally raised in Belfast, Ireland in 1701. George Monro was commissioned as a lieutenant in August of 1718. The 35th Foot would spend the next forty-eight years in Ireland. George Monro never married, but he advanced in rank steadily, to captain in September of 1727, then major in August of 1747, and finally lieutenant-colonel and commander of the regiment in January of 1750. The regiment saw no action in the field in any war until the soon to be called Seven Years War was declared between England and France in 1756. They were sent to England to be fully equipped for fighting in North America and transported to Nova Scotia.

In March of 1757, Lord Loudon had ordered the 35th Regiment of Foot to the relief of the 44th Regiment at Fort William Henry. Monro marched five companies of his regiment into the fort: about five hundred fifty men. It would be this regiment's first test in battle. They had drilled for decades in line infantry tactics, all of which were useless now in the wilderness style of fighting in North America. Survival would depend more upon the individual courage of soldiers in vicious hand-to-hand fighting.

Before the end of June, the 35th would be joined by two independent companies of men from New York, plus an additional eight hundred provincial soldiers from New Jersey and New Hampshire. In total, Lieutenant-Colonel Monro commanded fifteen hundred men for the defense of Fort William Henry.

Late in June, two English prisoners who had recently escaped from the French brought Monro a reliable report on the forces amassing near Fort Carillon. It was a regular French army that, combined with native warrior support, totaled some eight thousand. And they were coming.

Québec City

Major Péan had confronted Captain Trieste and shared this information with Captain Gerrard.

"Trieste claimed not to know what I was talking about. That he'd seen no official missives in the dispatch pouch carried by *La Comète* concerning Lady Corrinne VanderMeer."

Philippe frowned. "Do you believe him?"

"No. Even presuming Trieste did not see the one addressed to Intendant Bigôt, and further presuming the governor destroyed or ripped that one into little pieces, Trieste would have seen the one addressed to the governor. Governor Vaudreuil must reply to it."

Philippe's frown turned angry. "Now what?"

"I still recommend you ask the governor directly about the missive, claiming you saw and read its duplicate in Louisbourg. Ask Governor Vaudreuil if he has any questions, that you are concerned for your wife's safety. It is the truth and you deserve an answer."

"Well, I'm heading to the council of war right now. I will have an opportunity to speak with the governor privately. What about you?"

"Me? How kind of you to ask," he answered drolly. "In a few days, I will sail to Brest, take a coach to Paris, where I will be given trident and net and sent into the arena."

"How do you make jests about this?"

Péan smiled. "I can provide the names, the dates of the transactions, and the amount of monies involved. I have it memorized. And *everybody* knows this."

"You should worry about being assassinated," Philippe offered.

"Ah, yes. A worthy observation. I've also written this down and will give it to somebody I trust, who will give it to the tribunal investigator, should anything happen to me."

"You better ascertain *everybody* knows about this. Or they might kill you out of ignorance."

Major Péan nodded. "That's true. I'd not thought of that. Thank you."

"Then you sail for Brest on *La Comète*?"

"No. *La Comète* will return to Louisbourg. I will enjoy opulent accommodations aboard the *Falcon Queen* and Captain LaTour's sophisticated wit during my voyage. *La Comète* will escort the *Falcon Queen* until we reach the eastern coasts of Newfoundland. The frigate will sail south and LaTour will sail east."

Philippe said wryly, "Does Captain LaTour know this?"

"He will tomorrow! I have the privilege of handing him an order to provide me passage, signed by Governor Vaudreuil."

*

The participants for Governor Vaudreuil's council of war to review the planned attack on Fort William Henry filled the war council room in the citadel to its capacity. This would be the most formidable commitment of warring resources the French would field since the beginning of the war. Scout Captain Philippe Gerrard's forces had grown to a hundred sixty veteran *coureurs de bois* and native warriors. Vaudreuil and Montcalm had decided not to mention his promotion to colonel until after the battle, since it would invite too many questions better left unanswered. After the fort was taken, *Colonel* Gerrard would continue his journey to see Sir William Johnson.

General Montcalm announced he would conduct a classic Vauban-style siege. They would take the proper siege cannon, howitzers, mortars, and smaller caliber weapons, almost fifty artillery pieces in all. The army would stage and advance from Fort Carillon in two divisions. General François de Gaston de Lévis, Montcalm's second-in-command, would advance first with two thousand five hundred elite troops. They would march on foot down the west side of Lac du Saint-Sacrament and occupy the lands to the west of Fort William Henry, where the closest siege trenches would be dug. General

Montcalm's five thousand-plus main force would follow a day behind in a flotilla of bateaux, birch-bark war canoes and specially designed two-pontoon bateaux to carry the heavy artillery.

Each officer commanding a specific battalion or specialized unit of men presented when their name was called. Captain Philippe Gerrard presented for his scout battalion. It would go forward with General de Lévis and defend a place of ambush on the seventeen-mile road leading south to Fort Edward. When the main forces arrived, the siege would begin with an encirclement of Fort William Henry and the large battle entrenchment built to house other provincial troops added to the garrison to reinforce the 35th Foot inside the main fort.

A lot of planning had been completed for this siege and General Montcalm was very confident of its success. The French officers at the war council were confident they would succeed as well, but all of them were less confident of their tribal allies. These native warriors were difficult to control even in small numbers. In this campaign, there would be almost two thousand of them. Aware of Governor Vaudreuil's opinion, and the governor's penchant to boast how the tribes' wilderness fighting skills could be used against the English, the French officers were reticent about voicing any opinion to the contrary. They were weeks away from conducting this attack. The warriors were already here. There was nothing to gain from voicing this complaint.

Before the battle commenced, nineteen tribal nations, with twice as many sub-groups, had arrived north of Fort Carillon. The Abenaki, Malecite, Mi'kmaq, Nipissing, Caughnawaga Mohawk, Menominee, Ojibway, Ottawa, Chippewa, Mississauga, Potawatomi, Winnebago, Huron, Algonquin, Sauk, Fox, Miami, Delaware, and even the Iowa from the plains, a tribe never seen in Canada before. Nearly a thousand from the Pays d'en Haut, the upper country, and an equal number dubiously referred to as *domesticated*, since many of them were converts to Catholicism. This religion of *peace* had little influence on their barbaric behavior when it came to war.

So great was the consensus among these tribes that the French now dominated the lands against the English, some of them had marched fifteen hundred miles to take part in what they expected to be a huge quantity of plunder from a major English fort and settlement. The tribal warriors were not in this for any money or land, or to gain any favor with the French. They were in it for the spoils. The scalps, human prisoners, parts of people's bodies, and other gruesome trophies, articles of uniforms, weapons, and any possessions they could plunder from the baggage carried by the white man. Ironically, they would leave gold and silver coinage lying on the ground. They understood this was a white man's battle fought with the great thunder guns. They would agree to follow the orders of the French commanders, and even obeyed them for a time. They had come from far away for a share of this booty. When the clash was over, they would not be denied their reward.

Before the war council was adjourned, Governor Vaudreuil gave a rousing speech about the importance of this battle.

"This victory may, in fact, cause the English-Americans to sue for peace. The role you play in this will give you something to celebrate for the rest of your lives."

To many of the more senior officers, the scarred veterans of many battles and years of wilderness warfare, Scout Captain Philippe Gerrard included, the governor's words had little merit. This battle remained to be fought. Many things could happen that might turn the events. For instance, the recent arrival of the French fleet in Louisbourg may have induced Lord Loudon to move a brigade of his regulars to the defense of Fort William Henry. It was well known that Lord Loudon was confident he now had sufficient troops to make a campaign against the French forts on Lake Champlain. Victory there, followed by a march on Québec City and Montréal, was realistic in less than a month. He could win the war this year.

The meeting ended with a prayer from Jean-François Hubert, the Sulpician Bishop of Québec City. Everyone knelt to accept his blessing.

The same bishop would travel to Fort Carillon to bless the troops. Next to the soldiers, the Catholic tribal warriors would also kneel.

*

Governor Vaudreuil gestured for Philippe to remain behind as the room emptied out. He followed the governor to his private office.

"*Colonel* Gerrard...what do you think of this overall strategy to invest Fort William Henry?"

"Unless the English have seven thousand regulars already on the march in relief, we will invest Fort William Henry within a week of its encirclement."

"Good! That's exactly what I anticipate. Immediately after the surrender, I want you to proceed with your mission to Sir William Johnson. Captain Trieste will give you the prepared documents, with extra copies for you and General Montcalm. You have the freedom to negotiate with Sir William if you choose to do so. Your main objective is to get them to consider a negotiation is worth exploring."

"Yes, sir."

"Any other questions?"

"Yes, sir. When I was in Louisbourg, my wife and I had a discussion with Governor Drucour and Commodore du Bauffremont about a missive from Versailles, questioning the legitimacy of Lady Corrinne VanderMeer. This missive indicated you had also received the same inquiry and mentioned a copy was sent to Québec City addressed to you. We resolved this before I left Louisbourg. I wanted to know if you have any questions for me regarding this matter?"

Vaudreuil measured Captain Gerrard's words before he answered in even tones. "What was the resolution?"

"That Lady Corrinne is legitimately and publicly Lady Corrinne VanderMeer, wife of Lord Charles VanderMeer, the son of Louis Ernest, Duke of Brunswick-Wolfenbüttel. That was the commodore's written reply to Versailles. Known to the Governor Drucour and now Commodore du Bauffremont, Lady Corrinne is also a spy for the French government disguised as a wife of this Dutch lord. Now you know this, too. Her invented identity must be protected for her to return to Boston. On the eve of my departure for Fort William Henry and my mission to see Sir William Johnson, I am anxious about her safety here in Québec City. I do not know how many other people from your office read the official mail. Intendant Bigôt, for instance, would arrest her if he ever sees an inquiry like this from Versailles. The way the missive is written, he is authorized to take independent action by the direct authority of the King."

Vaudreuil did not reply for several seconds. They stared at one another.

"Is that all, Captain?"

"I would like to hear your opinion on this, sir."

"I see. Based on what you just imparted to me, my response will be the same as Commodore du Bauffremont's."

"Do I have assurance that no one else has read this particular missive?"

"Of course. And I look forward to dining with you and Lady Corrinne upon your return to Québec City."

"Thank you, sir." Philippe stood and saluted.

Vaudreuil dismissed him with the wave of his hand.

*

Philippe left the palace and went straight to Michelle's house. Michelle and Madeleine were at work in the hospital. Marcus lay in bed still recovering from the terrible cough that had developed a week earlier. Philippe sat by his side. Marcus was asleep. He had no fever. He hardly coughed anymore, but Michelle directed that Marcus must stay in bed until a full day went by without any further coughing. Philippe went to the cuisine.

Corrinne was waiting for him, sipping coffee. Constance was making a pie of some kind and Calypso was helping her, with face and clothes dusted in flour, like a light snowfall.

Philippe took hold of Calypso and hugged her tightly in his arms.

"God, you are beautiful," he told her. She giggled. "Just like your mother."

"You met with him?"

Philippe heard the tension in Corrinne's voice. He knew who she meant.

"Yes. I just came from there."

Corrinne arose from her chair. "Constance, please excuse us."

Philippe followed her into the library. They took sitting chairs across from one another, pulled closer together, and talked in low voices. Their knees were almost touching.

"Tell me."

Philippe told her word for word what was said.

"Do you believe him?"

Philippe shook his head. "Even if I did, I don't trust him. And after tomorrow, I will be gone for at least three months, maybe four. We should think about this."

"Philippe, I have been thinking about this for *days*. There is nothing for me to do in Québec City or Montréal except wait. Wait, until the war closes in on us. Wait, while you are gone all the time in the fighting. In the meantime, Intendant Bigôt will *never* stop trying to arrest me or extort me or worse. And Henri was right. Assassins from the other great houses will come again to Louisbourg. People in Louisbourg know that I've gone to Québec City. These killers will come here to search for me. Or the never-ending wraith will send its servants to find me, looking for the châsse. Or both. We have the children to worry about now. Michelle told me this morning there was a report of an outbreak of smallpox in Rimouski. It's been isolated to a farm. But with widespread famine expected in the winter, other diseases will come with it."

Philippe tried to read her thoughts. *She will not stay here. She cannot go back to Louisbourg. Montréal is only deeper into the problem. Boston?*

"Corrinne, you cannot go back to Boston, if that's what you're thinking. You might be accused of being a spy."

"I know. But let me ask you something first. Do you think I should stay here?"

Philippe looked at the floor for several seconds before he answered. The thought of not having her by his side at night almost made him stop breathing. Then it occurred to him. He looked up. He could see it in her eyes. *She has a plan. She always has a plan.*

"No. I don't. But I see you've already decided. So just tell me."

"I want to leave secretly with the children, so no one knows where I went. The châsse is well hidden on the *Falcon Queen,* and it will be over water. Charles was right. The wraith cannot see the châsse while it is over water. Or see me for that matter. Therefore, all our enemies will be searching for me in Canada…but not in France."

"Not in France…what?!"

"I can live with my sister in Brest. No one knows what I look like there. If anyone sees me in Brest, they will presume I am Margaux. Philippe, it is a perfect hiding place. No, that is selfish of me to say. Not perfect. You won't be there. But the children will be safe with me until this is over. I can write letters to Michelle. And you can send me letters addressed to Margaux-Lyneth Dubonnet in Brest. They will be our go-betweens. We can communicate as regularly as the dispatch ships sail."

Philippe exhaled wearily. Any sense of optimism he harbored was demolished by this idea. France was an ocean away. It was not a place Philippe could reach on foot, by an overland journey, no matter his willingness to sacrifice or suffer pain. His expression sagged to despair.

"I will never see you again." His heart was breaking. He felt forsaken.

Tears spilled down Corrinne's cheeks.

"Don't you dare say that, Philippe! This war! This curse! These assassins! None of these things will prevail against us. This will all end. We have a destiny together, Philippe. Our children are proof of that."

Philippe's wrenching sadness remained. It was devastating to see. Corrinne took his face in her hands and placed kisses on it everywhere.

"My love! My love! Do you remember the letter you sent me so long ago that found its way to me in Connecticut, even after passing through the hands of so many strangers? It arrived with the wax seal still intact. You said in your writing, if that happened, it proved we share a destiny. I believed it then. I believed it when we first met in Le Havre. I believe it now. I believe going to Brest to live with my sister is the right decision for our safety. But Philippe, oh, Philippe, my love! We *both* must believe this. If you believe it is safer for me to stay in Québec City, then I will stay. I will stay and never question your judgement. And I will dream of you every night we are apart, until we are together again. Because no matter how long we are separated, or how wide the distance between us, we *will* come together again." *It does not matter that I am in France*, she did not say.

Philippe's heart was pounding at the thought of being apart from Corrinne, made worse that he was completely in love with these two beautiful little people that came from her body. He had barely gotten to know them. They loved him now. They called him *Papah*. These miraculous little spirits, who could heal every part of him with just their simple hugs and kisses. The thought he'd be apart from them, too? It left him empty. He had no words. His strength waned.

Gripped with emotional exhaustion, Philippe leaned forward to rest his forehead against Corrinne's. They clasped hands in silence. Her tears dripped on their fingers. But as their heads touched, Corrinne experienced a rushing sensation ripple through her body. In all their years together and the variety of ways she'd embraced this man she loved so much, they had never simply touched their heads and hands together like this. The connection felt very natural, very familiar, and very intense.

Our souls are touching, she thought.

Philippe was affected no less. This silent touch he shared with her evoked a sense of peace within him, as if nothing else mattered. It was a potent type of intimacy, a bond that could be stretched but never broken.

They remained in this embrace, it seemed, for a long time. Then Philippe said, steadily and softy, "This war won't last much longer. General Montcalm knows this. We don't talk about it aloud. Even though we win all the battles, this is the *fourth war* in New France. The Americans in Boston were upset that England gave back Louisbourg after the Americans shed so much blood taking it in the last war. Those Boston men boasted they knew how to do it. They boasted they will do it again. I heard them promise one another that they will not allow England to make peace this time with the Canadians. They don't care about France. Next year, the redcoat regulars will outnumber the French metropolitan troops five or six to one, maybe even more. The English don't have to make peace. And there are a million Americans living in the colonies. It is only a matter of time until the English navy anchors in Québec's harbor. If they take Louisbourg this year, it could happen as early as next year. And I have no idea where I will be when that happens. But I know I don't want you here alone, without me by your side."

Philippe raised his head and gazed into Corrinne's anguished green eyes.

"You are right. You are always right. It's just that I will miss you all so much," he said in a tormented voice.

*

Philippe Gerrard rose early in the morning and went out to Captain LaTour's ship before he reported to military headquarters. The captain met him as he stepped off the ladder onto the helm deck.

"Philippe! You came to say good-bye to me?"

"Not exactly, Captain. I understand you are sailing to Brest."

"I am indeed. And I will carry *his royal rudeness*, Major Michel Péan, as a passenger. Can you believe that? He has arrested me, what, three times in the last ten years? How times have changed for all of us. But I carry a full load of the best furs I have seen in over two years. The Grand Société agent overcharged me by a factor of two for them, but I will sell them for three times that amount, if not more. Oh...I am glad you are here. I still have Lady Corrinne's standing clock, her chair, and her bathing tub in the main cabin. I was going to move these pieces to a warehouse somewhere, but I am not certain where. Do you know what to do?"

Philippe was subdued as he said, "As a matter of fact, I do." Philippe spent the next five minutes explaining the revelation by Major Péan and the conversation with Governor Vaudreuil the day before. "We have decided Corrinne, Marcus, and Calypso should reside with her sister in Brest."

Captain LaTour eyes widened. "God's balls," he whispered.

"Yes. My reaction exactly." Philippe further explained Corrinne's logic on her safety.

"Well. All right. It will be our pleasure to take her, of course. I will be leaving when the tide turns mid-morning tomorrow. *La Comète* will be my escort for part of the way."

"Can you send Victorio and another man to Michelle's house to pick up Corrinne's baggage today? We want to do this in a way that does not draw too much attention. I will stand outside in uniform and make people think the baggage is mine as a diversion. Then after sunset, I will bring Corrinne and the twins aboard in the dark, so they are out of sight when you sail. Can you have your launch wait for us on the dock?"

"Of course. What about the major?"

"Well, he warned us about the danger from Bigôt. I think Michel Péan will be pleased to have Corrinne dining with him during the crossing. Oh, and have some extra fresh water kegs brought aboard, ones she can use to bathe the children."

"Of course. What will you do?'

"Me? I march south to war tomorrow morning after you sail. Hopefully, I will survive," he added lightly.

Boston

The *ghost* flew from a tree near the fort at the first glimmer of sunrise. It came in high over the water city, well above the range of muskets, until it found the house. Then it glided silently in a circle down and down to land atop the roof of the structure behind the house without making a sound. The *ghost* had to make physical contact with this man, the one who conducted the ritual. This would be dangerous. There were armed men standing guard nearby. The *ghost* would have to be patient, keep the female from screeching, wait for someone inside the house to notice its presence, and trust they would tell the man. The *ghost* could see his brightness moving inside the house.

Molly had little Conor on a sling around her neck. He was happy and very animated with this arrangement. "For him it's like having front row seats at a theater," Molly said. Captain Conor Martyn was back at sea somewhere. Molly would wait patiently, like she always did for his return. His return was always a surprise. It would happen at a random time. It could be in an hour or months from now. Molly had Little Conor to keep her company. He smiled at her a lot. He had his father's eyes and hair.

Dianamora tickled Conor at the top of his shoulder. He squinted and giggled.

"Molly, can you see if there is any corn left on the stalks in the garden, and pick a few squashes for me to slice up. The bread is hot. I am ready to fry the bacon and the eggs."

Molly took up a small basket and headed out into the back garden. She waved at the guards.

"We'll bring you some food in an hour," she told them. "Coffee or tea?"

"Coffee," one of them proclaimed.

Molly found three ears of corn that were ripe. Another six that might be ready in a week. She stooped and, with her paring knife, cut six fresh squash from the plants—two green, two yellow crooknecks, and two elongated, light orange squash, good for making a pie. Little Conor was cooing with excitement and reaching with his fingers. She followed his gaze and saw the huge white eagle perched atop the carriage hangar.

"Oh, my God," she whispered.

Molly had not seen this magnificent, intimidating creature since the incident in Connecticut. But Sentry had mentioned it often, assuring her and Dian the animal had good intentions, so he claimed. It gazed at her with piercing yellow eyes. Conor made noises and waved his little fingers at the animal. She dared not draw the guards' attention to it. No telling what they might do.

She picked up her basket and walked slowly up the stairs and in through the back door, before turning around to look back. The raptor had not moved and still stared in her direction.

"It must want something," she whispered to Conor. "We need to tell Uncle Sentry."

"Oh, these look good," Dian complimented at seeing what Molly brought in the basket.

Conor made a louder noise and was wiggling his fingers toward the door.

"Is Sentry awake?"

"Yes. He's drinking coffee in the library. Is there a problem?"

"I don't know. The white eagle is perched atop the carriage hangar."

"It is?" Dian gasped.

"Yes. I'm worried the guards might see it and shoot at it."

"Oh no! I'll get Sentry."

Molly went back to the mudroom and looked out the window. Conor *oohed*. The eagle had not moved.

Sentry crowded into the room with Dian.

"Isn't it beautiful?" Dian enthused.

"Bloody hell," Sentry whispered.

"Why is it here?" Molly asked.

"I dinnah' knoo'."

"You need to go out and see it," Dian said and pushed Sentry towards the back door.

"Wait! Jist go slow. Deeya' see the bloody talons on tha' thing?"

Dian regarded the eagle's appearance as something to be hallowed.

"Sentry, it's not going to hurt anyone. Go out into the garden at the side of the hangar and wait. It will fly down to you. You'll see."

"And dah' wha' tah' me?"

"What? It came to see you, Sentry." Dian pressed. "Now go."

"Me? How deeya' yah' knoo' it wants tah' see me?"

"I can barely understand what you're saying. Calm down. It will not hurt you. If it does not glide down to you, then I will go out. If not me, then Molly."

"M-me?" Molly said with uncertainty. "It doesn't know me! And I'm holding Conor."

"It has come to see one of us," Dian insisted firmly. "Sentry, you go first. And tell the guards not to interfere."

"Oh, bloody hell," Sentry grumbled as he went out the door.

Sentry told the incredulous guards what he was going to do. "If you want to watch, leave your muskets here. And move slowly. Dinnah' make any sudden movements. Dinnah' stand close tah' me. I dinnah' knoo' wha' it will dah'. And I dinnah' want to get scarred."

"Did he say scared?" one guard asked the other.

Sentry took a deep breath. He saw Dian and Molly just outside the door, standing on the top porch step. Dian was smiling and gesturing him to go forward.

"Yeah, yeah, yeah," he groused under his breath. He made a wide move to the outside of the carriage hangar to leave plenty of distance between him and the raptor.

The eagle turned in its perch to keep facing him.

"Hold out your hand to it," Dian said in a voice just below a shout.

"Yeah, yeah, yeah," Sentry grumbled, but did as she suggested.

Then to the collective surprise of all watching, the white eagle extended its magnificent six-foot wings. In a graceful movement, it glided to the ground directly in front of Sentry.

"Holy Mary, Mother of God, protect me," Sentry whispered.

"Hold out your hand," Dian urged.

"Oh, bloody hell," he whispered. "Jist' look at the gaze of tha' beast. It looks pissed! Good boy, uh, er, good bird! Dinnah' bite me!"

The white eagle gazed up at Sentry and tilted its head as if examining him. It touched its hooked yellow beak to the back of Sentry's trembling fingers for several seconds. Then in one movement, it turned, flapped its wings, and went back up to the top of the carriage hangar and perched again.

"Holy shit," said one of the guards. "Sentry? Are you all right?"

Molly stayed on the porch, but the guards and Dian approached Sentry.

"That was marvelous. What did it do?" Dian asked with excitement.

Sentry seemed confused. "I dunnoo'. But I had an impression it said ello' tah' me. I need some brandy."

The eagle screeched loudly. As if a musket shot was heard, everyone stiffened. The screech brought the guards from the front of the house running. The raptor flapped it wings rapidly and flew upwards in a circle, higher and higher, and at a certain height, it flew inland. They watched until it was out of sight.

"What happened?" one of the front guards asked.

"That bloody eagle kissed Sentry."

"It dinnah' kiss me, yah' nitwit. It only pecked my hand."

"Color Sergeant, those birds can carry rabies, yah know. I saw it in Ireland."

"Rabies! Get on with you, Private! Get back to yah' posts, you bloody Irish morons!"

They went back into the cuisine. Sentry asked Dian quietly. "They dinnah' have rabies, dah' they?"

"No! Of course not! Tell us what you thought or felt." She was anxious with excitement.

Sentry sat in a chair. "I need some brandy."

Dian took down the bottle and a glass and poured him a double. "Now, tell us everything."

Sentry swallowed the brandy in one gulp. "You saw it. It touched my hand with its beak...God, tha' beak is big up close. It could rip my arm off at the shoulder. It tilted its head funny too. Yah' knoo'? Like this...like a dog does sometimes? I had this friendly feeling, almost like it said hello. Then a whole bunch of images came to my mind. They came fast. I saw Henri and Lady Corrinne and Anamosa, except Anamosa seemed much older. And that's all."

Dian's expression became thoughtful. "Then it's not over," she said. "It will visit your dreams."

"My dreams?! How deeya' knoo' tha'?"

"Because the bad spirit haunted my dreams," said Molly, provoked by the memory.

That got Sentry's attention. He looked at Dian. "Wha'…but you said it's a good eagle."

"Don't fret, Sentry. It is a good spirit. But it's magical too. If it comes into your dreams, it will not come to frighten you. It will bring you a message."

"A message?" Oh, God. That meant it *would* come into his dreams. "I need more brandy."

❦

Atlantic Ocean

Captain Martyn's sixteen-gun light frigate, the *Anamosa,* cruised off the coast of Louisbourg, just out of cannon range from the fortress. It was one of three frigates escorting Captain John Rous' command ship, HMS *Sutherland,* a fifty gun ship-of-the-line of the Royal Navy. Their orders were to assess the strength of the Louisbourg fleet anchored in the harbor. They'd not had much success trying to observe it from high in the crow's nest of the *Sutherland,* so a scout was put ashore.

Three days later, the *Sutherland* flag-signaled the *Anamosa.* Captain Martyn decoded the message from his code book.

"One. Man. Beach. South. GB. Flag."

"Coming left!" he shouted. The crew scrambled to adjust the sails. "Come left. Steer two-zero-zero," he told the helmsman.

The *Anamosa* peeled away from the other frigates.

"Keep watch for a man on the beach waving a flag," he told Lieutenant Carson, his second-in-command. "He is supposed to be just south of Gabarus Bay. Bosun, make a boat ready to lower in the water."

Captain Martyn only knew of one place to the south of Gabarus Bay where the shoaling ended close to the beach, where he could put a boat ashore to pick someone up. Twenty minutes later, sure enough, he saw a man standing in that spot, waving a small flag above his head in a circle. The flag was a Union Jack, no less. Dangerous thing to do in a wilderness patrolled by French scouts.

"There!" He pointed. "Bosun, go get him."

After another forty minutes of rowing through rough surf, they brought the man aboard. He saluted the captain and introduced himself.

"Sergeant Douglas Stearns, second New Hampshire rangers, sir."

"Captain Martyn of the *Anamosa*. You're a brave man, Sergeant Stearns, waving that Union Jack in a French wilderness," he said. The sergeant's features looked native.

The sergeant felt complimented. "Aye, sir. Thank you, sir."

"You have a feather knotted to your hair."

"A good luck charm from my mother. My father's a Scotsman."

"Any trouble?"

He shrugged. "Early this morning, three Mi'kmaq scouts picked up my trail. They're all dead now. I have your count. Louisbourg harbor is full of heavy man-o-wars."

"Good work, Sergeant Stearns. Bosun, take Sergeant Stearns below and give him a double ration of rum. Coming left!" Martyn shouted to the deckhands. "Steer zero-two-zero!" The helmsman repeated the order. "We will rendezvous with the *Sutherland*. Captain Rous will want to talk with you personally."

The sergeant saluted again. The bosun took the man below to share some rum rations with him. No man should drink alone. It would not be polite.

Captain Martyn felt the wind direction shifting behind him. "Come right to zero-three-five." The sail billowed tight with the course change. "We'll be flying now!"

Lieutenant Carson stood next to him. "One of the oarsmen said the ranger-sergeant counted eighteen ships-of-the-line and five frigates. Will that do it?"

"It would if I were Admiral Holburne," Martyn replied. "His fleet is not as big as the French. And why would the French leave the harbor anyway? Just to come out and fight? All they need to do is sit there until the end of September. Then the fighting season will be over, and we can all go home for Christmas. French and British alike."

"Amen to that," said his second. "We'll go to Boston then, after this?"

"Not after this patrol. Maybe a few days in Halifax for resupply. We need continuous squadrons on patrol until October. The *Anamosa* is the fastest ship out here. I'd rather log a lot of patrol time now, and try to get us more time in Boston over Christmas."

The Fortress of Louisbourg

Panther Claw found reason to linger near the Queen's Bastion barracks every morning, while the German mercenary companies drilled, performing line infantry movements. He was not standing conspicuously in the open, but found a place where the overhang from the rampart wall gave him shade. The summer days were bright with sunshine. The shadow of the overhang offered him a small degree of comfortable camouflage. Many soldiers walked by him, but after one look at his face, they averted their gaze. That was just fine for Mkuigen Malsum. He would stay and watch until the drilling companies went back into the barracks, usually when the sun began to set.

On the sixth day of doing this, the entire mercenary regiment was drilling, all seven hundred of them formed ranks. Panther Claw finally spotted the man he'd been waiting to see: Lieutenant-Colonel Karl Krieger. The Abenaki warrior straightened from his leaning position and stared intently at this man. He chanted the words taught to him by his mother. An incantation to the snake spirit, meant to fill a man with fear. But the thing he saw was an evil spirit of the dark, thus it would not be filled with fear. Instead, the chanting resulted in drawing the man's gaze to his.

The regimental commander left his position with the other officers and started walking slowly towards the person in the shadows across the marshalling yard. Panther Claw started walking towards him, too. They met halfway, stopping two paces away from one another.

Panther Claw knew this was not the time for fighting. He would not be permitted to cut the man's face from the body anyway. But it was the time to meet this adversary he vowed to stalk for the rest of his life.

The vulnax surged to full dominance and glared cruelly at this offending creature.

Panther Claw glared back. He saw the eyes of a demon. But he was not scared. Demons were only dangerous in the dream world. They became vulnerable when they possessed someone. The body they possessed could be killed.

The subordinate German officers hurried to stand beside their commander, not liking nor understanding this confrontation in the middle of the yard.

"What is your purpose here?" Major Sauer bellowed at Panther Claw. "How dare you show disrespect to Colonel Krieger!"

Panther Claw took a step closer to the demon and gazed without fear into the demon's eyes. He spoke to it in German. "*Ich werde dein gesicht nehmen.*" I will take your face.

Malsum turned and walked away. There followed a chorus of shouts, curses, and insults by the other German officers. Malsum ignored the insults. He concentrated on sensing the rage in the thing behind him as he crossed out of the marshalling yard. That is what he had intended to provoke. He could still feel it: the heat of this unnatural rage. It was distinctive, not of a man, not of any animal. Now he would be able to recognize this rage in the future, even from a distance. The rage would ensure they'd meet again. They would be drawn to one another. Panther Claw must be patient and choose the right time and place. He'd promised Lady Corrinne he would make it suffer. Of course, the demon would not suffer. Demons do not feel pain. But the man would. He had made a promise to Lady Corrinne.

A demon cannot be killed. The body the demon possessed must be consumed in a fire so hot, even the bones would reduce to fine ash. Not just a pyre to burn the dead. *Hot as a fire made from the black rocks.* He recalled the sweating man in the white man's village, pounding with an iron hammer on the glowing metal, white with heat so fierce you could feel its burning power at several paces. A blacksmith, he was called. Once burnt to an ash pile of white dust, he would scatter the ashes upon a flowing river. And the demon's spirit would possess pieces so tiny and far apart, it would cease to exist.

The demon was here for a purpose, its actions controlled by its obsession to achieve this purpose. This made the demon predictable. Predictability was the demon's weakness. Lieutenant Gerrard and the girl called Anamosa wore talismans to repel this evil. He must learn more from Lieutenant Gerrard about this.

Panther Claw looked forward to conquering this demon. He knew of no other warrior who boasted about doing such a thing. The shamans could boast about the spells they chanted to cast an evil one back into the blackness from whence it came. Yet the shamans' only proof of their feats were the stories they would exaggerate before the council fires.

But I will cut away its face and wear it on my belt. What little shard of magic this shriveled piece of skin contained will be mine to command.

Of course, Panther Claw had not been invited to speak at the Abenaki council fire in over eight seasons. He had been preoccupied, cutting away the faces of warriors, some of them still alive, and wearing them on his belt. Unless that changed, his boasts would only be heard by the chittering squirrels. To be accepted by the Abenaki again, to be invited to a council fire, Panther Claw must not be feared, or banished, or hated. The Abenaki must...*like* him?

I'll have to think on how to do that.

Québec City Waterfront

Very little was said by anyone during the embarkation out of respect for the quietness and privacy required. It was dark. Lines from the cargo launch were looped to the cleats on the dock and tied off to the oarlocks. Another seaman, Vincente, held up a lantern for light. Philippe held the twins while Corrinne was helped into the launch by Victorio. Once she was seated, Victorio turned around and Philippe carefully allowed Victorio to take Marcus first. Victorio handed him to Corrinne. Then Philippe stepped into the launch while holding onto Calypso. He sat next to Corrinne. She tilted her head and rested it on his shoulder in solidarity.

Vincente set the lantern in the forward posthole on the bow made for this purpose. They loosened the lines, took in the loops, and pushed off from the dock.

Corrinne saw the lantern lights of the city ablaze. This time she was happy about leaving. As the distance to the city widened, a great weight lifted from her spirit. *If I ever come back again, it will only be to visit*, she thought. *This is no longer my home.*

Victorio and Vicente each took a set of oars and by glancing backwards occasionally, they guided the launch next to the *Falcon Queen*'s port-side ladder, making contact with barely a bump. Bosun Linard helped Lady Corrinne from the boat. Victorio handed up Marcus. Philippe grabbed Linard's hand and pulled himself up. Captain LaTour was waiting for them along with Major Péan.

"Welcome aboard, my lady! And who is this handsome lad? Marcus?"

She embraced the captain. "Thank you for this, Beauregard."

"No need to thank me. I am thrilled and relieved to be taking you away from all this war, conflict, and danger. We've already placed the baggage in your cabin. The small beds are ready, and all the linens are clean."

Corrinne turned to Michel Péan. "Well, Michel, it appears we will be having many dinner conversations."

"I am elated at this prospect. I echo the captain's words, my lady. The future here is in great peril. Maybe you should consider coming with us?" Péan said to Philippe.

"Major, as you've said to me often enough, I follow orders. Tomorrow I go with the army to invest Fort William Henry."

"No! No talk of war tonight," Corrinne interjected quickly. The breeze on the river carried delicious food aromas wafting up from below. "Something smells good. Let's go down and enjoy a peaceful, happy meal together."

Pierrik, the steward, was proud to present the food to them as his guests. Captain LaTour sat at the head of his table, Michel Péan on his left. Corrinne on his right. The twins sat between Corrinne and Philippe.

"Two bottles of Roman Beaujolais from vineyards first planted by the Romans in the Saône valley," Pierrik explained as he pulled the corks. "Though not quite that old," he added quickly.

Toasts were made to each person's future with wishes of good fortune and luck. Appetizers of saltwater oysters were served on their shells, garnished with herbs, salt, and a tart vinegar sauce. He'd kept them fresh in a canvas bag hanging over the side in the coldest water, he told them. The children were served bite-size cream-filled biscuits, oven-warmed, brushed with sweet chocolate, and dusted with powdered sugar.

The main dish was an oven-roasted beef, simmered in a red wine sauce enhanced with aromatic leeks, wild mushrooms, crushed cloves, and other spices collected over the years from around the world, Pierrik confided. On the side was a dish of mixed squash and mashed roots, drenched with butter, seasoned with a dash of precious ground peppercorns.

Calypso imitated her mother, using a fork gracefully to choose small pieces of the beef. Marcus ate every piece of this rare meat they put on his plate and would have eaten more until Corrinne became concerned and intervened.

"He's eating like a wolf," she complained.

"I know!" Philippe was proud to see his son's appetite.

Dessert was individual dishes of Saint Honoré cake. Pierrik proudly described the creation. "It has a flat base of pâte à choux, topped with layers of puff pastry balls, intermixed with thickened cream laced with sugar, and crowned with mixed berries. Sweetness in every layer."

Soon Marcus' lips, face, and nose was covered in gooey sweetness, which had everyone laughing. Calypso looked fondly at her brother, and removed some cream on the verge of dripping off his cheek with a finger.

After dinner, Pierrik poured drams of Chartreuse liqueur. "A bottle I obtained the last time I was in Le Havre. Made by monks, I was told. Hard to get. Now seemed like a good occasion to share it." Then for the children, he poured small cups of sweet juices, obtained from a mixed berry mash, strained to remove seeds and skins.

More toasts were made.

Coffee and tea was served with tiny sticks of cinnamon on the saucer. "From a trade ship in the Antilles. They claimed it comes from Egypt. Who knows? But I tasted one. Nothing bad happened. Spicy, sweet taste. The trader said people often put the stick in their hot drinks. I leave that up to you to decide."

During the dinner, Captain LaTour entertained them with stories of the various places he'd sailed around the world. "When you're older," he teased Marcus, "I will tell you about a mermaid that rescued me from drowning... and other things." He winked.

"*Much* older, I think," Corrinne said with raised eyebrows.

Soon the twins were yawning.

Corrinne thanked Pierrik. "This might be the best dinner I've ever been served. Certainly, the most flavor-filled. I loved hearing about the preparation and the history of it all. But you will have to excuse me now. My little angels need their beds."

Captain LaTour, Major Péan, and Philippe went up on deck to take in the cold river air. Philippe explained the plan of siege to them.

"It should be overwhelming for that fort. The road to Fort Edward will be guarded and blocked. No relief will be possible. They will surrender in less than a week, or two days after the first siege cannons are fired. I am more concerned about after the surrender."

"After the surrender?" LaTour asked.

"Two thousand tribal warriors have gathered at Fort Carillon. Some have come from as far as Detroit. They've been promised plunder. I don't know how we will control them."

Major Péan shook his head in the darkness. "They will not be controlled. This will be worse than Fort Oswego. General Montcalm realizes this, yes?"

"He does. But they were invited by the governor."

Philippe excused himself to go down to bed. He wanted to spend his last night with Corrinne and go ashore at the first sign of sunrise.

When Philippe undressed in the darkness and slipped into bed, he found the twins already asleep between them at her side. He reached an arm over them to Corrinne in the darkness. Her hands were wet with tears.

Philippe rested his palm on little Callie's back. Corrinne laid her hand atop his. He would march off to war in the morning. She would make a journey by sea. Both were heading into unknown dangers. Both trusted in their destiny.

*

The cabin had the light of a single candle as Philippe dressed. He knelt by the bed and embraced Corrinne. He reached over her and gently touched the sleeping heads of the twins.

"I will return to the dock to wave when the tide turns," he whispered.

"Remember, this is not forever, my love," Corrinne whispered, tears fell silently down her cheeks. "You'll see."

"I know. Write to Michelle as soon as you are there. We need to know how and where to address our letters."

"Yes. I promise."

They kissed. The stone in Philippe's ring was glowing softly.

"Look at this. We've not seen that for a while."

Corrinne gripped his hand and touched the stone with a finger. It was cool to the touch. "What does it mean?"

"Let's agree it means good luck and Godspeed to both of us."

They kissed again.

"I love you," she said, gazing at her beloved.

"I love you, too." Philippe left the cabin. He could not say more.

The *Falcon Queen*'s cargo launch took Philippe to the dock in the twilight of a burgeoning golden sunrise. He looked back at the ship. Corrinne had followed him up. She stood on the deck, with a shawl wrapped around her shoulders. Her shadowed silhouette looked lonely against the backdrop of the impending sunrise.

The tide would turn at nine forty-two that morning. Captain LaTour said that was when the *Queen* and its escort, *La Comète*, would weigh anchor and start downriver.

Philippe walked rapidly up the hill to the citadel headquarters to gather his pack and collect the remaining scouts. He would meet with General Montcalm to discuss troop deployment during the march to Fort Carillon. Dozens of heavy bateaux were already in transit upriver with the artillery to the mouth of the Richelieu River. Militia troops were marching overland from Montréal to join the main forces.

There were nearly a hundred bateaux anchored all over the harbor area, each one waiting for the load of men or supplies to be delivered before rowing upriver as well. Corrinne would not appear on deck while it was daylight. She would stay in the shadows of the helm deck house so as not to be seen by anyone. By that time, the dock area was overloaded with troops and voyagers waiting to depart Québec City. She'd hoped to catch a glimpse of Philippe's wave of farewell, if possible, as the ship set sail.

Unfortunately, Philippe was attending General Montcalm's final war council to be certain everyone understood the orders of march to Fort Carillon. His scouts would provide much of the advance protection for the march. His opinion was petitioned continuously. The time for the *Falcon Queen*'s departure came and went. Philippe could not leave the council without announcing a good reason why.

*

As the bells of Québec City began tolling in farewell to the army of New France, Captain Trieste went to Intendant Bigôt's office as planned.

"I don't have much time," he told the intendant. "The governor still has your missive. It was missing from the pile of documents to be destroyed. He's either locked it away somewhere I don't know about, or he has destroyed it himself. But I read it. It was identical to the one sent to the governor, except it was addressed to you, and you alone, with a separate order for an investigation of Lady Corrinne VanderMeer."

"With arresting powers authorized by the King?"

"Yes, sir. Clearly stated. A reply from you is expected."

"Very well, Captain. Tell me if you see it again, or bring it to me when you find it to receive your gold."

After Trieste left, François Bigôt took out a fresh piece of paper and wrote back to Versailles, explaining that recent correspondence sent to him had been intercepted by someone else and was possibly destroyed. He requested another missive be sent, wrapped inside a false address, to prevent its interception, or have a courier assigned to hand deliver it.

He added a few more paragraphs regarding the army's march on Fort William Henry. He would personally drop this missive in the dispatch pouch of the fast courier schooner still waiting at anchor. It would sail the next morning with numerous pieces of official mail related to the army's campaign against the English.

Intendant Bigôt planned on waiting until Governor Vaudreuil was preoccupied with the new campaign and its aftermath before beginning any campaign against Lady de Chanaye. He certainly wanted her deadly dangerous husband, Scout Captain Gerrard, to be far away before his wife was incarcerated in the bastille. There was time for a new missive to reach Versailles and receive a response. Probably six weeks, but less than two months.

She isn't going anywhere.

CHAPTER 31
THE WILDERNESS LAKES
JULY 1757
Faces

The Electorate of Hanover was a small German state, formerly one of several dozen states, in the mish-mash collage known as the Holy Roman Empire. Hanover was bordered in the north by the North Sea and the kingdom of Denmark. The Dutch Republic bordered them in the west. Prussia surrounded them to the east, the south, and the southwest. There were at least seven other small German territories touching Hanover's borders that were of little consequence during the war. Consequently, the shape of the Hanover "territory" was so irregular, some historians found it bewildering that people were willing to identify, fight, and die for it. Yet, they did.

The English House of Hanover regarded this German state as its ancestral home. This was *English territory*, they vigorously asserted. It was subject to the absolute rule of George II, King of England. It was defended by Prince William Augustus, Duke of Cumberland, the third and youngest son of George II. The Duke was also known as the Butcher of Culloden for his role in putting down the Jacobite Rebellion in 1746, and more affectionately referred to by his Tory opponents in Parliament as Butcher Cumberland.

George II gave Butcher Cumberland only one order for his current assignment. "Do not lose Hanover!"

France occupying Hanover at the end of the current war would give them a huge bargaining chip they could use for the trading of territories that would take place in the peace treaty process.

Let the Austrians fight with Prussia! Hanover was France's primary target.

Accordingly, Versailles sent fifteen hundred more soldiers to General Montcalm for the defense of New France. In Europe, the French sent two entire armies to invade the central German states in April 1757.

Both French armies were dedicated to the occupation of the Electorate of Hanover. Its capital city was called, of course, Hanover. One of these armies was commanded by Charles de Rohan, Prince of Soubise. The second was commanded by Marshal Louis Charles d'Estrées, a more professional and experienced military man. In total, the French forces numbered *a hundred thousand troops*. But Marshall d'Estrées' army was the larger of the two, consisting of fifty thousand infantry, ten thousand cavalry, and supporting artillery.

In comparison, the Duke of Cumberland's Army of Observation consisted of thirty thousand infantry, five thousand cavalry, and supporting artillery. Very prudently, Cumberland intended to fight a defensive battle and planned to search for good ground to establish his defense after the enemy invaded. Most of the soldiers in this Army of Observation, about seventy percent, were men from Hanover. These soldiers were ostensibly English subjects. The balance of the army consisted of paid mercenaries from Hesse-Kassel, and a few other minor German states.

Cumberland had no English redcoats.

The French were allied with armies from Austria, Russia, Sweden, and Saxony.

Prussia, alone, opposed France and its allies in Europe.

Unlike Prussia, who'd been attacking the Austrians for months, the hundred thousand strong French army had been plodding towards Hanover since April, citing logistical problems to Versailles for its slowness. They blamed a long delay they experienced in the siege of Geldern. This was a fortified settlement town and castle, with walls and a moat built in the thirteenth century, situated near an old Roman road. This border city to France seemed a popular place to invade and occupy over the centuries, changing hands repeatedly among Spain, Austria, Prussia, and the Netherlands. According to legend, a fire-breathing *dragon* was killed there around the year 880. The dragon yelled out the word *Geldern* three times as it died, thus infusing this particular piece of ground with mystical warlike powers... some would say.

Whatever the reason, the Geldern fortification was fiercely defended by only eight hundred Prussian soldiers. It took the French army three months to defeat them.

Versailles did not care that Geldern was captured. Versailles was obsessed with preserving its monarchy. With the fighting season now half over, Versailles ordered Marshal Louis Charles d'Estrées to attack Hanover, now, without delay. On the seventh of July, the strong advanced guard of the

French crossed the river Weser. Nine days later, the main French army crossed the Weser. This advance by the French into the Electorate of Hanover's acknowledged territory forced Butcher Cumberland to leave his capital to engage them. He marched thirty miles southwest from his capital city to a place called Hastenbeck, near the town of Hamelin. Once the fighting started a week later, it would last three days.

In contrast, at this point of the fighting season, Frederick II had already engaged three Austrian armies, defeated two, lost to one, laid siege to Prague, and withdrew from Bohemia to reform his armies before attacking again.

When Cumberland neared the enemy, he selected his good defensive positions. He placed his artillery on the high ground of the battlefield where it could oppose any maneuver by the French. The French recognized the danger this artillery position posed to its forces. It sent four brigades to attack Cumberland's right flank. Cumberland sent his elite grenadiers, who were protecting the artillery, to oppose this flank attack. The undefended artillery position was now attacked by the main French infantry charging at it from the center of the lines. The direct attack on the entrenched artillery position resulted in heavy French casualties, but the artillery position was overrun.

Cumberland committed his infantry reserves to push back the French temporarily, while he began withdrawing his army to reach a stronger defensive position.

The Hanover artillery was destroyed. But Marshal d'Estrées observed his attack falter with the arrival of Cumberland's reserves.

Marshal d'Estrées gave the order to withdraw his army to a stronger defensive position.

Both commanders withdrew to defensive positions, each thinking they had lost the battle.

Days later, after realizing their mistake, the French declared a victory.

Among the French wounded in the attack on the Hanover artillery was the commander of the Auvergne Regiment from Amiens, Colonel Gustave Dubonnet, who lost his left leg to a cannon ball. A tourniquet rapidly administered by one of his men saved the life of the admired and respected commander. He was evacuated from the field.

Lake Champlain Wilderness

Scout Captain Philippe Gerrard could not stop worrying about Corrinne, Marcus, and Calypso. Within weeks, an ocean would separate them. If anything went wrong in France, Philippe was powerless to help. He would not even know about it, possibly forever. These were depressing thoughts. Maybe he should have embraced Major Péan's suggestion to go with them to France? Captain LaTour would have taken him, without protest.

"Like you," he'd told Major Péan at the time, "I follow orders." That sounded like a noble thing to say. *I should have said…Like you, I am stupid!*

Known for leading at the forefront of his scouts, Philippe paddled along with the others, matching the hard-stroking pace of the other five paddlers in the canoe, absent of his normal enthusiasm.

His subordinate officers and sergeants saw his preoccupation. The captain hardly spoke, remaining aloof most of the time, even when they camped at night, avoiding most questions. When they entered the Richelieu River, they started to worry. Their worries dissipated after they entered Lake Champlain and came abreast of Fort Saint-Frédéric. The extraordinary leader that was Scout Captain Gerrard appeared as if nothing unusual had occurred.

Philippe saw the large concentration of tribal warriors camped along the western banks of Lake Champlain. The marine scouts had not planned to stop at Fort Saint-Frédéric and pressed on towards Fort Carillon. Every mile further, he saw more encampments. He tried counting them, until they counted up to hundreds, then more hundreds, and even more hundreds. Over a thousand was his rough count and they'd not yet reached Fort Carillon. Warriors stood up along the shore of the lake in response to their passing. A few of them raised a hand in greeting.

Very few of them.

Philippe shouted an order to the other five men in his war canoe to pick up the speed. He moved his vessel to the front of the scouts.

"I hardly recognized any of these tribes since we passed Saint-Frédéric," one of the sergeants in another canoe shouted over to him. "Do you know them?"

"Some of them are Ottawa from Fort Detroit," Philippe shouted back. "But far too many of them are new to these lands." This was not a good situation in Philippe's thinking. The warriors were hard to control once the battles started, even when they had personal relationships with a tribe. Lacking even that influence, there was no telling what they might do. "Once we land at Fort Carillon, ask around, start learning who they are, and what languages they speak."

The population of the encampments grew denser the closer they got to the fort. All the lands north of the fort used for farming had been picked clean of any crops.

Upon reaching the boat landing on the south side of the fort, Philippe remained there long enough to gather and give orders to his lieutenants and senior sergeants after they arrived.

"Get these canoes portaged around La Chute Falls. Post a guard on them. Establish our main camp up there. Get scout patrols deployed over on the peninsula and down the west side of Lac du Saint-Sacrament, all the way to Fort William Henry. Post sentries by twos at appropriate intervals on both sides of the lake. We must be alerted if Fort William Henry starts showing signs of preparation for our attack."

Philippe headed up the hill to Fort Carillon and reported his arrival to his former commander, Commandant-Captain de Lusignan. After friendly greetings, he was offered quarters inside the fort.

"Thank you, sir. But I will be camping with my men from now on until the battle is over. What can you tell me about these tribal encampments? I counted well over a thousand native warriors that I could see from my canoe."

"It is probably closer to twice that many by now."

Philippe shook his head slowly with concern. "General Montcalm will arrive before the day is over. He will ask you for a full report on what tribes have arrived and how many they are. I must see to the deployment of my scout patrols, but I will come back."

Philippe searched around the fort's interior barracks, watching for any of his scouts still lingering inside. The four he encountered, he sent off to the forward camp. At the same time, he introduced himself to battalion officers he'd not met from among the regular regiments now marshaled. Not counting the regiments of Louisbourg, all the regiments assigned to Governor Vaudreuil were represented by battalions, including La Reine, Languedoc, La Sarre, Guyenne, Royal Roussillon, and Béarn. These totaled nearly two thousand six hundred regular infantry.

Philippe left the fort to the tent encampment on the western side, where the overflow from the regiments bivouacked. He skipped them and roamed among the Troupes de la Marine tents where he was well known. There were about six hundred of these marines assembled. By Philippe's estimation, this almost amounted to every one of the marine companies available in Québec and Montréal. He found a few more stragglers from his scouts among the marines and sent them to the forward camp. For these marine officers, he took time to brief them on what was said at the governor's war council and answered their questions. He knew the marines would not hear as much from the regular officers of the metropolitan regiments.

"I trust you to keep this information secret to yourselves. It would not surprise me to learn there are fighters of the American Rangers scouting us right now. If anyone is captured by these enemy raiders, the types of torture they will use to extract information from you quickly will be quite hideous. And then you will tell them whatever they want to know, of that you can be sure."

The militia battalions from Montréal and Québec, as they were referred to euphemistically, had gathered haphazardly in a wide scattering of tents. They numbered some three thousand farmers, merchants, tradesmen, voyageurs, and *coureurs de bois*. All of them were used to being called upon to defend the borders of New France against the Americans and their native allies, as they had for decades. They were especially excited about this campaign. The opportunity to penetrate or capture something that had been considered American territory had not occurred for over a century. That after investing Fort William Henry, the city of Albany was named as the goal of the next campaign. That was a startling rumor to hear, even from the militia. Philippe did not validate or deny any of their assertions, except an even wilder one soon made the rounds, claiming a bateaux assault was planned to go down the Hudson River and capture the port of New York. Where would they even get this idea?

"Why would we do that?" Philippe asked the farmer. There were a dozen other militiamen standing around, now anxious to hear the answer.

"Um…because we can?"

"How many people live in the port city of New York?"

A blank stare.

"Over fifteen thousand!" Philippe told them. "How would you even feed them?" He hoped to appeal to their common sense as farmers.

After a short pause, another farmer replied. "We wouldn't. We'd do like the tribes, eh? We just carry back the better-looking women," he offered with a leer.

The rest of the militia started laughing. More ribald jests followed.

The militia gossiped worse than wives at a parish meeting. Satisfied he'd given them something different to jaw about, Philippe left the crowd. Then to his utter surprise, he found three more of his scouts sitting drunk among their farming friends. He personally led them on a long uphill trek until they were above the La Chute rapids and pointed at the campfire smoke in the distance.

"Go there!"

Philippe returned to Fort Carillon, anticipating that General Montcalm would call another war council as soon as he arrived.

The Gulf of Saint Lawrence

The HMS *Sutherland* flag-signaled the *Anamosa* to come alongside with the other four escort frigates for a captain's council. They did this one at a time, leaving the captains on the flagship, while the frigates circled in the area until it was over.

Commander-Captain John Rous kept the council short. He was anxious to get back to Halifax.

"Gentlemen, my orders were to continue this patrol until today. If we are not engaged by the enemy by now, we are to return to Halifax. Have any of you spotted any enemy to engage? No? I did not think so. Since we are at the northeast point of Île Royal, I would like one frigate to cross over to Newfoundland just to be sure the French are not attempting any mischief in the gulf, then turn around and follow us back to Halifax. So, it's your chance to boast. Who among you captains the fastest ship?"

The other four captains turned their gaze to Conor Martyn.

"Oh, so now you all admit to being the masters of inferior, worm-eaten scows."

They did not take the bait.

"Captain Martyn, it appears your fellow captains acknowledge the *Anamosa*'s main armament is its speed...unless you deny this accolade."

The other captains laughed good-naturedly.

Captain Martyn smirked. "May I remind my fellow captains, the *Anamosa* successfully engaged and destroyed the Cap Noir battery in Louisbourg."

"Did it sink?" one of them replied.

"No, I think he captured it," said another.

More friendly laughter.

"All right, gentlemen. That's enough. I will attest the Cap Noir battery was never rebuilt. With that as the result, it is fair to conclude, based upon the audacity of the *Anamosa,* the sea defenses of Louisbourg were weakened permanently."

The other captains conceded. Conor Martyn was stunned by Commander Rous' unexpected compliment.

Rous continued. "So, Captain Martyn will have the honor of performing this last patrol of the gulf, which I anticipate he will accomplish before the sun sets today. Any questions?"

"Yes, sir. If I may. What do you think happens next, after we return to Halifax?" Captain Martyn felt he'd earned the temerity to ask.

"The French fleet does not seem inclined to leave the port. I am not Vice-Admiral Holburne, but soon it will be August. If we are to have this battle, we must persuade the French to come out and engage us. That suggests we bring the entire fleet within range as a lure to Admiral de la Motte."

When Conor Martyn was back aboard the *Anamosa*, he came about and steered due north, expecting this to be a short mission. He'd transited only two hours when the lookout posted atop the main mast shouted through a speaking trumpet.

"Ship! Horizon! Port bow!"

Captain Martyn scanned the horizon with his watch glass. He saw it.

"Come left, steer three-five-zero. Beat to quarters!"

The crew of the *Anamosa* reacted instantly. Men came on deck to man all the guns.

The ship Martyn saw was flying the white ensign of the French navy.

Lieutenant Carson came up from below. He stood alongside his captain and looked through his glass. "It doesn't look like a very large warship," Carson said with excitement. "Maybe a courier schooner? It's in our class. Yes?"

"It might be," Captain Martyn agreed. "For once, we might engage in a fight at sea."

"Ship! Port beam!" the lookout called again through his speaking trumpet.

Captain Martyn and Lieutenant Carson pivoted to the left.

"It's a frigate! A big one! Right full rudder! Coming right," he shouted to the crew.

They left their guns to work the sails.

Captain Martyn strode to the helmsman. He kept his glass on the frigate. "Call out your headings!"

"Passing zero-four-zero!"

"Steady zero-nine-zero! Bosun, raise all sail!"

Martyn continued to watch the other ship. A few seconds later, he saw the bow cannons on the frigate puff and flash.

"Get down!"

The sounds came next and the shots fell short of the stern. Captain Martyn took the helm.

"Lieutenant Carson. Count the seconds. Watch the frigate. Shout out when he fires again! Speed?!"

"Sixteen knots, Captain."

"We can do better than that," Martyn said to himself. He changed course slightly to the right, five degrees.

"Get down!" Carson shouted. "I counted thirty-two," he said to the captain.

Martyn was already counting. Everyone lay flat on the deck but Martyn. He looked back over his shoulder. He didn't see it, but he heard it as one ball passed through the main sail. The other splashed wide to the left.

"Damn! He's found our range!" He steered right to one-one-zero to put the wind directly on the stern.

"Speed!"

"Seventeen knots!"

"Come on, *Anna*! Show them your legs! Come on!"

"Get down!"

This time, Conor did not bother to run around. He prayed for a few seconds. He heard the balls' angry lowing sound. But that's all. He did not see any splashes to either side of the ship.

They fell short! He came left again just a few degrees. "What's he doing?!"

"He's still following," Carson replied. "I'm not sure where the shots went."

"Not through us! That's what counts! He fell short. He'll adjust his range! Speed?!"

"Twenty knots, Captain!" The bosun did not believe it. "I'll take another."

"Get down!"

Martyn stared straight ahead, eyed his course, and prayed. He heard the lowing sound again. He turned and looked. The shots fell well short. "Speed?!"

"Twenty-one!" Bosun Linard had never seen the *Anamosa* fly like this before. "I'll take another!"

"Watch his heading now, Mr. Carson. Either he has more sail to raise, or throws some of his cannons overboard. Load the stern guns!"

"Captain, I don't believe we have the range," Carson said, doubt on his face.

"I don't care. He fired at me. I'm returning fire. That's what I will write in my log, and you will witness."

Carson grinned. "Aye, aye, sir."

"Take charge of the guns, Mr. Carson. Fire when ready."

Twenty seconds later, the *Anamosa*'s two stern guns fired. A cheer went up from the crew.

"What's he doing, Mr. Carson?"

"He's changing course to the right."

"Mark the time. Helmsman take back the helm. Steady on this course."

"Steady as she goes, aye, sir."

"Speed?"

"Twenty-one, Captain!"

"And that's with a hole in our main sail! But we'll leave that out." He winked at his second. "Confidential information."

Captain Martyn continued sailing east southeast for half an hour to give the frigate time to sail towards Louisbourg harbor, which presumably was its destination. Then he turned southwest to sail for Halifax.

*

Captain LaTour looked through his long glass and recognized the sails he saw heading straight for him.

"God's balls," he whispered to himself. "What are the chances of seeing the *Anamosa* again! What is she doing out here?"

Then *La Comète* began its pursuit, firing its bow guns.

Captain LaTour hooted with laughter. "Well, sorry, Captain Martyn. Fate requires that one of Lady Corrinne's ships be cannoned! Better you than me!"

"Who is that?" Victorio asked.

"That's the *Anamosa*. Can you believe our luck?"

"The *Anamosa* is no match for *La Comète*'s thirty-two guns."

"Aye. But *La Comète* will never catch her. The *Anamosa* might even be faster than the *Queen*. Don't tell anyone I admitted this. In fact, don't tell Lady Corrinne about this at all. She's miserable enough."

y

The Fortress of Louisbourg

Anamosa gloried in the sublime sensation of night-gliding with the owl as it hunted in the grassy fields surrounding the fortress. A *screech* occurred without warning. It came from higher up and behind the owl.

The raptor reacted instantly, banking hard to its right. It dove into the nearest trees as the *screech* was heard again. It perched within the safety and protection of the branches to wait for the other hunter to pass by.

Anamosa knew it was the eagle. Her dreaming mind was flooded with images of the face she loved and of the fierce tattooed face of the warrior who now possessed the spirit of the eagle. The images repeated several times before a stronger thought interrupted.

Bring them!

Anamosa awoke with a start, disoriented for several seconds, until she remembered it was only the large bed she slept upon in the governor's quarters of the King's Bastion. It was still dark. She got up and went over to the tall window to sit in its seat. The room was warm, almost too warm, but the glass of the window was cool to her cheek.

Her bedroom was on the second floor of the governor's quarters. Madame Drucour was kind and seemed very happy to have her living with them.

"This room is reserved for special guests," she had told Anamosa. "And I cannot think of anyone more special than you."

From the window seat, Anna could see the lensed beam of the lighthouse. When she saw it, she thought of Corrinne, prayed, and whispered words of love, and that she missed Marcus and Calypso.

Her thoughts returned to flying with the owl and the appearance of the eagle.

"*Bring them*. The eagle said, 'Bring them,'" she whispered aloud and wondered what this meant. "Bring Henri and Monsieur Malsum?" Those were the faces she'd seen when she heard the whispered words.

Anamosa left the window seat and found the standing clock in the darkened room. She turned up the wick on the lantern. It was four and seventeen minutes in the morning. She went back to her bed.

Bring them? Bring them where?

She decided to tell Henri of her dream. Raining or not, they would usually meet at Frédéric Gate at seven every morning. And if he did not meet her there, she would walk down the quay wall street to the Dauphin barracks.

The marine guard on duty there would tell her where he was. Every few days, Henri would leave the fort and go to Gabarus Bay. But they would always have a meal together when he returned.

Anna fell asleep and awoke again when the clock gonged seven chimes. "Oh, no!"

She leaped from the bed, slipped a dress over her head, pulled on some high-top shoes, wrapped a shawl around her shoulders, and hurried through the governor's quarters.

"*Bonjour*, my lady." Lieutenant Christophe was at his desk as usual.

"*Bonjour*, Lieutenant." She did not stop and started running as soon as she got outside.

She could see Henri in the distance already waiting by the gate. She hurried down Rue Toulouse. He smiled and opened his arms wide as she approached. This was her favorite part. He didn't just hug her. Henri would lift her up and spin her around while she giggled.

"What happened to your hair?" he asked when he put her down.

"My hair?" Anamosa had not taken time to comb her hair before she ran out. "Does it look bad?" She smoothed it with her hands.

"It could never look bad. Just a little wild," he teased.

"I had a dream last night!" She told him about it.

"Bring them? The eagle said *Bring them*?"

"I think so."

"Malsum and me? Where?"

"I don't know."

Henri knew these dreams Anamosa experienced were important. Messages from the white eagle must not be ignored. Maybe it had something to do with the battalion of mercenaries?

"Well, I have to go to Gabarus today. I will take Malsum with me. If the eagle is nearby, I am certain it will show itself. Come. Can you smell the fresh bread? Let's go to the bakery and share some buttered slices."

These past few weeks after Corrinne had sailed were the best Anamosa had ever known. She had Henri all to herself now, when he wasn't doing his marine things. He was nice to her and talked with her, and sometimes bought her trinkets. Twice he ate with her at the governor's table.

Three times she had walked out on the high ramparts of the Dauphin Bastion in the afternoon. There was a spot that was shaded along the wall. She'd crouch there quietly in the shade and watch the marines down in the marshalling yard, training with their swords. Henri would teach them. He was the best one, by far. There were twenty-eight marines now. Henri said he expected more to join.

Henri was savoring the warm bread with butter. Anamosa asked for some honey to be spread on hers.

"How are things with Madame Drucour?"

Anamosa nodded. "Good. I see the tutor every morning. Madame usually eats with me. She worries about me. Her maids come by to sit with me sometimes and ask questions about living in an Indian village. Madame asks questions about the attack. If I am in pain. If there is anything I want. I tell her no, but I think she wants to do something more. So yesterday I told her my shoes hurt my feet. I think she will buy me some new ones. She asks if you are nice to me. I told her you hit me a lot."

"What?!"

Anamosa started giggling. Henri smiled at her teasing.

"Maybe I should tickle you a lot?"

She giggled even more. "How long will you be in Gabarus?"

"Just until tomorrow. I should be back before the day is over. Oh, before I forget. In three days, Admiral de la Motte has invited the fort's senior officers, and their wives, to dine aboard *La Formidable*. I was invited, too." Anamosa eyes widened so much, Henri had to stifle his laugh. "I wanted to see if you would like to go."

Anamosa jumped from her chair and hugged him. "Yes! Yes! Yes!"

"All right! I shall escort you. Tell Madame Drucour you are coming with me. I'm sure she will see you are dressed properly." He stood. "But I must go now." He kissed her lightly on the lips. "I will be back tomorrow."

Anamosa hugged him tightly before letting him go. As he walked away, she felt a tightness in her chest.

"Where's your handsome lieutenant going?" the baker's wife asked with a sympathetic smile.

"Gabarus," Anamosa said with regret.

"I think Lieutenant Gerrard likes you," the baker's wife offered in a kind voice.

Anamosa glowed. "I know. I love him."

*

Henri went to the Dauphin barracks and told Corporal Luc Chapelle to saddle a second horse for Malsum.

"I want you to come with me to Gabarus," he told the Abenaki warrior. But he did not tell him why.

Panther Claw nodded and collected the small pack from his bunk. They went outside.

"What will I be doing?" the warrior asked once they'd left the fort.

"I want to explain the different artillery and fallback positions we've planned to repulse any landing. Maybe you will see some weakness we've not noticed."

As they rode towards the battlements, Henri stopped at a certain point and pointed at a different trail he'd blazed through the woods.

"That trail connects a mile further with three others that lead down to the trench lines. If we must fall back, those trails begin at the points of retreat. They all lead to right here. From here, it's the same road back to the Dauphin Gate."

When they reached the center of the Gabarus Bay battlements, Henri rode to an elevated position. He gestured and explained how the troops would be deployed. What they would do if the English managed to get ashore at different places.

"I did not know you had that many men."

"We don't," Henri replied grimly. "Even with the new mercenaries, we will be spread very thin. If the English manage to get ashore and hold a position, we will be forced into a fighting retreat back to the fort."

Malsum thought about his. "The English will consider this too. If I were attacking, your weakness is there"—he pointed to their left—"at the end of the battlements. That is the closest point to the fort."

"Yes. If they can land there, they flank our entire line. But that is where we have our reserves waiting in the trees. There will be a strong artillery battery hidden back among those trees. The English would have to climb in a line, up a cliff, against enfilade fire."

Malsum could see it. He nodded. "Only until the rest of your lines retreat. Then that position in the trees will be flanked, too."

*

The *ghost* sat at the top of a tall tree, hidden within its leafy branches. It watched the movements of the boy become man and the warrior. It could not get too close. The fort bristled with muskets and idle men. It must wait and follow them, until they were far away from the fort before making its presence known.

The *ghost* saw them get off the horses at an elevated spot many paces back from the place where armed men patrolled among battlements. It circled high above them. They were talking and gesturing. After a long enough time, the *ghost* decided this would be the place.

"*Screech!*"

Henri and Malsum looked up together.

"The white eagle." Henri spoke first. Anamosa was right.

Malsum could not believe his good fortune at seeing this creature again. The eagle circled right above them.

"It's going to land right in front of us," Henri said. "No sudden movements."

The *ghost* landed ten paces away. The female was very agitated at being so close to these men and the horses. The beak opened and closed as if trying to screech but no sound came out. The *ghost* increased its dominance. It cut the distance between them by half.

Henri handed over the reins of his horse to Malsum. Then he walked slowly to the raptor with a hand extended until he was right in front of it. The eagle touched its beak to Henri's hand. Henri closed his eyes and saw images of Sentry Cheever.

When the images stopped, Henri opened his eyes and backed away slowly. He accepted the reins of both horses from Malsum.

"Do as I did. Close your eyes, once you stand before it."

Malsum walked slowly with his hand extended until he was a pace away. He closed his eyes.

The eagle lifted its beak into the palm of the warrior's hand to strengthen their connection.

Malsum saw images of Lady Corrinne, Anamosa, Lieutenant Henri Gerrard, and Captain Gerrard. Then the face of the mercenary commander came forth from his memory.

The eagle screeched suddenly and Malsum lifted his hand away as if it were burned.

The *ghost* took flight again. *Now I know the face of It.*

They watched the eagle circle higher and higher before it flew inland.

"What did you see?" Henri asked.

"Faces. Yours. Lady Corrinne's. Anamosa and Captain Gerrard. And it forced me to recall the face of the mercenary commander."

"Colonel Krieger?"

"Yes. He is the dark one following Lady Corrinne. I told him I would take his face."

"You did what?!" Henri was shocked by this revelation. "When did you do that?"

"Three days ago."

Henri handed back the reins. "Let's go. We're going back." Henri's heart pounded with the fear that Anamosa was in the fort, alone, and unprotected, so close to this horror.

They galloped to the Dauphin Gate. Henri left his lathered horse with the guard and quick-stepped up the streets to the King's Bastion. He burst into the foyer.

Lieutenant Christophe saw an uncommon expression of panic on the marine officer's face. He stood with surprise.

"Lieutenant Gerrard? Is something wrong?"

"Have you seen Lady Anamosa?"

"Yes. She is in the governor's quarters."

"I must see her right away!"

"Yes, sir. As you wish."

Christophe moved in a hurry. He went down the hallway to the door leading into the governor's quarters. Henri paced back and forth in the foyer. His back was tuned when Anamosa appeared with Lieutenant Christophe.

"Henri?"

Henri exhaled with great relief and took her up in his arms. "Oh, *Dieu merci*. Thank God!"

Anna could smell his sweat and sense his great concern.

Henri set her down. "Lieutenant, I need to speak with Lady Anamosa in private."

Christophe pointed towards the war council room's door. "That room is empty."

"*Merci*." He led Anna through the double doors and had her sit in a chair. He took the chair next to her. "We saw the white eagle," he whispered and motioned with his finger she should speak quietly, too. "It touched our hands." Henri explained what he saw and what Malsum saw. "That mercenary commander is evil. He is looking for Lady Corrinne. We must warn her somehow and you need to be guarded."

"When I fly with the owl, I see him. He is not looking for me. And Lady Corrinne is not in Québec City anymore."

Henri leaned back in the chair with surprise. "How do you know that?"

"She sailed again. The eagle saw this. She went somewhere on Captain LaTour's ship."

"Where?"

"I don't know. But the evil will not find her."

Governor Drucour opened the council room door with a very annoyed expression on his face. Lieutenant Christophe was right behind him.

"Lieutenant Gerrard? Is everything all right?"

Henri stood and saluted. "Yes, sir. I just wanted to warn Anamosa about the mercenary commander, Lieutenant-Colonel Krieger."

"Yes. Admiral de la Motte apprised me that this man had threatened a woman in Brest. That he is aggressive and offensive. I have ordered the colonel, unless performing his military duties, he should not stray from the confines of the Queen's Bastion. And he is never to socialize with any of the citizens in Louisbourg, particularly with any women. I've also ordered him to take passage on the next fast schooner back to France."

"*Pardon*, Governor. I was not aware of this."

"Has he been disrespectful to Lady Anamosa?"

"No, sir." Henri looked at Anna.

"No, Governor. I've not seen him."

"Good. Is there something more, Lieutenant?"

"No, sir." Henri felt he should explain more. "Given what happened before…I just wanted to be certain—"

"I understand. That was your purpose in coming here and issuing orders to my aide. You can plainly see Lady Anamosa is not in danger."

"Yes, sir."

"Carry on with your other duties, Lieutenant."

"Yes, sir."

Lieutenant Gerrard left the King's Bastion but did not return to his other duties as ordered by Governor Drucour. Instead, he walked directly to the Queen's Bastion and took a watch position beneath a portion of the ramparts that provided heavy shade at this spot for that time of day.

Henri hoped to glimpse Lieutenant-Colonel Krieger from there. His thinking was in turmoil. His first instinct was to simply kill this host of the wraith and eliminate the threat to Anamosa. But thinking more about it, he was uncertain this was the right thing to do. As Henri had argued to his father and Corrinne, this evil came here seeking the *Falcon Queen* and Corrinne. Not Anamosa. Not him. By now, It likely learned from anyone it asked in Louisbourg of the ship that had carried Corrinne to Québec City weeks earlier.

Just killing the host did nothing to the wraith. It would simply possess another of its servants. So, nothing permanent would be accomplished.

The governor ordered the Hessian commander to take the next fast schooner back to France. That could be tomorrow or any day after that. Then It would be gone. Was it better to let him go? Probably. For now.

It seeks the châsse, he reminded himself. It did no good to stay in Louisbourg. *Killing me or Anamosa, God forbid, does not bring It any closer to that goal. Just the opposite.*

Still, Henri would not take chances. He would post a discreet marine sentry on the Queen's Bastion and keep watch for this colonel. The marines would trail the Hessian's movements in Louisbourg until the man boarded a ship, as Drucour had ordered.

But there were other dangers. The large regiment of mercenaries might harbor assassins from the other great houses, as Lord VanderMeer would often refer to them. They were hired looking to kill Corrinne, Calypso, and Marcus. This danger would also follow Corrinne wherever she went. It was not practical to explain any of this to Governor Drucour, particularly the presence of the wraith. The idea of something so occult and evil being present in the fortress would be dismissed outright and would damage his reputation. Sentry Cheever had firsthand knowledge of the demon from his participation in the sealing, and the color sergeant still did not want to believe it. The wraith was a curse for his father, Corrinne, and himself to resolve. Captain LaTour revealed that the host of the wraith, probably Lieutenant-Colonel Krieger, boarded his ship in La Rochelle harbor, killed his bosun, and searched the ship for the châsse. But Victorio and the ship's carpenter had it cleverly hidden. The wraith was unable to "see" the châsse. The new seals were working. Good thing, too. Right now, keeping the châsse over water kept the ship's location hidden. For that matter, Corrinne being over water protected her. Corrinne had a plan: the vault she established in Old Saybrook. Presumably, it would be the final tomb of imprisonment. It was not yet clear to Henri how this would be done. He guessed another sealing ceremony. But whatever Corrinne devised, it would require them all to be present again in Connecticut, not possible to do until this war was over. That was years away. A lot could happen before then. They must all live and deal with the perilous war dangers until then.

Fortunately, Anamosa could *see* the wraith and its servants when she dreamed. But if she could see the wraith, It could see her too. That alone placed Anamosa in great danger until the mercenary commander left Louisbourg.

Unfortunately, assassins from the great houses would only become visible when they attempted to kill someone. That was more of a danger to Corrinne, not Anamosa.

Henri decided to write a letter that day to his mother, Michelle, in Québec City. Wrap that missive around another one addressed to Corrinne, with all this new information. Lieutenant-Colonel Krieger had been ordered back to France. When Corrinne stood on land, she would be visible to him again. She should be aware of this. And the *Falcon Queen* must not come out of the water.

*

Lieutenant-Colonel Karl Krieger stood in front of the window in his quarters on the second floor. He was invisible to anyone looking in from the outside, his body shrouded in the shadows created by the sunlight coming through the window at an angle. He could clearly see Lieutenant Gerrard, Adaelric's scion, standing in the shadows of the rampart across the marshalling yard.

The ship was gone. For a short time, the whore queen had been in Québec City. The vulnax had glimpsed her presence there. Then It could not see her at all. And It had no servants in Québec City. She must have boarded the ship again. To go where? *The girl has the sight. She may know something. Adaelric's spawn may know something, too.* He had killed all the other servants. He resolved to attack again. But it was very dangerous to attempt anything. The vulnax must not get trapped inside a dead host.

Lieutenant-Colonel Karl Krieger was effectively isolated to the Queen's Bastion. He'd brought some blood servants here with him, but there was little they could do of any value that was worth sacrificing their lives. There was a large fleet in the port. It did not appear the English would attempt an invasion this fighting season. It seemed likely they would try again the next year. Krieger could not go to Québec City or Montréal. The authorities there might recognize him, or question him about the death of Archbishop Nicolet. This would cause delays. From what he'd been told by the fort's other officers, the English would assault one of two places next fighting season: Louisbourg or Fort Carillon. Maintaining this identity was not bringing him closer to the châsse as he planned. Louisbourg would eventually become a prison under siege. Governor Drucour offered him the opportunity to go back to France. Krieger decided to do that. It might also prove a better decision to provide mercenary services to the English. If the English started winning, as a mercenary officer in the English forces, It could use that status to force the French to reveal Lady de Chanaye's location.

Better than staying here. This fighting season was almost over.

*

La Comète entered Louisbourg's harbor. Captain Severyn Peltier made his report to Admiral de la Motte.

"The ship was faster than mine and got away. But the *Falcon Queen* sailed east on its way to Brest, its intended destination."

"Sailed to Brest?" The admiral was irritated. "By whose orders?"

"I did not ask. I presume by Governor Vaudreuil or Intendant Bigôt."

"And its cargo?"

"My watches observed it being loaded with furs."

"Passengers?"

"Just one. Major Michel de Péan was given passage aboard. He is on a mission to Versailles."

Admiral de la Motte did not like anyone issuing orders to one of his warships. He would send Captain LaTour a message to that affect by courier. He would also give the captain papers to present to the governors of New France, stating this ship was not part of their private navy.

However, the engagement by *La Comète* with an escort frigate of HMS *Sutherland* in the waters off Newfoundland? The English may be contemplating a strategy to engage his fleet from two directions, if the time comes.

The same day Admiral de la Motte received the report from Captain Peltier of *La Comète*, Admiral Holburne's squadron of twenty-three heavy warships appeared off the coast of Louisbourg. Holburne's command took up firm blockade positions, daring the French to come out and engage them.

Admiral de la Motte regarded the daily reports on Holburne's fleet with smugness.

Holburne must think I am foolish enough to sail forth from my comfortable harbor anchorage. The admiral pondered this with amusement. *Maybe I will? Maybe in October? By then the English will be out of food and fresh water.*

This stand-off would continue well into September until a heavy gale appeared without warning and drove the English away. In the interim, no French ship would either enter or leave the harbor, including the fast courier schooners.

G eneral John Campbell, 4th Earl of Loudoun, studied the information on
the limited strength of the French metropolitan army, commanded by
General Louis-Antoine de Montcalm. The information was a month old. But
it confirmed what he had expected, moreover what he had hoped, that the
French had no plans to follow-up on their successful spring campaign that
destroyed the boat-building works located at Fort William Henry. The French
forts on Lake Champlain, Fort Carillon, and Fort Saint-Frédéric were manned
by small garrisons, the intelligence confirmed. More important, Montcalm
had withdrawn three full regiments back to the Saint Lawrence River valley,
presumably to defend the cities of Montréal and Québec from an invasion
by that route. Loudon would later learn this redeployment was temporary.

Lord Loudon's main strategy towards winning this war had not changed.
He intended to march his large army of professional redcoats in a relentless
assault straight up Lake George and Lake Champlain and on to the Richelieu
River valley. He would surround and isolate the French garrisons at Fort
Carillon and Fort Saint-Frédéric, using the provincial militias and rangers.
He considered them competent enough to do that, at least. To this strategy,
he had staged eleven thousand redcoats in the port of New York. They only
needed the order to do one of two things: boat north up the Hudson River
valley, or get loaded aboard ships for transport to Halifax in preparation for
the invasion of Louisbourg.

Loudon considered the logistics of the sea invasion of the Fortress of
Louisbourg extraordinarily complicated and unnecessary. It required a large
dedicated Royal Navy fleet, equipped with the proper boats for landing a
ten-thousand-man army, or more, with artillery, on the beaches of Gabarus
Bay. Over the last two years, the French had prepared those beaches, building
battlements designed to repulse such landings. Worse, in his viewpoint, it

would strip the New York colonies of sufficient forces necessary to inhibit French aggression south towards the city of Albany.

Lord Loudon was convinced he could beat this French army in a land battle and win this war. He did not want to invade Louisbourg, not in 1757.

Not everyone agreed with him.

Lord William Pitt, 1st Earl of Chatham, became Secretary of State for the Southern Department in December 1756, which meant he was in charge of North America. He was also the elected Leader of the House of Commons.

Lord Pitt wanted to invade Louisbourg by April 1757.

In January, Pitt had issued orders to that end and developed a plan with the army and navy to do just that.

However, Lord Pitt's vocal opposition in Parliament towards spending any monies or providing any troops for the defense of the Hanover territory, the ancestral home of the House of Hanover, got him suspended as Secretary of State by George II in the spring of 1757. This action by King George was protested by the people of England and resulted in overwhelming public support from all the English cities. The support was so strong, they demanded Lord Pitt's restoration as the senior minister of government. Reluctantly, King George II did this in June. Lord Pitt then lambasted the senior officers of the army and navy for not carrying out his orders issued back in January to invade the seaport of Louisbourg, which in June, still sat undefended!

Lord Pitt had his eye on defeating France across the globe. Let the French fight land wars in Europe. America was the most important prize in the world. Acrimonious missives flew off Pitt's desk and the courier ships sailed. Priorities changed for everyone. Rear Admiral, Sir Charles Hardy shipped the New York troops to Halifax. The English fleet arrived at Halifax, albeit late.

Lord Loudon received an acerbic missive asking him why he was not in Halifax. Loudon now realized he was in danger of being recalled for his inaction on Louisbourg. He must go to Halifax without delay. But he did not want his troops at Fort Edward and Fort William Henry to remain idle. He ordered Brigadier General Webb to send provincial raiders to the north point of Lake George and destroy any boat building works the French may have erected. He dismissed General Webb's protest there were not enough boats to do this. In Lord Loudon's thinking, destroying the French boat works would forestall any rumored intentions by the French to make a foray against his forts.

Then Lord Loudon left for Halifax…in a hurry.

But before July, the French would augment their naval strength at Louisbourg with three full battle squadrons commanded by Admiral Dubois de la Motte, the best commander in the French navy.

The movement of two regiments of French troops from Fort Carillon to Québec City was only temporary. But Lord Loudon left for Halifax as a result. The invasion of Louisbourg was supposed to start in April. Lord Loudon would not arrive in Halifax until the ninth of July! He did not convene a council of war until two weeks later. Once there, Lord Loudon ordered the Halifax troops to conduct mock landings against hastily constructed mock coastal entrenchments for training.

A senior military officer on Lord Loudon's war council, Major-General Lord Charles Hay, a favorite of King George II, criticized Lord Loudon's gross inaction in writing. Lord Loudon had the general arrested for making disrespectful speeches. Lord Loudon further suggested to London, that the seasonal weather and climate was prejudicial to his lordship's health, describing Lord Charles Hay as a man out of his senses.

King George II was not happy with this assessment.

Neither was Lord William Pitt.

It was one of the rare occasions when these two men agreed on something.

*

Brigadier General Daniel Webb considered his position of command over Fort William Henry and Fort Edward to be extremely precarious. For every report of French inaction around Lake Champlain, two other reports arrived suggesting the French were on the march with thousands of soldiers and native warriors. The thought of being assailed by these vicious savages gave Webb nightmares or sleepless nights. When Fort Oswego had fallen to the French the year before, word came down the Oswego River to then Colonel Webb at the Great Carrying Place. The message? The victors were surging up the Oswego River towards him. At that time, Colonel Webb commanded the 44th Regiment of Foot. The same regiment involved in the massacre at the Battle of Monongahela in 1755. Colonel Webb panicked at the thought of these howling monsters who intended to perpetrate all manner of torturous activities. The surviving veterans of the 44th Foot recalled the mutilations of their fellow soldiers at Monongahela. They needed no encouragement to embrace Webb's emotional orders. Webb ordered the complete destruction of the supply forts at either end of the Great Carrying Place. Then he ordered the men to chop up the bateaux, burn the wagons, kill the horses, and foul the river passages with blockades of fallen trees, as Webb made his retreat all the way back to Albany.

Fort William Henry and Fort Edward were fixed fortifications. There was no retreating from these places. They were the last defense to prevent the invasion of Albany. Now in command of these pox-ridden, weakly protected forts, with intelligence suggesting not hundreds, but thousands of native warriors descending on them, Brigadier General Webb could barely keep his pants dry.

Commandant Lieutenant-Colonel Monro of Fort William Henry received daily intelligence reports. It was raw, frightening, and confusing. Fort William Henry was closer to the French than Fort Edward, which was situated some seventeen miles further south. Each new report of the same event, this day or the next, added more vagaries or gross embellishments to the last. By the twenty second of July it became impossible to separate the truth from fiction. But one thing was for certain, the French were on the move. Colonel Monro was desperate to learn when the enemy could be expected to arrive and in what strength. The ambushes and abductions occurring among the smaller scout patrols he'd sent forward convinced Monro to conduct a much stronger reconnaissance. Three whaleboats of ranger scouts were dispatched as the lead of a larger force. The rangers were supposed to scout the approach at the foot of Lake George, then turn back and rendezvous with the main force at a place on the lake they called Sabbath-Day Point, twenty miles north of Fort William Henry.

On the twenty third of July, Commandant Monro ordered Colonel John Parker to go forward with men from his regiment of Jersey Blues, three hundred of them, plus fifty men from the New York regiment using all the remaining boats available at the fort. The orders were simple. Go to the foot of Lake George. Assess French strength. Burn the French sawmills. Capture and return with prisoners.

*

Scout Captain Philippe Gerrard saw three whaleboats approaching. He was on the western shore with sixty-two of his scouts. They'd pulled their canoes up out of the water into the trees the night before to camp. His remaining hundred scouts were camped two miles further back. They were leap-frogging their way up the lake in strength as they approached Fort William Henry. They were more than halfway there.

"Those are rangers," he said grimly. He turned to a sergeant, his fastest runner. "Sergeant Jubert. Run back up the trail and alert the others. We will allow the ranger boats to pass our position and deploy our canoes behind them. They should attack as soon as they see them. That way we will have them trapped, between us. We want to *capture* these men," he emphasized.

The sergeant repeated the instructions as Philippe ordered.

"Good! Go!"

The *coureur de bois* scouts stayed hidden in the trees as the English whaleboats rowed by them in the morning twilight. The rangers favored the whaleboats. They were pointed on both ends and keeled, in contrast to the flat-bottom bateaux the French used. These boats were fast, and the rowers could move in the opposite direction, simply by turning around in their seats.

Philippe wondered why three boats full of rangers would be traveling so far down the lake, where they were certain to be seen. They should have beached the boats by now and be walking within the cover of the trees.

"Bait for a trap? Well, we will soon find out." Addressing his subordinate officers and sergeants, he said, "Spread out across their rear as we move forward. I'll be in the middle. Watch for my flag signals. Don't let any of these boats escape."

The breathless Sergeant Jubert reached the rest of the scouts and repeated Captain Gerrard's orders. Among this group of scouts was Captain Louis-Antoine de Bougainville, who had come along with Philippe's permission to make entries in his diary. The lieutenant leading the scouts ordered his men to push their war canoes into the water to prepare for the sprint. Another scout canoe left the rest and went down the lake another mile to alert Captain Michel de Langlade about what was to take place, as they were certain to hear the musketry. Captain Langlade commanded a mixed group of militia and tribal warriors. He had been present at the Battle of Monongahela, leading the Ottawa and other western tribes, and participated in the massacre that occurred afterwards. He was an Ottawa war chief. His father was French. His mother was Ottawan.

"It's their way," he'd told Philippe afterwards. "But you know this. Why are you so angry?"

"It's not my way," Philippe had answered.

"Then you should not be here," Langlade had retorted.

Captain Langlade was a loyal Canadian and a member of the Troupes de la Marine. Despite their disagreements, he admired Scout Captain Philippe

Gerrard. Like Philippe, Langlade followed orders. Especially the orders of Governor Pierre de Vaudreuil.

Scout Captain Gerrard and his men moved out on the lake and turned north. He could see the three whaleboats close ahead. As he watched their reaction at seeing them following, another surge of war canoes came at them from the other direction. From front and back the whaleboats were surrounded and disarmed and were captured without a shot being fired.

"Take these prisoners to Fort Carillon," Philippe ordered.

Captain Bougainville used this lull in the fighting to join more directly with Philippe's small vanguard.

"That went well," Bougainville complimented him.

Philippe was not listening. He scanned the lake behind him with his glass and saw three more boats in the distance.

"To shore!" He pointed and led the remainder of his canoes to a place behind a tip of land, where they could wait to conduct another ambush.

As the next three English boats went by, Philippe raised his flag to signal the attack, when an even larger group of boats burgeoned into view. He counted sixteen more boats, loaded with armed men, fifteen to twenty men per boat. It was an attack force! Philippe waited as long as he could. He wanted to get behind them all. One of the boats spotted his canoes and opened fire. Philippe signaled the attack and the scouts surged out on the lake, screaming war cries, firing muskets.

Captain Michel de Langlade had been waiting for this larger group of boats, too. His war canoes were filled with over three hundred warriors from the far western tribes: the Iowas, Winnebagoes, Miamis, Weas, Peorias. Over half the number were members of the Ottawa. He waited until he saw Captain Gerrard's scouts attack, then gave his own signal to attack. Captain Langlade's orders were much less complicated.

"Kill them until they lay down their arms. Take those that surrender prisoner."

At seeing the powerful ambush emerging from the front and his left, and more sporadic shots occurring from the coastal forest on his right, Colonel Parker ordered a retreat. Only half the boats heard the command and turned. So swift was the attack by the native war canoes, only five of the sixteen vessels escaped back to Fort William Henry. Out of the three hundred fifty men from New Hampshire and New York, less than a hundred of them returned. The stories they told were horrific. They were, in fact, outnumbered. And the horrific reports of torture they reported were not even close to the truth.

Captain Antoine de Bougainville recorded some of the horrors he witnessed in his journal.

After one volley of musketry, most of which flew wild, the English boats were overrun by a multitude of war canoes filled with screaming men. Their heads were adorned with feathers and bones, hair cut short into scalp locks, and skin of their naked bodies covered with designs of colored paints. They shot waves of arrows. Some of the English jumped overboard, presuming to swim their way to safety, only to be speared in the water like fish. They would be the lucky ones. I estimate a hundred and fifty were taken prisoner, at least for a time. What happened to many of these men, my pen trembles to describe. I fear these memories will haunt me forever. One interpreter from the west indicated there were warrior fathers with their sons who wanted to demonstrate how an enemy should be carved up before cooking them in a pot, urging their sons to drink of this detestable broth. This, they did to three prisoners and forced at least a dozen other prisoners to watch and hear the screams. I cannot...

There may have been more. I averted my eyes and laid down my pen to cover my ears. Even now, the next morning, I cannot force myself to write about the other monstrous acts that occurred.

Captain Bougainville told General Montcalm of what he witnessed. Montcalm called a war council above the La Chute cascades in a place cleared of trees, at the end of the broad portage cut to the upper lake from the lower sawmills. Montcalm was regaled as the venerated white father who brought the children victories. Through a dozen interpreters, Montcalm praised the warrior allies, telling them of his plans, how he would attack Fort William Henry, stressing the importance of the parts they would play, and the need for them to follow his orders for the plan to work.

Scout Captain Gerrard listened cynically to Montcalm's speech. He understood what the general was hoping to do. The warriors basked in a glow of self-adulation following the victorious lake battle, where only four of them were wounded. These allies would follow orders for a time. But after the anticipated victory at Fort William Henry…it would be Monongahela all over again, only much worse.

During this war council, Snow Hair took aside one of the Caughnawaga Mohawk chiefs he knew and asked this chief to send a messenger to a certain member of the Mohawk council.

"He is called Peter Blue Jacket. Tell him to find me at Fort Carillon after the battle."

For doing this favor, Philippe gave the Caughnawaga chief two silver ounces. The Caughnawaga Mohawk had come to appreciate the value of silver, at least what it could do in trading with the French.

"Keep one of these. Say my name to the commissary sergeant at Fort Carillon and give him the other ounce. Tell him I ask you be given a keg of brandy."

*

Brigadier General Webb conducted an inspection of Fort William Henry in the aftermath of the disastrous expedition by Colonel Parker. He was angry with Commandant Monro for sending such a large force of men forward without his permission. But the crushing, brutal defeat confirmed the French were on the march. They had but a day or two at most to prepare. Webb ordered another thousand men sent forward from Fort Edward: a hundred and twenty redcoats, eight hundred ten provincials from the Massachusetts regiment, and sixty more men from New York. Behind them they dragged six whaleboats, to replace some of the ones lost, and six cannons to place inside the large retrenchment to the east and south of the fort. The main fort could hold almost six hundred, but ten percent of those lay sick and infected with smallpox. The remainder of the twenty-three hundred total fighters Monro commanded, about seventeen hundred, occupied the large retrenchment along with women and children.

With the realization that reinforcing Fort William Henry would leave Fort Edward reduced to only sixteen hundred defenders, with a French army of ten thousand approaching, General Webb had sent urgent missives to the governors of the nearby states, describing the size of the advancing French army, asking for militia reinforcements. He also petitioned Sir William Johnson for any Iroquois allies he could gather to defend Albany.

*

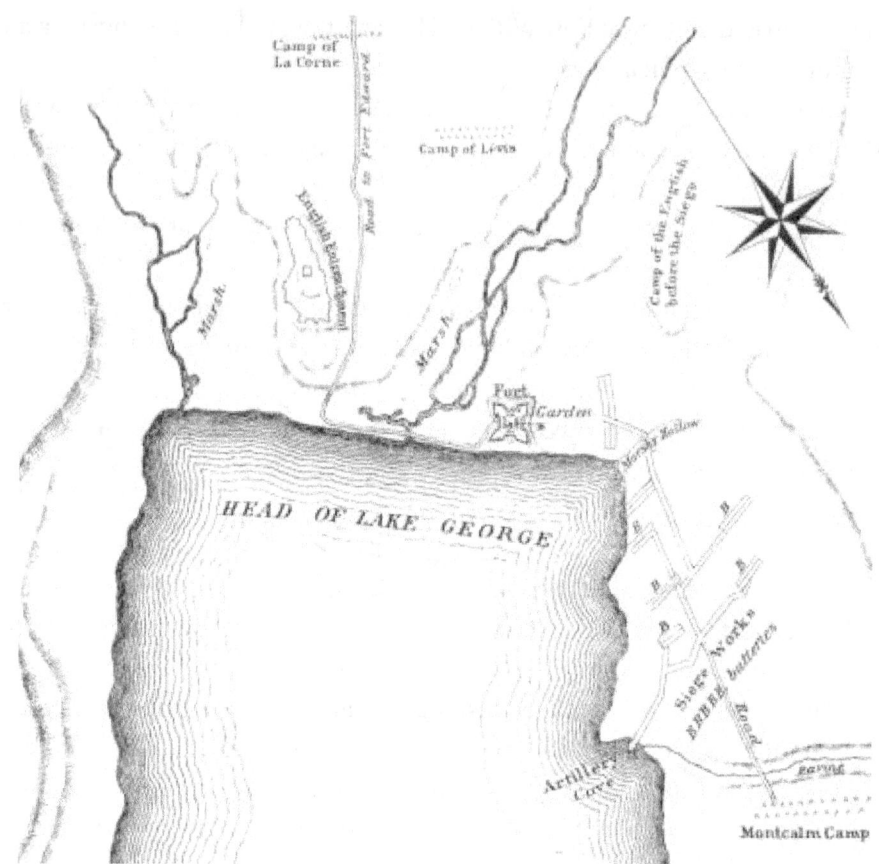

Siege of Fort William Henry

On the second of August, Montcalm's second-in-command General Francois-Gaston, Chevalier de Lévis, with his vanguard forces of twenty-five hundred elite fighters arrived a half mile west of Fort William Henry and began occupying positions. The force included grenadiers from each of the regular French regiments, piquets from these companies, the *coureur de bois* scouts, veteran militia, and several hundred "trusted" warrior allies.

Montcalm's main forces, with siege cannons, began arriving by bateaux the next day. The commander began redeploying his army immediately to complete an encirclement, returning the grenadiers to their regiments.

Chevalier de Lévis' remaining forces were deployed further to the south of the fort where they could threaten and assault the English retrenchment, plus guard the road coming north from Fort Edward. Lévis' troops engaged a company of Massachusetts Provincials in a fierce musket fight among the trees and drove them back inside the retrenchment. They seized all their horses and a hundred fifty oxen. The oxen were slaughtered and distributed among the warrior allies.

*

Two days later, Montcalm's forces started digging trenches to establish the siege batteries to fire on the fort. The fort began firing on the French sappers and engineers to disrupt this activity. Commandant Monro sent the first of several missives to General Webb describing the enemy's slow but relentless progress and his concern that the fort's capitulation was inevitable unless it received relief.

Under a red flag of truce, an aide of Montcalm was brought inside the fort, blindfolded, and delivered a message to Lieutenant-Colonel Monro. Essentially, it said they were surrounded by superior forces supported by tribal fighters, the cruelty of which they had recently experienced. At present, Montcalm had the power to restrain these warriors if Monro surrendered the fort, but could no longer be held responsible for what would happen if Monro persisted in defending his hopeless position. He asked Monro to surrender.

Monro rejected Montcalm's messenger and prayed that Webb's relief forces would arrive as promised. Except Webb had not promised anything that was not already there.

General Webb had sixteen hundred men fit-to-fight. Reports from his scouts came back with intelligence that reported General Montcalm's strength somewhere between eight to eleven thousand. He'd used the higher number when he petitioned the provincial governors for help. But even with the lowest number cut in half, the French outnumbered Fort Edward's strength by three to one. To weaken Fort Edward further would be to open Albany and northern New York to invasion. In fact, there was nothing Webb could do if Montcalm decided to march south after investing Fort William Henry and demand his surrender, except negotiate the best terms.

General Webb decided to send a missive to Commandant Monro with his honest advice. He had his aide write it.

Sir,

The General has ordered me to acquaint you, he does not think it prudent, as you know his strength at this place, to attempt a junction or to assist you till reinforced by the militia of the colonies, for the immediate march of which repeated requests have been sent. The General has learned that the French are now in complete possession of the road between us. A prisoner just brought in and questioned, revealed the enemy assails you with a force cannon and men, upwards of eleven thousand strong, who have you entirely surrounded to a distance of five miles. The General wishes you to be informed, so that, if the militia he requested arrives too late to march to your aid, the person in command of Fort William Henry better seek to obtain the best terms of surrender possible.

The missive was carried by an experienced wilderness courier, but despite his expertise, the man was stalked by one of the Scout Captain Gerrard's Caughnawaga scouts watching Fort Edward. He was killed before he reached Fort William Henry. The bloodstained missive was cut from a seam in the man's coat and delivered to General Montcalm.

*

At Montcalm's forward command next to the artillery, with two full batteries of siege cannon and mortars now in place on the left and right, he ordered a bombardment to begin at six in the morning.

The cannons of Fort William Henry were made of iron. After two days of continuous firing at the French trenches, over half of those cannon had overheated and burst from failure. This included all the fort's thirty-two-pound guns, the *black bitches* as Major Eyre affectionately referred to them. As a result, the response from the fort against this bombardment had little effect.

Montcalm felt certain the capitulation of the fort would happen soon. As a show of goodwill, he invited the chiefs of his warrior allies to each take turns lighting a fuse of a siege cannon. Afterwards, they would hoot and brag how their particular shot was the one that convinced the English to surrender. For three hours, twenty-one French cannons belched iron balls in a rain of death and terror.

Lieutenant-Colonel Monro ran around the fort shouting encouragement to his men, telling them relief was on the way. But secretly he was filled with doubt. He should have received a message from General Webb by now—any kind of message! Then seeing all the dozens of women and children still inside the fort, the families of the men from the New Hampshire Regiment, all huddled in one of the safer corners of a bastion, their faces twisted with terror, the commandant wished he'd insisted they obey his order, that they be taken to Fort Edward on the day they arrived. But their husbands in the

New Hampshire militia had protested. Monro relented. Now he was terribly afraid of what might lie ahead for them.

The severe hammering by the French artillery looked to continue all day long. But at nine in the morning, three hours later, the French bombardment stopped. For several minutes, a prolonged silence drew the fort's attention. Men hazarded a glance over the walls. There followed a ratatating drum beat. Another red flag of truce was raised above the French trench line.

"Sir, a party of French approach under a red flag of truce," shouted an officer on the ramparts.

Monro ordered a ceasefire throughout the fort. He charged to the top of the rampart. A French officer approached and announced he carried a letter for the fort commander. The officer was blindfolded and guided inside the fort until he stood inside Monro's quarters.

"What do you want?" Monro asked tersely.

The French officer spoke excellent English.

"Sir, I am Captain Louis Antoine de Bougainville, aide-de-camp of General Montcalm, who extends his respects and directs me to hand you his personal letter, in which, hoping to spare the further spilling of blood and to preserve the lives of your men, he asks for your surrender."

Monro did not hesitate in his answer. "I have already given your commander my answer to this request."

Captain Bougainville withdrew another letter from his pocket, wishing they would remove the blindfold so he could see the commandant's reaction.

"With respect, sir, I have another letter for you to consider."

The letter was wrinkled and bloodstained on the outside. The wilderness courier bringing it from Fort Edward had been intercepted and killed. The message was cut from a seam in his coat. It was dated three days earlier. It was from General Webb, saying no reinforcements could be expected, and urged Monro to get the best terms possible.

Monro waited until his emotions were under control. He answered the French officer in as calm a voice as he could muster.

"Captain Bougainville, please express to General Montcalm my genuine appreciation for his politeness in this matter. Further express that if and when I have a reply to send, the general will be so notified by our raising a white flag."

Once Bougainville regained the French lines, he reported to Montcalm, that the Fort William Henry commandant had no intention, at present, towards capitulation. Montcalm signaled the bombardment to continue, which it did. The logs on the fort eventually began to split and splinter.

*

As dawn broke over Fort William Henry on the ninth of August, the French siege artillery kept up a sporadic shelling consistent with what they had done all night long. The inhabitants of the fort were exhausted from the lack of sleep and their distress over their gloomy future. Those wounded over the last two days now shared the space lying next to others suffering from smallpox. There was no place else left to put them.

Overnight, the French had completed the final parallel trench of a classic Vauban-style siege and erected a battery of eighteen-pound guns only two hundred yards from the fort. At that range, the French siege cannons would reduce the wooden timbers of the walls to splinters.

Monro asked his engineer to survey the damage and report. The top of the bastions closest to the French lines had been reduced by three to four feet. The casements and bunkers beneath these bastions had all been heavily damaged, seriously caved in. Only four of the fort's seventeen cannons were still operable, and they were of small caliber. Stocks of ammunition were almost consumed. Reports from indirect fire on the entrenchment to the east were no better. They had suffered more casualties than the fort. With little to no cover to hide behind or beneath, the exhaustion from the pounding and relentless bombardment reduced some of the men to drooling madness.

Monro called a council of war and asked for options to consider. There was only one, and it was unanimous. Capitulation. Lieutenant-Colonel Monro stood and saluted his officers, thanking them all for their bravery under fire. He ordered the white flag to be raised.

The French bombardment stopped at seven thirty.

*

Montcalm quietly ordered Scout Captain Gerrard to take some of his men forward on the road to Fort Edward.

"Get out beyond our lines. Do you have men that will guard the English during their withdrawal?"

Philippe grimaced and shook his head. "Not many. Maybe sixty of my scouts feel the same as I do about protecting them. But they will not be much use against a thousand warriors rampaging for booty and trophies. I can guard maybe two hundred, but I will have to be ready to shoot the more aggressive warriors, to prove my earnestness. If I do not, they will all push through us with tomahawks. And then I will have to shoot more of them."

"And our militias?'

"Not good, General. Most of them have friends among these warriors, farms near the villages, or they are direct relatives by marriage. Your regulars might offer better discipline. Once the warriors collect something they consider respectable to carry away, they will turn and leave. The first day of the march will be the worst. They will loot everyone and everything. Many will try to take prisoners. God help such prisoners, if they do. They will kill them and take scalps. Or take scalps without killing them."

*

Lieutenant-Colonel Monro was directed to march the inhabitants of the fort to the retrenchment camp some nine hundred yards to the east, alongside the road leading to Fort Edward. Those sick and wounded were left inside the fort, assured by the French they would be cared for. This included those women and children from the families of the wounded and sick. Monro marched everyone else to the retrenchment, with more assurances they would be guarded on their march to Fort Edward the next morning by French regulars.

As soon as the garrison marched out, the warriors stormed inside to find it already empty of the plunder they'd been promised by Governor Vaudreuil. Most of the supplies had been carried away by the garrison when they marched to the retrenchment. What was not carried had been destroyed by the English, including all the kegs of brandy or rum that were smashed to prevent the natives from drinking it, which is what they had wanted most. They howled with anger at this discovery. But they continued searching. In the bottom casements of the eastern bastions, they found the pox-infected sick and severely wounded soldiers, together with their supporting families of women and children. Finding nothing else, they began taking human trophies. The screams and cries of terror did not last very long as every single person, no matter the age or the sex, was killed and scalped. A few of them lost their heads.

The ravagers then sprinted towards the retrenchment area guarded by a circle of French regulars. They burst by these soldiers as if they were trees and began assaulting the prisoners inside. The French regulars did nothing to stop them. It would have gotten worse, but Montcalm showed up with his personal guard and restored order, forcing the infuriated warriors out of the retrenchment.

Lieutenant-Colonel Monro protested that the terms of the surrender had been violated. Montcalm admitted he did not have control over his native allies. "Let them take whatever baggage they want, so they will leave the area before you march tomorrow morning."

Monro had no choice.

It was a worrisome day and a terrifying night for the English prisoners. Howls and screams in the dark of night signaled a murder was being committed just paces away. No one dared sleep lest they be next. Before nightfall, the wounded in the retrenchment were moved to the side of the road, to make it easier to load them into wagons purportedly coming for them in the morning. French regulars were assigned to guard them until then. These guards abruptly vanished in the twilight before sunrise. Warriors immediately appeared to kill and scalp these hapless men.

The day grew brighter when the sun appeared, and with it the French escort of three hundred regulars marched up to take positions on the English column that was forming. As the camp began to march forward, the regulars rearranged to form a protective semi-circle behind them. There was over two thousand people in this march. The line was long. At the front, Canadian militias took the lead. In front of them, searching the trees to either side of the road was Scout Captain Gerrard and the seventy-eight scouts he trusted for this assignment, more than he expected to volunteer, but not enough. Still, it was something.

Those marching were encouraged by the officers to move swiftly. Safety was only sixteen miles away. Travel was by road all the way. It could be done in a day. They simply had to keep going. One foot, then the next foot.

The soldiers and the vulnerable civilians knew they did not dare leave the road. Beyond the thin line of French soldiers, brutal agony awaited with a merciful death at the end.

The French soldiers were not happy about this duty. They had survived the battle. They did not plan to lose their lives now. The English were their traditional enemy. They'd been fighting them for centuries and had fought them intensely for the last two weeks. Now they were supposed to defend them? Even kill their native allies in such defense? Not likely.

When the line of marchers became extended and thinned out, the spacing between the French regulars became larger and larger, until they, too, felt isolated and exposed. Consequently, they did not try to stop the screaming, painted, and tattooed warriors who darted through the ever-widening spaces. Even if the French soldiers attempted to intervene for the English, the savages no longer heeded any orders. They wanted to loot, to plunder, to kill, to take scalps and even heads as trophies. They wanted to strip the English of everything they carried, including their clothing. Children were snatched from the arms of their loved ones before anyone could react. These unfortunates were taken back to the home villages to become slaves to various tribes. Some of the men taken as prisoner were later sold to Governor Vaudreuil, the French father, the great mountain, the Onontio, waiting for them in Montréal, by his promise of even greater rewards. These prisoners were herded as a sort of cattle, a few of them eaten along the way, the Catholic captors saying grace over the gruesome repast. Others were tortured for entertainment, the traditional penalty for being one of the defeated. Their arms and legs staked out over shallow fire pits, slow roasted in traditions exquisitely refined after centuries of practice involving fire, to produce the greatest pain...as was their way. Still others were hacked into pieces and boiled in a large pot.

The warriors prowled the forest on either side during the march, in step with their prey. Mid-morning, when the line was stretched to its thinnest, a howling cry arose from a war chief. It was a signal. The savages attacked all at once from both sides. Pandemonium ensued. The remaining women and children disappeared. They had been grabbed and carried off. Anyone who resisted was tomahawked and scalped. The French guards stood aside using their bayonets to defend themselves. English soldiers were stripped of every article of their uniform except for their pants, a shirt, or their shoes. Some ended up with only their shoes. It was not long before the dead lay everywhere. Many of the would-be victims ran off into the woods and became lost. This saved them, but it would be days before they managed to reach Fort Edward, starved, thirsty, eaten by insects and delirious, relating horrific stories of what they'd seen and experienced.

A large group at the front of the column speeded ahead of everyone else, about a hundred in all. A mix of women carrying children, some soldiers, some provincial militiamen, a few officers. At hearing the screams rising from behind, they surged forward, pushing past the Canadian militia guards in a panic. The Canadians stood aside passively and let them pass. Hearing the screams and panic, Captain Gerrard's scouts came in from the woods they'd been scouting on either side. Thinking they were being ambushed, it took a few minutes for Philippe to bring the prisoners to order. He heard the entire column behind them collapse in massacre and disarray. The scout captain was determined to get these few, at least, escorted alive to Fort Edward. He reposted his men at the front, the back, and along the sides. They walked quickly for the next few hours.

At the far rear of the line, General Montcalm along with his second- and third-in-command, Generals Lévis and Bourlamaque, and their personal guards of grenadiers, once again came to the rescue and surrounded five hundred of the prisoners, directing them to march them back into the retrenchment, where they would be guarded again, this time properly. The other marchers, spread over miles of forest road were left to survive on their own.

For a time, Scout Captain Gerrard thought the handful of survivors he guarded would be delivered safely to Fort Edward when a commotion began at the rear of his column.

"Don't stop! Keep them moving," he ordered his men loudly. Then he ran to the rear to confront the problem. And it was a big problem.

An Abenaki chief named Neealouska and some sixteen of his warriors had caught up to the small group advancing at the front, only to be stopped by the grim faces of the *coureur de bois* scouts. Almost half of Philippe's men, about thirty, took positions on either side of their captain, their muskets held at the ready.

Among the scouts but standing in the back, was an English captain, very conspicuous in his red uniform. Captain Kendall Tipton. If there was going to be a fight, he'd already promised himself to take a few of the savages with him. He was just waiting for weapons to be dropped that he could pick up and use.

Neealouska's head and shoulders were painted red. He carried a tomahawk in each hand. His men were similarly covered in paint, feathers, and bones and brandished muskets, pistols, knives, bows, and tomahawks. The warriors were aching for a fight. All of them carried bloody scalps, like so many fish on a string, tied around their waists. The Abenaki chief looked around Philippe's head and saw the end of the line he was trying to reach dwindling in the distance.

He scowled at Philippe and pointed. "They were promised to me."

The chief was mission-raised, a Catholic. His French was not perfect, but it was good enough.

"Not on this day," Philippe replied firmly. "General Montcalm gave me orders to guard them all the way to Fort Edward. That is what I will do."

"Governor Vaudreuil promised me rewards for bringing them to Montréal," Neealouska replied. "You are *stealing* from me."

The muskets on both sides elevated menacingly.

Philippe was revolted by this slaughter. His men outnumbered the Abenaki, and the *coureurs de bois* were better marksmen and equal with knife and tomahawk. It would be so easy to allow this to escalate. But even if Philippe killed them all, this would not be over. There were over a hundred Abenaki fighting alongside the French. If he killed one of their chiefs, they would go to war.

"Sergeant Jubert," Philippe called loudly.

"Sir!"

"How many prisoners do we escort?"

"Eighty-six men, eleven women, four boys, two girls, and three infants, sir!"

"That makes one hundred six. Neealouska does not need these prisoners. Neealouska can go see Vaudreuil in Montréal and tell him you gave one hundred six prisoners to Snow Hair. When Vaudreuil sees me, I will say Neealouska spoke the truth. He will reward you. Or...we can all start fighting right now, and you will receive no reward because you and I will both be dead."

Neealouska stared hard at Snow Hair. He glanced around the *coureur de bois* and saw the British officer standing in the back. He pointed at the officer.

"I want his coat," he demanded.

Philippe turned around and was surprised to see this soldier, too. He advised the officer in a grim tone, speaking English.

"Take off your coat, Captain, and gift it to this Abenaki chief."

Captain Tipton balked. Philippe spoke more tersely. "If you do not do this, you will insult this chief in front of his men. And I will not defend your insult." Philippe motioned the officer forward. "Do this respectfully, Captain, and this confrontation will end."

Captain Tipton was seething but slipped off his uniform coat and handed it to the Abenaki chief. Neealouska slipped it on and smiled proudly. His braves hooted with approval. The chief regarded Snow Hair one more time.

"Neealouska will tell the Onontio of Snow Hair's promise." Then he gestured his men to reverse direction.

"What is your name, sir?" Captain Tipton asked.

"Scout Captain Philippe Gerrard, at your service. Let's go," he ordered his men, waving his hand in a circle above his head. "Catch up to the rest. I want these people delivered before sundown."

As they began to trot, the officer persisted. "Have we met before, sir? Your name is familiar."

"That is unlikely, Captain."

Seven hours later, when Fort Edward came into view, Philippe and his scouts halted and let the English column go forward on its own. One of the terrified women carrying an infant came up to Philippe and thanked him.

He looked at the baby. "What's her name?"

"*Him*," she corrected tenderly. "His name is Barry."

"God go with you, Barry."

*

Montcalm kept the five hundred prisoners in the retrenchment for four more days. During this time, his troops tore down the timbers of the fort and began throwing any dead bodies they found littering the fighting field, be they French, English, or tribal, atop the heap. The pile of logs became one large funeral pyre. It was disgusting work.

By the end of the fourth day, none of the warriors remained. They were on their way home carrying trophies, human or otherwise. General Montcalm no longer needed to guard the English. The remaining prisoners went forward without escort to Fort Edward. They would march these sixteen miles without stopping, passing the dead lying in ghastly poses alongside the road. Even when they could not see them, a great stench would indicate those places where bodies were decaying among the nearby trees.

When the English were out of sight, a mile or more away, Montcalm ordered the pile of logs that was formerly Fort William Henry, set on fire. The bodies added to the pile became a fuel of sorts. It burned fiercely. The odors of the smoke and fumes were nauseating.

General Louis-Joseph de Montcalm-Gozon, Marquis de Saint-Veran, felt greatly ashamed. This was the most loathsome victory he'd ever perpetrated. He hoped the great fire would obliterate this foul stain from history.

It would not.

Fort Carillon

Scout Captain Gerrard intended to contact Sir William Johnson after delivering the prisoners he'd guarded to Fort Edward. But the outrage over the massacre was so great, he worried about the safety of his men. Hundreds of Mohawk allies of Sir William had gathered near Fort Edward. The main encampment of the rangers was nearby. Purportedly, another two thousand men of the New York militia were marching up the Hudson River and were already at Saratoga. They all wanted revenge. Philippe would not gain the slightest reprieve for the mercy he'd shown the handful of Fort William Henry prisoners he'd escorted. He withdrew all his scout companies back up the lake.

By the time he reached Fort Carillon, the great celebration was in its third day. The victory over Fort William Henry had succeeded beyond any expectation. French casualties amounted to sixteen killed and fifty-four wounded. By European measurements, it was an astonishing result. But General Montcalm remained subdued, mortified, and ashamed of the grisly massacre he'd been unable to control. The generous terms of the Fort William Henry's surrender had not been honored. The tribal warriors had been promised a reward. The French knew full well what would happen. They had expected this to take place and even abetted the action. General Montcalm had permitted the atrocities to take place without reprisal. It was Montcalm's responsibility to prevent such a slaughter from occurring. It did not matter what his personal intentions had been.

*

Philippe shared quarters in the fort with Captain Bougainville. His thoughts now dwelled on Corrinne and his children. He worried about the future. Until Corrinne wrote to Michelle in Québec City, he would not know how to address a letter to her.

Captain Bougainville was frenetic about getting his journal entries of the battle enhanced with more detail. Philippe helped his friend understand those portions of the battle where he was present to witness what happened, including the atrocities that occurred on the march to Fort Edward.

Captain Bougainville stopped writing and implored Philippe for an explanation.

"I do not comprehend such abject cruelty. There is no purpose to it. I recognize war is appalling in the extreme, full of villainy. It perverts compassion, emptying men of any human decency. Both sides perpetrate unspeakable crimes. But after the battle is over? This behavior," Bougainville expressed plaintively, "this propensity to take pleasure in torture, devising dreadful cruelties, the callous slaying and defilement of women and children! Celebrating cannibalism as a tradition to be revered, as if it were a rite of passage? These heinous characteristics are not natural. Our mission tribes from the villages along the Saint Lawrence River—they've been baptized Catholic for almost a century! They take communion! Yet they enthusiastically took part in this. It is sinfulness most foul! And they know it!"

Philippe was at a loss to explain any of it. "I know. I lived among them. These scars." He gestured at his face. "They gave them to me. And afterward they cared for me with the greatest kindness. They helped me heal."

"What are you saying? That they should be forgiven?"

"No. I am saying, we were like them once."

"Nay! Nay! Not me," Bougainville replied firmly. He refused to accept that.

Philippe had heard such arguments wrapped in self-righteous tones many times before. He abhorred what had occurred. He could not forgive it. It was too primitive. He could never understand it. And he could not defend it. He'd given up trying.

The nature of the discussion filled the small room with a dark pall. Philippe excused himself to eat. But instead of eating, he went up on the stone ramparts of Fort Carillon to gaze out at the beauty and serenity of Lake Champlain. He was not there long before a familiar voice intruded.

"Oho, Snow Hair."

It was Peter Blue Jacket, standing and smiling as if they'd been apart for only a moon, though it had been years.

"Oho, Peter!"

Philippe embraced this sometimes-friend warmly. He'd know the man for over a decade.

"The white Frenchmen are victorious again," Peter stated the obvious. "So, when Snow Hair calls, Peter must come."

"I am grateful you came. You are a good friend."

Peter held up a palm. "Be careful. The greatest part of me is Mohawk. The English may start winning someday."

Philippe smiled. "I called you to talk about peace."

"Peace?! After the French victory and slaughter that just occurred?"

"I plan to leave Fort Carillon and visit my Oneida father, Tall Mountain Among Trees. I hope to speak with Sir William...*Warraghiyagey,* while I am in the Oneida village. I ask that you give him written papers from Governor Vaudreuil concerning peace."

"Peace?" Peter said the word again in a dubious tone. He frowned. "And this you ask me to do after my travel for ten days in the middle of a battle, just to find you?"

"You are the most important Mohawk chief I know."

Both knew Philippe was exaggerating. Peter was not a chief. He could not vote on the council. But Peter Blue Jacket sat on the council of chiefs anyway. He was considered a wise counselor and an ambassador. As far as Philippe was concerned, Peter could speak for the entire Mohawk nation. Peter Blue Jacket knew this too. He appreciated the exaggeration.

"And what would you say to me that you would not say to a Mohawk chief?"

"I will tell Peter Blue Jacket what these papers say." He pulled the sealed missive from inside his coat. "That he might ask me questions. So, he might tell the Mohawk council first, before they hear it from anyone else. If the Mohawk do not see the benefit that the French see, they will not tell Warraghiyagey to travel to the Oneida village and meet with Snow Hair. And I will spend a pleasant month with my Oneida father before returning to Québec City, where I will tell Onontio that the Mohawk refuse to accept this treaty. But if Sir William comes to see me, then it will be the English who refuse the treaty. After this victory, I assume the English will refuse and may even try to kill me in front of my father. But in truth, I want to tell the Mohawk first. The offer from Governor Vaudreuil is genuine. And this is Mohawk land."

Peter Blue Jacket nodded. "Snow Hair is very clever. Do you have brandy to share with a chief of the Mohawk?"

Philippe smiled broadly. "I do, my friend. I will have a feast prepared for us. And we will smoke together and speak all night of the old times, and the now times, and the times of tomorrow."

They ate together outside the fort, where they could be alone. Because of Philippe's rank, food and drink was brought out to them. Peter Blue Jacket could read some French, but was not literate. Using the light of a lantern, Philippe pointed and read every single word of Governor Vaudreuil's proposal for peace. He took great pains to explain the reasons behind each sentence, answering Peter's questions as clearly and honestly as he could.

"The white Frenchmen have won all the battles," Peter argued. "Why would they offer this now?"

"Because we are going to lose this war to the English," Philippe admitted firmly. "Next year, the English will bring a great army of redcoats to this place. It will number ten times the size of any army ever seen in these lands…and maybe more. The French numbers will not change. We cannot win against an army of that size. We will withdraw to the lands north of the lakes and the great river."

"The French give Mohawk lands to the English? They are not yours to give."

"Yes. We know that. We are not giving anything to the English. As I said, we are withdrawing from these lands. That is why I want the Mohawk to know this first. In trade for our withdrawal, the fighting with the English will stop."

Peter snorted and scoffed. "You think it will be that easy?"

"No. But we will make the offer anyway. If the English agree, they will need to respond to us in writing."

"And if the English and the Mohawk do not give you an answer?"

"Then nothing changes. We will continue to fight."

Peter asked the same questions in different ways. Philippe gave him candid answers. Amid the back and forth, Philippe realized that Peter Blue Jacket would indeed speak on his behalf to the council.

Philippe thought of another point to make. "No matter what the Mohawk argue, I think it would be good for the Mohawk to know what the English think of the French proposal. Force the English to reveal their future intentions to the Mohawk. That an army of redcoats is coming."

Before the night was over, they even managed to laugh.

In the morning, they shared food again before Peter Blue Jacket marched south. Philippe gave him the copy of the truce that was to go to Sir William Johnson. He held a second copy in his hand.

"I will keep this copy with me to give to Sir William, if you decide to keep that one for the Mohawk. I will stay in my father's village for two moons. Then I will travel to Montréal…with or without an answer."

The two old friends clasped arms together.

"I hope to see you in the spring," Philippe said.

"Tell me the place, Snow Hair. I will be there."

*

At midday, Philippe sought out General Montcalm and was invited to eat a meal with his commander. As they ate, Philippe related what had happened with Neealouska and the Abenaki warriors near Fort Edward and his overnight discussions with Peter Blue Jacket.

Montcalm did not seem interested enough to comment on either revelation. The general's mood was somber despite the celebrations of victory over Fort William Henry that was moving into its fourth day.

Receiving only polite nods of acknowledgment from his commander, Scout Captain Gerrard began concluding his report.

"My scouts will resume their patrols next week. Today, I plan to start my march to the Oneida village on the Oswego River to await Sir William Johnson. At the end of September, I hope to be in Montréal and will stay there for a few weeks before returning to my scouting duties here at Fort Carillon. That is, unless you have other orders for me, sir."

"No, Captain. I agree with your plans. I am certain Governor Vaudreuil will be most anxious to hear your report when you return." Montcalm abruptly pushed aside his untouched plate of food and regarded Captain Gerrard more formally.

Philippe stopped eating and moved his plate aside.

"Captain, I've made a decision that I have not shared with anyone else… not yet anyway. I would like your honest opinion."

"It would be my honor, General."

"I will no longer use our native allies as units in my army when we engage the English again. I recognize there will be difficulties in prohibiting their participation, but if it comes to that, I will order them not to fight alongside any of my regulars or the Troupes de la Marine. Do you have counsel for me on this?"

"Candidly, sir, Governor Vaudreuil will encourage them to ignore your orders."

Montcalm's lips tightened.

Philippe had an idea. "But I anticipate Sir William Johnson will refuse the governor's proposal for an armistice."

"You know this already?"

"Peter Blue Jacket sits on the Mohawk Council. Governor Vaudreuil's armistice refers to lands that have been traditionally Mohawk for centuries.

It is an insulting presumption the English and French can barter these lands in trade. The Mohawk are the most powerful tribe of the Iroquois League. They will not tolerate this. The French cannot offer something they do not own, nor can the English accept ownership. Sir William is a Mohawk chief. He knows this. If Sir William meets with me at the Oneida village, he will say this to me. He might also cite the massacre at Fort William Henry as another reason why there can be no peace…if I ask him directly."

Philippe left the implication hanging in the air, that he could steer Sir William Johnson to say any of this.

Montcalm nodded thoughtfully. "That might be enough. The governor will want your personal report of the meeting with Sir William Johnson. When you return, command a scouting foray south that includes Fort Edward, and Albany, too. Collect an accurate assessment of troop build-up and English intentions for the spring. Then come to Québec City and make your report. Is that possible to do by the end of November?"

"Yes, sir."

Montcalm stood. Philippe followed his lead.

"I will be visiting Montréal before I go to Québec City. General de Lévis will assume command here for the winter. Governor Vaudreuil is still in Montréal. If you plan to visit there before continuing your mission, you should leave now and be gone from there before I arrive."

*

After assigning one of his lieutenants to take command of scouting activities, Scout Captain Gerrard left Fort Carillon with four of his most trusted *coureur de bois* scouts, including Sergeant Jubert. They reached the former Dunemoore Company warehouse in Montréal in three days. After a brief reunion with the chief clerk, Paulus Legates, Philippe arranged for his scouts to stay in the small quarters at the back of the warehouse.

"I am going into the city for two days at most and will rendezvous here with you before going on a mission assigned to me alone. Monsieur Legates will pay you and I will reimburse those payments. Questions?"

Philippe did not go into the western gate of the city, but instead walked the road outside the walls, clockwise, to enter the city through the northern gate to minimize being seen by anyone who might recognize him. It was also the gate closest to the Terrain des Jésuites. He came to the back gate of the compound and asked for Monsignor Eric Nicolet. He was immediately escorted to the monsignor's quarters.

"Philippe!" The Jesuit was very pleased to see him.

After sharing all the recent news and refreshing themselves with a small meal, Philippe explained he was going west until the end of September under special orders from General Montcalm.

"Is the city house available?"

"Available, clean, and ready for occupancy."

"That is good news. May I stay here overnight? I need the privacy and anonymity."

"Of course."

"I have letters to write. One of them is to Michelle de Propei in Québec City, telling her to pay you any monies I owe you, for the house and any expenses. If you think it wise, I would like to bring Denis and Mary, along with Joshua and Leah, to the city house so I can meet with them for a few weeks after I return to Montréal. But I do not want to do that until after the governor and Intendant Bigôt have left the city for Québec. Or, if you consider the city house too conspicuous, find a place more discreet. I leave that up to you. I also have a letter to send to Governor Vaudreuil, but I prefer it be dropped at the government house in Québec City."

"I can do that," Eric offered.

"I must change my appearance for the mission I am about to undertake. I will adopt traditional native dress, including war paint. It would be better if no one remembers seeing me this way. Can you lend me Jesuit garments with a hood that I can use tomorrow morning? And can you accompany me to the Dunemoore Warehouse before the sun is up?"

"Yes. Anything you need."

"Just a private room and that someone wakes me an hour before sunrise."

Monsignor Nicolet escorted Philippe to a large guest room where he would have the privacy requested. They agreed to leave together in the morning while it was still dark.

When he was alone, Philippe opened his heavy pack and removed some native clothing he'd brought with him. Standing in front of a mirror, he took out a tin of crushed charcoal mixed with deer fat and carefully lined his face, following the more prominent scars he'd collected over the years. The black lines zig-zagged left and right, running from above his hairline down to his chest. The purpose was to show the face of a warrior the Oneida would respect. He'd never done this before and had no idea how fearsome this looked until he was done. There were many more scars he could use, but he'd done enough. He stared for several minutes at the stark, visible evidence of the pain he'd endured.

From the pack, he withdrew three feathers he weaved into his hair in the manner of the Oneida. One of them was a red-tipped eagle feather, Chittaqua's feather, a symbol to others he was also a member of the Erigh tribe. To these adornments, he added a necklace of mountain lion claws given to him by his adoptive father, Tall Mountain Among Trees.

Philippe went to sleep this way. It was a fitful sleep, as if the change in dress evoked memories long ignored. When the knock on his door came in the morning, he was relieved to get up. He finished dressing and then folded and refilled his pack with the articles of uniform and other clothing. His saber would dangle on the outside of the pack. He wore a skinning knife, a tomahawk, a pistol, and carried his musket.

Another knock at his door brought Eric Nicolet into his room, carrying the hooded black robe of a Jesuit missionary. The monsignor stared with wonder at Philippe's face but did not say anything. Philippe put a finger to his lips to caution they should remain quiet. He slipped on the robe, pulled the cowl up around his face, shrugged the heavy pack over his shoulders, and they left the Terrain de Jésuites.

In the morning darkness that blanketed the city, they cut across the interior streets and left through the western gate. The half-asleep guards paid little attention to the two Jesuits, opening the gates and letting them pass. At the Dunemoore Warehouse, Sergeant Jubert and the three other scouts gathered in the front with Paulus Legates. When he dropped the cowl, their reaction to Philippe's appearance was no less surprised.

"I'd hate to encounter you in the forest," Jubert jested softly.

"I plan to stay with the Oneida until I return in late September. My mission is confidential. You are the only people who know where I am going. No one else must ever be told. I need three scouts to speed my transit to the mouth of the Oswego River. We will drag a small canoe behind us that I will use on my own from there. Questions?"

There were none. Philippe reached into his pocket and withdrew the letters for the monsignor to deliver.

"And if you do not return?" Jubert asked.

"Do not try to follow me. Just make your report to General Montcalm."

Jubert selected two other scouts to go with him. Philippe shook hands with Paulus Legates and Monsignor Nicolet. He returned the Jesuit robe.

"God go with you," the monsignor offered, his hand gesturing a blessing.

The *coureurs de bois* moved quickly into the night to the trail going upriver to get beyond the Lachine rapids before purchasing the war canoes required for the trip. The *coureurs de bois* were robust wilderness men with powerful oar stokes. Nevertheless, it would take them five days to reach the mouth of the Oswego River.

They found the burnt ruins of Fort Oswego eerily quiet. It had been a year since the fort had fallen to the French and already the environs were being reclaimed by small trees and other vegetation. They saw no sign of any animals, not even birds. They drew ashore at the former fort's boat landing. The men were on guard.

"Ghosts linger here still," one of the scouts muttered nervously.

"I will not argue with you," Philippe agreed.

They quickly transferred Philippe's pack and belongings to the single-man canoe.

"Go straight back to Montréal. Wait for me there. Rest and stay out of trouble. Don't be conspicuous. If you need counsel, Paulus Legates and Monsignor Nicolet will help you. Don't worry too much about me. I will come back."

Philippe shook their hands and pushed off in the smaller canoe. The scouts watched until their captain disappeared around the first bend in the river, before they pushed off in the larger war canoe to head back east.

Now alone, Philippe made strong steady strokes and allowed his thoughts to once again dwell on Corrinne and the twins, wondering where they were at that moment. Philippe had never been to the city of Brest. All he knew was its reputation as a powerful naval seaport. Corrinne would see her twin sister for the first time after being separated as small children. What would that be like? She might even be there by now, he speculated. To his surprise, he felt comforted at this thought.

Who better to defend Corrinne, then another Corrinne? Talk about formidable.

The skies were blue and clear, but the temperature was cool, hinting at the approaching turn of seasons. A few of the trees had yellowed leaves. It suddenly occurred to him it had been a very long time since he had been so alone. Dressed as he was, he was going back in time in a way. He would reach the Oneida village in two days, maybe three if he did not hurry. It might be better to arrive mid-morning, so his sudden appearance would be clearly visible—better to not arouse suspicious motives.

He passed by the Oswego River islands known for ambushes and stayed clear of the few places where he saw skeletal remains from the battles of the previous year. He camped early. Dug a fire pit, warmed some food, and slept in the surrounding darkness. The night was peaceful. Almost too peaceful.

The next morning, Philippe started upriver as soon as there was enough light to see where he was going. He had not paddled a mile before encountering a hunting canoe coming from the other direction, carrying two Oneida warriors. The carcass of a deer between them. Philippe back paddled until he stopped moving and held up a hand in a sign of peace. The Oneida approached him slowly, their muskets at the ready, their eyes searching the riverbanks, cautious of an ambush. When the canoes bumped, the warrior in the front spoke first.

"Why are you here?"

Philippe answered in the Oneida tongue. He had become fluent in his period of captivity after surviving the gauntlet.

"I am Snow Hair. Son of Tall Mountain Among Trees. I come to visit my father."

The warrior pointed at the feathers Philippe wore in his hair. "The eagle feather with the red tip?"

"It is the feather of an Erigh shaman. He was a friend and gave it to me."

"You are Erigh?"

The warrior's question was answered by the loud screech of an eagle, a white eagle flying directly over them.

"Yes," Philippe replied. He pointed at the magnificent creature. "And so is Chittaqua."

CHAPTER 33
NORTH ATLANTIC OCEAN
SEPTEMBER 1757
Changing Winds

A very strong gale from the south slammed into Île Royale, Louisbourg, and Admiral Holburne's blockade squadron with winds well over a hundred knots. The unprotected British fleet were ravaged by the full force of the winds. It took almost a day and a half for the storm to pass on to the east, sinking one ship-of-the-line, HMS *Tilbury*, and damaging nearly every other British vessel. Holburne's forces were effectively scattered and began limping back to Halifax.

Admiral de la Motte's flotilla was less damaged, protected by the coverage of the harbor, and completely seaworthy. The intense martial inclination of the seventy-three-year-old admiral was to sortie in pursuit of the English, to sink or capture any of the stragglers. However, the French fleet was weathering a different type of storm, an outbreak of typhus. It sat weakened and quarantined, delaying any departure. Nearly every ship was affected, including all the courier schooners. None of them had crews healthy enough to sail. With the British blockade effectively terminated, Governor Drucour pressed the admiral to send a frigate with the overdue, bulging satchel of dispatches without delay.

Of Admiral de la Motte's five frigates, *La Comète*, was least affected by the outbreak of disease which began after it set sail as escort to Captain LaTour's *Falcon Queen*. It had anchored away from the other vessels and, so far, had not contracted the disease.

Captain Severyn Peltier was summoned before Admiral de la Motte. He came aboard the flagship with a mask covering his nose and mouth. The admiral ordered the captain to sail without delay to deliver news of the successful defense of the fortress at Louisbourg.

"Your mission is more important than you might think, Captain," the admiral explained. "The official dispatches regarding the outcome of the

English blockade of Louisbourg will be eagerly awaited in Versailles. I do not mention our debilitating typhus. You are to avoid engagement with any enemy ship, even ones easily captured. You will be trailing the gale, counter to its winds, forcing many course changes. But you must find a way to sail as direct a route as possible to Brest. I also have my confidential missive for you to give personally to the port commandant in Brest."

*

Rumors spread quickly in Louisbourg that *La Comète* would be the only ship to put to sea after the storm. This was to satisfy the urgency of getting dispatches delivered to France. It would be going to Brest and was sailing as soon as it was provisioned for the crossing. The rest of the fleet would remain quarantined until the typhus epidemic had run its course.

Henri was anxious to warn Corrinne about Lieutenant-Colonel Krieger and intended to send her a warning through his mother in Québec City. That could take months. But from Anamosa's dreams, he knew Corrinne had left Québec City and sailed again on the *Falcon Queen* to an unknown destination. He speculated it might be one of the French naval ports, or maybe Amsterdam, though that was far less likely. Certainly not back to Boston. No, it had to be a French port. It could not go anywhere else for safe harbor.

But *La Comète* was going to Brest! This was one of several ports the *Falcon Queen* might visit. It was the nearest port and most direct.

Hearing that, and knowing *La Comète* would also be transporting Lieutenant-Colonel Krieger, he decided to warn Captain LaTour that the host of the wraith would disembark in Brest, too. No other French captain knew the *Falcon Queen* better than Captain Severyn Peltier. Henri hastily wrote a confidential missive to Captain LaTour relating all this information, and gambled the *La Comète* and Captain Peltier would come across the *Falcon Queen*, or could at least determine which port was LaTour's destination.

The missive signed, addressed, and sealed, Henri and two of his marines rowed out to *La Comète*. The deck officer shouted through a speaking trumpet for them to halt short of the boarding ladder, tie off to the cargo raft, and remain aboard their launch.

"We are quarantined! What is your business?"

"I am Lieutenant Henri Gerrard of the Troupes de la Marine. I have a missive for Captain Peltier!" Henri waved the missive aloft in the air.

A few minutes later, Captain Peltier appeared wearing a mask over his face and nose. He came down the ladder and walked to the end of the raft. Henri stood inside the boat and saluted. Peltier accepted the missive.

"But this is addressed to Captain LaTour?"

"Your passenger, Lieutenant-Colonel Karl Krieger, has tried to kill Lady Corrinne VanderMeer more than once. We've just learned she has sailed again from Québec City on the *Falcon Queen*, but the destination is unknown. Since you know both the ship and Captain LaTour, I am hoping you can deliver this missive to him if you encounter his ship, so he can be warned of the danger."

Unbelievable. Behind the scarf mask, Captain Peltier smirked. "Captain LaTour seems to invite all sorts of intrigue to follow him wherever he goes. I know he sailed from Québec City carrying a full load of furs for delivery to Brest. I escorted him to the Gulf of Saint Lawrence. But I am unaware he carried any passengers."

"I feel certain Lady VanderMeer was aboard the *Falcon Queen* in secret with her children, intending to seek refuge somewhere confidential. There have been three attempts on her life, including the most recent one here in Louisbourg. These killers were Colonel Krieger's men. Many have died defending her. Colonel Krieger does not know where she is, but he is still searching for her."

Captain Peltier slipped the missive inside of his coat. "I cannot promise I will encounter the *Falcon Queen*. But if I do, I will deliver your message."

Henri saluted the officer. "Thank you, Captain."

*

The next day, *La Comète* left Louisbourg bound for Brest. Lieutenant-Colonel Karl Krieger stood to one side of the bridge, away from Captain Peltier, and gazed back at the fortress port as it receded from view. He had left Major Sauer in charge of the mercenary regiment with a recommendation of promotion for the major to that of lieutenant-colonel.

Over water, the wraith was essentially blind. It did not know the location of the *Falcon Queen* and had lost sight of the whore queen. Krieger's facial appearance was known in Québec City. He could not go there. And he could no longer return to Louisbourg. Major Sauer would be his eyes in Louisbourg going forward. The French military expected England to invade Louisbourg or attack Fort Carillon in the next fighting season, possibly both. If the English attacked in force, the French would lose. The English had a standing request to Frederick II, the Prussian sovereign, for more mercenary regiments. Krieger decided to raise another German regiment after he returned to the middle kingdoms. But this one would be offered to the English for assignment to America to fight alongside the English. Next time, he would face the French as a conqueror.

The *Falcon Queen* could not hide forever. The wraith had servants all over France and Amsterdam watching for it. It would be seen. It was only a matter of time. The châsse was aboard that ship. This time, *It* would dismantle it piece by piece.

*

The *Falcon Queen* was more than halfway across the Atlantic when the winds shifted more from the south. There was a darkness gathering on the horizon behind the stern. A type of darkness Captain LaTour had seen before. The winds were building in strength and carried the faint tropical aromas of sun-kissed palm trees and mangoes. Instinctively, he knew it to be one of the devil storms from the south Atlantic. Those storms could move as fast as he could sail. They could overtake him. If it did, the cross-deck winds from the south would drag him inexorably towards the crushing maw that awaited at the storm's center.

LaTour could not take the chance. He must assume the gale would catch him.

Victorio saw the captain staring aft. He stared that way, too.

Almost at the same time, Major Michel Péan bounded up the ladder to the helm deck. He'd sensed the sudden change in the wind, the temperature, and in the roll of the ship. *Bad weather?* The major's uniform was heavily soiled with vomit. He stunk. The vomit was from Marcus. Péan had been helping Corrinne care for her seasick children.

After several seconds looking aft, Péan looked at Captain LaTour with concern.

"Yes. A tropical gale. A bad one." LaTour confirmed the major's suspicion. "We cannot go north. This gale might go north. We cannot continue east. The storm could go in that direction, too. And we cannot outrun this. We will sail southeast to stay outside the ring of stronger winds and gamble the storm weakens and does not follow."

Without being ordered, Victorio directed the crew in resetting the sails as LaTour took the helm and changed course.

With the course change, Captain LaTour now traveled against stronger winds coming from the south. His speed would be slower.

"Where will this course take us?" Péan asked.

"Well...not to France. Hopefully, one of the islands off the coast of Spain to the south. We need a harbor."

Major Péan went below. Victorio returned to the helm deck. LaTour gave him the wheel.

"Stay on this course while I check the charts."

LaTour went below and plotted various course possibilities; how the wind would set the *Queen*. It was a difficult prediction. He did not have a way to correct for this. The winds might also gain strength. *Better to just run with the present heading and guess where it will take us at several speeds.* Half the possibilities took him to the same general landfall. He decided to inform Lady Corrinne of the reason for the course change.

He found her sitting in the dining cabin with Major Péan. They were sipping something hot. Mercifully, the twins were sleeping. Corrinne's clothing was also stained with vomit. She looked haggard.

"My lady, the storm that approaches is too dangerous to face at sea. We must find a port and let the storm weaken before we continue. I've plotted a new course. If we maintain this course, our landfall will be in northern Spain."

"Spain! Should I be worried?"

"No, my lady. I've been to Spain before. The Spanish port authorities are just as corrupt as the French or Dutch port authorities. I just don't know how much money they will require."

"Marcus and Calypso are terribly seasick, constantly vomiting. They cannot keep anything down."

"We can hear their misery, my lady. I am sorry."

Corrinne was exhausted and worried about the future. Spain was not in her plans.

"Just pay whatever they ask."

"That's what I intend to do. The good news is, from northern Spain, Brest is only a four-day sail, maybe less."

Three days later, the violent tropical gale indeed pushed further east and was now to Captain LaTour's north. It would have caught them. Captain LaTour had made the right decision. Like his charts indicated, they reached northern Spain and entered the city port of *A Coruña*, in the Galicia province. There, the *Falcon Queen* would sit at anchor for almost ten days, hostage to the Spanish authorities.

It was deemed unwise for Major Péan to be seen in a uniform, and he was forced to shed his marine uniform and dress like a crewman. "These clothes smell even worse," he complained.

The delay in the safety of the harbor gave them some respite. The harbor waters were calm. They replenished the ship's fresh water and purchased food and bread from the local vendors. They all took baths. Corrinne washed their soiled clothes and linens. In a way, it was a blessing.

The Spanish inspected Captain LaTour's ship and cargo almost every day, asking new questions, trying to ascertain the value of the furs and determine the amount of money they could extort.

Finally, the Spanish harbor master presented Captain LaTour with an ornate document levying the ship with a fine. Captain LaTour could not read Spanish, but his eyes found a number at the bottom of the document.

"One hundred twenty?"

"Silver ounces. This is a penalty, Captain, for entering *A Coruña* illegally. By treaty, Spain must not permit any vessel of warring nations to enter a Spanish port and sail forth again while a state of war still exists. In fact, we should seize your ship and cargo. However, if you pay this fine, and in consideration you merely sought safe harbor from a storm, Spain will excuse your trespass."

Captain LaTour paid the fine, and by the end of the day they left port sailing northeast towards Brest. As predicted, within three days the *Falcon Queen* approached the Rade de Brest, the anchorage outside the main harbor entrance of the heavily defended naval port. But they did not disembark immediately. Ships intending to enter the port must wait in the anchorage until the harbor master's schooner boarded, inspected the vessel, and assessed the captain's credentials and intentions. Even then, a ship must wait until it received the proper flag signals to enter.

Captain LaTour scanned the anchorage with his glass and counted nearly fifty vessels waiting for permission to enter. Almost all of them were warships, and at least half of those were ships-of-the-line.

"I've never seen this port entrance so crowded with vessels waiting for entry. Certainly not warships."

Major Péan was using the other watch glass. "Looks like a fleet on parade."

"It's because of the storm," he told the major. "The port is probably full."

*

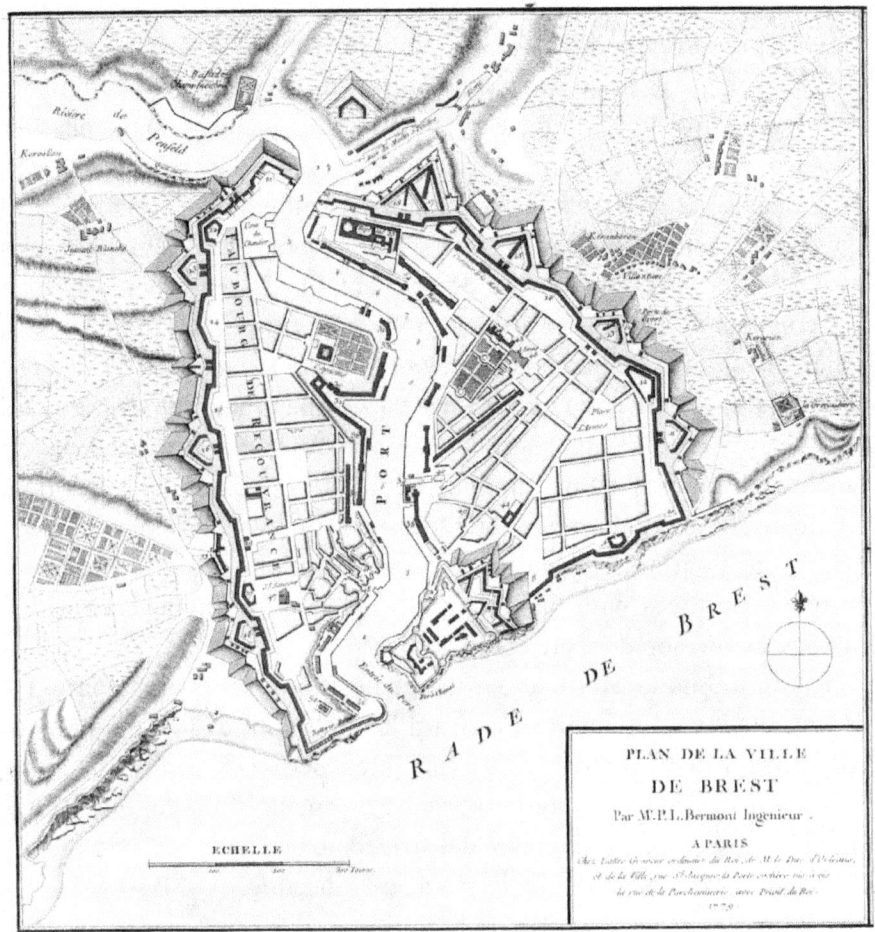

Rade de Brest

Captain Severyn Peltier was patiently waiting his turn to enter Brest. He'd been there a day already and wanted to finish this mission. He raised the "courier" pennant atop his main mast that morning to garner special privileges for a ship carrying official mail. The harbor master's schooner was just leaving a seventy-four-gun ship-of-the-line. He watched the schooner change course in his direction.

"Excellent!"

Captain Peltier scanned the Rade de Brest while he waited the twenty minutes it would take for the harbor master to arrive. He noticed a smaller ship anchored outside the warships. It looked familiar.

"*Incroyable!*" It was the *Falcon Queen*.

"What is so surprising?" asked the voice of Lieutenant-Colonel Krieger.

"Half the French navy is waiting here," Peltier answered without hesitation to cover his outburst. He turned to his second-in-command, Lieutenant Bertolet. "Have the harbor master brought down to my quarters as soon as he is aboard. Arrange your own relief on deck and come now."

Captain Peltier left the bridge and went below. Krieger's voice had a revolting tone. It had made him wince to hear it. His mannerisms were so crude, his officers would not share a table with him. The man was constantly grunting, almost growling as he ate. And there was a stench about him. He had no choice but to make the man eat alone. The mercenary did not seem to mind. Since the German came aboard, he heard daily reports by the ship's surgeon about recurring nightmares among the crew, or seamen waking up with debilitating sickness one morning, only to awake cured the next. The superstitious crew whispered of seeing apparitions floating through their quarters at night. After spending so many weeks at sea with this man, he wanted to be finished with him. The day he anchored in the Rade de Brest, he read the personal orders from Admiral de la Motte about the disposition of this mercenary. He also recalled what Lieutenant Gerrard had told him. He was a threat to Lady VanderMeer. He had to take this threat seriously.

Peltier sent his messenger to bring the captain of the marines to his cabin. When his second-in-command arrived, to be joined seconds later by the marine commander, Peltier began a hasty meeting.

"We have a dangerous problem." He explained the history of Lieutenant-Colonel Krieger. "The *Falcon Queen* is waiting in the anchorage with us. Lady Corrinne VanderMeer is aboard that ship. She is a member of the House of Brunswick. That information must remain confidential." He looked at each of the men until they nodded with acknowledgement. "No harm must come to her. This is what we will do."

*

"*Que se passe-t-il?!*" LaTour said aloud. His heart began pounding with anxiety. "That's *La Comète*! What is that ship doing here?"

Major Péan looked, too. "Let's pray it's not searching for us!"

"Victorio, keep a glass on that ship and the harbor master's schooner. Major, we need to talk with Lady Corrinne."

They went below and found her eating a pleasant meal with the twins, who looked happy for once. Calming his voice, Captain LaTour explained what he just saw.

Corrinne's eyes widened. "So, what does this mean?"

"My lady, instincts tell me that *La Comète*'s presence here is more than a coincidence. Captain Peltier knows the counts and shapes of my masts, and my rigging. I know his as well. We must assume he sees us."

Corrinne replied with exasperation. "After all of this misery...am I to worry about being arrested?"

"No, no, my lady. That is not going to happen," LaTour affirmed quickly. "Major, do you carry any type of documents that we can claim as official dispatches?"

Péan hesitated to answer for a few seconds. "I have documents meant for specific people in Paris that I do not intend to share with anyone else."

"Good. Then you can claim they are confidential, and you are the personal courier, yes?"

"What are you getting at, Captain?"

"I will raise a courier pennant on my main mast. That might help us gain immediate entry into port. I think it is better that we get in there first before *La Comète*. My lady?"

"I agree."

"You should both pack baggage you can carry by hand. You may have to disembark as soon as we tie up at the commercial docks."

*

Captain Peltier pointed at the *Falcon Queen* and explained to the harbor master, "I have been escorting that ship from Québec City. We were separated by the storm. It carries passengers of great importance, whose identities must remain confidential. If I might ask your indulgence, please inspect that ship next and clear them to enter port without delay. I will send two of my marines with you to be posted aboard as guards for the passengers."

The harbor master was used to being bullied by the ship masters. But no one entered into this port, by ship, without being identified and authenticated. He did not care how important they claimed themselves to be. He would be the judge.

"If the ship and its cargo pass my inspection, I will clear them for entry. But France is at war. My orders are specific, Captain. By order of the crown, I must log the identities of any passenger entering this port, by any ship, without exception. If the master of the ship tries to hide their presence, he is guilty of treason."

"Of course. May I respectfully request you keep their identities confidential to your log."

We'll see.

*

"The harbor master approaches!" Victorio shouted out.

Captain LaTour turned his glass to the approaching vessel. On its main mast flew the flag of an anchor, crossed by keys, above the *fleur-de-lis*; the sigil of the port authority. This port was effectively a fiefdom of the king. The harbor master was the vassal. He bowed only to one man: Louis XV. In addition to the schooner crew, and the usual inspectors, he saw two armed marines and another naval officer on board.

Marines! Why are there marines?

"*Merde*! Lower the port-side ladder! Prepare to be inspected!"

The crew dispersed to their inspection stations. The *Queen* carried no contraband. This was routine as far as they were concerned.

Captain LaTour and Major Péan stood side by side as the harbor master and two scribes came up the ladder first, followed by the naval officer and two marines. The harbor master was all business.

"Your name, Captain. The name of your ship. The port from which it sailed and its cargo."

LaTour handed the man a copy of his cargo manifest. "Captain Beauregard LaTour, master of the *Falcon Queen*. I carry a full load of furs from Québec City in New France. I seek permission to moor at your commercial wharf to unload my cargo."

"And you, Major?" the harbor master said with an edge of rudeness. He was not intimidated by the uniform.

"Major Michel de Péan, military attaché to Governor-General Pierre de Rigaud, Marquis de Vaudreuil. I am a courier to the Court of Versailles and will require further transport to Paris."

The harbor master regarded the marine major as just another royal who flaunted a title to get people to be deferential. He was not impressed.

"During times of war, I report directly to King Louis XV. Captain LaTour, your ship is known to me, along with its tarnished reputation. I acknowledge Admiral de la Motte as your superior. Major Péan, you are not known to me. So, let me speak plainly. I will record in my log the passengers carried aboard this ship. If either of you intend to smuggle someone into this port, or if you do not answer me truthfully, you will both be guilty of treason, subject to the penalty of death. I understand you have more than one passenger."

Captain LaTour opened his mouth to answer but Major Péan spoke first.

"I have given you my name, rank, and diplomatic association with Governor Vaudreuil of New France. Down below in the dining cabin you will find my wife, Corrinne, and two small children who accompanied me on this mission. The crossing has been very hard on them. The children are sick. Please treat them accordingly. Come with me and I will introduce them to you."

Captain LaTour looked as if his ass had just been stuck with a long hat pin.

The harbor master handed the cargo manifest to his scribes who went below with Victorio through the forward deck hatch to conduct an inspection and inventory. The harbor master followed Major Péan down the helm deck ladder to the dining cabin.

Just another port welcome with a threat of being hung, Captain LaTour thought. He followed last, his mood that of someone on a death march.

Corrinne was surprised to see the unexpected visitors. Péan slipped into the bench on the opposite side of the table, held out his arms to Marcus, who moved into the embrace happily as if he'd done it all his life.

"As I told you, sir, my wife, Madame Corrinne de Péan, my son Marcus, and my daughter Calypso."

Mon Dieu! Corrinne managed a courteous smile. "*Bonjour*, Monsieur. I hope the weather remains favorable. None of us are feeling very well just now. Particularly me!"

The harbor master bowed politely. "*Bonjour*, Madame Péan. The sky is blue and filled with sunshine. The temperature is cool. October weather. Welcome to Brest. Will you be traveling to Paris with your husband?"

"I hope to. But we may stay behind in the city first, for a few days of rest."

"*Merci*, Madame. Very good. Sorry to bother you." He smiled at Calypso who beamed back at him.

The harbor master left the dining cabin and proceeded aft to join his scribes inspecting the cargo.

"What. Was. That?!" Corrinne glared at the major and Captain LaTour.

LaTour was innocent of this. He glared at Major Péan. "I will let him explain."

The captain went back to the helm deck to speak with the naval officer and the two marines. He traded salutes with the officer.

"Lieutenant Jean-Claude Bertolet, second officer of *La Comète,* at your service."

"Apologies for the wait, Lieutenant. The port authority comes first."

"Of course, Captain. Captain Peltier sends you his respects. My captain instructs me to tell you that he carries Lieutenant-Colonel Karl Krieger as a passenger. Furthermore, by order of Admiral de la Motte, this mercenary officer will be escorted out of the city of Brest under guard, as soon as he disembarks. These two marines from *La Comète* are now posted aboard your ship until further notice to provide protection for your passengers. We presume you will see to their quartering. Once you have moored, *La Comète* will send over two more marines. These four guards are at your service to safeguard your passengers until such a time that you feel comfortable to dismiss them." The lieutenant withdrew a missive from inside his coat. It was addressed to Captain LaTour. "This is for you. It was given to my captain by Lieutenant Henri Gerrard of the Louisbourg garrison before we sailed. The seals are not broken."

What? LaTour did not know any Lieutenant-Colonel Karl Krieger, but he accepted the letter with both hands as if it were a silver bar.

"Should I read this now?"

"That is up to you, sir. We have no knowledge of the contents."

The harbor master, his two scribes, and Victorio appeared at that moment, climbing out of the forward hatch. They marched aft.

"Any problems?" Captain LaTour asked.

"No, Captain. Everything appears in order. Your cargo of fur appears to be of high quality." The harbor master signed a document and gave it over to LaTour. "Do not misplace this. It must be returned to the port authority on the day you leave port. Do you need a harbor pilot?"

"No, sir. I visited Brest twice before, though that was almost ten years ago. The commercial wharf is still at the northern end of the city, yes?"

"Yes, it is. Good, then you are cleared to enter Brest without delay. Lower your courier pennant and raise these three pennants instead." He pointed to the pennant designations on the document. "Tell Major Péan he is free to arrange his own travel to Paris. There are overland coach drivers by the northern gate."

The harbor master left the ship with his assistants. Lieutenant Bertolet saluted the captain and left as well, sailing in the direction of *La Comète.*

"Weigh anchor!" Captain LaTour wasted no time. "If you please," he told the marines. "Stand against the helm deck house and try to remain out of the way. The deck will get very busy. And welcome aboard."

"Aye, aye, sir."

"Victorio, raise these entry pennants. Make sail for river travel!" he shouted to the crew. "Take in the port ladder!"

Captain LaTour took the wheel from the watch and rotated it to port. The ship moved slowly at first and picked up speed as the sails were adjusted for the course. Major Péan appeared by his side.

"Did Lady Corrinne accept your explanation?" LaTour asked curtly.

"Of course. She is logged into the harbor master records as my wife and children."

"You do know the identities will eventually be found to be false?"

"That is months away and by then you will have several explanations that will be considered acceptable. The objective was to safeguard her anonymity, yes? Well, we've done that. I think Lady Corrinne is more upset the official record states she's been married three times. I know Angélique will try to have me killed if she hears of this. They were never friends."

Protected by the pennants they were flying, the *Falcon Queen* sailed down the line of anchored warships and beneath the heavy cannons of the harbor forts. LaTour could feel the eyes of at least a hundred watch glasses trained on them.

"Look sharp!" he shouted to the crew. "The elite of the French navy are watching you."

They minimized speed to four knots as they entered La Penfeld River that divided the city east and west. LaTour steered to the starboard side of the channel. Victorio managed the sails to maintain a constant speed without waiting for a command by the captain. The rigging was full of crewmen waiting for shouted orders.

The stone towers and walls to either side of the channel brimmed with cannons of every caliber. The cannoneers watched the passage of the small trading frigate, their arms draped lazily in the embrasures.

"Any one of those heavy rifles could reduce the *Queen* to burning splinters with only a few rounds," LaTour remarked to Péan.

On the right bank were dozens of naval and military buildings: multiple barracks, cannon foundries, and arsenals. In the gaps between the fortifications, they could see the ship-building works: shops of every kind, rotary cranes, smoke belching from elevated chimneys, signs of metalworks, and forges. On the left bank of La Penfeld River, the western half of the city referred to as the Recouvrance, the land sloped upward and was filled with hundreds of two or three-story buildings, many of them residences of the city dwellers.

The piers and wharves to either side were loaded with warships, moored three deep in many places. But that became less frequent as the *Queen* wended its way by the ship-building ways and yards. The bends and turns of the large river seemed to go on for a long time when they finally reached the commercial wharf in the north, one long commercial dock. To LaTour's surprise it was not full. Brest was a navy port. Only commercial traders with specific business with the port city of Brest were permitted to dock there, so said a large sign at the head of the dock.

"My business is not specific to this city," he remarked to Major Péan. "These furs are bound for the markets in Paris, yes?"

"Yes, but don't worry, Captain. It has all been arranged. After you tie up, a man will come aboard to inspect your cargo, and, based on what he estimates the value to be, he will offer you a price…which you will accept without further bargaining."

"That's not how this works!" LaTour replied with irritation.

"It will work thus today. Let him tell you the price he will pay, and you can tell me if it is fair or not."

"Tell you? Why you?"

"The buyer is my brother. I think you will find his price very reasonable."

"Your *brother*! Am I supposed to feel good about that?"

"This trade has been arranged by Bigôt's company, the Grande Société. Stop worrying."

It proceeded as Major Péan predicted. The buyer did not embrace the major as a brother, but it was apparent by their jests they knew one another. And the price Captain LaTour was offered was six times what he paid for the furs in Québec City. And that price was already inflated several times above normal because of the war. LaTour gave no argument. The unloading began. It would take another day to get the cargo transferred to the warehouse.

"*Merde*! I forgot about the missive!"

Captain LaTour drew the missive from inside his coat, broke the seal on the single page, and read Henri's message of warning. The captain's eyes bulged with alarm as he read what it said.

"I need to speak with Lady Corrinne," he told Major Péan. "Do you mind watching this unloading for me, since he is your trusted brother?"

"Not at all."

Captain LaTour went below and found Lady Corrinne and the twins still sitting in the dining cabin. She saw the anxious expression on his face.

"What's wrong now?"

LaTour held up the missive. "This sealed missive addressed to me was carried by *La Comète*. It's from Henri."

"Henri!" She held out her hand.

> *Captain,*
>
> *I am writing this with haste before I row it out to La Comète. The frigate sails today for Brest. La Comète carries Lieutenant-Colonel Karl Krieger. This mercenary officer is the host of the wraith. Anamosa has seen It multiple times in her dreams. I suspect It came to Louisbourg, looking for Corrinne. But Krieger is being expelled from Louisbourg because of his threatening reputation and behavior, which evidently followed him to Louisbourg from Brest. He did something in Brest, I know not what. But I do not believe he is aware Lady Corrinne is aboard the Falcon Queen. No one knows. I only know because Anamosa saw Corrinne on your ship in her dreams. Since your destination port may possibly be Brest, I wanted to warn you that It could be there, too. Remember, while over water, the wraith cannot see any of you. But as soon as Corrinne steps ashore on land, that might change. I don't know what to advise, except to tell you to stay aboard the ship until you somehow determine if Lieutenant-Colonel Krieger is there or not.*
>
> *I love you all. God protect you.*
> *Henri*

Corrinne's mouth hung open with shock. "After all this way? That *thing* is here? In Brest?"

"Captain Peltier's second-in-command, Lieutenant Bertolet, told me Lieutenant-Colonel Karl Krieger is indeed a passenger on *La Comète*. But Admiral de la Motte has already ordered the mercenary officer escorted out of the city of Brest under guard. There are two marines from *La Comète* posted on the helm deck topside, until further notice, to act as our guards. *La Comète* intends to send two more marines before the day is over."

Corrinne's breath had quickened, overwhelmed by this unexpected, crushing revelation.

"If it learns I am here. Then I am not safe here either. Where would I go now? I don't know what to do."

"My lady, we have marine guards posted. Stay aboard…until I can find out what happened to this mercenary colonel. If Henri…Anamosa for that matter…is right…the thing cannot see you when you are over water. It cannot see you!" he asserted more firmly.

"I cannot stay on this ship forever."

"I know, my lady. Just stay here for now. Let me find out what happened to the mercenary. And I will also go into the Recouvrance section of Brest to Madame Dubonnet's house…"

"You cannot leave me here alone, Beauregard!"

"You will be safe with these marines guarding us. And Major Péan will stay here until I return."

"He said that?"

"Yes, my lady. He did. I will get him to come down and tell you himself." He went back to the helm deck and found the major idly watching the precision movements of the crew, using winch and davit, to lower pallets of furs to the pier.

"We have another problem," LaTour said. He explained about Lieutenant-Colonel Krieger without mentioning the detailed contents of Henri's missive and the allusion to the wraith.

"What?! I am not a guard! I have my own travel to Paris and business to arrange."

"Just for a few days, Major," LaTour implored. "Until I can make safe arrangements for Lady Corrinne to go ashore."

Péan gestured vigorously. "Have these marines guard her!"

"This mercenary colonel is a professional assassin. He tried to kill her in Louisbourg. He may have confederates in this city. But right now, he is unaware she's even here. Captain Peltier has orders to have the man escorted out of Brest under guard."

Péan frowned, annoyed at the inconvenience.

"Major, please. Just act like any good *father* would act."

"Oh, *merde*! Don't play that tune to me!"

"Lady Corrinne is terrified. This assassin was trying to kill her children, too. They are the heirs to the House of Brunswick. Go down and assure her you will stay and help me for two days. Just two days! That's all I am asking."

Péan exhaled, resigned. "I should have arrested you years ago!" he grumbled.

Péan went below. Corrinne was in the dining cabin. Her eyes were red from tears, which she sniffed back at seeing him. He took his usual seat across the table from her. This time Calypso joined Marcus at his side.

"So, you will do this? You have people and contacts here, yes?"

"Of course, I will," Péan said, adopting the tone and attitude of a gallant. "These are my children, after all."

Corrinne knew Péan did not want to do this. "I am not certain which of us is due more favors by the other, but I will make certain Philippe knows the risk you have taken."

"Yes, well, just pray I am not tossed into the Bastille when I reach Paris. I stand accused of corruption, if you've not heard. Corruption! Of all things! Can you believe that? Me! A chevalier of the Order of Saint Louis!"

His ridiculous sarcasm punctured the tension and Corrinne started laughing. Péan started laughing, too.

*

La Comète moored at a special dock reserved for courier ships near the front of the harbor by the stone fortress of the port authority. Lieutenant-Colonel Karl Krieger was already on the main deck, anxious to get off the ship and be about his business. He was confronted at the head of the brow by Captain Peltier.

"You must wait like everyone else, Colonel, until the dispatch pouches are safely delivered to the magistrate's office of the port authority for further handling. At that point, they will send a representative back to the ship who will clear *La Comète* for access. They will also tell me how long I can maintain my mooring here before I must return to the anchorage. Your name is already being logged as our only official passenger. When the magistrate's representative comes aboard, you must disclose your intended destination."

The colonel's glare of annoyance was hard to miss. Already the wraith was reaching out with his senses searching for signs of any servants nearby. There weren't any.

"This may take a few hours. You may prefer to wait below. We will call you."

"I will wait on deck by my baggage."

"Very well. Please stay out of the way of the crew. There will be much activity associated with our arrival. Water and fresh food will be brought aboard."

The wait was almost three hours. Lieutenant Bertolet carried the dispatch pouches to the magistrate and, with others doing the same thing, waited to be called up by the magistrate. When it was his turn, he pointed out Admiral de la Motte's specific orders concerning Lieutenant-Colonel Karl Krieger.

"He is our only passenger."

The magistrate read the first sentence of the order aloud.

"This mercenary officer will be escorted, under guard, out of Brest, transported by military coach across France to the border of the nearest German electorate state, and further advised never to return to France."

The magistrate-major had never seen so specific an order for someone so inconsequential, in his opinion. And by Admiral de la Motte himself, no less. He regarded Bertolet with elevated brows.

"Why not just execute him? Save us trouble?"

Lieutenant Bertolet pointed at a sentence further down the page. "The colonel raises mercenary regiments for France. It was part of our agreement that on the last regiment he supplied to Louisbourg, we would provide transport to France and he would be escorted to the border."

The magistrate-major stood. "Very well. If the admiral wrote this order, it's the first one I administer. I will see to this myself." He gave orders to one of his aides to make the arrangements for the military coach transport and the guarding arrangements. "I want this obvious nuisance out of the city today."

Lieutenant Bertolet marched back to La Comète in the company of the magistrate-major and four marine guards. They went aboard the frigate, saluted Captain Peltier, and he pointed the magistrate towards Lieutenant-Colonel Krieger.

Standing before the mercenary officer, the magistrate-major recited Admiral de la Motte's specific orders aloud. When he finished, he regarded the man's menacing glare. *No wonder*, he thought.

"Colonel, this marine sergeant and his men will escort you to the military courier stables. Once there, you will board the next military coach heading to Paris with cavalry escorts, and further, by other coaches as necessary until you reach the border of France, where you will be free to go wherever you choose. These orders will follow you. If you disobey your escorts along the way, they are authorized to execute you. Do you understand this order, Colonel?"

Lieutenant-Colonel Krieger considered this to be a minor inconvenience. He was going back to the German states anyway. The eyes of the wraith appeared.

"*I understand,*" It grumbled.

The mercenary left the ship and with the marines to either side of him and began walking north through the shipyard buildings, towards the military coach stables at the city's northern end.

"Did you see that?" Captain Peltier asked when the colonel finally stepped off his ship and become someone else's problem. "His eyes?"

"Yes," the magistrate-major replied in strong agreement. "I still say, we should execute him now, yes?"

"Orders are orders," Captain Peltier reminded the magistrate. "Particularly when they are the admiral's orders."

*

Captain LaTour hailed one of the city carriages waiting at the foot of the wharf. "Are you familiar with the residence of Madame Margaux Dubonnet?"

The carriage driver squinted. "I am familiar with the residence of La Chevalier Lucais de Clermont. His daughter is named Margaux. She is staying at that house. Could this be the person you seek?"

"I don't know, Monsieur. But let's try that home first."

The driver proceeded at a leisurely pace. Brest was a centuries-old French city with buildings made of stone, many of them covered with climbing vines. There were numerous fountains, outdoor cafés, ornate churches, pots of flowers, overhanging balconies, and many people walking up and down the narrow streets, just wide enough to permit two carriages to pass by in opposite directions. Captain LaTour had forgotten the quaint beauty of such cities, very unlike the raw, chaotic sprawl of the cities in New France. The only thing that spoiled the autumn sunshine of the day was the sulfurous odors wafting up occasionally from the waterfront.

"That stench is strong," he mentioned to the driver.

"The smell of money, Captain. There are good days and bad, depending which way the wind blows. Much the same for you at sea among the storms, yes?"

Captain LaTour nodded. "Yes."

The carriage stopped at a house near a corner. It had a stoop of five polished sandstone steps that spread like a hand in invitation to someone standing at the bottom.

"Can you wait for me?"

"Will you pay me to wait?"

"Of course."

"Then I will eat my noontime meal and take a nap, Captain. Take as long as necessary. I will be right here."

Captain LaTour went to the top of the steps and lightly tapped the brass door knocker. In less than a minute, an officious-looking man appeared. He was tall, stately, white-haired and dressed in the livery of a chamberlain.

"May I help you?"

"*S'il vous plaît*, Monsieur. My name is Captain Beauregard LaTour. I am master of the frigate the *Falcon Queen*."

As LaTour explained who he was and why he was there, the chamberlain's expression softened with surprise.

"Come in, Captain. My name is Marshall DeBarge, chamberlain to Chevalier Lucais de Clermont. Madame Margaux Dubonnet has mentioned your name to me many times. I am very pleased you have visited us. Your ship is in Brest?"

"Indeed, Monsieur. I arrived this morning and have moored at the commercial docks. I am hoping to visit with Madame Dubonnet."

"Unfortunately, Captain, Madame Dubonnet is in Amiens to be with her husband, Colonel Gustave Dubonnet. He was wounded in the Battle of Hanover. I do not know when she will return."

Oh no, LaTour thought. His expression sagged.

Seeing the captain's immediate disappointment, the chamberlain asked politely, "May I help you in some way?"

LaTour looked at the man hopefully. "Yes, Monsieur. But I have a story to tell you first. It is very confidential."

"Confidential? Then let us take a seat together in the reception area." The chamberlain led the captain a few steps away to a small room, nicely appointed with a table, a couch, and a few cushioned chairs. LaTour sat in one of them. "A glass of brandy, perhaps?"

After pouring them each a small goblet, the chamberlain took another chair and made a toast to their health.

"Please continue."

"Has Madame Dubonnet mentioned the name Corrinne de Chanaye?"

The chamberlain laughed lightly. "*Mentioned?* She speaks of her sister with great joy. Do you know her, too?"

Captain LaTour nodded with relief. "Yes. And I have brought Lady Corrinne with me to Brest with her two children. She is waiting on my ship."

Marshall Debarge was rendered momentarily speechless by this astounding revelation.

"Corrinne de Chanaye is here? Now?"

"Yes, Monsieur."

"Then I insist, you must bring Lady Corrinne and her children to this house, now, without delay!"

"I am very pleased to hear you say this. But let me tell you the rest of the story."

Marshall Debarge did not interrupt, except to suggest the captain have some more brandy. But at the mention of Lieutenant-Colonel Karl Krieger's name, the chamberlain reacted with angry contempt.

"This bastard is here, too?"

"Yes. He is still pursuing her. But he is likely not aware of Lady Corrinne's presence. The mercenary came to Brest on another ship. She seeks refuge here, but her identity must remain a secret. The three assassination attempts on her life have taken a great toll on her, and the incidents have killed many people she cared about, including her husband, Lord Charles VanderMeer."

Marshall Debarge said firmly, "Bring Lady Corrine to this house. She no longer needs to fear or flee from anyone. We will protect her. Bring her here, tonight. We will have a room prepared for them all. It will be good to have small children in this house again."

Captain LaTour exhaled with relief. "She will be so pleased to hear this, Monsieur. What about Madame Dubonnet?"

"I will send a private courier to Amiens and tell Madame the good news. She will be overjoyed. There will be happy, happy times in this household after being struck by so much tragedy. Bring Lady Corrinne and her children, Captain, with all her baggage, to stay as long as she wants. This will be another home for her. Come at the hour of eight. It will be dark enough by then. I will send a carriage big enough to carry all of you."

*

Captain LaTour delivered the exciting good news to Corrinne with the other details of what the chamberlain disclosed about Margaux. She was disappointed to learn Margaux was not present, and wished she been around to console Margaux about the terrible injury to her husband. But she was relieved to know her journey was ending, that she was welcome.

"A carriage will arrive to transport us just before the hour of eight."

Corrinne took a bath and gave her children a fresh bath, too. She began packing everything, her mood elevated to one of celebration.

As the sun went down in Brest, it was apparent there would be no moon that night. *All the better*, Captain LaTour thought. It would make the city travel more discreet. After several trips by the coachmen to load Lady Corrinne's baggage, one of the last heavy articles brought out to the coach was a keel chest, with enough gold and silver to last Lady Corrinne for years.

She said good-bye, once again, to the crew, their faces sad as they lined up on the *Queen* to accept her farewell embrace. These simple seamen she cared so much about were her heroes and rescuers. It was a nostalgic farewell. She wished them good fortune.

"I promise, I will see you all again."

Finally, it came time for Corrinne, Marcus, Calypso, and Captain LaTour to board the coach. To their collective surprise, Major Péan also boarded.

"What are you doing?" Corrinne said, as he squeezed in next to Captain LaTour.

"Well...since I am part of this charade...that of being your husband...I think I should introduce myself to the chamberlain, so that he may say he met me personally...if ever he is asked, yes?"

Corrinne smiled. "*Merci*, Michel. If it is no trouble. It could get you hung, you know."

"Trouble? Hung? Must I remind you again that I am a Chevalier of the Order of Saint Louis, renowned for my courage and bravery in battle! Take advantage of my title. It's got to be good for something."

The ride through the quiet residences of the Recouvrance did not take very long. The carriage stopped in front of the cascade porch steps of the house. Excited servants came down the steps carrying hand lanterns to help, quietly saying words of welcome to them all. Michel Péan carried Marcus in his arms. Captain LaTour carried Calypso. Nervous with apprehension, Lady Corrinne led the way up to the open doorway where the impressive figure of Marshall DeBarge was waiting to greet them. The carriage pulled around the house to the back before unloading the baggage. The chamberlain stepped back from the doorway several steps as the visitors began to enter.

In the brighter lights of the foyer, the other household servants lined up to be presented to Lady Corrinne. The servants included a valet, two maids, and two female cooks. At seeing her remarkable likeness to Margaux, they emitted gasps of wonder.

Marshall DeBarge bowed deeply to welcome her. He was also overcome. To his surprise he was uncertain how to react. He had known Margaux since she was a small girl. The chamberlain straightened his posture. He vividly recalled the anguished expression of fear and vulnerability on Margaux's face when her adoptive father, Lucais de Clermont, had suffered a heart attack years ago. Margaux had been only twelve at the time. Her mother had been completely occupied at her father's bedside. Margaux had no one else to turn to for comfort, except for the devoted chamberlain she'd grown to depend upon so much.

The chamberlain saw this exact expression on Lady Corrinne's face, amplified further by the feelings of uncertainty over the new people and surroundings she was experiencing. Seeing her evident distress, the chamberlain's instinctive reaction was the same as it had been for Margaux so many years before. He extended his arms in an invitation to embrace her.

Corrinne had never known anyone like a father in her life, except for maybe the old abbot at the orphanage of her youth and Archbishop André Nicolet, but neither of them had ever said anything to her that matched the deep comforting resonance that she heard in the voice of Marshall DeBarge.

"Welcome home, Lady Corrinne."

Her breathing shallowed. She trembled, took the last few steps, and surrendered to the warm, reassuring arms of someone she bonded to instantly. She gripped the front of his livery coat with her hands. Corrinne de Chanaye laid her head on his chest and closed her eyes.

"Thank you. Thank you," she whispered. The restrained angst of the last several years rushed forward, seeking release. She managed to hold back the tears.

The chamberlain patted her trembling back in a soothing manner.

"Don't worry, my lady. You're all safe here with us."

Seeing the unexpected actions of their mother, Marcus and Calypso began weeping. The female servants of the Chevalier Lucais de Clermont household crowded forward around the children, cooing and offering words of comfort. Soon, both children were being held and coddled by the women.

Captain LaTour was too choked up to say anything.

THE MERCENARIES

Major Michel Péan leaned his head towards Captain LaTour and whispered, "I'll wager you've never smuggled anything as precious as this. Well done, Captain. I feel privileged to witness this."

END OF BOOK 5

EPILOGUE
BREST, FRANCE
OCTOBER 1757
The Vulnax Wraith

Lieutenant-Colonel Karl Krieger took his seat inside the military coach for the long trip to Paris. There were two other passengers, but after introductions, Krieger declined to engage them in any further conversation. The other two officers, one an army major, the other a captain, were chilled into silence by the brooding, menacing insolence of the mercenary with whom they would share the carriage house.

The coach stopped twice to receive fresh horses before sunset. They had traveled fifty miles east of Brest by then. They would continue travel throughout the night, changing horses routinely at the relay stations. The well-traveled road to Paris was illuminated by the overland coach's lanterns, equipped with nautical lenses to create a focused beam in front of the horses.

It was a moonless, dark night. During the first leg of the overnight travel, the vulnax wraith surged to dominance and reached out from the colonel's dream-like trance. It identified the places where the nearest servants could be available for use. Those closest were at the border within the German states. Many others were in Amsterdam. The wraith intruded on their dreams to begin drawing them closer. The wraith turned its gaze back towards Brest and was surprised to see the brilliant glowing light of the whore queen!

The whore queen!? That was not possible! Was it? It must be the other woman, the twin. She lived there. Was this the twin? How was this not seen before?

The location of the ship and the châsse dwelled foremost in the wraith's thoughts. The whore queen had answers to all these questions. The vulnax decided to send a servant back to that city just to be certain. Because if the whore queen somehow was present, the ship would not be far away.

Glossary

10th Century Characters from Daenial's Tale.
(* implies the name was invented by the author)

*Adaelric	(Ah-del-rick) Celtic warlord of Normandie
*Aermorgen	(Air–morgan) Danish warlord of Normandie
*Brevelaer	(Brev-lahr) Catholic bishop of Normandie
Daeniel	(Daniel) high druid priest in Normandie
Maeve	(May-eve) wife to Lord Adaelric
*Vaelblez	(Vall-blez) warlord of Normandie and practitioner of the black arts

THE MERCENARIES
Note: Some of these entries are aliases or adjusted names to previous characters and not necessarily a new character in the book series.

Anamosa	meaning "white fawn"; Okeanneh's daughter by an unknown French fur trader (not Philippe Gerrard)
Comte Marc-Pierre d'Argenson	French Minister of War
Joseph du Bauffremont	commander of the first squadron of French warships to come to Louisbourg's relief in 1757
Bertolet	lieutenant, second-in-command to Captain Severyn Peltier of the French frigate *La Comète*
François Bigôt	intendant general of New France, corrupt minister of Governor Vaudreuil, and enemy of Philippe Gerrard and Corrinne de Chanaye
Rutger van Boekel	colonel, primary aide-de-camp, counselor, confidante, and friend to Duke Louis Ernest
Charles de Bourlamaque	colonel and third-in-command to General Montcalm
Michel du Bourzt	lieutenant-colonel and commander of the Bourgogne regiment of grenadiers

Louis Antoine de Bougainville captain, scientist, author, explorer, and aide-de-camp to General Montcalm

Cabrelle color sergeant and Major Péan's battalion sergeant for the Québécois militia

John Campbell 4th Earl of Loudoun, general, and commander in chief of British forces in North America

Jimmy Cantlin Boston gang boy who escapes with Rachel Bristol

Rachel Cantlin assassin, servant of the vulnax wraith, and sister of Caroline Bristol

Desiree Cardon senior nurse at the Louisbourg hospital

Joshua and Leah Carlisle ages 12 and 13, rescued by Philippe from the Delaware

Carson lieutenant and first officer of the *Anamosa*

Chanter mother of Mkuigen Malsum

Sentry Cheever color sergeant of the Carlisle Marine Regimental, martial-at-arms trainer, mentor to Henri Gerrard, and husband of Dianamora

Chittaqua (Chi-tock´-qwah) Iroquoian name believed to mean "one lost in the wilderness"; Erigh shaman, the Ghost Eagle

Lucais de Clermont father to Margaux Dubonnet and French warship designer in Brest

Constance maid to Michelle de Propei and nurse to Crispin, Michelle's son

C. Bernard Conway lawyer for Thomas Hancock, oversees Winter House

coureur de bois (coo-ruhr´ deh bwah) bushloper or bush master, name given to the famous French forest men of the 18th century

Prince William Cumberland Duke of Cumberland and son of King George II, also known as the Butcher of Culloden, royal benefactor to General Edward Braddock

Marshall Debarge chamberlain to Lucais de Clermont and Madame Dubonnet in Brest

Denis and Mary Corrinne's former chamberlain and his wife in Montréal, caretakers for Joshua and Leah Carlisle

Dian short for *Dianamora*, native of Saint-Domingue, and wife to Sentry Cheever

Dimmette first officer of Captain Vauquelin's ship *L'Valkyrie*

Augustin de Drucour governor of Île Royale in Louisbourg

Marie-Louise de Drucour wife of Louisbourg governor, Augustin de Drucour

Margaux-Lyneth Dubonnet sister of Lady Corrinne de Chanaye

Gustave Dubonnet de Arras   colonel and commander of Auvergne Regiment, husband of Margaux-Lyneth Dubonnet

Erigh   (Ear-ee) also Erie, the great lake of Ohio tribal people known as "the cat people" also "the people of the panther"

Louis Ernest   Duke of Brunswick-Wolfenbüttel, father of Charles VanderMeer

Brockaert Eschwege   Hesse lord; enemy to House of Brunswick Wolfenbüttel; Dutch lord allied to Anne, the Queen Regent of the Netherlands

William Eyre   major and commanding officer of the 44th Regiment of Foot and commandant of Fort William Henry during its first attack

Fleurant   captain of the river trade ship *Proud Recluse*

Louis Franquet   colonel and engineer for Fortress Louisbourg

Frederick II   Fredrick the Great, sovereign of Prussia

Fürst   lieutenant officer of 1st Battalion Volontaires Étrangers Regiment

Henri Gerrard   (Awn-ree´ Jurr-rard)

Philippe Gerrard   (Fill-leap´ Jurr-rard)

Gosse   color sergeant of Le Guyenne Grenadier Regiment, Lieutenant Henri Gerrard's second, and head of the Louisbourg Marine Grenadiers

John Griffin   12-year-old ranger captured by Philippe

Haas   private of 1st Battalion Volontaires Étrangers Regiment

Thomas Hancock   wealthy Boston merchant, partner to Charles VanderMeer, and uncle to John Hancock

Sir Charles Hardy   admiral of the English Navy and New York provincial governor

René Hilaire   assistant ship designer to Lucais de Clermont

Karl Hollenberg   major general and military aide to Louis Ernest, Duke of Brunswick-Wolfenbüttel

Intendant   title of chief administrator of any of the appointed postings in New France

Iroquois   (Ear-row-kwoy´) one of the most successful native confederations in North America

Sir William Johnson   also known as Warraghiyagey, or a Man Who Does Great Things, crown-appointed Indian agent in the American colonies, Mohawk sachem, and Major-General in the English army

Wilhelm von Kleinfels   Hessian colonel, possessed by the vulnax-wraith, special ambassador for Frederick II, secret liaison from Frederick II to the French Naval Minister

Kohring	first sergeant and soldier of 1st Battalion Volontaires Étrangers Regiment
Karl Krieger	lieutenant-colonel, host of the *vulnax wraith*, and commander of the 1st Battalion Volontaires-Étrangers Regiment
LaCorne	sergeant of the Black Rock cannoneers
William LaFont	scholar hired by Madame Dubonnet to research family history
Seirian l'Aigle	Welsh mother of Margaux-Lyneth and Corrinne; died after childbirth
Charles de Langlade	French captain in the Troupes de la Marine at Fort Detroit, leads Ottawa Indians in support of Fort Duquesne, and fights at Battle of Monongahela
Beauregard LaTour	(Lah-toor´) French merchant ship captain of *William's Queen*, also called the *Falcon Queen*
Paulus Legates	clerk for The Grand Company of Traders
Legrande	doctor of Lucais de Clermont
François de Lévis	brigadier general and second-in-command to General Montcalm
Madeleine Louvet	Henri's lover in Québec City
Paul-Louis de Lusignan	commanding officer of Fort Carillon
Jean-Baptiste de Machault	(Ma-sho) French financial wizard, statesman, and Minister of Marine
Mkuigen Malsum	(key-gun) Abenaki warrior and Philippe's friend, also called Panther Claw
Marcel	bodyguard of Madame Dubonnet
Alain Marcoux	the primary host of the vulnax who later becomes Lieutenant-Colonel Karl Krieger
Mariel	secret wife of Duke Louis Ernest and mother of Charles VanderMeer
Conor Martyn	English naval officer, husband to Molly Shreve, and captain of the *Anamosa*
Conor Gwyn Martyn II	child of Conor Martyn and Molly
Mathilde	deceased, beloved maidservant to Corrinne de Chanaye
Angélique des Méloizes	wife of Major Michel de Péan
Mettler	lieutenant and Swiss mercenary assassin collaborator for Captain Stoecklin
Pernell Michaux	attending doctor at Louisbourg hospital

George Monro	lieutenant-colonel and commandant of Fort William Henry during its second attack, commander of the 35th Regiment of Foot
Louis Joseph de Montcalm	commanding general of all French forces in New France
Comte Dubois de la Motte	senior admiral of the French Navy
Neealouska	Abenaki war chief
Father Eric Nicolet	André Nicolet's son, recipient of André Nicolet's cross after his death, and new scion of a Great House
Carlton North	courier secretary of Lord Pitt
Okeanneh	(Oh-key´-ahh-nay) meaning "princess", first wife of Philippe Gerrard, mother of Anamosa
Oneida	(Oh-knee´-dah) meaning "stone people", a tribe of the Iroquois League of which Philippe Gerrard is a member
Michel de Péan	(Pay-awh) commander of gendarmerie in Québec City and Montréal, decorated major in the Troupes de la Marine
Severyn Peltier	captain of the French frigate *La Comète*
William Pitt	Secretary of State for America, 1st Earl of Chatham, and future Prime Minister of England
François Grillot de Poilly	deputy engineer to Franquet
Jeanne Antoinette Poisson	Madame de Pompadour, courtesan mistress of Louis XV
Róbert	bodyguard of Madame Dubonnet
Robert Rogers	major and commanding officer of Robert's Rangers
Charles de Rohan	Prince of Soubise, French general attacking Hanover
Roos	lieutenant and assassin collaborator for Captain Stoecklin
Sauer	major and second-in-command to Colonel Krieger in the 1st Battalion Volontaires Étrangers Regiment
Seneca	(Sen´-nick-kah) meaning "stony place"; the westernmost tribe of the Iroquois League of five tribal nations
Molly Shreve	wife to Captain Conor Martyn
Skenando	Pine Tree chief of Oneida tribe
Bergen Stoecklin	Swiss mercenary captain and assassin
Tall Mountain Among Trees	high chief of the Oswego Oneida, adoptive father of Philippe Gerrard
Nicolas de Saulx de Tavannes	archbishop of the Rouen Cathedral
Pierre Trémoille	captain adjutant-aide to Admiral Dubois de la Motte
Carter Trevathan	vulnax servant
Marcel Trieste	captain and aide to Governor Vaudreuil

Jean Vauquelin	captain of *L'Valkyrie*
John Winslow	senior American general reporting to Lord Loudon
Jacob and Louise de Witte	retired friends of Margaux Dubonnet in Antwerp
Charles VanderMeer	(Van-der-mere´) court artist to the crown of France, jewel trader, heir to the Dutch House of Brunswick-Wolfenbüttel, son of Duke Louis Ernest
Calypso Alexis VanderMeer	twin of Marcus, daughter of Corrinne and Philippe
Marcus Valerious VanderMeer	twin of Calypso, son of Corrinne and Philippe
Sébastien le Prestre de Vauban	famous French military engineer, marquis
Pierre de Vaudreuil	governor-general of New France, marquis
Rigaud de Vaudreuil	Troupes de la Marine captain and brother to Governor-General Vaudreuil
Victorio	sail maker, surgeon, carpenter, and second-in-command on the *Falcon Queen*

Crew of the Falcon Queen

Bosun Linard *the Lanyard*
Etienne *One Ear*
Gilles *of the Rope Burn*
Geron *the Toothless*
Remy *of the One Crossed Eye*
Tinidor *the Unwashed*
Caiden *the Guilty*
Audrik *the Tall*
Vernon *Pox Face*
Reynard *Bushy Beard*
Martin *the Shy*
Pierrik *Red Scarf*
Leon *the Bald*
Vincente *Curled Mustache*
Stefan *Tool Belt*
Dragon *Tattooed Cheeks*
Eric *Braided Hair*
Knute *Wearing Knots*
Monty *the Huguenot*
Killian *Island Man*
Turiau *Old Wrinkled*

Troupes de Marine
Louisbourg volunteers

Color Sergeant Gosse *formerly of the Guyenne Regiment*
Private Nicolas Vallier
Corporal Luc Chapelle
Private Pieter l'Alcyon
Private Costin Méchins

References

With the advent of the Internet, a huge amount of research for this book was obtained from standard Google searches and the extraordinary trove of information available from Wikipedia queries.

With a respectful nod given to the modern search-engine databases mentioned, I also relied heavily on the list of references below to keep my imagination from getting too far astray from recorded history. *Wilderness Empire* by Allan W. Eckert (noted historian and seven-time Pulitzer Prize nominee), the second book in a series, is an extraordinary read, and was a primary resource of facts and information. I also relied on several works by René Chartrand who has created a series of books covering various years and aspects of the French and Indian War.

Parkman, Francis *Montcalm and Wolfe*, De Capo Press, member of the Perseus Group, 2001.

Anderson, Fred *Crucible of War*. Vintage Books, a Division of Random House, 2000.

Hamilton, Edward P. *Adventure in the Wilderness: The American Journals of Louis Antoine De Bougainville, 1756–1760*. University of Oklahoma Press; Edition 1990.

Warden, G.B. *Boston 1689–1776*. NY: Little, Brown, and Company Limited, 1970.

Baxter, W.T. *The House of Hancock, Business in Boston, 1724–1775*. Russell & Russell, Inc., 1965.

Kirby, William. *The Golden Dog (1897)*. Colonial Press, C.H. Simonds & Co. 1911.

Baugh, Daniel. *The Global Seven Years War 1754–1763*. Routledge, Taylor and Francis Group 2014.

McLennan, J.S. *Louisbourg, From its Foundation to it Fall*, The Book Room Limited, 1979.

Chartrand, René. *Montcalm's Crushing Blow*, Oxford: Osprey Publishing, 2014.

Lincoln, Charles Henry, PhD. *Correspondence of William Shirley V2: Governor of Massachusetts and Military Commander in America 1731–1760*. The MacMillan Company, 1912.

Johnson, Michael. *Tribes of the Iroquois Confederacy*. Oxford: Osprey Publishing, 2003.

Eckert, Allan W. *Wilderness Empire*. Ashland, KY: Jesse Stuart Foundation, 2001.

Snow, Dean R. *The Iroquois*. Oxford: Wiley-Blackwell Publisher, 1994.

Graymont, Barbara. *The Iroquois*. New York: Chelsea House Publishers, 1988.

Hutchens, Alma R. *A Handbook of Native American Herbs*. Boston: Shambhala Publications, 1992.

About the Author

Quentin Grady was born in Hartford, Connecticut, and raised in Cleveland, Ohio. Upon receiving a scholarship from the U.S. Navy in 1970, he graduated from the University of Utah in 1972 with degrees in computer science and mathematics. Subsequent to that he completed graduate studies in nuclear engineering. He served as a naval officer on nuclear submarines until 1980. After leaving the service, he held several senior management positions in the software industry for companies like Oracle, specializing in utility applications and engineering solutions. Passionate about fiction writing from an early age, he has devoted the last four years towards getting his first five novels published with several more in production.

The Mercenaries is the fifth book in the *Tales of the Ghost Eagle* series. Book 6 is expected to be published in 2018.

He lives in Tacoma, Washington.

A Note From the Author

Quentin Grady is merely my pen name. My official name is Papa-Q, as declared by the president of my fan club, seen in the picture above, as she graciously allows me to accompany her to a matinee performance of *Disney on Ice*. I just do what she tells me to do. Her name is Corrinne, by the way. Go figure.

www.ingramcontent.com/pod-product-compliance
Lightning Source LLC
Chambersburg PA
CBHW071329020726
47502CB00001B/13